PENGUIN BOOKS

TALKING PICTURES

A native of Philadelphia, Richard Corliss
earned his B.A. degree at St. Joseph's College
and his M.A. in film at Columbia University.
He did film research at the Museum of Modern
Art in New York City for two years, leaving
in 1970 to become editor in chief of the much
admired journal *Film Comment*—a post he
still occupies. Articles by him have appeared
in the *New York Times*, the *Village Voice*,
Commonweal, the *National Review*, *Variety*,
Film Quarterly, and other publications, and he
is editor of the recently published anthology
Hollywood Screenwriters. Mr. Corliss lives in
New York, where he serves on the selection
committee of the New York Film Festival.

RICHARD CORLISS

TALKING PICTURES

Screenwriters in the American Cinema

Preface by Andrew Sarris

Penguin Books Inc
New York · *Baltimore*

Penguin Books Inc
72 Fifth Avenue
New York, New York 10011
Penguin Books Inc
7110 Ambassador Road
Baltimore, Maryland 21207
Penguin Books Canada Limited
41 Steelcase Road West
Markham, Ontario, Canada L3R 1B4

First published by The Overlook Press, Inc.,
Woodstock, New York, 1974
Published by Penguin Books Inc, 1975
This edition published by arrangement with The Overlook Press, Inc.
Copyright © Richard Corliss, 1974

Printed in the United States of America

Portions of this book have appeared in somewhat different form in *The New York Times, The Village Voice, Commonweal, National Review, Cinema, Film Comment, Film Quarterly,* and the Avon book *The Hollywood Screenwriters.* Grateful acknowledgment is made to the publishers for their permission to reprint that material. "The Pen Is Mightier Than the Gun" reprinted by permission of The Village Voice, Inc., 1971. "The Hollywood Screenwriter," "The Front Page," "Two Affairs to Remember," and "Capra and Riskin" copyright © Film Comment Publishing Corporation, 1970, 1971, 1972. All rights reserved. Used with permission. "I Admit It, I Didn't Like M*A*S*H" and "Who Says All the World Loves 'Love Story'?" copyright © The New York Times Company, 1970, 1971. Reprinted by permission. "Southern Discomfort" copyright © Commonweal Publishing Co., Inc., 1970. "Red Hot and Medium Cool" reprinted by permission of *National Review.* "Bad Company" (review of) copyright © The Regents of the University of California, 1973. "Preston Sturges" first published in *Cinema,* Vol. 7, No. 2 (1972).

The task of accreditation in any collaborative art form is a frustrating journey into the darkness of lost records, foggy memories, old grudges, office politics, and a dozen other obscurants. To assign correctly the contributions of all the participants in all the more than one thousand movies included in this book's text and filmographies would require the film equivalent of the Senate Watergate Hearings—and would likely yield the same result: well-documented chaos.

One point, made repeatedly in the following pages, is worth making up front. A filmography can only suggest; it cannot define. And a screenwriter's filmography, involving Guild myopia and critical shortsightedness, may mislead as often as it enlightens. Even if all the credits herein were "correct," words such as *story, screenplay, adaptation,* and *dialogue* would capture only the silhouette of what is, at best, the communal combustion of many crafts, many minds and spirits.

Nonetheless, every attempt has been made to assemble here the most accurate possible filmographies. When feasible, the screenwriters themselves were asked to amend and append the lists; and, for their assistance, the author expresses his deep gratitude. He would be pleased to receive further corrections from readers and to incorporate them into any future editions of *Talking Pictures.*

Acknowledgments

This book was begun with the help of a grant from the American Film Institute.

For generous assistance above and beyond the call of duty (or even friendship), I am most grateful to Charles Silver, Barbara Shapiro, and Stephen Harvey of the Museum of Modern Art's Film Study Center, Melinda Ward of *Film Comment,* Joanne Koch of the Film Society of Lincoln Center, Michael Kerbel of Brandon Films, Diane Solomon of Warner Brothers, and Marion Billings of Billings Associates.

Help in forming and reforming many of this book's less outrageous opinions came, in expressions of support and outrage, from such valued colleagues as Richard Roud, George Amberg, Gary Carey, Howard Koch, John Hanhardt, Stuart Byron, Molly Haskell, Elliott Sirkin, Paul Jensen, Ted Perry, William Yushak, Brooks Riley, Robert Benton and David Newman, and Dalton Trumbo. Their insights—some of which appear uncredited herein—were nonetheless valuable.

The idea for a critical survey of Hollywood screenwriters first came in 1969, as a response to and expansion of Andrew Sarris's *The American Cinema*; what emerged as this book would simply not have begun without his pioneering work and heroically tolerant guidance. Without Austin Lamont, the idea would have been there, but not the impetus; soon after I became editor of his *Film Comment* magazine, he allowed and encouraged me to devote one mammoth issue to the screenwriter, and since then has continued to pamper the most delirious of my editorial whims. Without Peter Mayer, my own editor at Avon Books and the Overlook Press, I would have had ideas and impetus, but no books; his personal enthusiasm and publisher's energy were crucial in turning the *Film Comment* issue into *The Hollywood Screenwriters,* and a sheaf of discursive opinions into this book. Finally and ultimately, without my wife Mary I would have had two boxes of index cards but no manuscript; she not only typed the whole thing, but through patience and prodding was as responsible as I that there was anything at all to type. With gratitude and love, I dedicate this book . . .

. . . TO MARY

Contents

PREFACE FOR A DIALECTICAL DISCUSSION
BY ANDREW SARRIS

Richard Corliss has kindly invited me to write a preface to his revisionist enterprise of enthroning screenwriters where once not so long ago only directors reigned. I accept the invitation not so much out of a perverse delight in its ironic implications as out of a firm conviction that what unites us (the poetics of the cinema) is infinitely more important than what divides us (the polemics of craft contributions). Indeed, I can think of no higher tribute to pay Corliss than to say that he communicates an enjoyment of movies with none of the constipating prissiness of the mere pedant, the catatonic euphoria of the mere enthusiast, or the crabby superciliousness of the mere snob. Even where we disagree, it is a matter more of dialectics than of diatribes, and, more often than not, more of nuance than of substance. Nonetheless we do disagree, and therefore before I deliver my formal benediction on this book I would like to review my own position as a frame of reference.

When I wrote my first "auteurist" article about a hundred years ago, I had no idea that the term would stick to me like glue. Nor that I would eventually be credited with an army of followers, the alleged number of which would make Leavis's legions seem Luxemburgian by comparison. I had hoped that my articles might stimulate some debate, but I was not really prepared for the nuclear holocaust that followed. Now that the radioactive dust has settled somewhat, it becomes clear that the original outbursts over "auteurism" were not concerned so much with auteurs as such, or directors as such, or screenwriters as such, but rather with the proper mode

of expression to be used in the discussion of Hollywood movies.
What linked the not-so-grand alliance of anti-auteurists in their
acrimony was their unwillingness to abandon their lofty position
of moral and intellectual superiority to their supposed subject.
Auteurism and the Cahierism that had spawned it proposed a
thoughtful perception of style in even the lowliest flick. And this
proposition, reasonable as it seems today, managed to enrage the
Kaels, the Macdonalds, the Kauffmanns, the Alperts, the Knights,
the Crists, and the Simons to the point that this particular cultist
proceeded overnight from obscurity to notoriety. However, none of
the original anti-auteurist diatribes went to bat for the poor,
neglected Hollywood screenwriter. That particular brand of hypocritical concern for one class of God's creatures in the collaborative
process of the motion picture came much later after dozens of
books on individual directors had poured off the presses, thus establishing that a serious interest in old Hollywood movies was
here to stay. So let us not forget that it was auteurism and not anti-
auteurism that established the very existence of an artistically valid
field of study, and if screenwriters are suddenly coming out of the
woodwork of the Algonquin Bar, it is because Hollywood does not
automatically evoke horselaughs among the literati as it once did
in the pre-auteurist era. Suddenly the old Hollywood movies are
something in which to take pride instead of the Fifth, and the
screenwriters want their share of glory. I don't blame them, but
now they'll just have to take their turn behind the directors they
maligned or allowed to be maligned for so long. Also, screenwriters
will have to learn to take the blame for their bad movies if they
want credit for their good ones. This is the encyclopedic aspect of
auteurism that even so systematic a scholar as Corliss seems unwilling to invoke on a won-lost basis for the ultimate ranking.

I bring up the polemical past also because even Corliss seems to
be purveying some of the more dubious debating points of the
anti-auteurists as straight auteurist doctrine. I certainly never meant
auteurism to be a running advertisement for the Screen Directors
Guild, and I was very careful to point out that the "auteur" theory,
such as it was, was more the first step than the last stop in the re-
discovery and revaluation of the American Cinema. But my disclaimers and qualifications were completely ignored, and I was
vilified, in FDR's old lament, for a phrase here and half a phrase
there. Well, now the shoe is on the other foot, and nothing would

be easier than to ignore Corliss's very reasonable disclaimers and qualifications, and zero in on his spicier passages of snide partisanship. However, I realize better than most people that nothing could be duller than a piece of critical writing full of disclaimers and qualifications. I realize also better than most people that it is far easier to tear down some one else's unifying aesthetic theory than to build up one of one's own. Hence, I shall try, as I have promised, to keep my debate with Corliss on the level of dialectics rather than diatribes.

A few preliminary distinctions might be in order at this point. Corliss notes very considerately: "Sarris wasn't the first American to argue that the director is the author of the film. . . ." As it stands, this attributed statement strikes me as almost meaningless in its abstractness. How can anyone say a priori that any director is automatically the author of the film for which he is credited as a director? We are then simply making two words do the job of one, and it is thus very simple to argue in rebuttal that the director is obviously not the author on the grounds that directors are people who wave their arms around and throw tantrums whereas authors are people who pound away on their typewriters in creative solitude. As it happens, the first examples Corliss provides of this separation of functions are so loaded against the director that one wonders only why directors are ranked even above hairdressers as creative agents of the medium. I agree with Corliss that it is ridiculous to speak of Arthur Hiller's *Love Story* and Herbert Ross's *Play It Again, Sam*. Even I, arch auteurist that I am alleged to be, consider Erich Segal both author and auteur of *Love Story*, and Woody Allen both author and auteur of *Play It Again, Sam*. But then I don't consider either Hiller or Ross quite on the same level as Max Ophuls, John Ford, Alfred Hitchcock, Howard Hawks, Fritz Lang, Ernst Lubitsch, Jean Renoir, F. W. Murnau, or Orson Welles, to name but a few of the directors who deserve stylistic analysis above and beyond the not inconsiderable contributions of their scenarists. Still, even with Hiller and Ross, very different movies might have emerged from different directors. And it is especially interesting to note how much slicker *Play It Again, Sam* seems when compared to Allen's self-directed scenarios, and yet how much less elegantly wistful than the Clive Donner–directed and Woody Allen–written *What's New, Pussycat?* But why descend to such intermediate depths to discuss the diminishing returns of directorial auteurism. Why not slither all the way down beneath the manhole covers to the Bowery Boys and their wretched directorial collaborators? Obviously, a little common sense and critical perspective can go a long way in avoiding the absurdities of cut-rate dialectics.

But even if we confine ourselves to the top rather than the bottom of a critical scale of movie values, certain practical problems remain to confound us. I have recently examined Donald E. Knox's fascinating collection of interviews with most of the participants in the production of *An American in Paris.* The interviews run for thousands and thousands of words, and it is frightening to think that film critics and historians seeking to apportion proper credit for each and every one of the thousands of interesting movies ever made would have to immerse themselves in thousands of such manuscripts. There has to be some middle way between functional presumption by the critic about creative roles and endless recollections poured into a tape recorder. I still think that a very tentative form of auteurism is the best approach. In this way, the director is the hypothetically dominant figure in the filmmaking process until a pattern of contributions has been established. The director-auteur is not even a real person as such, but a field of magnetic force around which all agents and elements of the filmmaking process tend to cluster. If his magnetic force is strong enough and selective enough, he can come to be regarded after a time as an authentic auteur. If his magnetic force is weak and erratic, he will be denigrated in time as a mere *metteur-en-scène.* Similarly, writers, players, cinematographers, set designers (*vide* Teresa Wright's revealing insight on the crucial contribution of William Cameron Menzies to the career of Sam Wood), producers and all other contributory artists and craftsmen have to be evaluated for their own patterns of achievement. I wrote something like this about a decade ago, and now Corliss is taking me to task for not having worked hard enough in the meantime to unearth nondirectorial auteurs.

I can defend myself in various ways: (a) The apotheosis of the screenwriter is premature since we have not yet finished doing the job on the director. After all, how many more, if indeed any more people know that Michael Curtiz directed *Casablanca* than that Howard Koch and Jules J. and Philip G. Epstein wrote it? A rather weak argument to be sure, and fainthearted in the bargain. (b) I have been waiting for someone sophisticated to take up the cudgels for the screenwriter to see what sort of blows could be struck against the notion of directorial dominance. (c) I have become increasingly conscientious about mentioning screenwriters as hypothetical auteurs largely under the influence of Corliss's noisy crusade in the pages of *Film Comment*. (d) I still feel the gravitational pull of the director in those regions of cinematic expression that are the highest and the deepest, but I am prepared to concede many points to Corliss in the pleasant middle regions. (e) We seem to be fencing around with the roles of the director and screenwriter in that I would grant the screenwriter most of the dividends accruing from dialogue, and Corliss would grant the director the interpretive insights of a musical conductor. Where we grapple most desperately and most blindly is in that no man's land of narrative and dramatic structure. And here I think the balance of power between the director and the screenwriter is too variable for any generalization.

I tend to agree with Joseph L. Mankiewicz that every screenplay is a directed movie, and every directed movie a screenplay. That is to say that writing and directing are fundamentally the same function. As a screenplay is less than a blueprint and more than a libretto, so is directing less than creating and more than conducting. Most movies can best be understood in terms of an aesthetic tending toward the adhesive rather than toward the abstract. In the cinema, unlike the theater, players adhere forever to characters, images to words, backgrounds to human figures, and the time past of production to the time eternal of projection. That I believe in a dramatist's theater at the same time as I believe in a director's cinema is thus, at least in my own mind, not so much an inconsistency as an insight.

Fortunately, Richard Corliss is one of our most scrupulous film scholars as well as one of our most perceptive film critics, and through a blend of scruple, perception, and compassion he has managed to detoxify the debate between director and screenwriter, between auteurist and authorist, and between the frame-by-frame school and the scene-by-scene school. And oh yes, he has a rather formidable sense of humor, and that helps matters considerably in this age of plastic absurdism. I should add that he was one of my students at NYU, and that I suspected from the very beginning that he was going to be a troublemaker. And here is his book to fulfill my prophecy. I recommend it to everyone seriously interested in film, and especially to the millions and millions of my fellow auteurists. We must face up to its challenge.

Introduction: Notes on a Screenwriter's Theory, 1973

1. *Thesis: The Director as Auteur*

> *I was driving by Otto Preminger's house last night—or is it "a house by Otto Preminger"?*
>
> —BURT KENNEDY, 1971

It's a full decade now since Andrew Sarris published, in *Film Culture* magazine, his two-part Americanization of the *politique des auteurs*. At the time it could be taken as a thoughtful and provocative challenge to that near-monopoly in serious English-language film criticism, the Social Dialectic. Refreshingly, Sarris examined films as the creations of artists rather than of social forces—whether capitalist, communist, or fascist—and, in doing so, he helped liberate the scrupulous study of American film from the numbing strictures of solemnity. We could finally admit without shame that the best Hollywood movies succeeded not only as delightful entertainments but as art works rivaling those from the culture capitals of Europe.

Sarris wasn't the first American to argue that "the director is the author of a film." Hollywood itself had accepted this policy in the silent days, when directors received billing just below their stars; *The Rise of the American Film* and *The Liveliest Art* devote long chapters to the careers of Hollywood *metteurs-en-scène;* even Bosley Crowther, back in 1940, seconded William Wyler's assertion that "the final responsibility for a picture's quality rests solely and completely upon the shoulders of the man who directed it." But it was Sarris's call to arms that started the auteur revolution. First the specialized journals, then the mass-market magazines, then *The New York Times, Cue,* and *TV Guide* began crediting directors not only with authorship but with ownership: "Arthur Hiller's *Love Story.*" By the time the trend had reached Hollywood, it had become something of a joke. Thus *Play It Again, Sam*—starring Woody Allen, screenplay by Woody Allen, from a play by Woody Allen—is heralded in the screen credits as "A Herbert Ross Film."

Sarris's version of the *politique* was extraordinarily helpful in calling attention to neglected American directors in a fistful of infra dig genres, but it may have done more harm than good in citing the director as the sole author of his film. What could have begun a systematic expansion of American film history—by calling attention to anonymous screenwriters, cinematographers, art directors, and, yes, even actors—bogged down in an endless coronation of the director as benevolent despot, in his enshrinement as solitary artist, with his collaborating craftsmen functioning merely as paint, canvas, bowl of fruit, and patron.

By establishing the director as the Creator of a Work of Art, the auteurists were falling into the same critical traps that had snared the no-less-well-meaning Social Realism crowd some thirty years earlier. The notion persists that a work of art is the product of one man working alone to carve a personal vision out of the marble of his sensibility. Ideally, perhaps, but not invariably—and, in Hollywood, not even generally. Yet this notion, very romantic and very American, is the basis upon which most recent film histories stand. It is so basic that it is taken for granted: in the standard book-length studies of Sternberg and Stevens, Hitchcock and Hawks, the critics' auteur bias is a given that needn't be proven.

A number of critical labels have to be spindled and mutilated before we can begin to appreciate the collaborative complexity of American cinema more fully. ART VS. ENTERTAINMENT: a rather precious distinction by now, since any supremely entertaining movie should reveal deeper (or at least broader) levels upon further viewings, and since any work of art cannot help but entertain, if only in the viewer's delight in discovering it. SOLITARY ART VS. CORPORATE ART: The fact that Chartres, or *Charade,* was the work of a number of individuals contributing their unique talents to a corporate enterprise doesn't necessarily make either work less "artistic" than, say, Van Gogh's "Wildflowers" or Snow's *Wavelength.* It just makes it more difficult for the critic to assign sole authorship, which is more a critical convenience than a value judgment—or should be, any-way.

THE CREATIVE ARTIST VS. THE INTERPRETIVE ARTIST: Both Stan-ley Donen and Michael Snow are, shall we say, artists; but Snow is a creative artist and Donen an interpretive artist. Snow is almost literally a film *maker*, collaborating with his film strips and his Movieola in an intimate, incestuous way that has very little to do with the way Donen collaborates with his scriptwriter, actors, and technicians. The traditional view was that the solitary, creative artist produced Art, while the corporate, interpretive craftsman produced Entertainment. It would seem that the auteur theory, which one might have assumed would demolish this old canard, is actually re-inforcing it. If Donen is worthy of sustained critical study (and I believe he is), so are, say, Arthur Freed, Gene Kelly, Betty Comden and Adolph Green, Richard Avedon, George Abbott, Cary Grant, Peter Stone, Christopher Challis, and all the other talented men and women whose careers intersected Donen's at mutually felicitous points.

Cinema is not the only medium in which authorship is bestowed upon the director (or, for that matter, the art director—as witness John Simon's recent critical study, *Ingmar Bergman Directs,* which the title page describes, in a type size equal to Mr. Simon's credit, as "a creation of Halcyon Enterprises"!). Determining authorship in the theater can be a complicated business. Is Harold Pinter the "au-thor" of *Old Times*? Most assuredly. And yet the difference between the London and New York productions of the play amounted to more than a subtle shift in tone, or even in effect; it was a difference in *meaning.* As played by Colin Blakely (London), the Deeley char-acter was the audience's very vulnerable identity figure; as played by Robert Shaw (New York), he was a self-deceiving boor. As played by Vivien Merchant (London), the Anna character was menacing, predatory; as played by Rosemary Harris (New York), she was helpful, sympathetic. Same author, same director, same pauses—but different casts and, almost, two different plays.

It's probably fair to consider Tom O'Horgan the prime mover (whether as creator or defiler) of his later theatrical extravaganzas, because he shapes, packages, controls his productions as completely as, say, Ken Russell controls *his* films. In a less mannerist vein, the Broadway career of Elia Kazan—whose collaborations with Ten-nessee Williams, Arthur Miller, and S. N. Behrman, among others, were both intense and enduring—could be profitably studied for Kazan's personal approach to themes and styles. But could he exercise "directorial authority" as powerfully on Broadway as in Hollywood? In one case at least, *yes*: at his insistence, Williams wrote an entirely new third act for *Cat on a Hot Tin Roof*. To be sure (and to be lamented), one can*not* study Kazan's theater work, because his productions died on closing night, while his playwrights' scripts live on in book form. One reason for directorial supremacy in the cinema may be that, there, the reverse is true: screenplays are rarely published (and barely consulted even then), while the films made from them are available at the flick of a TV channel selector.

William Wyler was absolutely right to hold the director responsible for "a picture's quality"—just as a conductor is responsible for the composer's symphony, or a contractor for the architect's plans. But he must also be responsible *to* something: the screenplay. With it, he can do one of three things: ruin it, shoot it, or improve it. (Scattered throughout this book are instances of all three possible results.) Realizing a screenplay is the director's job; transcending it is his glory. Despite the Writers Guild's immemorial gripes, directing is a fine art, not a lead-pipe cinch (as too many screenwriters have proved when they tried to direct a picture). It's no coincidence that most of the films selected for praise in this book were directed by Hollywood's finest auteurs—no more a coincidence than that these same films were scripted by Hollywood's finest authors.

Andrew Sarris has said that the directors he prefers are those with an unconscious—who, presumably, speak from the soul, and not from the scenario. I think that this statement also suggests why Sarris prefers a director's cinema to a writer's. One restraint on the poetic tendencies of a screenwriter-oriented critic, as opposed to those of an auteurist, is that the screenwriter *makes* words and situations occur, while the director *allows* actions to occur. Thus, the process of creating a screenplay is more formal, less mystical than the image, which is created by the director, photographer, designer, and actors. This inexactness of the visual process gives the auteurist an opportunity to infer reams and realms of metaphysical nuance. Typewriter keys seem to spring to the paper with grandiose generalizations: "a world of . . . ," "the cinema of . . ." And since the director allowed these filmic epiphanies to take place, who's to say he didn't *make* them happen?

This is the notion of the artist as inspired dervish—literally "inspired." The Muse breathes the spirit into a director, and he exhales this inspiration, filling the sound stage with a magic that affects cast and crew and results in a privileged moment. To the great directors, making their greatest films, this fantasy may apply. One gets the feeling that John Ford creatively controlled every moment of *The Searchers*, from first opening door to last closing door. But the greatness of even so controlled a film as *Psycho* is partly due to Anthony Perkins' performance, which at least extended, and probably transcended, Hitchcock's understanding of Norman Bates's character.

The director *is* right in the middle of things. At the very least, he's on the sound stage while the cinematographer is lighting the set that the art director has designed and, later, while the actors are speaking the lines that the screenwriter wrote. At best, he steers all these factors (story, actors, camera) in the right *direction*, to the extent that many films are indeed dominated by his personality—though not, perhaps, in the way the auteurists mean. The phrase "directorial personality" may make more sense if it's taken quite literally. Anyone who's seen Stanley Donen or Sam Peckinpah or Howard Hawks or Radley Metzger in action knows that the effective director is usually a man with a strong, persuasive personality. He has to combine the talents of salesman (to get a job in the first place), tough guy (to make the technicians respond to his commands), and best friend (to coax a good performance out of a volatile actress). Whether he directs with a riding crop (Stroheim), an icy stare (Sternberg), or some lightweight banter (Cukor), his personality is often crucial to the success of a film. The importance of a director's personal—or even visual—style is not at question here, only the assumption that he creates a style out of thin air instead of adapting it to the equally important styles of the story and performers.

Indeed, if auteur criticism had lived up to its early claim to be truly concerned with visual style, there would be no need for any systematic slighting of the screenwriter. Given a certain text, or pretext, the director could be said to weave the writer's design into a personal, visual subtext through the use of camera placement and movement, lighting, cutting, direction of actors, etc. Such a *politique* would go far toward elucidating the work of superior *metteurs-en-scène* on the order of Cukor, Donen, Michael Curtiz, Mitchell Leisen, and Don Siegel. But visual style is not the auteurist's major

interest. Auteur criticism is essentially theme criticism; and themes
—as expressed through plot, characterization, and dialogue—belong primarily to the writer.

2. *Antithesis: The Screenwriter as Auteur*

> *In my opinion, the writer should have the first and last word in
> filmmaking, the only better alternative being the writer-director,
> but with the stress on the first word.*
>
> —ORSON WELLES, 1950

The cry *"cherchez l'auteur"* can lead unwary film scholars astray
when the auteur happens to be the author—or rather, when the
script is the basis of a film's success. As often as not, when a fine film
is signed by a middle-rung director, the film's distinctive qualities
can be traced to the screenwriter. There's no need to rescue Mitchell
Leisen, Garson Kanin, Sam Wood, and William D. Russell from the
underworld of neglected directors simply because each was fortunate enough to direct a comedy written, in his best period, by Norman Krasna (*Hands Across the Table, Bachelor Mother, The Devil
and Miss Jones,* and *Dear Ruth,* respectively). The direction of
these films *is* usually adroit and sensitive, and the presence of charming comediennes enhances them even further; but the delightfully
dominant personality behind the screen is undoubtedly Krasna's.

Krasna's "mistaken-identity" theme, which he milked for more
than thirty years, is as unmistakable as an Eric Rohmer plot—but
he's hardly the only Hollywood screenwriter with thematic or tonal
obsessions. Ben Hecht's penny-ante cynicism, Preston Sturges's
apple-pie-in-the-face Americana, Frank Tashlin's breast fixation,
Peter Stone's schizophrenia, George Axelrod's impotent Svengalis,
Howard Koch's *liebestod* letters, Borden Chase's wagon trains of
Western Civilization, Abraham Polonsky's economic determinism,
Billy Wilder's creative con men, Samson Raphaelson's aristocratic
bourgeoisie, Garson Kanin and Ruth Gordon's eccentric marriages,
Dudley Nichols' instant redemption, Joseph L. Mankiewicz's endless
articulation, Dalton Trumbo's gilt-edged propaganda, Robert Riskin's demogogic populism, Sidney Buchman's democratic republi-
canism, Jules Furthman's noble adventurers, Charles Lederer's sassy
misanthropy, Ring Lardner, Jr.'s brassy misogyny, Terry Southern's
practical joking, Erich Segal's ivy-covered sentimentality, Jules Feiffer's cartoon morality plays, David Newman and Robert Benton's

likable losers . . . look at the films of these screenwriters half as closely as an auteurist would examine the work of Otto Preminger or Robert Mulligan, and chances are you'll find yourself staring at some dominant theme or style or plot or mood—some strong personal trait of film authorship. After all, film is (as Andrew Sarris has observed) essentially a dramatic medium; and the screenwriters are the medium's dramatists.

It's clear that some method of classification and evaluation is necessary, both to identify and to assess the contribution of that overpaid but unsung *genus* known as the screenwriter. But that is a game that conceals even more pitfalls than does the Sarris Hit Parade of Directors. Once the auteur scholar accepts the myth of the omnipotent director—that nonexistent Hawks or Stevens who writes, produces, photographs, acts in, and edits every film he makes—his game is won. Indeed, even the stanchest adherent of the *politique des collaborateurs* can be fairly sure that the director of record is the man who hollered "Action!" and "Cut!"—though his importance in controlling what went on between those two commands may be disputed. But the size of a screenwriter's contribution to any given film is often more difficult to ascertain.

A writer may be given screen credit for work he didn't do (as with Sidney Buchman on *Holiday*), or be denied credit for work he did do (as with Sidney Buchman on *The Awful Truth*). The latter case is far more common than the former. Garson Kanin co-wrote *The More the Merrier,* but his name didn't appear on-screen because he had already been inducted into the wartime Army. Ben Hecht toiled for seven days rewriting the first nine reels of *Gone With the Wind*, but David O. Selznick wanted Sidney Howard's name to appear alone on the screenplay. Michael Wilson wrote the screenplay for *Friendly Persuasion* and co-scripted *The Bridge on the River Kwai* and *Lawrence of Arabia,* but the Hollywood blacklist kept his name off all three films, and the writing Oscar for *Kwai* was awarded to Pierre Boulle, who had nothing at all to do with the film adapted from his novel.

The American Screen Writers Guild has a ridiculous rule that disallows screenplay credit to any director who has not contributed at least fifty per cent of the dialogue—ridiculous if only because it permits auteur critics to infer that their favorite directors consistently contributed, say, forty-nine percent. (When the Guild discovered that *Bad Company*, a script by the writing team of Benton

and Newman, was going to be directed by Benton, it routinely sched-
uled an arbitration hearing to determine whether director Benton
was stealing a credit on poor writer Newman's script!) In Europe,
the auteurists tell us, things are more enlightened: there, the director
receives screenplay credit whether he wrote anything or not. Certainly
Bergman, Fellini, Antonioni, Chabrol, Truffaut (all writers before
they were directors) work either as sole authors or as collaborators—
and not just as editors—on their screenplays. But reliable sources
indicate that *Tout Va Bien,* the new "Godard" film, was written
solely by Jean-Pierre Gorin; and Luis Buñuel has admitted in print
that he contributed not one word of dialogue to Jean-Claude Carrière's script for *Le Charme Discret de la Bourgeoisie,* although
Buñuel is listed ahead of Carrière as an author of the screenplay.
Joseph Losey, who never takes screenplay credit, says he works as
closely with the screenwriter as he does with the cinematographer,
editor, and actors—should he share official credit with these collaborators as well? Losey needn't worry: auteur critics would have him
share credit with *nobody.*

In the Golden Age of Hollywood, things were a bit different. A
director would be given a script and instructed to start shooting
Monday; so much for shaping a personal vision through creative
rewriting. But what about the screenwriter who specializes in adaptations? Who's the auteur then? It's true that, in the case of a Donald Ogden Stewart, the problem is more subtle. Few screenwriters
can boast a more impressive list of credits than Stewart's. As with
George Cukor, the director for whom he produced his finest scripts,
Stewart's "filmography is his most eloquent defense." Both Stewart
and Cukor, however, had the good luck to be assigned adaptations
of some of the wittiest and most actable theater pieces of their time
—*Holiday, The Women* (for which Stewart received no screen
credit), *The Philadelphia Story,* and *Edward, My Son*—and Stewart's transferrals of these works from stage to screen adhered closely
to both the spirit and the letter of the originals.

Stewart's achievement should not be dismissed; many screenwriters failed at the delicate craft he mastered. But, as with directors,
one can distinguish several layers of screenwriting authorship: the
indifferent work of a mediocre writer, whether it's an original script
or an adaptation (which we may call procrustean); the gem-polish-
ing of a gifted adapter like Stewart (protean); and the creation of
a superior original script, like Herman J. Mankiewicz's *Citizen*

Kane or Abraham Polonsky's *Body and Soul* (promethean). When faced with the career of a Stewart, the critic who has discarded the convenience of the auteur theory must compare Stewart's adaptations with the source works, in hopes of detecting such changes as plot compression or expansion, bowdlerization, addition or deletion of dialogue, and differences in theme and tone. At worst, this research will exhaust and discourage the critic; at best, it will convince him that the creation of a Hollywood movie involves a complex weave of talents, properties, and personalities.

When a screenwriter, like Preston Sturges or George Axelrod, has a distinctive authorial tone, his contributions to films with multiple script credits can usually be discerned. But the hallmark of many fine screenwriters is versatility, not consistency. Subject matter dictates style. Given the Cheshire Cat nature of these writers, how are we to know which part of the *Casablanca* script is the work of the sophisticated but self-effacing Howard Koch, and which part was written by Julius and Philip Epstein? Well, recent archaeological studies have indicated that the Epsteins began to rework the plot of an unproduced play, *Everybody Comes to Rick's* (which has, in sketch form, most of the film's characters, including a Negro named Sam who is told to "Play it, Sam," and plays "As Time Goes By"), but then were called to the War; and that Koch developed these contributions into the final, full-blooded screenplay.

We don't have many of these memoirs, though—screenwriters being a notoriously underinterviewed breed (ever read one with Herman Mankiewicz?)—and since most Hollywood egos are approximately the size of the Graf Zeppelin, the accounts of screenwriters may be taken with the same pillar of salt we keep handy for directors' interviews and actors' autobiographies. Nevertheless, a screenwriter's work should and can be judged by analyzing his entire career, as is done with a director. If a writer has been associated with a number of favorite films, if he has received sole writing credit on some of these films, and if we can decipher a common style in films with different directors and actors, an authorial personality begins to appear. The high polish and understated irony of Koch's other work—from his script for the Mercury Theatre *War of the Worlds*, through his ten-year tenure at Warners, to his late-forties scripts for *Letter from an Unknown Woman* and *No Sad Songs for Me*—and his fulfillment of our three conditions, give credence to this account of the writing of *Casablanca*. In fact, most of the best

Hollywood screenwriters were sole authors of a substantial number of scripts.

The paucity of critical and historical literature makes all screenwriters "Subjects for Further Research." The cavalier group headings on the following lists are meant only to emphasize the tentative nature of the classification (as opposed to the groupings of screenwriters in the body of this book, which attempts to categorize without polemicizing). As more films are seen from the writers' point of view, names will be shuffled from one list to another. Ultimately, each of them, and many more, should have an artistic identity clear enough to make such capricious classification unnecessary. Until that enlightened time comes to pass, we must make do with an Acropolis of Screenwriters something like this one—which considers only the writers who are evaluated in this book.

Parthenon. Borden Chase, Betty Comden and Adolph Green, Ben Hecht, Nunnally Johnson, Garson Kanin (and Ruth Gordon), Howard Koch, Frank S. Nugent, Samson Raphaelson, Preston Sturges, Billy Wilder.

Erechtheion. George Axelrod, Sidney Buchman, Jules Feiffer, Norman Krasna, Ernest Lehman, Herman J. Mankiewicz, David Newman and Robert Benton, Abraham Polonsky, Casey Robinson, Peter Stone.

Propylaea. Charles Brackett, Delmer Daves, Jules Furthman, Buck Henry, Ring Lardner, Jr., Charles Lederer, Joseph L. Mankiewicz, Robert Riskin, Morrie Ryskind, Frank Tashlin.

Outside the Walls. Edwin Justus Mayer, Dudley Nichols, Erich Segal, Terry Southern, Dalton Trumbo.

All of these screenwriters—even those infidels muttering curses outside our Acropolis walls—deserve monographs or books devoted to their Hollywood careers. If the critical winds reverse themselves, and if publishers' generosity to unsalable film books continues, dawn may yet break over a bookshelf stocked with such titles as *The Cinema of Samson Raphaelson* and *The Collected Letters of Howard Koch.* It seemed to me of primary importance, however, to provide a general but detailed introduction to as many screenwriters as possible. The result (three and a half years later) is this book, with its arbitrary but perhaps panoramic consideration of one hundred films scripted by thirty-five prominent writers or writing teams. Within the bounds of available films and the limitations of my own prejudices, I have tried to select representative works of each writer's career, and representative writers from the several genres, periods, and styles of the Hollywood talkie. My aim has been to avoid facile generalizations by confronting specific films, thus not merely pin-pointing a writer's themes but discovering how he related his preoc-cupations to the job at hand.

In the main, the screenwriters who appear in this book are those who, by adapting their conspicuous talents to the Byzantine de-mands of the trade, developed the most successful screenwriting techniques. Success usually begat power, and power begat authority. By authority is meant the right to complete your own script without being forced to surrender it to the next fellow on the assembly line, the right to consult with any actor or director who wants changes, and the right to fight for your film through the taffy pull of front-office politics, pressure groups, and publicists. If directors have been pre-eminent in Hollywood since long before the arrival of the auteur theory, it is probably because, among all of Tinseltown's employees, they were the ones with the most power.

3. Synthesis: The Multiple Auteur

> There was the era of the actor, when a film was its star, and we had Mary Pickford, Douglas Fairbanks, Greta Garbo. Then we had the era of the director, and the films of King Vidor, Stern-berg, Feyder and Clair. A new era is beginning: that of the author. After all, it's the author who makes a film.
>
> —JEAN RENOIR, 1939

Despite their own kvetching about functional impotence in the moviemaking process, and despite the criminal negligence of a new breed of critics, screenwriters have done so much in making a film entertaining, moving, even ennobling. But such has been the factory nature of the Hollywood movie that writers can still do *only* so much. A screenwriter is, as often as not, the middleman between the author of the original property and the director—and the man who gets his hands on the flypaper last is the one whose fingerprints will show up first. The writers' movement in the thirties and forties, in-extricably bound up with inter-Guild hostilities and jealousies as it was, drew its limited power by sucking as much blood as possible from the *metteur-en-scène* as the Directors Guild would allow. The effect of the auteur theory was to steal back whatever authority (and authorship) the writers had usurped: at best, it was proposed, the writer writes a script but the director makes the film. The two crafts were seen as riding on opposite sides of a seesaw, with the weight of contemporary critical opinion deciding which group was to be left stranded in the air.

Perhaps a synthesis of these presumably antithetical functions is in order. The films that receive the highest praise in this book are those whose writers and directors—in creative association with the actors and technicians—worked together toward a collaborative vision. You could call *Citizen Kane* either the culmination of Herman Mankiewicz's dreams or the beginning of Orson Welles' nightmares, but it would be silly to ignore either man's contribution. Who is the auteur of *Ninotchka*: Ernst Lubitsch, or the Charles Brackett–Billy Wilder–Walter Reisch team, or Greta Garbo? Obviously, all of them. I've tried in this book to make a case for the screenwriter without libeling either the director or the actor. Once the contribution of all these crafts—individually and collectively—have been accepted and examined, studies of other vital film collaborators could begin and be meshed into a giant matrix of coordinate talents. One ultimate result of this process of synthesis should be to open the critical shutter a few more stops upon that strange and glorious hybrid: the artistic-entertaining, solitary-corporate, creative-interpretive talking picture.

RICHARD CORLISS

I. *The Author-Auteurs*

BEN HECHT · PRESTON STURGES · NORMAN KRASNA · FRANK TASHLIN · GEORGE AXELROD · PETER STONE · HOWARD KOCH · BORDEN CHASE · ABRAHAM POLONSKY · BILLY WILDER

Such was the insidious power of the Hollywood assembly line that it would take an expert graphologist to decipher the artistic signatures of most screenwriters (or, for that matter, of most directors). Not so these men. To a degree rare in the commercial cinema, their personalities are indelibly stamped on their films. In their fidelity to idiosyncratic themes, plots, characterizations, styles, and moods, they won the right to be called true movie auteurs. Seven of the ten were eventually able to direct, thus nursing their visions onto the sound stage and through the editing room.

Occasionally—as with Preston Sturges, Norman Krasna, Frank Tashlin, and Abraham Polonsky—this fidelity approached fanaticism. That the work of our author-auteurs was most distinctive doesn't necessarily mean that it was more distinguished than that of, say, Samson Raphaelson (a stylist) or Herman J. Mankiewicz (with his themes in search of a style) or Frank S. Nugent (a card-carrying chameleon) or Jules Feiffer (a breath of the new wind from the East). But even the failures of an auteur can be instructive: not only as critical fodder for a volume such as this, but also as proof that the American movie machine was resilient enough to endure the excesses and eccentricities of its most creative craftsmen.

I

BEN HECHT
(1893–1964)

1927 UNDERWORLD (Josef von Sternberg) story
1928 THE BIG NOISE (Allan Dwan) co-screenplay (uncredited)
1929 UNHOLY NIGHT (Lionel Barrymore) story
1930 ROADHOUSE NIGHTS (Hobart Henley) story
THE GREAT GABBO (James Cruze) story
1931 THE FRONT PAGE (Lewis Milestone) from his and Charles MacArthur's play
UNHOLY GARDEN (George Fitzmaurice), co-screenplay [1]
1932 SCARFACE (Howard Hawks) story
BACK STREET (John M. Stahl) co-screenplay (uncredited)
1933 HALLELUJAH, I'M A BUM (Lewis Milestone) story
TOPAZE (Harry d'Abbadie d'Arrast) co-screenplay (uncredited)
TURN BACK THE CLOCK (Edgar Selwyn) co-screenplay
DESIGN FOR LIVING (Ernst Lubitsch) screenplay
QUEEN CHRISTINA (Rouben Mamoulian) co-screenplay (uncredited)
1934 UPPER WORLD (Roy Del Ruth) story
THE TWENTIETH CENTURY (Howard Hawks) co-screenplay,[1] from his, Charles MacArthur's, and Charles Mulholland's play
SHOOT THE WORKS (Wesley Ruggles) from his and Gene Fowler's play, *The Great Magoo*
CRIME WITHOUT PASSION (Ben Hecht and Charles MacArthur) story,[1] screenplay [1]
VIVA VILLA! (Howard Hawks and Jack Conway) screenplay
1935 THE FLORENTINE DAGGER (Robert Florey) from his novel

[1] Written with Charles MacArthur.

2

ONCE IN A BLUE MOON (Ben Hecht and Charles Mac-Arthur) story,[1] screenplay [1]

THE SCOUNDREL (Ben Hecht and Charles MacArthur) screenplay,[1] from his and Rose Caylor's play, *All He Ever Loved*

BARBARY COAST (Howard Hawks) story,[1] screenplay [1]

SPRING TONIC (Clyde Bruckman) from his and Rose Caylor's play, *Man-Eating Tiger*

1936 SOAK THE RICH (Ben Hecht and Charles MacArthur) co-screenplay,[1] from his and Charles MacArthur's play

1937 NOTHING SACRED (William A. Wellman) screenplay

THE HURRICANE (John Ford and Stuart Heisler) co-screenplay (uncredited)

1938 THE GOLDWYN FOLLIES (George Marshall) story, screenplay

1939 LET FREEDOM RING (Jack Conway) story, screenplay

IT'S A WONDERFUL WORLD (W. S. Van Dyke) co-story, screenplay

SOME LIKE IT HOT (George Archainbaud) from his and Gene Fowler's play, *The Great Magoo*

LADY OF THE TROPICS (Jack Conway) story, screenplay

GUNGA DIN (George Stevens) co-screenplay [2]

WUTHERING HEIGHTS (William Wyler) co-screenplay [1]

GONE WITH THE WIND (Victor Fleming) co-screenplay (uncredited)

1940 HIS GIRL FRIDAY (Howard Hawks) co-screenplay (uncredited),[3] from his and Charles MacArthur's play, *The Front Page*

ANGELS OVER BROADWAY (Ben Hecht and Lee Garmes) story, screenplay

FOREIGN CORRESPONDENT (Alfred Hitchcock) co-screenplay (uncredited)

COMRADE X (King Vidor) co-screenplay [3]

THE SHOP AROUND THE CORNER (Ernst Lubitsch) co-screenplay (uncredited)

1941 LYDIA (Julien Duvivier) co-screenplay

1942 TALES OF MANHATTAN (Julien Duvivier) co-story, co-screenplay

THE BLACK SWAN (Henry King) co-screenplay

CHINA GIRL (Henry Hathaway) screenplay, producer

ROXIE HART (William A. Wellman) co-screenplay (uncredited)

[2] Written with Charles MacArthur, Joel Sayre, and Fred Guiol.
[3] Written with Charles Lederer.

1943   THE OUTLAW (Howard Hughes and Howard Hawks) co-
        screenplay (uncredited)
1945   SPELLBOUND (Alfred Hitchcock) screenplay
1946   SPECTER OF THE ROSE (Ben Hecht and Lee Garmes)
        screenplay, from his short story
        NOTORIOUS (Alfred Hitchcock) screenplay
        GILDA (Charles Vidor) co-screenplay (uncredited)
1947   HER HUSBAND'S AFFAIRS (S. Sylvan Simon) co-story,[3]
        co-screenplay [3]
        KISS OF DEATH (Henry Hathaway) co-screenplay [3]
        DISHONORED LADY (Robert Stevenson) co-screenplay (un-
        credited)
        RIDE THE PINK HORSE (Robert Montgomery) co-screen-
        play[3]
        THE PARADINE CASE (Alfred Hitchcock) co-screenplay
        (uncredited)
1948   MIRACLE OF THE BELLS (Irving Pichel) co-screenplay
        ROPE (Alfred Hitchcock) co-screenplay (uncredited)
1949   WHIRLPOOL (Otto Preminger) co-screenplay
        LOVE HAPPY (David Miller) co-screenplay (uncredited)
1950   WHERE THE SIDEWALK ENDS (Otto Preminger) screen-
        play
        PERFECT STRANGERS (Bretaigne Windust) from his and
        Charles MacArthur's play, Ladies and Gentlemen
1951   THE THING (Christian Nyby and Howard Hawks) co-screen-
        play (uncredited) [3]
1952   ACTORS AND SIN (Ben Hecht) producer, screenplay, from
        his short stories, "Actor's Blood" and "Concerning a Woman of
        Sin"
        MONKEY BUSINESS (Howard Hawks) co-screenplay [4]
1953   ROMAN HOLIDAY (William Wyler) co-screenplay (uncred-
        ited)
1954   LIVING IT UP (Norman Taurog) from his musical play,
        Hazel Flagg, and his screenplay for Nothing Sacred
1955   ULYSSES (Mario Camerini) co-screenplay
        THE INDIAN FIGHTER (André DeToth) co-screenplay
        THE COURT-MARTIAL OF BILLY MITCHELL (Otto Prem-
        inger) co-screenplay (uncredited)
1956   MIRACLE IN THE RAIN (Rudolph Maté) screenplay, from
        his novel
        THE IRON PETTICOAT (Ralph Thomas) screenplay (un-
        credited)

[4] Written with Charles Lederer and I. A. L. Diamond.

1957   LEGEND OF THE LOST (Henry Hathaway) co-screenplay
      A FAREWELL TO ARMS (Charles Vidor) screenplay
1958   THE FIEND WHO WALKED THE WEST (Gordon Douglas)
      from his and Charles Lederer's screenplay for *Kiss of Death*
      QUEEN OF OUTER SPACE (Edward Bernds) "story" (Hecht,
      though officially credited, did not work on this film)
1962   BILLY ROSE'S JUMBO (Charles Walters) from his and
      Charles MacArthur's play, *Jumbo*
1964   CIRCUS WORLD (Henry Hathaway) co-screenplay
1967   CASINO ROYALE (John Huston, Ken Hughes, Val Guest,
      Robert Parrish, and Joseph McGrath) co-screenplay (uncred-
      ited)
1969   GAILY, GAILY (Norman Jewison) from his novel

Ben Hecht *was* the Hollywood screenwriter. Nearly every facet of that talented and haunted breed—from the street-corner wit and inexhaustible articulateness to the sense of compromise and feelings of artistic frustration—can be found in Hecht's dazzlingly contradictory career. Indeed, it can be said without too much exaggeration that Hecht personifies Hollywood itself: a jumble of talent, cynical and overpaid; most successful when he was least ambitious; often failing when he mistook sentimentality for seriousness, racy, superficial, vital, and *American*.

The Hecht legend assures that any attempt at a comprehensive filmography will be both incomplete and overly generous. That Hecht worked uncredited on many films is unquestioned; that he left many other projects to be developed by members of the "School of Hecht" is just as certain. What is difficult to ascertain with most screenwriters—and is especially maddening in Hecht's case—is the size of the writer's contribution to any particular film. The filmography included here (compiled by Steven Fuller with the cooperation of Rose Caylor Hecht) credits Hecht with just about every entertaining movie in the Hollywood sound era. This would tally with Pauline Kael's assertion that, between them, Hecht and Jules Furthman wrote most of the best American talkies. But objections raised by Gary Carey (that *Gone With the Wind* virtually reproduced Margaret Mitchell's dialogue verbatim), Arthur Laurents (that, on *Rope,* Hecht "wasn't responsible for one word of the screenplay used"), and others suggest that Hecht's influence on some of the uncredited scripts, at least, was marginal.

The most accurate filmography is at best a map that helps film archaeologists unearth the secrets of a filmmaker's career. Hecht's movie career may be defined by about twenty credited screenplays he wrote for Hawks, Hitchcock, Hathaway, Lubitsch, Wellman, Sternberg, and himself. Any further consideration of his career— with all its omissions and disputed claims, still one of Hollywood's most remarkable—must await the solution to two mysteries: What films did he substantially write, and what were the roles of his regular collaborators? For, just as Hecht is too often ignored in discussions of Hawks or Hitchcock, so are Charles MacArthur, Charles Lederer and Gene Fowler forgotten on those rare occasions when Hecht's work is seriously appraised.

Underworld (1927) and Scarface (1932)

These two films act effectively as the alpha and omega of Hollywood's first gangster craze. Underworld romanticized the criminal with Sternbergian soft-focus and what Hecht himself called "moody Sandburgian sentences"; by the end of the film its hero, Bull Weed, has acquired enough rudimentary moral sense to surrender himself to the police and leave his leading lady in the care of a friend who is star-billed two notches below him. Tony Camonte of Scarface is less sympathetic but more pitiable; the oblique angles and marshmallow edges have given way to a brittle, eye-level, unflinching mise-en-scène, and the script indicts not only the mobster but also his cynical accomplices in the big-city pressrooms. Like so many of his films, Underworld and Scarface are "stories" that ace-reporter Hecht loved to cover, as much for the larger-than-life qualities of his headliners as for the enormity of their crimes. Love-hate . . . fascination-revulsion . . . exposé-glorification . . . these are the polarities that make Hecht's best films deliciously ambiguous. But it is his crisp, frenetic, sensational prose and dialogue style that elevates his work above that of the dozens of other reporters who streamed west to cover and exploit Hollywood's biggest "story": the talkie revolution.

Despite the differences in visual and thematic mood, Underworld and Scarface share that disturbing Hechtian combination of penny-ante cynicism and the tendency to place his "realistic" characters within the brackets of a romantic cultural reference. Hecht has written that he envisioned Tony Camonte and his sister Cesca as Prohibition-Era equivalents of Cesare and Lucrezia Borgia, though the film never makes this analogy explicit. And in *Underworld* the following conversation takes place between Bull Weed and his refined friend, Rolls Royce:

> ROLLS ROYCE: [You're] Attila, the Hun, at the gates of Rome.
> BULL WEED: Who's Attila? The leader of some wop gang?
> ROLLS ROYCE: You were born two thousand years too late.

But Hecht gives his mobsters even more distinct antecedents. The title *Underworld* suggests rivers of blood and death, while adding a soupçon of mythological elegance to the film. Hecht's introduction, which is nothing if not moody and Sandburgian, describes "A great city in the dead of night—streets lonely, moon-flooded—buildings empty as the cliff-dwellings of a forgotten age." Pluto keeps a watchful eye on the Underworld's denizens; the "upper world," about which Hecht would later write, rarely intrudes. The rival gang lords are known only as "Bull" and "Buck"—Taurus and Aries, a fatal conjunction.

Tony Camonte is more animal than human, an ape man. He possesses the instinct to survive, which expresses itself in the reflex to kill. And yet even Tony has intellectual pretensions, although they function merely as embellishments to his atrocities, as a curlicue windup to a ferocious flourish of bullets. Tony has to leave a performance of *Rain* after the second act to gun down a rival; his "secretary" stays behind to find out how the play ended (he reports that Sadie "climbed back in the hay with the army"). And his signature tune is the sextet from *Lucia di Lammermoor, "Chi mi frena in tal momento?"* ("What restrains me in such a moment?"). Obviously, nothing restrains, let alone soothes, this savage breast in such a moment. Carnage and culture go hand in hand.

The most noticeable link between the two films—which also suggests a link between Hecht and Howard Hawks, his collaborator on at least eight films—is the neon sign that blinks on and off in the Chicago night. In *Underworld* it reads:

THE CITY IS YOURS
A.B.C. INVESTMENT CO.

In *Scarface* the message is subtly altered and enriched:

THE WORLD IS YOURS
COOK'S TOURS

Bull Weed's sign evokes the cautious megalomania of a fairly benign gangster who "invests" in people the way a flamboyant broker might gamble on an erratic stock. Hecht's respect for the professional, whose knowledge of his "territory" includes an awareness of its boundaries, is significantly close to Hawks's preference for a man who knows his job and does it, with maximum efficiency and minimum fuss. Indeed, the disinterested critic may wonder whether the Hawksian chicken actually preceded the Hechtian egg.

What is more likely is that this pair of supreme technicians— Hecht the wordsmith and Hawks the engineer—shared the masculine ethic that auteur critics have labeled "Hawksian." The difference between a Hawks film written by Hecht and a Hawks film by some other writer is usually the difference between the cynical side of Hawks's outlook (*Scarface, The Twentieth Century, His Girl Friday, Monkey Business*) and the noble, elegiac aspect (many of which were written by Jules Furthman). The three Hecht-Hawks films discussed in Robin Wood's book on Hawks are all grouped under the title, "The Lure of Irresponsibility"—an ideal subtitle for a book on Hecht.

Ultimately, Bull Weed resists this lure, while Tony falls victim to it. Again, responsibility means in large part knowing your place: Bull knows his (THE CITY); Tony doesn't know his. The second line of Hecht's neon fortune cookie—COOK'S TOURS—is the one Tony ignores at his peril. The world is yours, it implies, but only to travel through. Tony's ambition is based on his belief in machines, specifically the Thompson submachine gun. His downfall is announced by the breaking down of a machine: "I got nobody!" he cries. "I'm all alone, Li'l Boy's gone, Angelo's gone—my steel shutters don't work. . . ." (Ambition and the loss of another Little Boy would defeat Preston Sturges's tycoon Tom Garner a year later in *The Power and the Glory*.) Bull Weed is also trapped, by the police, with the girl whom he loves but who loves another. His steel doors jam, too. And yet Bull is saved by his feeling for the girl. Tony's "girl" was his sister, toward whom he was less wisely protective than wildly possessive. In demanding exclusive rights to her love he sealed her doom, for she is killed by the police in Tony's porous hideout. Bull generously surrenders his girl Feathers to Rolls Royce once he becomes convinced of his friend's loyalty.

And here we find another thematic thread shared by Hecht and Hawks: what Andrew Sarris has identified in Hawks films as "the love story between two men." In his autobiography, *A Child of the Century,* Hecht even wrote about "Why Men Like Each Other"— and, in a few hundred words, reduced the Hawksian ethic to its essentials.

> No matter how close I have been to a man I have never made a a jackass of myself over him, which is to say a poet or a fantast. . . . In loving a man, one does not have to contort oneself into a hundred pretenses of devotion and fidelity in order to wrest a cry of ardor from his lips; not unless one is looking for ardor. I have loved men for their looks, their talents, their spiced personalities, their gallantry, their verbal style, but never because I needed them.
>
> And I have never felt jealousy toward a man. As a result, I have never been cruel, mean, dishonest or vengeful to males, nor have I ever uttered an hysterical word in a man's presence. No wonder men like each other and swear by each other as nobler animals. They see only each other's best sides. . . .
>
> These are the secrets of the charm men can have for each other—a sort of love without pain or anger. Friendship between men is a goad to their gallantry, a stimulation of their virtues and seldom a locked-horns conflict of their insecurities. . . .
>
> Of the things men give each other the greatest is loyalty.

The vital dramatic question in *Underworld* is not whether or not Bull will be killed, but whether he'll die thinking Rolls Royce is a traitor—loyalty over life. The two are reconciled, and comradeship saves Bull's soul (if not his life) by shielding him from the isolation that drives Tony insane. Cesca's dying condemnation of Tony as weak—because he killed her lover, who was Tony's best friend— leaves the gangster alone and seals his spiritual doom.

The Rolls Royce was (until recently) a machine that signified not only opulence, but a craftsmanship approaching artistry—qualities that define Hecht and Hawks as well as Hecht's *Underworld* co-star. Unlike Machine-Gun, Steel-Shuttered Tony, Rolls Royce will not break down. Even when he is discovered, early in the film, as a bum, Rolls Royce as played by Clive Brook possesses all the unshaven aristocracy of a Jean Gabin, whom Brook resembles. (Bull saves him from humiliation at the hands of Buck Mulligan in a situation that Furthman and Hawks duplicated almost exactly in *Rio Bravo:* Buck throws a wad of money into a spittoon for Rolls to retrieve.) Rolls Royce's nobility is such that, in winning Feathers' love, he refines her morals to the extent that she cannot leave Bull, because "you taught me to be decent." Though Bull "leaves" her at the end, we feel that Feathers will think of Rolls as a custodian of Bull's affection, and that Rolls will respect her new-found decency at arm's-length.

Rolls Royce has become the humane professional in Bull's image, the man who knows when he has enough. Tony Camonte's first boss, Louie Costillo, delivers a short homily on this topic: "A man-a always gotta know when he's gotta enough. I gotta plenty. I got-a house—I got-a automobile—I got-a nice girl—[Belches] I got-a stomach trouble, too." Bootlegging is a business, and an ulcer is the universal badge of the successful businessman. But Louie signs his own death warrant when he refuses to take his own advice: "Gonna have-a much more music—a-much more girls—a-much more everything—Everybody she say, 'Ah, Big Louie [Laugh], he sit on top of the world, eh?'" As with Cody Jarrett in White Heat, the top of the world for a gangster is only a great height to fall from.

Hecht manages both to congratulate journalism for its importance and to chastise it for its chicanery, by underlining the newspapers' complicity in promoting the underworld image. "It's gonna be just like war!" a Walter Howie-type editor exults when he hears of Louie Costillo's abrupt demise. "That's it! War! You put that in the lead. 'WAR—GANG WAR!'" In Underworld the newspapers fuel Bull's jealousy by misreporting Feathers' fondness for Rolls Royce. In Scarface Tony comes on like the Dean of the Columbia School of Journalism when he proclaims that "The News has got-a best story. Pictures of you—and one of me, too." Does Tony kill, in part, to get famous, to get in the papers?

Scarface's all-but-suffocating vitality is a kind of cinematic version of tabloid prose at its best, so it's cheekily appropriate that two legendary newspapermen—Hecht's first boss, Duffy, whom he immortalized in The Front Page, and a certain "MacArthur, from The Journal"—make unexpected but not unwelcome cameo bows. This subplot culminates in a ludicrous inserted scene that begins with a charge of reportorial culpability and ends with a brazen call to action. Hecht must have known this scene offered little more than popcorn time for the Scarface audience; people read the front page, not the editorials. In this context, Underworld was a prose poem masquerading as an editorial, while Scarface was a brutal comic strip in the form of a 90-point headline.

Design for Living (1933)

In Noël Coward's 1932 play, Leo the successful writer is asked by a reporter if he thinks the talkies will kill the theater. "No," he replies, "I think they'll kill the talkies." This is Coward's typically oblique, superficially bantering warning—which, in *Design for Living*'s original production, he delivered as well as wrote—to a Hollywood voracious for his talky, actable plays. Of the three Coward plays filmed in 1933 alone, only *Cavalcade*, which lent itself superbly to Babylonian elephantiasis and thus won the year's Oscar for Best Picture, was a hit. Herbert Wilcox's production of *Bitter Sweet* proved too tart for moviegoers' tastes, and the Ben Hecht–Ernst Lubitsch remodeling of *Design for Living* merely proved that there were occasions when even Lubitsch should have known to leave well enough alone.

It's one thing to buy the rights to Hungarian plays by such as Laszlo Aladar and Nikolaus Laszlo, to tell Samson Raphaelson to throw away the scripts and write new ones, and to come up with *Trouble in Paradise* and *The Shop Around the Corner*. It's quite another to let Coward's remarkable juggling act of three blessedly ballsy bohemians fall into the comparatively calloused hands of Ben Hecht. The story is that Lubitsch wanted to retain only the name, and have Hecht write a new scenario. Lubitsch should have resisted the impulse to exploit the Coward title, and instead commissioned an entirely different work from Hecht; for the film version of *Design for Living* is not only bad Coward, it is even bad Hecht—and, as a result, bad Lubitsch.

The three "elements" in Coward's play are literally that: mercury (writer Leo Mercuré), silver (painter Otto Sylvus), and gold (their mistress Gilda). Though the two men are often considered interchangeable, Leo is certainly the slipperier, the moodier, the one with a lower moral weight. Otto's character is summarized by Webster's New World Dictionary definition of silver: "extremely ductile and malleable, capable of a high polish, and an excellent conductor of heat and electricity." Gilda, the precious fulcrum keeping these two variable, vulnerable elements in balance, also bears the responsibility for keeping Coward's eccentric plot in motion and on course. Gilda is an interior decorator—an apt metaphor for her role as spiritual patroness of two sloppy but comfortable male souls—and the settings of the play reflect her evolving state of mind as well as her progressively more chic professional style. Otto's "shabby studio in Paris" (the setting for Act I) reverberates with the most carefree kind of *la vie de bohème,* if also a life that is made more exhilarating by the careerist ambitions of the studio's inhabitants. Act II takes place in Leo's "very comfortably furnished" London flat; Leo's play is successful and Gilda's spirit is restless. By the beginning of Act III Gilda has married Ernest, the ménage's conservative confidant, and moved into his "luxuriously furnished . . . penthouse in New York," from the genteel conformity of which Leo and Otto finally extricate her.

The play's situation, its problem and its resolution are set down in Leo's early speech to Gilda: "The actual facts are so simple. I love you. You love me. You love Otto. I love Otto. Otto loves you. Otto loves me. There now! Start to unravel from there." When Gilda, who has been first Otto's and then Leo's paramour, finds herself in the "degrading" position of being morally indecisive about sleeping with Otto again, Otto retorts: "Our lives are diametrically opposed to ordinary social conventions; and it's no use grabbing at those conventions to hold us up when we find we're in deep water. We've jilted them and eliminated them, and we've got to find our own solutions for our own peculiar moral problems."

Coward's resolution is no solution, however; his denouement refuses to unravel. Leo and Otto save Gilda from Ernest, but their own peculiar moral problem is as perplexing as ever: How can Gilda retain the friendship of the man she happens *not* to be sleeping with? Like its appealing characters, Coward's extraordinarily well-made play is conventional at heart, sympathizing with if not absolving the trio with that hoariest of curtain lines, the convulsive explosion of laughter (a climax that has served such ambivalent movies as *The Treasure of the Sierra Madre, Five Fingers,* and *Le Souffle au Coeur*). In the case of *Design for Living,* the theatrical mechanism that triggers this explosion finds its echo in an earlier situation that, as Gilda explains it, "made a picture, you see—an unbearably comic picture—we were both terribly strained and unhappy; our nerves were stretched like elastic, and that snapped it." So the play doesn't really end. It just breaks up, with its heroes, and thus breaks down.

As is well known, Coward wrote *Design for Living* for Alfred Lunt, Lynn Fontanne, and himself. Whether intentionally or not, he generously gave the Lunts the best lines. Moreover, though the play is hardly a biographical sketch of the three, Coward created Otto and Gilda (the Lunts) as a virtually married couple—quite liberal, to be sure—whose invisible ties are stretched "like elastic" but not snapped by their bizarre friendship with Leo. One can assume, without too much stretching of one's own, that at play's end Gilda will return to Otto, her original bed partner, and Leo will bear up manfully. (The same impression is conveyed by the recent revival of the play starring Robert Stephens and Maggie Smith, the Lunts of the seventies, in the Lunts' parts.) One can also assume that Coward intended the play that makes Leo a success—*Change and Decay*—as a humorous equivalent to *Design for Living*. As Gilda describes it, "Three scenes are first-rate, especially the last act. The beginning of the second act drags a bit, and most of the first act's too facile—you know what I mean—he flips along with easy swift dialogue, but doesn't go deep enough." This was the received intellectual consensus of Coward's work, and though it's much too facile a judgment itself, it may have encouraged Hecht to uncage his own talent for "easy swift dialogue" of a more intense, ultimately laborious and moralizing kind.

Hecht did follow the play's basic plot line, and even traced Gilda's journey westward from Paris to New York. But the psychological and moral coordinates are missing. Hecht took the play's verbal sophistication, which Coward meticulously traced in a parabola from Paris (rising) to London (its apogee) to New York (decadent), and reduced it to the snappy patter of his own bourgeois bohemia, the energetic pressrooms of Jazz Age Chicago. Vladimir Nabokov's observation that "nothing is more exhilarating than Philistine vulgarity" applies perfectly to the most vigorous, most indigenous American movies, from Mack Sennett's early slapstick to Russ Meyer's late sexploiters; and the phrase rings especially true when applied to the Hecht of *The Front Page, Scarface,* and *Crime Without Passion.* Hecht in the raw—the cynical, dishonest, sentimental reporter-writer—is Hecht at his best. He's disappointing only when he strains to be lofty (*A Farewell to Arms*) or classical (*Wuthering Heights*) or outrageous (*Nothing Sacred*), when he speaks in a voice other than his own.

Hecht's idea of Cowardly sophistication is to throw a "rather" into a line like "I'm afraid you've behaved like a rather common, ordinary rat." The closest he comes to Coward's epigrammatic elegance is "Delicacy, as the philosophers point out, is the banana peel under the feet of truth." As for flaunting the Hollywood Production

Code's prissy standards, a phrase such as "sitting on Lady Godiva's historical background" now seems more risky than risqué. And his attempt at mimicking Coward's genial devastation of carping reviewers is a paltry "I hate stupidity masquerading as criticism"—which sets him up for critics who may well hate banality masquerading as wit.

Unfortunately, Fredric March (in the Leo role, but called Tom) and Gary Cooper (in the Otto role, but called George) are the perfect personifications of Hecht's leaden heroes. They deliver their lines, which are impeccably free of subtlety to begin with, in cadences and tones just as impeccably free of nuance. They are really old-time newspapermen pretending to be continentals, and in this sense Hecht's *Design for Living* trio can be seen as himself (Leo), Charles MacArthur (Otto), and MacArthur's wife, Helen Hayes (Gilda)—a triangle that sounds far more intriguing than the Cooper–March–Miriam Hopkins group.

Only Hopkins, a comedienne as brilliant in the early thirties as she was neglected before her death, conveys the charm, vitality and drive of the original. Significantly, though Gilda's vocation has been degraded from interior decorating to commercial illustrating (placing her in the hands of boring capitalists from the word go), her character underwent the fewest changes. In one intense speech, she comes across as both Earth Mother and Red Hot Mamma. "Let's forget about sex," she says to March, who is suffering from the kind of writer's block that never affected Hecht. "I'm gonna tell you how bad your work is until you do something good, and then I'm gonna tell you it's rotten until you do better. I'll be a mother of the arts." They kiss, twice. She shakes her head. "No sex." And she even sparks a moribund March to life in a nicely written scene that takes place, over March's neglected typewriter, upon his return to the flat she now shares with Cooper.

> MARCH: You didn't keep it oiled.
> HOPKINS: I did, for a while.
> MARCH: The keys are rusty—shift is broken—
> (*He pushes down a few keys. The "return bell rings.*)
> HOPKINS: But it still rings! It still rings!
> (*They stand facing each other, their hips touching.*)
> MARCH: Does it?

Coward's play is really an ode to star quality. The three unprincipled principals have it, and their "time-honoured" friend Ernest doesn't. But Edward Everett Horton, for whom Hecht wrote an unrewarding fourth-wheel part, has a movie presence here that Cooper and March sadly lack, making his role often more sympathetic than theirs. If the play had had a slightly different focus, it could have been called "The Impotence of Being Ernest." Coward's Ernest is likable, generous, even witty when forced. Hecht developed the role's pomposity at the expense of its pathos, and turned a tolerant (if bewildered) gentleman into an old prune. "Immorality may be fun," he is made to say, "but it isn't fun enough to take the place of one hundred percent virtue and three square meals a day." It is against this grain that Horton constructs an intermittently *understandable* character. And when Horton (who in the movie is called Max) is finally alone with Gilda in their bridal suite, and says, "Now that it's all over—the excitement, et cetera—I'd like to know: do you love me?" he almost *is* lovable. Gilda's response is unusually gentle, for her and for Hecht: "People should never ask that question on their wedding night. It's either too late or too early. I'm your wife, Max."

Hecht obviously wasn't satisfied with the mellowness of this sexual compromise, so he sent Cooper and March in to liberate Gilda in their own stifling fashion. In the original, Leo and Otto played a mild variation of Get the Guests, shocking Gilda's wealthy New York friends with some deft, fey repartee. Hecht's vision of Manhattan society is peopled with oafish millionaires who play Twenty Questions, and who need a put-down that approaches psychodrama in its abrasive violence. Cooper wins Gilda back, even as he will win Jean Arthur's love three years later in *Mr. Deeds*, with "a sock in the jaw" of a few fall-guy businessmen. It is ultimately a punch directed at that smug, effete limey—Noël Coward —but its effect is to knock any favorable reaction out of the audience, and to boomerang back, demolishing the film.

Nothing Sacred (1937)

Nothing Sacred belongs in the company of *Theodora Goes Wild, The Awful Truth, His Girl Friday,* and a handful of other Hollywood pictures that gave the industry's big-city screenwriters a chance to vent their cynicism about the prevailing rural-American dream. What Hecht didn't put into his script, which has a girl preferring death by radium poisoning in New York to life in a moribund Vermont village, director William Wellman added in the *mise-en-scène*: the town's stationmaster drops a visiting reporter's fifty-cent piece, to test if it's real; a group of local children stone the reporter from the back of a covered wagon; another little blond-haired boy rushes out from behind a picket fence and *bites* him in the back of the leg. This is a small town filled with Transylvanian tightwads who treat the reporter as both vampire and victim; and Hecht and Wellman have a good time arguing that rural virtues evaporate when an intruder pricks the placenta.

But Hecht has not set the small town up as some small-minded villain, the better to celebrate the excitement and extravagance of the city. His prologue makes that clear, in its description of a New York "where the slickers and know-it-alls peddle gold bricks to each other—and where Truth, crushed to earth, rises again more phony than a glass eye. . . ." Later in the film Wallace Cook, star reporter for *The Morning Star,* looks at a pair of wrestlers and declares: "They're a symbol of the whole town, pretending to fight, love, weep and laugh all the time—and they're phonies, all of them. And I head the list." The small town, personified by Hazel Flagg and her Doctor Downer, who parlay a false report of radium poisoning into a grand tour of Manhattan, is as phony as the Big City, personified by Cook and Oliver Stone, the newspapermen who give their dear readers "a chance to pretend their phony hearts were dripping with the milk of human kindness." For once, Hecht's cynicism was undiluted by a conventional nod to the heroine—or even to the happy ending. The script, which he wrote "in two weeks . . . on trains between New York and Hollywood," was evidently delivered to David O. Selznick, and Hecht had returned to Nyack before the producer discovered that Hecht had tacked on a facetious and wholly unsatisfactory ending. Hecht had retained his artistic integrity by displaying his usual disinclination to finish anything he started.

Though *Nothing Sacred* is probably the definitive Hecht newspaper picture (fewer hands intervened here between him and the finished product than on *Underworld, The Front Page, Scarface,* or *His Girl Friday*), it's not one of his best. The Walter Howie-type managing editor, who is "sort of a cross between a ferris wheel and a werewolf—but with a lovable streak, if you care to blast for it," and the Hechtian ace reporter himself are written with the author's customarily sneaky admiration, but they aren't played (by Walter

Connolly and Fredric March, respectively) with anything like the manic energy needed to bring these snarling dervishes to life. March in particular is so much the gentleman—changing Hecht's "pretty kid" to "pretty girl," and refining "ain'ts" into " 'tisn'ts," and at other times treating Hecht's zippy dialogue with a ponderous respect more suitable to Tolstoy or O'Neill—that the moxie of a scoop-hungry reporter degenerates into sullen, maladroit winsomeness. March has always possessed the vegetable magnetism of Hubert Humphrey crossed with Merv Griffin; what he does not have, and what is needed when toiling in the Hechtian underworld of press lords and prostitutes, is a little of the "coarseness or aggression" Pauline Kael identifies as being "so essential for an actor's sex appeal." In a Hecht role, good manners usually means bad acting. Instead of fulfilling the script's vision of Cook as the vibrant, immoral center of an irresistibly heartless milieu, March plays the reporter as a wounded faun, a klutz, a Ralph Bellamy!

Carole Lombard (as Hazel Flagg) and Charles Winninger (Dr. Downer), in providing some of the zest that March and Connolly lack, throw the film off balance; it seems perversely weighted in favor of the small-town shysters—at least *they* have style. There's a moment when a furious Winninger slams his office door shut after a departing Cook. It snaps back at him. He slams it again. It comes back again. He kicks it vengefully. Back it comes. He starts at it, then snaps his fingers at it, as if to say "So much for *you!*" and walks off-screen. This is intuitive acting—or reacting—of a resourcefulness beyond March's Broadway gentility. Like the moment later on when Maxie Rosenbloom casually folds back a cauliflower ear so it will fit around a telephone receiver, Winninger's gesture is one that economically defines a character instead of grammatically declining it, as March does.

Maybe Lombard didn't need to be aggressive *and* coarse because back in the thirties, aggressiveness in a woman was considered coarse. Whatever the reason, the combination of the plot's iconoclastic stance and the players' iconographic imbalance gives Lombard the propulsive force usually lavished on the leading male character, as well as the complimentary camera angles customarily lavished on the female star—leaving March in the shadows, thematically and visually. Given the opportunity, Lombard makes the best of such props as an oversized slicker and fireman's hat, which turn her into a little girl in daddy's coat even as they invest her with the

uniform of a dominant male. And the rib-shattering way she em-
braces big-city corruption makes her the perfect object for New
York's evanescent, spurious sentimentality.

The city seems unconsciously to sense the phoniness of both her
plight and its own warm-hearted response. HAZEL FLAGG LUNCHED
HERE, reads the sign in a delicatessen, and underneath: CHEESE &
BOLOGNA OUR SPECIALTY. A newspaper headline blares: HAZEL
SETS NEW HIGH POINT IN COURAGE, and we see a construction worker
read this, sitting nonchalantly on the steel beam of a skyscraper
skeleton high atop Hecht's "Niagara of stone and steel pouring out
of tomorrow." Another Hazel Flagg headline is used as the wrapper
for a particularly grotesque-looking fish. Two wrestlers pause in
their simulated carnage as the Madison Square Garden announcer
asks the crowd to "observe ten seconds of silence for Miss Flagg"—
and the knockdown bell peals ten mournful times.

Ultimately the dollops of cynicism, spread over every plot twist
and line of dialogue, every major character and bit player, thin
out; and the devices with which Hecht tries to shock us become as
tiresome as those he will use to uplift us, two years later, in his and
MacArthur's "respectful" adaptation of *Wuthering Heights*. His
viewpoint turns from brutal purgation to captious cruelty, and we
are left with an uncharacteristically Olympian disinterest on the
part of a screenwriter-reporter who was usually happy—and honest
—enough to implicate himself in the cheerful venality of his news-
worthy protagonists.

Angels Over Broadway (1940)

One argument against the idea of the screenwriter as author is
that the film script—the writer's creation—is a mere halfway house
between original idea and final image; that the moviegoer responds
to the parade of light and shadow, to the moving picture itself, and
not to the word a screenwriter has typed out as suggested notes
which the director may consult or ignore as he sees fit. Of course,
the same objection applies to the preservation and reading of play
scripts or sonata scores: a drama achieves its final, completed form
only when performed, a musical composition when it is played, and
a film when it is shot, cut, and released. And yet, not only have we
continued to "read" Shakespeare and (especially before the advent
of the phonograph) Beethoven, but we consider them, and not their

interpretive performers, the authors of their work—while a screen-play such as Ben Hecht's *Angels Over Broadway* is still thought of less as an art form than as an embryonic form of the final film. As Arthur Barron has said of *Citizen Kane:* "The script is marble, and the film is David, and Welles is Michelangelo."

Much of this mystical nonsense is rooted in the simple, madden-ing unavailability of film scripts. The production of a play dies on closing night, its ghost haunting the precarious memories of a few theatergoers. But a "film" is what we see at the local Bijou, or in a museum auditorium, or on television; we think of it as what is printed on film, not on paper. Fewer than one hundred American screenplays have been published, many of these being films of marginal scholarly interest, to say the least. (The admirable efforts of John Gassner in the forties were easily extinguished by a combi-nation of studio resistance and publishers' indifference.) As a result, there is very little source material to study, and researchers must make do with the same scribbled notes and fallible memories used by those who would reconstruct a play production. Film students may be forgiven for thinking that, because there are so few scripts available, the rest simply aren't worth considering.

Some important screenplays have found their way into public libraries—the Museum of Modern Art has about five hundred, Lin-coln Center's Library and Museum of the Performing Arts Theater Collection a thousand—and there the screenwriter freak can dis-cover, to his surprise, not only that many scripts include minute camera directions which a viewing of the films reveal to have been explicitly followed, but that some scripts actually read better than they play. *Angels Over Broadway* is one of these screenplays. (Other examples in this collection are *Ball of Fire, My Man Godfrey,* and *The Fortune Cookie.*) The dialogues as well as the script's descrip-tive passages are chock full of brittle Hechtian similes that sparkle on the page but turn leaden when delivered. Hecht was an endlessly articulate raconteur. In his novels and memoirs, articulation dom-inates; but in the films he directed and wrote, "endless" is the opera-tive word.

While this makes for sporadically tedious moviegoing, it guar-antees superb reading—if one knows how to read a script, a task less thankless or demanding than it may seem at first. A screenplay combines the authoritative terseness of a blueprint with the tradi-tional dialogue-style of a play script, but it's probably best to aproach it more as a novel in skeletal form. As we read a novel, we unavoidably make our own mental movie adaptation. We cast the characters, give importance to certain scenes by slowing down our reading pace, choose the sets (from some remembered home or guided tour) and even call the shots—which are usually close-ups, for descriptive detail and emphasis of dialogue. This process holds for reading a script, especially one, like *Angels Over Broadway*, with such voluptuous verbal character sketches.

The average reader of *Angels Over Broadway* is likely to have a surer sense of pace, a fresher "staging" of the acting and action, than Hecht did when he transferred his words to the screen. This doesn't mean that a script reads well *only* when its realization is unsuccessful; *Casablanca, Mr. Smith Goes to Washington, Ninotchka,* and *Citizen Kane* satisfy both as screenplays and as films. The "making" of a film script—the direction—is not a mystical process, but it *is* mysterious, and any man who can be simultaneously a dreamer and a lion tamer, a painter and a field marshal—in sum, a director—deserves as much respect as the creative screenwriter. He simply should not receive deification at his collaborator's expense.

Two members of the quartet in *Angels Over Broadway* are, like Hecht, addicted to talk. The hero, a two-bit, would-be gangster named Bill O'Brien, is really a Richard II of the Manhattan demi-monde, searching for the perfect metaphor for rain while his life drains away—like those dirty raindrops trickling into the sewer. (Hecht's prose style, while inimitable, is contagious.) "That's the way the horses run in the home stretch," he muses as the raindrops fall. "They look like arrowheads. No, more like dice rolling." O'Brien describes playwright Gene Gibbons, his cohort in volubility, as, "three years ago, the white hope of the theatre. Today, a mug. That's New York for you. Puts you on a Christmas tree, and then—the alley." Gibbons (an amalgam of Herman J. Mankiewicz's spirit and Eugene O'Neill's reputation) calls himself "one who has destroyed himself a score of times . . . a veteran corpse . . . an epitaph over an ashcan." Or, as Hecht puts it in the script: "Gibbons is a man full of pain and violence. On this night, there is a Witch's Sabbath in his heart. Storms are blowing his world to bits and great troubles are pounding him on a reef." On paper it is obvious that Hecht saw these two as a misguided knight errant and a silver-tongued jongleur; on film, as personified by Douglas Fairbanks, Jr. and Thomas Mitchell, they come across almost as the seedy hustler and the boozy failure the prosaic world takes them for.

Nina Barone is the heroine. The script tells us: "She has danced in a chorus, clerked at Macy's, been a sweetie. She is in the last line of moths fluttering around the city's lights . . . a girl who knows her place, who knows there is little to expect, and who is always ready to smile." All of Hecht's affection for New York's hard-luck girls, from Molly Malloy of *The Front Page* to Margo of *Crime Without Passion,* went into this passage. But the only way Hecht could make a character eloquent was to make him loquacious; and since Nina isn't as quick with similes as she is with smiles, her individuality keeps receding even as her function in the film's plot becomes more clumsily evident. (And this was the young Rita Hayworth!) As for Charles Engle, the suicidal box manufacturer around whom these three tarnished Broadway angels gather, first to sucker and then to save, he is so indistinct—perhaps "ill-defined" is more apt—that Hecht doesn't even bother to describe him. Thus, John Qualen, who was memorable in so many small parts (including Hecht's *Upper World, Nothing Sacred,* and *His Girl Friday*), is utterly forgettable in one of his few leading roles.

Hecht's photographer and co-director (either officially or actually) on *Crime Without Passion, Once in a Blue Moon, The Scoundrel, Angels Over Broadway, Specter of the Rose,* and *Actors and Sin* was the brilliant cinematographer Lee Garmes. All of the Hecht-Garmes collaborations are moody and oppressive, looking as if they were lit with a couple of flashlight batteries. In Hecht's script for *Angels Over Broadway,* and in Garmes' lighting, the two experimented with "reflections of life—as if a ghost were drifting in the rain." These "reflections" of sidewalks, bridges, glass, and neon make the film a visual prototype of the forties *film noir*; thematically, though characters are indeed looking for solutions to dilemmas from their troubled pasts, *Angels Over Broadway* is a recapitulation of the familiar Hecht terrain. As the only film he directed, produced, and wrote originally for the screen, *Angels Over Broadway* can't help but be one of his most personal works. It is only the perversity of a collaborative medium that makes it also one of his most frustrating, for its ideal form is as a screenplay. It offers the screenwriter critic a rare chance to suggest that students of Hecht "read the script, don't see the movie."

Miracle in the Rain (1956)

The Hechtian blend of lighthearted cynicism and unregenerate sentimentality is here attached to a fragile story of wartime romance in New York rather like that of *The Clock,* the 1945 film directed by Vincente Minnelli—except that the Hecht novel on which he based his screenplay was written two years before *The Clock* was released. *The Clock* was a fantasy set in the realistic mode: a soldier and a working girl meet, fall in love, and get married, all within three days and with the help of every New Yorker they stumble across, from milkman to marriage-license clerk. Hecht is as sentimental as Minnelli and *his* writers were romantic, but he knows enough about The City to make any story about the natural generosity of New Yorkers into a fairy story—or, in this case, a miracle play.

It's impossible for anyone who didn't live through World War II in New York to know if the natives did indeed display the courtesy that seemed so freakish during the 1965 blackout; the tendency is to favor the pessimistic vision of *Little Murders* over the optimistic one of *The Clock* and *Miracle in the Rain.* But whatever the reality, New York's benevolence to soldiers in wartime is undiminished (if not entirely untarnished) a decade after *The Clock,* even as filtered through the tougher sensibilities of the fifties and Ben Hecht. Maître d's seat Van Johnson and Jane Wyman without reservations, waiters treat them to expensive hors d'oeuvres, priests in St. Patrick's let Jane Wyman light votive candles for free, and Jane can put her nose to the Central Park ground and say, "Isn't it wonderful the way the grass smells?" (Perhaps, three decades ago, even dog owners had a sense of community pride.) Van Johnson makes a little speech about lovers in the city, the theme of which is: "Walking in the Park is an act of Faith"—a demonstration of how the creamy, dreamy idealism of one generation can become the nightmare reality of the next.

But there are differences. Hecht's dreams are much closer to the asphalt surface, his sleep less sound, than Minnelli's—perhaps because, though both worked in New York, Hecht was a newspaperman and playwright, while Minnelli confected set designs for Radio City Music Hall. Thus, one finds Negroes and Jews in Hecht's fantasy. The Negro is a doorman, sad and stoop-shouldered; and the camera lingers on this bit player, in life and in the film, just long enough to impress us with his insignificance in both. The Jews are Alan King and Barbara Nichols as a honeymoon couple; nothing sinister, mind you, but vulgar in an off-putting way. Further, Jane Wyman's mother has attempted suicide because her husband deserted her. And an obstreperous neighbor makes a remark that sounds more like a cliché of Bronxian fatalism than the premonition it turns out to be: "You're such a nice boy," she tells Van Johnson. "What do you want to go off and get killed in the War for?"

So the "miracle" of the title refers as much to New Yorkers' selflessness as it does to the lovers' first and last meetings. Johnson and Wyman are introduced in what is possibly the shoddiest example of "meeting cute" in the annals of American romance: he simply starts talking, first to anyone and then to her. So much for Hecht's interest in constructing a well-made comedy. Nor does he seem to care about clever bits of business or witty dialogue. Johnson is amiable enough, and Wyman thinks he's funny because he's quick, and because his interest in her has made her happy for the first time in her life; but there's no straining for laughs, as in *The Scoundrel* (which *Miracle in the Rain* somewhat resembles, even down to the "miracle" at the end of each film).

Hecht's sentimentality is, for once, unabashed, and thus unobjectionable, but he does attempt to conceal his own feelings toward the material by putting *Miracle in the Rain* in the form of a human-interest newspaper story, just as Van Johnson does in the film. (Indeed, through some improbable convolutions, Hecht manages to maneuver his young lovers into the city room of *The New York Times*!) When Johnson leaves Jane Wyman to go to war, he promises, "I'll be back as if I never left you, and I love you as if I've always known you"—a weepie line delivered and filmed with such conviction that it comes across as one of the most honest moments in a Hecht film. Sure enough, Johnson comes back from the dead, in the rain, in front of St. Patrick's, and leaves a token of his appearance. The camera discreetly pulls back from this revelation for the obligatory long-shot fade-out—but, Hecht, always pretending to be the disinterested observer, has the last word: "Thus," Hecht's narrator states, "a story of New York and of an antique Roman coin. That's the way we heard it. We'd like to believe it's true."

As pleasant as it is, *Miracle in the Rain* hardly comprises the Author's Testament; Hecht was too much the journeyman-cynic to provide us with anything as neat as that. Late in his career, however, Hecht did offer a backhanded defense of the craft he loved and the restrictions he loathed. "It is as difficult to make a toilet seat as a castle window," he wrote in 1962, "even if the view is a bit different." During his long tenure in Hollywood, Ben Hecht made both. But at his best, he could make a porcelain privy glisten like stained glass on a sunny day.

Preston Sturges

(1898–1959)

1930   THE BIG POND (Hobart Henley) co-dialogue
       FAST AND LOOSE (Fred Newmeyer) dialogue
1931   STRICTLY DISHONORABLE (John M. Stahl) from his play
1933   CHILD OF MANHATTAN (Edward Buzzell) from his play
       THE POWER AND THE GLORY (William K. Howard) story, screenplay
1934   THIRTY DAY PRINCESS (Marion Gering) co-screenplay
       WE LIVE AGAIN (Rouben Mamoulian) co-screenplay
       IMITATION OF LIFE (John M. Stahl) co-screenplay (uncredited)
1935   THE GOOD FAIRY (William Wyler) screenplay
       DIAMOND JIM (A. Edward Sutherland) screenplay
1936   NEXT TIME WE LOVE (Edward H. Griffith) co-screenplay (uncredited)
       ONE RAINY AFTERNOON (Rowland V. Lee) lyrics
1937   HOTEL HAYWIRE (George Archainbaud) story, screenplay
       EASY LIVING (Mitchell Leisen) screenplay
1938   PORT OF SEVEN SEAS (James Whale) screenplay
       IF I WERE KING (Frank Lloyd) screenplay
1939   NEVER SAY DIE (Elliott Nugent) co-screenplay
1940   REMEMBER THE NIGHT (Mitchell Leisen) story, screenplay
       THE GREAT McGINTY (Preston Sturges) story, screenplay
       CHRISTMAS IN JULY (Preston Sturges) story, screenplay
1941   THE LADY EVE (Preston Sturges) screenplay
1942   SULLIVAN'S TRAVELS (Preston Sturges) story, screenplay
       THE PALM BEACH STORY (Preston Sturges) story, screenplay
1943   THE GREAT MOMENT (Preston Sturges) screenplay [1]

1944   THE MIRACLE OF MORGAN'S CREEK (Preston Sturges)
       story, screenplay
       HAIL THE CONQUERING HERO (Preston Sturges) story,
       screenplay
1947   I'LL BE YOURS (William A. Seiter) remake of *The Good Fairy*
       MAD WEDNESDAY [*The Sin of Harold Diddlebock*] (Preston
       Sturges) story, screenplay, producer [2]
1948   UNFAITHFULLY YOURS (Preston Sturges) story, screen-
       play, producer [2]
1949   THE BEAUTIFUL BLONDE FROM BASHFUL BEND
       (Preston Sturges) screenplay, producer
1951   STRICTLY DISHONORABLE (Melvin Frank, Norman Pan-
       ama) from his play
1956   THE BIRDS AND THE BEES (Norman Taurog) from his
       screenplay, *The Lady Eve*
1957   LES CARNETS DU MAJOR THOMPSON [*The French They
       Are a Funny Race*] (Preston Sturges) screenplay
1958   ROCK-A-BYE BABY (Frank Tashlin) remake of *The Miracle
       of Morgan's Creek*

[1] Released in 1944, after *Hail the Conquering Hero.*
[2] Released in 1950.

In the handful of screenwriters whose influence was crucial to the
craft, Preston Sturges deserves at least two fingers and a thumb. He
was Hollywood's greatest writer-director, with the emphasis on the
former. He created a racy, malapropriate idiom whose deceptive
ease would prove inimitable and, more important, a vision that was
sometimes profound, often petty, but always worthy of the term
"Sturgean." While his direction, especially of extended dialogue
scenes, shows far more control than contemporary critics were willing to grant it, Sturges's direction would be of only the most esoteric
concern today if he had not written eight or ten of Hollywood's best
screenplays; a Sturges script like *Remember the Night,* directed by
Mitchell Leisen, is certainly more personal (let alone more successful) than Sturges's direction of an unsympathetic project like *Les
Carnets du Major Thompson.* His last decade was spent in a decline
that is still only partly explicable. Perhaps his talent simply burned
out, since, for five years in the early forties, Sturges's star blazed as
brilliantly as any in Hollywood's Golden Age.

   The emphasis here is on the Sturges vision as it emanated from
his typewriter—especially since four of the ten films appraised in

this chapter were directed by others—and not on Sturges's visual style. In their *Film Culture* article, Manny Farber and W. S. Poster ("Bill Poster" sounds suspiciously like the name of some sub-Sturgean bit player, but Farber has said that Mr. Poster actually exists) so perceptively evoked the director's frenzied pace and cluttered *mise-en-scène* that further discussion of the subject may seem superfluous. Nevertheless, a few additional points might be made here.

Sturges's films fall, with surprising grace, into "light" and "dark" categories—thematically and chromatically—and this applies even when he did not direct. *Easy Living, Remember the Night, The Lady Eve, The Palm Beach Story, Hail the Conquering Hero, Mad Wednesday, The Beautiful Blonde from Bashful Bend*, and *Les Carnets du Major Thompson* all have a flat, thirties look that allows the dialogue and actors to roam authoritatively, for better or worse, through studio sets and set-ups. The memories provoked by *The Power and the Glory, Diamond Jim, Port of Seven Seas, If I Were King, The Great McGinty, Sullivan's Travels, The Miracle of Morgan's Creek*, and *Unfaithfully Yours* are shadowy, nocturnal, opaque, the mood often somber and melancholy, the theme one of loss through either aristocratic renunciation or plebian frustration. Sturges's bridge between these tonalities is *The Great Moment*—a predominantly reflective, even morose film until its sublime-ridiculous climax, in which divine approval of Dr. Morton's selflessness is signified by an abrupt flood of Kleig lights.

The temptation to construct elaborate dialectics on biographical, professional, and artistic levels seems particularly acute when critics try to deal with Sturges, so I'll stop short of developing a case for the "dark" films over the "light" ones, or even suggesting that the categories are absolute. What can be said is that the dark films are visually more interesting, beginning with *The Power and the Glory*— that startling if embryonic *film noir*—and culminating in the technically accomplished self-immolation performed by Rex Harrison (read: Sturges) in *Unfaithfully Yours*. Consciously or not, Sturges underlit Harrison's grotesqueries with such relentlessness that some of the actor's more painful pratfalls were muffled in the darkness— though Sturges made up for this generosity by dubbing in some especially unpleasant and counterproductive sound effects.

In *Unfaithfully Yours*, Sturges built audience sympathy for the lovable co-stars by shooting them in cheery close-ups that con-trasted adroitly with the medium shots he used to frame the comically astringent featured couple. No such distinction was made for the respective pairs in *The Palm Beach Story*; nor was it needed, since all four of the major characters are pretty unstable. In general, though, Sturges let any moral or thematic distinctions arise from the dialogue, and relied on what might be called "the proscenium frame" to express the author's disinterest in his puppets' manic meanderings.

Sturges's remoteness from the numbing activity of his films helps explain the failure of his endless succession of slapstick sequences. To call his attitude "classical" would be to slur genuine Hollywood classicism as exemplified by Hawks and McCarey. Sturges never had the control over a physical scene that Hawks demonstrates in, say, *His Girl Friday*. Instead, his disinterest borders on the documentary, and makes his slapstick seem crueler than it was probably intended. His shots remain as static and noncommittally medium-range as ever; even the tempo is hardly accelerated. His preoccupation with the pain in slapstick when it's attempted by the uncoordinated begins to look almost anthropological. Perhaps Sturges was just as fascinated by members of the *sucker sapiens* when they were humiliated physically as when they tripped malapropriately over the English language. In the end, Sturges's visual-physical style expressed only the perversity of his world, whereas his dialogue expressed both that world's perversity *and* its resilience.

The Power and the Glory (1933)

Sturges's first original screenplay—and the only one, except for *Hotel Haywire*, before 1940—proposes the unstartling Hollywood thesis that, as professional power increases, personal glory diminishes. What distinguishes *The Power and the Glory*, making it so relentlessly somber and, for the ultralinear thirties, virtually unique, is Sturges's "narratage" technique, a complicated series of Chinese-box-puzzle flashbacks that casts a pall of determinism over the film's early, joyous sequences. We are led back and forth over four periods of tycoon Tom Garner's life: childhood, early manhood, middle age, and the day of his death; a friend of Tom's narrates the story on the evening of his funeral.

In its present condition (the film had been lost, and was reconstructed from existing scraps into a truncated but not emasculated print), the narrative of *The Power and the Glory* can be broadly traced in the following fashion, with "A" representing childhood, "B" early manhood, "C" middle age, and "D" the day of death; "E" is the burial day.

E. Funeral, with elegy; Henry, Tom's friend, begins the narration that night, in the form of an argument with his wife over Tom's merits and faults; the action frequently returns to the present;

A(1). Henry meets Tom at a rural waterhole; they become friends;

A(2). A few years later, Tom is quiet, moody, and confesses he has no intellectual ambitions;

C(1). Tom, now president of a railroad company, bullies his board of directors into approving the purchase of another line he had actually bought ten minutes earlier;

B(1). Tom learns to read and write, to make Henry "sore"; he proposes to his teacher, Sally;

C(2). Tom meets Eve, the daughter of the president of his new subsidiary, and becomes infatuated;

B(2). Sally, now Tom's wife, prods his ambition;

C(3). Sally tells Tom of her regret that she ever encouraged him to be a success, and Tom tells Sally of his love for Eve; Tom, Jr., now a young man, has become a wastrel;

B(3). Tom is named chief of a construction crew, and Sally becomes pregnant;

B(4). Tom, Jr. is born; Tom expresses his high hopes for the boy;

C(4). Tom divorces Sally and marries Eve, but spends their honeymoon night breaking a strike; Eve spends it on the town with Tom, Jr.; Sally commits suicide;

D(1). Five years later, Tom discovers that his son is the father of Eve's child; Tom commits suicide;

E. The film ends, at Henry's house, in the present tense.

The Power and the Glory is, in several ways, a film out of its time, a unique precursor of forties filmmaking in Hollywood—though, oddly, not of the kind of film Sturges himself was to make. Not only does it bear striking thematic similarities to *Citizen Kane* (Herman Mankiewicz was head writer at Paramount when Sturges began working there in 1929), but its oppressive sense of prede-termined pastness became the hallmark of all those examples of the *film noir* a decade later, films whose copious use of the flashback and of the implicated narrator helped drench nearly every optimistic or noncommittal scene in the mists of irony and fatalism.

Andrew Sarris might argue that *The Power and the Glory* betrays a very thirties-like preference for the evanescent *plaisir d'amour* over that ultimate *chagrin d'amour* we associate with films of the forties. He refers specifically, in his *Film Comment* article on Sturges's early screenplays, to a sequence in which Spencer Tracy, as Tom, "holds up [his] newborn babe proudly and the music swells and he rousingly declares his hopes and dreams for his son—hopes and dreams that we have long since learned are to be horribly disappointed. And yet the scene is played for all it is worth as if Sturges were trying to tell us that no matter how things end (and they always end badly), we must act as if they were going to end well."

If—what an if!—there is any moral lesson to be learned from Sturges's later comedies, it is that no matter how things end (and they always end well), we must act as if they were going to end badly. Witness the heroes of *The Lady Eve, The Palm Beach Story, The Miracle of Morgan's Creek, Hail the Conquering Hero,* and *Unfaithfully Yours,* to name only the most obvious examples; every one of them is a congenital defeatist doomed to final good fortune by the conventions of Hollywood comedy. Now, it may be unfair to use Sturges's later comedies to rebut a point about an early tragedy, but I think there's a simpler dramatic rule at work in the sequence Sarris describes: namely, the greater the hopes, the deeper the depression—a corollary of the film's thesis. The higher Tom holds his son, the more profound will be the psychic injuries when Tom, Jr. falls. Tom's son, who grows up suffering from the spiritual acrophobia that traditionally infects sons of men-in-high-places, is the repository of Tom's only great hope (his financial greatness was thrust upon him by Sally); so it is appropriate that the bursting of this dream will lead to his suicide. But the sequence in question, though "played for all it is worth," conveys less golden optimism than rhinestone irony. We are not meant to share the character's hopes, but rather to appreciate the dereliction of parental responsibilities that triggers their disillusionment. Far from showing "the affirmative, idealistic side of Sturges that came to the fore in *The Great Moment*," as Sarris argues, this sequence is *The Great Moment*'s opposite, in theme if not in tone. The later film is indeed optimistic and affirmative because, although Dr. Morton's life ended in "ignominious death and humiliation," Morton was led to a tragic end by the criminal ignorance of his colleagues, and not by the inability to live up to ideals that condemns Tom Garner. Tom is a rough sketch of Charles Foster Kane; Morton is an earlier, more satisfying version of Sister Kenny. Tom and Kane betray themselves; Morton and Elizabeth Kenny are betrayed by others.

The designation of Henry, the narrator, as Tom's "friend" has to be qualified: Henry is a true friend to Tom, but Tom doesn't reciprocate. He never lets Henry get very close to him, either professionally (Henry was Tom's secretary, not his partner) or personally. Henry is a duller Jed Leland, filling Leland's functions of whipping boy and part-time conscience. At one point, Henry captures exactly the bemused, rather smug tone we will associate with Jedediah: "When Tom bought the Santa Clara," Henry recalls, "he got more than he bargained for. The Santa Clara had a president, and the president had a daughter." Like Leland, Henry is a "sourpuss"; in the person of Ralph Morgan, he even looks like an older Joseph Cotten.

Still, as Jed said of Kane, "Maybe I wasn't his friend—but if I wasn't, he never had one." And Henry is Tom's only friend. Their first meeting reveals Tom's exploitation-education of Henry: Tom throws the younger and smaller Henry into the waterhole and, in desperation, Henry learns how to swim. Is this an act of bullying or a practical lesson in self-reliance? Henry says, "He was teaching me to die." By this definition of "teaching," Tom, Jr.'s cuckolding of his father could be taken as postgraduate instruction at its most chillingly effective. The difference is that something in Henry, the weakling, made him swim, whereas Tom, the strong man, could only sink into suicide.

Sally is accused (by Henry and by herself) of responsibility for Tom's ruin because she instilled in him a desire for success that he resisted at first. Henry says, "Tom might be a track-walker yet, happy and satisfied, if it wasn't for her." Sally depicts herself as a bourgeois Lady Macbeth: "I wanted the power and the money," she says ruefully to Tom; "you wanted to go fishing." And: "You've built so many miles of railroad, and every mile has taken you further away from me." Yet, in the earliest childhood sequence, Tom is shown to be a born leader, or at least a born climber. He dares to climb to the top of a forbidding-looking tree overhanging the waterhole, then dives off, catches his hand under a rock at the bottom of the pond, and fights his way out of the predicament by himself—

but with a scar on his hand that will last a lifetime. In later life, the pattern will repeat itself: Tom will have to be resourceful, because he is so foolhardy.

Climbing up . . . tumbling down. There are four of these "exceptionally strenuous metaphors" (Sarris's phrase) in the film, all foretelling or dramatizing the rise and fall of a "great man," all illustrating Sturges's moral: "The power and the glory—what they can do to a man!" The most delirious ascension has Tom dragging Sally up an endless mountain. Here, his ambition is born of indecision; he is simply stalling to get up the nerve to propose. "Tom," Sally asks, "couldn't you have asked me at the foot of the mountain?" Tom's desire to succeed in business is specifically triggered by his impending parenthood: "I'll make so much money that we'll be able to buy the Southwestern"—which he eventually does. All these incidents tend to absolve Sally from much of the guilt that drives her to suicide.

The final "ascension" sequence is related, with genuine poignancy, to the scene where Tom lifted up his son and his hopes. It comes at the end of the film, when Tom learns of his second wife's adultery. Stricken, he slowly mounts the stairs from his living room to the bedrooms above, gasping, "Where's Little Boy? Want to see Little Boy. . . ." His last hope, we can infer, is to hold Little Boy up in ironic completion of an action begun thirty years earlier—even though it is not *his* little boy, as he had believed until that moment, but his little boy's little boy. When he reaches the top of the stairs he mutters, "Why shouldn't you be in love? And do as you want just once in your life?" This is meant less to forgive his young wife for her sins than to recall the exact words Sally used to forgive *his* adultery with Eve. Both Sally and Tom have accepted the responsibility for driving their respective spouses to infidelity. Tom's recollection of Sally's words preordains the denouement, since Sally committed suicide soon after absolving Tom. He shoots himself, and utters one word: "Sally!"

Tom's retrospective reverence for Sally closely parallels Charlie Kane's love for the memory of his mother, while Emily Norton and Susan Alexander reflect various facets of Tom's second wife, Eve. With Emily, Eve shares wealth and breeding; with Susan, she shares youth and the lure of self-destruction. Tom's dying word, like Kane's, indicates where his sympathies lie, as well as expressing painful nostalgia for some kind of paradise lost. In Tom's case the pain is complicated by the memory that Sally helped thrust ambition—and success, with the sexual advantages its usually entails—upon a complacent naïf who ended up losing everything he never wanted.

What distinguishes Tom Garner from Charles Foster Kane is Tom's use of power and people (which, for both men, are one and the same thing). Garner never tries anything but straightforward intimidation. He's a grown-up version of the toughest kid in town, and since he missed the moderating, corrupting influence of "good schools," he doesn't know how to get what he wants through seduction rather than rape. (Tracy's portrayal of a tycoon in *Edward, My Son* is slightly more polished, just as his hoodlum executive in *Quick Millions* is even more brutal; and Colleen Moore's—Sally's—ill temper in her last years prefigures Deborah Kerr's Grand Guignol tour de force in *Edward*.) When the railroad workers threaten to strike, Tom threatens them with worse; and when they do strike, he strikes back, with 406 deaths resulting. Nor does Tom hide his infatuation for Eve from Sally. Henry says, "Tom fell in love, that's all. He couldn't help it. He was too honest." Though Henry's wife retorts, "He was too selfish, you mean," we get the point. Unlike Kane, Tom is too honest to hide his selfishness.

Kane, an *émigré* of Princeton, Harvard, and Switzerland, is suaver, more oblique, preferring cajolery to cracked skulls. But his velvet-glove technique fools no one. His colleagues know that an iron fist is encased within, ready for use if the occasion demands—as it does with Boss Jim Gettys. Kane, however, is compromised by his need for "the love of the people," which forces his ruthlessness into subterranean channels. Garner, the financial gangster, strove for power and got it; Kane, the newspaper warlord, wanted glory—and, though he tried to buy it, it was never fully his.

Despite its remarkable resemblance to *Kane* in outline and situations (Mankiewicz's early drafts of the script were even closer, with Kane's son originally growing up into a profligate parody of his father, and Susan taking a young lover), *The Power and the Glory* emerges on celluloid as little more than a primitive ancestor, or a fetus to Welles' child-prodigy of a film. As directed by William K. Howard, the film is desolate and desperate in contrast with Mankiewicz's racy, journalistic cynicism and Welles' love of chiaroscuro magic that together form the mark of *Kane*. In tone and form, *The Power and the Glory* presents us with the skeletons of seven

people (Tom, Sally, Tom, Jr., Eve, her father, Henry, and his wife),
whereas the portaits in *Kane* give the illusion of being fully fleshed
out, at least in relation to the protagonist. Tom Garner's rise and
fall is narrated by a loving, rather dull friend; Kane's story—told
by three not-so-dull men who had the advantages of wealth
(Thatcher), old-country wisdom (Bernstein), and journalistic experience (Leland), and appended by one unimaginative woman—is
filtered through the lively if less-than-poetic sensibility of a news-
magazine reporter. Henry is given a dash of individual existence
early in the film, when his wife tells him that she has been happy
enough with "you, and a home of our own, and—well, I have
everything I really wanted"—as if to keep herself from prodding
Henry, Sally-like, into Tom's world of success and excess. But in
general, Sturges's characters are arid, and they make the film as life-
less as *Kane* is incorrigibly vital.

Undoubtedly, we feel a sympathy for Tom that Kane never earns,
because Henry (or, rather, Sturges) saves Eve's adultery for the
climactic revelation. The crises in Tom's life build to a fairly conventional crescendo, for all the shuffling of tenses, and the climax is
at least dramatically compelling. But Kane's last years were unevent-
ful; indeed, the film touches upon them only in the opening newsreel. The climax of the film—Susan's departure and Kane's demolition job on her room, followed by the mention of "Rosebud"—
comes eight years before Kane's death, and the absence of a chrono-
logical climax in his life story helps validate Mankiewicz's "narratage" framework. Perhaps we respond more immediately to the
simple discovery of Tom's cuckoldry than we do to the complex
and partially misleading import of a childhood sled, that "missing
piece of a jigsaw puzzle." If so, the difference in cinematic stimuli
is the difference between a well-manipulated plot device and the
lingering, mystical aura of an elusive symbol. Unfortunately,
Sturges's most ambitious early film suggests neither the power of a
"great man" nor the glory of a great film—both of which distinguish forever the kingdom of *Kane*.

Diamond Jim (1935)

The arrival of "narratage" did not exactly revolutionize Hollywood; that privilege would be granted to Orson Welles and Herman
J. Mankiewicz some eight years later. So Sturges went to Universal,

where he toiled without credit on the scripts for *Imitation of Life* and *Next Time We Love*. His most prestigious official project there was *The Good Fairy*, a Molnar play Sturges adapted for William Wyler. At the time, *Diamond Jim* was considered little more than double-feature filler; even now, Eddie Sutherland and Edward Arnold are hardly a charismatic director-star parlay. But a reasonable familiarity with Sturges's career reveals this forgotten film as one of the writer's most personal works and, until his rise at Paramount two years later, certainly his most successful.

Although Harry Clork and Doris Malloy, two screenwriters of deservedly modest repute, are credited with the "adaptation" of Parker Morell's biography of Diamond Jim Brady, the screenplay and, indeed, the entire film are pure Sturges—more Sturges, in fact, than Brady. The most obvious connection with his later films can be found in the cast list: Arnold and Jean Arthur from *Easy Living*, Eric Blore from *The Lady Eve*, Cesar Romero from *The Beautiful Blonde from Bashful Bend*, and those charter future members of the Mighty Sturges Art Players, William Demarest and Alan Bridge. But there are many other references, both vagrant and meaningful, to his other films. Like the hero in Sturges's first screenplay credit, *The Big Pond*, Brady makes his fortune by selling an ingenious invention (there it was spiked chewing gum, here it is undertrucks for railroad cars). As in *The Lady Eve*, the leading lady is given a double-crossing double role, and a person with an English accent mispronounces "Connecticut." Sturges's fascination with railroads—which he uses comically in *The Lady Eve* and *The Palm Beach Story*, heroically in *Hail the Conquering Hero*, and tragically in *The Power and the Glory* and *Sullivan's Travels*—is reflected in Diamond Jim's rise from a station hand to an industrial magnate, just as Tom Garner discarded the minor glory of a trackwalker for the forlorn power of a railroad president.

But whereas Garner and, for that matter, J. B. Ball, "The Bull of Wall Street" played by Edward Arnold in *Easy Living*, are ruthless and crude, figures of either fear or fun, Brady is sympathetically composed and played. Though he hangs on the ticker tape as tenaciously as Ball does, Brady doesn't take its fluctuations too seriously. When the market crashes, his response is to "grab a sandwich." He is Sturges's generous, somewhat Freudian version of the rich fat man, who has as compulsive a need for food as Tom Garner has for power and Charles Foster Kane has for the love of the people. In each case, the need is an unsatisfactory substitution for mother love (remember that Garner's wife Sally really fills the function of mother to a headstrong, overgrown boy). *Diamond Jim*'s opening scene has Jim's father come downstairs to announce the birth of a boy who will grow into a tycoon of Garneresque proportions; more important, his father completes the action—*The Power and the Glory*'s final ascension-descension—that Garner's suicide interrupted. Jim's true emotional allegiance, however, is to his mother, and here some more of Sturges's eerie portents of *Citizen Kane* begin.

Like Kane, Jim is separated from his mother at an early age: she dies when he is ten. The year is 1876, about the time Mrs. Kane died. Jim's only memento is a photograph, inscribed "To my dear son James on his 10th birthday—Mother." His only abstention in adulthood is from liquor, which he promised his mother he would never drink. Instead, he drinks orange juice and, to wash it down, eats every kind of food. Since Brady has, subconsciously, renounced all women out of respect for his mother, his courtships are quaint, absurd, worshipful, and irrevocably platonic. His sexual drive is diverted to making money and spent in an orgy of overeating. The woman he thinks he loves (Jean Arthur) is the image of another woman he thinks he loved (also Jean Arthur), who is really a distorted image of his mother. When she finally tells him that she has always loved another man, Brady fumes that the couple has been "double-crossin', two-timin' . . . eatin' my food!" His food is his sex, and sharing his table while sharing someone else's bed is a treasonable act.

Like Kane, Brady gives a great deal of money and personal attention to a singer (who turns out to be Lillian Russell), although here the friendship he shares with Miss Russell is deeper, and more loving, than the infatuation masquerading as love that he feels for Jean Arthur I and II. Like Kane, Brady and his would-be wife argue across a dinner table whose length comically expresses the psychic chasm that divides them. Brady isn't detestable, like Garner, nor enigmatic, like Kane. His proposal of marriage—"I'll give you more diamonds than there ever was. . . . I'll give you a million dollars for a wedding present"—is affecting and appealing, for all its short-sightedness. Kane's irony doesn't make him self-aware, only self-conscious; but Jim's self-deprecating good humor is surely one of the keys to his good fortune.

Nevertheless, at the end Jim is left alone to die, just as Kane and

Garner had been. Before she walked out, Lillian Russell had said, "I guess you only loved one person in your life"—thinking of the first Jean Arthur but meaning, intentionally or not, Jim's mother—and Jim had nodded sagely. Now, in an Americanized hara-kiri, he prepares a ritual in which he will literally eat himself to death, ordering oysters, green-turtle soup, lobster, and guinea hens with truffles. Earlier in the film, the expansion of both his business and his waistline was suggested by a comical left-to-right tracking shot, long and fast, through a busy kitchen preparing one of Mr. Brady's dinners. For his last supper, the shot is reversed: it is somber, slow, and abrupt, moving from right to left over the edible implements of a macabre self-immolation. Jim takes his mother's photograph out to look once more at the only person he loved in his life and, without a word ("Sally!" "Rosebud!"), walks into his dining room/ mausoleum, and closes the big doors. This final, elegiac gesture, graceful and audacious, tragic and farcical, heroic and grotesque, captures perfectly a schizophrenic mood that Sturges will evoke again nearly a decade later in his saddest, most ironic film, *The Great Moment*. There are ironies in Sturges's career which this critic would prefer to ignore.

Easy Living (1937)

Easy Living has the reputation of a glossy, genteel romantic comedy, purring serenely in the fashion of Hollywood's best collaborative comedies instead of lurching and growling like the choleric farces Sturges himself would later direct. The presumed triumph of smooth execution over slapstick form is credited to Mitchell Leisen, who steered potentially erratic scripts by Norman Krasna (*Hands Across the Table*), Billy Wilder (*Midnight*), and Sturges (*Remember the Night*) into the calm course of the Paramount-Lubitsch comedy style. *Easy Living*'s aftertaste is undeniably mellow, but this has less to do with the precision comedy for which Leisen is respected than with the extraordinarily persuasive comic presence of its star, Jean Arthur. As the moral center of the film, she puts its inanities (delightfully personified by Luis Alberni) and insanities (gratingly personified by Edward Arnold) into bit-player perspective—a feat well beyond the powers of dour Joel McCrea or craven Eddie Bracken in Sturges-directed films. McCrea and Bracken simply lack the strength of character and characterization to hold

Sturges's stable of supporting actors in rein. Of course, Sturges loaded the dice against the leads in his own films by creating deterministic plots that moved at hurricane speed. In *Easy Living*, though, he let Miss Arthur take refuge in the hurricane's eye, a vantage point from which she could "direct" the chaos with a bit more assurance than Sturges showed in most of his own films or Leisen demonstrated here.

The carnage to which Sturges subjects stockbroker Edward Arnold must appeal less to *cinéastes* than to armchair psychoanalysts who earnestly study every Sturges film for evidence of a split personality that resulted from the conflict between his stockbroker stepfather Solomon and his aesthete mother Mary. In *Easy Living,* it's Daddy who gets it. The first five minutes' action has Arnold tripping down a long flight of stairs, falling resoundingly into a closetful of mink coats, crashing through a door only to land under a cocktail table he's broken, and having a bunch of brooms thrown down at him through a stair well; he spends most of the final two reels encased in a straitjacket of ticker tape. (Sturges took a subtler revenge on mother Mary by turning that intellectuals' favorite, the Pagnol trilogy, into the clumsy farce *Port of Seven Seas,* with bleary Wallace Beery as Cesar and milquetoast Frank Morgan as Panisse. Even Joshua Logan would do better than that.)

Arnold's son, played with casual charm by Ray Milland, could perhaps be taken as a Sturges alter ego, if he didn't fit so neatly into the thirties mold of the impoverished-scion-with-nothing-to-do-who-receives-direction-and-affection-from-a-poor-but-pert-leading-lady. When the action slows down and concentrates on the Arthur-Milland love affair, *Easy Living* is as effortless and lively as its title would suggest. And when Miss Arthur acts as a wall of sanity off which Alberni can bounce his inventive malapropisms and rages, the film carries that balanced comic tone for which it is happily, if improperly, remembered.

Maybe Sturges would argue that the film has to begin violently, with Arnold's brutal pratfalls acting as metaphors for the marital malevolence existing between him and his acquisitive wife, so that the audience would feel relief and release when Arnold finally throws his wife's sable coat over the edge of his penthouse patio and it sails gloriously downward to land on Miss Arthur's lovely head. This wonderful plot twist does help atone for the chaos that has preceded it, and there's a strong temptation to rationalize the opening sequence as an unpleasant situation that Miss Arthur can oppose and obliterate with her working-girl common sense. But too often in the film, chaos overwhelms common sense, and we are treated to visions of Depression-bound New York in all its hectic aimlessness. It's hard to decide which is more dispiriting: a roomful of poor people going selfishly manic over the ejaculations of a deranged automat, or a roomful of rich people going selfishly depressive over the fluctuations of a deranged steel stock.

The mordant social satire implicit in these two sequences tends to be obscured by the fact that both are triggered by our hero and heroine. In the first, Milland tries to sneak some food through an automat window to the famished Miss Arthur and, in an ensuing fight with the restaurant's detective, accidentally kicks a switch that opens all the other windows. In the second sequence, Milland gives Miss Arthur an offhand stock-market prediction which an optimistic investment man takes too seriously, setting off a Wall Street panic. And that's how Cynicism rouged itself up as Romance in movies of the thirties. The romantic could believe that love could make the stock market beat as fast and as steadily as Jean Arthur's heart; the cynic could claim that any economic system based on something as capricious as Ray Milland's endocrines was far too fragile to endure. Sturges was to develop this disquieting dialectic in his more raucous forties films. In 1937, he could evade the implications of his love-and-money philosophy, and let Jean Arthur's incandescent charm carry *Easy Living* breezily past the uneasy few who would question its theme.

Remember the Night (1940)

Aside from a vague family resemblance—in the regeneration of a petty crook—to the plot of *The Great McGinty,* plus an occasional Sturgean aspiration ("Piffle!") and the ribbing of a few Morgan's-Creeky rubes, Sturges's last film as screenwriter-only seems hardly as personal as *McGinty* and the seven succeeding films he would make as Paramount's most protean writer-director. In its idealizing of small-town America and its reconciling of two opposite personalities, *Remember the Night* looks more like some of Sidney Buchman's pleasantest comedies, especially *Theodora Goes Wild.* But these were not so much conventions in Hollywood as the town's commandments. Though it is accepted as fact that all Hollywood moguls were raised within a three-block radius on New York's Lower East Side, few of these men ever allowed the urban sophisticate's notorious condescension toward rural America to appear in their pictures. One radiant exception came in *The Awful Truth,* supposedly co-written by Buchman. In it, Cary Grant learns that his estranged wife, Irene Dunne, is thinking of marrying Oklahoma cattleman Ralph Bellamy. What fun you'll have in Oklahoma City, Grant effuses—"and if it should get dull, you can always go over to Tulsa for the weekend!"

The Freudian side of Sturges, which is painfully probed in *The Power and the Glory* and playfully poked at in *Easy Living,* is spotlighted by his implication that Barbara Stanwyck, the heroine of *Remember the Night,* would not have turned into a cleptomaniac if only her mother had loved her a little. Stanwyck is redeemed by a Christmas vacation, spent with lawyer Fred MacMurray's wonderfully warm family, during which she takes a cram course in Vicarious Happy Childhood I & II. The love she gets from mother Beulah Bondi, coupled with the love she feels for MacMurray (who also manages to act as a father figure both for his own family and for Stanwyck), turns her from a life of crime. Indeed, she not only gives up shoplifting, but she even refuses to let MacMurray—the prosecutor—lose a case to win her freedom. MacMurray has sacrificed his principles for love. Stanwyck, wiser perhaps, sacrifices immediate love for a principle that may win Fred's ultimate devotion.

The "family weepie" would seem to be a genre totally inaccessible to the Sturges touch. The Christmas Eve reunion is an even more questionable plot staple, susceptible only to the blandishments of a Leo McCarey, and now rendered especially trite by the inevitable glut of variety-hosts' holiday get-togethers. (Johnny Carson has defined Christmas as the time of year when TV stars get custody of their families so they can do their annual holiday shows.) But Sturges and Mitchell Leisen treat this fragile material with a delicacy and, more important, a conviction that make it believable and affecting. Sturges judiciously kept from making any blasphemous analogies to the first Christmas and its First Family until 1944 and *The Miracle of Morgan's Creek.*

By now he had shown Paramount that he could write farces (*Hotel Haywire*), screwball comedies (*Easy Living*), historical spectacles (*If I Were King*), and lighthearted romances (*Remember the Night*). It was time that he be allowed to direct his own work.

Diamond Jim, the two Leisen films, and *If I Were King,* with its Justin McCarthy stage eloquence so gracefully assimilated by Sturges, may actually be preferred to a few of the rasping, rapacious pictures he was to direct—*The Beautiful Blonde from Bashful Bend,* and *Les Carnets du Major Thompson* spring to mind in this context, though in blessedly few others. Too often, Sturges-directed scripts substituted monomaniacal force for well-modulated ambiguities, and his subtle, quixotic sense of humor was lost in a mad comedy of humors. But *Easy Living* and *Remember the Night* fit snugly into traditional genres; if they were so satisfying, it may have been because they were so unsurprising. Sturges yearned to be outrageous, and Paramount gave him his chance. Later, his audacity would harden into an attitude, and become a genre all its own. But he had filled the mold so artfully in his apprentice years that he certainly deserved the opportunity to crack it—which he did, all things considered, with smashing success.

The Lady Eve (1941)

The comedies that Sturges wrote and directed for Paramount are rather evenly divided between social satire (*The Great McGinty, Sullivan's Travels, The Miracle of Morgan's Creek,* and *Hail the Conquering Hero*) and screwball romance (*Christmas in July, The Lady Eve,* and *The Palm Beach Story*). In the latter genre, *The Lady Eve* is undoubtedly the richest. It is also the most perfectly realized of all his films, as smooth, hard, and cutting as the diamonds in Barbara Stanwyck's jewel-digging eyes. The dazzling quartet of *Mr. Smith Goes to Washington, His Girl Friday, The Lady Eve,* and *The More the Merrier* manages to epitomize and apotheosize Hollywood comedy in its several formulae and attitudes: social-idealist (*Mr. Smith*), social-cynical (*His Girl Friday*), romantic-cynical (*The Lady Eve*), and romantic-idealist (*Merrier*). Sturges wrote films in each of these subgenres, but never did feeling meet formula with the sublimity expressed in *The Lady Eve.*

Sturges seemed to enjoy tailoring Western Civilization's most revered masterpieces (*Gulliver's Travels,* in *Sullivan's Travels*), mysteries (The Nativity, in *The Miracle of Morgan's Creek*), and myths (The War Hero, in *Hail the Conquering Hero*) to fit his own cynical, small-eyed vision. Though he deserves praise for his courage in throwing stones through the stained-glass windows of chauvinism and self-righteousness, Sturges's aim was not always precise. In *Sullivan's Travels* and *Hail the Conquering Hero* he demonstrated a great wind-up but a weak follow-through; and the denouement of *Morgan's Creek*—admirable in its audacity but chaotic in character resolution—proved Sturges to be a fine starting pitcher who tired in the stretch, in need of strong relief (rewriting). *The Lady Eve* mocks and milks another sacred cow—the Garden of Eden story, with gullible Henry Fonda as Adam, con-artiste Barbara Stanwyck as Eve, and slippery Charles Coburn as the serpent—but here (to send this baseball conceit to the showers once and for all) Sturges's grip on his material is surer, if only because there is as much polish as spit on his screwball.

The Lady Eve is a screenplay in two acts and an epilogue. The first act—the longest and strongest part—takes places on a luxury liner, where ophiologist Fonda is heading for home after a snake-hunting sabbatical from his position as scion of the Pike family, producers of "the ale that won for Yale." Fonda is described with some acuity later on as "the tall, backward boy who's always toying with toads and things." A scientific education and a domineering father have conspired to inject qualifications into his every sentence. "Snakes are my life, in a way," he conditionally confesses soon after meeting Miss Stanwyck, whose reply bears no trace of circumspection: "What a life!"

Fonda is charmed (in both senses of the word) by Stanwyck's easy authority, and she is amused by his naïveté. Urged on by Coburn, her snake-in-the-grass of a father, she gulls Fonda out of part of his fortune, only to recoup it for him after they have fallen in love. "You're certainly a funny girl for anybody to meet who's just been up the Amazon for a year," Fonda says, in a voice that pinches its phrases with painful plaintiveness until the end of a sentence, when it releases all tension with a froggy gulp. The scene in which Fonda falls in love with Stanwyck, and her amusement ripens into affection, is beautifully shot—in one three-minute take—and played, with the two sitting on her stateroom floor, both facing the camera at oblique angles. The outward signs of Fonda's lovesickness are a catatonic, glazed-doughnut stare and that monotonous, constricted speech, while Stanwyck tousels his hair and transforms her smile from one of irony to sympathy to understated ecstasy.

Our feelings toward the bad-good-bad girl Stanwyck are more ambiguous, and thus richer, than our fondness for Fonda. She is the card shark snapping up Fonda's only bait, his numbing innocence. He has stumbled through life loving only snakes, so it is appropriate —indeed, it is *The Lady Eve*'s grand conceit—that untouched Adam should fall for the first woman he really meets. Stanwyck is different. She has toyed with men in the line of duty before, so her love is bestowed with a stinginess that makes it rare. Byron was wrong: in her first passion all a woman loves is love, in others she loves her lover. Stanwyck is closer to Lilith than to Eve in this first act. To her all men were "marks," and thus not yet human. But now she has met a *man*—so defined by his innocence and vulnerability —tempted him, and fallen.

When Coburn learns that Fonda ("as fine a specimen of the *sucker sapiens* as I've ever seen") is in love with his daughter, he exults: "Who is he not to be in love with you who beautify the North Atlantic!" And when Fonda asks him for her hand ("It was my intention to—uh—ask Miss Harrington—I mean your daughter— to—uh—be mine"), Coburn plots his final swindle. Though Stanwyck saves Fonda from penury by topping her father's legerdemain, she realizes that Fonda will soon have to know the truth, and prepares him for the inevitable dejection by saying, of women in general, "The best ones aren't as good as you think they are, and the bad ones aren't as bad—not nearly as bad." This apothegm is the rest of the film's plot as well as its moral, for our hero isn't sophisticated enough to accept this relativistic optimism in theory or in fact, and when he discovers his inamorata's profession he turns on her viciously, and she plots sweet revenge. To begin with, she and Coburn sneak away with the thirty-two-thousand-dollar check she'd shamed Coburn into "tearing up." Curtain on Act One.

The rest of *The Lady Eve* is not quite so perfectly sustained. There's a little too much slapstick, always critical for Sturges; Bosley Crowther tabulated six Fonda pratfalls. And while Stanwyck's revenge—in a diaphanous disguise as Eve, the British noblewoman who isn't as good as Fonda thinks she is—is indeed as sweet as it is bitter, the love-hate-love story is forced to compete with family shenanigans that are funny in themselves (and, for Sturges, surprisingly well realized) but tend to defile the formal purity of the shipboard romance section. Stanwyck's retaliation is justified by her feeling that she, the sharpie, has for once been made the sucker, and that she is thus entitled to professional as well as personal satisfaction.

And it is appealing to watch Sturges pull the lovers farther apart after their breakup, rather than reuniting them as soon as possible. Stanwyck-as-Eve seduces Fonda into marriage, only to reveal a list of former lovers as long as a Sturges cast sheet. "Vernon! I thought you said Herman!" Fonda gasps upon hearing of her third or fourth affair. "He was Herman's friend." "What a friend!" Fonda moans, finally succumbing to Stanwyck's early sarcasm.

Sturges gets the lovers back together by sending the estranged Fonda on another cruise to heal his connubial blisters—whereupon he meets his first love, Stanwyck-as-Jean, and their romance is resumed. By closing a stateroom door on the happy pair (with Fonda as delirious and deluded as he had been on the first cruise, and Stanwyck secure in her knowledge that the Garden of Eden is no place for a worm like Coburn), Sturges tips his cap to the discretion and formal elegance of the Lubitsch tradition. It was a tradition he would attempt to repudiate in the characteristically Sturgean films to follow—with matchless energy and mixed success.

Sullivan's Travels (1942)

In this, Sturges's most ambitious film, all the elements of his later, more successful social comedies can be found, as well as his directorial trademarks of density (but not depth) of composition and recklessness of pace. By now he had assembled nearly all of his matchless stable of character actors; William Demarest, Jimmy Conlin, Porter Hall, Franklin Pangborn, and Alan Bridge all appear in Sullivan's Travels. Part of the Sturges congestion was due to a surfeit of sterling character actors. There were so many in the forties that directors had an incredibly rich source to tap, and they were so good that writers worked hard to give them some special lines, because the bit players always gave them a special delivery. Whether the bits seemed so good because of the players, or vice versa, is open to question; but this richness was certainly symptomatic of a healthy industry. Today, studios can hardly afford to make films, let alone support contract players of this caliber for the one or two pictures a year they could be used in. And the dearth of good roles—of any roles—has made the character actor's easy finesse a thing of the past. Now you can see them pampering their roles the way a bum "works" his cigarette butts. In this desperate market, unheroic free lances like Warren Oates and even Don Knotts are easily promoted to star status, something a Jimmy Conlin would never have dreamed of.

No writer or director was more generous to these gifted spear carriers than was Sturges as writer-director, but then no writer or director was as dependent on them to propel his picture. He used them as a chorus to carry his hero, kicking and screaming, away to the burial ground. They were raffish, cynical small-timers in themselves, but when unified in opposition to the hero—which is what Sturges always did with them—they forgot their differences and banded into a powerful force for intimidation. Individually, they were bull throwers; collectively, they were a bulldozer. And it took the Sturgean hero a full ninety minutes to free himself, however tentatively, from their grasp. John L. Sullivan, the Hollywood director who is *Sullivan's Travels'* protagonist, asserts himself more positively than, say, Eddie Bracken's 4-F flunkie in *The Miracle of Morgan's Creek* and *Hail the Conquering Hero*. Moreover, Sturges has split his cabal into two complementary but less effective camps: Sullivan's producers and his press agents. So Sullivan comes closer to being a free spirit than most of his successors. But even here, the typical Sturges framing appears over and over, acting in collusion with the cabal: a medium shot, with five or six versions of the Sturgean shyster fast-talking the implacable but slower-talking hero.

Sullivan has directed a string of frothy hits that include *Hey Hey in the Hayloft* and *Ants in Your Plants of 1939*. (*Hotel Haywire?* *Never Say Die* with Bob Hope and Martha Raye of 1939?) But now he wants to make a more "meaningful" film—an adaptation of the best-selling novel, *O Brother Where Art Thou?* Sturges's attitude toward both the frivolous flicks and the serious, symbolic world of Hellman and Steinbeck is painfully obvious from the very absurdity of his parody titles. He doesn't like either. But Sturges is setting up a false dilemma for his hero, who doesn't really have to make either kind of film. Sullivan himself says that he wants to make movies "like Capra"—not exactly the most exalted of ambitions for Sturges, whose sensibility if not sentimentality was remote from Capra's. Maybe Sturges thought *The Lady Eve* was too mild and irrelevant a film for 1941, "with Grim Death gargling at you." But *The Lady Eve* was no *Hey Hey in the Hayloft*. Indeed, it is wittier, stylistically more coherent, far more beautifully sustained and sure of itself than is *Sullivan's Travels*.

But it may be unfair to compare two films that are fitter subjects for contrast. *Sullivan's Travels* is endearing, even admirable, in the way it lurches from sardonic comedy to deterministic tragedy as violently as the film's greedy, desperate derelict, with a fistful of green dreams, falls from blind ecstasy into black eternity when he loses his money and his life under the wheels of a train. Certainly Sturges was trying to touch different nerves with the two films; his choice of actors says as much. Whereas both films' leading ladies are refreshingly cynical opportunists (Barbara Stanwyck in *Eve,* Veronica Lake in *Travels*), Henry Fonda's pig-headed innocence acts as a tender foil to Stanwyck's designs. But in *Sullivan's Travels,* dour Joel McCrea uses Lake to reinforce his own cynicism.

Much of the audacity implicit in the film can be traced to the title Sturges has given it—a title naturally designed to provoke comparison, not with one of his own light comedies, but with the most revered satire in the language. Like Gulliver, Sullivan makes four voyages to lands peopled with mirrored distortions of himself. And both works ask to be accepted as entertainment *and* polemic. *Gulliver's Travels* deserves that acceptance, appealing successfully to both the child's appetite for adventure *in extenso* and the adult's desire for satire *de profundis.* Under its childlike surface lies Swift's compassionate misanthropy. In *Sullivan's Travels,* however, the intellectual quest is on the surface, while at its heart is a childlike—though no less compassionate—sentimentality. Certain correspondences can be made between the tiny Lilliputians and the "little people" Sullivan meets on the roads and rails; between the huge Brobdingnagians and the Hollywood big shots; between the Yahoos and the studio's likably rapacious press agents; and between the Houyhnhnms and that muse of social enlightenment who sent Sullivan on his slumming pilgrimage in the first place. But these similarities can't bear much scrutiny.

Swift sliced man and his institutions apart with a blazing stiletto; Sturges just gives man an elbow in the ribs. Far from "glaringly highlight[ing] . . . the distorted values, the essential inhumanity of the film colony," as Richard Griffith wrote in *The Film Till Now,* Sturges all but celebrates this inhumanity by giving it a succulent style, just as Hawks and Lederer did with the cynics and psychotics of *His Girl Friday.* And far from exposing the moral myopia of his mountebanks and clowns, Sturges dedicates *Sullivan's Travels* to them. Sturges is much closer to Sullivan and the film's gargoyles than Swift was to Gulliver and the inhabitants of those "several remote nations of the world." Whereas Swift was polemical, Sturges is autobiographical, so that his exposure of the hero's foibles evokes the ambiguous response we reserve for the later, more self-conscious protagonists of Bergman's *The Magician,* Fellini's *8½,* and Buñuel's *Tristana.* Rather than simply identifying his hero as a man too much like other men, Sturges obviously identifies *with* him—not only in his position and disposition, but also in the awareness that any celluloid attack on Hollywood will have to be financed by the victim. Maybe that thought wouldn't have corrupted Dean Swift, but it might have cowed him a little.

Swift taught that man's institutions were an extension of his capacity for bestiality. For Sturges, the system—whether the movie system or the economic system or the penal system—is evil, but man is good, or at least not so bad that you couldn't share a drink and swap some stories with him. Is it cynicism or realism to believe that every guy has to make a buck in this world, fast or slow, honest or not, and that every con artist is at least half artist? (*Easy Living* provoked the same dilemma.) Maybe it *is* the forties Hollywood equivalent of Swift's philosophy, as explicated by Samuel Holt Monk: "that human nature is deeply and permanently flawed, and that we can do nothing with or for the human race until we recognize its moral and intellectual limitations."

At the end of Gulliver's last voyage, Swift's hero discovers that his Portuguese sea captain has more humanity than he. At the end of Sturges's film, Sullivan discovers that a good laugh at a Mickey Mouse cartoon can ease the pain of seven days' slave labor far more effectively than any Marxist or humanist palliative. Neither Sullivan nor Sturges stops to wonder why a man must be starved before he can swallow a punchline, or if he must be exhausted by meaningless labor before he can be revived by the sweet breath of comedy. Swift wept at man's disdain for reason, and from this outrage wrote a masterpiece. Sturges winked at his own and his fellow man's chicanery, and accommodated himself very well, thank you.

The Miracle of Morgan's Creek (1944)

If *Sullivan's Travels* was audacious in its ambiguous attack on Hollywood and its ambitious attempt to modernize and modify Jonathan Swift, *The Miracle of Morgan's Creek* is no less than blasphemous in its retelling of the Nativity story—with the Virgin Mary as a fun-loving World War II party girl, Saint Joseph as an adenoidal 4-F stuck on the home front, God (or the Angel Gabriel) as an unseen soldier whose name may be Ignatz Ratzkiwatzki, and the baby Jesus as sextuplets! Sturges must have drugged the Hays Office to get this one through, especially since the title spells out any symbolic subtleties that might have camouflaged the Biblical allusions. Trudy, the Mary surrogate, gives birth on Christmas morning, and although she doesn't quite deliver her litter in a stable, she does get her first labor pains in a farmhouse, with a restless cow in the kitchen mooing to be milked.

When Roberto Rossellini tried something similar, though incomparably more deeply felt, sublime, and religious, in *The Miracle* a few years later, he and the film were crucified by Cardinal Spellman and the Legion of Decency, only to be resurrected by the Supreme Court. Billy Wilder is often accused of pacing his dialogue so fast that the viewer doesn't have time to decide whether each witticism is actually witty. Here it's Sturges who paces his *Miracle* so fast— and, more important, builds it steadily to a manic crescendo with almost no restful adagios—that the viewer is more concerned with seeing the situation resolved happily, and then escaping from it himself, than with speculating on its theological ramifications. Nevertheless, the film can be enjoyed, and its memory savored, even by those completely unaware of its submerged Arianism. It would just be less fun to write about if that element were missing.

By 1944 Sturges was without peer as an auteur, at least in the sense that he directed his own *original* screenplays. His nearest rivals in the writer-director sweepstakes—Billy Wilder, Orson Welles, and John Huston—either directed screenplays written by others or based their own screenplays on successful books and plays. Sturges not only wrote singlehandedly all the films he directed but, with the exceptions of *The Lady Eve* and *The Great Moment* in his Paramount period, was also responsible for the original ideas—with occasional uncredited nods to Dean Swift and the Evangelist Luke. With Sturges there was no question of outside or conflicting interest in the person of Charles Brackett, Herman J. Mankiewicz, or Dashiell Hammett. A Sturges film was undeniably his in a way no Hitchcock, Hawks, or Ford could boast (although their current champions can).

But even if his films had been made under the signature of "The Paramount Filmmakers Commune," the Sturges flourish would be unmistakable, if only (though not only) for the presence of his repertory company of ganefs and no-goodniks. As this endearing assortment of character actors kept working together in the Sturges series, the characters they played seemed to get to know each other better. By *Miracle* time, they were as coherently malignant as any Hawks group was coherently noble, and strong enough to send any Sturges hero into a tailspin. Eddie Bracken was the perfect *sucker sapiens* for this crowd. In *Miracle* he is sucked into a whirlpool of situation so fierce that individual members of the cabal can intimidate him simply by shuffling into the frame. But then, Bracken is as easily scared by Trudy's kid sister as by her booming papa William Demarest.

Bracken is so mousy, shrill, negligible that Sturges puts him through nearly two full films before allowing him to show any pluck at all. Not until the end of *Hail the Conquering Hero* does Bracken confront the Sturges vortex. At the conclusion of *Miracle* he's no more formidable than he was ninety minutes before. It's just that, for most of the film, he is the victim of circumstance, while at the end he is the beneficiary. His one virtue, a heroically self-effacing love for Trudy, remains constant. He had nothing to do with getting either Trudy or himself in trouble (for that, blame Private Ratzkiwatzki), and has nothing to do with getting her out (blame Ratzkiwatzki, Trudy, God, and Sturges for the sextuplets). Only in the eyes of the character-actor cabal does Bracken change: from a rapist, or a cuckold, or something, to a hero.

If there is any moral to be found in the two Bracken films, it is "Innocent Bystander, Beware!" Although Bracken is a genuine innocent, circumstances make him stagger through his films with a weight of guilt worthy of Kafka's Joseph K. Psychological critics need delve into Bracken's past only as far back as his Army physical. He obviously sees his rejection as a curse he somehow deserved, and every subsequent misfortune as a fulfillment of the curse. In the early forties everybody had to make war films, and most comedy heroes were either going to war (*The More the Merrier*), on leave (*The Clock*), too old to fight (*Woman of the Year*), or blessed with occupational deferments (*Going My Way*). So Sturges constructed a pair of films around a "conquering hero" who was unfit for service. And Bracken was as apt an icon of the forties 4-F as Joe Namath and Muhammad Ali would be of the sixties.

All this pontificating should not obscure the happy fact that *The*

Miracle of Morgan's Creek is Sturges's funniest black (and blue) comedy, with several scenes—such as Norval's declaration of love for Trudy, their attempt to recall Ratzkiwatzki's name, and their abortive wedding—that qualify in concept and execution as comedy classics. William Demarest's performance is possibly the most devastatingly choleric in American screen history, rivaling Saro Urzi's father in *Seduced and Abandoned*. Sturges entrusted Demarest not only with the film's choicest role, but also with an important function in its *mise-en-scène*: many dialogue scenes that might go on, in the Sturges tradition, forever are broken up only when Demarest takes violent pratfalls out of the frame, and the camera follows the carnage.

Hail the Conquering Hero (1944)

This, the last of the seven comedies he wrote and directed for Paramount, reveals Sturges at his most frenetic and ferocious. His "group" is split in two, as in *Sullivan's Travels*—one part is a Marine contingent that accompanies a reluctant 4-F (Eddie Bracken) back to his home town as a heroic veteran of Guadalcanal, and the other part consists of the home-town gentry who are so pleased to have a real hero that they almost propel him into the mayor's chair —but their effect is complementary rather than contradictory, so that Bracken has even less mastery over his fate than in *The Miracle of Morgan's Creek*. This is not really a comedy. Rarely is a joke allowed to impede the movement of Sturges's snowballing situation. Indeed, in its reckless force, its characters' descent from eccentricity into a kind of insanity, and its development of a minor misunderstanding into a town crisis, *Hero* most resembles *Seduced and Abandoned* by Pietro Germi, the Sturgean Sicilian—though, in particulars of plot (choleric father, pregnant girl, weak suitor, conspiratorial town), that hilariously pessimistic film is closer to the Sturges *Miracle*.

As pomposity and circumstance encircle our hero, who looks as if he holds the losing ticket in Shirley Jackson's lottery, Sturges's camera moves in on him, pinning him down so the town can eviscerate him of any vestigial courage. This is a formal departure from the static frame Sturges had found so congenial; here he implicates himself in the conspiracy through the *mise-en-scène*. (In *Sullivan's Travels* he had thoroughly implicated if not indicted himself by the autobiographical nature of its content, but his visual style remained noncommittal.) It is only at the climax, when Eddie Bracken has finally freed himself from his shame at being represented as a hero (thus becoming a hero) and rushes out onto the town's Main Street, that Sturges's camera draws back—for the first time in two nerve-racking films—and lets Bracken take a few good, deep breaths and long, proud strides.

What is Sturges telling us in this ending? Bracken expresses contempt for himself and his neighbors. "My cup runneth over—with gall," he says. "You didn't know a good man [kindly Doc Bissell, mayoral candidate for the Progressive Party] when you saw one, so you always elected a phony [pompous Mr. Noble, mayor of the Regular Party] instead. Until a still bigger phony [Bracken] came along—then you naturally wanted him." And yet, he swears to the same crowd that "your affection means a great deal to me," and goes on to tell his story. For once, Bracken has the situation in rein, rather than being tied to its tail; and for once, the bit players and backbiters are easily swayed by his honesty. (Frank Capra didn't let his "John Doe" off so simply, to that film's ultimate ruin.) The crowd follows Bracken to the train station, not to lynch him, as he thinks, but to elect him mayor by acclamation. The Marines leave for the front—"We still got a little work to do in our own line"—and, as the band plays "The Halls of Montezuma" and Bracken reverently whispers, "Semper Fidelis," the scene dissolves to the United States Marine emblem, and fades out.

This ending is extraordinarily effective emotionally, but it can't bear much disinterested analysis. *The Miracle of Morgan's Creek* seemed to stress the crucial role of civilians in providing more cannon fodder for the Nips and Nazis—"They also serve who just stay home and mate"—but, since Our Hero wasn't the father of Our Heroine's sextuplets, Sturges could be presumed to have tongue firmly a-cheek, if he wasn't actually thrusting it out at the War Department's population specialists and at his approving audience as well. On this superficial level, the moral of *Hail the Conquering Hero* is that youthful civilians needn't be ashamed of their status as long as they confess it freely: "They also serve who only stand and prate." Here, however, no Sturgean irony imposes itself. There is as much apparent conviction in this relatively preposterous cop-out as Sturges had shown in his pleasant weepie, *Remember the Night*. Is this Sturges's belated contribution to the war effort? Or is it simply the "Hollywood ending" that so often was the price we had to pay for the preceding ninety minutes of cheerful cynicism—a quality which, like nuance, was a precious commodity in the early forties. *Mildred Pierce* had been like that—unredeemed squalor and double-dealing until the very last shot, when Mildred and her reconciled husband blow the whole mood of the picture by walking off into a glorious Warner Brothers sunrise.

It's probably better to ignore *Hero*'s uplifting conclusion, or to accept it as the dues Sturges felt he had to pay to an industry that had subsidized his freewheeling satires for so many years. The rest of the film gives us enough to be grateful for. Its twist on that popular comedy subgenre, the postponed marital consummation, has Bracken and his girl friend being constantly diverted from telling each other the truth about themselves—what might be called *veritas interruptus*. The fulcrum of Sturges's plot pirouettes is an orphaned, mother-loving brute named Bugsy. It is he who becomes so outraged by Bracken's lying to his mother about being in the Marines that he phones her to say her heroic son is coming home. It is he who blocks Bracken's attempts to worm out of trouble. And it is he who, with a stern look that Bracken surprisingly returns, triggers the worm's turn into an honest and honorable man. Freddie Steele, the ex-prizefighter who plays Bugsy, invests the character with a freakish authority that helps give the film its almost documentary authenticity of forties middle-Americana.

The Great Moment (1944)

Endings in Sturges films tend to be schizophrenic showdowns between the two sides of the writer-director. On one side is Preston the Pride of Paramount, laughgetter and moneymaker, stepson of millionaire stockbroker Solomon Sturges; this is the Sturges who gave audiences the endings they wanted, in *Sullivan's Travels, The Palm Beach Story, The Miracle of Morgan's Creek,* and *Hail the Conquering Hero.* On the other side, frowning at his alter ego like Jekyll at Hyde, is Sturges the artist, adapter of Tolstoy, Molnar, and Pagnol, joy and despair of James Agee, only son of the notorious aesthete and adventuress Mary Desti; this is the Sturges who sent Tom Garner and Jim Brady to their lonely deaths, who dazzled the Hays Office with *The Lady Eve*'s double-lutz plot turns, whose studio advertised his pictures as the works of a genius.

Too often, Sturges's artistry would carry a film until the last reel, when the happy hack would take over, turning the fade-out into a cop-out. Too rarely does a Sturges film possess any consistency of tone, and when it does it is often somber and monotonous like *The Power and the Glory*, or easy and impersonal like *If I were King*. The only important Sturges films with sustained, affecting moods are *Diamond Jim, Remember the Night*, and (precariously) *The Lady Eve*. The characters are developed with as much sense as affection; the dialogue serves the situation instead of tyrannizing it; the climaxes have an aura of inevitability about them, whether dirgelike, teary, or wry. In only one other (very uneven) film did an ending exalt both Sturges and the viewer, and not demean them. This was *The Great Moment*, the last Sturges film Paramount was to release before he left the studio for Howard Hughes and one of the most precipitous pratfalls in screen history.

Sturges had written the script for *The Great Moment* (his only adaptation, besides *The Lady Eve*, as a writer-director at Paramount) several years earlier, soon after the publication, in 1940, of René Fulop-Miller's biography of Dr. W. T. G. Morton, discoverer of ether. Paramount evidently didn't like Sturges's treatment —a bizarre blending of low comedy and high tragedy—from the start, and suggested that another director film it. Finally, the studio relented and Sturges began filming it in 1943, right after *The Palm Beach Story*. But the Front Office (B. G. DeSylva, probably) still didn't like the project, and its release was postponed until after *The Miracle of Morgan's Creek* and *Hail the Conquering Hero* had premiered to general acclaim. By this time (according to Andrew Sarris, who talked with the director in 1957), Sturges had decided to leave Paramount in the wake of a contract dispute which, in the dark shadow of the director's decline, seems absurdly insignificant: the studio offered him a seven-year contract, demanding the right to decide at the end of each year whether or not he would continue; Sturges wanted a seven-year contract where *he* would have the option to terminate.

All this niggling hardly suggests heroic *hamartia*, and it's worth reporting only because the artistic freedom Sturges thought he had won when he left Paramount turned out to be a virtual dead end, with Harold Lloyd Alley and Darryl Zanuck Circle offering only the most frustrating of side streets. For most directors who find Hollywood congenial, freedom is like the Labyrinth. Many get lost in the maze of intransigent producers and incompetent technicians and, like Sturges, are eventually devoured by a Minotaur on the order of Howard Hughes or Raymond Hakim; a few, once they are trapped, have the resourcefulness to make the entrapment their subject matter, like Welles; a rare director will rise to the challenge of this freedom, and triumph, as Murnau did with *Tabu.* Sturges was not Murnau. He needed the sympathetic cast and crew he had assembled at Paramount, who took care of the details while he worked on his script and its direction. Once that concentration was broken—once he began spending more time in a production conference with Hughes or Zanuck than in a script conference with himself—the Sturges spell, the lucky streak, the five-year spurt of creative energy went too. Although released out of sequence, *The Great Moment* seems chillingly appropriate just where it is as a chapter in Sturges's artistic autobiography. The writer is reaching up; the machine is breaking down.

The Great Moment is consciously reflective and unconsciously prophetic. It recalls the form (and thus, at least in part, the mood) of Sturges's first important film, *The Power and the Glory.* Both begin in "the present," with the protagonist's funeral; both shift through various stages of the past to tell a story whose conclusion we already know, and to justify a mood we might prefer to escape. But *The Great Moment* returns to the past only twice, and on its second visit stays there for most of the film; Sturges, perhaps committed to subject over form more firmly than he had been a decade earlier, avoids shifts in tense to concentrate on daredevil shifts in mood. As with *The Power and the Glory,* Sturges is again far ahead of his time. These shifts are jarring, atonal, especially for a forties film, and the humor is sudden and abrupt, giving the film an uneasy, very modern feeling that is totally at odds with the presumed seriousness of a biographical subject that Warners would surely have treated with a reverence befitting the Gospel According to Saint Paul Muni.

Sturges's hero is Joel McCrea, survivor of *Sullivan's Travels* and *The Palm Beach Story.* McCrea's bilious stubbornness deprived him of genuine stardom, even in the hunk-hungry war years (though he was certainly handsome enough). But this quality was perfect for a heroic but imperfect medical giant *malgré lui.* Dr. Morton is certified as a hero in the first scene, when his wife receives the Government's posthumous tribute "To the Benefactor of Mankind,

With the Gratitude of Humanity"—and even earlier, in the film's introduction, which describes great men towering on the horizon of history: "Morton seems very small indeed, until the incandescent moment he ruined himself for a servant girl, and gained immortality." The film that follows this peculiar tribute is itself so peculiar that we don't know whether to take the line "he ruined himself for a servant girl"—which sounds like a preface for *Dr. Chatterley's Lover*—as a dangerously phrased but honestly felt elegy, or as a Sturgean jibe at the self-important prose style affected by the writers of biographical films. At any rate, we know within five minutes that the Government's testimonial is a sham. President Pierce himself (whom Sturges skewers far more devastatingly than, say, Theodore Flicker will work over Lyndon Johnson in *The President's Analyst* a generation later) turns Morton down. In a memorable exchange, Morton notes that the country is at war with Mexico, and that his discovery might be put to use immediately in Army hospitals.

> MORTON: [Of course] I'd hate for it to look as if I were trying to make the Government pay to relieve the pain of wounded soldiers.
> PRESIDENT: The Government pays for the guns, don't it? (*Laughs.*)

So much for executive compassion and idealism. So much, too, for Morton's hope of a patent on his discovery. He is rebuked and disgraced. He dies. End of first flashback, and return to the present for a description of his death. Now, when the film reverts to past tense to trace Morton's courtship, marriage, early practice, discovery of ether and its success, we are aware of the doom, and thus the heroism, that weighs down each forward step. Not *ultimate* doom—since ultimately, in the pages of medical history, Morton's discovery was accepted, and the film itself is a kind of centennial celebration—but *irrevocable* doom, of the sort that finally caught up with Tom Garner. Doom should not be confused with destiny.

Morton is heroic in deed, but not in manner. As McCrea plays him, he is genial, determined, but a little dense (he gets a simple formula wrong the first time)—"Morton seems very small indeed." And he is handicapped by the assistance of William Demarest, who reprises his characterization of Muggsy, Henry Fonda's bodyguard in *The Lady Eve*. Demarest is the fulcrum for most of the film's comic explosions, which not only break the mood but shatter it into as many pieces as the glass beakers Demarest is constantly dropping. Sturges seems to be testing a theory of comedy as vicarious pain, ruthlessly observed. He switches so often from the pain of of a surgical patient without anesthesia to the pain of Demarest with a sore tooth or a hurt expression that Sturges's intentions are inescapable. There is little verbal comedy here, and what there is is strained, severe. ("The Wells Method!" one surgeon mocks. "The half-ass-phixiated method!" What unnecessary work Sturges went to, just to sneak that rotten pun into his script!) Sturges has tried to make his slapstick an object of both pleasure and pain, but the only sound it makes is off-putting, off-pitch, flat.

The film's conclusion—The Great Moment itself—is as peculiar as its preface. Here, though, we know that Sturges means to be taken seriously, and the sequence succeeds almost in spite of itself. Morton, who has been imperfect enough to deny surgical use of his discovery because he continued to demand an exclusive patent for it, is walking out of the operating room when he sees the servant girl who is to be the patient. The hall is suffused with a heavenly spotlight; Victor Young's music works hard to undercut any genuine emotions by underlining obvious ones. As the choir builds to a messianic crescendo, the doors to the operating room open magically, and Morton walks through, his patient behind him—she to be saved, he to be condemned. It is a scene Douglas Sirk would be hard pressed to bring off without a giggle, but Sturges nearly does it, through sheer directorial conviction.

Is it melodramatic to point to this as Sturges's own great moment? In five years he had written nine scripts and directed eight of them himself, averaging close to two films per year for which he bore complete responsibility. In fifteen years in Hollywood he had been credited with twenty-one screenplays, almost half of which were original stories—a scandalous achievement among the membership of Writers Guild West. Now Sturges was leaving Paramount, scene of his greatest triumphs, for Total Artistic Freedom under Howard Hughes. A generation later, this clarion call would result in *Myra Breckinridge, Alex in Wonderland,* and *Brewster McCloud.* Sturges was too jealous a custodian of his talent to produce one of these spectacular fiascoes endemic to a dying Hollywood; his decline was to be much more tasteful. And even here he blazed an erratic trail that other filmmakers in the suicidal twilight of their careers could follow: John Huston, Joseph L. Mankiewicz, Nunnally Johnson, and Frank Tashlin were just some of the writer-directors who would trace the same sad parabola a decade or two later.

Among that strange breed, the hyphenate, Sturges had been first-est with the mostest, so it was appropriate that he lose it the fastest —throw it away, almost, as he had made Dr. Morton seem to throw away all chance for reputation and security on the hunch that he might "gain immortality." Sturges wasn't to have even that satisfaction: like Tom Garner, his doom was his destiny. It's as if Sturges walked through those doors and fell victim to the ultimate prank. The doors were the entrance to Diamond Jim's mausoleum, and not the portals to an immortal, great moment.

Unfaithfully Yours (1948)

As the first picture Sturges made for Twentieth Century–Fox, and the first to be released since he had left Paramount in the wake of the *Great Moment* debacle, *Unfaithfully Yours* was the beneficiary of sympathetic critics' hopes for a successful return to studio production. Several factors were familiar, if not altogether comforting. The modest twist of the title recalled Sturges's first success, the play *Strictly Dishonorable*. The film version of that stage hit had starred Paul Lukas as a flirtatious opera star; *Unfaithfully Yours* had another charming European, Rex Harrison, as a volcanic symphony conductor. Sturges had wooed some of his prized character actors, notably Rudy Vallee, Alan Bridge, Torben Meyer, and Julius Tannen, back into his stable. The film's first sequence featured the filmmaker's favorite dialogue retort, the "What a ———!" gag. (In this case, Lionel Stander, upon being told that Harrison's plane is stranded "in the general neighborhood of Nova Scotia," moans, "What a neighborhood!") And his old cinematographer, Victor Milner, was there to anchor the camera at its usual medium range and move it whenever kinetic violence threatened to explode outside the frame.

However odd the result may appear today, contemporary critics treated it favorably, or, rather, kindly. An exception was the *Time* reviewer (possibly James Agee), who complained about the turgid build-up for a good two-reel gag idea. Today, the first few reels look to be the film's best. The Sturges staccato, operating in the seemingly uncongenial milieu of the artistic *haut monde,* still performs expertly. Vallee, again the insecure plutocrat of *The Palm*

Beach Story—though his exact identity has been altered from John D. Hackensacker the oil billionaire to August Henschler the mortgage millionaire—is given a few lovely slurs on American industry to deliver, including the gem: "There is one very reassuring thing about airplanes—they always come down." Harrison fulminates attractively and purrs seductively. He is seen, from the credit shot on, as a conductor of energy as well as of music, his shadow looming over the music in a Mephistophelian manner reminiscent of Mickey Mouse in *The Sorcerer's Apprentice*. "All I do is wave a little wand a little," Harrison says, "and out comes the music." And while Harrison, who remained sexy into his sixties, is inappropriately cast as a middle-aged man suspecting his wife of dalliance with a pomaded pup, he imbues the part with enough electric charm to make such reservations academic.

For the first hour or so, even the film's sound effects are handled with some wit and discretion. A wallet zipper, a slice of bread, and especially a wastebasket all provoke chuckles instead of the expected groans. When Vallee first tells Harrison that the conductor's wife may be straying, he sets a detective report on fire, throws it into a nearby basket, and kicks Vallee and the wastebasket out with a climactic crash.

Unfaithfully Yours can also boast a delicate, exquisitely detailed performance by Edgar Kennedy as the flatfoot (or "footpad," as Harrison rather derisively calls him) who is assigned by Vallee to "keep an eye on" Harrison's wife. This impertinence outrages Harrison, especially when he begins to suspect that there may have been some justification for the surveillance, but he is gradually disarmed by Kennedy's admiration and sympathy. The detective is one of those Sturges characters whose sensibilities far outstrip their diction. Kennedy refers ecstatically to Harrison's American "debutt," and effuses, "Nobody handles Handel like you handle Handel! And your Delius! Delirious!" At first Harrison is typically apoplectic: "I always hoped that music had certain moral and antiseptic powers, quite apart from its obvious engorgement of the senses, which elevated and purified the society." But Kennedy's compassion—for a predicament Harrison has not cared to believe himself in—soon silences him. As Harrison's opinion of his wife diminishes, his respect for Kennedy increases. Kennedy is an unwilling sleuth, whose own marriage was destroyed by a private eye and a public wife. But the misery of cuckoldom has taught him to appreciate the mystery of womanhood: "I'd just be grateful for whatever they was willing to give me. A year, a week—an hour. . . ." This line is delivered with near-Chekhovian melancholy. Its closest equivalent in a Hollywood comedy is Frank Morgan's philosophical acceptance of the same cross in *The Shop Around the Corner*. Kennedy's performance alone would be enough to rescue *Unfaithfully Yours* from the scrap heap of a fallen idol's final films.

There is another, sadder metaphor that applies here, though: as Harrison's opinion of his wife diminishes, so does his moral stature, and so does the film. Even Harrison's shadow shrinks, and by the time he has plotted her early demise, the shade of his rival towers over him. The revenge Harrison plans manages to destroy himself and Sturges too. The reason is Sturges's old bête noire, physical comedy, which for some reason he kept as a pet. This problem had arisen as far back as *Easy Living*, with its crazed automat presaging by some three decades Stanley Kubrick's far more likable HAL 9000. It surfaced occasionally in the films he directed for Paramount—*The Palm Beach Story*, some of *Hail the Conquering Hero*. In *Mad Wednesday* it was personified by a lion who dragged Harold Lloyd around Wall Street even as it dragged the film down from a melodious comedy to a malodorous farce. It would achieve its purest expression—which is to say, its most monotonous and painful elaboration—in a perplexing shootout in *The Beautiful Blonde from Bashful Bend*: a villain is shot and crashes down on a roof, and this finger-in-the-throat gag is repeated three times without the slightest development. As a kind of premature *hommage* to the cinema of Frank Tashlin, this sequence has some weird appeal. It is more appropriate, however, as an epitaph to Sturges's ventures into the silent-movie roughhouse.

Sturges's affection for the physical comedy of the twenties is as commendable as his application of silent-comedy principles to his own films was calamitous. In his Paramount films the profusion of slapstick was usually softened and saved by the profundity of his wisecracks. But in *Unfaithfully Yours* Sturges submits us to a fifteen-minute sequence in which Rex Harrison falls through a chair several times, trips over a phone cord several times, hurls a roulette wheel out of his apartment window, dismantles—and is dismantled by—an insane voice-recording machine . . . the catalogue is unnerving, and endless, and the sequence is so grating that it demolishes the cumulative appeal of the film. Its only value is in the opportunity it affords us to analyze Sturges's most notorious weakness.

Silent comedy is comparable to thirties romantic comedy in that it emanated from some sublime virus that infected most of its practitioners; it was, if you will, a privileged momentum. A surprisingly large number of comedians mastered its rules, and the result was a sizable body of exceptional work. The early romantic-comedy talkies (whose most able directors, like Lubitsch and McCarey, adapted silent techniques brilliantly to the demands of sound) also had a remarkably high consistency. If the thirties films have acquired fewer mythological trappings, it may be because they derived as much from the stage as from the "film essence" and were thus less amenable to apocalyptic generalizations. Sturges was so adept at verbal comedy that one wonders why he chose to humble and degrade his art by attempting sustained slapstick. Unarguably, he and his performers were terrible at it. But who in the sound era could bring it off? Lloyd's *Professor Beware,* many of the Laurel-and-Hardy talkies, even Chaplin's *Monsieur Verdoux*—all are cursed with painful sequences that would have been funny if shot silent, because the screams of agony and the graceless pratfalls would have been transformed into mime and ballet. Buster Keaton is unintentionally heartbreaking in one of his early talkie two-reelers when he rolls down a steep hill inside a tubeless tire, wailing pathetically at every bump; those groans age him instantly before our eyes from the noble Nijinsky of *The General* to the beach-party buffoon of forty years later.

Rex Harrison is no Keaton, so his disgrace at the hands of some demoniacal objects evokes only fear, and not the wrenching pity we feel watching an ignominiously abrupt end to Keaton's art. Harrison is merely forced to undertake a lot of strenuous, maniacal activity that falls (with a thud) somewhere between exercise and exorcism. There is the vague impression that Sturges, by murdering Harrison, is committing career suicide; the sound effects are trite and obtrusive, the music is overexplicit and cute, the humor is strained and inept. An attempt to give some humorous contrast to an ideal murder plot and a real one falls short even of the modest entertainment provided by the 1966 *Gambit.* In *Unfaithfully Yours* Sturges could still do well the things he did best. The failure of the film is ominous because it seemed for once as if Sturges himself didn't know what these things were.

Unfortunately—as much for film historians as for film history—Sturges's career did not follow that graceful directorial curve which leads, in the auteurist view of things, from the early, unpretentious *film bien-fait* to the final, melancholy masterpiece. For a filmmaker whose hallmark was always more energy than equivocation, Sturges's last film, *Les Carnets du Major Thompson,* is nonetheless a particularly sad end. Vapid and flatulent, it can be distinguished as a Sturges film only by the director-writer credit; the most devoted Sturgean would be hard put to identify any verbal, stylistic, or behavioral niceties.

He died two years later in the Algonquin Hotel, his New York home, where memories of an early stage success and of full filmic pre-eminence must have sweetened and saddened his last days. Perhaps we should grant Sturges the courtesy he gave Tom Garner, Diamond Jim Brady, and Dr. Morton, and end this consideration of his work with a flashback to his great years. But even in the hectic forties, Sturges didn't transcend the era as much as he was its most perfect and personal expression. And any historian of the screenwriter's craft could look at his best films now, and accept—if not anticipate—the inevitable decline of a brilliant, burnt-out career.

NORMAN KRASNA

(1909–   )

1932   HOLLYWOOD SPEAKS (Edward Buzzell) story, co-screen-
        play, co-dialogue
        THAT'S MY BOY (Roy William Neill) screenplay
1933   SO THIS IS AFRICA (Edward Cline) story, adaptation
        PAROLE GIRL (Edward Cline) story, adaptation, dialogue
        MEET THE BARON (Walter Lang) co-story
        LOVE, HONOR AND OH BABY! (Edward Buzzell) co-adap-
        tation
1934   THE RICHEST GIRL IN THE WORLD (William A. Seiter)
        story, adaptation, screenplay
        ROMANCE IN MANHATTAN (Stephen Roberts) from his
        play
1935   FOUR HOURS TO KILL (Mitchell Leisen) screenplay, from
        his play, *Small Miracle*
        HANDS ACROSS THE TABLE (Mitchell Leisen) co-screen-
        play
1936   WIFE VERSUS SECRETARY (Clarence Brown) co-screenplay
        FURY (Fritz Lang) story
1937   THE KING AND THE CHORUS GIRL (Mervyn LeRoy) co-
        story, co-screenplay
        AS GOOD AS MARRIED (Edward Buzzell) story
        THE BIG CITY (Frank Borzage) story, producer
1938   THE FIRST HUNDRED YEARS (Richard Thorpe) story,
        producer
        YOU AND ME (Fritz Lang) story, co-adaptation
1939   BACHELOR MOTHER (Garson Kanin) screenplay
1940   IT'S A DATE (William A. Seiter) screenplay
1941   MR. AND MRS. SMITH (Alfred Hitchcock) story, screenplay

62

THE DEVIL AND MISS JONES (Sam Wood) story, screenplay, co-producer

THE FLAME OF NEW ORLEANS (René Clair) story, screenplay

IT STARTED WITH EVE (Henry Koster) co-screenplay

1943   PRINCESS O'ROURKE (Norman Krasna) story, screenplay

1944   BRIDE BY MISTAKE (Edward Wallace) story

1945   PRACTICALLY YOURS (Mitchell Leisen) story, screenplay

1947   DEAR RUTH (William D. Russell) from his play

1949   JOHN LOVES MARY (David Butler) from his play

1950   THE BIG HANGOVER (Norman Krasna) story, screenplay, co-producer

1951   DEAR BRAT (William A. Seiter) based on characters in Krasna's play, *Dear Ruth*

1956   THE AMBASSADOR'S DAUGHTER (Norman Krasna) story, screenplay

BUNDLE OF JOY (Norman Taurog) remake of *Bachelor Mother*

1958   INDISCREET (Stanley Donen) screenplay, from his play, *Kind Sir*

1960   WHO WAS THAT LADY? (George Sidney) screenplay, from his play, *Who Was That Lady I Saw You With?*; producer

LET'S MAKE LOVE (George Cukor) story, screenplay

THE RICHEST GIRL IN THE WORLD (Lau Lauritzen) Danish remake of the 1934 film

1962   MY GEISHA (Jack Cardiff) story, screenplay

1963   SUNDAY IN NEW YORK (Peter Tewksbury) screenplay, from his play

1964   I'D RATHER BE RICH (Jack Smight) remake of *It Started with Eve*

For most comedy craftsmen, the "mistaken identity" ploy is a reliable convention; for Norman Krasna, it was a career-long obsession. In *Hands Across the Table,* She (a manicurist) thinks He (an impoverished playboy) is rich. In *Fury,* They (the mob) think He (an innocent man) is a kidnapper. In *You and Me,* He (an ex-con) thinks She (also an ex-con) has never been to prison. In *The Devil and Miss Jones,* She (an employee) thinks He (the boss) is a co-worker. In *The Flame of New Orleans,* He (a rich man) thinks She (a poor adventuress) is a noblewoman. In *It Started with Eve,* He (a dying tycoon) thinks She (a total stranger) is his son's fiancée. In *Princess O'Rourke,* He (a soldier) thinks She (a princess) is a commoner. In *Practically Yours,* She (an office worker) thinks He (a pilot) sent her a love message. In *Dear Ruth,* He (a soldier) thinks She (a home-fire kindler) sent him love letters. In *John Loves Mary,* She (a Senator's daughter) thinks He (her fiancé) is still single. In *The Ambassador's Daughter,* He (a soldier) thinks She (the ambassador's daughter) is a Paris model. In *Indiscreet,* She (an actress) thinks He (a bachelor) is married. In *Who Was That Lady?,* She (the wife) thinks He (her civilian husband) is an FBI agent. In *My Geisha,* He (a movie director) thinks She (his American wife) is a Japanese actress. And in *Sunday in New York,* He (a man of the world) thinks She (a virgin) isn't.

These Krasna heroes, heroines and imposing father figures, deceiving themselves or allowing themselves to be deceived, are not merely stock characters—though, as they kept appearing in script after script, Krasna too often recycled them into cardboard. They are really creatures of habit, in bondage to the first impression, trapped by their own prejudices and presumptions to the extent that they prefer to accept the idea of a mistaken identity (however horrifying) rather than admit to the real one (however respectable). In the thirties, Krasna was willing to examine the consequences of his characters' myopia in both comic and dramatic terms. Of the comedies, *Hands Across the Table* remains the most enchanting, *Bachelor Mother* the most deft in juggling complicated plots and sympathetic characters; Krasna's two stories for Fritz Lang, *Fury* and *You and Me,* suggest the tragic and pathetic aspects of mistaken or assumed identity.

None of his later work is as engaging as these comedies or as ambitious as the Lang melodramas. There are sunbursts of behavioral humor in Krasna films throughout the forties; but by 1956, with *The Ambassador's Daughter,* he was giving evidence of turning into a minor Labiche, with that farceur's convolutions of plot but without his formal inventiveness. A one-man comedy machine was sputtering to a standstill after three productive decades. It is the nature of machines to run down.

Hands Across the Table (1935)

The most difficult and vital part of a director's job is to build and sustain the mood indicated in a screenwriter's script—a function that has been virtually ignored while critics concerned with "visual style" trot off in search of the themes a director is more liable to have filched from his writers. The ghost of literary criticism haunts and pervades much of today's auteur work. Perhaps the next generation will put into practice what the current crop eloquently preaches. It should restore respect for the writer's contribution and perspective for the director's.

When it comes to the mood men, the *metteurs-en-scène*, auteur critics start tap dancing away from the subject. George Cukor is a genuine auteur; Michael Curtiz is a happy hack; Mitchell Leisen is actually despised by some critics for "ruining" films like *Midnight* and *Arise My Love*. Yet what Leisen and the writers of *Hands Across the Table* did to make that film the most amiable of thirties screwball comedies is a prime example of sympathetic collaboration. As with so many delightful comedies, it is the writers who create the characters and establish a mood in the first half of the picture, and the director who develops both in the second half. The story line of *Hands Across the Table* isn't flimsy, it's downright diaphanous: Goldbrick Fred MacMurray meets and moves in with Gold digger Carole Lombard; each intends to marry for money and live off the fat of the spouse; and when they fall inevitably in love, they resolve instead to get married to each other and go to work. But the characters of these would-be layabouts are created (by the writers), developed (by the director), and personified (by the stars) with enough élan and good humor to hold our attention and affection with gentle assurance.

The script rarely strains to push a punchline, and when it does, the stars bring it off with a wry smile or a look of charming chagrin, which neatly emphasizes our willingness to indulge characters who are so personable they needn't try to score with one-liners. The following may give some idea of the effortless and effervescent aura created by Krasna & Co.'s dialogue. Carole suspects Fred of crying poor but being rich.

> FRED: It's amazing how people differ. No matter how hard I try to convince my tailor I have money, he thinks I haven't. And no matter how hard I try to convince you I haven't, you think I have. If only you were my tailor, how simple life would be. Say, can you sew?
>
> CAROLE: No. What about your father?
>
> FRED: He can't sew either. (*Mild wince.*) He lives abroad.

You know, he has an amazing ability to get people to give him
their money. Unfortunately, that ability isn't hereditary.
CAROLE: How could the Drews be broke?
FRED: You remember that thing called The Crash? Well, that
was us.

Carole is a manicurist (hence the title), gardening the nails of
people rich enough to keep their hands out of dirt. The fact that a
young man named Theodore Drew III is patronizing a place like
that interests Carole enough to send him out with a bandaged hand
("Stabbed in the cuticle," he says, wincing for more than one reason
this time; "this isn't your first manicure by any chance, is it?") and
an evening's date. The film's easy authority is such that it can even
handle the treacherous "hiccup routine" that would later demolish
stalwart stars like Irene Dunne and Douglas Fairbanks, Jr. (in *Joy
of Living*) and Barbra Streisand and George Segal (in *The Owl
and the Pussycat*).

Carole's and Fred's conquest of this difficult routine clinches the
attachment, so it is time for the complications to be introduced.
Fred is engaged to an heiress, who has her own telephone exchange
and a maid who wears her furs. Carole is being pursued, in a sense,
by a rich cripple. (Ralph Bellamy, who naturally plays the cripple,
shrugs off his infatuation by saying, "Some play golf to pass the time,
some go tap dancing, some destroy clay pigeons. I have mani-
cures.") Bellamy is charmingly cruel about his misfortune, but so is
the film. Carole first sees Fred hopscotching down a hotel corridor
as she leaves her crippled courtier's room; the contrast couldn't be
more jarring. This is comedy where the loser is a paraplegic! After
Carole jilts Bellamy for Fred, the lovers climax the movie by
dodging gaily through traffic to chase a flipped and flippant coin.
They skip into wedded bliss while Bellamy laughs himself half-
hysterically off-screen.

This is also a movie about two unmarried people in love who
live together. The writers eluded a frontal attack from the Legion of
Decency by pairing innocent situations with indecent proposals—
that is, before Fred and Carole fall in love they say things to each
other like, "Are you going to get undressed or do I have to undress
you?"—and later reversing the ploy: once they realize they're in
love, what seemed innocent before (like Fred's asking Carole,
"Aren't you going to tuck me in?") becomes a piquant proposition.

Their blithe banter makes an intrusion of some genuine sentiment more refreshing than the same dialogue would be in a weepie:

> FRED: You know, you'd be very beautiful with blonde hair.
> CAROLE: I *have* blonde hair....
> FRED (*laughs*): I know it.

Under Leisen's direction, Lombard and MacMurray have a chemistry between them that approaches alchemy. Leisen handles the comedy with relaxed assurance; surely a couplet like Carole's suggestion to Fred that "You must have a lot of friends who'd give you a job" and his retort that "It'd be a fine friend who'd give you a job!" would be less affecting had it been supervised by a lesser director. The romantic climax is heightened—and softened—by Leisen's oblique movements of the actors and the camera. No director ever did more for Carole Lombard than Leisen did when he photographed her in a luscious, three-quarter-profile close-up, and with a creamily soft focus that caressed her with a seductiveness that the Hays Office would never allow Fred MacMurray. *Hands Across the Table* was Ernst Lubitsch's first film as Paramount's production chief. For once, the School of Lubitsch—which was attended, consciously or not, by most of Hollywood's best romantic-comedy writers and directors—produced a work eminently worthy of its master.

Bachelor Mother (1939)

Polly Parrish is one of those spunky working girls, often played by Jean Arthur, Carole Lombard, or (as in *Bachelor Mother*) Ginger Rogers, who made the typical heroine of thirties comedies more "liberated" than any movie female throughout Hollywood's next thirty years—in the sense that her intelligence, forthrightness, and careerism were taken as seriously as the hero's. She was attractive, but no sex symbol: does anyone remember, or care, what kind of figure Jean Arthur had? She was romantic, but no Victorian symbol of fragile purity. If she became involved in a compromising plot twist, it was probably because she needed the rent money. Poverty persuaded Jean Arthur to accept Luis Alberni's devious offer of easy living in a penthouse suite; and poverty, overriding a concern for her reputation, foils Polly Parrish in her persistent attempts to return or dump the baby she found on the steps of an orphanage—a baby everyone in the movie believes to be hers.

The Foundling Home officials *want* Polly to be the baby's mother, so they can lavish upon her their special brand of condescension masked as professional sympathy for an unwed mother. Freddy, her barnacle boy friend, wants to believe the worst about a girl who's obviously too good for him, first so he can get a promotion, second so he can get revenge. Mrs. Weiss, Polly's landlady, wants a surrogate grandson—and Polly's "baby" fills the bill. J. B. Merlin, the president of the department store where Polly works, wants a *real* grandson—and thus is anxious to believe not only that Polly is the mother, but that his son David is the father. And David, the likable, fast-living scion, wants a chance to behave first like an executive (he threatens Polly with ignominy and starvation to force her to take the child back), then like a know-it-all (he is certain that to feed a baby you "take a spoonful of food and place it on a piece of gauze"), then like a father (he gets to like Little Johnnie), and finally like a husband (he gets to love Polly). All are eager to believe the unimaginative worst instead of the improbable truth. In the end, J.B. accuses David of parenthood (as David had accused Polly); David's vehement denials meet with vehement disbelief (as Polly's had); and David finally realizes (as Polly did) that it's easier to admit to something he didn't do.

> DAVID: Dad, I want to confess something. I'm the father of that child.
> J.B.: Those are the first true words that have passed your lips in forty-eight hours!

Thus, Krasna doesn't resolve his well-made plot in the usual well-made way—with Polly finally blurting out the truth, and everyone asking, "Why didn't you say so in the first place?"—but with the hero and heroine still lying to save face, to simplify misunderstandings, and to beat the band. In fact, until the final line, David continues to believe that Polly is lying, that she *is* an unwed mother.

> DAVID: I've got a surprise for you—we're getting married tonight.
> POLLY: You still think I'm the mother of that baby?
> DAVID: Certainly.
> POLLY: Then have I got a surprise for you!

Bachelor Mother has already carried comic echoes of the Nativity (Polly became a "mother" on Christmas Eve, and when she tells Freddy that "I got it for Christmas," he gulps and asks, *"This* Christmas or *last?"*). For Krasna to conclude his film with a pointed reference to Polly's precarious maidenhood must have stretched the Hollywood Production Code's guidelines to breaking, for, in the film as released, Polly merely answers David's "Certainly" with a mirthless "Ha! Ha!"

This revised ending is indirect, but it's hardly evasive. Earlier in the film, David had arrogantly assumed he could return one of the "defective ducks" (mechanical Donald Duck toys) which it was Polly's job to sell. Polly could only respond to David's intention to get satisfaction at the store's exchange counter with a sarcastic laugh: "Ha! Ha!" To David, Polly is like the duck: a piece of broken merchandise that he, without knowing it, was responsible for breaking. Ironically, David will be convinced of Polly's virginity only when he has deprived her of it. For attentive viewers, this supposedly euphemistic curtain line may be one of the raunchiest in Old Hollywood history.

But the mechanical duck isn't just part of an elaborate setup for the final gag. It is a symbol and a symptom of Polly's maddening, automaton routine at Merlin's. While waiting on customers, she must keep three display ducks in perpetual motion, with the first running down just as the third is wound up. After she gets stuck with the baby, Polly's routine becomes cyclical, and endless. She spends all day winding up mechanical ducks to keep them quacking, and all night turning Baby John over on his stomach to keep him from crying.

POLLY: Do you know how you get a baby to sleep on its stomach? You turn it on its stomach. Then you go to bed. Then the baby turns over and starts to cry. Then you get up and turn the baby over. Then you go to bed again. Then the baby turns over and starts to cry again. Then you get up and turn it on its stomach. Pretty soon it's nine o'clock and you're winding ducks.

Gradually, the duck comes to symbolize Polly's baby, for it is as noisy, troublesome, cute, and endearing as Little Johnnie. Just as gradually, David stops looking on Polly as a willful but mechanical employee and begins to see her as a mother and (thus) a human being. In the process, he is himself humanized. At first David is drawn as a spoiled and presumptuous rich boy ("Any motorcycle cop who can afford to turn down a hundred-dollar bribe must be in some crooked racket") who nevertheless works hard and loves his father. David's nervous reaction, when the orphanage investigator tells him "a baby has been left at the Foundling Home that is, frankly, your responsibility," clearly indicates that David could have fathered an illegitimate child—if not this one.

The rest of *Bachelor Mother* is a crash course in the bourgeoisification of David Merlin: he gets mauled at a dance contest, contradicted at the Merlin & Son exchange counter, mugged as a shoplifter in his own store, lost in a snake-dancing crowd at Times Square on New Year's Eve, and infatuated with a stubborn, *seasonal* employee. By the end of the film, his capitulation to middle-class humanism is complete: he allows a certain millionaire capitalist to bully him into admitting to a "crime" he didn't commit—and makes his father "radiant, grateful and tearful." Earlier J.B. had roared: "I don't care who the father is. *I'm* the grandfather!" Polly has long since become so devoted to the child that she really is its mother, and David has acquired enough rudimentary maturity that he is finally willing to accept moral paternity for a child whose actual paternity he first thought might have been his.

This humanizing process also worked on Krasna himself. Although *Bachelor Mother* is as meticulously constructed as any of his later films, the construction is less deterministic. There's a generous, relaxed quality to this film that can be attributed partly to Garson Kanin, who created the same easy feeling in his and Ruth Gordon's comedies for George Cukor; partly to Ginger Rogers and David Niven, who always seem to be in command of the material, instead of being manipulated by it; partly to the whole aura of thirties comedy, in which writers, directors, and actors had high standards to meet, and so often met them. And yet, the initial and final credit is Krasna's. All of the author's fondness for the mistaken-identity plot and the elaborate mechanisms of romantic farce can be found here, in glorious detail. But, as typical as *Bachelor Mother* is, it avoids stereotypes; and, however characteristic, it exults in defining vibrant, living characters.

Sunday in New York (1963)

In the thirties and forties, Norman Krasna's virtue consisted in transcending a particularly vital Hollywood genre: the situation screwball-comedy. In the late fifties and sixties, his vice consisted in succumbing to a rather venal Broadway genre: the situation lechery-comedy. *Who Was That Lady?* and *Sunday in New York,* both of which he adapted for the movies from his own plays, employ his standard plot devices (assumed identity in the former, mistaken identity in the latter), but here they are forced, distended, and far too mechanical. The absence of any strongly drawn and genuinely likable characters further emphasizes the emptiness.

Oddly enough, the nuclear trio in these late films (boy, girl, friendly letch) echoes the far more benign trios (boy, girl, friendly father figure) in *Bachelor Mother, The Devil and Miss Jones, It Started with Eve,* and *Dear Ruth.* Dean Martin (in *Lady*) and Cliff Robertson (in *Sunday*) are not without their charms as the good-natured satyrs, but their very amiability tends to rob them of any moral weight and to expose them as weaker than Krasna may have intended. This sounds more like a Legion of Decency condemnation than a disinterested critical judgment. Still, the films do suffer from the lack of a strong situation or character for the hero and heroine to act against.

Charles Coburn (in *Bachelor Mother* and *The Devil and Miss Jones*) and Charles Laughton (in *It Started with Eve*) fulfilled this function admirably. Indeed, Laughton threatened to overwhelm poor Bob Cummings and Deanna Durbin, and did. Cummings and Durbin are actually less attractive mates than Tony Curtis and Janet Leigh (in *Lady*) or Rod Taylor and Jane Fonda (in *Sunday*) —a fact that only makes the failure of Krasna's material more depressing. The stars are forced to suppress their natural moxie, appeal, and vitality so that the author's steam-roller plots can press them into the kookie cutouts of dehydrated farce. When a middle-class genre such as farce is drained of all human eccentricities, the inevitable triumph of popular morality turns hollow and smug. A moral imposed on a machine is only a slogan.

But Krasna's decline was not entirely self-inflicted. The failure of *Bundle of Joy* (a remake of *Bachelor Mother*) and *I'd Rather Be Rich* (a remake of *It Started with Eve*) can be traced largely to those paragons of pointless energy, Debbie Reynolds and Sandra Dee. Both actresses were too tough to make it as Audrey Hepburns and too angular to be Marilyn Monroes; wide-eyed aggression would have to do. If that was enough to keep their careers afloat longer than their talents deserved, it also helped sink their movies. Debbie rarely transmitted a feeling of joy in her work; it was all work, reworking, and overworking. Norman Taurog, her *Bundle of Joy* director, must have sensed this. He punctuates her punchlines with the movie equivalent of a drummer's rim shot after the burlesque comic has told a particularly bad joke: a long pause and a startled-reaction shot. Taurog is a gut fighter in a film that demands an expert masseur. Sandra Dee is a bit blander than Debbie, and her co-star, Robert Goulet, looks like the Tin Woodman and acts with as much grace; so director Jack Smight surrounds and submerges them in a swamp full of double-takers and karate-choppers. The effect is the same: at best, antipathy; at worst, antagonism.

Perhaps we should blame the era rather than the individuals. The thirties was Hollywood's great age of dialogue comedy, both sophisticated and screwball, just as the forties was the decade of the psychological melodrama, and the fifties that of the melancholy western. Most comedies of the fifties and sixties were forced, whether they tried to be cute or adult, and the Krasna films were as typical of an unfortunate era for comedy as the earlier successes were of a wonderful one. *Who Was That Lady?* is a bit worse than its norm; *Bachelor Mother* is quite a bit better than its. The sad fact is that Norman Krasna, who had helped talkie-comedy scale its peak, chose to accompany it on its descent into the Valley of Vacuity.

FRANK TASHLIN
(1913–1972)

1945 DELIGHTFULLY DANGEROUS (Arthur Lubin) co-story
1947 LADIES' MAN (William D. Russell) co-screenplay (uncredited)
     VARIETY GIRL (George Marshall) co-story, co-screenplay
1948 THE FULLER BRUSH MAN (S. Sylvan Simon) co-screenplay
     ONE TOUCH OF VENUS (William A. Seiter) co-screenplay
     THE PALEFACE (Norman Z. McLeod) co-story, co-screenplay
1949 MISS GRANT TAKES RICHMOND (Lloyd Bacon) co-screenplay
     LOVE HAPPY (David Miller) co-screenplay
1950 KILL THE UMPIRE (Lloyd Bacon) story, screenplay
     A WOMAN OF DISTINCTION (Edward Buzzell) additional dialogue
     THE GOOD HUMOR MAN (Lloyd Bacon) screenplay
     THE FULLER BRUSH GIRL (Lloyd Bacon) story, screenplay
1951 THE LEMON DROP KID (Sidney Lanfield) adaptation
1952 THE FIRST TIME (Frank Tashlin) co-screenplay
     SON OF PALEFACE (Frank Tashlin) co-story, co-screenplay
1953 MARRY ME AGAIN (Frank Tashlin) screenplay
1955 ARTISTS AND MODELS (Frank Tashlin) co-screenplay
1956 THE LIEUTENANT WORE SKIRTS (Frank Tashlin) co-screenplay
     THE SCARLET HOUR (Michael Curtiz) co-story, co-screenplay
     THE GIRL CAN'T HELP IT (Frank Tashlin) co-screenplay
     HOLLYWOOD OR BUST (Frank Tashlin) co-screenplay (uncredited)

1957   WILL SUCCESS SPOIL ROCK HUNTER? (Frank Tashlin) screenplay
1958   ROCK-A-BYE BABY (Frank Tashlin) screenplay
       THE GEISHA BOY (Frank Tashlin) screenplay
1960   CINDERFELLA (Frank Tashlin) screenplay
1962   BACHELOR FLAT (Frank Tashlin) co-screenplay
1963   WHO'S MINDING THE STORE? (Frank Tashlin) co-story, co-screenplay
1964   THE DISORDERLY ORDERLY (Frank Tashlin) screenplay
1967   CAPRICE (Frank Tashlin) co-screenplay
1968   THE SHAKIEST GUN IN THE WEST (Alan Rafkin) from his screenplay, *The Paleface*
       THE PRIVATE NAVY OF SERGEANT O'FARRELL (Frank Tashlin) screenplay

Tashlin directed, but did not write, the following films: *Susan Slept Here* (1954), *Say One for Me* (1959), *It's Only Money* (1962), *The Man from the Diner's Club* (1963), *The Glass Bottom Boat* (1966), *The Alphabet Murders* (1966).

Like Federico Fellini, Alfred Hitchcock, Gregory LaCava, Norman McLeod, James Whale, and Jules Feiffer, the late Frank Tashlin was first a cartoonist. All these filmmakers share a visual facility, a talent for the swift sketching of characters, and a tendency to show contempt for the figures they have so adroitly animated. What distinguishes Tashlin from this distinguished group is that, almost invariably, the films he wrote and directed remain on the level of cartoon work—alternately sophisticated and childish, inventive and monotonous, humane and robotoid.

One is tempted to add "personal and mechanical," except that, perversely, Tashlin was most personal when his films were most mechanical. He was a visual-gag technician who loved nothing more than to construct baroque elaborations upon some standard comic premise. More elaborate, not funnier: his gags weren't really developed, but rather driven to their logical, chaotic conclusion. His punchlines were often eschatological demolition jobs. This is the humor of predictability, of inevitability, of determinism. And so one doesn't laugh much during his films; one simply steps aside and watches them move, at hurricane force, leaving actors, scenery, and plot in aesthetic carnage.

Tashlin followed this creed so fervently that his films are also easily distinguished from those of his rivals in forties and fifties comedy. In verbal pacing, Tashlin usually played Soupy Sales to Preston Sturges's wise-cracking Rocky and His Friends. In form, his films are hit-and-run comic strips compared to Norman Krasna's cause-and-effect anecdotes. In tone, Tashlin preferred the custard-pie approach to that of Billy Wilder's Viennese pastry. And temperamentally, Tashlin was the sarcastic press agent to George Axelrod's cynical playwright. Sturges, Krasna, Wilder, and Axelrod just might deserve the tag of "moralists," but Tashlin's point of view was so vague, and his fidelity to the well-made plot so tenuous, that there's little surprise in discovering that his career ended where it began: with the mechanics of the lovingly drawn-out, endlessly repeated, inevitable, and finally exhausting sight-gag.

The structures of Tashlin's films break down rather neatly into two types: the pastiche (a series of related gags, or cartoon panels, on a general topic) and the more traditional plot movie. Protagonists in the latter type of film—Bob Hope in *The Paleface, The Lemon Drop Kid*, and *Son of Paleface*, Tom Ewell in *The Girl Can't Help It*, Tony Randall in *Will Success Spoil Rock Hunter?*, Terry-Thomas in *Bachelor Flat*—are variations on the weak, middle-aged male. Whether they are desperately brash (Hope), likably jaded (Ewell), or just psychologically unable to cope with the buxom women Tashlin throws at them as both temptation and challenge, (Randall and Terry-Thomas), the heroes of his plot movies are at least borderline adults with enough maturity to discover whatever optimistic truism is being saved for their films' denouements. In his story films, Tashlin is relatively accessible, conventional, and successful.

But Tashlin's reputation, such as it is, and his unique filmic personality are rooted in the pastiches—the cartoon films. Here the protagonist is a bumbling naïf whose sheer ineptitude catapults him through a series of frantic gag situations. Often the films' titles describe the milieu: *The Fuller Brush Man* (Red Skelton), *Kill the Umpire* (William Bendix), *The Good Humor Man* (Jack Carson), *The Fuller Brush Girl* (Lucille Ball), *Artists and Models* (Dean Martin and Jerry Lewis), *The Geisha Boy* (Jerry Lewis), *Rock-a-bye Baby* (Jerry Lewis as a babysitter), *Who's Minding the Store?* (Jerry Lewis as a department-store clerk), *The Disorderly Orderly* (Jerry Lewis). *Miss Grant Takes Richmond* pits Lucille Ball against a mélange of thugs; *Love Happy* does the same for Harpo

Marx; *It's Only Money* (for which Tashlin did not receive writer's credit) does the same for Jerry Lewis. *Variety Girl* sends Mary Hatcher and Olga San Juan to Hollywood; a decade later, Tashlin gave Martin and Lewis the same itinerary in *Hollywood Or Bust*.

Jerry Lewis's precarious pre-eminence in auteur circles came at Tashlin's expense, and distracted from the task of putting Tashlin, as writer and director, into some sensible critical perspective. Lewis, as actor and director, has been the object of so many sneers and *hommages* that it's probably best to refrain from jumping into the fray, and simply to point out that the characteristics of any Lewis-Tashlin film are the same as those of many pre-Lewis-Tashlin pastiches. Lewis's goony character was the cul-de-sac culmination of Tashlin's gallery of naïfs. The mock-heroic, pre-credits précis of *The Disorderly Orderly* has its antecedent in several of Tashlin's fifties plot films. And the string of silent-comedy gags that marked nearly all of Lewis's later films, with or without Tashlin, is the rickety structure upon which Tashlin scripts as far back as *The Fuller Brush Man* are built.

With Preston Sturges as a valiant predecessor, and Jerry Lewis as a manic successor, Tashlin was one of the few directors of the talkie era obsessed with dragging the silent-comedy tradition kicking and screaming into sound films. It's no coincidence that the climactic chase in *The Fuller Brush Man* is the most satisfying of Tashlin's many attempts to sustain comic momentum through purely visual means, for the film's "adviser" was none other than Buster Keaton. (One of the picture's best gags—the frame of a house collapsing around Red Skelton—is a direct quote from Keaton's masterful *One Week*.) Tashlin's career is a monument to the hard work he put into creating sequences that might rival Keaton's in their comedy and complexity. But, with one exception, his films betrayed the effort instead of displaying the effect.

The exception is Tashlin's first film as a director, appropriately called *The First Time*. Here he was developing characters and not simply manipulating caricatures. One cared about the young parents, and responded to the gag situations not as demonic mechanisms but as moral dilemmas. And this, of course, was the secret of silent comedy that Tashlin otherwise never learned: Keaton, Chaplin, and Lloyd were human beings first, and fulcrums of visual humor second.

Perhaps, working with Skelton, Bendix, Carson, Hope, Ball,

Lewis—hardly the most galvanic or affecting troupe ever assembled under one writer-director—forced Tashlin to rely on predetermined pratfalls, and not on behavioral nuance. But the feeling persists that Tashlin found in their severe limitations exactly that quality of lumpy, proletarian inflexibility that would express his own view of comedy as submission to pain, and not—as the greatest silent-comedy artists demonstrated—its sublime, effortless transcendence.

The First Time (1952)

Tashlin is one of four writers who received screen credit on his first directorial venture. The other credits of two of the writers help us to rationalize dismissing them in favor of Tashlin: Jean Rouverol has written only five films in thirty years, and the best of these were collaborations with her husband Hugo Butler, while Dale Lussier's most characteristic titles are *Mexican Spitfire's Blessed Event, The Lady and the Monster, The Falcon's Alibi,* and *Dick Tracy Vs. Cueball.* Hugo Butler, the other credited writer, is best known for his work with Joseph Losey (*The Prowler, Eva*); he also wrote some family pictures for Joseph L. Mankiewicz back at MGM. But none of these careers do much toward dissuading us from the suspicion that this is as much a Tashlin film as any of his later, more notorious efforts—though *The First Time* may surprise those who know him only from his Jerry Lewis farces. Tashlin is undeniably sympathetic, even gentle, with Robert Cummings and Barbara Hale, the new parents in *The First Time.* And his invention has rarely been more impressive.

The film is narrated by the couple's first-born, who is as flip as his parents are sentimental: "My father paid for a bouncing baby boy with a bouncing rubber check." If his jokes are old, even more so are some of his references: he describes one of his grandmothers as "a sophisticated divorcee, the poor man's Gloria Swanson"—an example of the cinema of memory that would please L. Ron Hubbard. Mostly, though, this Groucho in diapers remains in the background, crawling forward only when Tashlin wants to place the loving ineptitude of the young couple in a lightly ironic perspective. When Cummings and Hale are on their own—which is most of the time—*The First Time* radiates a casual glow we associate with the nicest romantic comedies of the twenties: not much plot, no villainous conflict, and lots of inspired but seemingly improvised "busi-ness," all emerging from two modest, likable young people.

The film is studded with engaging comic routines that could be played, almost without change, in a Gloria Swanson, Mary Pick-ford, or Laurette Taylor silent film. One routine is constructed around Baby's first four-a.m. feeding: Daddy groggily opens one eye, notices Mommy sound asleep; leans over her, snaps his fingers in her ear, jumps up and down on her mattress, no response; he feels his way out to the kitchen, blindly opens the refrigerator door, pulls out a beer bottle, places it in a pan to heat; notices his mistake, gets Baby's bottle, trudges toward Baby's room; now Mommy wakes up, goes to the kitchen, opens the refrigerator, gets a bottle, and trudges toward Baby's room . . . fade-out. There are other delightful "silent" sequences involving the choice of a babysitter, a trip to the drive-in movie, and—most effective and affecting—the problem of feeding Baby on schedule.

The nurse has just left, giving Barbara Hale a short sermon on the importance of feeding Baby precisely on time. But Baby has been crying all morning, and it's still ten minutes before his ten-a.m. bottle. With equal measures of desperation and guilt, she moves the living-room clock forward so that it reads ten o'clock, and rushes into Baby's room . . . only to find the bedroom clock (a duck with huge, dilating eyes) threatening her with the correct time. Finally, she calls her husband, and sobs that she's tried everything—being sweet, being tough, ignoring the wails—but Baby is still crying, and every clock in this house tells a different time. Papa Joe looks up at his office clock; it reads ten minutes to ten. He looks back and tells his wife: "It's ten o'clock right now. Go feed him." Barbara, laugh-ing and crying with the understanding that he is fibbing out of love for her, can only whisper, "I love you, Joe."

This sequence—indeed, the whole movie—suggests Tashlin's warmth *and* inventiveness; and both are far more impressive here than they are in the Jerry Lewis equivalent, *Rock-a-bye Baby,* which had the head start of a Preston Sturges story. Even when the couple is generating argumentative heat instead of their usual lovelight, Tashlin's ideas spark generously. Cummings and Hale, in the midst of a fight, are having a candlelight supper. After medium shots of each, there is a full shot of the table: the table's length (just slightly ridiculous) and the attitudes of Bob and Barbara suggest, with de-licious understatement, the last shot in the *Citizen Kane* dinner-table montage. They begin to argue; the candles are set about a foot in front of each, and the force with which each flame is bent neatly indicates the furious hostility they feel.

Tashlin even makes an oblique comment on that most beloved of situation-comedy staples, the "meeting cute" routine. The archetypal example of "meeting cute" was devised by Charles Brackett and Billy Wilder for *Bluebeard's Eighth Wife*: Gary Cooper is shopping for the bottom half of a pair of pajamas and Claudette Colbert is shopping for a pajama top; their decision to split a single pair leads to romantic entanglement. (George Axelrod cites this in the play version of *The Seven Year Itch*.) Cummings and Hale can hardly "meet cute"—they've been married for a year when the film begins—but, as Cummings packs his clothes to walk out on his wife, Tashlin lets them "leave cute": Cummings looks at the pajamas, gives the tops to Hale ("your half") and throws the bottoms in his suitcase ("my half"). Aside from the *hommage* aspect, this gesture implies the closeness of their marriage and the feeling that they were of one spirit as well as one flesh. It is another example of the "character" Tashlin's script and direction infused into what could easily have been a tiresome programmer.

Son of Paleface (1952)

Tashlin's early films, as a director, are not only promising; more important, they often deliver on their promises. In hindsight, *The First Time* may seem more remarkable than it really is because Tashlin so rarely chose to make traditional romantic comedies. Nevertheless, the success of both the romantic *The First Time* and the farcical *Son of Paleface* pastiche bequeaths a retrospectively ominous tone to Tashlin's middle-period comedies, and gives the final eclipse of his artistry and his career a "melancholy twilight" aspect it may not quite deserve. One is angered when superior directors like Renoir, Riefenstahl, or Welles are deprived of their filmmaking tools; but when Tashlin can't get backing to continue his monotonous comic experiments, the reaction can only be one of pity.

In the postwar decade, Bob Hope was still an actor and not yet an institution (as Pauline Kael has perspicaciously observed about Rosalind Russell's evolution from *His Girl Friday* to *Auntie Mame*). His lifelong portrayal of the petty, cowardly shingle salesman, wisecracking his way into and out of grim situations, fits perfectly into

Tashlin's shallow world view of life as a series of slot-machine gags. Tashlin peculiarly insisted on rather large, ungraceful comedians to act as repositories for a very demanding brand of visual humor. Hope, at least, had some physical resilience to match his verbal resourcefulness. His repartee was so quick that villains rarely got a chance to lean on him; and when they did, he was malleable enough to bend back, if only in a windup for his next comic pitch. As long as Hope could choose weapons—which were always one-liners—he was willing to back into any fight. And he was more than willing to use his verbal advantage to humiliate any antagonist who might be slower on the drawl.

In *Son of Paleface* Hope and Tashlin spend an inordinate amount of time mocking Roy Rogers' love for his horse—and, incidentally, revealing Tashlin's own love for phallic humor. As Jane Russell sings a torch song, Hope sneaks a peek at Rogers' crotch and asks the cowboy if he doesn't like women. When Rogers indicates that he only has eyes for Trigger, Hope just stares at him, sucking away furiously at his long pipe, and mutters, "That's ridiculous." More stares. More sucking. And finally, when the sequence has long since stopped making a comic point and begun to wallow in directorial preoccupations, it fades out. The typical Tashlin topper for a gag is some kind of ejaculation: the deranged washing-machine hose in *The First Time,* the spurting milk in *The Girl Can't Help It,* the reverse vacuum cleaner in *Who's Minding the Store.* It's as if Tashlin's all-but-impotent heroes can find vicarious fulfillment only in chaos. *Son of Paleface* plays a switch on this joke by having Hope's pipe curl up as Russell approaches (cf. *Will Success Spoil Rock Hunter?*), and by screwing Hope's head down between his shoulders—literally and quite dextrously—when he drinks a deadly alcoholic concoction to prove he's a man.

If Tashlin's Lewis films strove to maintain an intolerable stridency, his pictures with Hope are characterized by a more genial but still reckless energy. Only periodic injections of gushy sentiment slowed the Tashlin-Lewis machine, but *The Paleface* and *Son of Paleface* made well-timed use of songs (most notably "Buttons and Bows") to give the film some formal rhythm. Lewis's sentimentality acted as intrusions into the soulless frenzy of the action; the Hope songs were easy entr'actes that, as much as anything else, identify *The Paleface* and *Son of Paleface* as entertainments instead of Tashlinian endurance tests.

The Lieutenant Wore Skirts (1956)

This extraordinarily unpleasant service comedy tries to blend the situations of Tashlin's gentle, generous *The First Time* with the theme and temperament of Hawks's *I Was a Male War Bride*—chaotic and choleric. The result is what is thought of, disparagingly, as a Tashlin comedy. Tashlin's leads (Tom Ewell and Sheree North) are not unsympathetic in themselves. Indeed, the story—of the brainwashing to which a husband will submit his wife in order to have her declared insane and unfit for the military duty that keeps them apart—would be less grotesque if Ewell, the middle-aged man with a "springer spaniel" face, and North, his young and sexy wife, were more grotesque. But they very plainly, and very warmly, love each other; and it is love, Tashlin argues, that makes Ewell so monomaniacal in his attempts to drive his wife temporarily insane. The insecurity he feels as an average, fortyish man whose voluptuous wife is surrounded by handsome young officers—her peers—while he plays bridge with the other housewives, lends desperation to Ewell's scheme, and makes the Ewell-North difficulties more pathetic, if less poignant, than those experienced by *The First Time*'s young parents.

The difference between Bob Cummings' schemes in the earlier film and Ewell's here is the difference between plot and ploy, and gives *The Lieutenant Wore Skirts* a sadder but wilder (not wiser) tone that removes it from the comic realm and places the Ewell character in the unheroic company of Tashlin's other heroes in *Son of Paleface, The Girl Can't Help It, Will Success Spoil Rock Hunter?, Bachelor Flat, The Man from the Diner's Club, The Private Navy of Sergeant O'Farrell*, and, of course, the Jerry Lewis movies. Not all these "heroes" are cowards like Bob Hope, or simpletons like Jerry Lewis; Ewell in his two films and Tony Randall in *Rock Hunter* are blessed with a charm that matches (and springs from) their vulnerability. They possess a kind of vegetable magnetism. But Tashlin chooses to emphasize their shortcomings by opposing them with comic-strip Valkyries like Jayne Mansfield and Anita Ekberg. Again, he doesn't treat his busty starlets with the myopic contempt that these ladies (and Joi Lansing and Barbara Nichols) received at the hands and lenses of other filmmakers; Lieutenant Sheree North, though big-bosomed, is idealized as the faithful, understanding wife. But only so much can be done with a Dagwood, however traumatized, and a Daisy Mae, however devoted. When a cartoon character cries, we worry only that the ink will smudge.

Some of the same gag situations appear in *The First Time* and *The Lieutenant Wore Skirts,* but the affectionate ingenuity Tashlin applied in the earlier film is subject to melancholy modifications in the later. A reference as minor as the shared pajamas becomes an even sadder metaphor for incompleteness in *The Lieutenant Wore Skirts.* When Sheree North flies to Hawaii to join her regiment, Ewell is left to share a wolfish friend's bachelor apartment *and* his bachelor pajamas, with Ewell wearing the top (female) half in a distraught way that presages his later role as housewife in the man-woman relationship. More than once Ewell is caught with his pants either down or off, and he is rarely allowed the dignity with which Cummings parlayed the humiliation of being fired into the triumph of principle over interest. Ewell must humiliate himself *and* his wife to get her released from the service, and when he does, any sense of triumph is overwhelmed by a sense of relief—felt by the characters and the audience—that the ordeal is over. Ultimately, *The Lieutenant Wore Skirts* has less to do with the depth of the couple's love than with the depths of degradation its hero (not to mention its writer-director) will descend to for a chance to secure his wife's love and his own self-respect. But did he have to destroy that self-respect in order to save it?

The Girl Can't Help It (1956)

The pulsating energy of early rock-and-roll appealed to mid-fifties teen-agers because of its liberating vitality, and appalled middle-aged parents because of its anarchic lack of discipline and variation. True to its faltering reputation as a weather vane of popular psychology, Hollywood movies of the period reflected these contradictory feelings. Not surprisingly, most of the films were "exploitation" pictures aimed toward a gullible, voracious teen market; these films featured a dozen or more R'n'R acts and the inevitable climactic moment when, with Bill Haley and His Comets belting it out at the sock hop, the town meanie would irresistibly begin to tap his foot and sway to the infectious beat. Then there was the Elvis Presley series. Presley, who oozed so much animal authority that Ed Sullivan dared photograph him only from the waist up, was neutered by Colonel Tom Parker and Hal Wallis, and his movies quickly degenerated into VistaVision equivalents of the thirties backstage musicals, with only an occasional suggestion (as in *Jailhouse Rock*) of the pulsating pelvis that had made him famous. Finally, there were the straight, big-budget films, like *Blackboard Jungle,* which wove the minor motif of an R'n'R score into some sociological theme.

Tashlin was the only major director to make a rock "exploitation" movie. Typically, though, *The Girl Can't Help It* embraced the other subgenres (backstage musicals and underworld corruption), started a few of its own (the rock comedy, the Jayne Mansfield movie), and parodied them all. Tashlin obviously had fun treating R'n'R not as an art form, or even a form of primitive entertainment, but as a commodity—like gambling or drugs or sex—ripe for both exploitation by gangsters and satire by a corrupt, irreverent Hollywood filmmaker. He was naïve enough to assume that rock fans, mostly girls whose idolatrous response to the sexual danger of male singers ranged somewhere between the visceral and the masturbatory, would accept the premise that Jayne Mansfield's forty-inch chest could become the next icon of American adolescence. (After all, it was Tashlin who had the breast fixation, not the typical teen-ager he imagined.) But he was also cynical enough to assume that, with twenty songs by Little Richard, Fats Domino, Gene Vincent, Eddie Cochran, and other R'n'R stars, the kids wouldn't care how satirical or naïve the framing story was; one picture of a sexy rock star, accompanied by a raucously familiar sound track, could drown out a thousand words.

Tashlin's sensibility was made for the fifties; if those years had not existed, one hopes (fears) that he would have invented them. In fact, his films—and the decade—can be summarized by the epithet "Grrross!", a fifties expression that indicted the excesses of conspicuous consumption even as it retained some sneaky admiration for its, well, grossness.

In Jayne Mansfield, Tashlin found the ultimate image of everything fifties capitalism cherished: quantity over quality, shallowness over style, the machine over the individual, the immediate over the sublime. Not that Tashlin rejected these values. His was a satire that epitomized its subject rather than eviscerating it; that's one thing that makes his career fascinating. His plot and *mise-en-scène* for *The Girl Can't Help It* are cluttered with artifacts of the Gadget Age— tape recorders, TVs, jukeboxes, telephones, recording equipment, slot machines. When he has Mansfield hold two quart bottles of milk against her breasts, and then say, "Everybody thinks of me as a sex-pot—nobody thinks of me as equipped for motherhood," he is defining his own obsessions as well as those of the consumer culture.

Although Mansfield is given a final touch of humanity (when it turns out she's really a *good* singer, not just a rock phenomenon), Tashlin is primarily interested in two throwbacks to the forties: Tom Ewell (an alcoholic agent) and Edmond O'Brien ("Fats" Marty Murdock, a big-time gangster on the skids). Both are mired in the memories of their past successes: Ewell hallucinates that Julie London, his former client and wife, is singing "Cry Me a River" to him; O'Brien runs March-of-Timey newsreels of himself, and bursts into tears. Ewell wears Eddie Bracken-style bowties; O'Brien composes songs with Cole Porterish intros. They are obviously made for each other, more than either one is suited to Julie or Jayne. It is also obvious that O'Brien is the only character in *The Girl Can't Help It* aggressive enough to become a rock-and-roll star, and that his delivery of "Rock Around the Rock Pile" will propel an essentially late-forties bop song onto the R'n'R charts. If Mansfield embodies Tashlin's bracingly gross vision of the monster only a fifties culture could create, O'Brien suggests the filmmaker's fantasy of a middle-aged rage the fifties just might accept.

Will Success Spoil Rock Hunter? (1957)

For a brief period in the middle fifties (from *The Lieutenant Wore Skirts* through *The Girl Can't Help It,* and ending with *Will Success Spoil Rock Hunter?*), Tashlin flirted with the story film—as opposed to the gag films he had made with Jack Carson, Red Skelton, Lucille Ball, and Martin and Lewis. If these films now seem more successful, it is because concentration, however sporadic, on a plot line gave some added comic point to his repetitious gags, and put his obsession with phallus and breast symbolism into a more acceptable perspective. In *The Girl Can't Help It* and *Will Success Spoil Rock Hunter?,* Tashlin also had the advantage of proven comedy material by Garson Kanin and George Axelrod, respectively. Although he used little more of Kanin's "Do Re Mi" than the premise, and threw out virtually everything but Axelrod's querulous title, the spirits of these comic craftsmen can be felt hovering, a bit uneasily, over Tashlin's adaptations.

In *The Girl Can't Help It,* Tashlin paired Jayne Mansfield, the ultimate young exhibitionist, with Tom Ewell, the ultimate middle-aged voyeur. For all of Ewell's presumed avuncular disinterest, the situation still smacked unpleasantly of *The Immoral Mr. Teas*—sexuality and impotence exploiting each other's weaknesses. Ewell would have to wait until the seventies, and an off-Broadway revival of *Waiting for Godot,* to give eloquent expression to the sense of embraceable failure he conveyed in his fifties films. Mansfield's next Tashlin co-star, Tony Randall, was both vulnerable enough *and* attractive enough to present a strong moral opposition to Mansfield's sexual suasions. Randall's voice—a melodious baritone on the cutting edge of puberty—and his world-weary, near-hysterical grace epitomized the depression of fifties New York as surely as Tashlin personified the mania of fifties Hollywood. So Randall was a natural for Tashlin's affectionate burlesque of the TV–Mad Ave. axis. In return for Tashlin's perspicacity of casting, Randall contributed a human quality sorely lacking in the director's work—and, in the process, helped humanize the Mansfield homuncula.

Just as Harry Cohn "created" Kim Novak partly to bring a cantankerous Rita Hayworth back in line, so one can assume the brass at Twentieth Century–Fox encouraged Mansfield's sex-star parodies as a way of making Marilyn Monroe more tractable. But the ploy backfired. Monroe proved inimitable, and Mansfield wound up parodying herself. *Rock Hunter*'s Rita Marlowe *is* Jayne Mansfield. One fan tells her, "I've seen all your pictures, and I'm going again to see *The Girl Can't Help It.*" Later, Rita Marlowe is described as "the girl with those oh-so-kissable lips, soon to be seen with Cary Grant in *Kiss Them for Me*"—a triple joke: (1) the kiss-kiss gag; (2) the interoffice plug for Mansfield's next Fox film; and (3) an even more "inside" gag, since the line is concluded as Betsy Drake, Randall's movie-fiancée and Cary Grant's actual wife of the moment, walks on-screen. Tashlin's movie-within-movies gags predated and prematurely satirized the *hommages* of the *nouvelle vague*. Mansfield's Hollywood boy friend, Bobo Branigansky, the TV "Jungle Man" with false chest hair, is played by Mickey Hargitay, her real husband; and Groucho Marx, for whom Tashlin had co-scripted *Love Happy* a decade earlier, appears as Georgie Schmidlap, Jayne's true love. True to his nature, Tashlin's references are almost always *hommages à* Tashlin; why sound a fanfare for some other filmmaker when you can blow your own horn? (Here, Tashlin was

working within the established, if not exalted, tradition of the
Crosby–Hope Road pictures—notably *The Road to Utopia,* with
its reference to the Paramount mountain as "our bread and butter.")

It is a mark of Tashlin's uncharacteristic softness that Mansfield,
who was only naïve in *The Girl Can't Help It,* is actually innocent
in *Rock Hunter.* Her assumption that words like "seclusion," "en-
dorsement," "vice-president," and "titular" are dirty, and her offhand remark that "all my lovers and I are just good friends," serve
to domesticate Mansfield even as they consigned her forever to the
Mamie Van Doren substratum of starletdom. That the Monroe persona took itself seriously, even if moviegoers didn't, helped build
and sustain her remarkable appeal. Monroe's sexiness was added to
the roles she played; it was an aura and not, as in Mansfield's case,
the whole character. Monroe *delivered* gag lines; Mansfield *was* one.
Thus, Monroe was delightfully appropriate for Billy Wilder's habi-
table story films, and Mansfield was pathetically perfect for Tashlin's string of one-liners. Tashlin could bring a human aspect to the
Mansfield caricature only by first taking it at face value.

Just as Tashlin gives the Randall character enough leeway to
allow the metamorphosis from schlep to sex-star (which Randall
carries off deliciously, with the simple line, "Well thank you very
much, Miss Marlowe," his voice lowering authoritatively, his shoulders straightening), so does John Williams as Mr. LaSalle, the ad
agency president, effect a graceful change from haughty executive to
happy gardener, who had always wanted "to develop new roses,"
and instead developed neuroses behind the president's desk. In Axelrod's play, Irving LaSalle had been based on the agent Irving Lazar,
and developed into a Hollywood-and-Vine Mephistopheles who buys
Faust's soul for ten per cent of the take. Tashlin's Rock Hunter does
nearly sell his soul for the sake of the agency, but Mansfield's cartoon measurements and Randall's inept aplomb turn the mechanics
of demonic seduction into the merest accouterments of situation
comedy.

The real "problem" in *Rock Hunter* is yet another one of Tashlin's
phallic gags: not "Will success spoil Rock Hunter?" but "Will Rock
Hunter, cursed with an incipient case of sexual and career impotence, be able to keep his long-stemmed pipe lit?" In an eerie premonition of *Carnal Knowledge,* our hero learns that breast fixation is
not the answer, and turns to the saving grace of love with a flat-
chested fiancée. If it is encouraging to see Tashlin approaching,

however tentatively, a solution to the problem of his own films—a fixation on overdeveloped gag lines and ponderous physical humor —it is even more discouraging to trace his career through another decade that can be characterized, like the films themselves, as a case of repetition without development.

Bachelor Flat (1962)

More than once, Tashlin has been accused of expressing the middle-aged, middle-class man's inhumanity to woman. Thus, Andrew Sarris: "To ridicule Jayne Mansfield's enormous bust in *Will Success Spoil Rock Hunter* may be construed as satire, indulgent or otherwise, but to ridicule Betsy Drake's small bust in the same film is simply unabashed vulgarity. Although Tashlin is impressively inventive, particularly with gadgets and animals, he has never been sympathetic enough to any of his characters to forgo a laugh at their expense." The argument seems to be that, if Tashlin were a greater humanitarian, he would be a better filmmaker, and that, by treating his females as something between a gadget and an animal, parody becomes vulgarity, and impressive invention turns into callous manipulation.

Tashlin's peculiar view of women is unlikely to be canonized by Women's Lib, but this isn't because he is antifeminine—or profeminine. His outlook is too ambiguous and ambitious to be categorized so simply. The subject of his non-Lewis films was usually the bourgeois, suburban man's image of voluptuous womankind, and his blond heroines—Jayne Mansfield, Sheree North, and, in *Bachelor Flat,* Tuesday Weld—were sweet, gentle, often intelligent women who had to pretend to be sexy and brash in order to fulfill the image their men had of them. Tashlin gives these women a sympathetic ribbing, and saves his ridicule for the weak-chinned men—Tom Ewell, Tony Randall, and, in *Bachelor Flat,* Terry-Thomas—whose breast fixation Tashlin simultaneously shares and deplores. When Betsy Drake parades before Randall in a tight sweater bulging with Jaynesque falsies, she is mocking his attraction for big bosoms; far from satirizing her, Tashlin is siding with her in her war against the lure of overdevelopment. It is the writer-director's obsessive self-aggrandizement and self-hatred (to overstate the case) that makes his films so maddeningly repetitious and, ultimately and unconsciously, so perversely poignant. These obsessions increase our respect for Tashlin even as they diminish our response to his films.

Terry-Thomas's gat tooth serves as the perfect iconographical metaphor for the impotence that underlies all of Tashlin's breast and penis gags. Again and again, he uses milk as either suckling food (Mansfield's "motherhood" joke in *The Girl Can't Help It*) or semen (the milk that spurts out of its bottle when a milkman sees Mansfield in the same film). At one point in *Bachelor Flat*, Terry-Thomas flattens himself against a door, presses two white convex dish lids (with button "nipples" at the appropriate spots) against his chest, and shouts, "I've run out of milk!" Later he is told, "And if you have any bad dreams, I'll make you some hot milk." As Molly Haskell has observed, Terry-Thomas receives the adoration and pampering of Southern California's most curvaceous cartoons precisely because he poses no sexual threat. He is the winsome child engulfed in aggressive smother love—until he begins to act not like a child but like a lover, waving his ubiquitous umbrella around like the phallus in a Greek satyr play. "You and your ridiculous umbrella!" one woman finally tells him. "When I first met you, I thought that umbrella was charming." Exactly: when it wasn't "erect."

Terry-Thomas's young male rival, or counterpart, is Richard Beymer. Beymer, a poorly-minted Warren Beatty with the overbite and Asian eyes of early Gene Tierney, just might have become a suitable Tashlin hero of the sixties, if their respective careers had flourished for a few more years. Here, he is the friendly young letch of the later Norman Krasna comedies, with a soupçon of Tashlinian sexual insecurity that manifests itself in a nervous, high-pitched laugh. Indeed, most of the film's characters have to laugh at their own jokes, partly because there's so little genuine rapport between them—*Bachelor Flat* is a comedy of communal isolation—but also because there's very little rapport between film and viewer. It occasionally suggests a mediocre comedian bombing in some cavernous, almost empty night club: Archie Rice Goes to Southern California.

Movie comedies that exploit sexual impotence or embarrassment —*Bringing Up Baby, Vivacious Lady, I Was a Male War Bride, The Family Way, M*A*S*H*—have never lacked a receptive audience. Theories of comedy are ultimately rationalizations for whatever the theorist happens to think is funny. My own bias is toward comedies that emphasize surprise, and away from those which emphasize pain. This may help explain why I find Tashlin's comedies fascinating as a critic—they're naturals for screenwriter-as-auteur analysis—but disappointing as a viewer. His recurrent use of themes, plots, situations, gags, and actors recommend him as worthy of serious study. His writing over two decades has an undeniable, nearly unique consistency. He is certainly a director who, following Jean Renoir's dictum, made the same film over and over. His films epitomize burlesque comedy in the movies, and his middle-fifties work virtually defines the decade's brassy humor. It may be too much to ask that Tashlin's films also provoke the joy, the delight, the spontaneous laughter of great screen comedy. So I will not ask. I will simply say: they are not funny.

GEORGE AXELROD

(1922–   )

1954 PHFFFT (Mark Robson) story, screenplay
1955 THE SEVEN YEAR ITCH (Billy Wilder) co-screenplay, from his play
1956 BUS STOP (Joshua Logan) screenplay
1957 WILL SUCCESS SPOIL ROCK HUNTER? (Frank Tashlin) from his play, sort of
1958 RALLY 'ROUND THE FLAG BOYS! (Leo McCarey) adaptation [uncredited]
1961 BREAKFAST AT TIFFANY'S (Blake Edwards) screenplay
1962 THE MANCHURIAN CANDIDATE (John Frankenheimer) screenplay, co-producer
1964 PARIS WHEN IT SIZZLES (Richard Quine) screenplay, co-producer
      GOODBYE CHARLIE (Vincente Minnelli) from his play
1965 HOW TO MURDER YOUR WIFE (Richard Quine) story, screenplay, co-producer
1966 LORD LOVE A DUCK (George Axelrod) co-screenplay, producer
1968 THE SECRET LIFE OF AN AMERICAN WIFE (George Axelrod) story, screenplay, producer

Like many of the characters created by Norman Krasna, Frank Tashlin, and (as we shall see) Peter Stone and Billy Wilder, the protagonists of George Axelrod's comedies are also role-players— but not through choice so much as through the dictates of some sub-Shavian genie. The Axelrod male is usually a middle-aged, Apollonian Pygmalion; the female, a young, Dionysian Galatea. As

William Holden (cynical screenwriter) tells Audrey Hepburn (spritely secretary) in *Paris When It Sizzles*, "*Frankenstein* and *My Fair Lady* are the same story." All of Axelrod's most important films are fantasies involving dreams (the dream affair in *The Seven Year Itch*, the dream politician in *The Manchurian Candidate*, the dream movie in *Paris When It Sizzles*, the dream murder in *How to Murder Your Wife*, the dream girl in *Lord Love a Duck*) that, more often than not, turn into nightmares. In his love-hate attitude toward both his horny, ineffectual writers and his all-American girls who "express the total vulgarity of our time," Axelrod comes close to defining the post-Kinsey, pre-Reichian male who has become aware of sexual alternatives to which neither Hollywood nor society would let him respond—except with brittle wisecracks, bashful leers, and bleeding ulcers.

Axelrod's 1971 novel, *Where Am I Now—When I Need Me?*, is as good an introduction as any to the writer's highly varnished world of wish-fulfillments and want-frustrations. The leading character, Harvey Bernstein, is a jaded writer whose sexual and career frustrations are hopelessly intertwined, and for whom the only way out is through the dream mirror. His dead-end, correspondence-course job introduces him to one of those "tall girls, with long, sun-tanned legs and blond hair flying, that I dreamt of in my youth"—the sort of girls Axelrod has been imprinting onto dream-ribbons of celluloid for the past two decades. "Cathy," he writes, "if you *are* real, there is no limit! You know life. I know grammar and sentence structure. Together we can own the world." After Harvey's wife runs off with best-selling author Max Wilk (Axelrod's real-life collaborator on two Broadway revues in the early fifties), he and Cathy move to Hollywood, where they buy one of the major studios at an auction of memorabilia and proceed to sweep the Oscar race by filming a trashy novel Cathy has written under Harvey's disgusted tutelage. But Harvey finds being a success harder than being a failure (a role he had learned to play with assured, if morose, panache), and resolves, as he has done continually throughout the book, to commit suicide with a gun that "to my knowledge has not once been fired in joy, much less in anger."

In the fifties and early sixties, Axelrod's triple-sec wet dreams ended (as wet dreams will) just before climax: the hero never got the heroine to bed. But all of his film scripts read like suicide notes, for which the morning-after hangover—and not the night-before revelry—has provided the inspiration. Though his films are as fliply facile as any written by Hecht or Sturges or Wilder, the sense of self-pity and self-loathing that pervades Axelrod's characters is uniquely strong. *Paris When It Sizzles* ends with a typical hymn of self-hate. In what sounds suspiciously like a confession directed to Axelrod's friends back East, William Holden laments that "there've been too many years of too much dough, too many bad scripts, and too much whiskey." This peroration has been preceded by Holden's (read: Axelrod's) vision of the ideal "writer's movie." And so it is, with a story-and-screenplay credit that grows larger and larger until it has to be squeezed to fit into the frame—and with no director's credit. But it's a "writer's movie" in another, more depressing way: a surfeit of cute ideas and strained-sophisticated dialogue, and a fatal absence of any directorial style. As usual when Axelrod points a satirical finger at some Hollywood banality, the other four fingers point back accusingly at himself.

Axelrod is nothing if not ambivalent about *all* his targets, himself included. In *Paris When It Sizzles,* there's a swipe at auteurs that has the dream-movie director attempt a few visual flourishes, after which Holden observes: "And now that the director has distracted the audience with these wholly irrelevant vignettes, he returns reluctantly to the story." This is surely a needle with two points—one for the self-important director, the other for the kind of self-pitying screenwriter the Holden character really is. This uneasy combination of identification and satirical distance tends to dilute the final apologia, which ends up sounding like a halfhearted apology for an indulgent film idea made into a mediocre movie. But the self-administered goosing had a purgative effect: it cleared Axelrod's creative passages for the more honest, bilious mysogyny of his ultimate wish-fulfillment movie, *How to Murder Your Wife*, and for the stunning if erratic synthesis of his dream movies and his nightmare plays: the triumphantly bizarre *Lord Love a Duck*.

Lord Love a Duck (1966)

A decade of spasmodic success and pervading frustration as a Hollywood screenwriter seems to have left the early-sixties Axelrod in a deep funk. His most popular films (*Breakfast at Tiffany's* and *The Manchurian Candidate*) were, for all their brilliance as adaptations, perhaps his least personal projects. But popularity breeds power in Hollywood, and Axelrod had finally acquired enough power to write his own ticket—and his own scripts. He entered into a trial movie marriage with director Richard Quine, who had just separated from Blake Edwards after a decade of close collaboration, and produced two rambunctious offsprings: *Paris When It Sizzles* and *How to Murder Your Wife.*

Quine is one of those passive directors who neither improve nor ruin the scripts they are handed—the amiable sort of "contract artiste" that powerful screenwriters have a weakness for (cf. Nunnally Johnson). Axelrod seems to have needed a competent "employee" like Quine to soothe his ego and his spirit following a series of enervating associations with Edwards, Frank Tashlin, Leo McCarey, and John Frankenheimer. But the results of his partnership with Quine—pallid in the case of *Paris When It Sizzles,* pleasant in the case of *How to Murder Your Wife*—must have convinced Axelrod that he could do as well, if not better, on his own. For Nunnally Johnson, this move into the director's chair was a tacit admission of defeat; for Axelrod, it was a bracing challenge which, with *Lord Love a Duck,* he met head on.

Lord Love a Duck is a reckless, eccentric, infuriating movie. Its weaknesses are so obvious because its strengths are so dazzling, and because (as usual) Axelrod is unable to resolve his ambivalent feelings about the American woman. Is she a siren or just a loudmouth? a temptress or just a slut? vital or vulgar? demonic or demented? And is she really aware of the havoc she wreaks on the poor American male? Axelrod's obsession with American vulgarity (like that of Tashlin, Sturges, and, occasionally, Wilder) prevents him from attaining the distance we generally think of as being necessary for satire. Instead, we get a picture of the writer-director grappling and groping with his subject, resisting an embrace with one hand while he pinches a ripe buttock with the other.

Norman Mailer's biography of Marilyn Monroe, a book of vertiginous insights, contains this epiphany on the Axelrod-Wilder *Seven Year Itch*: "In Eisenhower years, comedy resides in how close one can come to the concept of hot pussy while still living in the cool of the innocent." Mailer's observation certainly holds true for the pictures Wilder made with Monroe, and Tashlin with Jayne Mansfield; beneath the 37- and 40-inch busts, these films told us, beat the heart of a greedy child. But the sixties was a very different decade. The same summer that witnessed the death of Norma Jean Mortenson gave birth to the screen incarnation of Dolores Haze. And from 1962 on, the haunting vulnerability of Lorelei Lee would be eclipsed by the calculating presence of Lolita. Imaginary seduction—the dream life of an Axelrod male—was now in danger of degenerating into statutory rape. Little wonder that in *Lord Love a Duck* we have the sensation that one hand is warily watching the other.

Axelrod succeeds in confronting his artistic schizophrenia to the extent that he can actually split the film's male and female personalities into self-contained stereotypes. Thus, among the men are a middle-aged high-school principal, sapless and slavering over the luscious teen bodies under his care, and fondling a series of phallic symbols; a father who tries to repress certain unspeakable urges for his teen-age daughter by going on an orgiastic shopping spree for cashmere sweaters (sample shades: Grape Yum Yum, Papaya Surprise, Midnight à Go-Go, Peach Put-Down); and a brutish, constantly perplexed football star whose overactive glands lead him down the bridal path and into a marital bed designed by Procrustes of Hollywood. The film's women range from Barbara Ann Greene (Tuesday Weld), the ambitious sweater-girl who's not quite sure whether immediate moviestardom is best achieved through exciting men or through emasculating them; to Barbara Ann's mother (Lola Albright), a bar-room bunny whose cottontail droops in direct proportion to her daughter's increasing perkiness; and, at the far right of this spectrum, a dotty old crustacean (played by Ruth Gordon in a style she has since congealed into kooky Kabuki) who tells her prospective daughter-in-law that "in our family, Miss Greene, we don't divorce our men—we bury 'em."

Hovering over this Sturgean mélange, making lazy circles in the sky and appraising the Southern California ethos with an admirably lofty condescension, is Mollymauk—"a bird thought to be extinct," a malefic Brewster McCloud—who occasionally assumes human, earthbound form as Alan (Roddy McDowall), a classmate of Barbara Ann's. Career-wise, they are the perfect match, with her voraciousness ("Everybody has got to love me—*every*body!") and sense of destiny ("This little girl is gonna cause a lot of trouble—that's what the gypsy said") complementing his awareness that male marionettes love to have their strings pulled by peroxided puppeteers. Inevitably, Alan's (and Axelrod's) attempt to inhabit some metasexual realm where one manipulates others, and is only massaged in return, may lead to a Hollywood contract for Barbara Ann; but it must end in psychotic loss of identity for the high-flying dirty bird.

Woven into this Dayglo tapestry are vignettes of L.A. *dolce vita*: the high school whose curriculum includes such courses as Adolescent Ethics, Commercial Relationships, Making and Taking II, and Plant Skills for Life (Botany); the First Drive-In Church, with loud-speaker attachments for hearing the sermon ("The Lord sure-as-shootin' answers prayers"); and a beach-party frug that appears to be staged only so some randy producer can make a movie out of it. There *is* a producer in *Lord Love a Duck*—who keeps losing his script in the Pacific shallows—but I suspect that the frug scene goes on as long as it does simply because Axelrod (his own producer here) enjoys gazing at boundlessly bountiful girls in motion. The vivisectionist in him wants to cut away and make some satirical point; the voyeur insists on long takes of those "long sun-tanned legs . . . that I dreamt of in my youth." And the voyeur wins. And the scene goes on and on.

To be sure, *every* scene in *Lord Love a Duck* goes on past the point where disinterested parody ends and obsessive revelations are exposed. Lola Albright's confession of her menopausal miseries sustains a chord of aching abrasiveness as she descends from histrionics into hysterics. The sweater-buying scene extends its shaggy-lamb premise to include a wry comment on the acquisition of child love through conspicuous consumption. And Axelrod directs all of this with an edgy intensity that suggests a more controlled, more radical Frank Tashlin. Today, the film has an uncompromisingly modern look to it, from the plastic people who fit perfectly into its "functional" *décor,* to the whites and grays that blend Barbara Ann's blond hair and creamy clothes into the school's institutional sterility and the smoggy monochrome of the new Hollywood sky.

In its visuals (surely intentionally) and its vision (perhaps unintentionally), *Lord Love a Duck* almost *is* what it's satirizing—and Axelrod is both creator and victim of his sad-eyed men and sadistic women. If imitation is the sincerest form of flattery, then complicity is the highest compliment a satirist can pay the objects of his nominal scorn. And if *Frankenstein* and *My Fair Lady* really are the same story, then Axelrod's males may be defined as genial Henry Higginses whom sexual frustration turns into impotent mad scientists; and his women are lovely Eliza Doolittles whose naïve use of their erotic Life Force is—dare we say it?—monstrous!

PETER STONE
(1930–   )

1963   CHARADE (Stanley Donen) co-story, screenplay
1964   FATHER GOOSE (Ralph Nelson) co-screenplay
1965   MIRAGE (Edward Dmytryk) screenplay
1966   ARABESQUE (Stanley Donen) co-screenplay [1]
1968   THE SECRET WAR OF HARRY FRIGG (Jack Smight) co-screenplay
       JIGSAW (James Goldstone) story, screenplay [2]
       DARK OF THE SUN (Jack Cardiff) co-screenplay [2]
1969   SWEET CHARITY (Bob Fosse) screenplay
1971   SKIN GAME (Paul Bogart) screenplay [1]
1972   1776 (Peter M. Hall) screenplay, from his musical play

[1] Under the pseudonym "Pierre Marton."
[2] Under the pseudonym "Quentin Werty."

In *Charade* the hero has five separate identities, all of which appear simultaneously on the screen at the finale. (Andrew Sarris complained of "a plot that smells of red herrings.") In *Mirage* the hero loses his identity through amnesia. (Howard Thompson called the film's flashbacks "a truly tangled web of 'teasers,' some never clarified.") In *Arabesque* the heroine may be working for any one, or all, of four Middle East Machiavellis. (*Variety* wrote that the "audience is never sure where it stands.") In *Jigsaw,* an informal remake of *Mirage,* the hero gets entangled in even more plot strands. (Leonard Maltin's *TV Movies* book calls it an "utterly confusing yarn.")

The leads in *Skin Game* are two friends, one white and one black, who survive in the antebellum Southwest by posing as slave trader and slave; Private Paul Newman in *The Secret War of Harry Frigg* poses as a general on an escape mission; Shirley MacLaine in *Sweet Charity* falls in love with a succession of frauds; and, in *Father Goose*, Cary Grant undertakes the most audacious disguise of all: that of a grizzled old beach bum. The musical *Kean* portrays an actor who is never quite sure of the difference between "acting" and "being"; and the 1972 musical *Sugar*, an adaptation of *Some Like It Hot*, features a male musician who, when he starts "acting" like a girl, almost "becomes" one.

Clearly, in Peter Stone's world and world view, *nothing* is true—as is indicated by some of his films' titles (*Charade, Mirage, Arabesque, Jigsaw*). Indeed, for many of the critics, precious little is even clear. Stone delights in constructing scripts in which every sinister plot twist signals another identity crisis. The psychological disorientation that haunted Hollywood's postwar *film noir* has become so pervasive, so inescapable, Stone's films seem to say, that the only rational response is to laugh at the existential absurdity of it all. Fortunately, Stone's technique is as distinguished as his theme is distinctive, or *Charade, Arabesque*, and *Skin Game* would merely be tantalizing footnotes to the *Zeitgeist*, and not three of the most elegant entertainments Hollywood has produced since the assembly line broke down.

Charade (1963)

Charade is a film steeped in so many ambiguities, intrigues, and deceptions that it's almost to be expected that some of its mistaken-identity games would take place behind the camera. Stone's script is credited as originating in a story by himself and Marc Behm (who also worked mysteriously on *Help!*). Soon before the film was released, a novel appeared under the title *Charade* and the byline of Peter Stone, but dedicated to Marc Behm. The Writers Guild of America cites "The Unsuspecting Wife," "a published story by Peter Stone and Marc Behm," as the source material. And, in a *New York* magazine article written in 1964, Stone described the difficulty he found in selling his original idea to Hollywood, and the decision to rewrite the screenplay as a novel, thereby creating a salable property —which is (it would seem) what happened, except that the final screenplay is more dexterous and delicious by far than the novel, which is missing important sequences, and which gives away the film's surprise ending ten pages too early.

No one in *Charade* is to be trusted, or, for that matter, *is* trusted. The villain, a man first known as Carson Dyle, turns out to be the hero, a CIA agent; and the heroine's protector, a CIA agent, turns out to be the villainous Carson Dyle. The heroine's name is Reggie Lambert, until she learns that her deceased husband Charles had at least three other names (Voss, Fabrii, and Moreno); the CIA agent (that is, the bad Dyle) refers offhandedly to her as "Mrs. Voss." A trio of Lambert's (that is, Voss's) war buddies believes Reggie is the villainess (that is, that she has the money for which her husband was murdered), and they are right (that she has the money, in the form of stamps), but she doesn't know it. She is too busy (1) trying to avoid being murdered herself, and (2) falling in love with "Carson Dyle," alias Alexander Dyle, alias Peter Joshua, alias Adam Canfield, who is really Brian Cruikshank, the CIA man, but whom Reggie suspects is the murderer. But she is deceiving Carson/Alexander/Peter/Adam/Brian by working for the man she believes to be a CIA agent, who is really the murderer, the "real" Carson Dyle. In a showdown between the two Dyles, Reggie saves her life by trusting her instincts—as Gregory Peck will do when confronted with the equally perplexing personality of Sophia Loren, in *Arabesque*—and believing the man she loves instead of the man she trusted. Love, intuitive and irrational, is the only clue to ending a devious, deadly charade.

Stone's (and Behm's?) labyrinthine plot might have made an intricate but empty film if Stone had not taken as much care developing his characters as he did assembling his story line. The three menacing Army pals exemplify humors as well as purvey terror: James Coburn is tall and genial, Ned Glass is short and nervous, George Kennedy is big and brutal. Each has an evil personality strong enough to earn him star status as the real villain, and enough personal charm to make the viewer regret his passing—one by strangulation (in an elevator), one by suffocation (in a cellophane bag), and one by loss of blood (from the throat)—and not only because, as each suspect departs, it becomes increasingly clear that the real murderer must be Cary Grant! Walter Matthau, the "CIA agent" with dandruff and dyspepsia, seems simply too bumbling to be a mass murderer. But, in the great tradition of detective stories, the murderer is the character we least suspect; and, as in

Agatha Christie's *The Mousetrap,* we least suspect the "detective."

Stanley Donen here directs script, players, and camera with a panache worthy of Hitchcock at his best. Perhaps this explains the attacks on Donen's "Hitchcock" films by royalists Andrew Sarris and Robin Wood, who see Donen as an arrogant pretender to Hitchcock's crown. (The same charge is applied to Donen's "Minnelli" musicals.) Other critical eyes, untouched by auteur clairvoyance or myopia, may see in *Charade* and *Arabesque* the craftsmanship of early Hitchcockery (*The Lady Vanishes, Shadow of a Doubt*) wedded to the complexity of the Master's later suspense films (*Rear Window, North by Northwest*). If Donen occasionally shows a tendency to flex his cinematic muscles, as in *Arabesque*'s LSD sequence, his films at least never turn to flab, the way long stretches of *Torn Curtain* and *Topaz* do. And yet, for all his facility in a wide variety of genres, "the Donen 'touch,' " according to Andrew Sarris, "remains as elusive as ever"—a failing which, if it denies Donen entrance to the auteur pantheon, certainly qualifies him as the perfect director for that most "elusive" of screenwriters, Peter Stone.

Skin Game (1971)

The heroes (and, in *Arabesque,* the heroine) of Stone's comedies generally assume identities; the heroes of his melodramas usually lose them, a problem summarized by this dialogue, from *Jigsaw,* between scientist Jonathan Fields and the detective Fields has hired to trace the missing person within him:

> FIELDS: I don't know who I am.
> DETECTIVE: When did you start not knowing who you were?
> FIELDS: I don't know.

Quincy Drew, the engaging con man in *Skin Game,* has no such problem. No matter what role he happens to be playing—slave trader, horse trader, Oriental fortune teller, Army surgeon, priest— Quincy retains an easy assurance of his own identity because the personality is always the same. Quincy's partner in duplicity, the black freeman Jason O'Rourke, is slightly less at ease as an East Indian, American Indian, domestic slave or African tribal prince, since the racist realities of Kansas, Missouri, and Texas in the 1850s make his role-playing slightly more precarious: Quincy could never be a priest, but with a little bad luck Jason could be—and does become

—a slave. Quincy is perceptive enough to spot a "natural-born bunko artist" beneath Jason's ebony exterior, but just shortsighted enough to ignore a skin-deep difference which means, as Jason says, that "I can be bought and sold like a horse, and you can do the buying and selling."

This is exactly how Quincy and Jason make their living in the small Western towns where slavery is not only rife but also ripe for exploitation by a clever black-and-white confidence team. Quincy "sells" Jason to avaricious slave owners, pockets the money, and then escapes with Jason and heads for the next outpost of gullibility. Before this ruse can wear thin as a plot device, it backfires, throwing Quincy for a loop that lands him, fortunately, on his wits. The local marks are no match for Quincy, so Stone introduces an antagonist worthy of his protagonist's wiles: fleet-fingered Ginger, who beats Quincy at his own game by trading on the traditional honesty of her sex. Quincy is proud enough to believe that no woman could resist his charms, and Ginger is smart enough to realize that the theme of wide-eyed coquetry can be played with a few cunning variations, resulting in both fun and profit. Intelligence and style go hand in hand here (literally, once Quincy and Ginger fall in love), obliterating any questions of morality for those few viewers who couldn't accept the proposition that stealing from slave owners is an honorable, if not a revolutionary, profession.

Quincy, the antebellum Bret Maverick, is a part tailor-made for James Garner, with his mischievous eyes belying the phony slow-wittedness in that most characteristic gesture of his: the receding, slack-jawed look of duped innocence. Garner has an amiable familiarity that might have made him a major star in the thirties and forties, but on today's manic-catatonic movie scene, good-natured resourcefulness without a compensating sense of neurotic danger doesn't quite spell star quality. Because of this, *Skin Game* may find its rightful audience only when it appears on the home screen—if its inexhaustible inventiveness doesn't seem too supercharged to television viewers for whom comfortable boredom is the natural state of being.

One thing about Hollywood's Golden Age that made moviegoing (as opposed to movie criticism) so much more enjoyable than it is now was the high level of entertainment in those middle-ground pictures which Andrew Sarris and Pauline Kael rightly identified as the glory of the American commercial cinema: the crisp action movies, the four-hankie romances, the fast-paced comedies. Today those one-time rhinestones have the sparkle of genuine movie gems, which seem all the more precious now because, with the industry's prolonged suicidal tendencies and the defaulting of quickly made, low-budget filming to TV, the doctrine of the excluded middle has taken effect. Millions for *Papillon,* but barely one decent budget for a high-quality programmer. When Hollywood does try to invoke its treasured tradition, the results are often stale and cadaverous, demolishing what was good in the old, and flattening by imitation what is good in the new. And on those even rarer occasions when a major "minor" film like *Skin Game* sneaks through, the studios forget how to publicize it for moviegoers who have forgotten such films still exist. *Skin Game* thus quickly, and unjustly, achieved the anonymity Peter Stone has so long sought for himself, though not for his films.

The problem of identity, which Stone has probed with such ingenious ambiguity, extends to the author himself. Nearly half of his films have been written under pseudonyms. *Skin Game,* credited on the script to Peter Stone and David Giler (who authored the original, supposedly clever screenplay for *Myra Breckinridge*), is credited on the film to one "Pierre Marton," the alias Stone used for his dialogue-polishing job on *Arabesque.* Marton is the surname of Stone's stepfather; Pierre is the French for "Peter"—and also the French word for "stone." The questions inevitably arise: Who is Peter Stone? And does *he* really exist?

HOWARD KOCH
(1902–   )

1940   VIRGINIA CITY (Michael Curtiz) co-story (uncredited)
       THE SEA HAWK (Michael Curtiz) co-story, co-screenplay
       THE LETTER (William Wyler) screenplay
1941   SHINING VICTORY (Irving Rapper) co-screenplay
       SERGEANT YORK (Howard Hawks) co-screenplay
1942   IN THIS OUR LIFE (John Huston) screenplay
       CASABLANCA (Michael Curtiz) co-screenplay
1943   MISSION TO MOSCOW (Michael Curtiz) screenplay
1944   IN OUR TIME (Vincent Sherman) co-story, co-screenplay
1945   RHAPSODY IN BLUE (Irving Rapper) co-screenplay
1946   THREE STRANGERS (Jean Negulesco) co-story, co-screen-
       play
1948   LETTER FROM AN UNKNOWN WOMAN (Max Ophuls)
       screenplay
1950   NO SAD SONGS FOR ME (Rudolph Maté) screenplay
1951   THE THIRTEENTH LETTER (Otto Preminger) screenplay
1961   THE GREENGAGE SUMMER [LOSS OF INNOCENCE]
       (Lewis Gilbert) screenplay
1962   THE WAR LOVER (Philip Leacock) screenplay
1967   THE FOX (Mark Rydell) co-screenplay
1974   THE WOMAN OF OTOWI CROSSING (Daniel Mann) screen-
       play

Literally and figuratively, Howard Koch is Hollywood's premier
man of letters. The most cursory glance at his filmography reveals a
passion bordering on obsession with messages of every kind, from
the Martian signals in his "War of the Worlds" radio play for Orson

Welles' Mercury Theatre in 1938 to the photograph with which Susannah York betrays her middle-aged beau to the police in *Loss of Innocence* in 1961. Koch's golden decade was the forties, when he helped create such memorable films as *The Sea Hawk, Sergeant York, Mission to Moscow, Three Strangers*, and *No Sad Songs for Me.*

His most characteristic work involved a curious quartet that included a resourceful adaptation of Maugham's *The Letter*; his and Max Ophuls' affecting elegy to memory and movement, *Letter from an Unknown Woman*; and the Canadianization of Clouzot's *Le Corbeau* into one of Otto Preminger's few understated melodramas, *The Thirteenth Letter.* The last member of this quartet is not only Koch's most famous film but also perhaps Hollywood's most durable hit, with those notorious "letters of transit" in *Casablanca* serving as the tantalizing MacGuffin for a film whose nonpareil reputation ill-conceals the happy fact that it boasts some of the best dialogue to be found in an American film—which Koch wrote. The blacklist (a sort of poison-pen letter from the House un-American Activities Committee to Koch and several hundred other filmmakers) retired our prolific correspondent earlier than the eminence of his credits would have indicated. His definitive re-emergence came only in 1971, with the first performance of a one-act drama that plays like a misanthropic summation of his lifelong theme. The play's title is *Dead Letters.*

Casablanca (1942)

When *Casablanca* first appeared, toward the end of 1942, few movie-wise people would have bet that screen history was about to be embossed on the Warner Brothers shield. Hal Wallis had a topical subject on which to base another hit production; but everybody was making war-effort movies. Moreover, the script—which bore some recognizable traces of *Everybody Comes to Rick's,* "one of the world's worst plays," according to James Agee—was completed at breakneck speed and under appalling pressure by a junior member of the Warners writing pool, Howard Koch, after the studio's prolific Epstein brothers had been called to Washington for an important war assignment.

The stars and supporting players were indeed first-rate; certainly the film would not enjoy its present reputation if it had starred

Ronald Reagan, Ann Sheridan, and Dennis Morgan, as originally planned, instead of Humphrey Bogart, Ingrid Bergman, and Paul Henreid. Although *Casablanca* defines Bogey for all time as the existential-hero-in-spite-of-himself, several of his roles just preceding this one (notably *High Sierra* and *The Maltese Falcon*) had prepared his fans for the misanthropy and climactic selflessness he would embody as Rick Blaine. Bergman (as Ilsa Lund) and Henreid (as Victor Laszlo) are hardly incandescent lovers—neither, for that matter, are Bergman and Bogart—but their turgidity as sexual partners works, intentionally or not, to the film's advantage. Claude Rains had played a perplexing variety of roles: some sympathetic (*Now, Voyager*), some unsympathetic (*Crime Without Passion*), and some in which he was a good man weak enough to fall prey to overwhelming forces (scientific megalomania in *The Invisible Man*, political corruption in *Mr. Smith Goes to Washington*); audiences weren't sure of the proper moral attitude to assume toward Rains, and this made him perfect for the suave, enigmatic Louis Renault.

The outrageously dense supporting cast of Conrad Veidt, Peter Lorre, Sydney Greenstreet, Dooley Wilson, S. Z. Sakall, Leonid Kinsky, John Qualen, Curt Bois, Marcel Dalio, and dozens of others would have lent a certain spurious sense of resonance to *Deep Throat*, let alone to a film in which each player is adroitly cast and allowed a privileged moment or two all his own. Michael Curtiz had directed forty-two films in the previous decade for Warners and, when one considers the restrictions on shot-planning and script-doctoring inherent in such a prodigious output, the generally high quality of his work is impressive. Undoubtedly, much of the film's verve and terse efficiency—as well as its occasionally hurried, perfunctory *mise-en-scène*—can be traced to Curtiz.

But the real success of *Casablanca* derives from the writers' character development and from the dialogue which Bogart and Bergman complained about to the press, and which James Agee so flippantly dismissed in his *Nation* column. Warners would again assemble attractive casts, and assign Curtiz to direct them—as with *Passage to Marseille*. None of the sequels was as richly textured, as effortlessly witty, as complex in characterization, as entertaining or, consequently, as popular as *Casablanca*. On the other hand, when Koch had the opportunity, five years later, to work with Max Ophuls on *Letter from an Unknown Woman,* he produced a script as drenched in delicate Viennese irony as *Casablanca* was suffused with the more pungent irony of an occupied city where all roles are uncertain, and thus played to the hilt—and where the only values are the shifting ones of the Vichy franc, and thus gambled on with a stylish desperation that tries to pass for insouciance.

Casablanca is concerned with the reconciling of opposites: comradeship and love, realism and idealism, war and resistance to warmakers. Its plot bears an amusing resemblance to Casey Robinson's script for the 1937 Warners romantic comedy, *It's Love I'm After* (*q.v.*). In that film the polarities are represented by two engaged couples. One pair (Leslie Howard and Bette Davis) is bantering and sophisticated; the other (Patric Knowles and Olivia de Havilland) is naïve and headstrong. De Havilland thinks she's in love with Howard, a stage star, although she's really fallen for his portrayal of Romeo to Davis's Juliet. After nearly succumbing to de Havilland's ravenous innocence—he even pretends attempted rape, hoping *that* will shatter her illusions, only to find her an ecstatically willing victim—Howard finally convinces Olivia that Knowles is the man for her, and this leaves him free to pursue his relationship with Davis, a truly suitable partner.

In *Casablanca* the Howard and Davis roles are taken by Bogart and Rains, and the de Havilland and Knowles parts by Bergman and Henreid. Bogart chooses Rains over Bergman less because he finds a fellow cynic more compatible than an inexperienced idealist than because, in wartime, the man of action must accept comradeship (i.e., pragmatic patriotism) over love (i.e., political idealism). To a nation that had just entered the war and was considering the prospects with some reluctance if not resistance, *Casablanca* acted as both an explanation of its causes and an exhortation to America's young men to pack up their sweethearts in an attic trunk and smile, smile, smile—wryly, of course. The men (Bogart and Rains) would do the fighting while the women (Bergman) and idealists (Henreid) would keep the home fires of freedom burning until their return.

The vigorous stoicism with which Rick Blaine surrenders Ilsa to Laszlo, and the pleasure he exudes in walking with Renault into the final fade-out, have given rise to two intriguing theories about the film, one pertinent and one impertinent. The first is that *Casablanca* is a political allegory, with Rick as President Roosevelt (*casa blanca* is Spanish for "white house"), a man who gambles on the odds of going to war until circumstance and his own submerged nobility force him to close his casino (read: partisan politics) and commit himself—first by financing the Side of Right and then by fighting for it. The time of the film's action (December 1941) adds credence to this view, as does the irrelevant fact that, two months after *Casablanca* opened, Roosevelt (Rick) and Prime Minister Winston Churchill (Laszlo) met for a war conference in Casablanca.

The other theory proposes *Casablanca* as a repressed homosexual fantasy, in which Rick rejects his token mistress for an honest if furtive affair with another man. Well, Rick isn't exactly "rough trade," and Renault's exhaustive string of conquests attests to his performance, if not his preference. Still, they make an intriguing active-passive pair. Renault flirts with Rick—indeed, he flirts with everyone—throughout the film, and at one point he tells Ilsa, "He is the kind of man that . . . well, if I were a woman, and *I* were not around, I should be in love with Rick." The pansexual sophistication of the seventies makes such inferences as these appealing, especially when we can attach them to artifacts from our own primitive past. But we should be careful when we paint yesterday's picture in today's colors; tomorrow they may seem gaudily inappropriate. At the time Renault speaks to Ilsa, he doesn't know that she was and is "in love with Rick." Ilsa, however, loves an *idealized* Rick—a socialist adventurer, who fought on the right sides in Ethiopia and Spain—while Renault loves or likes or admires the *real* Rick, who uses his financial and sexual authority to throw Nazis out of his café and idealists out of his life (the latter more gently, to be sure). For Rick, women are an occasional obsession; for Renault they are a perpetual diversion. Both want companionship more than they need love. If audiences did not intuit this preference, they wouldn't accept the film's ending with such supreme satisfaction.

Besides, Renault's presumed ambisexuality is of less interest than his genuine ambiguity. When Renault's tongue is not in his cheek (a place of relative repose), it is darting out to catch the weary or unwary females who buzz into Casablanca hoping for a visa. Renault is not rapacious so much as he is pleased by the power that he wields, and amused at the indignities men must endure—and women must enjoy—for him to use that power to their benefit. He is radiantly corrupt. He has style. What Rick thinks of, early in the film, as political realism, Renault knows is expediency. In Rick, American pragmatism has soured into phlegmatism, while in Renault French charm has degenerated into coquetry. But Rick can give Renault a sense of values, and Renault can give Rick a sense of proportion; both have a sardonic sense of humor. In Jungian terms, Rick is the *animus* of this split personality and Renault is the *anima*. Or, as they used to say at Schwab's, the two are made for each other.

Rick and Renault share the economic and spiritual leadership of Vichy-ruled Casablanca with Signor Ferrari (Sydney Greenstreet), the black-market boss who can say simply, "As leader of all illegal activities in Casablanca, I am an influential and respected man." This odd troika presides over a populace that is either flourishing or desperate, depending on their ability to hustle persuasively, and regardless of their former status. Thus, a beautiful woman tells her companion, an old letch: "It used to take a villa at Cannes, or the very least, a string of pearls. Now all I ask is an exit visa." (Her plight was even more serious than she had feared: her dialogue was cut from the completed film.) When the manager of "the second largest banking house in Amsterdam" tries to bully Carl, the head-waiter, for a drink with Rick, Carl replies that "the leading banker is the pastry chef in our kitchen." Carl, whom the script describes as the author of books on "mathematics . . . astronomy . . . the greatest professor in the whole University of Leipzig," represents the humanistic—that is, the Jewish—side of the German psyche.

Of Rick's other employees, Sascha the bartender (Leonid Kinskey) had been "the Czar's favorite sword-swallower"; Abdul the doorman (Dan Seymour) adds some local color to the café, if not to the film; and the croupier of Rick's illegal gambling table is given no specific past, but since he is played by Marcel Dalio, reverberations of his tainted aristocracy in *The Rules of the Game* may appear on the seismographic memories of some moviegoers. The only member of Rick's retinue who indicates any integrity with his own past is Sam, the piano player (Dooley Wilson), who had been Rick's companion four years earlier in Paris—when Rick and Ilsa fell in love—and shares the same relationship with him in Casablanca. The continuity of Sam's function suggests that the lighthearted Rick of Paris and the pessimistic Rick of Casablanca are closer to one another than his crude bitterness toward Ilsa later on in the café would imply. At any rate, Rick's role to the rest of his staff is that of the curt if protective patriarch, whereas he shows Sam a courtesy that he reveals to few others, usually prefacing requests with a gentlemanly "do you mind." Indeed, Ferrari's offer to "buy" Sam, along with Rick's sa-

loon, drives Rick to a rare flight of self-righteousness—"I don't buy
or sell human beings"—which leads us to believe that, at this point
in the film at least, Sam is one of the few beings in Casablanca whom
Rick would consider human.

After a brief montage of animated maps describing the European
émigré's route through Casablanca (an undistinguished chore that
has won Don Siegel more attention than Koch ever got for his work
on the script), the film's irony and the city's duplicity are immediately established with the entrance of the Dark European (Curt
Bois). The term is both literal and metaphorical: this guy is doubly
shady, pursuing the pickpocket's profession by warning his suckers,
with a great show of concern, about the many pickpockets in town.
With a pithiness typical of both characters and dialogue, the script
not only establishes the sinister dexterity of this Dark European—
and, by extension, of all those who thrive in Casablanca—but also
imparts some crucial plot information. "Two German couriers were
found murdered in the desert. (*With an ironic smile* [says the
script]) The . . . unoccupied desert." They had been carrying letters
of transit, the visas which cannot be questioned, and whose fateful
power will bring all who touch them—beginning with the doomed
black-marketeer Ugarte (Peter Lorre) and ending with Rick himself—close to death, like the sexual love that turns to syphilis in
Schnitzler's *La Ronde*.

The sign by the door of Captain Renault's *Palais de Justice*—
itself an ironic title—reads "LIBERTÉ, ÉGALITÉ, FRATERNITÉ." The
film will place a fairly grave accent on Liberty (as personified by
Ilsa and Laszlo) and a cute accent on Fraternity (as exemplified by
Rick and Renault). As for Equality . . . well, this is an African
country run by white Europeans; there is a Dark European in the
film, but no blackamoor. Economic and sexual equality are also
ignored. As the Dark European says (in the script), "The rich and
beautiful sail to Lisbon. The poor are always with us."

Even Major Strasser (Conrad Veidt), Laszlo's formidable pursuer and the chief representative of the Third Reich's arrogance and
humorlessness, is entertaining in a verminous way—a quality that
would be lacking in later Hollywood Nazis, once the makers of war
movies decided that putting a two- or three-dimensional villain on
the screen was a creative act of treason. Strasser can't help but be
affected by the irony that laces Casablanca's humid air, and he occasionally jousts with Renault and, later, with Rick and Laszlo. But

he always loses in these contests of wit, if only because of his grim, heavy-handed determination to win.

Whenever a long-lost love emerges from the machine-made mists of a Hollywood hero's past, an "other woman" is needed to add a little dramatic tension to the confrontation in the present. Rick's present is clouded by such a smoke screen of cynicism that an alluring third party would be redundant—but we are given one anyway: Yvonne (Madeleine Le Beau). Her main function, aside from ever-so-tenuously indicating Rick's vacillation between German power and Allied positive thinking, is to act as foil for two of *Casablanca*'s most quoted lines. More than any other, this bit of dialogue established Rick and Bogart as early existential heroes.

> YVONNE: Where were you last night?
> RICK: That's so long ago, I don't remember.
> YVONNE (*after a pause*): Will I see you tonight?
> RICK: I never make plans that far ahead.

With the merest suggestion that his stoic rejection of Yvonne will save her a lot of heartache (and save him a few annoying hysteria scenes), Rick sends her home—with Sascha, who really loves her. Rick seems to throw away women with the same assured carelessness he evinces in throwing away lines; but there is hardly ever a waste motion in either his actions or his dialogue. Here he has obliquely stated his philosophy, ended a tedious affair, and made a match. He has also lured Renault into the conversation, for the Captain, after chiding Rick on his extravagance with women (Rains says, "Some day they may be scarce," but the script's phrasing is wittier and more relevant: "Some day they may be rationed"), allows that he is interested in Yvonne himself. Rick, it would seem, can have any woman he wants—and yet he doesn't seem to want any.

> RENAULT: I've often speculated on why you don't return to America. Did you abscond with the church funds? Did you run off with a Senator's wife? I'd like to think you killed a man. It's the romantic in me.
> RICK (*sardonically*): It was a combination of all three.

For some, Casablanca is a purgatory where their worldly sins (money, jewels, political connections) must be bartered away in order to escape. For others—the omnipresent but unseen poor—Casablanca is sheer hell, with no hope of redemption. For Rick it is Limbo, a state of suspended spiritual animation. We never do find

out about Rick's distant past, although he finds out about Ilsa's; perhaps this is one reason why the Bogart character lives today, while
Bergman's Ilsa has lost co-starred billing (for at least some *Casablanca* devotees) to Rick's partner in enigmatic ambiguity, Louis
Renault. But if Rick's sardonic evasion doesn't tell us about his
past, it does portend future events which only he can control. The
film's climax will have Rick "abscond with the church funds" by
selling his saloon to Ferrari, "run off with a Senator's wife" by leaving Casablanca in the company of the coquettish representative from
Vichy, and "kill a man"—Major Strasser.

> RENAULT: And what in Heaven's name brought you to Casa-
> blanca?
> RICK: My health. I came to Casablanca for the waters.
> RENAULT: The waters? What waters? We are in the desert.
> RICK: I was misinformed.

The Pinteresque understatement of Rick's ludicrous "explanation"
explains his presence—at least, it telegraphs to Renault elements of
pastness that point to Rick's reluctance to explain them, as well as the
nimble absurdity with which he chooses to evade the question—as
eloquently as will the long, informative Paris flashback.

Rick is even nimbler, and more oblique, about his dormant political nobility. We know he ran guns to Ethiopia in 1935, and fought
for the Loyalists in 1936, long-shot activities that make his current
political and sexual neutrality look more counterrevolutionary than
it would otherwise. But when Strasser tries to intimidate Rick by
reading him a Nazi-researched dossier of these adventures, Rick
simply glances at the German's little black book and, with a bland
expression that perfectly reveals his contempt for the obviousness
of Strasser's methods, asks, "Are my eyes really brown?" This
blending of the modest and the arrogant, the casual and the ballsy,
stamps Rick as a man of courage and offers a presentiment of his
climactic heroism. Here, he has nothing to gain by his bravado except an affirmation of his self-respect—and an offhand solicitation
of Renault's respect, which one doubts Rick values very highly.
Nevertheless, when Renault (in the same conversation) says of
Laszlo, "Of course, one must admit he has great courage," it is a
tribute that Rick has already earned for himself.

Laszlo *is* courageous. True, the oratorical skills necessary in a
Resistance leader—not to mention his lame-duck role in the plot—
frequently draw him into pomposity and self-righteousness. But

Laszlo can be ironic when irony is needed, if only to Advance The
Cause. (Humorless men, like Laszlo, like Strasser, indeed like
Charles Foster Kane, can use humor to their advantage: to convert,
to threaten, to *seem* human. These three men, superficially so different, are tied together by their use of power and people. They are
all public men; only their goals distinguish them.) Thus, when an
Underground contact (John Qualen) tells Laszlo that he has "read
five times that you were killed in five different places," Laszlo replies, "(*smiling wryly*): As you can see, it was true every single
time." In fact, the life of a fugitive has sapped enough of Laszlo's
vitality so that he must channel all of it into politics, and too little
of it to his love, his wife, Ilsa.

Four years earlier, in pre-Occupation Paris, Ilsa had been only a
mystery woman ("I know so little about you—just the fact that you
had your teeth straightened"). Now, in Casablanca, she is a phantom. Once she had been the repository of Rick's romantic love and
political idealism, to such an extent that distinctions between personal obsessions and political affections blurred and then merged.
When the Nazis moved into Paris, she moved out of his life; Rick's
idealism and love, because they had become inseparable, were
fatally dissolved on the same day. The death of romance left a rancid
crust of cynicism upon Rick's soul, and over the years the crust
hardened to form a casket for his optimism and nobility. *Casablanca*'s crucial dramatic question is whether her reappearance after
such a long time—a lifetime, a death time—will help revive that
Parisian optimism or bury it for good; and whether, once Ilsa has
resurrected Rick's romantic love and political idealism, he will be
able to suppress the former for the sake of the latter.

In the 1937 flashback, Rick bombards Ilsa with the kind of questions his Casablanca acquaintances would later ask him: "Who are
you really, and what were you before? What did you do, and what
did you think?" His famous toast—"Here's looking at you, kid"—
can be read as meaning, "Here's trying to look into your soul, kid, to
figure out who you really are." For most of *Casablanca,* Rick and
Ilsa and Laszlo are defined not only by their pasts but by the suspicions other characters have about these pasts. Ilsa in 1937 and Rick
in 1941 are evasive for the same reason: for each, a love affair
melded into international affairs so imperceptibly and overwhelm
ingly that telling one's confession would amount to a chaotic, person-
alized history lesson. The film's denouement will, for Rick, be literally

that—an "unraveling" of future conditional from past imperfect, of
Western Civilization from autobiography, of duty from love.

Ilsa is basically a simple country girl; *her* irony is platitudinous.
"With the whole world crumbling, we pick this time to fall in love,"
she says to Rick in Paris (it will be as appropriate in Casablanca).
And, later: "Was that cannon fire—or is it my heart pounding?"
These are presumably two of the lines whose vapidity drove Miss
Bergman to carp to the press. It's a shame the actress didn't realize
that Ilsa was simply written to character; perhaps she was too close
to Ilsa, a character whose veins simply couldn't hold enough ice
water (Strasser), Pernod (Renault) or *sang-froid* (Rick) to banter
brilliantly and disinterestedly with the movie's heroes, villains, and
fence straddlers. Ilsa is the sort of serious, naïve young woman who
would express the most exalted of emotions in the rhetoric of a
Hollywood love story—unlike Rick and Renault, whose diction and
delivery indicate a more genuine, more assured compatibility.

Miss Bergman's petulance over the lines she had to read may be
understandable if we realize that the deeper ironies in Ilsa's dialogue
are apparent not to the character but only to the viewer. As sign-
posts to the film's plot and characterization, these lines have meanings they lack as stabs at rapier wit. When Ilsa dodges Rick's probes
into her past and his demands on her future—even saying, in response to Rick's suggestion that they get married as soon as they
arrive in Marseilles, that "That's too far ahead to plan"—she is unknowingly clarifying Rick's abrupt dismissal of Yvonne; Rick's
quest for a past and hope for a future with Ilsa had inflamed a love
that disappointment turned to ashes—once burned, twice shy.
When she tells Rick that "you must leave Paris" and he replies, "No,
we must leave," Ilsa (or, more precisely, the film itself) is preparing the viewer for Rick's final choice of the greatest good for the
greatest number over an easy solution to "the problems of three little
people."

Of course, Rick leaves Paris alone, with the Paris rain smudging
Ilsa's farewell letter as a considerate substitute for Rick's (and Bogart's) reluctant tears. The flashback ends with Rick drunkenly
bleary instead of heroically teary—the cynic's attempt to becloud
pain with a dull gauze rather than letting it all drip out. When Ilsa
interrupts Rick's masochistic reverie to tell him about her marriage
to Laszlo then and now, Rick accuses her of literal and political
prostitution—the loser's attempt to punish himself by hurting some-

one he may still love. As Ilsa walks out, Rick surrenders to one of those rare waste motions that reveal the unwinding of his coiled composure: he collapses, heartbroken and instantly hungover, like the sort of drunk "M'sieur Rick" would throw out of his café without breaking his stride, his composure, or the silky pattern of his dialogue.

The galaxy of supporting characters in *Casablanca* constitutes a dazzling and baroque hall of mirrors that reflect facets and distortions of the leading characters' lives and life styles. Ugarte and Ferrari are various corruptions of Rick, as peddler and panderer, respectively; Carl is a cuddly, less ostentatious Laszlo; Sascha is an unseductive Renault; Yvonne and the Dark European share Rick's indecision between Free France and the Third Reich; Strasser is a German version of Renault, a prosaic scientist of war to Renault's master of the boudoir arts, the crazy-mirror image of an *übermensch* as opposed to Renault's *homme moyen sensuel*. The film is almost symphonic in the way its reflections of plot and reverberations of dialogue help to reinforce themes and deepen our understanding of Rick and Renault, Ilsa and Laszlo. One of these variations, which almost amounts to a subplot, involves Rick and Annina, a young Bulgarian woman determined to get herself and her calf-like husband to America—even if it means meeting Captain Renault's stiff price. Annina's plea to Rick for advice is practically a précis of the film's dilemma. (The dialogue is straight from the original play.)

> ANNINA: M'sieur, you are a man. If someone loved you—very much, so that your happiness was the only thing that she wanted in the world—but she did a bad thing to make certain of it, could you forgive her?
> RICK: Nobody ever loved me that much.
> ANNINA: And he never knew—and the girl kept this bad thing locked in her heart—that would be all right, wouldn't it?
> RICK (*harshly*): You want my advice?
> ANNINA: Oh, yes, please.
> RICK: Go back to Bulgaria.

There's nothing neat about the analogy of subplot to plot here. What is clear is that the Rick-Annina dialogue acts both as echo and as prophecy. Annina's forthrightness and bravery, as much as anything else, convince Rick to revise his estimation of Ilsa's attachment for him; perhaps, at the moment he mutters "nobody has ever loved me that much," Rick realizes how much Ilsa loved and admired him—enough to believe he had the strength to survive a bitterly cruel disillusionment. Rick "never knew"; Ilsa "kept this bad thing locked in her heart"; and ultimately she "went back" to Czechoslovakia, as personified by Victor Laszlo. Of course, Ilsa didn't guarantee Rick's (or Laszlo's) happiness by leaving him to join Laszlo. And, when she comes to his apartment later to get the letters of transit, it won't be because she loves Laszlo "very much," at least not romantically, or even personally: only as the embodiment of a great cause. Indeed, as she finally realizes, she loves Rick beyond all scruple—unaware that Rick will settle for her admiration. The Rick-Annina analogy is more fitting as a portent of this climactic decision of Rick's, to send Ilsa away with Laszlo—for Rick, by fixing the roulette wheel, helps Annina get the visa money without capitulating to the *capitaine*.

Renault has his revenge when, at the suggestion of Major Strasser, he orders Rick's saloon closed. Earlier, Renault had told Rick that he allowed the place to stay open partly because Rick let him win at roulette. By assisting Annina, Rick made Renault lose. Now, Renault gestures dramatically toward the back room he has patronized for so long and says, "I'm shocked—*shocked* to find that gambling is going on in here!" Thus, in one foul sweep, Renault satisfies Strasser with a genuine excuse for closing Rick's; indicates to Rick, through the absurdity of the charge, that it was Strasser's idea to close it, and not his; and pleases himself by taking revenge on Rick for depriving him of an evening's horizontal pleasure.

The café shut down, Ilsa returns for the letters of transit which she knows are in Rick's possession. Every ploy she tries—invoking the name of the Resistance, stirring the ashes of their Paris affair, calling him a coward, pleading with him, and finally threatening him—aggravates her barely suppressed hysterical love and increases his morose fatalism. "Go ahead and shoot," Rick says. "You'll be doing me a favor." It is here that Ilsa realizes not how much she overestimated his ability to withstand her departure in Paris, but how crushingly it affected his spirit. The man who, four years earlier, said of the Nazis, "I left a note in my apartment; they'll know where to find me," is now a handful of pulp waiting to be tossed away. Laszlo, the saint, has won her admiration, while Rick's terse admission of his weakness, his humanity, wins her love. "How much I loved you . . . how much I still love you!"

But Rick has a ploy—noble, to be sure—of his own. Ilsa thinks she can stay with Rick and send Laszlo off to convert the masses, so Rick devises several artful decoys. *Someone,* he lets it be known, is going to use those letters of transit to leave Casablanca. Ilsa believes Laszlo will go alone; Renault believes Rick and Ilsa are going; and poor Laszlo believes he and Ilsa will be the lucky pair. Rick tells the truth only to the person he knows and likes least; again, admiration is the operative motive. Rick contributes to The Cause by telling his rival the truth, and prolongs his mistress's love by lying to her. In both cases he is preserving illusions as well as saving lives—and, as regards Ilsa and Laszlo, preserving an illusion about Rick's "gesture" toward Ilsa may be the only way to save their life together.

Rick is as adept as Renault at the multiple ploy. It would appear he is about to make Strasser and Renault happy by promising to turn Laszlo over to them; make Ilsa happy by promising to leave with her; make Ferrari happy by selling the saloon—and Sam—to him. Actually, he is making himself happy by fooling all of them. Renault, ever the professional, tries to stop Rick from stepping into selflessness; but throughout the film, we have sensed indications that the Vichy-suave Captain, who shares with Rick a vaguely liberal wartime past, may be just corruptible enough to be bribed into political, if not stylistic, nobility. And so, when Rick dispatches Strasser and sends Ilsa and Laszlo off to the remote continent of North America, Renault orders his gendarmes to "round up the usual suspects." True to form, Renault is incorrigibly corrupt: where he once evaded the law for sex, he now evades it for comradeship.

As for Rick, his generosity masked the removal of an obsession whose poignancy had degenerated into the dull pain of an abscessed truth. We have known all along that Rick's nobility consisted mainly in setting spilled glasses aright, asking Germans about the color of his eyes, and squeezing a profit out of a café whose specialties were Molotov cocktails of political intrigue. Renault's order to his gendarmes is the password into Rick's exclusive new club: The Order of the Heroic Pragmatist. What better place than the edge of the Sahara, and what better man than Renault, for "the beginning of a beautiful friendship"?

Like the very best Hollywood films but unlike works by the European commercial *avant-garde, Casablanca* succeeds as allegory, popular myth, clinical psychology, or whatever, *and* as a superb romantic melodrama. Koch and Curtiz don't ruin the epiphanies

—nearly all of which, as I have tried to show, rise from the script's development of the characters and not from an inspired directorial effort—with overexplicit dialogue or long pauses that give us time to consider double and triple meanings. Superficially, *Casablanca* is another Bogart vehicle, driven at Warners' usual reckless pace, and shifting emotional gears at the climax so we can be sure enough of Bogey's softhearted tough guy to return in a few months for his next picture. Rich as it is—though not terrifyingly deep—the film is so damned entertaining that we don't need the spur of cultural insecurity to prod us to see it again and again. Ultimately, perhaps, both the *Casablanca* script and Howard Koch's development of it come close to defining that rarest of attitudes: Grace Under Pressure, Hollywood-style.

Letter from an Unknown Woman (1948)

With a little research and even less generosity, the disinterested film critic can trace a line reading "Jules Furthman" between the seeming polarities of Josef von Sternberg and Howard Hawks. A screenwriter is often the shortest—and the most stubbornly ignored —distance between two directorial sensibilities. Now, few films of the forties would at first seem as opposite in mood, pacing, and characterization as *Casablanca* and *Letter from an Unknown Woman*: the former is cynical, brisk, and brittle, the latter romantic, eccentric, and profound. And yet this pair of films does have something in common. The first is a screenplay credited to Howard Koch; the second, less obvious, is that peculiarly ironic and graceful Kochian attitude which helped make *Casablanca* so perfectly balanced and *Letter from an Unknown Woman* so completely drenched in what has become revered, with some distortion, as the Ophulsian ambience.

Letter from an Unknown Woman, both as an exquisite set of reverberations from Koch's best early films and as a virtual master plan for the later, more famous Ophuls pictures, is a most convincing case for multiple authorship. Not only is *Letter* crucial to the careers of both writer and director, but it is also the perfect conjunction of these powerful proponents of film romance. Ophuls' woman-in-love theme achieves perhaps its most beautiful expression here; but the film reveals at least as many Kochian obsessions, most significantly the letter as a transmitter of intonations of love and intimations of death—a *memento mori* that can cleanse the receiver even as it kills the sender.

Stefan Brand (Louis Jourdan) is introduced as a Viennese man of the world whose cynicism runs much deeper than that of his blood brother Rick Blaine. Cynicism was imposed on Rick as punishment for trusting a woman once; it is a passing virus. As we learn later in *Letter,* Stefan has endured no equivalent of Rick's Ethiopian and Spanish campaigns; he has never proved himself unworthy of the self-hatred that takes the form of self-inflicted irony. Upon meeting him we discover that he has been challenged to a duel—"one engagement I have no intention of keeping," since "Honor is a luxury only gentlemen can afford." Still, for his hedonistic friends he sustains an insouciant pose. "I don't mind so much being killed," he drawls, "but you know how hard it is for me to get up in the morning."

A letter, from an unknown woman, will change all this. "By the time you read this letter, I may be dead." Of all Koch's explorations of his theme, from Leslie Crosbie's in *The Letter* (his 1940 film) to Willoughby's *Dead Letters* (his 1971 play), the opening of Lisa Berndl's message is its tersest summation. Lisa is a dreamer, cursed with an insatiably pragmatic mother who attaches herself to a small-minded businessman and tries to attach a small-minded soldier to Lisa. Koch's dialogue conveys with brevity and good humor the too-common common sense of Lisa's mother ("think about it sensibly . . . good business . . . pension . . . military . . ."), the new stepfather ("I've lost half-a-minute . . . how much will that be? . . . one krone should be enough . . . send them third class . . .") and the more verbose lieutenant ("since you came to my attention I've been most favorably impressed . . . I have every reason to believe that your parents are not opposed to my keeping company . . . as far as my prospects are concerned . . . outstanding military career . . . we should know each other for a reasonable time. . .").

But Lisa is not "favorably impressed" by reason or pragmatism or prospects, or with Linz, the military town to which her mother has taken her. She is in love with a Viennese pianist, and for her, Stefan embodies the lilt of Vienna as surely as Leopold symbolizes the ponderous pomp of Linz. Ophuls' camera gently underlines these traits with tracking shots which, in Vienna, are witty and a little delirious, and in Linz are measured martial. Lisa's rejection of Leopold—she tells him she is engaged to Stefan, although she has never met him—is a small and delightful *opéra bouffe,* complete with a final flourish

and vigorous applause as the estranged couple exits into a court-
yard.

Vienna, before and after Lisa's abortive stay in Linz, is as much
a repository of *her* hopes and frustrations as Koch's Casablanca had
been for *its* denizens. The greater the hopes (whether for a visa to
America or a visit to Stefan Brand's apartment), the more severe
the frustrations as the hopes are further deferred. When Lisa returns
alone to Vienna, she is more than ever a spiritual refugee from the
military dictatorship of stodgy Linz. ("So I waited . . . waited . . . ,"
she writes, echoing *Casablanca*'s opening narration.) Like Rick
Blaine's atelier, Stefan's apartment will be either beautiful or tawdry
depending on the attitude of the woman entering it—although here
the attitude is complicated by an Ophulsian overview, literally an
overhead shot, that reveals several ladies being compromised on the
stairway to Stefan's rooms. (The first such shot, usually forgotten,
is of Lisa's mother kissing her businessman fiancé; this shot, with
its merging of love and commerce, colors the later views of an un-
named woman whom Lisa sees, and then of Lisa, whom we see
from the same vantage point.)

When they finally meet, the promising prodigy who never lived
up to his promise or his promises is intrigued by this lovely girl's
forthrightness and generosity ("I have no engagements. . . . Please
talk about yourself. . . . How could I help you?"). Stefan seems to
want someone—a mother, perhaps, or even a daughter, but not just
a mistress—who will impose upon him the discipline he feels he
needs to realize his ambition. Lisa tucks his scarf in his coat, in a
maternal gesture, and Stefan says wistfully, "It's a long while since
anyone did that for me." In the next scene, she is reaching for a
candy apple: "And now, I see you as a little girl." The highlight of
their brief courtship is a whirlwind "world tour" on a Prada amusement ride, with its rumbling coach and backdrop "foreign" scenery.
Lisa talks of trips she took with her father to Rio and other exotic
locales, and then confesses, "There weren't any trips." But the connection has been made: Stefan can envision the understanding, encouraging father who might have helped him fulfill his promise. And
Lisa is her father's child. Talking about him, she becomes a wall-
flower opening up, her gestures more informal, even careless, childlike; she is talking *to* her father, almost. "My mother used to say
that he knew what the weather was everywhere except home."

STEFAN: Tell me more about your father.
LISA: He had the nicest eyes.
STEFAN: Yes, I can see them.

Stefan is looking for a moral beacon. He thinks he may see it somewhere behind Lisa's eyes. Can he fix his restless attention span on it long enough to keep from drowning in condemnation and mediocrity? He leaves the coach to order the "conductress," who has run out of countries, to "begin all over again . . . we'll revisit the scenes of our youth!" Jourdan delivers this line with the direct and winning theatricality that makes Stefan as irresistible (though shallow) as John Boles' *Back Street* lover was shallowly resistible.

The entire courtship sequence recalls the similarly foreboding Parisian affair of Rick and Ilsa in *Casablanca*: the backdrop "world tour" suggesting the lovers' ride through a back-projected Paris; Ilsa's wavering between idealist Laszlo and realist Rick, which mirrors Lisa's awareness of two Stefans, the lover and the louse; even Rick's poignant jibe about knowing nothing about Ilsa "except that you had your teeth fixed," which is given an additional ironic turn in *Letter* when Stefan says, "I know almost nothing about you—except that you've travelled a great deal." Both affairs will end in misunderstanding at a train station one late afternoon. "It won't be long, just two weeks," Stefan promises Lisa in all evanescent sincerity. He is as ignorant of his own other side, his fickleness, his weakness, as Rick had been of Laszlo's existence. "Two weeks," Lisa writes in her letter. "Stefan, how little you knew yourself. That train was taking you out of my life." The first time one of Lisa's trains actually moves, it heads in a tragic direction; the second time, ten years later, its movement will prove fatal.

Stefan leaves her, but with a child. (If there were no other differences between the roguish Romeos of *Back Street* and *Letter from an Unknown Woman*, this child, this living lover's icon, would be enough to separate the sterile affair of Boles and Irene Dunne from this life-giving romance.) The boy is named Stefan, and when he is nine he keeps his mother's bed warm while she goes to the opera with the older man she has married to protect Stefan, the boy and the memory. Johann, Lisa's husband, combines the qualities of two other men in her life: he is as prosaic as her mother's businessman and as pompous as Lieutenant Leopold. But Lisa is older, too, and common sense has its attractions now. She marries Johann for what, presumably, were her mother's reasons for marrying the merchant of Linz: security for her child.

But here is Lisa dragging Johann to an opera—*The Magic Flute*, in fact. Lisa had once said, "The morning review compared you to a young Mozart," and Stefan had replied, "I was, very young. There was that much resemblance." Indeed, the first remark she had ever heard about Stefan (a moving man's grunt, as he hoists Stefan's piano up the stair well to his apartment: "Why does he have to play the piano? Why not the piccolo?") conspires to reunite the two at a performance of Papageno and his *zauberflöte*. So Lisa's avowal in her letter—"I know now that nothing happens by chance. Every moment is measured. Every step is counted"—has a trace of disingenuousness in it. She has directed her steps toward the moment when she and her life's love will meet again.

Stefan seems to remember her; but is it as conquest or as confessor? Johann sees and is not pleased. Again echoing Leopold and the "adult" world Lisa had once rejected, Johann coldly says, "There are such things as honor and decency." We can almost see Johann formulating a challenge to duel Stefan, and Lisa's offhand remark earlier in her letter—"You know who my husband is"—now makes a threat out of what had seemed a mere truism. Lisa ignores Johann. She is both somber and ecstatic imagining her dual role of mother and lover to the two Stefans: "I now know that he needs me as much as I've always needed him." But Johann is resolute: "Isn't it a little late for him to find that out?" And we understand that Johann means now that Stefan is about to lose his life in a duel. If Stefan loves Lisa as much as she thinks he does, he won't hesitate to answer Johann's challenge, and be killed. Ophuls emphasizes Johann's cold honor and steely decency by placing crossed sabers on the wall behind Johann as he mutters, "I warn you, I shall do everything in my power to prevent it."

Lisa delays her plans for a holiday with young Stefan to meet with the boy's real father and confess her eternal love; she sends him on alone. Unwittingly, the boy speaks his own death sentence: "You'll see. Two weeks will go like an express train." The coach they sit in for a moment has carried a typhoid victim, and it infects them both, so that Lisa is already dying when she visits Stefan at his old apartment. The aging lover is all professional charm: "Now this is just the hour for a little late supper. Or is it too late? Well, it makes no difference. You're here, and as far as I'm concerned, all the clocks in the world have stopped." This time, Jourdan's diction, carriage, and smile convey the falseness, the hollow theatricality to which his dissolution has led him. Indeed, he confesses his cynicism so expertly that it is simply another seducer's "line." Still, the high life has its advantages: Stefan has visited America, where "the men are fond of money, and their wives are fond of Europeans"— and, undoubtedly, Europianists.

We begin to see Stefan through Johann's small, suspicious eyes. When Lisa, ignoring her lover's dissoluteness as she had evaded her husband's resoluteness, interrupts his world-weary aphorisms by saying, "Stefan, I came here . . . I have something to tell you. . . . It has to do with us," Stefan waves her off—"Now we can't possibly be serious this early in the morning"—and this frivolous response condemns the old Stefan to death at the sword tip of an outraged husband. Lisa becomes just one of many women to whom Stefan was the love of a life; Stefan becomes a casual despoiler, more cruel because he is so casual; and Johann becomes an avenger for all the misdirected lives and loves. "Early in the morning" in Stefan's response calls up another echo—that of his first remark about getting up in the morning—of the duel-doom that we can now appreciate. How can he be so glib? "Are you getting lonely out there [for Stefan the seducer]?" he asks. Lisa answers, softly, "Very lonely"— for the Stefan she loved—and leaves. At the precise moment her image of Stefan dies in her heart, young Stefan, the image of her idealized Stefan, dies of typhoid. And Lisa herself will soon die.

"If this letter reaches you, believe this—that I love you now as I've always loved you. My life can be measured by the moments I've had with you and our child. If only you could have shared those moments. . . . If only you could have recognized what was always yours . . . could have found what was never lost. . . . If only . . ." Lisa's belief in the power of a letter (a belief Howard Koch fervently shares), as much as her belief in the Stefan she loved, keeps her love alive after her death, and transforms Stefan as Lisa never could while she lived. Johann was wrong: it is *not* too late for Stefan to find out that "he needs me as much as I've always needed him." Stefan needs Lisa to kindle a sense of honor he has avoided, to convince him of a love that can reach its fulfillment only in his death.

As he prepares to meet death at Johann's hand, he walks down his apartment steps—the scene of so many frustrations and hopes— and passes the spot where Lisa, then a young teen-ager, first saw and fell in love with Stefan. She appears; "And now, I see you as a little girl." Stefan will give this little girl the fatherly affection Johann attempted by challenging Stefan to a duel. Stefan has killed the playboy in himself; Johann will have to kill Stefan the redeemed lover, Stefan the man of honor. And the duel will act as an elegy, a memorial tribute to the woman whose goodness doomed them both. The two Stefans become one, as do Stefan and Johann and, indeed, Koch and Ophuls: for *Letter from an Unknown Woman* is a supreme, seamless collaboration between two film artists, one a noted director, the other an unknown screenwriter.

Borden Chase
(1900–1971)

1935 UNDER PRESSURE (Raoul Walsh) co-screenplay, from his and Edward J. Doherty's novel, *Sand Hog*
1937 MIDNIGHT TAXI (Eugene Forde) from his short story
1938 THE DEVIL'S PARTY (Ray McCarey) from his novel, *Trouble Wagon*
1941 BLUE, WHITE AND PERFECT (Herbert I. Leeds) from his short story
1942 THE NAVY COMES THROUGH (A. Edward Sutherland) from his short story, "Pay to Learn"
      DR. BROADWAY (Anthony Mann) from his short story
1943 HARRIGAN'S KID (Charles F. Reisner) from his short story
      DESTROYER (William A. Seiter) co-story, co-screenplay
1944 THE FIGHTING SEABEES (Edward Ludwig and Howard Lydecker) story
1945 THIS MAN'S NAVY (William A. Wellman) story, screenplay
      FLAME OF THE BARBARY COAST (Joseph Kane) story, screenplay
1946 I'VE ALWAYS LOVED YOU (Frank Borzage) screenplay, from his short story, "Concerto"
1947 TYCOON (Richard Wallace) co-screenplay
1948 THE MAN FROM COLORADO (Henry Levin) story
      RED RIVER (Howard Hawks) co-screenplay, from his serialized novel, *The Chisholm Trail,* later published as *The Blazing Guns on the Chisholm Trail*
1950 THE GREAT JEWEL ROBBERY (Peter Godfrey) story, screenplay
      MONTANA (Ray Enright) co-screenplay
      WINCHESTER '73 (Anthony Mann) co-screenplay
1951 IRON MAN (Joseph Pevney) co-screenplay

1952   LONE STAR (Vincent Sherman) story, screenplay
       BEND OF THE RIVER (Anthony Mann) screenplay
       THE WORLD IN HIS ARMS (Raoul Walsh) screenplay
1953   SEA DEVILS (Raoul Walsh) story, screenplay
       HIS MAJESTY O'KEEFE (Byron Haskin) co-screenplay
1954   VERA CRUZ (Robert Aldrich) story, co-screenplay
1955   THE FAR COUNTRY (Anthony Mann) story, screenplay
       MAN WITHOUT A STAR (King Vidor) co-screenplay
1956   BACKLASH (John Sturges) screenplay
1957   NIGHT PASSAGE (James Neilson) screenplay
1958   RIDE A CROOKED TRAIL (Jesse Hibbs) screenplay
1965   GUNFIGHTERS OF CASA GRANDE (Roy Rowland) co-
       story, co-screenplay
1969   A MAN CALLED GANNON (James Goldstone) remake of
       Man Without a Star

Borden Chase's story, repeated throughout a decade of films that
stretched from *Red River* (1948) to *Night Passage* (1957), was
that of the civilizing of the American West. His films were minia-
ture epics of westward movement and colonization, with the forces
of Good and Evil in an embryonic age often battling within the
same person, whether hero or villain. The stalwart figures of Montgomery Clift (*Red River*), Gregory Peck (*The World in His Arms*),
Burt Lancaster (*His Majesty O'Keefe*), and especially James Stewart (*Winchester '73, Bend of the River, The Far Country*) were
ideal repositories for the precarious values of civilization that Chase
tested relentlessly as his cattle drives, wagon trains, and traveling
vendettas headed into the wilderness. His Stewart–Anthony Mann
films epitomize the social (but antisocialist) westerns of the fifties,
with each step toward an uncharted land revealing more of the characters' equally uncharted psychologies. Chase's "message" was that
only under the pressure of savagery, at a far remove from the trappings of culture, can we ever really know if a man is truly civilized,
or if he is only a beast in a ruffled shirt.

Red River (1948)

The influence of the *New Yorker* school on Hollywood films of
the thirties and forties was established, and possibly exaggerated, by
Pauline Kael in her long essay on *Citizen Kane*. But *The New*

Yorker wasn't the only magazine to send its writers and their stories out West. *The Saturday Evening Post* may not have been able to provide its contributors with an Independence Square equivalent of the Algonquin (Bookbinders?), but it nevertheless sired a school of fiction which, in its exaltation of rural virtues and the American historical legend, may have had a more pervasive influence on Hollywood—if only because it carried the already outmoded ideals of silent movies credibly, and creditably, into the fast-talking, amoral talkie era.

Whatever the reason, the *Post*'s Clarence Buddington Kelland (*Mr. Deeds Goes to Town*), David Goodis (*Dark Passage*), Paul Gallico (*The Clock*), Norman Reilly Raine (*Tugboat Annie*), C. S. Forrester (*The African Queen*), Robert Carson (*A Star is Born*), Dorothy M. Johnson (*The Man Who Shot Liberty Valance*), Ernest Haycox (*Stagecoach*), James Street (*Nothing Sacred*), and A. B. Guthrie, Jr. (*The Big Sky*)—all *Post* regulars in the late forties—stamped the magazine's moral and craftsmanlike imprint onto virtually every movie genre. As is evident from the preceding list, the *Post*'s influence on the western was especially great. James Warner Bellah's stories of the American Cavalry ("Massacre," "The Big Hunt," "War Party," and "Mission with No Record") were developed with surprising fidelity by John Ford and his screenwriters into the "cavalry trilogy" of *Fort Apache, She Wore a Yellow Ribbon,* and *Rio Grande;* when Bellah came to Hollywood, Ford teamed him with Willis Goldbeck to script *Sergeant Rutledge* and *Liberty Valance*. The other major postwar graduate of the *Post* school was Borden Chase, whose serial, *The Chisholm Trail,* became the grandest of forties westerns, *Red River*—and who reworked the theme of "The Chisholm Trail" in a dozen important westerns over the next decade.

Chase's films were mostly concerned (as Chase himself was largely obsessed) with the building of the West. In recreating a "Western" civilization, he was in effect creating an American fantasy of how the more general Western Civilization should have been built. From the early lines in *The Chisholm Trail*—a vision of Conestoga wagons "crawling snakelike across the face of a continent. Heading west. Always west"—to his final, unrealized project about the first wagons heading over the Sierra Trail to California, Chase eulogized westward movement, expansion, colonization. In a word, Civilization.

Interwoven with this theme was that of a love-hate relationship between two strong men: "That I believe is the greatest love story in all the world," Chase told Jim Kitses in an interview just before his death. "I have always believed that a man can love and respect another man more so than he can a woman." In the same interview Chase recalls competing with another screenwriter on *This Man's Navy* in 1945: "I said . . . 'I'm trying to write you off this thing, aren't you trying to write me off it? If you're not, you're stupid!' " This raw mixture of camaraderie and combat marked Chase's films as well as his life, and distinguishes his signature from those of other writers in a genre often thought to be sole property of the director.

Most of Chase's films trace a journey westward, with a benign dictator imposing rudimentary civilization at gunpoint. *Red River* is different: the trek is north by northeast, from the wild plains of Texas to the streets and shops of Abilene, Kansas, and the hero's role is transferred from Thomas Dunson, the intransigent, reactionary loner, to Matthew Garth, a more liberal social being—"an image [of Dunson] that had grown taller and straighter and equally strong." The climax of *The Chisholm Trail* had Matthew defeat Dunson not by outdrawing him, but by *not* drawing on him. Dunson, already mortally wounded, keeps firing away at Matthew, and with every missed shot Matthew establishes his own moral supremacy and that of the civilization Dunson had rejected. In this aspect and in others, *Red River* is a particularly satisfying "late" film that comes, perversely, early in Chase's Hollywood career.

As they fight, Dunson thinks of Matthew as a traitor to the unwritten code of savage nobility the older man had instilled in him; afterward, Dunson realizes that his own primitive justice and Matthew's civilized mercy are complementary tools needed if the West is to be built and not merely claimed. Dunson had implicitly understood this interdependence when he first met the boy, a generation earlier, wandering orphaned through Texas with only his pet calf. "My bull and your calf," Dunson had proclaimed. "My gun and you at my back. We'll build an empire, Matthew! We'll build an empire!" Dunson's bull (animal force) and Matthew's calf (human reason) drive thousands of cattle and scores of men from Texas to Kansas. The same parlay will "win the West" (subdue the Indian nations) and construct a society on fertile new ground. Dunson remembers first seeing Matthew, "dragging a cow across a continent. God knows where he expected to go. California, I suppose." And just as Dunson epitomizes Texas frontier pride, Matthew prefigures the eclectic resilience of the Golden State.

(Today, we can see in the film a spectacularly bizarre prefigurement of the political relationship between Lyndon Johnson and Robert Kennedy. Bobby was no adopted son of Johnson's, and there was never any shred of reconciliation between the two. But Johnson's foray into the Big Muddy of South Vietnam, and Kennedy's role in diverting that tragic cattle drive toward the civilized path of withdrawal, bear such striking metaphorical similarity to the plot and characters of the Chase story that, had the film been made in 1968 instead of 1948, a title like *Red River* would have seemed too baldly, politically pointed. John Wayne's uncanny resemblance in the forties to Johnson—even more evident in *She Wore a Yellow Ribbon*, when he dons a pair of LBJ rimless spectacles—and Clift's to the Kennedy clan make this comparison iconographically as well as thematically apt.)

Howard Hawks made a characteristically tense, uncharacteristically handsome film from Chase's script, by sticking close to the author's master plan; a lot of dialogue from *The Chisholm Trail* survives intact in the film. But Hawks made two major changes which even Robin Wood identifies as "weaknesses in the construction of *Red River* as we now have it: one, that the intriguing relationship between Montgomery Clift [Matthew] and John Ireland [Cherry Valance] is so little developed. . . . The second, more important, is inherent in the conception of the film: Tess Millay (Joanne Dru) is introduced so late that the development of her relationships with the two men (Wayne and Clift) seems contrived"— and that, because of this, "the ending of *Red River* has been much criticized." An investigation of the film's history may uncover the reasons for these weaknesses, and indicate besides some of the difficulties inherent in attributing thematic cohesion to works of art based on collaboration and compromise.

In *The Chisholm Trail,* Cherry Valance is a likable gunman and cynical middleman between Dunson, the obsolescent idealist, and Matthew, the new-and-improved idealist. Cherry and Matthew personify the alternatives available to the young West: anarchy with a smile, or clear-eyed order. Their introduction is shot portentously, with sparks of anticipated dramatic conflict careening off them into the audience; and Chase increases the tension between the two by suggesting a personal, reciprocal attraction. In the serial, Chase had

Cherry break off from the cattle drive once Matthew assumed control, the better to raid it and take the spoils for himself—which is exactly what the revenge-crazed Dunson planned to do. But Cherry's and Dunson's interests have merged so completely that one of them is now superfluous, and must be eliminated: in a showdown, Dunson kills Cherry, but sustains a bullet wound that will ultimately prevent him from killing Matthew.

In the film, Cherry's crucial role "was chopped completely," according to Chase. "Duke called me one day and he said . . . 'We're dumping Cherry Valance.' I said, 'What do you mean?' 'Well,' he said, 'He's fooling around with Howard's girl.' I can't remember her name, she's married now. I said, 'What the hell has that got to do with making a picture? I don't care if he's fooling around with the Virgin Mary, you've got a picture to make and the guy is good.' 'Well,' he said, 'look, he's out. That's it.' . . . Talk about a crucifixion, that was it." The guy was John Ireland; the girl was Joanne Dru, who played Tess Millay. They were married a year later.

Chase's Tess Millay is not only a pivotal character; she is a central character, appearing throughout the serial, beginning before Matthew returns to Texas from the Civil War. Dunson notes a change in Matthew, a truculent independence from his foster father's iron rule, and the difference is Tess: his love for this New Orleans saloon siren forces him to consider, for the first time, a West that a woman can live in. Tess's movement toward Abilene—first with Cherry, then with Matthew, and finally with Dunson—lends formal as well as narrative excitement to Chase's plot, and it is appropriate that she is regenerated by the composite Western spirit of Matthew and Dunson even as she saves both the pride of the man she admires (Dunson, the stern patriarch) and the life of the man she loves (Matthew, her eventual spouse).

Hawks's Tess enters only in the final third of *Red River*. Instead of allowing her to help Dunson complete a moral progression from savagery to civility, Hawks created an *Ur*-Tess in the person of Fen, Dunson's young fiancée whom he had abandoned early in the film to the same Indian massacre that left Matthew an orphan. Dunson is thus an *homme maudit* throughout *Red River*, and Tess's affectionate words comprise an incantation that breaks the spell of his loneliness. All this makes sense, but the viewer's interest has been focused for so long on the Dunson-Matthew conflict that Tess's sudden appearance comes as an unwelcome intrusion—the *dea ex machina* whose clumsy contrivances will tidy up a more complex dilemma.

Once Hawks got hold of Tess (or Miss Dru), he refused to let go. Chase's original epilogue—with the fatally wounded Dunson being taken back to Texas by Tess and Matthew, and standing up to die on Texas soil just after they cross the Red River—had already been thrown out. (According to Chase, Hawks simply said, "Look, Wayne isn't going to die.") But Hawks also rewrote Chase's version of the Dunson-Matthew gunfight, so that Tess's intervention —with the words, "Now you two boys stop fighting!"—turns a showdown between two kinds of nobility into the melodramatic setup for a comic punchline worthy of *Bringing Up Baby*. No wonder Chase calls the film's climax "garbage"! With a few scribbles on his famous yellow lined pad, Hawks nearly ruined *Red River*; for surely, if the protagonists' conflicts can be resolved with one schoolmarmish scolding, they can hardly have had much dramatic stature to begin with.

It takes a strong effort of will to ignore this resolution, or at least to see it as one flawed piece in the ambitious and serene mosaic Chase and Hawks had created up to then—a vision most vibrantly expressed in Chase's description, in *The Chisholm Trail,* of the building of Abilene and, by extension, the West itself:

> And so a town was born. It wasn't planned. No dreamers in Congress sketched its streets. Men built it! Hard men. Americans! Built it with gall and guts and sweat. Built it for profit and built it for fun. It was good to build. Good to spread their country across a continent. They made mistakes. Hundreds of mistakes. Thousands of mistakes. But they set out to build a country, and they got the job done.

ABRAHAM POLONSKY
(1910–   )

1947 GOLDEN EARRINGS (Mitchell Leisen) co-screenplay [1]
BODY AND SOUL (Robert Rossen) story, screenplay
1948 FORCE OF EVIL (Abraham Polonsky) co-screenplay
1951 I CAN GET IT FOR YOU WHOLESALE (Michael Gordon)
screenplay
1968 MADIGAN (Donald Siegel) co-screenplay
1969 TELL THEM WILLIE BOY IS HERE (Abraham Polonsky)
screenplay

Polonsky directed but did not write *Romance of a Horse Thief*
(1971).

[1] "I know there isn't a single scene or word of mine in it." —Abraham Polonsky.

Of all the Marxists who came to Hollywood, Polonsky was the most
successful—single-minded, if you like—in setting the capitalist ogre
within a gilded narrative frame. The scripts for his late-forties trilogy on the profit motive (*Body and Soul, Force of Evil, I Can Get
It for You Wholesale*) reveal characters so obsessed with money as
to make *Greed,* by comparison, look like *A Christmas Carol.* As
described by Roberts, the malignant, manipulative force of evil in
Body and Soul, life is just "addition and subtraction. Everything
else is conversation." *Body and Soul,* directed by Robert Rossen, fits
securely into Polonsky's very personal urban Hellmouth, with its
Breughelesque, subway-at-rush-hour density, its stylized but fiercely
realistic dialogue, and its cheeky characters who seem to carry both
a chip and an albatross on their shoulders. But defining *Body and
Soul,* and to a diminishing extent *Force of Evil* and *I Can Get It for
You Wholesale,* are the soundless voices whispering through the

tenements and boxing clubs, through the bookie joints and garment centers, like the whispering house in D. H. Lawrence's "The Rocking Horse Winner": *"There must be more money!"*

Body and Soul (1947)

Body and Soul shares many of the generic conventions of Clifford Odets's 1937 play, *Golden Boy*: the ambitious youngster who leaves an ethnic home for the excitement and notoriety of prizefighting, the avuncular manager and rapacious gangster who grab "pieces" of him, the Negro champ he accidentally kills, the final decision to make a clean break; even the presence of John Garfield in both roles. Whatever Garfield brought to the role of Odets's Joe Napoleon is lost in the mists of theatrical memory-history. With all the critical good will in the world, it's hard to imagine how Garfield could have breathed much more life into Odets's moribund clichés than an ill-starred William Holden was able to do in the risible movie version. Ironically, Odets would work more pleasing arabesques around Garfield and the theme of a corruptible violinist in the Hollywood *Humoresque* of 1946, when the most intractable social force opposing Garfield would be Joan Crawford.

Polonsky's dialectics are more basic than violins and violence, or, as Odets identified them, "the fiddle and the fist." Charlie Davis has no musical genius to suppress for the sake of pugilistic renown. He's out of work; his only conservatory is a pool hall. And his only choice is between Money and No Money. And all it takes to make him decide is a look at his mother answering embarrassing family questions to get a loan for her son's education. Over his mother's adamant objections, he tells his friend to set him up for a fifty-dollar bout—and mother and son explode at each other like cheap fireworks in a slum hallway.

> CHARLIE: Get Quinn. I want that fight! I want money, *money,* MONEY!
> MOTHER: Better you go buy a gun and shoot yourself!
> CHARLIE: You need *money* to buy a gun!

Charlie tells his mother, "I wanna be a fighter." "So fight for *some*thing," she barks back, like a good Jewish mother cherishing The Cause over The Cash, "not for money!" . . . When Charlie begins rising through the middleweight ranks, his friend Shorty snorts: "You know what they're making of Charlie? A money ma-

chine." . . . Roberts asks Charlie who Shorty is. "That's my friend."
Yeah? "For how much?" (As a matter of fact, Shorty gets ten per
cent.) . . . Later, Shorty mutters that Charlie's "not just a kid who
can fight. He's money. And people want money so much they make
it stink." . . . Roberts offers a bill to Ben, the former champ whom
Charlie, unknowingly, had almost killed in the ring. "I don't take
blood money, Mr. Roberts," says Ben, "mine or anybody else's."
Roberts drops it on the floor in front of him: "You only have to
bend down to pick it up, Ben." Roberts leaves, and Charlie picks it
up. "Here, take the money," he says gently. "It's not like people. It's
got no memory. It don't think." He hands the money to Ben, who
finally pockets it. . . . When Charlie condemns Roberts for his
scornful treatment of a man with a bad heart, Roberts replies, "I
don't care where his heart is. Only the money." . . . Charlie tries to
explain the roller-coaster polygraph of a boxer's life: "That's the
way things are, Ben. That's the way they are. There's a lot of money
—and then it's over."

Death and money, money and death. You kill somebody (one
way or another) to get money, then somebody kills you to get yours.
Throughout the movie, Roberts keeps reminding, warning, threatening Charlie that "everybody dies. Ben—Shorty—even you." By
the time Charlie decides not to throw the fight that could let him
retire rich, Ben and Shorty have died, at Roberts's hands; so Charlie
knows his life won't be "worth much" when he steps out of the ring
as the undefeated champ. Only his realization that two years of
success and money have made him less his own man, and have
brought him dangerously closer to Roberts's scrap heap, gives him
the courage to walk up to his boss after the fight and ask, "What
are you gonna do, kill me?" Roberts doesn't answer. But Charlie
does. "Everybody dies." And he walks away.

Robert Rossen was neither the most forceful nor even the most
adroit of the Directors Guild's leftists. Where his intent was to go
for the jugular, as in *All the King's Men,* his execution too often
pandered to the obvious. Where his material was lyric (as in *Lilith*),
Rossen's treatment inevitably called to mind the sight of Phil Sil-
vers, in *A Funny Thing Happened on the Way to the Forum,* singing a mock-romantic "Lovely" to Jack Gilford in drag, as the two
traipse clumsily through an impeccably sylvan setting. But, as happens more often than auteur philosophers would dream of, something clicked when Polonsky, Rossen, Garfield, James Wong Howe,

and the rest of the *Body and Soul* troupe converged: there's a claustrophobic concentration of mood and dialogue, of character and characterization, that makes *Body and Soul* not only the bleakest (and, perversely, the most exhilarating) of boxing movies, but also the blackest of the decade's *film noir*.

To say, for example, that Anne Revere conveys an almost hysterical intensity as Garfield's concerned, possessive mother is to understate the case, and to underestimate her achievement. It would be more precise to credit her with restoring, in a few short scenes, a literary concept of the Jewish mother that had been thrown out of balance by three decades of well-meaning, soft-edged, hypocritical Hollywood matrons. Revere (who, like just about everybody else who worked on *Body and Soul,* was blacklisted from movie work) is both the real spur to Garfield's undefined ambitions and the overpowering rival to recessive "co-star" Lilli Palmer, for her son's love and loyalty.

It is just as demeaning to credit Polonsky with writing, on his first try, dialogue that ranks with the tersest and fiercest a screenwriter has ever produced. When a cocky contender for Garfield's crown looks the champ over, and snorts, "All fat. Night-club fat. Whiskey fat. Thirty-five-year-old fat," Polonsky is giving us more than a neat précis of the protagonist's condition, distorted only slightly by the callow perception of a young punk; he is creating a kind of urban, cinematic poetry, a language that builds its richest effects out of the rhythms and images of street-smart poverty. The film's labyrinthine contradictions (of prose-poetry and ghetto toughtalk, of saintly motherhood and a woman's demonic ambition for her son, of money hate and money obsession) find their ironic apogee in the climactic fight, which is photographed and edited so excitingly, so involvingly, that it explains our hero's fascination with "the game," and nearly makes us regret that he has to give it up. Charlie may think he finally demolished Roberts with a verbal cut to the jaw ("Everybody dies"), but Charlie's last fight helps us realize that he had to put his body on the line before he could pick up the chips of his soul.

Force of Evil (1948)

If *Force of Evil* looked out of place as MGM's 1948 Christmas attraction at Loew's State Theatre—like a bookie in a lineup of

Santa Clauses—it must feel even stranger residing, after two decades of obscurity, among "the great films of the modern American cinema" (Andrew Sarris's nomination, seconded by William Pechter, Martin Rubin, and others). For the truth is that *Force of Evil,* like Polonsky's other writer-director effort *Tell Them Willie Boy Is Here,* makes numbingly explicit all the subdued currents of self-corruption under *Body and Soul*'s and *Madigan*'s plot clichés.

Though the film is chocked—perhaps even choked—with handsome dialogue and eloquent images, too often they are repetitious instead of reinforcing, like the shot of Joe Morse trudging hundreds of feet down to the banks of the East River to find his brother, which is overlaid with the narration: "It was like going down to the bottom of the world—to find my brother." Both *Body and Soul*'s Charlie Davis and *Force of Evil*'s Joe Morse regenerate themselves only when there is no possibility for further degeneration, when there is no way to go, ethically and literally, but up. Charlie's change of heart, however, has a bracing, dramatic inevitability lacking in the textbook visuals of *Force of Evil*'s climax, with Joe Morse's descent into hell followed and reversed by the film's last shot, indicating the Calvary-Resurrection ahead of him.

Force of Evil is a much darker film than *Body and Soul.* The corruption it defines is immediately established as the norm, and not as a contagious aberration personified by Roberts, the fight boss. The temptation for Joe Morse to go straight is as elusive and perverse as the offer of big money had been for Charlie Davis. Since both characters are played by John Garfield, and since Robert Blake in *Willie Boy* is an obvious Garfield descendant, Polonsky's three most typical films finally seem to chart the course of Sisyphus, and not the tragic-heroic *peripateia* of an Oedipus. At the end of *Body and Soul* Charlie has begun to push his boulder up the hill; when *Force of Evil* begins, we find him (under the pseudonym Joe Morse) back down in the valley of corruption; at the end of *Force of Evil* Joe has "decided to help," and the process begins again; but, with *Willie Boy,* we are trapped again—and this time there is no escape. Perhaps this explains why the moral uplift in *Force of Evil*'s conclusion seems halfhearted, resigned, unfelt: Polonsky has drawn his picture of urban corruption with such bold black strokes that to erase them takes more than some swelling violins and an elegiac, uptilted long shot. His pessimism is so pervasive throughout the film that his final, guarded optimism, however strongly felt on the author's part, comes over like a studio-imposed afterthought.

The role of Garfield's "mother"—the nagging, righteous family voice in *Body and Soul*—is here taken by Thomas Gomez as Garfield's older, less successful brother. Because Gomez runs a modest community service (the neighborhood numbers parlor), he can tell himself that he's just a "businessman," whereas Garfield, the corporation lawyer on a retainer to make numbers legal, is a gangster. We know enough from Polonsky's other films to infer that Gomez's designation of himself as a businessman—like Roberts in *Body and Soul*—condemns him to stick his fingers into his brother's messy pie, even if he winds up with smaller pieces. Any moral distinctions in the Cain-and-Abel story that Polonsky tells over and over in his films are murkier here: Garfield's remark that "I didn't have the strength to resist corruption, but I was strong enough to fight for a piece of it," applies to Gomez as well, although Garfield (as in *Body and Soul*) is a slick club fighter, while Gomez is too pudgy to exert himself for more than a few "businessman's" nickels.

Gomez is middle-class enough to find conspicuous success distasteful, if not immoral. When Garfield tells him, "You lost a crooked little peanut stand, now you can open up on Fifth Avenue," Gomez retorts with one of the few unequivocal statements in the film: "My final answer is no. Finally and absolutely no. Absolutely and positively no. No, *no*, NO! N-O!" He won't let Joe turn him into a crooked success; he needs to be a crooked failure—a mark of self-deception, not of incorruptibility. All I want, Gomez tells his brother, is "to look in a mirror and see my face, not yours." For a little man with the underworld equivalent of the corner store, independence from the chain is just too much to ask. But there's no reason why Garfield should have any better chance of beating the mob than Gomez. *Force of Evil* can be optimistic only if it ends in the split second after Garfield has "decided to help," and before his resolution is broken by a vindictive, murderous mob.

William Pechter's quietly passionate defense of *Force of Evil* is intimidating but not quite convincing, because he asserts the film's greatness rather than proving it. To another, more prosaic mind and ear, *Force of Evil* remains in the category of ambitious films which achieve an underground reputation largely because so few people have seen them. And Polonsky remains a graceful screenwriter—with a talent for the flavor and rhythms of city speech matched by few of his Hollywood colleagues—whose direction of his own material tends to the obvious and self-indulgent. Polonsky's dialogue has less the chiseled, smart-aleck quality of Sturges, Wilder, and other long-time denizens of Tinseltown, and more the reckless pungency of Odets and Daniel Fuchs. Like Odets and Fuchs, Polonsky was at his movie best when he thought he was selling out. When he was left on his own (as in *Force of Evil* and *Willie Boy*), the themes turned pedagogical, the images verged on the ponderous, the dialogue often surrendered epigrammatic cheekiness for muted soliloquies and voluptuous self-contempt.

Madigan (1968)

Most of the Hollywood Ten and their blacklisted brethren had drifted back to Tinseltown by 1968, when Polonsky's name finally cropped up on the credits of *Madigan*. In the two decades since *Force of Evil*, the cops-and-robbers movie had grown more acerbic, and Polonsky had possibly mellowed, to the point where the man and the genre could peacefully coexist. As a result, the writer's pet obsessions of plot and prose were so successfully submerged in the weave of a Don Siegel action movie that neither Pauline Kael nor John Simon nor Renata Adler deemed *Madigan* worth writing about.

Madigan is certainly, recognizably a Siegel film, uncharacteristic only in that it may also be his best. It begins with a flurry of sex and violence that will keep an action audience glued to their seats through two hours of less violence and no sex. *Madigan* also fulfills Andrew Sarris's dictum that Siegel's best films "express the doomed peculiarity of the antisocial outcast"—although this definition would seem to fit Barney Benesch, the film's psychopathic murderer, more snugly than Richard Widmark, the tough cop who finally guns Benesch down at the cost of his own life. But these elements have been present in other Siegel movies, notably *Coogan's Bluff*, without assuring their success. Polonsky's responsibility for the screenplay is far from clear—producer Frank Rosenberg hired Polonsky to rewrite the script, perhaps over Siegel's objections—but *Madigan* does transcend the director's other urban melodramas precisely because of a complexity of characterization, and an ambiguity of motivations, that we associate with the best of Polonsky's early work.

Madigan was based on Richard Dougherty's novel, *The Commissioner,* and the film's change of emphasis can be seen in its change of title. The Commissioner is the man at the top, whose ability to make important decisions quickly is founded on a devout adherence to The Rules; "with him," Madigan says, "everything's right or wrong." Madigan treats the rule book less as a religion than as a pretty girl—something to wink at—and in deciding to concentrate on the street cop instead of the desk cop, the film is forced to recognize the contradictions Madigan has to face in order to bring in his man. "What he wasn't getting wholesale, he was getting for nothing," snorts the Commissioner. "Policeman's discount!" But that's just the price Madigan figures the community should be happy to pay for the service of his life, on the line, every time he steps out of his unmarked car or barrels into a killer's hideaway. And the film not only consents to these contradictions, it elaborates on them. Indeed, its structure is built on them.

The film's first sequence shows Benesch, in bed with a whore, being awoken by Madigan and his colleague Rocco Bonaro; its second sequence shows the Commissioner, at dawn, receiving the news that Benesch managed to elude the two detectives, taking their guns in the confusion—as his mistress enters the room. The Commissioner is a pillar of the Establishment, and Benesch is a mere rodent under the floorboards, but they share a need for sexual companionship that vaguely embarrasses them both. The same "contrast-and-compare" dichotomy is established between the wives of Madigan and Bonaro, as well as between the cold, efficient Chief of Detectives and the warm, effective Chief of Inspectors; both pairs develop the tension between tight-assed liberal authority and free-swinging urban reality.

Around these polarities Polansky & Co. put in motion a carousel of Manhattan no-goodnik guys and good-bad girls. In any other movie, tenth billing might have seemed an insult to falling-star Sheree North, but Polonsky gives her a good New York joke ("Hey, take it easy on that stuff," she advises Madigan as he takes one drink too many, "there's water in it") and the chance (as Madigan tells her, "Next to my wife, I love you best") to convey a feeling of devalued middle-aged love that it took Anne Bancroft's Mrs. Robinson half a picture and some juicy close-ups to put across. Harry Bellaver has an even smaller part, as a punch-drunk ex-fighter, but Polonsky and Siegel atone by giving him a few seconds at the end of his scene to suggest the hearty hypocrisy and aching loneliness of a man who has to send an old friend off the trail of a killer, just to get some attention. "Once more, huh, Chuck?" Bellaver calls out to the bartender, while his voice breaks on the cutting edge of a hollow laugh.

But there's more than sentimentality, however noble, in *Madigan's* New York. This is a town with a gun under every tuxedo and a connection (for illegal drugs or police information) on every corner. The city's palpable nervous energy makes *everybody* edgy, whether it's a guy they mistake for Benesch (and when Madigan tells him he thought he knew him from Cincinnati, the guy explodes: "Nobody tells me I look like I'm from Cincinnati!") or Hughie, a personable pimp on the Upper West Side. Hughie is spending the afternoon in a ratty Broadway moviehouse ("waitin' for night," as one acquaintance puts it) when Madigan and Bonaro catch up with him, slap him around a little ("I was just trying to explain a little law to him, that's all"), and send him back inside, apologizing: "Hope you didn't miss too much of the movie." "Aaaah," Hughie spits out, "I seen it before." It is surely to Polonsky's credit that all these "characters" are as crucial to the final complexion of his Manhattan mosaic as they are to the film's propulsive if Byzantine plot.

Madigan's matter-of-fact acceptance of the city's heathen catholicity gives a starkness and believability to the few expressions of emotion, as when Rocco cries over the dying body of his friend and partner. The climactic confrontation between the Commissioner and Madigan's hysterical widow is formally appropriate as well. Throughout the film, Madigan's wife has come closest to the Commissioner in wanting her husband to conform to a few well-defined (conjugal) rules. The night before his death, she had come perilously close to breaking one of them by plying an amiable cop with the unfulfilled promise of some long-deferred sex; and Madigan had died before she could confess her sins and release her desires. In blaming the Commissioner for her husband's death, she is really blaming herself—and the rules. Her tirade hardly exorcises her agony, but it does reveal to the Commissioner the fatal flaw in his rigorous code of ethics. Though this "revelation" is as underplayed as the rest of the film, it acts as a cool, sixties equivalent to the volcanic reversals of Polonsky's forties *film noir*.

Tell Them Willie Boy Is Here (1970)

At first glance, *Willie Boy* might seem "relevant," even trendy. Its subject is, after all, that first and last neglected minority, the American Indian. With a few exceptions—notably George B. Seitz's and Lucien Hubbard's richly and sometimes unintentionally ironic adaptation of Zane Grey's *The Vanishing American*, a 1926 film starring Richard Dix—redskins were portrayed as our westerns' all-purpose bad guys, the soulless beasts we had to cage or kill to tame the early West. Only in 1950, when Jeff Chandler played a sympathetic Cochise in Delmer Daves' *Broken Arrow*, did Hollywood hint that there might be some nobility in the Savage. As the movie western became "adult"—some would say "neurotic"—in the fifties, the white man was often more an exploiter than an explorer, and the red man gradually acquired civilized characteristics that made him almost white.

Now, in 1973, the Indian has finally made it onto the list of Liberal Causes just behind Blacks, Homosexuals, and Women. *Willie Boy* skips much of the facile moralizing that would convert the Indian into a totem of white racism; the leading character is no Sidney Poitier, and no Superfly. He's something more: an individual who commands respect as an individual, and not as the collective hero, whether benign or rabid, of a long-silent minority.

Willie—the "boy" is used as a diminutive, a pejorative, and an expletive—is no noble savage, although the fear turn-of-the-century whites feel toward him is provoked both by his savagery and by a fierce independence that suggests nobility. Mainly, he is very strong, very smart, and very angry, three traits that make his would-be oppressors furious as well as afraid. When Willie kills his girl friend's father, a motley posse (patriarchal rancher, proletarian cowhand, promethean deputy sheriff) is organized to track him down. Polonsky's film is the story of this pursuit, and in telling it he uses the most traditional of genres—cowboy chases Indian—in an exciting and possibly radical way.

Part of *Willie Boy*'s strength comes from the strengths of the protagonist, Coop, the archetypal sheriff, and those of his crafty antagonist Willie. As played by Robert Blake (who is sort of a compact John Garfield), Willie has an arrogant, admirable sense of legend about himself, whereas Coop (Robert Redford), the proud son of a "great Western marshal," stoops under the combined weight of being the repository of Western Civilization and not quite living

up to his legendary father. The reverberations here are really those
of the forties and more specifically of Polonsky's Garfield films, with
their urban textures and tensions. Garfield was tough, cagey, resilient—but never the hero that Willie becomes when allowed to expand during his flight for life. Though *Willie Boy* is set in the
California desert, Polonsky has suffused the film with a remarkable
open-spaced tension. That familiar forties odor, crossing stale sweat
and cigarette smoke with cotton candy and roadhouse gin, somehow sticks to the rocky landscape that Coop should feel at home in,
and give Willie a slight edge.

Willie *is* the smart forties gangster, stripped of any vestige of
civility (with minority coloration for audience sympathy), but Coop
is only the *son* of "that great Western marshal"—Gary Cooper, of
course, the tight-lipped lawman. In the Old West and the old western, old Coop was good and true, so the Law was assumed to be,
too. Old Coop symbolized both might and right. But young Coop is
cursed with the modern liberal's self-doubt and equivocation; so the
Law, which young Coop himself is carrying out, becomes questionable, and its final satisfaction is less a very mixed blessing than the
white man's terrible curse.

Polonsky is to be commended for the masterful *mise-en-scène*,
the silver-blue cinematography, and the genuinely radical sympathies of *Tell Them Willie Boy Is Here*. And yet it remains primarily
a thesis film, complex but not compassionate, angry but not an-
guished, thought out but not quite felt. Polonsky obviously admires
Willie, but he doesn't—he can't—get inside him. No turn-of-the-
century Indian, however updated, however "Jewish" (especially as
played by Robert Blake), can provide Polonsky with the sense of
spiritual complicity, if not identity, that Garfield offered. There are
moments when Willie has to look off into space to deliver one of his
"white man's guilt" lines, and you know neither Blake nor Polonsky
can take the line seriously. If they could, Blake would spit it out
with all the fratricidal force of Garfield and Gomez tearing each
other apart, back in an era when rhetorical fury was as bracing as
the genres it inhabited and enhanced.

Billy Wilder
(1906–   )

1929   MENSCHEN AM SONNTAG (Robert Siodmak) co-screenplay
1930   SEITENSPRÜNGE (Stefan Szekely) story
1931   DER FALSCHE EHEMANN (Johannes Guter) co-screenplay
      EMIL UND DIE DETEKTIVE (Gerhard Lamprecht) screen-
      play
      IHRE HOHEIT BEFIEHLT (Hanns Schwarz) co-screenplay
      DER MANN, DER SEINEN MÖRDER SUCHT (Robert Siod-
      mak) co-screenplay
1932   DAS BLAUE VON HIMMEL (Viktor Janson) co-screenplay
      EIN BLONDER TRÄUM (Paul Martin) co-screenplay
      ES WAR EINMAL EIN WARZER (Viktor Janson) screen-
      play
      SCAMPOLO, EIN KIND DER STRASSE (Hans Steinhoff) co-
      screenplay
1933   MADAME WÜNSCHT KEINE KINDER (Hans Steinhoff) co-
      screenplay
      ADORABLE (William Dieterle) remake of *Ihre Hoheit Befiehlt,*
      using the Wilder screenplay
      WAS FRAUEN TRÄUMEN (Geza von Bolvary) co-screenplay
      MAUVAISE GRAINE (Billy Wilder) story
1934   MUSIC IN THE AIR (Joe May) co-screenplay
      ONE EXCITING ADVENTURE (Ernst L. Frank) co-story
1935   LOTTERY LOVER (William Thiele) co-screenplay
1937   CHAMPAGNE WALTZ (A. Edward Sutherland) co-story
1938   BLUEBEARD'S EIGHTH WIFE (Ernst Lubitsch) co-screen-
      play [1]
1939   WHAT A LIFE (Jay Theodore Reed) co-screenplay [1]
      MIDNIGHT (Mitchell Leisen) co-screenplay [1]
      NINOTCHKA (Ernst Lubitsch) co-screenplay [2]

1940   ARISE, MY LOVE (Mitchell Leisen) co-screenplay[1]
        RHYTHM ON THE RIVER (Victor Schertzinger) co-story
1941   HOLD BACK THE DAWN (Mitchell Leisen) co-screenplay [1]
        BALL OF FIRE (Howard Hawks) co-story, co-screenplay [1]
1942   THE MAJOR AND THE MINOR (Billy Wilder) co-screen-
        play [1]
1943   FIVE GRAVES TO CAIRO (Billy Wilder) co-screenplay [1]
1944   DOUBLE INDEMNITY (Billy Wilder) co-screenplay
1945   THE LOST WEEKEND (Billy Wilder) co-screenplay [1]
1948   THE EMPEROR WALTZ (Billy Wilder) co-story,[1] co-screen-
        play [1]
        A FOREIGN AFFAIR (Billy Wilder) co-screenplay [2]
        A SONG IS BORN (Howard Hawks) remake of *Ball of Fire*
1950   SUNSET BOULEVARD (Billy Wilder) co-screenplay [2]
1951   ACE IN THE HOLE THE BIG CARNIVAL (Billy Wilder)
        co-story, co-screenplay, producer
1953   STALAG 17 (Billy Wilder) co-screenplay, producer
1954   SABRINA (Billy Wilder) co-screenplay, producer
1955   THE SEVEN YEAR ITCH (Billy Wilder) co-screenplay
1957   THE SPIRIT OF ST. LOUIS (Billy Wilder) co-screenplay
        LOVE IN THE AFTERNOON (Billy Wilder) co-screenplay,[3]
        producer
        WITNESS FOR THE PROSECUTION (Billy Wilder) co-
        screenplay
1959   SOME LIKE IT HOT (Billy Wilder) co-screenplay,[3] producer
1960   THE APARTMENT (Billy Wilder) co-story,[3] co-screenplay,[3]
        producer
1961   ONE, TWO, THREE (Billy Wilder) co-screenplay,[3] producer
1963   IRMA LA DOUCE (Billy Wilder) co-screenplay,[3] producer
1964   KISS ME, STUPID (Billy Wilder) co-screenplay,[3] producer
1966   THE FORTUNE COOKIE (Billy Wilder) co-story,[3] co-screen-
        play,[3] producer
1970   THE PRIVATE LIFE OF SHERLOCK HOLMES (Billy
        Wilder) co-story,[3] co-screenplay,[3] producer
1972   AVANTI! (Billy Wilder) co-screenplay,[3] producer

[1] With Charles Brackett.
[2] With Charles Brackett and another writer.
[3] With I. A. L. Diamond.

Some appraisals of Billy Wilder's career are too critical to be taken
seriously as criticism. John Simon's and Andrew Sarris's dismissals
of Wilder sound like the filmmaker himself on one of his bilious

binges. The virulent reaction to Wilder's work at least indicates the unavoidable presence of an auteur—if the word is to have any meaning at all—who has investigated the theme of role-playing for over four decades. It's no coincidence that Wilder's best films involve various forms of deception (*Ace in the Hole, Witness for the Prosecution, Some Like It Hot*), detection (*Emil and the Detective, Double Indemnity, The Private Life of Sherlock Holmes*), dementia (*The Lost Weekend, Sunset Boulevard, The Apartment*) and, finally, transformation (*Hold Back the Dawn, Ball of Fire, Love in the Afternoon*). His women often begin as victims of directorial misogyny and end as vessels of Christian regeneration, while his attitude toward those polar opposites of fifties child-women, Audrey Hepburn and Marilyn Monroe, vacillated from the cruel to the caressing.

Wilder is one of the few strong-willed screenwriters who function best with a genuine collaborator (as opposed to the rewrite men and studio hacks who often received shared credit on-screen). But the films Charles Brackett and I. A. L. Diamond, Wilder's most frequent partners, have written on their own enforces the belief that their role has been that of the resourceful private secretary to an immigrant never completely confident in his grasp of English. Thus, though he may have used other men as mediums, Wilder's message comes through loud and clear—from the avant-garde *People on Sunday* in pre-Hitler Germany to the backward-glancing *Avanti!* of forty-three years later.

Ball of Fire (1941)

Superficially, *Ball of Fire* can be placed within the framework of the Howard Hawks "group" film: eight men, united in one coherent activity, and a girl, the equal of any or all of them. But this definition applies just as aptly to *Snow White and the Seven Dwarfs*—of which *Ball of Fire* is a peculiar and endearing sequel. The Brackett-Wilder script (from an idea by Wilder and Thomas Monroe) clearly sets the tone and dominates the film. There are fewer Hawksian digressions than usual, perhaps because the director was working for Samuel Goldwyn for the first time since he was fired from *Come and Get It*, five years earlier; or perhaps because he simply found the script to his liking. At any rate, the "group feeling" among *Ball of Fire*'s innocent academics is far closer to the gentle camaraderie of Comrades Buljanoff, Iranoff, and Kopalski in *Ninotchka* than to the more standard tight-lipped heroics of the Hawks groups in his westerns and air epics. If Robin Wood finds the film's "mellowness" somewhat "surprising," it is probably because Hawks recognized that his trademarked tempo would be inappropriate to the temper of this particular group, and adapted his style accordingly—with mixed results.

I mentioned that *Ball of Fire* bore comparison with the Disney cartoon feature, and also that the film was about *eight* men and a girl. There's no contradiction here, because although Gary Cooper, as Professor Bertram Potts, masquerades as the eighth (and youngest) dwarf throughout most of the picture, his final victory over Dana Andrews' Damon Runyon version of the wicked queen proves Cooper to be a budding Prince Charming. Cooper is as likable here as he had been ludicrous in *Mr. Deeds Goes to Town,* although there is a vague family resemblance. In *Ball of Fire,* however, Bertram's use of "fisticuffs" to defeat Joe Lilac is merely an extension of his research: he prepares for the fight by speed-reading *The Manly Art of Self-Defense.* Moreover, his identification with an eccentric group of professors helps to make him more absurd and more attractive. That he dares to fight an underworld bruiser at all is due to his love for the pugnacious Sugarpuss O'Shea. Their late-blooming love gives him physical courage and her the potential for a gentler life; emotional interaction makes both of them complete.

Barbara Stanwyck was in danger of becoming typecast: as with two of her other 1941 films, she spent most of *Ball of Fire* playing her leading man for a sucker. Even her shills' nicknames are alike: in *The Lady Eve* she called Henry Fonda "Hopsy"; here she calls Cooper "Pottsy." Again she falls in love with her sucker. Again her ruse is discovered just as she is about to confess and reform. But Brackett and Wilder refrained from the delicious complexities of Sturges's film. In that one, the plot went: Boy Meets Girl, Boy Loses Girl, Girl Plots Revenge and Gets It. Here things build up to a fairly traditional confrontation between the two men—one all-good, the other all-bad—who want the girl. Since conflicts (such as the Potts-Lilac rivalry) are less interesting in *Ball of Fire* than the various aspects of community spirit (the professorial "group," and then Sugarpuss's initiation and acceptance into it), the denouement is more let down than build-up.

But Hawks has problems of pace throughout the film. Part of this is imposed: the film stops dead for seven or eight minutes while

Stanwyck is introduced singing a monotonous boogie-woogie and Gene Krupa beats out a couple of interminable drum solos. (Robin Wood would be hard put to make the eloquent case for this interlude that he made for Ricky Nelson's song in *Rio Bravo*.) There's a more basic difficulty, however. The professors set a benign and reflective pace in the opening scenes that Sugarpuss's intrusion jars. We like the relaxed tempo of the movie so much that we don't want it shattered by Sugarpuss. For a few scenes after her arrival, Stanwyck seems unpleasantly incongruous, like a cheerleader at a chess game. There is a tension, of rhythm as well as of character, that Hawks surely did not intend.

I'm not sure that the director could do much about this. The script reads beautifully, and it plays well; the characters are full enough to make gag lines unnecessary. It's the sort of comedy one smiles through, not the kind that strains for explosions of laughter. But the finished work does seem slow—contemporary reviewers noticed this—and, since no other director worked on the same script (though Hawks's remake, *A Song Is Born*, was a failure), any speculation on Hawks's culpability would be idle at best, and captious at worst. And yet, I can't help but blame Hawks for making anything less than a memorable film out of one of Brackett-and-Wilder's most civilized and congenial screenplays.

A Foreign Affair (1948)

This is the kind of film that can turn one away from a director's or writer's entire body of work. *A Foreign Affair* offers Wilder at his most vile, both in his construction of story and dialogue and in his handling—or, rather, manhandling—of performers. The rise and fall of the Third Reich is capsulized into a monologue on Nazi architecture, with each building prompting a puerile gag from that most reptilian of "sympathetic" character actors, Millard Mitchell. More than the depravity and megalomania of Hitler's Germany, it expresses in the coarsest possible terms the self-righteous brutality of the American occupying force.

But then, brutality, conscious or otherwise, is the theme and, indeed, the style of this tawdry jape. How else describe Wilder's treatment of Jean Arthur and Marlene Dietrich? Miss Arthur, making her first film appearance in four years, is photographed with all the gentleness of a mug shot. Her hair is pulled back into a corona that suggests less Flemish portraiture than medieval torture. Her character—that of a Congresswoman on a European fact-finding tour—is smug and prissy, so suspicious of a philandering soldier that we are supposed to feel pleased when he corners her and pretends some romantic interest.

A star is usually deglamorized like this in the first half of a film so that she can blossom into her familiar, movie-star self in the second half. Though Miss Arthur is let loose, it is not to blossom but to fester. She is made to wear what, after much morbid consideration, I can describe as the ugliest dress in a forties movie. She is not allowed to let her hair down (literally) so that, in that outfit, she looks really grotesque. And she sings one of those hooch numbers with which, late in their careers, too many stellar performers (Jean-Louis Barrault in *Chappaqua,* Ingrid Bergman in *Cactus Flower*) have degraded themselves and our memories of them. Nowhere is there evidence of the insouciance, easy wit, or working-girl grace that made Jean Arthur the most accomplished and affecting comic actress of the thirties and early forties. No wonder it was her last comedy picture!

Dietrich, ever as indestructible as she was corruptible, fares better in a role that combines facets of Eva Braun and Leni Riefenstahl with choice bits of Marleniana, notably that most cynical of all Frederick Hollander songs, "Black Market." But while her character might have been expected to blend Wilder's Viennese mordancy with her own Berliner opportunism, the director has the final say, and the role winds up implying an Austrian's nasty revenge on a Germanic institution.

I can hear my critical voice rising to an unnecessarily strident pitch. Surely, any film that provokes such moralistic outrage can't be all bad. And, truth to tell, I'm of two minds about the film. If the viewer is willing to abandon all scruples upon entering the cheerfully decadent world of *A Foreign Affair,* he may find himself sneakily admiring Wilder's moxie in making, within three years of V-E Day, a film that not only celebrates the German survival instinct in the midst of hunger and humiliation, but sees this desperate tenacity as the European equivalent of America's pioneer individualism. And if he can stand back a few disinterested paces and accept the defacing of Miss Arthur's charming screen persona as an inventive example of casting-against-type, the viewer may even decide that she is simply playing, to the hilt, a role unique in its pile-driving unpleasantness.

Indeed, there's something wickedly salubrious in having the constipated Congresswoman lure her cynical Captain away from his ex-Nazi mistress, not by elevating him to her level with a patriotic peroration, but by lowering herself to his! I can't think of another Hollywood movie that so boldly and baldly preaches the gospel of emotional redemption through sexual degeneration. John Lund, the officer who uses both ladies for his own selfish ends, is perhaps the most amoral hero ever to escape Production Code absolution or damnation in the last reel. As for his love-play with Dietrich (She: "I have a new Führer now. You. Heil Johnny." He: "You 'heil' me again and I'll knock your teeth in." She: "C'mere. Bruise my lips." He: "I think I'll choke you."), it's so raw and raunchy, it almost sounds real.

I suppose the film's black-market heart is in the right place. It certainly makes all those noble Hollywood war romances seem as phony as they probably were. But, in the end, *A Foreign Affair* fails to resolve its ambivalent attitudes toward downtrodden Germans and uptight Americans. Perhaps, then, I can be forgiven for my own inability to choose here the proper critical role to play—hanging judge, or hung jury.

Sunset Boulevard (1950)

Sunset Boulevard is the definitive Hollywood horror movie. Practically everything about this final Brackett-Wilder collaboration is ghoulish. The film is narrated by a corpse that is waiting to be fished out of a swimming pool. Most of it takes place in an old dark house that opens its doors only to the walking dead. The first time our doomed hero (William Holden as an unemployed screenwriter) enters the house, he is mistaken for an undertaker Soon after, another corpse is buried—that of a pet monkey, in a white coffin. Outside the house is the swimming pool, at first filled only with rats, and "the ghost of a tennis court." The only musical sound in the house is that of the wind, wheezing through the broken pipes of a huge old organ.

The old man who occasionally plays it calls to mind Lon Chaney's *Phantom of the Opera*—that and other images of the Silent Era. The old man is Erich von Stroheim, playing himself as he plays the organ, with intimations of melancholia, absurdity, and loss. In the house on Sunset Boulevard, Stroheim is the butler, ex-husband, and former director of Gloria Swanson, who *is* actress Norma Desmond in a way that Diana Ross never *is* Billie Holliday. Desmond and Swanson were both Mack Sennett bathing beauties. Both made a dozen pictures with Cecil B. De Mille, who calls both "Youngfellow." Both were responsible for the success of Paramount Pictures in the twenties: "Without me there wouldn't be any Paramount studio."

I may be making too much of the similarities between Norma Desmond and Gloria Swanson. Miss Swanson was and is a very spunky lady, whose overestimation of her box-office appeal in the thirties and forties fell far short of Norma Desmond's certified dementia. Nor is her performance the pathetic job of self-parody John Barrymore indulged in, beginning with *Dinner at Eight* and reaching its nadir with *Playmates,* the Kay Kyser musical in which Barrymore's once-heroic Hamlet degenerates into a beery ham. No; Swanson's "acting" is remarkable. Her body movement, hand gestures, and facial nuances prove her worthy of the "return" she long desired. Her descent into insanity is as technically adroit as Hepburn's in *Long Day's Journey into Night,* and far more grotesque, audacious, moving. Unfortunately, the last two decades, in which she has made only one film and several plays on the road, have come closer to fulfilling the Norma Desmond curse than the Gloria Swanson promise.

Desmond-Swanson is Dracula, or perhaps the Count's older, forgotten sister, condemned to relive a former life, sucking blood from her victim (Holden). Life for her was the silent film, and her projected "return"—not "comeback"—is a pathetic stab at life after death. Not that she could ever breathe freely in this new, wordy world, because all those words distract the audience from the pictures and, even more important, the faces.

Holden says, "You used to be big," and tiny Swanson replies, "I *am* big. It's the pictures that got small." She looks at one of her old films (Swanson's *Queen Kelly,* directed by Stroheim) and says, "We had faces. They don't have faces like that any more"—a statement of simple fact, revealing pride of the era as much as of the individual. Holden tells her he's a screenwriter, and Swanson pronounces the death sentence: "You made a rope of words and strangled this business." But however great a star Desmond-Swanson may have been, she is now dead: when she takes Holden as a kind of lover, the camera fades out just before they kiss, a discretion that recalls the traditional directorial attitude taken toward Dracula's jugular seductions; and, when visiting a sound stage, a microphone boom brushes against her hat, and the old star recoils as if from wolfbane.

Our response to this macabre picture is unique, perhaps because the film acts as autobiography on several levels. Its star is a faded actress played by a fading actress; its "hero" is a failed cynical screenwriter created by two successful cynical screenwriters. And now, when as much time has elapsed between *Sunset Boulevard* and 1973 as had elapsed between *Queen Kelly* and *Sunset Boulevard,* the "realistic" attitude of the screenwriter seems as great a pose (though certainly not as grand) as the "romantic" style of the Silents. This distinction is beautifully demonstrated in the sequence of the *Queen Kelly* screening: the close-up of Swanson, who has covered herself with a veil (the romantic actor), draws back to reveal her encircled in a corona of candles (the romantic director). But we see all this through yet another filter, Holden's cheap cigarette smoke (the cynical writer), and Wilder's framing of this scene is so detached that we are wary of coupling the writers of the film with the writer in the film.

As Norma correctly indicates, there are too many "words" in *Sunset Boulevard.* The narration is often drenched in cheap sarcasm; Holden's relationship with nice-girl Nancy Olsen is the only "romantic" aspect of the film. But Brackett and Wilder are not narrating *Sunset Boulevard;* the two-bit hack played by Holden is. And the Holden-Olsen romance is very likely the authors' comment on the decline and fall of movie romance, from the stylish shenanigans of something like Swanson's own *Manhandled* to the glum lumbering of "realistic," plebeian comedies and melodramas in the late forties. The polarities are Has-Been vs. Never-Was; decayed grandeur vs. festering sarcasm; Old Hollywood of the twenties vs. New Hollywood of the forties. Both were illusions, delusions: the Old thinking it can buy anything or anybody, the New thinking that there is anyone left to buy what they're so willing to sell.

Now both are dead. Hollywood of 1950 could hardly have realized that it was fatally ill, that the studios would soon be turned into parking lots and TV sausage factories. But the conclusion of *Sunset Boulevard* may serve as a fitting elegy and epitaph for both Eras. Swanson-Desmond, "still waving at a parade that had long since passed her by," is given a final Big Scene—a mad scene, to be sure—before the newsreel cameras, which Stroheim directs. She glides

down the grand staircase of her old dark house majestically, in slow
motion, like the flip-card books from an even earlier epoch in film
history. Her Medusa gaze has petrified the camera, so she walks
toward it, head high, eyes flaming. The focus softens, then dissolves
—literally—into gauze.

Love in the Afternoon (1957)

Paris is the geographical setting of *Love in the Afternoon,* but the
ambience is unmistakably Viennese. The film reverberates with
Lubitsch touches, Ophulsian caresses, and the gentle fatalism characteristic of both these directors at their worldly-wise best. At its
own best, *Love in the Afternoon* is worthy of these associations.
Wilder has decelerated his pile-driving pace to the point where
actors are given a few moments after important lines to register their
own—or their characters'—reactions to the jokes. Thus:

> MAURICE CHEVALIER (*the father*): Your *maman* was a mar-
> ried woman.
> AUDREY HEPBURN (*the daughter*): I'm so glad. (*Pause. In-*
> *genuous smile.*)

> Or: MAURICE CHEVALIER (*referring to philanderer Gary*
> *Cooper's many male enemies*): Do you know what happened to
> Lincoln? And right in the middle of a performance. (*Hepburn*
> *slams door. Camera holds interminably on Chevalier's concern.*)

> Or: GARY COOPER (*to Hepburn*): What are you, a religious fa-
> natic or something? (*He shrugs at his ineptness with the line.*)

Wilder has been criticized for misusing Cooper as the tired and
tiring Pepsi-Cola playboy. To this jaundiced eye, Cooper's Frank
Flanigan is the logical middle-aged extension of the actor's preening, prating studs from *Morocco* through *Desire* and *Beau Geste* to
The Fountainhead. Always too clumsy to be taken seriously as a
sexual threat, never sufficiently self-aware to infuse his roles with
the saving grace of vulnerability, Cooper possessed a lifelessness and
an artlessness that made him the perfect image of a loathsome Lothario in decline—and the ideal co-star for Audrey Hepburn, the
fragile gamin whose fate it was to be courted by most of Hollywood's durable but no-less-fragile senior citizens (Bogart, Grant,
Astaire, Fonda, Harrison).

Although Hepburn and Cooper are tugging at each other from

opposite ends of the life line, it is Hepburn who possesses the maturity and, ultimately, the protectiveness necessary to save her frivolous, childish pursuer. Perhaps Wilder, despite his film's intentions, is not the rightful heir to the tradition of genteel continental comedy, and is simply trying to turn his own sour grapes into the heady Lubitsch wine. But it is certainly unfair to contrast thirties Lubitsch with fifties Wilder, especially since, as *Ninotchka* proves, the prejudices and preoccupations of the two filmmakers could mesh so beautifully. Still, Cooper and John McGiver, as a choleric cuckolded husband, can be seen as the bitter, postwar equivalents to Joseph Schildkraut and Frank Morgan in Lubitsch's *The Shop Around the Corner*. McGiver is oafish where Morgan was endearing, but the two share a genuine passion that puts the pseudo-suave insincerity of Cooper and Schildkraut to shame. And who is to say that, had Lubitsch lived to make films in the Atomic Age, one of his characters would not have been allowed to muse, in all seriousness, "If people loved each other more, they'd shoot each other less"?

If McGiver is finally denied the opportunity to engage our sympathies as well as our pity, both Hepburn and Chevalier function, with supreme grace, through veils of irony and chagrin. Whether wide-eyed (Audrey) or wizened (Chevalier), they seem to intuit that they are traveling on tracks that will intersect in pathos; and that, only after having tacitly agreed to keep following their separate roads, will they end, apart, in exaltation. Chevalier knows that his daughter's naïveté will lead her into Cooper's clutches, but Audrey believes just as strongly that her innocence will save her even as it redeems her played-out playboy. It is no coincidence that the film's plot carries melancholy echoes of *Letter from an Unknown Woman,* or that Cooper's rainy, five-p.m. departure from a Paris train station evokes memories of the Bogart-Bergman estrangement in *Casablanca.* Wilder is operating in the same area of old-young, cynical-idealist, bitter-sweet romance, where love must be frustrated before it can be fulfilled, and the attraction of opposites is strong enough for an aging, jaded filmmaker to respond to its irrational, irresistible force.

Some Like It Hot (1959)

It begins with a mad car chase—gangsters, cops, bootleg whisky and a funeral. After all this, a superfluous title card flashes on: CHICAGO 1929. The scene of *Some Like It Hot* is America's largest small town in a year whose memory evokes both the pinnacle of Prohibition and the depths of the Depression. Its theme song is a jazzy, jarring antiphony of the roar of the Roaring Twenties and the pratfalling crash of the stock market. And its film style straddles two eras: "movies," with a frenetic pace and strategically placed chases, and "talkies," with a pair of male stars who manage to apotheosize, in different ways, the early-talkie actor—brash, flamboyant, show-tough; in a word: effeminate. Just as Marilyn Monroe combines the raunchiness of the silent-movie vamp with the resilience of a Colleen Moore flapper, so do Tony Curtis and Jack Lemmon combine to produce a set of variations on the acting style of the talkies' most durable and archetypal romantic-comedy actor, Cary Grant—and to put his brutal good looks and flossy gestural extravagance into a sensible critical perspective.

Wilder had played off voluptuous female against ineffectual male before (notably in *The Seven Year Itch*), and would do so again (ignobly in *Kiss Me, Stupid*). Time and again Wilder heroes set out to transform an earthy heroine, only to be transformed themselves in the process, from the traditional *Ball of Fire* to the transcendent *Sherlock Holmes* thirty years later. When Wilder worked with Monroe (*Itch* and *Hot*), he reaffirmed her guileless sexuality even while kidding it, and both times by casting her against harmless satyrs who were as childish in pursuing her gifts as she was in dispensing them. Wilder could tap Monroe's sex as no director of her dramatic films would dare, because the censors would say "it's only comedy" and shrug it off. But, like Garbo in *Ninotchka*, Monroe played comedy with a bizarre intensity—neither actress seemed to make any distinction between what was to be played for laughs and what was not —so that her "seduction" of Tony Curtis on "his" yacht reveals Monroe (looking pendulous, diaphanous, and great) at her most erotic as an exuberant missionary for sexual rebirth.

Tony Curtis was young and pretty when he came to Hollywood, so his studio, Universal, cast him "visually," in Fairbanks-Flynn swash-buckling epics. But what he had, lurking beneath those cartoon looks, was a spine-wide streak of Bronx moxie; he was always more a Bernie Schwartz than a Tony Curtis. The essence of moxie is hustling and, in marled twilight of Broadway, hustling is best expressed by a show-bizzy amalgam of tough talk and sweet talk ("You want a perforated stomach?" and "I love ya, sweetie baby"). Curtis finally got a chance to play himself—Bernie Schwartz—in the sublimely titled *Sweet Smell of Success*: peripatetic, rodentoid, ulcerous, and almost Jewish. The film was a financial flop. But meanwhile Curtis had been honing a desire even keener than playing himself: namely, playing—being—Cary Grant. Blake Edwards, who had turned a Grant film, *Mr. Lucky*, into a successful TV show, and built another series, *Peter Gunn*, around the resemblance of star Craig Stevens to Grant, helped Curtis achieve his ambition by starring him in a string of lightweight comedies—the last one (*Operation Petticoat*) co-starring Cary Grant. But by this time *Some Like It Hot* had intervened, and Curtis had gotten his chance to *pretend* to do what he had been *trying* to do for years: play a nearsighted, impotent Cary Grant.

Even when Curtis is not playing his Grant-like millionaire intentionally, there's enough of Grant's manic, hand-on-hip, moi-good-mayin bantering (from *His Girl Friday*) in his performance to establish spiritual kinship. In his early scenes with Jack Lemmon—who in turn is busy mimicking Joe E. Brown, with a touch of Jimmy Durante's head-shaking pant—the two flirt with each other and everyone else. Curtis, the Lothario, is romantic-effeminate, Lemmon, the kvetch, is whiny-effeminate. As Curtis seduces a girl out of her car keys, Lemmon looks into the camera and effuses, "Isn't he a bit of terrific!" In a way, *Some Like It Hot* tells how Monroe helped Curtis shrug off the accouterments of an early-talkie acting style—to become the more subdued, sophisticated Grant of *An Affair to Remember* and other late films—and how Joe E. Brown trapped Lemmon into the awful transsexual consequences of an effeminate movie presence.

To escape from some Chicago mobsters, Curtis and Lemmon don matted wigs and padded bras and join an all-girl jazz band. "Being" a girl—and falling in love with a real girl whose love life has been pocked with fast-talking heels like himself—teaches Curtis generosity; his role as the Grant millionaire is a distorted mirror image of his own character, since both avoid contact with the girls who chase after them. At any rate, Curtis is far more comfortable as Grant than as a girl. Lemmon "lives" his part too well: he becomes the role he plays, a flapper in search of a millionaire. When Lemmon takes off his wig, he looks ridiculous and incomplete, like the girlish second bananas in many early-talkies (Glenn Tryon). At first Lemmon had to convince himself that he was a girl; after becoming engaged to Brown, he keeps repeating: "I'm a guy, I'm a guy. I wish I was dead."

Curtis's masculinity is asserted for good when, again dressed as a girl and in the middle of the final chase sequence, he stops to hear Monroe singing "I'm Thru With Love." Music was hardly the making of Monroe's career, and yet that sad and remarkable decade of stardom can be summarized by two songs she performed. "Diamonds Are a Girl's Best Friend" (in *Gentlemen Prefer Blondes*) expresses a delicious comedy timing that was too often exploited and distended by Hawks, Wilder, and her other directors. And "I'm Thru With Love" is worth all the Method performances she never gave; it encapsulates a tawdry childhood, three disappointing marriages, the adulation-mockery of curious fans, even a final, abortive phone call. Astoundingly enough, Monroe's singing builds audacious swirls of tremolos and breathiness on the solid foundation of a confident vocal technique.

It's this combination of audacity and assurance that marks a great performance—one thinks of Garbo in *Camille,* Vivien Leigh in *A Streetcar Named Desire,* Anna Magnani in *The Miracle.* Because these actresses excelled in other roles, while Monroe played simple parts well and difficult ones insecurely, the tendency is to shrug off her few epiphanies as happy accidents. Say rather that Monroe's more obvious attributes, at least as they were apprehended by moviemakers and moviegoers alike, deprived her of the chance to exalt instead of merely to excite. Twenty years later, when Hollywood had died and been replaced by Nashville, she might have been a greater singer than she was an actress—and as great a star.

Wilder caps this brilliant sequence with Curtis's entrance. He steps onto the stage, holds her face in his hands, kisses her, and, seeing her tears, says, "None of that, Sugar. No man is worth it." It is a moment as bizarre and powerful as anything in *Sunset Boulevard,* and yet as tender and tragic as the Garbo-Douglas apartment scene in *Ninotchka.* For the gabby, grabby little men whose portraits Wilder so often drew, it marks a coming of age, almost a redemption. And those who think of Wilder as a smalltime cynic, peddling imitation Berliner *Weltschmerz,* will find their definitive refutation in the conviction, technique, assurance, and audacity of a simple kiss between an aging sex queen and a Bronx boy in drag.

The Fortune Cookie (1966)

The theme, plot, and tone of *The Fortune Cookie* is summarized in a line that Willie Gingrich (Walter Matthau), a resourceful shyster-lawyer, delivers to his schmucky brother-in-law Harry Hinkle (Jack Lemmon), for whom Willie, exploiting an injury Harry received on the sidelines of a football game, has devised a plan to defraud the insurance companies. "I'm handing you a quarter of a million dollars," Willie says, handing Harry a bedpan, "on a silver platter." In its posing of the question, "How much of Willie's unethical crap will Harry have to endure in order to collect?", *The Fortune Cookie* explores the same cynical terrain Ben Hecht went over in *Nothing Sacred*. Both films concern sympathetic persons whom circumstances cajole into feigning a medical disability. Both Harry Hinkle and Hazel Flagg agree to the deception as a means of escaping dead-end lives, Hazel to get out of a stultifying Vermont village, and Harry to win back his sexy, slutty wife. Both are even examined by the same actor playing a Viennese specialist: Sig Ruman, who pronounces each of them a "Fake!"

More importantly, both films betray a sneaking admiration for any con artist who dares to perpetrate so outrageous a fraud. As Stephen Farber has written of Whiplash Willie's grand scheme: "Taking on a professional football team and the city of Cleveland and almost making his phony claim stick is a *creative* achievement of real substance. Another director would condemn the dishonesty and heartlessness of it all; Wilder pays tribute to the imagination behind the swindle." And Wilder pays through the nose. Willie demanded so much of his attention that top-billed Jack Lemmon was turned into a straight man, a Ralph Bellamy patsy for the actor who has called himself "the Ukrainian Cary Grant." Matthau not only bilks the insurance company, he steals the show—and ultimately robs the film of any genuine comic balance.

There's no question of our sympathizing with those Establishment figures (lawyers, network officials, insurance men, and doctors) who unite to fight that cur of an underdog, Whiplash Willie. As he says of the insurance company, "They've got so much money they don't know what to do with it—they've run out of storage space —they have to microfilm it." Any moviegoer who has ever realized that insurance men are mere speculators of disaster will root for Willie's ploy to succeed, while hoping that his fancy footwork doesn't crush Harry. Nor do we sympathize with Purkey, the shabby private-eye who triggers the film's reversal. By making racist remarks about the Negro athlete who was inadvertently responsible for Harry's injury, Purkey goads Harry out of his wheelchair to sock the investigator on his flabby jaw. Willie's manipulation of Harry's selfish romantic love pales beside Purkey's manipulation of his idealistic brotherly love. A couple of hundred thousand dollars hardly calls for nigger jokes—especially when the person telling the jokes has no higher motive than saving his own professional reputation. Cliff Osmond, who plays Purkey and also appeared in *Kiss Me, Stupid,* projects a small-minded seediness that fits the mood of these two films like a ratty glove.

But Purkey's unsavoriness differs only in degree, and not in kind, from that of the film's other characters. Just about everybody wants something out of the fortune cookie. Willie wants the "creative achievement"—and the money. His wife wants a mink coat. His mother-in-law wants to "bake her chest" in Florida. Harry wants his wife back. *His* wife wants twenty thousand dollars so she can buy a classy night-club act, and leave Harry again. The one exception is Boom Boom Jackson, the honest, devoted, scrupulous, *nice* Negro. Wilder is often ill-at-ease in writing "good" characters. Since Boom Boom is not only decent, but also black, his role teeters over the brink of the believable into a curiously undefined, unconvincing caricature of the noble Negro. Hinkle, who has faked his injury to regain his ex-wife's love, reveals the fraud to regain Boom Boom's friendship. But, instead of easy Hawksian camaraderie, Wilder can only give us an awkwardly playful romp down the football field. He may be as sincere as his protagonist in atoning for the ploy by wallowing in sentiment but, as played and directed, this final gesture seems as fraudulent as any of Whiplash Willie's—and a lot less "creative."

The Private Life of Sherlock Holmes (1970)

Much good will, if too much glibness, has been lavished on the proposition that the best film directors—like the great auteurs in other arts—produce their most mature works in those "melancholy twilight years" defined with such affection by Andrew Sarris. The dawn of a new decade brought a handful of "late works" from four American masters: Alfred Hitchcock's *Topaz,* Howard Hawks's

Rio Lobo, Blake Edwards' *Darling Lili,* and Billy Wilder's *The Private Life of Sherlock Holmes.* The dichotomy here is intriguing. The first two are films by directors who, though not usually credited with the screenplays for their films, have both the power to select "meaningful" material and the interest to work closely with the writers of record in making the property more "personal." The second pair of films are original stories (though based on popular, public-domain themes) which were created and developed into screenplays by the men who would direct them.

A truly dogmatic critic can talk himself into liking—or, at the very least, making a sophisticated case for—just about any film that appeals to his prejudices. So, although I continue to affirm my resistance to any formal theory that claims the screenwriter as an auteur, any reader deserves to be skeptical when I simply state that the pair of writer-director films, *Darling Lili* and *Sherlock Holmes,* can be recommended as more meaningful, more personal, and even, to the disinterested viewer, more satisfying than the offerings of our two Pantheon residents.

All of these "late" films are streaked with a sense of loss and a sense of the past that virtually define the state of melancholy. Indeed, three of them are wistful excursions into a fifty- or hundred-year-old past, and *Topaz,* though it takes place in the early sixties, has a spy plot as venerable as that of *The 39 Steps.* But none of them have the spareness, compression of form, serenity, or ruthless expulsion of the inessential that marks what we tend to think of as late masterworks—Beethoven's Quartets, Beckett's recent plays, Bresson's and Bergman's last few films. Rather, they bear some comparison to a different kind of "late" work: Nabokov's *Ada*—florid and sometimes flaccid, ambling and often rambling. As precious as the last book (or film) of a superior artist is, we sometimes wish Nabokov (or Hawks) would tell his story at a slightly accelerated pace, choose his words (or images) with a bit more precision, and in general keep us from confusing a last testament with a last gasp.

One is readier to indulge Nabokov, the supreme stylist, than Hawks, the ultimate technician, since in *Ada* the style is merely distended, whereas in *Rio Lobo* Hawks's famous pacemaking machine has just about broken down. Even if we grant Nabokov and Hawks equality in their respective fields—an assumption so gross it makes my typing fingers tremble at the keys—*Ada* is still the more reward-

ing, exhilarating experience, because it gives us a leisurely glimpse of
the author on vacation, as it were, from a string of dark masterpieces, writing a mellow, generous memoir, a kind of White Russian
Claire's Knee. Rio Lobo is simply, sadly, the work of a tired old
man. To attempt to justify this footnote to an exceptional movie
career is to pretend to serve the artist at the expense of demeaning
his greatest works of art.

My intention here is not to weigh in with a detailed critique of
the four films, but merely to identify the distinguishing traits they
share and suggest the advantage that Wilder and Edwards, as filmmakers (that is, writer-directors) of the first order, have in their late
work over Hitchcock and Hawks, who are directors first and script
doctors second. *Topaz* and *Rio Lobo* can hardly be seen as the cul-
minations of careers that *Darling Lili* and *Sherlock Holmes* surely
are. Edwards devoted two full years to his evocation of a form
(Julie Andrews') and a formula (the romantic spy film); Wilder
gave at least four years to Sherlock Holmes (in the decade before
beginning these projects, Edwards had made eleven films and Wilder
had written, directed, and produced nine); and we can see this prepa-
ration in Edwards' production and Wilder's script. The love of a
subject, as well as the love of filmmaking, enlivens and enriches these
films; *Topaz* and *Rio Lobo* lack the feeling that they're important,
let alone crucial, to their directors. There are heroic tensions in the
Edwards and Wilder films that finally make *Darling Lili* the greatest
"white whale" of them all, and *Sherlock Holmes* an uncompromisingly mellow work by a genuine Old Master.

The Private Life of Sherlock Holmes, eighth in the Wilder folio
of collaborations with I. A. L. Diamond, derives its ambience from
the lapidary Lubitsch years more specifically than any of Wilder's
post-Brackett films (including *Love in the Afternoon*). The film is
suffused with Ernstian civility and restraint all the more civilized
and restrained for its being made in the late sixties, when the temptation to literary libertinism must have been very strong. It is to the
Lubitsch Era—which is less a date on the calendar than a state of
mind—rather than to Holmes' Victorian England that the film owes
its ultimate allegiance.

Sir Arthur Conan Doyle portrayed Holmes, and Basil Rathbone
personified him, as the first realist, the great scientist. We recall Rathbone's clipped voice, eagle eye, and ta-pocketa-pocketa mind digest-
ing minutiae and disgorging motives. Wilder and *his* Holmes, Robert

Stephens, took other facets of the sleuth's personality—the moodiness, the cocaine, the rarely mentioned memory of Irene Adler from "A Scandal in Bohemia"—and fashioned a portrait of Holmes as the last romantic, an artist masquerading as a detective.

In the Doyle stories Holmes' divine aloneness, his tragic superiority, his vulnerability, and his erratic behavior were used only as motifs, pervasive but usually submerged and often forgotten. Wilder made them the theme, indeed the vertebrae in the spine of his plot. And Stephens' stylized make-up and acting—his face in a Kabuki pallor and his expressions evoking both *commedia dell'arte* and Madame Oglepuss—are so voluptuous, his diction so oleaginous, that Holmes' melancholy becomes palpably sensual; and "the most perfect reasoning and observing machine that the world has seen" (as Dr. Watson, with a mixture of admiration and resignation, described Holmes) is transformed into a Victorian male approximation of the screen's great tortured angel: Garbo.

It is thus appropriate that this private life—interior life would be closer—pits Holmes against a Garboesque Mata Hari (Genevieve Page), whose very angularity of figure comments as ironically on the conventions of spy-movie villainesses as Stephens' androgynous lushness mocks the curt propriety that Rathbone, Clive Brook, Peter Cushing, John Neville, Stewart Granger, and others have invested in the role. A plot, of the kind of complexity that undoubtedly gave Wilder and Diamond more pleasure in creating and realizing it than any viewer could possibly have in unraveling it, ensues. The film's wistful, wishful mood foredooms both Holmes and his lovely antagonist to defeat; the only question is which one will take defeat, and give it, with the surest grace. The duel ends in a tie. Both are mortally wounded, either with a rarefied almost-love, or with two professionals' mutual respect, of a delicacy and intensity that shame what, in Hawks movies, is called group solidarity. The dialogue, like the sensibilities behind it, is oblique:

> ILSA: I never had you fooled for a moment. . . . I failed miserably.
> HOLMES: We all have occasional failures. Fortunately, Doctor Watson never writes about mine.

Holmes' pride and his refusal to be sentimentalized keep him from directly answering Ilsa's confession. She *had* fooled him, completely. He *did* fail, miserably. The traditional Sherlock Holmes, invincible detective, is a role taken in this film by his brother Mycroft, whom we remember from the stories as an even more bloodless computer than Sherlock. It is Mycroft who has to explain Ilsa's duplicity, and indeed the whole plot, to our flatfooted gumshoe. As in "A Scandal in Bohemia" (to which Wilder makes a specific *hommage*, by lining the bottom of a mysterious bird cage with a newspaper whose date— March 1888—corresponds with the date of the Irene Adler case), Holmes is intrigued less by the mystery of the adventure than by the mystique of the adventuress. They are the only two instances of his "losing" a case, and the only two in which the human equation takes precedence over the objective deduction.

So Wilder does not distort Holmes, as some outraged Baker Street Irregulars have charged (while ignoring the 1932 version, in which Clive Brook not only plans marriage at the beginning and end of the film, but practically throws Watson over in favor of a loathsome Canadian houseboy). Wilder simply emphasizes what a later audience would find interesting about Holmes and the Victorian Era— the courtly cynicism, the sexual repression, the veddy English ideal of the sublime eccentric—and disposes of that sense of the ordered universe, with everything in its place and the sun at high noon over the British Empire, which was so indispensable to Holmes' (and Doyle's) art but now makes some of the stories creak with predictability. Holmes could have existed only in *fin-de-siècle* England, a nation of habits and traditions; it was his knowledge of these habits, as much as any scientific facility, that led Holmes to the solution of most crimes. Wilder elevates Holmes' stature as an artist by diminishing his standing as a detective, for he loses the case not only because of a woman but also because it involves international doubledealing and the advent of the great machine wars. The MacGuffin here is a submarine, a blunt weapon unlikely to amuse Queen Victoria or impress Sherlock Holmes.

The romantic in us doesn't *want* Holmes to solve this problem. We want him to drop his ironic detachment (for ironic involvement with Ilsa), *and* we want to see the cold light in his eyes when "the game is afoot." We want him still to feel the excitement of a spectacular challenge when he opens a coffin that contains a dead man whom Watson identifies, and to reply, "Obviously. But what is not so obvious is why his wedding ring has turned green . . . and why there are three dead canaries in the coffin . . . *white* canaries!" Wilder gives us all that, and more

But most of all, at this particular moment in *The Private Life of Sherlock Holmes* and the public life of Billy Wilder, we want Holmes to fail—and Wilder to succeed—by showing us how to transcend the demands of an age (Victorian or Space) for boring, mechanical perfection. Wilder himself showed some courage (as did Blake Edwards) by selecting a theme of such complete indifference to the "youth" and "sex" markets. We needn't take the film's conclusion—Holmes, upon reading of Ilsa's death, retires quietly to his room with a vial of cocaine—as an autobiographical statement from Wilder, turning his back on an audience that chooses to ignore him at a peak in his Alpine movie career. Such reading between the frames is tempting, but here, the mood is the message: that Wilder, the Brown Derby cynic whose wisecracks won Oscars, chose to make as melancholy and reflective a "late film" as one would care—or could bear—to see.

II. *The Stylists*

SAMSON RAPHAELSON   NUNNALLY JOHNSON   ERNEST LEHMAN
BETTY COMDEN AND ADOLPH GREEN   GARSON KANIN (AND RUTH
GORDON)

Webster defines style as comprising "distinction, excellence, originality, and character"—qualities that also define the work of the
screenwriters in this section. Indeed, we may say that "style" was
their common theme. Though they shied away from trying to redeem
the moviegoer (possibly because it never occurred to them that he
might be in the state of sin), they nevertheless found ways to explore
the range of human experience: through a Miriam Hopkins *moue*,
a Gracie Fields *mot*, a Cary Grant mumble, a Fred Astaire shrug, a
Judy Holliday shout.

How did the Stylists do it? How did they create the assured, reassuring movie mood that relaxed viewers even as it involved them
in an intricate plot? I suppose it's a bit like asking, "How do you
get someone to like you?" Whatever the secret (and, as the next
fifty pages attest, we won't quite let it go at that), the Stylists seemed
effortlessly able to establish an aura without sending a message—a
triumph of sociable context over social content.

To be sure, they were most fortunate in finding actors with the
felicity—and directors with the facility—to turn a mimeographed
manuscript into a gracefully realized film. When all these elements
work (as in *Trouble in Paradise, Holy Matrimony, North by Northwest, Singin' in the Rain,* and *Adam's Rib*), the result seems like a
gay, congenial party full of talented, charming people, to which we
the audience have miraculously been invited.

SAMSON RAPHAELSON
(1896–   )

1927 THE JAZZ SINGER (Alan Crosland) from his play
1930 BOUDOIR DIPLOMAT (Mal St. Clair) co-screenplay (uncredited)
1931 THE SMILING LIEUTENANT (Ernst Lubitsch) co-screenplay, co-dialogue
       MAGNIFICENT LIE (Berthold Viertel) screenplay, co-dialogue
1932 ONE HOUR WITH YOU (Ernst Lubitsch, George Cukor) screenplay
       BROKEN LULLABY [THE MAN I KILLED] (Ernst Lubitsch) co-screenplay
       TROUBLE IN PARADISE (Ernst Lubitsch) screenplay
1934 THE MERRY WIDOW (Ernst Lubitsch) co-screenplay
       CARAVAN (Erik Charrell) screenplay
       SERVANTS' ENTRANCE (Frank Lloyd) screenplay
1935 LADIES LOVE DANGER (H. Bruce Humberstone) co-screenplay
       DRESSED TO THRILL (Harry Lachman) screenplay
       ACCENT ON YOUTH (Wesley Ruggles) from his play
1937 THE LAST OF MRS. CHEYNEY (Richard Boleslawski) co-screenplay
       ANGEL (Ernst Lubitsch) screenplay
1940 THE SHOP AROUND THE CORNER (Ernst Lubitsch) screenplay
1941 SUSPICION (Alfred Hitchcock) screenplay
       SKYLARK (Mark Sandrich) from his novel and play
1943 HEAVEN CAN WAIT (Ernst Lubitsch) screenplay
1946 THE HARVEY GIRLS (George Sidney) co-screenplay
       THE PERFECT MARRIAGE (Lewis Allen) from his play
1947 GREEN DOLPHIN STREET (Victor Saville) screenplay

1948 THAT LADY IN ERMINE (Ernst Lubitsch, Otto Preminger)
      screenplay
1949 IN THE GOOD OLD SUMMERTIME (Robert Z. Leonard)
      remake of *The Shop Around the Corner*
1950 MR. MUSIC (Richard Haydn) from his play, *Accent on Youth*
1951 BANNERLINE (Don Weis) from his short story, "A Rose Is
      Not a Rose"
1952 THE JAZZ SINGER (Michael Curtiz) from his play
1953 MAIN STREET TO BROADWAY (Tay Garnett) screenplay
1956 HILDA CRANE (Philip Dunne) from his play
1959 BUT NOT FOR ME (Walter Lang) from his play, *Accent on
      Youth*

Samson Raphaelson's name deserves to be linked with Ernst Lubitsch's as surely as Robert Riskin's does with Frank Capra's, or
Dudley Nichols' with John Ford's. Indeed, the Raphaelson signature
was far more distinctive than Riskin's and far less disruptive than
Nichols'. In his work with the Immortal Ernst, he created the most
highly polished and perfectly sustained comedy style of any Hollywood screenwriter. Raphaelson possessed an unsurpassed talent for
writing dialogue that was sophisticated without being sophistical.
When this was coupled with Lubitsch's genius for coaxing humanity
out of the stiffest starched collar, the result was that sublimely comic
caress known as "the Lubitsch touch." Every writer who worked for
Lubitsch has described his pervasive, exacting influence on scripts,
and Raphaelson was no exception. But the sheer verbal brilliance
of *Trouble in Paradise* is certainly a writer's achievement, just as
Heaven Can Wait's serene death scene stands as the apotheosis of a
movie moment that both melds and dissolves the collaborative efforts
of writer, director, actor, and era.

Trouble in Paradise (1932)

Trouble in Paradise inhabits a world of bogus nobility and dis-
loyal family retainers, in which charm is acquired not for its own
sake but to give the swindler an acceptable upper-class façade, and
in which *noblesse oblige* is worth about as much as the failed stocks
kept sentimentally in the vaults of the still rich and the *nouveau*
poor. This milieu, uncharacteristic for Lubitsch, has led some critics
to argue that the director abandoned Ruritanian romance for elegant

muckraking *à la* Stroheim, allowing milady's mudpack to harden into an appropriately grotesque mask, and m'sieur's Vichy water to go flatter than his current bank account. Well, the milieu may have changed, but Lubitsch's tone did not. The Depression did not affect him nearly so deeply as Hitler's territorial imperatives would a decade later. *Trouble in Paradise* remains the most perfect expression of Lubitsch's—and Raphaelson's—urbanity, whereas *To Be Or Not to Be* possesses a tone determined to an off-putting extent by the boorish personality of Nazism.

There is even some question as to whether Lubitsch and Raphaelson are exposing the dishonesty of romance in Depression-ridden Europe or extolling the romance of dishonesty. The opening sequence is often taken as an image of disillusion and dissolution: "a romantic tenor . . . turns out to be the captain of a garbage gondola," as Richard Koszarski describes it. What the scene actually shows is a man with a garbage can who turns out to be a romantic tenor. Although the filmmakers may be robbing the upper class of its expensive pretenses (just as Gaston, the hero, and Lily, the heroine, are doing), they are also investing the working class— garbage men and con men alike—with romance and respect.

We know, almost from the start, that "Baron" Gaston and "Countess" Lily are opportunistic phonies. Later on, we learn that they are more gracious and graceful, more honest and honorable—in a word, more *noble*—than the nobility they are working so hard to impoverish. In this twilight of the aristocracy, manners are rules that can be played by the rich, the servants of the rich, and the would-be rich; so it's often difficult to know whether that distinguished man in the drawing room is the very model of a modern major-general, majority stockholder, major-domo, or master criminal (like Gaston). The first dialogue sequence finds "Baron" Gaston on his Venetian veranda, being met by a waiter.

> WAITER (*offering menu*): Yes, Baron. (*No answer.*) What shall we start with, Baron?
> GASTON (*absent-mindedly*): Hmm? Oh, yes. (*He scans the menu.*) That's not so easy. Beginnings are always difficult.
> WAITER: Yes, Baron.
> GASTON: If Casanova suddenly turned out to be Romeo, having supper with Juliet, who might become . . . Cleopatra . . . how would *you* start?

WAITER (*momentarily nonplussed—then, brightly*): I would start with cocktails.

GASTON: Mm-hmm. Very good. Excellent. (*He sees Lily—his assignation for the evening—in a gondola, and waves to her.*) It must be the most marvelous supper. We may not eat it—but it must be marvelous.

WAITER: Yes, Baron.

GASTON: And, waiter ...

WAITER: Yes, Baron?

GASTON: You see that moon?

WAITER: Yes, Baron.

GASTON: I want to see that moon in the champagne.

WAITER: Yes, Baron. (*He writes.*) Moon ... in champagne.

GASTON: I want to see ... (*His mind wanders back down to the canal.*) Umm ...

WAITER (*understands*): Yes, Baron.

GASTON: And as for you, waiter ...

WAITER (*expectantly*): Yes, Baron?

GASTON: I don't want to see you at all.

WAITER (*the slightest bit disappointed that the Baron has thought it necessary to mention this*): No, Baron.

The waiter's professional chagrin at this last remark is so beautifully understated that I can't be sure whether I'm inferring it or inventing it. What is certain is that Herbert Marshall's false *sang-froid* is far more assured here than the real thing would be a few years later in *Angel*. But of course Marshall—like nearly every other actor who ever played an aristocrat or a plutocrat—is a swindler himself, convincing his audience that he is to the manner born when he has really only snuck into it through the servants' entrance. Indeed, Gaston and Lily can be seen not as thieves but as thespians who are fooling viewers used to "defining essences in terms of surfaces" (Andrew Sarris's description of "the highest art of the cinema"), just as they trick their wealthy suckers into accepting them as equals so they can steal from them and *become* their equals.

Gaston and Lily may be able to fool their "marks," and us, but they can't fool each other. Gaston is the perfect gentleman-on-the-make, removing Lily's wrap with a panache that implies the most sensual seduction. But Lily is on to him. We know that Gaston has just robbed foppish Edward Everett Horton of twenty thousand francs, because the waiter has removed a leaf, which had clung to Gaston's coat during the getaway, from his dinner jacket. Now Lily says, "Baron, I have a confession to make. You are a crook. You robbed the gentlemen in 253, -5, -7, and -9. Would you please pass the salt?" The rest of a delightful dinner is spent filching things and returning them. Gaston steals Lily's pin, and appraises it for her. Lily pinches Gaston's watch, and regulates it for him. It is love—or, at the very least, mutual admiration and collaboration—at first sight, the perfect liaison of business and pleasure.

The Depression began in the banks, then put the poor out of work, and finally kept the rich from buying any new jewelry— which threatens to deprive Gaston and Lily of a livelihood. Stocks and lovers tend to depreciate without warning; only cash is trustworthy. So our plucky thieves switch to a "cash business," which Gaston doesn't mind but Lily does. Lily is an *amateuse,* and it takes the heart out of her work to steal something she can't wear. She is also slightly less secure in her role of noblewoman than Gaston is as a bankrupt baron (in fact, she *dunks,* a habit later Lubitsch-Raphaelson films will condemn as the nadir of gaucherie), so she needs jewelry as an emblem of the status that Gaston carries in his diction and his discretion. Whereas Gaston radiates the understated arrogance of the wealthy even when he works as private secretary to a woman he plans to swindle, Lily finds it easy to assume the working-class attitudes appropriate to Gaston's assistant, when he later hires *her.*

Mme. Colet, Gaston's employer and Lily's ultimate rival, is a woman with money enough to finance her exquisite taste. She finds a 3,000-franc purse too expensive, but buys a 125,000-franc purse because it's "beautiful." It is this handbag that Gaston steals, only to return it to its owner when the reward comes to twice its black-market value. Mme. Colet appraises Gaston—rather as Gaston and Lily had appraised each other—and, deciding he is worth more than a handbag, takes him on, first as a secretary, then as a lover. This arrangement infuriates Lily ("I wouldn't fall for another man if he were the biggest crook on earth!") and she plots her revenge on both of them.

The romantic and financial complications that ensue are too complicated to synopsize here. Suffice it to say that Mme. Colet discovers that her French lover is a Rumanian thief, but that he has saved her loss of both face and fortune by getting out of her life, after leaving her with a choice bit of information (namely that the family retainer—C. Aubrey Smith, no less—has been embezzling her husband's company for more than forty years). "Do you know what you're missing?" he asks, bidding an amorous adieu. "Yes," she says, expressing the ecstasy of things lost. "No," he replies. "*This* is what you're missing"—and pulls out a rope of priceless pearls—"a gift to Lily. . . ." She smiles and says, regally, . . . with the compliments of Colet . . . and Company."

As in *The Lady Eve,* the leads fall in love again as they had at first. In a taxi, Gaston reaches into his pocket for Mme. Colet's gift —but Lily has it. She pulls out Mme. Colet's 125,000-franc handbag—but something is missing. Gaston pulls out 100,000 francs (which Lily had threatened to rob, then thrown back at Mme. Colet)—and hands the notes to Lily. "Gaston!" They embrace. Fade-out on the first film in which Lubitsch's visual subtlety and Raphaelson's verbal sophistication combine to produce a triumphant immorality play.

Angel (1937)

"Let us pass over . . . *Angel,*" is the only comment Herman G. Weinberg's book-length "critical study" makes of the film which Andrew Sarris has rated the best of 1937. *Angel* should not be allowed to pass over these notes unremarked; nor should it really be considered superior to such delights of the same year as *Camille, The Awful Truth, The Prisoner of Zenda,* or even *Easy Living.* The film begins beautifully. Its "no names" love affair between Marlene Dietrich and Melvyn Douglas (a story convention repeated, with varying results, in *Casablanca, Phantom Lady,* and *Last Tango in Paris*) creates a spell that saturates the entire film and, perhaps perversely, forces one to judge it by a more severe standard. Once *Angel* leaves the romantic restaurants and parks of Paris for the stuffy drawing rooms of London, its psychological climate turns cold. The rest of the film is remarkable for its literal *sang-froid,* for the severe emotional chill it radiates and engenders; in it, the Lubitsch touch petrifies into a Medusa stare. Marlene Dietrich is her icy self, but she can hardly be blamed for playing to dull perfection the role of a calculating woman who barters for security instead of accepting love as a gift. Again, Marshall is at his most pompous and wooden, but (like Dietrich) Marshall had proved he could be charming in earlier Lubitsch.

Clearly, *Angel* is cold because Lubitsch and Raphaelson wanted it that way. And yet, at its conclusion, it is certainly meant to be moving. Marshall suspects that his wife has had an affair with his new friend, Melvyn Douglas, who had known her, during the affair, only as "Angel." He visits a salon where Angel is to be found, and finds his wife instead. Angel, she says, is in the next room—but please don't go in, if you value your marriage. He goes in, and returns soon after. He then tells his wife that she can leave with him immediately, and Angel's name will never be mentioned again; or she can remain behind with Douglas, and consider their marriage dissolved. After a brief pause, she follows him. The End.

If Marshall were to have evinced any nobility, even any style, he would have come out of "Angel's" room, said he had met the woman—"She is like you in many ways, my dear. The wisdom of experience shines in her eyes, but also the pain of remorse. And now that we've both met her, shall we go? Or would you prefer to keep Anthony company? He seems so depressed"—and walked out. If it seems the height of presumption to attempt to rewrite Lubitsch and Raphaelson, the presumption can only be explained by the disappointment the ending creates, especially for those viewers who have been anticipating it as some kind of redemption for a couple strangled by ennui and convenience, trapped in the jaws of a yawn. Maybe I'm wrong. Maybe Lubitsch means to suggest Dietrich's nobility in her accession to Marshall's unusually straightforward plea. But we can hardly be exalted, or even moved, by this victory for the *status quo*—and status is the one quality that Marshall, a Lord, possesses in spades.

Raphaelson's well-bred insouciance is, naturally enough, held in tight rein here. Most of it is funneled into the character of Marshall's manservant (Edward Everett Horton, in a beguiling switching of roles from *Trouble in Paradise*), who can divine the course of diplomatic relations from the manners of the ambassadors' servants. France, for instance, is headed for trouble because "the French delegate had not even one manservant!" And, although "the Russians may be going places," they are not yet ready for greatness: "They still dunk." The rest of Raphaelson's *soufflé* style is bestowed on Melvyn Douglas. In a conversation with Marshall, Douglas debates the philosophy and history of the boudoir.

DOUGLAS: If Caesar had ever met Angel, the history of the Roman Empire would have changed completely.

MARSHALL: Yes. It probably would have collapsed two hundred years earlier.

DOUGLAS: What are two hundred years in history? Twenty-five pages in a history book! But an hour with Angel . . .

MARSHALL (*not interested*): Sixty minutes.

DOUGLAS (*ecstatic*): Three *thousand* six *hundred* seconds!

This lovely dialogue reveals the cosmic chasm in the attitudes of two men drawn to one woman. For Marshall, history is an object he believes himself to be shaping, and two hundred years is a lot of history; for Douglas, history is a subject his university professors droned on about, while Douglas was enraptured by some Angelic prototype. For Marshall, time is a mechanism that ticks away as monotonously in the bedroom as it does in the board room; for Douglas, time is a creature that flutters and stops whenever his heart does—as it did when he fell in love with Angel, and as it did *not* when Marshall and Dietrich signed their marriage contract.

For Dietrich to have satisfied, even momentarily, these opposing visions, the actress would have had to express both facets—Angel and Lady Marshall—in her performance. Instead, to paraphrase the *Psycho* psychiatrist's appraisal of Norman Bates, "She was *never* all Angel, but she was *often* all Lady Marshall." Perhaps Dietrich's Lady Marshall is really more disposed to the life of a diplomat's wife than to the love of an uncommon commoner. If so, it's perverse of Lubitsch to have suggested any hope of redemption in the first place.

Twenty years earlier, Douglas and Marshall had both loved another woman, in a shabby Paris walk-up flat. Though they knew of each other—by affectionate nicknames only—they never met. And when they finally recognized each other, the aura of camaraderie by proxy, and of shared wealth, remained unblemished. How perfect a Lubitsch idea that is; and how preferable a film developed by Lubitsch and Raphaelson from that intriguing wisp might have been to the tarnished *Angel* they made instead.

The Shop Around the Corner (1940)

This film is as alive as *Angel* is aloof, as sweet as *Angel* is bitter-sweet, as redolent with the familial bond of a small business as *Angel* was with the business aspect of an important marriage. The warmth that pervades the Matuschek shop in Budapest, and the friendship

that enfolds its family of employees, are so complete, so moving that
the restrictions of what is essentially a one-set film all but disappear.
The famed Lubitsch touch is here more of a caress; rarely does a
visual effect call attention to the director instead of to the situation.
And Raphaelson's preference for a script full of nuances, not knee-
slappers, is matched by a cast of characters who radiate old-fashioned "character." (Of the Nikolaus Laszlo play upon which *The
Shop Around the Corner* was supposedly based, Raphaelson told
Herman G. Weinberg, "Nothing, not one scene, not one line of dialogue, coincides with the film.")

In the world of Lubitsch and Raphaelson, the difference between
"too much goose liver" and "a little too much goose liver" can
provoke an argument that may be crucial to the plot. Appropriately,
the man who misrepresented James Stewart's mild complaint about
goose liver has a good deal to gain from exaggerating the point, and,
ultimately, even more to lose. But more immediately, we know to be
wary of anyone who would play a shell game with the language that
Lubitsch and Raphaelson love and care for so well.

And in this gentle, honorable little world, each man, of whatever
station, is allowed a pride in himself and in his work. Thus, the
shop's errand boy describes his job to a doctor.

> PEPI: I'm a contact man. I keep contact between Matuschek
> & Co. and the customers—on a bicycle.
> DOCTOR: You mean an errand boy.
> PEPI: Doctor—did I call you a pill-peddler?

Pepi's oblique humility shows his sense of balance as well as his
sense of pride. This is as forthright a confession as you are likely to
draw from a Lubitsch-Raphaelson character, so it seems captious
for the doctor to try to deflate Pepi's bicycle tire when Pepi has at
least admitted that he rides on one.

Even though the shop-world is cheerfully (though not compla-
cently) bourgeois, there are distinctive substrata. Vadas, the goose-
liver man, is a social climber; indeed, he hopes to vault into the
moneyed class by climbing into bed with the boss's wife. Petrovich,
a sales clerk, is the noble servant, fond of the hero, doting, with a
sense of propriety that usually keeps him from contradicting his employer but forces him to chastise the hero's inamorata. (He describes her movements in a café: "There's a cup of coffee. . . . She's
taking a piece of cake. . . ." Then, severely: "Kralik, she's dunking!")

There are the hero and heroine, head salesman and novice clerk, respectively, upon whom Lubitsch bestows his approval by having them meet over a copy of his beloved *Anna Karenina.*

At the head of the family (or of the class) is Mr. Matuschek, pompous when he feels he is being attacked, generous and fatherly whenever possible. On learning that his wife has been unfaithful with Vadas, he reveals a melancholy that approaches wisdom. "Twenty-two years we've been married," he says softly. "Twenty-two years I was proud of my wife. Well . . . she just didn't want to grow old with me." This poignant observation-absolution is made half to himself and half to the private detective who has just uncovered his wife's adultery—an indiscretion over which this cuckolded husband draws a diaphanous veil with the greatest dignity and the noblest sense of irony.

Raphaelson's scripts for other directors—notably *Suspicion* for Alfred Hitchcock—were hardly negligible, but it is with Lubitsch that he is rightly associated. He wrote no credited screenplays before his first Lubitsch film (*The Smiling Lieutenant*), and only one after his last (*That Lady in Ermine*); and he contributed to Lubitsch musicals (*The Merry Widow*) and melodramas (*Broken Lullaby*) as well as to the divine comedies. During the fifties, Hollywood remade two of his most popular plays, *The Jazz Singer* and *Accent on Youth.* At last report Raphaelson was working with the infant Israeli film industry, perhaps to help it produce a movie as sensational as *The Jazz Singer* or, if the puckish spirit of Lubitsch hovers over Tel Aviv, as satisfying as *Trouble in Paradise, The Shop Around the Corner,* or *Heaven Can Wait.*

NUNNALLY JOHNSON

(1897–   )

1933   A BEDTIME STORY (Norman Taurog) co-adaptation
1934   THE HOUSE OF ROTHSCHILD (Alfred Werker) screenplay
      BULLDOG DRUMMOND STRIKES BACK (Roy Del Ruth) screenplay
1935   THE MAN WHO BROKE THE BANK AT MONTE CARLO (Stephen Roberts) screenplay, producer
1936   THE PRISONER OF SHARK ISLAND (John Ford) story, screenplay
1939   JESSE JAMES (Henry King) story, screenplay, associate producer
      WIFE, HUSBAND AND FRIEND (Gregory Ratoff) screenplay, producer
      ROSE OF WASHINGTON SQUARE (Gregory Ratoff) screenplay, producer
1940   THE GRAPES OF WRATH (John Ford) screenplay, associate producer
      CHAD HANNA (Henry King) screenplay, associate producer
1941   TOBACCO ROAD (John Ford) screenplay
1942   ROXIE HART (William A. Wellman) screenplay, producer
      LIFE BEGINS AT 8:30 (Irving Pichel) screenplay, producer
      THE PIED PIPER (Irving Pichel) screenplay, producer
1943   HOLY MATRIMONY (John M. Stahl) screenplay, producer
      THE MOON IS DOWN (Irving Pichel) screenplay, producer
1944   THE WOMAN IN THE WINDOW (Fritz Lang) screenplay, producer
      CASANOVA BROWN (Sam Wood) screenplay, producer
      THE KEYS OF THE KINGDOM (John M. Stahl) co-screenplay
1945   ALONG CAME JONES (Stuart Heisler) screenplay

1946 THE DARK MIRROR (Robert Siodmak) screenplay, producer
1948 MR. PEABODY AND THE MERMAID (Irving Pichel) screenplay, producer
1949 EVERYBODY DOES IT (Edmund Goulding) screenplay, producer; remake of *Wife, Husband and Friend*
1950 THREE CAME HOME (Jean Negulesco) screenplay, producer
THE MUDLARK (Jean Negulesco) screenplay, producer
1951 THE DESERT FOX (Henry Hathaway) screenplay
THE LONG DARK HALL (Anthony Bushell and Reginald Beck) screenplay
1952 PHONE CALL FROM A STRANGER (Jean Negulesco) screenplay, producer
WE'RE NOT MARRIED (Edmund Goulding) screenplay, producer
MY COUSIN RACHEL (Henry Koster) screenplay, producer
O. HENRY'S FULL HOUSE: THE RANSOM OF RED CHIEF (Howard Hawks) screenplay
1953 HOW TO MARRY A MILLIONAIRE (Jean Negulesco) screenplay, producer
1954 NIGHT PEOPLE (Nunnally Johnson) screenplay, producer
BLACK WIDOW (Nunnally Johnson) screenplay, producer
1955 HOW TO BE VERY, VERY POPULAR (Nunnally Johnson) screenplay, producer
1956 THE MAN IN THE GRAY FLANNEL SUIT (Nunnally Johnson) screenplay
1957 THE TRUE STORY OF JESSE JAMES (Nicholas Ray) remake of *Jesse James*
THE THREE FACES OF EVE (Nunnally Johnson) screenplay, producer
OH, MEN! OH, WOMEN! (Nunnally Johnson) screenplay (uncredited), producer
1959 THE MAN WHO UNDERSTOOD WOMEN (Nunnally Johnson) screenplay, producer
1960 THE ANGEL WORE RED (Nunnally Johnson) screenplay
FLAMING STAR (Don Siegel) co-screenplay
1962 MR. HOBBS TAKES A VACATION (Henry Koster) screenplay
1963 TAKE HER, SHE'S MINE (Henry Koster) screenplay
1964 THE WORLD OF HENRY ORIENT (George Roy Hill) co-screenplay
1967 THE DIRTY DOZEN (Robert Aldrich) co-screenplay

Johnson produced but did not write the following films: *Cardinal Richelieu* (1935, Rowland V. Lee), *The Road to Glory* (1936, Howard Hawks), *Cafe Metropole* (1937, Edward Griffith), *Slave Ship* (1937, Tay Garnett), *The Gunfighter* (1950, Henry King).

Nunnally Johnson, with a career that spans thirty-five years and some fifty films, was perhaps the busiest if not the most prolific screenwriter considered here. Only five of his screenplay credits were shared with another writer; he produced more than thirty films; he directed eight. His road to glory—the Twentieth Century–Fox back lot, site of so many Johnsonian period romances—was paved with Darryl Zanuck's good intentions. Zanuck, who had started in movies writing scripts for Rin Tin Tin, was known as a writer's producer. It's no coincidence that Johnson, Dudley Nichols, Philip Dunne, and Lamar Trotti—all Fox regulars in the late thirties—were among the most powerful as well as most respected of screenwriters.

Of these four, Johnson wears best. His early films demonstrate an uncanny ability to inhabit "historical" characters as disparate (and desperate) as Dr. Mudd, Jesse James, Tom Joad, Jeeter Lester, Roxie Hart, and Priam Farll. Johnson's original screenplay for *The Prisoner of Shark Island* has an openness and intensity of feeling worlds above the thesis films Nichols wrote for John Ford; his careful adaptation of *The Grapes of Wrath* gave Ford room to expand, visually and emotionally, in a way Nichols' script- and studio-bound rewrites of *The Informer, Mary of Scotland,* and *Stagecoach* never did. Johnson even extracted a superior film (*Jesse James*) from Henry King—a feat that should have qualified him for a degree in dental surgery, if not an Academy Award.

Johnson's decline—gradual, to be sure—came with his ascension to the role of independent producer. He has spoken of his frequent arguments with Ford, and it seems likely that, when Johnson became a writer-producer, his tendency was to choose directors he could handle. Unfortunately, while Irving Pichel, Sam Wood, Stuart Heisler, and Jean Negulesco are undoubtedly amiable gentlemen, they pale as moviemakers before that cantankerous old fart, John Ford. Johnson ultimately ended all writer-producer-director animosity by installing himself as writer-producer-director. But, without any personal friction on the set, precious little creative tension seeped through to the screen. Johnson had forfeited an ulcer and his reputation at the same time.

The Prisoner of Shark Island (1936)

Johnson wrote only two original screenplays, both in the thirties, both based on incidents in American Reconstruction Era history, both eulogizing reluctant but genuine rebel heroes and condemning the political/economic power structure of the period. If *The Prisoner of Shark Island* remains less intriguing, and possibly less successful, than *Jesse James*, it is not because Johnson's bias is conservative in the first film and radical in the second, but because the vestiges of his Southern (Georgia) heritage blinded him to dramatic ambiguities in the post-Civil War North-South antagonism.

The Prisoner of Shark Island is political romance of a high order, but in dealing with themes of misdirected generosity, justice outraged, and selfless heroism, it refuses to transcend the limitations of melodrama. Its characters are defined by either their morals or their humors, and once Johnson establishes them—with a few deft strokes —our response to them never changes. There are good guys (Dr. Mudd, the Southern physician who unknowingly treated John Wilkes Booth, and Mudd's family); there are bad guys (the military, penal, and bureaucratic cogs in an unfeeling Union machine); but there are no characters with any of Jesse James' complexity—a complexity that never lets us pigeonhole him as either a Robin Hood or a Baby Face Nelson.

Johnson might argue, with cause, that *The Prisoner of Shark Island* is not a demonstration of the seven types of ambiguity, but rather a retrospective case for the defense of Dr. Mudd, who was certainly the victim of a complex but unambiguous conspiracy on the part of the Reconstruction Era administration to impose order after Abraham Lincoln's death, whatever the price in civil liberties or judicial restraint. In this light, the film can be seen as a more accomplished and affecting Twentieth Century–Fox response to the social biographies emanating from Warner Brothers. All of Johnson's best characters (Dr. Mudd, Frank and Jesse James, Tom Joad, even Gracie Fields in *Holy Matrimony*) possess an easy, natural moral authority that makes them believable as leaders. This, plus the relaxed conjugal affection Johnson created in so many of his films, gives *The Prisoner of Shark Island* a naturalness that distinguishes it from the solemn, textbook biopics Warners was making.

Dr. Mudd's genteel manners and racial paternalism make him the apotheosis of the antebellum Southern aristocrat; his humanity —perversely, he freed the slaves on his plantation when the South seceded—and dignity make him the personification of that Confederate myth, the naturally superior white man whose slaves stay with him out of admiration, and whose vulgar Northern adversaries hate him out of envy. Johnson not only venerates Mudd, he seems to identify with him, and this makes the script's racism (slightly tempered in John Ford's direction) difficult to ignore. Negroes are given lines like "Who say so?" "White man say so, dat's who say so." Johnson may chide the supremacist oratory of Mudd's father-in-law (as he drones on about "the aristocracy of the South . . . founded on land and slavery," the camera pulls back to reveal his five-year-old granddaughter "gazing with rapt attention at the waggling of her grandfather's whiskers"), but Mudd and Johnson clearly share these sentiments, even if they don't often voice them.

At one point, after delivering a Negress' twelfth illegitimate child, the script pictures Mudd as he "sighs and shakes his head at the general irresponsibility of negroes." Later, when he has been convicted of treason and sent to Shark Island, he singlehandedly stops a strike of black guards by shouting: "Put down that gun, nigger"; it is supposed to be the only talk they understand. Indeed, since they know Mudd to be a Southerner, they assume he means business— and the revolt ends quickly, meekly, ignominiously. Johnson is careful to indicate that this tough talk is the ruse of a gentle man to save a medical mission of mercy, and just as careful to suggest that the Northern intruders want to manipulate blacks and not only enfranchise them. Johnson's image of a carpetbagger is that of a man who first tells Negroes, "You're as good as any white man," but who, when they approach him, screams, "Don't you dare lay your black hands on a white man!" The film's treatment of traditional white-black relations testifies to the old cliché that, in the South, whites don't care how close a black man gets, as long as he doesn't rise too high; in the North, they don't care how high he rises, as long as he doesn't get too close.

It's unfair, of course, to accuse Johnson of exploiting prejudices he merely exemplifies. Every Hollywood film dealing with Negroes was at least implicitly, and often explicitly, racist. (Filmmakers' condescension was just as noticeable—and less excuseable—in Marx

Brothers production numbers and in quasi-Marxist "problem" films
of the late forties.) In fact, Johnson is harsher on white trash, of both
Northern and Southern varieties. One brutish Union sergeant breaks
little girls' dolls and prisoners' spirits with equal dispatch, and
Mudd's Southern "co-conspirators" are characterized by the script
as "stupid, open-mouthed, low-browed, savage, giggling, bewildered,
disheveled, shabby, lunatic." Johnson's is as much a class as a racial
bias. *The Prisoner of Shark Island* is a hymn of praise to indomita-
ble human aristocracy, with Dr. Mudd towering over the moral
midgets, black and white, who try to reduce him to their own small
stature.

Johnson's cinematic stature is greatest in those sequences where
he concentrates on Mudd's heroism. The peroration to Mudd's
court-martial plea is written with such conviction, and acted with
such intensity, that it marks one of the high points in the careers of
Johnson, Ford, and (as Mudd) Warner Baxter.

> MUDD (*to his judges*): And till the day you die, ask yourselves
> in your heart three questions: Does an assassin confide his plans
> to anyone? Was I, a physician, in the plot because it was part of
> John Wilkes Booth's plan to break his leg and need me? Does a
> man whose first devotion is no longer to a lost cause, or to any
> flag that flies, but to his wife and child, risk any act that could
> only bring misery and heartbreak on their innocent lives? In the
> sight of the holy God I worship, I am innocent.

The simple eloquence of which Johnson was capable also informs
the short scene between Mudd, the Shark Island pariah, and the
prison commandant who finally begs him to fight the yellow fever
that is ravaging the island. "One night four years ago, sir," Mudd
softly replies, "I was a doctor. (*Smiling ironically*) I'm still a doctor." Rather than Mudd, it is the North that is reprieved here and
allowed to atone for its injustice to a doctor whose assistance to a
wounded man was taken as a war crime.

Johnson's screenplay describes very specific camera movements
and actors' gestures—as exhaustive in detail as those of any play—
which were followed carefully, for the most part, by Ford and his
cast. Indeed, Johnson describes the kind of familial tableaux which,
one and two decades later, Ford will stamp as his own. After Mudd
has been convicted, he sees his wife and daughter Martha for what
may be the last time. As the script puts it: "Mrs. Mudd comes
slowly to meet him, her eyes flooded with tears, and he clasps her

and Martha in one embrace." Their final, ecstatic reunion on the
plantation possesses all the exaltation, if not the pain, of *The Searchers*' last sequence; for Ethan Edwards is doomed to wander, while
the door that closes on Dr. Mudd and his family encloses them
forever in that one tender embrace.

Jesse James (1939)

"Would film history have been radically altered," Andrew Sarris
asks, "if Henry King had directed *The Grapes of Wrath* and John
Ford *Jesse James*, instead of vice versa? Not likely." He is probably
correct, radical alterations being rare enough when film history is
tailor-made to suit the director. What is likely is that *Jesse James*
would enjoy today the reputation mysteriously won by *Stagecoach*.
The puzzling pre-eminence of that mediocre western is the subject
of remarks in the chapter on Dudley Nichols. It was not even the
first in the string of "A" westerns, being preceded two months
earlier in 1939 by *Jesse James*. *Stagecoach* may have attracted more
historical attention originally because it had the look of a Republic
or Monogram oater, whereas *Jesse James* bore some resemblance
to Fox's pallid epics of American history, such as *Ramona, Alexander's Ragtime Band,* and *In Old Chicago*—all of which were directed, with remarkably consistent tepidity, by Henry King. Moreover, Dudley Nichols wrote rigidly schematized scripts filled with
characters who are initially ambiguous but usually resolve their
dilemmas by coming out so strongly, and verbally, on the side of
right that audiences could be moved to tears and critics moved to
anthologize. (The only script Arthur Knight quotes at length in *The
Liveliest Art* is Nichols' *The Informer*, perhaps because every gesture is obvious enough to be praised and parsed by novice film
students.)

Johnson's *Jesse James* screenplay is much more of a piece, which
would make it difficult to break into easily defined components. His
story line has a devious circuity lacking in Nichols' A-B-C plotting
which would be more appropriate as a model in a correspondence
course from the Famous Screenwriters School than as a milestone
in Contemp. Cinema I. In *Jesse James,* Johnson juggles the motivations of twice as many characters as Nichols does in *Stagecoach,*
and with far greater dexterity; the motivations are rarely simple,
and never spelled out with Nichols' schoolmarm perseverance. And,

while *Stagecoach* is content to be taken as a western with certain psychological obliquities (which aren't very well developed), *Jesse James* is a western with relatively audacious political and social ambitions, which are realized with admirable aplomb.

Jesse James is not only a defense of the notorious outlaw, it is practically a deification. The James Boys—Jesse and Frank—are portrayed as two amiable, if stubborn, farm boys, who turn outside the law only when the law fails to enforce justice. Their family is threatened, their house blown up, and their mother killed before they even think of holding up trains. The law defines them as criminals because they choose to fight back against the robber barons of the railroad, who buy land at a dollar an acre and beat up anyone who won't sell. Jesse is firmly enshrined in the movie tradition of Individual-vs.-Corporation; he's a nineteenth-century Nader's Night Raider, fighting corruption by whatever means necessary. Frank, in the strong, silent person of Henry Fonda, is an earlier version of his Tom Joad. But whereas Fonda the Okie moves west when "the bankers" seize his family's farm, Fonda the Outlaw stands his ground in order to save it.

Johnson is fiercely explicit in blaming the railroad interests for the James Boys' banditry, and just as fearless in imputing almost universal corruption to the forces of law and order. The railroad, one man tells Jesse, has "got this state hogtied. They got the police, they got the courts, they got everything. . . . The railroad's got too much at stake to let two little farmer boys bollix things up." Nevertheless, when the boys take to robbing trains, they are models of good behavior. After accepting a walletful of money from one frightened man, Frank reassures him: "Don't forget to sue the railroad for everything you give us, 'cause it's responsible. Thank you very kindly, sir." The robbery takes on the tone of collection time on a Sunday morning. Indeed, Jesse is a hero to the revivalist preacher who marries him later on. And audiences of the thirties, ill-disposed to social violence, could accept Jesse and Frank as heroes because of the film's elaborate respect for America's cultural and cinematic traditions. The romance of Jesse James and of the early West is equated with the romance of the country and its popular art form, the movies.

One of the firmest romantic traditions in Hollywood films was that Beauty is Good, and Ugly is Evil. Thus, the heroine was generally more beautiful than the Other Woman because a visual medium demanded visual correlatives for the popular moral code; it helped the audience to distinguish Good from Evil, and it simplified things for the movie's hero—it was easier to choose a good woman who was also more attractive, since he received immediate satisfaction as well as ultimate salvation. Tyrone Power (Jesse) and Henry Fonda are so beautiful that they can't possibly be bad. There is no conflict between Jesse's outlawry and our sympathy until Randolph Scott, who is also beautiful, intrudes on the scene as a representative of the law; in a tense dialogue with Scott, Power looks a little seedy for the first time. The conversation also leads Jesse into his first verbal evasion (although it's the truth). When Scott asks him, "What business you in?" Jessie replies tersely, "Guns . . . and horses."

But Johnson still follows his Hollywood logic faithfully. If Scott is beautiful, he must also be good; therefore, he will eventually side with Jesse. And this he does. Out of love for his wife (whom Scott also loves), Jesse agrees to serve five years in jail for his noble crimes; Scott has procured a written promise from the railroad president to that effect. When the president breaks his word and determines to have Jesse hanged, Scott balks. "Jesse played fair. He did everything he promised." But the president (the usually mild-mannered Donald Meek) has a blood vengeance that would astound the James Boys. Johnson lets this mouse's plot to trap Jesse fall apart with poetic (or perhaps balladic) justice. Just as it was Meek's avarice that led the brothers into banditry, it is his vengefulness that provokes Frank's determination to break Jesse out of jail, and his stupidity—in deputizing two members of the James Gang, who "arrest" Frank so he can help Jesse escape—that leads to the success of their venture. By this time Scott is on Jesse's side, and by the side of Jesse's wife, whom the outlaw is now neglecting. For Jesse's altruism has soured into an obsession; the farm boy has been traumatized into a revolutionary.

Violence is a contagion that infects those who fight it as well as those who foment it. This is a truism as applicable to the Westerner as to the Weatherman. Business associations become strained (Jesse's suicidal guilt and career ambitions make life difficult for the working-class men in his gang), and the tension affects in-laws as well as the outlaw (a robbery keeps Jesse away from his wife the day she has their first child). It takes his wife's desertion—with Scott —to shock Jesse into eventual retirement; it takes one glimpse of his son to convince him that he is more valuable at home than on the road. But Jesse's past and the railroad's inexorable lust for revenge catch up with him. A gang member turns traitor and—as Jesse reaffirms his familial solidarity by adjusting a HOME SWEET HOME sampler on his living-room wall—shoots him in the back. This scene is enclosed in one elegiac backtracking shot that is interrupted only by a close-up of the murderer, as if he is unworthy to be included in the frame of the film's ultimate, memorable portrait of Jesse. The shot is as effective as Arthur Penn's textbook montage of the Bonnie-and-Clyde massacre, and, in its simplicity, just as affecting.

The film's coda is a stirring peroration in Jesse's honor, delivered by the choleric editor of his home-town paper. "Jesse was an outlaw," he admits. "But I don't think even America is ashamed of Jesse James. Maybe it's because we understand that he wasn't altogether to blame for being what his times made him. Maybe it's because he was so good at what he was doing." In other words, Jesse offered sedentary America an image of everything it admired: vicarious thrills, righteousness, recklessness, professionalism—complete with sociological justification ("what his times made him"). Jesse believed that what he had to do was right, and we agree. He had the courage to do it, and we approve. In his second (and last) original screenplay, Johnson created an authentic hero out of treacherous material, and set him in a full-blooded, fully believable milieu. That his *Jesse James* is ignored, while *Stagecoach* is venerated, is a crime it may take a small revolution in film criticism to avenge.

Holy Matrimony (1943)

Johnson was producer-screenwriter on eleven Fox films between 1939 and 1944, beginning with *Jesse James,* including *The Grapes of Wrath, Tobacco Road,* and *Holy Matrimony,* and ending with *Casanova Brown.* He left Fox to pursue "independent" filmmaking at RKO, turning out *The Woman in the Window* and *Along Came Jones* (the latter being, with the exception of Neil Simon's *The Heartbreak Kid* in 1972, the only example that springs to mind of a screenwriter—who did not also produce or direct, or create the original story—receiving possessive credit: "Nunnally Johnson's *Along Came Jones*"). Through his own designs, or possibly those of his devoted superior, Darryl F. Zanuck, the bulk of Johnson's Fox films dealt with historical or sociological Americana, occasionally mixing the genres, as in *Jesse James*. But no Johnson script is more satisfying today than his adaptation of Arnold Bennett's *Buried Alive*, which he and director John M. Stahl turned into the delightful *Holy Matrimony*.

Johnson and Stahl graced the film with a bemused reverence for its aging hero and heroine—Monty Woolley and Gracie Fields— that reveals itself in the development, pacing, acting, and dialogue of the leading characters. Unlike Ben Hecht at his most indulgent, Johnson doesn't coast by making one character the author's mouthpiece and giving him all the best lines. Woolley and Fields are granted a sense of their past, an even share of comical or rhetorical "points" to score (points that are made with a gentleness suggesting comradely love and intellectual respect), and rich color and shading worthy of a painting by Priam Farll, the dashing recluse played by Woolley. Woolley's performance is a special surprise. Occasionally unbearable, he is here unbeatable, in a role you might suppose Coburn or Laughton would be given by right. Perhaps Johnson learned to tame Woolley after their other collaborations, *The Pied Piper* and *Life Begins at 8:30*. Perhaps Woolley responded to Stahl's direction; the care Johnson took in transferring Bennett's fragile tale to the screen is matched by Stahl's attention to the tiniest behavioral detail.

In one early scene, Woolley visits a shop where he keeps the brushes and canvases needed for his surreptitious avocation. The proprietor, a willing conspirator in this husband's secret, nevertheless warns him of the seductive dangers of amateur painting. The painter begins with still lifes, and graduates to dogs. "Next he wants to draw women. First with their clothes on, and then . . ." He finishes the sentence with a glance at Woolley that encompasses disdain for such degradation, cautionary advice not to be snared in this trap, and a certain suspicion that Woolley is ripe for a fall. It is another example of the kind of privileged moment that results from the perfect combination of script, direction, and acting.

And the dialogue! Gracie Fields, a working-class matron with equal measures of dignity and pluck, is casing the menu at a posh French restaurant. Having no success with the language, she collars a passing waiter with one hand and points to a phrase on the menu with the other. "What is that?" she asks. "That, madam," the waiter replies in a tone clearly meant to deflate, "is the name of the selec-

tion the orchestra is playing." Gracie, flung against the wall, re-
bounds with admirable resilience. "Well, there's not much nourish-
ment in that!" Later, when she discovers that her benevolent, doting
husband is in fact the nation's foremost painter, she muses about
her role as a notable's wife. "I don't know how I'd be. Not much,
probably—like I could never be a duchess or a bareback rider."
With this line, she expresses the mixture of a sensible sensibility and
a poet's understanding of the improbable that invests her with a life
that survives the final fade-out.

Woolley's character is almost as enjoyable—during one rage,
he says of an enemy, "I wouldn't throw a pot of tea on him if he
were on fire at my feet!" And after another rage he comments on
his polemical style: "It's just a dramatic way of expressing my exas-
peration with the whole affair"—but he is made memorable by the
subtle, sublime redemption he undergoes at his wife's bidding. It is
her softly radiant love for a sexagenarian hero that is reflected in the
viewer's eyes, and nudges us to think fondly of the film, its characters, and its creators.

Oh, Men! Oh, Women! (1957)

What does it say about the latter part of Nunnally Johnson's career that the two films he scripted, produced, and directed in 1957
were a romantic documentary about an analyst who cures a schizophrenic young woman (*The Three Faces of Eve*), and a sarcastic
comedy about an analyst whose fiancée is the subject of his patients'
sex fantasies (*Oh, Men! Oh, Women!*)? Do we infer that Johnson,
the salty but soft Georgia cracker, was so intrigued by the topic of
psychoanalysis that he turned two random properties into compelling personal statements reflecting the tragic and comic facets of
mind-probing? Or was he more interested in exploiting his material
than exploring it?

As applies to so many prominent screenwriters who were promoted from the impotent creativity of mere scriptwork to the studio
corridors of power as writer-producers, the truth for Johnson lies
somewhere boringly in between. Johnson was enough of a craftsman
to turn any hack play (like Edward Chodorov's *Oh, Men! Oh,
Women!*) into a highly competent, hack movie; and he was enough
of an artist to do his best work in response to involving material
(like Corbett H. Thigpen and Hervey M. Cleckley's nonfiction ac-

count, *The Three Faces of Eve*). Johnson's involvement with the latter, as well as his muted, documentary *mise-en-scène,* made *The Three Faces of Eve* his best job of direction, as well as one of the few postwar Johnson films to meet the standards set by his early work as a screenwriter. Generally, he seems to have been so relaxed as a director that his films now look slack, lax, with careless framing of scenes and directionless directing of actors. His fifties films tend to slouch, then droop, then amiably fall asleep.

Oh, Men! Oh, Women! is one of these films. Given the perfect subject for the CinemaScope screen—a patient lying on an analyst's couch—Johnson begins well, with a hysterical, horizontal Tony Randall monologue, but then scrupulously avoids any of the comic investigation of the wide screen that marked the contemporary films of Frank Tashlin and George Axelrod. He does share Tashlin's and Axelrod's fondness for the in-film parody, a form that evolved from TV-revue humor and developed into the "revue" movies of the late sixties (*The Troublemaker, The Producers, Bob & Carol & Ted & Alice*). But Johnson's use of this sketchy, embryonic form was itself too sketchy, too embryonic, without any of the audacity shown by its more assured practitioners. Johnson was a product of the "story" film—indeed, he produced some of the best of them— and his flirtation with the new, satirical-comic-strip humor was tentative at best, and thus embarrassing at worst.

Every once in a while Johnson forgets he's retooling an ersatz-hip, Broadway comedy machine, and sneaks in some romantic dialogue that is poignant as much for what it reminds us of the writer's strengths as for what it reveals to use about the characters' weaknesses. Throughout the movie, Dan Dailey has been treating the role of an overbearing ham actor as if it were really a sure-fire actor's part, chewing the scenery when he's on, trying clumsily to melt into it when he's not. (This is more Johnson's fault, for misdirecting, than Dailey's, for taking it.) But finally he begs the reluctant heroine, Barbara Rush, for "a kiss?" "Just one," she warns. "But one as long as my exile," he croons, "and sweet as my revenge." Here we have Johnson wittily composing some of that sweet dialogue he had renounced for too long, and Dailey taking revenge for his film's-length exile from a decent line.

Johnson's talent never completely deserted him. *My Cousin Rachel* (1953) has a lushness of mood and level of achievement worthy of his best prewar films; and *The World of Henry Orient* and *The Dirty Dozen,* his last two films, mark a surprisingly vigorous end to a long and distinguished career. But the record of his early successes promised a bright career for Johnson when he achieved the uncommon autonomy of a writer-producer-director. Instead of Sun-King brilliance, there were only a few vagrant rays peeking through an all-too-typical Hollywood eclipse.

ERNEST LEHMAN

(1920–   )

1948   THE INSIDE STORY (Allan Dwan) co-story
1954   EXECUTIVE SUITE (Robert Wise) screenplay
        SABRINA (Billy Wilder) co-screenplay
1956   SOMEBODY UP THERE LIKES ME (Robert Wise) screen-
        play
        THE KING AND I (Walter Lang) screenplay
1957   SWEET SMELL OF SUCCESS (Alexander Mackendrick) co-
        screenplay, from his novella, *Tell Me About It Tomorrow*
1959   NORTH BY NORTHWEST (Alfred Hitchcock) story, screen-
        play
1960   FROM THE TERRACE (Mark Robson) screenplay
1961   WEST SIDE STORY (Robert Wise, Jerome Robbins) screen-
        play
1965   THE SOUND OF MUSIC (Robert Wise) screenplay
1966   WHO'S AFRAID OF VIRGINIA WOOLF? (Mike Nichols)
        screenplay, producer
1969   HELLO, DOLLY! (Gene Kelly) screenplay, producer
1972   PORTNOY'S COMPLAINT (Ernest Lehman) screenplay, pro-
        ducer
1974   ONE PLUS ONE EQUALS ONE (Alfred Hitchcock) story,
        screenplay

Ernest Lehman's current reputation as Curator-in-Chief of the
Hollywood Museum of High-Priced Broadway Properties would be
unremarkable if Lehman had not established himself in the fifties as
a distinct movie stylist. At first glance, the personal signature on
Sweet Smell of Success and *North by Northwest* may seem less
obtrusive than elusive, and the films themselves seem as dissimilar as,

say, *Casablanca* and *Letter from an Unknown Woman*. And yet, Lehman's two original films are not only dissimilar, they are direct opposites: the first, a cautionary tale of degeneration; the second, a comic fable of regeneration. All *Sweet Smell of Success* and *North by Northwest* have in common are the craft, wit, and story sense of their author—which is why Lehman's close adaptations of *West Side Story*, *The Sound of Music*, *Who's Afraid of Virginia Woolf?*, and *Hello, Dolly!* (not to mention his flat-footed bawdlerization of *Portnoy's Complaint*) strike Lehman's admirers as acts of treason against his considerable talent. The master plot mechanic has become a mere service-station attendant of other writers' vehicles, inspecting them without correcting them, and allowing us to infer that it was his gas that made them move.

Sweet Smell of Success (1957)

Lehman had dealt with urban corruption before—in business (*Executive Suite*) and in boxing (*Somebody Up There Likes Me*) —but Evil had been relegated to feature-player status, and the triumph of Good was as predictable as it was predestined. In *Sweet Smell of Success* (which Lehman scripted from his own novella, and then turned over to Clifford Odets for some dialogue-spicing), the villains are front and center. Burt Lancaster, with horn-rimmed glasses and without his usual display of flexed biceps and flashing bicuspids, is the Winchellesque calumnist who epitomizes Absolute Power; and Tony Curtis, playing Bernie Schwartz for the first time in his career, is the press agent propelled by an Ambition for power that has already led to absolute corruption.

In several respects, *Sweet Smell of Success* is a Seventh Avenue version of *The Man with the Golden Arm*: the staccato score, the brilliantly depicted milieu, the good-bad girl who walks bravely into the final dawn. But *The Man with the Golden Arm* is basically the fantasy of an optimistic junkie. At the outset, Frankie thinks he can kick the habit with pure determination; at the end, he *knows* he can do it, with determination and the love of a good-bad woman. The film traces a line from crucifixion to resurrection. *Sweet Smell of Success* provides its characters with no such instant uplift. The needling here is verbal, but all the more devastating because it implies a psychological rather than physiological addiction.

Even in the lower depths of Manhattan nite life, however, style

is the man, and the Lehman-Odets dialogue is appropriately baroque. Lancaster may write his column with a stiletto, but his wit
must have a fascinating point; and the self-consciously colorful
dialogue of *all* the characters lends irony and a tinge of uncertainty
to their undisguised but understated power plays. "Sidney lives in
marled twilight," says Lancaster of Curtis; does Lancaster really
understand what makes Curtis drive himself so hard, even against
the traffic, or is he simply guying a rube? When Lancaster's sister's
annoyingly straight fiancé—an average Joe so righteous that he actually calls himself "an average Joe"—wants to state something as
simple as "Your brother made you say that," he comes out with,
"That's fish four days old. I won't buy it. It comes out of that mouth
I love like a ventriloquist's dummy. That's J. J. Honsegger saying
good-bye." The degree to which Average Joe spouts J.J.'s slang is
the degree to which he is potentially corruptible. Thus, only the
sister speaks direct Hollywood-heroine prose. It is a tribute to the
utter venality of Emile Meyer's fat, sweaty cop that he is given the
film's most memorable line: "Come back here, Sidney. I want to
chastise you." (At the end of the picture, he gets to chastise Sidney
black and blue.)

Only once does *Sweet Smell of Success* indulge in the overstressed
social symbolism that we identify as Odetsian. Susan Honsegger wears
a mink coat, a present from J.J., as a constant emblem of her
brother's power over her as well as his constant, felt presence
(whether actual or personified by Sidney). We see her without it
for the first time as she attempts suicide, which she imagines as the
only way to escape J.J.'s shroud of influence; and when she leaves
him finally, she has put on a trim suede jacket. This is a nice touch
as long as it isn't verbalized. So why did the filmmakers succumb to
the temptation to have her fiancé say in disgust, "This coat is your
brother. I've always hated this coat"? It's one difference between
serious American movies and the best European films that the latter leaves some things unsaid.

Every interesting character in this film is rotten—rotten with
style, of course, but without the immoral charm that seduces us into
liking, and accepting the values of, the con artists in *His Girl Friday*.
Perhaps this is why *Sweet Smell of Success* was a box-office failure
—and why, of all Lehman's fifties screenplays, it was the only one
not to receive an award nomination from either the Motion Picture
Academy or the Screen Writers Guild. Lehman learned his lesson:

in the next decade he would write (and sometimes produce) *West Side Story, The Sound of Music, Who's Afraid of Virginia Woolf?,* and *Hello, Dolly!* But it would be captious to invoke the spirits of J. J. Honsegger and Sidney Falco. In Lehman's case, when he "sold out," he did so in the direction Hollywood honors and rewards. Still, with the triumphant exception of *North by Northwest,* he never achieved the consistency of bile and banter evident in his writing here.

As with most of the best American movies, *Sweet Smell of Success* is an example of artistic collaboration in top form. A nod of thanks should go to the person responsible for interesting Tony Curtis in a screen character that touched facets of his off-screen personality (a coup that can be compared with Hitchcock's realization, in *Psycho,* of the homosexual vulnerability beneath Tony Perkins' ingenuous smile and gait.) Maybe it was Lancaster, who had hired Curtis the year before for his superproduction, *Trapeze*; maybe it was Curtis's own inclination. But I prefer to believe that the part was suggested by his agent—and that Curtis rewarded him, in a way that may not have been immediately appreciated, with the delineation of a rapacious agent that was both libelous and satisfying.

North by Northwest (1959)

"I am but mad north-northwest," Hamlet tells Guildenstern, just before The Mousetrap begins. "When the wind is southerly, I know a hawk from a handsaw." The maddest thing about Lehman's *North by Northwest*—surely the most successful original screenplay ever written for Hitchcock—may be Lehman's audacity in comparing Roger Thornhill, the indecisive adman played by Cary Grant, to Shakespeare's melancholy Dane. Comparison, normally odious, must seem sacrilegious here. And yet Thornhill, whose weakness of character stems partly from an Oedipal relationship so chummy one hardly dares to take it seriously, finds the resolve to become a man of action only when he plays a secret-agent role to catch that conscienceless king of spies, James Mason as the suave Vandamm.

Thornhill has been mistaken for one George Kaplan, an "agent" who never existed in the first place—who never was anything more than a role. To suggest the film's complications and the characters' confusion, it is only necessary to mention that, at their first meeting, Thornhill, whom Vandamm believes is Kaplan, believes Vandamm is UN diplomat Lester Townsend. After this Pirandellian juggling act, chaos is the only logical plot development. As Thornhill says in reply to a request for some top-secret information ("a simple yes or no"): "A simple no. For the simple reason I simply don't know what you're talking about." Hitchcock has related that Grant himself used that very line unconsciously in complaining about the bewildering sequence of events that propels him from the Oak Room at the Plaza into a maelstrom of espionage. Hitchcock might have replied that Lehman's script wasn't completely mad—just "mad north-northwest."

Both Thornhill, the super salesman, and Vandamm, the super-spy, are by trade consummate actors; their jobs—one of which involves selling disposable products to disreputable people, the other of which involves buying disreputable secrets from disposable people—demand it. The problem, as Thornhill discovers to his nearly fatal chagrin, is that, when one attempts to "be oneself," to assert one's "real" identity, there's less believability in the role. At a point halfway through the film, when our hero would like nothing better than to remove George Kaplan's dandruff-speckled jacket and become Roger Thornhill again, Vandamm merely chides him about his successive roles as advertising executive, fugitive from justice, and jealous lover—and puts Hollywood existentialism in a well-polished nutshell.

> VANDAMM: Seems to me you fellows [CIA agents] could stand a little less training from the FBI and a little more from the Actors' Studio.
>
> THORNHILL: Apparently, the only performance that's going to satisfy you is when I play dead.
>
> VANDAMM: Your very next role. You'll be quite convincing.

Though Thornhill and Vandamm are supposedly fighting over some ill-defined military secrets, their real object of contention is Vandamm's mistress, and Thornhill's ultimate beloved, Eve Kendall. "Object" is the operative word here: Vandamm strokes his sex-kitten's neck distractedly, and the closest Thornhill can get to a compliment is: "You're the smartest girl I've ever spent the night with on the train." (On the train! What a qualifier!) At this remark, Eve lowers her head in muted disappointment and then looks to the right in dismay—Vandamm's henchmen are following them. The scene displays not only Hitchcock's occasional mastery of what are thought of as "actors' moments," but also the subtlety of Bernard

Herrmann's score, which swoops and starts in perfect harmony with Eva Marie Saint's movements. Hitchcock, Saint, and Grant himself orchestrate the pair's "love" scenes (kissing scenes, actually) so that they reverberate with a tension that is more pathological than sexual. The famous circling kiss in Eve's train compartment describes both a mating dance and the wary preliminaries to some fatal ritual of combat; and Grant's suntanned hands, which suddenly look menacingly large, are both instruments of seduction and potential murder weapons. When they meet again later, after Eve has sent Thornhill away to die on a Midwestern prairie, Grant holds his hands out—to embrace her? to strangle her?—only to pull them back and mumble, "I need a drink."

Robin Wood has identified the serious theme of regeneration—exemplified by Thornhill's almost chronic dependence on alcohol—lurking beneath the veneer of a Hitchcock comedy-thriller. Lehman's triumph comes from his weaving of this theme with that of the antagonists' role-playing: Thornhill is "cured" and, we may assume, actually "becomes" Eve's husband at the film's conclusion; but Vandamm is incorrigibly the actor. Thus, when the henchmen attempting to dislodge Thornhill's hand from its precarious hold on a Mount Rushmore monument is shot by a real CIA agent, Vandamm can express only petulance: "Rather unsporting . . . using real bullets." The runaway sports car, the careening crop-duster and, indeed, the beautiful blonde Vandamm used to "defeat" Thornhill were, to the suave spy, so many tiddles in a game only gentlemen should play. Earlier, Thornhill had won a round by "shooting" Eve with blank cartridges; to Vandamm, *that* was imaginative, and thus "fair." But winning the game with such a hoary trick as a well-placed bullet at the right moment leaves the victors open to a charge of unsportsmanlike conduct. In a sense, Vandamm retains stylistic supremacy to the end, and we admire him for playing a morally meaningless game with Raffles-like wit and good humor.

Everyone concerned worked on *North by Northwest* at top form, from Hitchcock to Herrmann—who borrowed freely both from himself (the love scenes echo his "Salammbo" opera in *Citizen Kane*) and from, of all people, Charlie Chaplin (the "industrial" theme from *Modern Times* turns up underneath the credits). Because Cary Grant is never called upon to play Hamlet, except indirectly, applause and Oscars have eluded him. "He's *only* a movie star." And yet the range of his roles—manic managing editor in

His Girl Friday, desperate adoptive father in *Penny Serenade,* vulnerable charmer in *North by Northwest*—and the breadth he effortlessly brings to these roles suggest an acting ability as large as it is self-effacing. Try to imagine Grant instead of Frederick Stafford in Hitchcock's *Topaz* and you begin to understand Grant's contribution to the moral universes of Hitchcock, Hawks, Stevens, McCarey, Cukor, Donen, *et al.* Grant played against three of Hitchcock's ersatz Joan Fontaines; if Eva Marie Saint is less mysterious than Ingrid Bergman, and less voluptuous than Grace Kelly, she still possesses a remote but smoldering Snow Queen quality that gives her role an ambiguous tension neither Bergman nor Kelly—and certainly not Tippi Hedren—could convey.

But the ultimate, anonymous triumph is Lehman's. His script is both an anthology of Hitchcock spy movies *and* their apotheosis. Beyond this, Lehman's dialogue is so rich and so relevant that it recalls the diamond-hard repartee of classical Hollywood. Lehman doesn't consign his villains to stylistic perdition by giving them the worst lines and the most easily demolished arguments. Like Rick and Renault, the charming duelists of *Casablanca*—indeed, like adversaries in the best drama—Thornhill and Vandamm begin with equal strengths and weaknesses. They differ only in their susceptibility to regeneration at Eve's hands. When Thornhill wins Eve's devotion, he can change; Vandamm cannot. Thornhill becomes strong enough to (presumably) discard his dependence on a doting mother for a responsible relationship with his new wife. That Lehman can say all this in a light-comedy framework, without saying it out loud, is a mark of his—and the film's—own surprising strengths.

Lehman's only subsequent flirtation with originality—his adaptation of Irving Wallace's best-selling mastodon, *The Prize*—bears interesting family resemblances to *North by Northwest,* from the picaresque, spy-vs.-sucker plot to individual sequences. Thus, Cary Grant being flattened by a malevolent crop-duster is replaced by Paul Newman being knocked off a narrow bridge by a vicious Volvo; and Grant bluffing his way out of danger by getting arrested at a fine-art auction is replaced by Newman cheekily doing the same at a convocation of Swedish nudists. Because wise guy Newman lacks the great Grant vulnerability, we merely enjoy his adventures vicariously instead of empathizing with the reluctant adventurer. And Mark Robson is, shall we say, no Hitchcock. But Lehman's willingness to discard just about everything in the novel except the setting and the sketchiest outlines of Wallace's major characters indicated, even as late as 1963, that a spark of insouciance remained in the prestigious writer-producer—and encouraged the speculation that Lehman was marking time, prostituting his talents until the chance for a return to stylish form presented itself. (That's one of the reasons why *Portnoy's Complaint* was so discouraging: it seemed to demonstrate incontestably that there was very little talent left for Lehman to prostitute.) Maybe his renewed partnership with Hitchcock will provide such a chance—and prove again that one Pantheon director plus one stylish screenwriter can equal one superior film.

BETTY COMDEN (1919–   )
    and
ADOLPH GREEN (1915–   )

1947   GOOD NEWS (Charles Walters) screenplay
1948   TAKE ME OUT TO THE BALL GAME (Busby Berkeley)
        lyrics
1949   THE BARKLEYS OF BROADWAY (Charles Walters) story,
        screenplay
        ON THE TOWN (Gene Kelly and Stanley Donen) screenplay,
        from their musical play; lyrics
1952   SINGIN' IN THE RAIN (Gene Kelly and Stanley Donen) story,
        screenplay, lyrics
1953   THE BAND WAGON (Vincente Minnelli) story, screenplay
1955   IT'S ALWAYS FAIR WEATHER (Gene Kelly and Stanley
        Donen) story, screenplay
1958   AUNTIE MAME (Morton DaCosta) screenplay
1959   BELLS ARE RINGING (Vincente Minnelli) screenplay, from
        their musical play; lyrics
1964   WHAT A WAY TO GO! (J. Lee Thompson) screenplay, lyrics

Hollywood musicals are not generally remembered for their screenplays. Occasionally the hoariest cliché—"You're going out there a
youngster; you've got to come back a star!"—will worm its way
into the language. Once in a while an accomplished actor will take
a line—"I am reech and I am preety"—and turn it into a vagrant
privileged moment. But, in general, musical plots are minor func-
tionaries, carrying the action from hotel room to gazebo to ballroom
to Broadway stage; and dialogue serves merely to give actors and
audience a breathing spell between production numbers.

    The screenplays of Betty Comden and Adolph Green stand out

in this forgettable field like Joan Blondell in a chorus line. Their musicals, all spoofs of show-biz genres or milieux, are both affectionate and perspicacious, with a comic distance that keeps them from drowning in nostalgia. Although their films are often star vehicles, they are not *merely* star vehicles; Comden and Green had an uncanny sense of what each star—Kelly in *Singin' in the Rain,* Astaire in *The Band Wagon,* Judy Holliday in *Bells Are Ringing*—could do best, and what kind of plot structure he or she was most comfortable inhabiting. The only movie convention that worked against them was one over which they had no control: the requisite, climactic "ballets" in *On the Town, Singin' in the Rain,* and *The Band Wagon.* This may explain why *Bells Are Ringing,* with an incandescent star and a gallery of featured players worthy of a Sturges or a Kanin working at top form, wears as well as any of their films. Instead of Kelly or Astaire entangling themselves in Cyd Charisse's voluptuous gowns and gams, we are treated to Judy Holliday's awesomely hilarious and wrenching swan song to the cinema: "I'm gonna go back / to where I belong, / to the Bonjour Tristesse Brassiere Company!"

Singin' in the Rain (1952)

If *Singin' in the Rain* is the best original movie musical ever—and it is, it is!—it's because Comden and Green's script, Gene Kelly's and Donald O'Connor's complementarily exhilarating screen personalities, and Stanley Donen's silky *mise-en-scène* exude and evoke the kind of effortless high spirits that virtually define Hollywood moviemaking at its best. The decade beginning with 1925, which led America from Jazz Age childishness to adolescent Depression, served as the basis for some of Hollywood's finest and most characteristic films, from *His Girl Friday* to *Some Like It Hot,* from *Sunset Boulevard* to *Bonnie and Clyde.* This decade found its perfect prose expression, however, in Comden and Green's wisecracking and wonderfully knowledgeable behind-the-scenes plot, and an almost poetic synthesis of the era's demonic vitality in the grace and drive of the film's dances.

If Comden and Green laid the groundwork for laughs, Kelly, O'Connor, and Donen proved how serene a repository of sheer delight movies—and moviemaking—can be. Kelly's artistic ambition, which was to culminate in his unacceptable *Invitation to the Dance,* showed its swelled head only in that orgy of taffy and taffeta, the "Broadway Rhythm" ballet. But, in his *pas de deux* with O'Connor ("Fit as a Fiddle"), in his own solo ("Singin' in the Rain"), and in O'Connor's knockabout knockout ("Make 'Em Laugh"), the combination of comic invention, technical expertise and an exhausting manic energy produced elegant, surrealistic balletics worthy of a Ballanchine, a Nijinsky, a Keaton.

The film's generosity toward its period was as great as the filmmakers' affection for it. Kelly at his most studiously hammy possesses infinitely more charm and simple competence than Charles Farrell, Glenn Tryon, or Douglas Fairbanks, Jr. in their early-talkie incarnations. Comden-Green dialogue such as "You're a French aristocrat, and she's a simple girl of the people, and she won't even give you a tumbrel" or "Why, I make more money than Calvin Coolidge—put together!" or "*The Dueling Cavalier* with music— how about *The Dueling Mammy*?" might not have won them an Oscar (*Singin' in the Rain* wasn't even nominated for the Academy's screenwriting award), but its easy frivolity manages to elevate the standard of late-twenties dialogue even as it kids it. In the same way, Donen's camera, gliding around the stationary photographic equipment that froze so many early talkies, and Cedric Gibbons' extravagantly colorful art direction seem gently satirical to those who are familiar with this immobile, monochromatic period, while providing an agreeable fantasy-history to novices who would be excused for thinking, "If the first talkies were this good, why satirize them?"

In fact, Comden and Green, avid movie buffs both, are making a case for philistine vulgarity. The film's famous "elocution lesson" ("Moses supposes his toeses are roses, / but Moses supposes erroneously; / Moses he knowses his toeses aren't roses, / as Moses supposes his toeses to be") makes their bias clear. Whereas Lerner and Loewe, four year later, would argue the opposite point in their *My Fair Lady* "Rain in Spain" number, here Comden, Green, Kelly, and O'Connor demonstrate the triumph of Hollywood's kinetic exuberance over Broadway's verbal finesse. The song—indeed, the entire film—indicates that Comden and Green went west not to make a buck or a name for themselves, but to repay the movies with thanks, and with interest, for the delight it had brought them.

Kelly, O'Connor, and Debbie Reynolds are not, in themselves, the most appealing trio in Hollywood. On the basis of their performances before and after *Singin' in the Rain*, one would think the perfect musical might star, by something akin to divine right, Fred Astaire, Ginger Rogers, and maybe Edward Everett Horton. Kelly's Pepsodent grin usually looked as if it emerged from between clenched teeth; Debbie Reynolds' energy seemed directed more to her career than to the camera, and Donald O'Connor had become so adept at being inept in movies that one despaired of his ever leaving Universal (where he had been mired since 1942) for something more international. It is part of Comden and Green's genius that they recognized and manipulated these "weaknesses" in their script. Kelly is turned into a movie star whose grin is as phony as the studio-made romance with a dumb leading lady; Reynolds is an ambitious chorus girl who pretends to despise the stardom she fiercely desires; O'Connor is the hero's best friend, whose sappy banter is belied by his heroic footwork.

The fourth wheel on this merry tricycle, Jean Hagen (who would later "Make Room for Daddy" on sitcom TV), plays the silent-movie star with a shrill, Judy Hollidayish voice. Through most of the film, Hagen functions as a delicious marplot, a harridan whose dim intelligence is matched by her moral myopia. She becomes pathetically appealing only when Reynolds agrees to save Hagen's face by dubbing her own voice onto the sound track of Hagen's first talkie. As the coarse star, feelingly for once, mouthes the lyrics of a love song Reynolds is really singing to Kelly, the camera pulls back elegiacally, the color screen turns to sepia, and we see both the reason for her evanescent popularity and the beginning of the end of her career. It is a moment that suggests, without a wasted shot or twist of the plot, the same end of a sublime, ridiculous movie era that Billy Wilder painted, with broader, more delirious strokes, in *Sunset Boulevard*. The difference in tone is due as much to the two films' fidelity to their own themes as to the fact that Hagen is *Singin' in the Rain*'s comic villainess, and not its tragic heroine.

The theme of *Singin' in the Rain* is the birth pangs of a new Hollywood, not the death throes of the old. And, just as the town lured a new generation of talent when the talkies came in—when everybody was young—the Arthur Freed musicals of two decades later seemed to signal another onslaught, with the arrival of Comden, Green, Donen, Lerner, Betty Garrett, Jules Munshin, Debbie Reynolds, and Cyd Charisse. But the studios were beginning to fall apart, and not even this transfusion of talent could save them. With the possible exception of *Seven Brides for Seven Brothers, Singin' in the Rain* was the last original movie musical until *A Hard Day's Night* that expressed irrepressible optimism through its infectious vitality. The genre would soon be seized with an industry-wide depression that would be ideal for the melancholic sensibility of Vincente Minnelli. Thus, *Singin' in the Rain* might have been more appropriately titled *Whistlin' in the Dark*. But what dancing! What singing! What incomparable whistling!

The Band Wagon (1953)

For all of Gene Kelly's entrepreneurial skills, *Singin' in the Rain* remains an *hommage* to that brand of clubhouse camaraderie that breathes life into the old "Hey gang, let's put the show on right here!" canard. And although it borrows heavily from *Singin' in the Rain*'s backstage plotting, *The Band Wagon* is really an essay in melancholy aloneness, if not aloofness. Fred Astaire always possessed an air so casually aristocratic that most mortals were repelled and propelled into chorus-line impotence. His plainclothes roles in the forties suggested that the Man in the Top Hat was a self-exiled king masquerading as the amiable commoner; one dance step, even with a game Rita Hayworth or Joan Leslie, was enough to confirm Astaire's remote royalty. Gene Kelly, except in his flaky ballets, danced *with* his colleagues; in *The Band Wagon,* Astaire dances *around* them. The Comden-Green script pretends to draw the solitary patrician into a web of democratic creativity by having him rally a disconsolate stage company to save their show by throwing out all the arty stuff. But the film's first and lasting impression is that of Astaire shuffling off toward a Garboesque Valhalla as he sings, "No one knows better than I myself / I'm by myself / alone."

Elliott Sirkin has defined the typical Comden-Green movie climax as one that shows the villain foiled by a form of communication he had relied upon too arrogantly. In *Singin' in the Rain,* Jean Hagen is revealed as a voiceless phony when a curtain is drawn and Debbie Reynolds is seen singing for her. In *The Band Wagon,* highbrow director Jack Buchanan's attempts to legitimize the Broadway musical by infusing classical theatrics into it are disastrous, and Buchanan immediately turns into a swell guy willing to be just another song-and-dance man at Astaire's side. In the process, Comden and Green take a few swipes at a pretentious choreographer whom viewers may be forgiven for mistaking for Gene Kelly! He has the same unlined, Dorian-Gray face, and the same ambitions to transform show-biz terpsichore from ballroom classicism to ballet-stage baroque. The choice of Cyd Charisse (Kelly's partner in the "Broadway Rhythm" ballet) for the role of the ballet star whom Astaire finally wins over, heart and hoof, makes it even easier to spot the Kelly character. Oddly enough, though, the film concludes with an Astaire bow to the Kelly influence—or maybe just to an Arthur Freed memo, since Freed had produced *On the Town, An American in Paris,* and *Singin' in the Rain*—namely, the Mickey Spillaine–parody "Girl Hunt" ballet. (To conclude all these interior references, we may note that Spillaine himself later wrote a novel called *The Girl Hunters*—and starred himself in the movie version.)

The meticulous, exuberant energy that characterizes Kelly's best dancing also marks the Comden-Green script for *Singin' in the Rain.* Kelly was always more obsessed with his films' formal integrity than was Astaire, whose roots in the loosely framed, almost vaudevillian tradition of late-twenties musical comedy were reflected in the haphazard, often flaccid pacing of his RKO movies. In *The Band Wagon,* Comden and Green again wrote for their star. Consequently, the film bears the marks of intermittent grace and interminable longeurs symptomatic not only of Astaire's films, but also those of other Hollywood aristocrats such as Garbo, Fields, Chaplin, and the Marx Brothers. As Nanette Fabray and Oscar Levant (*The Band Wagon*'s Comden and Green surrogates) say of the script they are writing for Astaire, it has "just enough plot to let Tony [Astaire] do all sorts of gay and varied numbers." As might be expected, too little plot means too little gayness and variety. When the show-within-the-film is supposed to fall together, the film itself simply falls apart, as one pleasant number after another is unreeled.

Andrew Sarris credits Vincente Minnelli's fifties musicals with "a sympathetic *mise-en-scène*" that "lyricized loneliness." Certainly *An American in Paris* and *The Band Wagon* fit this description (its application to *Brigadoon, Kismet,* and especially *Bells Are Ringing* is more precarious), although I suspect that Alan Jay Lerner's lame script for *An American in Paris* and the Comden-Green pastiche for *The Band Wagon* help intensify the sense of depression Minnelli excels at conveying. One small but possibly significant difference between Minnelli and Kelly-Donen is the tendency of performers in *The Band Wagon* to play to the director, just at the left of the camera. (In *Singin' in the Rain* the actors sell their songs and dances *through* the camera directly to the audience.) Minnelli's own mordant loneliness combines with Astaire's mythic aloneness to produce, in *The Band Wagon,* a Broadway melody in a minor key. And Comden and Green refract their own sensibilities to contribute to the film's spirit of pastness and malaise. In *Singin' in the Rain,* a bunch of chorus boys, surrounding Jean Hagen at a happy Hollywood soiree, rush to light her long-stemmed cigarette; but there's such an abundance of flames that Hagen simply throws her cigarette away, gold-plated holder and all. In *The Band Wagon,* Astaire walks into an ornate but desolate hall, where a cast party was to have taken place. He pulls out a cigarette, and a team of waiters moves in to light it for him. Astaire lets them do it, but, surveying the scene of a ballroom that has become a mausoleum, he extinguishes it, and walks out—by himself, alone.

Garson Kanin (1912–   )
(and
Ruth Gordon [1896–   ])

1942 WOMAN OF THE YEAR (George Stevens) idea (uncredited)
1943 THE MORE THE MERRIER (George Stevens) story, co-screenplay (uncredited)
1945 THE TRUE GLORY (Carol Reed, Garson Kanin) co-compilation
1946 FROM THIS DAY FORWARD (John Barry) adaptation
1948 A DOUBLE LIFE (George Cukor) co-story,[1] co-screenplay [1]
1949 ADAM'S RIB (George Cukor) co-story,[1] co-screenplay [1]
1950 BORN YESTERDAY (George Cukor) from his play
1951 THE MARRYING KIND (George Cukor) co-story,[1] co-screenplay [1]
1952 PAT AND MIKE (George Cukor) co-story,[1] co-screenplay [1]
1954 IT SHOULD HAPPEN TO YOU (George Cukor) story, screenplay
1956 THE GIRL CAN'T HELP IT (Frank Tashlin) from his short story, "Do Re Mi"
1960 THE RAT RACE (Robert Mulligan) screenplay, from his novel
1961 THE RIGHT APPROACH (David Butler) from his play, *The Live Wire*
1969 WHERE IT'S AT (Garson Kanin) screenplay, from his novel
      SOME KIND OF A NUT (Garson Kanin) story, screenplay
      Kanin directed but did not write the following films: 1938 *A Man to Remember, Next Time I Marry.* 1939 *The Great Man Votes, Bachelor Mother.* 1940 *My Favorite Wife, They Knew What They Wanted.* 1941 *Tom, Dick and Harry.*

[1] With Ruth Gordon.

Garson Kanin directed films (*fl.* 1938–1941) before he wrote them (*fl.* 1948–1954). He knew performers, he married one, he was one

—and he could write dialogue for them that was incorrigibly actable. Like Betty Comden and Adolph Green, Kanin and Ruth Gordon found special inspiration in the personality and comic talents
of Judy Holliday (in *Adam's Rib, Born Yesterday, The Marrying
Kind*, and *It Should Happen to You*), the difference being that,
early in the actress's career, the Kanins emphasized her eccentricities of diction and dress, while, a decade later, Comden and Green
could afford to discover a warm, loving woman inside the star.
Verbal eccentricity as an index to a person's class and character is,
in fact, the Kanin trademark. From the political and sporting jargon
in *Woman of the Year* and Charles Coburn's mischievously dan-
gling prepositional phrases in *The More the Merrier* to Spencer
Tracy's tortuous colloquialisms in *Pat and Mike*, Kanin demonstrated a flair for phraseology that remained fresh and distinctive.
Because of Kanin's close collaboration with his wife on scripts written for another, very close couple—Tracy and Katharine Hepburn
—the "marriages" portrayed in *Adam's Rib* and *Pat and Mike* have
a sense of natural familiarity and mutual respect rare in Hollywood
domestic comedies.

The More the Merrier (1943)

The writing credit on this film reads: "Screenplay by Robert
Russell and Frank Ross; Richard Flournoy and Lewis Foster. Story
by Robert Russell and Frank Ross." It seems odd that such an undistinguished quartet (Russell's career high point was *Come Sep-
tember*, Foster's was the original idea for *Mr. Smith Goes to Washington*, Flournoy's was nine scripts in the *Blondie* series, and Ross's
was his marriage to Jean Arthur) should produce a screenplay with
characters and dialogue worthy of a Garson Kanin—so Kanin's
statement (in *Tracy and Hepburn*) that "I wrote it with Bob Russell;
and later, Frank Ross, Jean Arthur's husband, came in on it," can
be accepted without too much wish fulfillment or straining to find
internal evidence.

The Kanin touch is evident throughout: Connie, Joe, and Dingle
are fully and carefully drawn people with distinctive personalities
and patterns of speech. Dingle, the businessman-lobbyist (his precise occupation is never divulged), is the most eccentric in both
action and diction. His motto is "Damn the torpedoes! Full speed
ahead!" and he tends to barge into hotels, apartments, business

meetings, budding love affairs, and declarative sentences—always moving at full speed but often forgetting his direction. An inveterate "which" hunter, he seems to look on relative pronouns with the disdain a torpedo must feel for a shred of seaweed blocking its path. Thus, the following headlong circumlocutions: "Then how would you like it for her to spill a cocktail all over it at the party you couldn't go with her to, because she borrowed your dress to wear to it—in." And: "Of all times, Miss Milligan, this is no time to be indecisive—in." Dingle's good-natured and intuitively sensible bullying propels the plot through intricacies and toward a conclusion that neither our disinterested hero nor our disarming heroine could have had the slightest premonition—of. And Kanin's construction of Dinglesque diction neatly matches Charles Coburn's overbearing but genial performance.

Jean Arthur had long since perfected her star-image as the down-to-earth, slightly dithery working girl who hopes for romance around the next plot turn but is sensible enough not to expect it until the next-to-last reel. What made her especially endearing was the catch in her voice that could suggest more nuances than were dreamt of in the philosophies of her leading man, her scriptwriters, and the Hays Office. Though she had been extraordinarily well-served by Preston Sturges, Sidney Buchman, and Norman Krasna, Kanin's development of the Arthur persona in *The More the Merrier* may be the ripest of all. Connie Milligan is more serious than the typical Arthur heroine; she has to be, for us to accept her engagement to solemn, pompous Charles J. Pendergast. Such is their relationship that, when asked her fiancé's first name, she replies, "Charles J." (So pervasive is his influence that, in the script, even while Connie is falling for heroic Joe Carter, she talks of her future with Pendergast: "We've been looking at an awful nice—*awfully* nice house in Georgetown." Charles J.'s spirit hovers, as the diffident professor correcting her grammar.) But Dingle's spirit is not to be ignored; besides, unlike Charles J., he's always around.

And his language is as contagious as his manner. Dingle, who has cozened Connie into renting half of her apartment to him, has just rented half of his half to Joe. "Otherwise," he appeals, "my friend, Joe here, woulda hadda sleep in the park." At first, Connie doesn't budge: "Otherwise, your friend Joe here's gonna woulda hadda sleep in the park anyway." But Dingle's rhetoric has insinuated itself; and we know that Connie will never be the same. Dingle's real mission in Washington is to find a "high-type, clean cut, nice young fellow" for Connie. He mentions it once to her before Joe moves in, and once after. Before long, Connie has entered Joe in her diary, as an HT-CC-NYF. By now we know that, in this movie at least, words precede actions, and that the irresistible force and the immovable torpedo can meet with no further delay.

Because he is an HT-CC-NYF, and because he is played by the attractively glum Joel McCrea, Joe Carter is largely immune to Dingle's verbal duplicity. He tilts with the vernacular only when provoked. So, when Pendergast asks Joe if he's "crowded like everyone else in Washington," Joe assures him that—physically and psychically—"I'm crowded like *nobody* else." Once, he ventures the Dinglesque judgment that "marriage is okay, if you want to be." But his importance is primarily that of a prod to Connie's charming stubbornness. During Joe's seduction of Connie, Kanin suggests the deepening of her affection for Joe by the way she gradually extricates herself from her fiancé's influence through the slightest variations in sentence structure. Joe and Connie continue their conversation in adjoining beds; a wall separates them. Connie says she's been thinking about Mr. Dingle.

> CONNIE: People can't do like he says, can they?
> JOE: You mean "Full Speed Ahead"?
> CONNIE: A person can't just rush in.
> JOE: No, no, they can't.
> [CONNIE: *He* cant.
> JOE: Who can't?
> CONNIE: A person. You say "he" instead of "they" when you're talking about one person.
> JOE: Oh, yeah. Thanks a lot.
> CONNIE: You know what I mean, don't you, Joe.
> JOE: Sure.]
> CONNIE: It's all right for Dingle to talk. He hasn't any decisions to make. But for a person like *us* . . .

Joe's use of "they"—meaning Connie and Joe—instead of the impersonal and selfish "he," is tantamount to a proposal. And Connie's phrase, "a person like us," signals her acceptance of a Connie-Joe unity, as well as the purging of Charles J. Pendergast. The new engagement is practically made official when Joe whispers, "Good night—dear," and Connie, with a verbal wave goodbye to the stuffy man she almost married, replies, "Good night, Mr. C—*darling.*"

Dingle's conspiracy is finally consummated, as is our lovers' marriage—the latter with little of the annoying cloyingness of George Stevens' earlier film, *Vivacious Lady*. As Connie and Joe come together in their sawed-off bedroom, Dingle and his cronies wassail below:

> "In love and war with people like us,
> We've got to work fast or we'll miss the bus.
> If you straddle the fence and you sit and wait,
> You get too little and you get it too late . . .
> And our eighteen children will be glad we said:
> Damn the torpedoes! Full Speed Ahead!"

Here is a concluding sexual innuendo that makes Preston Sturges's curtain line for *The Miracle of Morgan's Creek*—"some have greatness *thrust upon them*"—seem downright spineless in its subtlety.

The Marrying Kind (1951)

Kanin's film characters are divided rather evenly between celebrities and anonymities, between nabobs and nebbishes. Katharine Hepburn was ill-equipped to play women of no importance, and Kanin put this understanding of her to work in his stories for her (*Woman of the Year, Adam's Rib, Pat and Mike*). But Judy Holliday's appeal—even more than that of Jean Arthur in *The More the Merrier* or Debbie Reynolds in *The Rat Race*—was incorrigibly plebeian; her star quality, however dazzling, could hardly be called heavenly. If we find Kanin at fault for emphasizing the roughness of this diamond-in-the-rough, we must still credit him and Ruth Gordon with shaping a screen personality Miss Holliday could use to advantage until another famous writing team, Betty Comden and Adolph Green, saw it mellowing with age and ripe for apotheosis—and wrote her most satisfying role in *Bells Are Ringing*.

The Marrying Kind has an earthiness rare for Kanin, and rarer for George Cukor. In that not-too-distant day when the American Film Institute compiles a catalogue of Feature Films, 1951–1960, one wonders how many listings there will be under such subject headings as "Spitting in the Sink," "Bus Sickness," and "Pulling Out Chin Whiskers"—domestic trivialities that Hollywood chose to ignore until the passing of the Star Era, and which are all the more surprising in *The Marrying Kind* because they are presented so casually. When Judy looks at her husband and says, "First you brush your teeth, then you drink beer—yucch," the viewer can easily imagine himself in a fifties neighborhood theater feeling a seismic shiver of recognition run through every couple in the audience.

And not just couples of the lower-middle class, which were as neglected filmically in the postwar decade as they were politically throughout the sixties. If this were the case—if *The Marrying Kind* spotlighted a way of living, or of enduring, applicable only to one class—then Gary Carey's charge that the Kanins "haven't the remotest knowledge of what they are writing about" would be valid. It's true that the film's title indicates a generic overview susceptible to the tinge of condescension, and that its episodic story line, which covers a decade of courtship, marriage, and separation, leaves little space for the supporting players to expand their characterizations much past the point of shrill caricatures. But *The Marrying Kind* is basically, almost exclusively, the story of two persons whose lives are determined more by inertia than by any grand movie scheme— who don't *move* into situations so much as they *fall*: fall together, fall apart, fall in love and out of love and maybe back in again. The Kanins' scenario, and their treatment of it, may not be cosmic, but it's hardly parochial. If there's a distance between these Manhattan sophisticates and their very Bronxian subjects, it's nonetheless a distance tempered with respect and informed by affection.

Judy Holliday was not a small woman, but Aldo Ray (as her husband) towers over and around her—formidably in love, threateningly in opposition. His raspy voice manages to be both aggressive and defensive, no matter what he's saying, and his tone suggests that of the neighborhood tough kid backtalking to an accusing fifth-grade teacher. The two-character story and claustrophobic *mise-en-scène* constantly pit Ray and Holliday against, and next to, each other, and in the process transform emotional tension into physical abrasion. Indeed, *The Marrying Kind* is one of the few Hollywood films in which the trump cards of the traditional marriage partners—the man's brute strength, the woman's wily vulnerability—are played instead of being merely implied. Who better epitomizes the domestic brute than Aldo Ray? And who the shrilly vulnerable wife than Judy Holliday?

Aldo is neither sadistic nor desperate enough to actually beat Judy up; he sublimates his drives through career ambition and sexual intimidation. It's enough for the Kanins' purposes that Aldo is shown practically flattening Judy on her tiny twin bed, asking her (and the Hays Code) why they can't have a double bed; that, to rouse him from a nightmare, Judy naturally shakes his pects, not his shoulders; and that, in a moment of humiliation, Aldo crawls out of the living room and the film frame on all fours, muttering, "Don't be surprised I never talk again." Postwar comedy was a genre unusually preoccupied with the American male's fears and feelings of impotence. But while Hawks and Tashlin were making sexual inadequacy the theme of their films, the Kanins managed to say as much through the choice and gestures of their actors. The difference between the Tracy-Hepburn films and *The Marrying Kind* may simply be the difference between Spencer Tracy, who is sure of his masculinity and thus can cope, almost successfully, with the sudden shift into a passive, "female" role, and Aldo Ray, whose belligerence masks both a rigid interpretation of his maleness and a suspicion that any articulated endearments would betray his concept of the macho ideal. It's no wonder that, as Aldo is literally pulled out of bed and into a nightmarish dream sequence, he grabs his trousers for protective coloration.

Aldo's dialogue is as grating, defensive, and primitive as his character. "I'm in a perfectly condition!" "What am I? Some peculiar?" "A week or ten." Nouns and adjectives are dropped like so many final "g"s, with the sense—if any—of his remarks left to be decoded by the listener, just as the depth of his fondness for Judy is left to be decoded, or merely assumed, by her. The fact that she's no more perceptive than he is in discovering undercurrents of love beneath the sea-level turbulence of an unspectacular marriage leads to their ultimate appearance in Judge Madge Kennedy's divorce court— where the film begins and from which we learn, through flashbacks, of events leading to their bourgeois catastrophe.

These flashbacks are occasionally subjective (we hear of their first meeting through his dialogue, but see it through her camera-eyes) and cleverly establish *The Marrying Kind*'s wavering between third-person omniscient and first-person myopic, as well as between romantic comedy and domestic melodrama. One of the film's most ambitious and ambiguous moments comes at a picnic, with Judy happily singing and strumming "Dolores" as a holiday crowd rushes toward her bringing the sorrowful news of her son's death by drowning. The couple had earlier been arguing about the blessing-burden of children, and part of the "Dolores" scene's special impact derives from the feeling that, in the open air and for once not within shouting distance of their kids, the temptation to shout at each other can be replaced by an irrepressible desire to sing. It is the one lyrical impulse the film encourages, only to turn it into a wail of strangled suffocation.

In its bourgeois-epic plotting, its daring mixture of exaltation and despair, its weird insistence that the admonition "till death do us part" means that a child must die before a movie marriage can be dissolved, *The Marrying Kind* stands up as a *Penny Serenade* of the tenements. But the Kanins' film came a decade later, and concerned a couple several social notches lower than Cary Grant and Irene Dunne in the Ryskind-Stevens film. Ray and Holliday never occupied the mythic (well, archetypal) superstar positions held by Grant and Dunne; so their marriage needs a less violent, less preposterous Olympian nudge to steer it on the rocks. Because their fall is from a lesser height, the sounds they make (except verbally) haven't the tragicomic reverberations of *Penny Serenade*. The resolution of their story must in part be one of resignation, for they rarely seem right for each other, and *that's* usually when they're scraping fingernails across each other's sensibilities.

Mickey Shaughnessy, a friend of Aldo's with fractured diction *à la Pat and Mike,* expresses the Kanins' "message" this way: "For my kind of type, I married Emily, who is the right kind of type for my kind of type." That Aldo and Judy are "the marrying kind of type" —that they are, in a sense, programmed for just this and no more— is a sobering moral to make in a romantic comedy-drama designed for the Aldos and Judys of the local Loew's. It may also be curiously bracing. "You aren't Cary Grant and Irene Dunne," the Kanins seem to be telling their audience, "and you never will be. At your best and worst, you are Aldo Ray and Judy Holliday, with all their arguing and making up, exhilaration and boredom, complacency and compromise—and acceptance." One dialogue between the Judge and Aldo Ray sums up the attitude of the film, and its characters, toward the perverse, heroic custom of two people choosing to live together forever:

> JUDGE: Did you love Florence?
> ALDO: Sure!
> JUDGE: How'd you know?
> ALDO: 'Cause she told me I did. (*Pause.*) And she was right!

Adam's Rib (1949) and *Pat and Mike* (1952)

When people talk about "Tracy-Hepburn pictures," they usually mean the ones co-written by Garson Kanin—either *Woman of the Year* (for which Kanin provided the story; *q.v.*), or *Adam's Rib* and *Pat and Mike* (written by Kanin and Ruth Gordon). With the exception of the underrated *Desk Set*, also scripted by a married screenwriting team (Phoebe and Henry Ephron), none of the stars' other films together seemed tailor-made for them. And because they looked uncomfortable in their roles, they were at a loss to project the feeling of relaxed control that distinguished their finest collaborations. *Woman of the Year*, for all its misogynous loading of points against Hepburn's feminist career woman, did capture on film the sexual/intellectual combustion that accompanied the couple's first movie meeting. And the script managed to combine two plot strands that the Kanins would develop more naturally and fruitfully in their own Tracy-Hepburn films: the attraction of opposites (Kate the aristocrat and Spence the Average Joe, which reappeared in *Pat and Mike*) and the rivalry of colleagues (journalists in *Woman of the Year*, lawyers in *Adam's Rib*).

Adam's Rib and *Pat and Mike* are both very funny, satisfying films whose most endearing achievement is the sense of spontaneity they effortlessly convey. One rarely feels an obtrusive directorial touch, or a writer's nudge, or a performer's sweeping gestural point being made. Indeed, some of the Kanins' dialogue seems less underwritten than overheard. What is one to make, for example, of the following preprandial exchange between Adam (Tracy) and Amanda (Hepburn) in *Adam's Rib*?

> ADAM: Hello, thing.
> AMANDA: Hello, at last.
> ADAM: Well well well.
> AMANDA: Well well well what?
> ADAM: Here we are.
> AMANDA: How true!
> ADAM: Home at last.
> AMANDA: You took the words right out. (*Pause.*) Darling . . .
> ADAM: Mmmmmm—mh?
> AMANDA: Are you all right?
> ADAM: How do you mean?
> AMANDA: In health—and so forth.

ADAM: Sure.

AMANDA: Oh good.

ADAM: In health, splendid. In so forth—fair. (*Indicating the cocktail shaker.*) What's this some of?

AMANDA: Some of daiquiris.

ADAM: Good.

Well well well. In cold print this dialogue reads like an unholy marriage between *Dick and Jane* and *The Bald Soprano*. But sparked by the absolute assurance of Tracy and Hepburn, and fanned by George Cukor's benign passivity, the colloquy takes on a palpable, naturalistic warmth. The Kanins knew this, of course; they were writing dialogue that could be delivered without being telegraphed. Grammatically if not dramatically, Adam and Amanda appear to be their least eccentric creations. Inhabiting some rarefied penthouse of the stars, they seem hardly adaptable to that posture of impersonal truculence that the script defines as being quintessentially New Yorkish. But when they meet their respective clients, Doris and Warren Attinger (Judy Holliday and Tom Ewell), Adam and Amanda begin to discover how dangerously intoxicating life can be when spiked with professional and sexual jealousy. And as the pressures of opposing each other in a proto-Women's-Lib trial become more and more acute, their rhetoric inches closer and closer toward a style we may easily identify as Kaninesque.

Adam reverts to apoplectic stuttering; Amanda seems incapable of finishing a sentence. The featured players join in: the judge's indistinct diction suggests an auctioneer who's chewing tobacco while he's selling it; Doris Attinger's sentences are either monosyllabic ("He used to not do that a lot—come home") or nonstop and unpunctuated ("So then I bought two chocolate nut bars and then I went outside of his office and I waited the whole afternoon and I kept waiting and eating the candy bars till he came out so then I followed him so then I shot him"); her husband enlivens his testimony with phlegmatic ejaculations ("She used to wait until I fell asleep then—pow! pow! So then an argument. So then I would go to sleep again. So then—pow! pow!"); and gum-chewing Beryl Caighn, the "other woman" in the case, tries heroically and unsuccessfully to camouflage her limited training in elocution ("So I think I must have started to conk out or—excuse me, to faint or somethin' and Mr. Attinger grabbed me so's I wouldn't fall down, I guess—so then she, Mrs. Attinger, tried to kill me"). Kanin obviously enjoyed writing dialogue for Beryl and the Attingers: he would mine the riches of the Bronx patios in his other Judy Holliday films, and even lend it to Debbie Reynolds for the duration of *The Rat Race*.

The sports promoter played by Tracy in *Pat and Mike* is virtually a one-man lexicon of Kaninisms. Some samples of his erratic speech patterns: "Let me give you a few statistics or two." "Of course, there's always the chance you could be an escaped fruitcake." To Hepburn: "You're a beeyouteeful thing to watch—in action." About Hepburn: "Not much meat on 'er, but what's there is cherce." And in reference to his colleagues in the boxing underworld: "Now, I am in no position to give you their names by name, but I can tell you this—they are the kind of type who have been known to get very hot-headed in their day and age." Tracy is eccentric enough for two, so Hepburn has to make do with some taut dialogue (Bartender: "What do you want to drink?" Dejected Kate: "Plenty." Bartender: "Lemonade." Kate: "Strong. Plenty of lemon. What do I care?") and a chance to display her unmatched gift for understated bravura performing—especially in one long take during the "lemonade" scene where she tacitly and incontestably rebuts Dorothy Parker by running the acting gamut from A (anguish) to B (beatification).

But *Adam's Rib* and *Pat and Mike* are no more *only* about language than is *Pygmalion*. Both films take in their easy stride the question of woman's equality with man. During the thirties, Hollywood had cast a sympathetic eye on the career woman, but by the final reel she had almost inevitably found a man who could set her up in a lifetime job: housekeeping. In the forties, it seemed as if movie women were too busy being predators to bother with being providers. *Adam's Rib* neither ignored Hepburn's aggressive intelligence nor turned it against her. She is always sympathetic, if occasionally overbearing. If anyone in *Adam's Rib* is made to look foolish, it's Tracy, for believing that Hepburn could reject him for a smarmy, ineffectual David Wayne. A variation on this grotesquely lopsided triangle appears in *Pat and Mike*: we can accept Hepburn's engagement to the intolerably smug William Ching only if we realize how little Hepburn thinks of herself—until Tracy begins his program to develop both her physical stamina and her depleted self-esteem.

In both films, Tracy plumps for equality of the sexes—on his own terms. In *Adam's Rib*: "I'm old-fashioned! I like two sexes! Another thing. All of a sudden I don't like being married to what's known as

the *new* woman. I want a wife—not a competitor! *Competitor!*
Com-pe-ti-tor! If you want to be a big he-woman, go ahead and be
it—but not with me!!" And, less virulently, in *Pat and Mike*: "I like
a he to be a he and a she to be a she. Five-oh five-oh." Throughout
most of *Pat and Mike,* Hepburn is looking to change men, not roles;
Ching told her what to wear and how to act, Tracy tells her how to
eat, sleep, work, and live. She doesn't realize that something's wrong
in this handler-athlete relationship until shortly before Tracy does.
And there won't be any problems after the final fade-out, because
she will never be his com-pe-ti-tor.

Adam's Rib is both more ambitious and more resourceful in confronting the woman's-rights dilemma. After Amanda has won her
court case, freeing Mrs. Attinger from the charge of a *crime de
passion,* the film doesn't take the easy way out by having Amanda
humiliated and finally absolved by a generous Adam. (Imagine the
penance that Ring Lardner, Jr. and Michael Kanin, authors of
Woman of the Year, would have extracted from her!) Instead,
Adam and Amanda are driven further apart through a ploy with
ironic echoes of the Attinger-Caighn ménage—and, in perhaps the
funniest scene the Kanins ever wrote, Adam waves a gun threateningly at his wife, and then takes a bite out of the barrel! ("Licorice.
If I'm a sucker for anything, it's for licorice.") The Kanins top this
with a climax that neatly reverses the failed-female denouement of
Woman of the Year: Adam wins Amanda back by bursting into
tears, "like a woman," and the reconciled couple finally agrees that
the sexes can be equal without being identical. As Adam says, *"Vive
la différence!"*

It's easy to imagine the merry quintet of Tracy, Hepburn, Kanin,
Gordon, and Cukor sitting around Kate's living room weaving the
stories of *Adam's Rib* and *Pat and Mike* in the gentle California
twilight. The evidence of the past two decades indicates that their
accomplishment wasn't all that offhanded. Perhaps it was simply a
magic moment that passed. The Kanins never wrote films together
again. Tracy and Hepburn wandered off toward a final, anticlimactic
assignation with Stanley Kramer. Cukor couldn't find collaborators
as talented or congenial. And the kind of comedy they created—wry
and generous, pertinent and impertinent, modest and rather serene
—died away, to be succeeded by the complicitous caricatures of
Billy Wilder, Frank Tashlin, and George Axelrod, and by the
numbing banalities of sitcom TV.

III. *Themes In Search of a Style*

ROBERT RISKIN   DUDLEY NICHOLS   JOSEPH L. MANKIEWICZ
HERMAN J. MANKIEWICZ   DALTON TRUMBO

There was a breed of screenwriter notorious for sticking stilettos of
social comment between the ribs of Hollywood's most bourgeois
films. Predictably, the handles still stuck out. Robert Riskin, Dudley Nichols, Joseph L. Mankiewicz, and Dalton Trumbo could all
write entertainingly—and more convincingly—when they relaxed
and let the characters and situations lead *them,* instead of trying to
collar the moviegoer and lead him down the road toward some fashionable "ism." They were praised by their more timorous colleagues
for ennobling the medium with decade-old sentiments from Union
Square; but for them, the message was the medium. As their careers
wore on, this preoccupation with Significance became an obsession.
Meet John Doe, Sister Kenny, The Barefoot Contessa, and *Johnny
Got His Gun* are obvious, obtrusive—and almost endearingly personal. The closet socialists and populists had finally made the films
they'd always wanted to, suffered for their beliefs, and, just possibly, were themselves ennobled.

Herman J. Mankiewicz is something of an anomaly here, as,
frankly, he would be anywhere else in this book. If we shoehorn
him into this section, however, it's not only so he can be near his
younger brother. It's because Herman was also frustrated in his
attempt to express what he believed in, and because one can trace
through his work in the thirties tentative stabs at expressing it. But
for him, the message was more elusive. Vitality and decay, power

and impotence, high hopes and the deepest despair—these were the themes he was able to investigate fully only once. Since his chance of a lifetime came with Orson Welles and *Citizen Kane*, that once seems quite enough.

ROBERT RISKIN
(1897–1955)

1931   ILLICIT (Archie Mayo) from his and Edith Fitzgerald's play
       MANY A SLIP (Vin Moore) from his and Edith Fitzgerald's play
       MEN IN HER LIFE (William Beaudine) co-screenplay, dialogue
       THE MIRACLE WOMAN (Frank Capra) from his play, *Bless You Sister*
       PLATINUM BLONDE (Frank Capra) dialogue
1932   THREE WISE GIRLS (William Beaudine) dialogue
       BIG TIMER (Edward Buzzell) dialogue
       AMERICAN MADNESS (Frank Capra) story, screenplay, dialogue
       NIGHT CLUB LADY (Irving Cummings) screenplay, dialogue
       VIRTUE (Edward Buzzell) screenplay
       SHOPWORN (Nick Grinde) co-dialogue
1933   ANN CARVER'S PROFESSION (Edward Buzzell) adaptation, from his story, "Rules for Wives"
       LADY FOR A DAY (Frank Capra) adaptation
1934   IT HAPPENED ONE NIGHT (Frank Capra) screenplay
       BROADWAY BILL (Frank Capra) screenplay
1935   CARNIVAL (Walter Lang) screenplay
       THE WHOLE TOWN'S TALKING (John Ford) co-screnplay
1936   MR. DEEDS GOES TO TOWN (Frank Capra) screenplay
1937   WHEN YOU'RE IN LOVE (Robert Riskin) screenplay
       LOST HORIZON (Frank Capra) screenplay
1938   YOU CAN'T TAKE IT WITH YOU (Frank Capra) screenplay
1941   MEET JOHN DOE (Frank Capra) screenplay
1944   THE THIN MAN GOES HOME (Richard Thorpe) co-story, co-screenplay

1947   MAGIC TOWN (William A. Wellman) co-story, screenplay, producer
1950   MISTER 880 (Edmund Goulding) screenplay
       RIDING HIGH (Frank Capra) remake of *Broadway Bill*
1951   HALF ANGEL (Richard Sale) screenplay
       HERE COMES THE GROOM (Frank Capra) co-story
1956   YOU CAN'T RUN AWAY FROM IT (Dick Powell) remake of *It Happened One Night*
1961   POCKETFUL OF MIRACLES (Frank Capra) remake of *Lady for a Day*

The image of Robert Riskin that Bob Thomas has sketched (in *King Cohn*) is that of a casual, amiable man sitting on the porch of his Columbia back-lot bungalow, and writing his dialogue in long-hand on a yellow pad, as if he were composing a letter to his friends back East. The man's quiet conviction and self-respect emanate from this scene in a way that almost suggests Marshal Henry Fonda, chair back, feet up, in *My Darling Clementine*. The ease with which Riskin is purported to have written his early films indicates a sympathy with his characters bordering on identity, and gives us a convenient gauge by which to evaluate his films: the closer the male lead to Riskin's own personality, the more successful the film.

His forays into fantasy (*Lost Horizon*), mob psychology (*The Miracle Woman*), rube psychosis (*Mr. Deeds Goes to Town* and especially *Meet John Doe*), criminal gentility (*Mister 880*), split personality (*The Whole Town's Talking*), and Broadway adaptations (*You Can't Take It With You*) offer less interest—and less the sense of Riskin's involvement—than do those films whose protagonists are New Yorkers of his old milieu: high-pressure bankers (*American Madness*), newspapermen (*Platinum Blonde* and *It Happened One Night*), Broadway sharpies (*Lady for a Day*) and race-track touts (*Broadway Bill*). Riskin seemed most comfortable when placing his characters in a familiar genre (such as the newspaper comedy), and least at ease when he had to invent, or adapt, a new one, as in *Mr. Deeds Goes to Town* and *Lost Horizon*.

The prototype for Riskin's most famous films with Capra was the writer's first original movie script, the still-fresh *American Madness*. Walter Huston, the very model of a quick-thinking capitalist, is faced with a Capran crisis no smaller than the Great Depression itself. His only reaction is immediate action, and through sheer rhetorical magnetism he convinces his panicking depositors to keep their money in his bank—a gambit the equally persuasive, if less overbearing, George Bailey will pull off in Capra's astonishing tour de force, *It's a Wonderful Life*. As the Riskin-Capra formula grew more rigid, the films' heroes became less resourceful, until we are left with the masochistic Longfellow Deeds and the suicidal John Doe.

Andrew Sarris has written that "the obligatory scene in most Capra films is the confession of folly in the most public manner possible." This was a staple of Riskin plots before, during, and after his association with Capra; his first directorial effort, the routine *When You're in Love*, ends with Cary Grant shouting apologies and endearments across a crowded backstage to opera star Grace Moore! Like fellow playwright-journalist Ben Hecht, Riskin was far more convincing tracing a character's degeneration than he was when he began winding up the inevitable *deus ex machina*. By this point in his scripts, Hecht had usually handed the work over to a more tractable acolyte. But Riskin's denouements required some well-written hysteria, a lightning conversion of the guilty, and a call to Central Casting for a few dozen extras whom the script and direction would whip into a combination of jury, mob, and movie audience. If this type of climax could be counted on to reduce the moviegoing Mr. and Mrs. Deedses to tears, it was also likely to raise a condescending snort from Riskin's early hero, banker Walter Huston. "They're not diagnosing American Madness," he might say. "They're helping to spread it!"

It Happened One Night (1934)

It Happened One Night can be summarized by a headline that might have appeared on a story bylined by Peter Warne (Clark Gable), about his adventures with madcap heiress Ellen Andrews (Claudette Colbert): STAR REPORTER TRAILS AND NAILS HEIRESS—FOR LIFE. The "Road of Life" metaphor is one that bookish critics used to think Ingmar Bergman invented for the screen with *Wild Strawberries*. Yet even *It Happened One Night* came in the middle of a contemporary cycle of "road" and "bus" pictures, and the nostalgic critic could trace this particular genre through the Chaplin films and that final, eloquent, enigmatic walk toward the horizon.

It's ideal for comedy because it allows the filmmakers to develop short comedy sequences without the monotony of a single location. If used inventively, as by Riskin and Capra, it can reveal the characters' resourcefulness in adapting to unusual situations, as when Peter assembles the Walls of Jericho in a motel room, or scares off a nosy salesman with threats of kidnapping the guy's children, or when Ellen demonstrates that "the limb is mightier than the thumb" by hitching a ride with an exposed left leg. (With Colbert, in everything from profile to toe, the left is always favored.) Since the story is essentially the taming of an uppity woman, Peter must be given most of the resourcefulness. Ellen's one coup, her hitchhiking ploy, backfires because it attracts a "road thief" who drives off with their bags at a rest stop, and Peter has to catch the thief himself—by running after him!

The combination of Gable's almost coquettish puckishness and Riskin's weakness for the strong to bully the weak risks turning Peter Warne into a citified Longfellow Deeds. Audiences of 1934 must have had pitifully short memories to laugh at Peter's "kidnapping" threat less than two years after the murder of the Lindbergh baby. Even today the scene is saved from its undertone of brutality only by Roscoe Karns' performance as Shapeley—garrulous but insecure, a portrait of the traveling salesman as evil twin brother to Warne's tough-talking but gold-hearted reporter—and by two lines that are not in the script, one of which has the petrified Shapeley, ever the salesman, lapsing into his routine even as he describes his children to their would-be kidnapper ("a little golden-haired boy . . ."); the other has him backing away, convinced Peter is a mobster, pleading, "You ain't gonna shoot me in the back, are you?"

If Riskin's character development isn't as subtle as it might be—when he wants to make Ellen's father sympathetic, he just changes the man's character—the rapport that gradually develops between Gable and Colbert, the major-studio stars being punished with a loan-out to Columbia, *is* utterly convincing. At first, Gable's sense of condescending irony, which he expresses mainly by sucking in his cheeks, seems more appropriate to Jean Harlow, his regular co-star, than to the spoiled brat Colbert is supposed to be playing. Whether because that part of the role was beyond her ability or because she didn't *want* to appear convincing as a spoiled heiress—or maybe because Riskin couldn't identify with her at that point—Colbert at first seems as ill at ease in the role as she must have felt working for

Harry Cohn. Gradually, though, the stars and their characters get to know each other, and the film strikes sparks that radiate behavioral warmth as much as situational heat.

With the exception of *Mr. Smith Goes to Washington* (which Sidney Buchman wrote), *It Happened One Night* is by far the most acceptable of those Capra films in which a reporter-type exploits someone in order either to get a story or simply to get even, perhaps because this time it's a man doing the exploiting. The situations are certainly Riskin's most inventive. Those Walls of Jericho still have the power to delight, if as much from the love of ritual it exemplifies in the newlyweds as from its use as a capricious symbol for their long-deferred rite of consummation.

Mr. Deeds Goes to Town (1936)

American Madness portrayed an activist businessman trying to hold on to his money. *It Happened One Night* concerned a newspaperman who falls in love with the girl he's been exploiting for the sake of a story. In *Mr. Deeds Goes to Town*, Riskin and Capra managed to retain their formula while turning a switcheroo on their plot: a passive tuba player tries to give his money away while being exploited by a newspaperwoman who finally falls in love with him. And, in *Mr. Deeds*, they added for the first time what were to become the First and Second Laws of Capracorn: (1) the city cynics must be converted to a faith in individual (usually rural) simplicity and eccentricity, and (2) the mob is (almost) always right.

There's no question here of siding against Longfellow Deeds. His adversaries are either pathetically weak (twitching Jameson Thomas) or sadistically strong (sneering Douglass Dumbrille), but they're always incarnations of evil, and decked out in broad, silent-movie postures worthy of a Stroheim villain. Although newspaper editor George Bancroft and ace reporter Jean Arthur begin the film as journalistic vultures trailing a particular vulnerable pigeon, *Mr. Deeds* is no precursor of *Nothing Sacred*, with its trio of sleek opportunists exploiting each other and every sucker in Manhattan. For all of Miss Arthur's manipulation of Longfellow Deeds, she is soon enough revealed as the puppet of some invisible force—probably the Hearst ethic, but, for Capra's purposes, really Bigcityism—and once we learn that Miss Arthur is a small-town girl herself, we realize that redemption is imminent. As for Bancroft, he effects an aston-

ishingly easy reversal with few if any guilt feelings and ends up as
cheerleader to the courtroom rabble.

Mr. Deeds offers the first example of an evil so pure that its main
desire is simply to crush goodness—a plot device that will reach its
absurd (and, ironically, compelling) apogee in the person of Lionel
Barrymore, the physically and spiritually crippled millionaire of
It's a Wonderful Life. But Riskin and Capra devoted so much energy to creating corrupt characters that they seemed to assume the
audience would sympathize with Longfellow Deeds almost by de-
fault. Deeds is generous, direct, tenacious—in sum, a repository of
the small-town virtues the filmmakers sought to eulogize—but he
is also less simple than simple-minded.

The poetry he writes is greeting-card doggerel, and his "solution"
to most moral dilemmas is a sock in the jaw of his nearest antagonist. The film cleverly insinuates that Longfellow's verse is superior
to *New Yorker* prose because Longfellow himself is morally superior to the Algonquin Round Table group, whom Riskin and Capra
slander as fulsomely as the Rossites rib Deeds in the film. Still, for
all of the filmmakers' talent and Gary Cooper's iconographic apt-
ness as the hero, Longfellow Deeds is no Billy Budd lashing out at
Claggart-like city-slickers when taunted beyond reason. Even back
in Mandrake Falls, Deeds had a habit of beating up people who dis-
pleased him; it was Longfellow's little quirk. The verdict of the
judges in Longfellow's insanity hearing first excuses the quirk, and
then condones it by letting h'm clout wicked (and relatively de-
fenseless) old Dumorille on the jaw. Cheers! Catharsis! The Triumph of Goodness! (The Law of the Jungle.)

Mr. Deeds is most effective, ironically, when it indicates areas
Capra will follow more successfully with Sidney Buchman in *Mr.
Smith Goes to Washington,* and with Frances Goodrich and Albert
Hackett in *It's a Wonderful Life*. Some of Deeds' Hallmark philosophy ("People here are funny: they work so hard at living, they
forget to live. . . . They created a lot of grand palaces here, but they
didn't create any noblemen to put in them") suggests that he might
have qualified as a speechwriter for Jefferson Smith. The Cooper-
Arthur antiphonal duet of "Swanee River" and "Humoresque" is
less a steal from *It Happened One Night*'s community sing of "The
Man on the Flying Trapeze" than an antecedent of the duet of "Buf-
falo Gal" that will bring Jimmy Stewart and Donna Reed together
in *It's a Wonderful Life*.

More important, Stewart is an actor far more capable of conveying idealistic intensity than Cooper, whose woodenness makes him right as the bucolic bumbler but woefully inadequate as an impromptu crusader for the rights of the undeserving poor. Capra and Riskin created a formula so precarious that aura and acting were crucial to making political fantasy a human reality. Stewart's nervous breakdowns at the climaxes of *Mr. Smith* and *It's a Wonderful Life* serve as the only possible response to the corrupt opposition his lifelong idealism provokes. The scripts for these films make his response logical, but Stewart's performances make it *felt*. Longfellow Deeds' only response to less substantial resistance is a virtually catatonic withdrawal. The film's evasions and simplifications have prepared us for this withdrawal, and we accept it. Indeed, we share it.

Meet John Doe (1941)

This was Riskin's last screenplay for Capra (although Capra would remake *Lady for a Day* as *Pocketful of Miracles,* and *Broadway Bill* as *Riding High*). Both the film itself and the way it was created are riddled with cynicism masked as desperation, or desperation masked as cynicism—it's difficult to tell where the phony sentiment leaves off and the real sentimentality begins. Capra and Riskin began with a story (by Richard Connell and Robert Presnell) that had no end, about a suicidal tramp whom a Machiavellian politician and his Borgiaesque public-relations girl turn into the mouthpiece for a boss-controlled Common Cause. Since the tramp was played by Gary Cooper, a happy ending would have seemed predestined, with John Doe's bum checks being countersigned in the final reel by stalwart Longfellow Deeds; and since the manipulative newspaper-type was played by Barbara Stanwyck, completing her two-year tetralogy of conscienceless schemers (shoplifter in *Remember the Night,* con artist in *The Lady Eve,* and gunman's moll in *Ball of Fire*), Cooper seemed assured of converting the glitter of gelt in Jane Dough's eyes into the serene lovelight of Mrs. John Doe —*omnia vincit amor,* vanquishing man's capitalism and woman's careerism with one swift thrust of the plot.

Capra and Riskin managed to maneuver their leads into an admirable fix: the "John Doe" movement was crushed, John Doe himself had disappeared, Stanwyck was exposed as a dupe of the do-gooders, and Evil Incarnate (played by Edward Arnold) held the firm, fascistic reins. The problem was, they had no ending. Either Capra was desperate enough to begin filming with no conclusion to his story—contractual disputes had kept him off the Columbia lot for almost two years, and now he and Harry Cohn were most anxious to come out with another golden kernel of Capracorn—or he and Riskin were cynical enough to think that the Capra formula, which had produced the *Deeds* and *Smith* films, would generate an ending all by itself.

Director and writer had already denied themselves one option by having John Doe's declaration of corruptibility drowned out by a contingent of the politician's private Gestapo. (Even Preston Sturges was wily enough to allow his unheroic Conquering Hero, who had been backed into a corner by circumstance and cowardice, to escape through the trap door of a Public Confession). All that was left was for John Doe to do what he had threatened at the film's outset: commit suicide. This act, as genuine and unpublicized as his first threat to kill himself had been full of blather and bally-hoo, will, he hopes, establish him as the Little People's very own martyr instead of the Big Bosses' tool, and make him a spotless standard of idealism instead of a Hazel Flagg.

This was a plot twist that Bernardo Bertolucci would transform into a metaphor for political myth-making in *The Spider's Strata-gem*. Maybe Welles would have tried it in 1941; certainly *Citizen Kane* was audacious enough on its own terms. But Capra was a man for immediate resolutions, not ultimate solutions. Just as John Doe is about to jump, Miss Stanwyck rushes in to save him from his grand gesture and condemn the film and its makers to a charge of criminal expediency. With a remarkable soliloquy—remarkable because Miss Stanwyck tries every histrionic trick in the actor's book but can't quite rescue her peroration from its suicidal bathos—John Doe is convinced to carry on his work among the living. But Capra can't stop at that. He has to stage his redemption scene at midnight on Christmas Eve. Thus, a new hope shines its light on the world: not the Christianity of Jesus, but the demagogic populism of Frank Capra and Robert Riskin.

DUDLEY NICHOLS
(1895–1960)

1930   MEN WITHOUT WOMEN (John Ford) screenplay
        ON THE LEVEL (Irving Cummings) screenplay
        BORN RECKLESS (John Ford) screenplay
        ONE MAD KISS (Marcel Silver) screenplay
        A DEVIL WITH WOMEN (Irving Cummings) co-screenplay
1931   SEAS BENEATH (John Ford) screenplay
        NOT EXACTLY GENTLEMEN (Benjamin Stoloff) co-screen-
        play, co-dialogue
        HUSH MONEY (Sidney Lanfield) dialogue
        SKYLINE (Sam Taylor) co-screenplay, co-dialogue
1932   THIS SPORTING AGE (Andrew W. Bennison and A. F. Erick-
        son) screenplay
1933   PILGRIMAGE (John Ford) dialogue
        ROBBERS ROOST (Louis King) screenplay
        THE MAN WHO DARED (Hamilton MacFadden) co-screen-
        play
        HOT PEPPER (John Blystone) story
1934   YOU CAN'T BUY EVERYTHING (Charles F. Reisner) co-
        story [1]
        HOLD THAT GIRL (Hamilton MacFadden) co-story,[1] co-
        screenplay [1]
        THE LOST PATROL (John Ford) co-screenplay
        WILD GOLD (George Marshall) co-story [1]
        MARIE GALLANTE (Henry King) co-screenplay (uncredited)
        CALL IT LUCK (James Tinling) co-story, co-screenplay [1]
        JUDGE PRIEST (John Ford) co-screenplay [1]
1935   MYSTERY WOMAN (Eugene Forde) co-story
        LIFE BEGINS AT 40 (George Marshall) co-screenplay [1] (un-
        credited)
        THE INFORMER (John Ford) screenplay

THE ARIZONIAN (Charles Vidor) story, screenplay
THE CRUSADES (Cecil B. De Mille) co-screenplay
SHE (Irving Pichel and Lansing C. Holden) co-screenplay (uncredited)
STEAMBOAT ROUND THE BEND (John Ford) co-screenplay [1]
THE THREE MUSKETEERS (Rowland V. Lee) screenplay

1936 MARY OF SCOTLAND (John Ford) screenplay
THE PLOUGH AND THE STARS (John Ford) screenplay
1937 THE TOAST OF NEW YORK (Rowland V. Lee) co-screenplay
THE HURRICANE (John Ford and Stuart Heisler) screenplay
1938 BRINGING UP BABY (Howard Hawks) co-screenplay
CAREFREE (Mark Sandrich) co-story, co-adaptation
1939 STAGECOACH (John Ford) screenplay
THE 400 MILLION (Joris Ivens and John Ferno) commentary
1940 THE LONG VOYAGE HOME (John Ford) screenplay
1941 MAN HUNT (Fritz Lang) screenplay
SWAMP WATER (Jean Renoir) screenplay
1943 THIS LAND IS MINE (Jean Renoir) story, screenplay
AIR FORCE (Howard Hawks) screenplay
FOR WHOM THE BELL TOLLS (Sam Wood) screenplay
GOVERNMENT GIRL (Dudley Nichols) screenplay
1944 IT HAPPENED TOMORROW (René Clair) co-screenplay
THE SIGN OF THE CROSS (Cecil B. De Mille) Nichols wrote a nine-minute prologue for the re-release of this 1932 film
1945 AND THEN THERE WERE NONE (René Clair) screenplay
THE BELLS OF ST. MARY'S (Leo McCarey) screenplay
SCARLET STREET (Fritz Lang) screenplay
1946 SISTER KENNY (Dudley Nichols) co-screenplay
1947 THE FUGITIVE (John Ford) screenplay
MOURNING BECOMES ELECTRA (Dudley Nichols) screenplay
1949 PINKY (Elia Kazan) co-screenplay
1951 RAWHIDE (Henry Hathaway) screenplay
1952 RETURN OF THE TEXAN (Delmer Daves) screenplay
THE BIG SKY (Howard Hawks) screenplay
1954 PRINCE VALIANT (Henry Hathaway) screenplay
1956 RUN FOR THE SUN (Roy Boulting) co-screenplay
1957 THE TIN STAR (Anthony Mann) screenplay
1959 THE HANGMAN (Michael Curtiz) screenplay
1960 HELLER IN PINK TIGHTS (George Cukor) co-screenplay

[1] In collaboration with Lamar Trotti.

It would be preposterous to deny Dudley Nichols attention, or even merit. Any man whose scripts have been filmed by John Ford, Howard Hawks, Fritz Lang, Jean Renoir, George Cukor, Cecil B. De Mille, Anthony Mann, Leo McCarey, René Clair, Elia Kazan, Michael Curtiz, Henry Hathaway, Delmer Daves, and Henry King, among others, must be doing something right—especially when the results are such registered masterpieces as *The Informer, Bringing Up Baby, Stagecoach, Man Hunt, Swamp Water, Air Force, Scarlet Street,* and *Heller in Pink Tights.* On closer inspection, however, Nichols' world is a rigorously schematized place where Good and Evil are rarely allowed to interact within one person, and where Big Brother Dudley is forever whispering slogans of moral uplift into the ears of the mass audience he sought to liberalize but ended up insulting. With the exceptions of *Judge Priest* and *Steamboat Round the Bend,* for which Will Rogers is said to have composed his own dialogue, Nichols' scripts for Ford are solemn, simplistic morality plays. With regular transfusions of Nunnally Johnson's warmer, more engaging screenplays, Ford would survive Nichols until he found Frank Nugent, while Nichols would coast through the fifties writing moderately good westerns for moderately good directors—a case of tepid cinematic water finally finding its proper level.

Stagecoach (1939)

It is 1885, and the West is still very wild. The name Geronimo hangs over the white settlements like an ominous war cloud, its very mention provoking "a silence that is heavy with doom." Into this parlous atmosphere rides Lucy Mallory, the wife of a U.S. Army captain; "she looks tired, yet there is great strength of character in her clear face." Alighting from a stagecoach, Mrs. Mallory directs a question to Buck, the blustering coach driver.

> LUCY: Is there any place where I can have a cup of tea?
> *Tea is not quite in Buck's lexicon. He scratches his head and speaks politely.*
> BUCK: Well, ma'am, you can get a cup of coffee right there in the hotel.

As these quotations from the script of *Stagecoach* may show, ambiguity is not quite in Dudley Nichols' lexicon. If asked for some, he'd probably dip into his bag of noble clichés, scratch his typewriter keys, and give you some "strength of character," two lumps of "heavy menace," the inevitable cup of "transfiguration"—and expect it to make do. What seems so surprising now is that this folksy, mass-market recipe proved so successful for Nichols; and that a director like John Ford (or, for that matter, Jean Renoir) would do so little to doctor it up—not adulterate it so much as make it adult. Despite the generosity and reverence a viewer brings to *Stagecoach,* the first classic Ford western, the picture turns out to be rather retarded, self-important but turgid, an entirely predictable film *bien fait.*

We can be grateful to thirties movie critics for praising such Ford-Nichols collaborations as *The Informer, Mary of Scotland, Stagecoach,* and *The Long Voyage Home.* They kept Ford solvent and his reputation secure until he could make the superior westerns which later critics would ignore. But we should also realize that what appealed to the Ars Gratis Politicae bunch in the Nichols-Ford films is what seems so bogus today: the character types whose every movement and motive we can predict as soon as they step on-screen; the manipulation of emotions and conventions in the safest, most traditional ways; the absence of any genuine eccentricity, of anything dangerous, innovative, irresponsible, or disturbing. The movie is so damned *academic.* It's as if *Stagecoach* had been manufactured specifically to be exhibited to future film students as *the* classic western—which it would be, if a 16mm distributor could get the rights to it.

Most annoying is Nichols' need to subject every one of his amiable leading characters to catharsis, not because they are tragically flawed but because they are socially gauche. In any other western of the period—John Wayne's earlier Singin' Sandy pictures, for example—the quartet of leads (Ringo, Dallas, Doc Boone, and Hatfield) would be accepted for what they are (a righteous revenger, a whore with a heart of gold, a tipsy but good-natured general practitioner, and a Southern *gentilhomme maudit*). Nichols has to prod these reprobates up to their own personal Calvaries before they can be redeemed in the eyes of Nichols, his audience, and the "good" characters his audience is supposed to identify with.

Though we are introduced to Dallas just as the bluenoses of Tonto are throwing her out of town, there's not a moment's doubt that she has "great strength of character" of her own. As Nichols' script direction puts it, "It is obvious that she is suffering inner distress, but her mouth is set hard in an attempt not to reveal her feelings." The Ringo Kid (Wayne) has killed a man and escaped from prison when we first see him, but "his manner is friendly. . . . His eyes smile up at Curly . . . with charm . . . a good-humored shrug . . . charmingly unaware . . . quiet authority unusual in a man so young. . . ." To be sure, there are reasons for the fall in station of such noble folk. Three bad guys had killed Ringo's brother. He explains it to Dallas.

> RINGO: I used to be a good cowhand a few years back. But —things happened.
> DALLAS (*thinking of herself*): Yes—things happen. That's it.

Dallas herself can't be just a professional who enjoys her work, or even a good-bad girl. There has to be a reason for her being "that way"—and there is. "My people were killed by the Indians. I was just a kid. There was a massacre in the Superstition Mountains."

> RINGO: That's tough on a girl. It's a hard country.
> DALLAS: You have to live, no matter what happens.
> RINGO (*chucking a stone somberly*): Yeah, that's it.

Having swapped revelations with Ringo, Dallas is ready for the mandatory Dudley Nichols *peripateia*. And sure enough, "Dallas seems transfigured." Falling in love has saved her soul, but she must undergo a public cleansing ritual to redeem her in the eyes of her fellow passengers on the stagecoach—Nichols' surrogate audience. So she and Doc Boone deliver Lucy Mallory's baby. Nor does transformation elude Doc Boone, who "is a different man now, a good professional man, sober as a judge"—from the town drunk to Marcus Welby in four quick gulps of black coffee. But, even more remarkable, "the last trace of hardness has vanished from Dallas as she holds the infant in her arms, and there is a glow of wonder in her face. . . . Dallas' voice is as proud as if the child were her own, her smile tender and maternal. . . . Dallas, seen close with the baby in her arms, is beautiful with the lamplight glowing on her face. . . . Her experience of the last few hours has deeply affected her, taken all the defiance out of her face, and softened it into beauty." Dallas, who has been treated so far like the coach nigger, especially by Southerners Lucy and Hatfield, wins the passengers' respect at about the same time Nichols forfeits the tolerance of his readers and viewers.

The only character who might hold any hint of ambiguity for the moviegoer is Hatfield, the gambler with a past. But by now we should realize that, for Nichols, this *Stagecoach* ride is a journey through Purgatory that will absolve all but the bad guy—a "bank manager who robs his own bank," in Ford's words—and the Indians. (Nichols was liberal, but he wasn't prophetic.) Hatfield is the only one who starts out bad and ends up good, if dead. Even here our lovable *raisonneur,* Doc Boone, tips us off as to how we should feel about Hatfield. When we're supposed to distrust him, Doc makes cracks about removing a bullet from the back of a man shot by a "gentleman" like Hatfield; later, when Hatfield has certified his gallantry and is about to put honor above life, Doc muses about a crippled Confederate whom he had "learned to like . . . mighty well." Next slide, please.

It's easy enough to mock Dudley Nichols' stage directions, and to condemn his screenplays for reading poorly. But is not the image the thing wherein you'll catch the conscience—nay, the very soul— of a film? Where's John Ford in this discussion? The sad fact is that Ford adds precious little to the Nichols schema. Although Thomas Mitchell occasionally breathes enough life into his stereotype to turn it into a tintype, in general the actors' gestures are not much more than attractive illustrations of those awful internal descriptions of Nichols'. Ford's *mise-en-scène* seems primitive in comparison with *The Grapes of Wrath* of only a year later. Even in the climactic Apache charge, which Nichols describes in great detail, Ford sticks closely to the script—except for the clumsy shot of a brave who is gunned down, dies, and then gets up before the scene ends.

Ringo's final showdown with his brother's murderers is not shown; but this isn't Ford's choice, only a practical example of one of Nichols' favorite theories, that "the stage is the medium of action while the screen is the medium of reaction." We see only Dallas's face as she *hears* the shots being fired: this is action three times removed. Nichols had wrapped a conventional *Grand Hotel* story in the shiny Corrasable Bond used for Award-Winning Screenwriting. At this point in his career, Ford chose simply to tie a bow of workmanlike style around it. Today the bow and the wrapping have nearly decomposed, and we are left with a box of faded Hollywood confections.

This Land Is Mine (1943)

By 1943, as a result of films which had been either critical or popular successes, and sometimes both, Nichols was approaching an eminence as the O'Neill of Hollywood screenwriters. Even by today's auteur standards, Nichols had built an enviable record by collaborating with more Pantheon residents and pretenders than any other Writers Guild member: John Ford, Howard Hawks, Fritz Lang, and Jean Renoir had all made films from Nichols scripts, and today these films are considered among the filmmakers' chefs-d'œuvre. Anyone whose knowledge of Nichols derives from a look at his virtually nonpareil list of credits and his thoughtful theoretical pieces in the Gassner screenplay collections of the forties might feel justified in anticipating *This Land Is Mine*—for which Nichols and Renoir were given (according to the former) "complete freedom to make a film, without any other impediment than our own shortcomings"—as the climax of a talented and powerful writer's career and the continuation of a great director's greatest period. But a closer examination of Nichols' strengths and weaknesses would prepare us for the disappointments of *This Land Is Mine*.

Nichols had become serious and important, and he took his importance seriously; thus the decision to make a "meaningful" (read: message) film with Renoir, who was known in this country primarily for the antiwar humanism of *La Grande Illusion* and the leftist politics of *La Marseillaise*. Nichols was a former court reporter and playwright *manqué*; thus the film's climactic setting of a courtroom for the defense of civil and national liberties. Too often Nichols mistook political rhetoric for moral significance, and sentimentality for moral rigor; thus his tendency for the somewhat smug peroration of *This Land Is Mine,* and the recurring descriptions of characters as "spellbound" (three times in the climactic scene) and "transfigured" (twice, in reference to the heroine). Finally, Nichols was a far more powerful figure than Renoir in the Hollywood of 1943. The screenplay is Nichols undiluted and utterly self-indulgent, and the film itself, despite what must have been Renoir's obvious sympathy for the material (if not for Nichols' treatment), has the feel of a commissioned work. With Nichols it could not be otherwise.

I suspect that Nichols misread Renoir's aristocrats in *La Grande Illusion* as elitists, and that he believed his own thinly disguised condescension for "the mass" would be shared by the director. In chronicling the development of *This Land Is Mine,* Nichols writes: ". . . to accomplish our purpose we knew we had to deal in ideas . . . and that was not easy; for ideas need words for their expression and . . . Words are not entertaining to the mass, who need simpler images." This disdain for the mass, and his curious coupling of the mass with images—the stuff of directorial art—are echoed in Nichols' script, with yet another link in the metaphor: children. The boys in Albert Lory's classroom clearly symbolize the silent, sleeping majority in Europe and the United States, as Nichols saw it in 1943. Albert's mentor, the saintly Professor Sorel, tells him: "We can keep the truth alive if the children believe in us and follow our example. . . . Love of liberty isn't glamorous to children. Respect for the human being isn't exciting. . . . But every one of us they execute wins a battle for our cause, because he dies a hero—(*smiling*) and heroism is glamorous for the children. (*Then he chuckles, seeing Albert's face illuminated by his words.*)" As obvious as Nichols' dialogue often is, the giveaway here comes in the stage directions. One can imagine him saying to Renoir: "We'll take a real schmuck—Charles Laughton would be perfect—and we'll turn him into a hero. Heroism is glamorous for the mass." (*Then he chuckles . . .*) Transfiguration and death: the old Hollywood switcheroo.

All this was undoubtedly done with the best intentions, even if today it seems like remedial political education for the masses. But Nichols and Renoir were not looking for an easy propaganda victory over Nazi oppression. "A good film against Fascism," Nichols wrote, "ought to seem shocking even to the German and Italian peoples." Perhaps the ultimate test of such a film is its emotional and intellectual validity thirty years later. By this standard *This Land Is Mine* is a failure. Though it suggests that tyranny is really an internal virus, and thus eschews any "foreign" sets or manners, it still gives the German Occupiers those comical-treacherous accents that instantly identify them as the pernicious villains, and all others as potential heroes. In attempting to transmit what they believe is a sophisticated message, Nichols and Renoir scrape all behavioral complexity from their characters and plot. The hero is a male Cinderella; the plot is "the worm turns." As with Mary of Scotland, Gypo Nolan, and *Stagecoach*'s Dallas, Albert is a victim of Nichols' Cinema of Exaltation: a truth is revealed to some character the audience can identify with, and the character, along with the audience (Nichols hopes), sees the light.

This theme is hardly a Nichols exclusive; it can be found in Aesop's Fables and Gibran's *Prophet*. Other screenwriters were known to work in the mold occasionally. But Nichols used it most boldly, most artlessly. No wonder the mass rejected *This Land Is Mine*. Nichols' attempts to bring an adult idea to the cinema ended in his treating the audience like children—children who were flocking to hear the same ideas explored with far greater sophistication, insight, and maturity in Howard Koch's *Casablanca*.

The Bells of St. Mary's (1945)

In attempting to trade on the good will engendered by *Going My Way*—and in doing it with such box-office success—Nichols and Leo McCarey not only produced a film that chokes on its own calculated treacle, but almost managed to cast suspicions on its genuinely appealing predecessor. In *The Bells of St. Mary's,* Bing Crosby pulls off a land-grab scheme for the greater glory of God and Sister Ingrid Bergman—an achievement less than heart-warming for any infidel aware that the Roman Catholic Church was New York's largest landowner at the time. It couldn't have been intended, but in this struggle between Church and Capital, the capitalist can't help but be the sympathetic party.

On one side are aligned the forces of Sweetness (Sister Ing) and Lightness (Father Bing) with their hosts of fresh-faced children, conspiratorial dogs, ornery construction workers, and whispered warnings from Above in the form of threatening heart murmurs in the capitalist's shriveled breast. On the other side stands one lone, rather stoop-shouldered, not very rapacious businessman and his new office building, both of which the Side of Right wants to appropriate. Henry Travers plays him as a mixture of Scrooge and Saint George. As long as he refuses to feed the Church's edifice complex, *The Bells of St. Mary's* retains some of the traditional McCarey spark. Unfortunately, it tries to palm off the breaking of Travers' spirit (through soulwashing instead of brainwashing) as his redemption. When he sells out to the Powers That Be—heavenly, directorly, and actorly—the movie loses its fragile hold on our sympathies, and the skeptical viewer loses someone with whom to identify.

Travers is disposed of with a few reels left to go (although he is given a more characteristic exit line when his benificence is made public: ". . . and a gift to the Church is always deductible"). This gives Father Bing a chance to chastise Sister Berg for flunking one of her students—a girl who, we learn later, failed her tests deliberately so she could stay in Sister's class. Bergman resists all of Bing's baritone benevolence and defies his will; but Crosby has his revenge. Sister is struck ill with tuberculosis and removed from her post as school principal. This phony conflict, which sets up the inevitable reconciliation, is a prime example of Nichols' (and McCarey's) cynical shuffling of emotions for an effective fade-out.

Sister Kenny (1946)

When *Sister Kenny* was released, reviewers were divided into two camps as hostile to each other as those in the medical profession who had debated the validity of the Kenny Treatment of infantile paralysis for almost forty years. The reviewers who accepted the film's brief for Sister Kenny praised the movie. Other critics, who shared the reservations (if not the animosity) of the Australian, British, and American orthopedic establishment that opposed the Kenny Treatment, opposed Nichols' treatment of Sister Kenny. Since her program of "alienation, coordination, re-education" had been ignored by British and American medical associations as late as 1944, the lay viewer of the seventies is never quite sure whether Sister Kenny is a distinguished predecessor of Jonas Salk or an earlier incarnation of L. Ron Hubbard—and whether the film is an honest appraisal of the Ehrlich of paralysis or a bland whitewash of Sister Kenny's Magic Bullshit.

Taken on its own terms, however, the film ranks with the best of Nichols' self-righteous works. If his direction is itself paralytic, forcing just about every secondary character to freeze in place while Rosalind Russell mimes outraged nobility, the leaden style is quite appropriate in suggesting Sister Kenny's ability to be both personally domineering and medically persuasive. In its rigid concentration on Miss Russell and its virtual exclusion of a compelling opposition, it unconsciously hints at a mild conspiracy on the parts of Nichols and Miss Russell to suppress any audience sympathy for a less sensational method of treatment.

The opposition isn't ignored; it's simply distorted, on human as well as medical terms. Sister Kenny would hardly be as sympathetic a figure if she weren't portrayed as the underdog attempting to unmask the arrogance of power among surgeons, as well as a woman condemned by her profession's male chauvinism. But Nichols & Co. cinch their argument by pitting the cured children of the Kenny Treatment against the pathetically smiling, crutch-ridden kids of her opponents. The only sop thrown to disinterested speculation is one small rebuttal which Dr. Brack—as domineering as Sister Kenny, but on the wrong side of the controversy—makes to kindly Dr. Mac-Donald (Alexander Knox), one of the Sister's supporters. "I wouldn't use the Kenny treatment on my own children," Brack states, and MacDonald rebuts, "I would," "You have no children," says Brack; and neither do any of Sister Kenny's other advocates —suggesting that it is his fatherly love for his children, and not a medical interest in them compounded by ambition, that leads him to accept a depressingly cautious method of therapy over Sister Kenny's flamboyant cures.

Still, it's refreshing to have one of Nichols' paragons behave with an arrogance commensurate to her conviction, for Nichols is at his most annoying when his heroes compound their self-righteousness with phony down-home humility (as in the prologue he wrote to Cecil B. De Mille's reissue of *The Sign of the Cross*). Miss Russell may not have tried to portray arrogance—she was a devoted follower of Sister Kenny, and sponsored a thirty-six-thousand-dollar short explaining the Kenny Treatment, as well as singlehandedly interesting Nichols and RKO in the project—but that's how it looks today, especially when compared to Knox's amiable eccentricity. And the script by Nichols, Knox, and Mary (E.) McCarthy (who wrote the story for *Theodora Goes Wild*) provides Miss Russell and Philip Merivale, as Dr. Brack, with some exciting "trial" debates in the Nichols style—with Brack's operating theater serving as a combination courtroom of ideas and theater of ideals.

Sister Kenny stands as one of Nichols' last forays into apocalyptic polemicism. Perhaps in reaction to the McCarthy Era—which hushed the voices of those liberals it didn't banish—Nichols spent his final Hollywood decade writing amiable adventure movies. These assignments might have earned him a modest reputation as a talented artisan if his earlier work hadn't condemned him to play the role of soporific salesman for Causes too noble to be dramatized in flesh, blood, and style.

JOSEPH L. MANKIEWICZ

(1909–   )

1929   THE DUMMY (Robert Milton) titles
        CLOSE HARMONY (John Cromwell) titles
        THE STUDIO MURDER MYSTERY (Frank Tuttle) titles
        THE MAN I LOVE (William A. Wellman) titles
        THUNDERBOLT (Josef von Sternberg) titles
        THE MYSTERIOUS DR FU. MANCHU (Rowland V. Lee)
        titles
        THE SATURDAY NIGHT KID (A. Edward Sutherland) co-
        dialogue (uncredited)
        FAST COMPANY (A. Edward Sutherland) dialogue
1930   SLIGHTLY SCARLET (Louis Gasnier and Edwin H. Knopf)
        co-screenplay, co-dialogue
        PARAMOUNT ON PARADE (Dorothy Arzner, Otto Brower,
        Edmund Goulding, Victor Heerman, Edwin H. Knopf, Row-
        land V. Lee, Ernst Lubitsch, Lothar Mendes, Victor Schertz-
        inger, A. Edward Sutherland, Frank Tuttle) dialogue for Jack
        Oakie sequence, directed by Sutherland (uncredited)
        THE SOCIAL LION (A. Edward Sutherland) co-screenplay,
        dialogue
        SAP FROM SYRACUSE (A. Edward Sutherland) co-screen-
        play (uncredited)
        ONLY SAPS WORK (Cyril Gardner and Edwin H. Knopf) co-
        screenplay
        THE GANG BUSTER (A. Edward Sutherland) dialogue
1931   FINN AND HATTIE (Norman Taurog and Norman Z. Mc-
        Leod) dialogue
        JUNE MOON (A. Edward Sutherland) co-screenplay, co-dia-
        logue
        SKIPPY (Norman Taurog) co-screenplay

DUDE RANCH (Frank Tuttle) co-screenplay (uncredited)
FORBIDDEN ADVENTURE (Norman Taurog) co-screenplay
TOUCHDOWN (Norman Z. McLeod) co-screenplay (uncredited)
SOOKY (Norman Taurog) co-screenplay

1932 THIS RECKLESS AGE (Frank Tuttle) screenplay
SKY BRIDE (Stephen Roberts) co-screenplay
MILLION DOLLAR LEGS (Edward Cline) story, co-screenplay
IF I HAD A MILLION (Ernst Lubitsch, Norman Taurog, Stephen Roberts, Norman Z. McLeod, James Cruze, William A. Seiter, H. Bruce Humberstone) co-screenplay, for Jack Oakie sequence, directed by McLeod

1933 DIPLOMANIACS (William A. Seiter) story, co-screenplay
EMERGENCY CALL (Edward Cahn) co-screenplay
TOO MUCH HARMONY (A. Edward Sutherland) screenplay
ALICE IN WONDERLAND (Norman Z. McLeod) screenplay

1934 MANHATTAN MELODRAMA (W. S. Van Dyke) co-screenplay
OUR DAILY BREAD (King Vidor) dialogue
FORSAKING ALL OTHERS (W. S. Van Dyke) screenplay

1935 I LIVE MY LIFE (W. S. Van Dyke) screenplay

1944 THE KEYS OF THE KINGDOM (John M. Stahl) co-screenplay, producer

1946 DRAGONWYCK (Joseph L. Mankiewicz) screenplay

1947 SOMEWHERE IN THE NIGHT (Joseph L. Mankiewicz) co-screenplay

1949 A LETTER TO THREE WIVES (Joseph L. Mankiewicz) screenplay

1950 NO WAY OUT (Joseph L. Mankiewicz) co-screenplay
ALL ABOUT EVE (Joseph L. Mankiewicz) screenplay

1951 PEOPLE WILL TALK (Joseph L. Mankiewicz) screenplay

1953 JULIUS CAESAR (Joseph L. Mankiewicz) co-adaptation

1954 THE BAREFOOT CONTESSA (Joseph L. Mankiewicz) story, screenplay, producer

1955 GUYS AND DOLLS (Joseph L. Mankiewicz) screenplay

1958 THE QUIET AMERICAN (Joseph L. Mankiewicz) screenplay

1963 CLEOPATRA (Joseph L. Mankiewicz) co-screenplay

1967 THE HONEY POT (Joseph L. Mankiewicz) screenplay

Mankiewicz contributed to but did not sign the scripts of these films, which he also directed: *The Late George Apley* (1946), *The Ghost and Mrs. Muir* (1947), *Escape* (1947), *Five Fingers*

(1952), *Suddenly, Last Summer* (1959), *There Was a Crooked Man* (1970), *Sleuth* (1972).

Mankiewicz contributed to but did not sign the screenplays of the films he produced at MGM: *Three Godfathers* (1936, Richard Boleslawski), *Fury* (1936, Fritz Lang), *The Gorgeous Hussy* (1936, Clarence Brown), *Love on the Run* (1936, W. S. Van Dyke), *The Bride Wore Red* (1937, Dorothy Arzner), *Double Wedding* (1937, Richard Thorpe), *Mannequin* (1937, Frank Borzage), *Three Comrades* (1938, Frank Borzage), *The Shining Hour* (1938, Frank Borzage), *A Christmas Carol* (1938, Edward L. Marin), *The Adventures of Huckleberry Finn* (1939, Richard Thorpe), *Strange Cargo* (1940, Frank Borzage), *The Philadelphia Story* (1940, George Cukor), *The Wild Man of Borneo* (1941, Robert B. Sinclair), *The Feminine Touch* (1941, W. S. Van Dyke), *Woman of the Year* (1942, George Stevens) *Reunion* (1942, Jules Dassin).

One of the characters in *Hubba-Hubba* (an unproduced script "reviewed" in the Robert Benton-David Newman chapter) is an out-of-work, over-the-Beverly-Hills romantic actor, about whom his earthy inamorata says, "Everything you say sounds like two writers worked on it all night." She might as well have been speaking about any character who opens his mouth in a Joseph L. Mankiewicz film. Articulate artifice is Mankiewicz's style; the Yups and frowns of Hollywood naturalism are the enemies he has fought throughout a four-decade career that traced an arc from Jack Oakie comedies in the early thirties, to the apogee of two successive Oscar-winning years as the writer-director of *A Letter to Three Wives* and *All About Eve*, and ending with a graceful descent into the Leisure Valley populated by *metteurs-en-scène* for hire.

Oddly enough, Mankiewicz's reputation has been revived by his recent association with two projects he directed but did not write: the Benton-and-Newman *There Was a Crooked Man* and Anthony Shaffer's *Sleuth*. To be sure, Benton and Newman have testified to Mankiewicz's brilliance as story editor of their script, and *Sleuth* lists as one of its characters a certain "Marguerite" played by a certain "Eve Channing"—a cunning double-reference to the role-players in *All About Eve*. But these assignments can hardly be considered as crucial to Mankiewicz's career as any of the six consecutive films, from *A Letter to Three Wives* to *Five Fingers*, which he describes as "a continuing comment on the manners-and-mores of our contemporary society in general, and the male-female relationship in particular." The irony of Mankiewicz's restored eminence is that auteurist critics who found his visual style pedestrian when he directed his own scripts now praise his commissioned work, saving their reservations for the screenplays he "transcends."

But if Mankiewicz has (inexplicably) retired from the writer-director grind, he has not stopped writing and talking in the only voice his characters ever really knew: his own. The introduction to his recently-published screenplay of *All About Eve*, which began as a tidy, twenty-page conversation between Mankiewicz and Gary Carey, eventually grew into a one-hundred-and-five-page disquisition on art, aging, acting, and *All About Eve*. It's a fascinating document, alternately wise and wise-cracking, with enough *mots* to propel any after-dinner plagiarist through an entire season. But, as Mankiewicz "reworked and expanded upon" his remarks, he polished all the spontaneity out of it. The resulting "colloquy" is about as close to an actual conversation, or even monologue, as was the notorious Mankiewicz interview that was translated into French, and then retranslated into "incoherent gibberish" in *Cahiers du Cinéma in English*—or as is his dazzlingly dense, richly unreal dialogue, which indeed "sounds like two writers worked on it all night." At its epigrammatic best, this dialogue is worth staying up all night for. At its garrulous worst, it can talk his characters to death, and his audiences to sleep.

A Letter to Three Wives (1949)

Working from a treatment by Vera Caspery, Mankiewicz turned a neat little story into an Oscar-winning film that reveals some of his talent as a director and his limitations as a screenwriter. Deluged by the fast, facile dialogue, the viewer appreciatively grabs for the film's visual and behavioral niceties. In one, tough-guy Paul Douglas, momentarily distracted by Linda Darnell's forthrightness on the make, lights a cigarette with his car lighter, shakes it out like a match, and throws it out the window. In another, Jeanne Crain, high on one drink spiked with self-pity, talks about her years as a WAVE: "That uniform," she sputters, "it's the great leveleleler."

Too often, though, Mankiewicz's admirable intention to write "screen plays" that can practically direct themselves leads him to dip into a patchwork bag of theatrical tricks. Ann Sothern laughs falsely at unheard punchlines; radios warm up immediately; even Addie Ross the omnipotent éminence grise, performs a hoary function served by Edward in *Edward, My Son* and Stephen in *The Women*. Of course, these conventions aren't nearly so idiotic as the countless movie stereotypes Mankiewicz avoided; and, if we can ignore *them*, we can see today that *A Letter to Three Wives* wears its comic sophistication as easily and jauntily as it did a generation ago. Even the ending—in which Paul Douglas confesses that it was he who planned to run away with the divine Addie, only to reject her finally for his lower-class Linda—allows for a touch of adult irony. We may infer, without distorting the screen evidence too far, that Douglas lied about his assignation in order to help Miss Crain (whose husband has *not* returned from town) make it through a suicidally lonely night.

There is, however, a real flaw in Mankiewicz's treatment of Kirk Douglas's professor, who is intended to be the one unequivocally sympathetic character in the film. He spouts Shakespeare constantly, so that both academe and *hoi polloi* can identify his species without any strain; and he wins his Mid-Cult stripes by fearlessly attacking—guess what?—radio soap opera, toward which almost any member of the movie audience can feel superior. "None of that bilge has the remotest relation to writing," proclaims this Profile in Courage as he launches into a pat diatribe against the vacuity of radio advertising and programming. Mankiewicz's stick men are so easy to flick over, of course, that the manifesto has no bite, and the moral victory that follows gives little satisfaction.

Throughout, Mankiewicz-the-writer pays scant attention to the details that provide real feelings with a real place to inhabit. Because the details are missing, the feeling is too. Howevermuch we may *want* to sympathize with Miss Crain's humiliation by her nouveau-riche friends, it's difficult to become involved because each character is playing such a rigidly defined part. It is left to Mankiewicz-the-director to develop skillfully the final episode (with Linda Darnell and Paul Douglas) into a slim but valid story of two recalcitrant individuals, which is capped by gold-digger Darnell's triumphant lapse into shanty-town slang: "Why don't everybody dance?"

All About Eve (1950)

This is the most famous, the most typical, and—alas!—the wittiest of Mankiewicz's "film plays." The overriding impression one has emerging from a Mankiewicz film may be summarized by one of his titles: *People Will Talk*. But *All About Eve* (emphasis on the "all") pretty well epitomizes what we hear in this film (emphasis on the "hear"). Not only do we learn enough about Eve Harrington to compose a cynical biography on the spot, but we are also told practically everything about the five people—fading star, directorial comet, bilious critic, important playwright, sympathetic wife of important playwright—into whose lives Eve brings a little sunstroke. If Mankiewicz's ambitions for the perfect film play were put in musical terms, it would approach a series of rhetorical cadenzas culminating in a dramatic cantata. Unfortunately, Mankiewicz indulged his rhetoric at the expense of his drama, and allowed the admirable formal shape of his flashback films (*Letter, Eve, Contessa*) to grow flabby and loose-skinned by force feeding an endless diet of bons mots. Even his nasty-but-nice epigrams tended to balloon into polemical essays on the banality of radio drama or the corruption of income-tax laws, so that he ultimately sounded less like the short-tempered wit and more like the long-winded lady.

Granting this, *All About Eve* still succeeds to an extent unmatched by other Mankiewicz films because its players—all servants and masters of the spoken word—can slip into garrulous bombast and set pieces of self-pity without slipping out of character. Theater people, Mankiewicz implies, are talkers, not listeners. Where a Hollywood star will make do with a sarcastic grunt or a petulant whine, the Broadway actress takes her cue for a page-long soliloquy; and while the movie star establishes his importance by saying as little as necessary to as few people as possible, the Broadway star massages her ego by co-opting stage center and reducing her colleagues to spear carriers.

Mankiewicz's style is much more appropriate to stage than to screen. The best film dialogue is tough and terse, suggesting the give-and-take of a good prize fight; its closest dramatic correlative is the stichomythia of Greek tragedy, with speakers alternating short, punchy lines. Theatrical dialogue—at least of the type favored by Mankiewicz—approaches the more distended point-counterpoint of a debate, with each speaker allowing the other to present and develop an argument. Mankiewicz showed a certain heroic intransigence in pursuing canned theater, but the sad fact is that his reluctance to edit his own scripts resulted in films whose monologues are less often elegant than elongated. He had the temperament to establish a distinguished alternative to staccato film dialogue, but not the talent. Too often, his characters were reduced to puppet messengers bearing the Author's Message.

Ironically, this tendency is made more obvious in *All About Eve* by the presence of a character who, in conception, diction, and acting, achieves the serenity of style that Mankiewicz strove so diligently to infuse into all his creations. This is George Sanders' Addison De Witt, the Nathanesque critic. Sanders' opening monologue—in which he sets the stage and introduces the players—carries an assurance of tone, a keen awareness and benign indulgence of the theme's essential triviality, and a rich, pithy rhetoric that kindles hopes for the kind of sophistication Mankiewicz is incapable of sustaining. "To those of you who do not read, attend the theatre, listen to unsponsored radio programs, or know anything of the world in which you live, it is perhaps necessary to introduce myself. My name is Addison De Witt. My native habitat is the theatre. In it I toil not; neither do I spin. I am a critic and commentator. I am essential to the theatre."

Would that this witty adder—even his name suggests the humors of Restoration comedy—had dominated the film, and all of Mankiewicz's films! As it is, he merely overwhelms it, and *Eve* never quite recovers from his lapidary introduction. Mankiewicz's best monologues were predominantly personal, and the Sanders character is as close an approximation of the director's persona as one can find. When Mankiewicz filtered one of his pet diatribes through a more "normal" character (Kirk Douglas in *A Letter to Three Wives* or Marius Goring in *The Barefoot Contessa*), we were aware that this was our pilot speaking, and this emphasized the mechanical nature of the loud-speaker system.

For better or worse, the film is not all about Addison. Perhaps such a film isn't feasible, since the *raisonneur* is rarely the protagonist. Addison occasionally pulls the plot strings—or rather *plays* them, a Menuhin of manipulation—but for discouragingly large chunks of the film he seems content to sit on the fifth row aisle and take notes. What *would* he have written about *All About Eve*? That the title role was miscast? In the first act, Eve is depicted as a selfless handmaiden of the theater, devoted past the point of idolatry to her patroness, the great Margo Channing. In the second act, Eve is revealed as a ruthless harridan, devouring the very people she had buttered up earlier. A star is born, but the mother, father, and godparents nearly die producing it.

The received wisdom about Anne Baxter's portrayal is that a more vital, actressy actress was needed to suggest Eve's amoral ambition, if not her acting abililty. I don't agree. Eve's greatest performance extended over some months, and consisted in convincing a troupe of old pros that the dew in her eyes was as genuine as the stars that more obviously shone in them. Eve's turnabout from ingénue to infighter may have seemed abrupt, but this can be traced to the complex scheme of Mankiewicz's original script, in which each of the other major characters told part of the story with *Kane*-like obliquity. Only gradually did they learn the extent of Eve's determination to light up Broadway, and it is fitting that we share their lingering gullibility. We never see Eve on the stage, but we don't have to. She has shown us she can act by making her colleagues believe she was not acting.

The flashback (which was begun and concluded not by the traditional gauzy dissolve, but by freezing the frame, a technique rarely used in Hollywood films of the forties) ends with Eve receiving the Sarah Siddons Award for excellence in the theater. Eve's speech of thanks is dishonest enough to keep her from attending a party in her honor. When she returns to her apartment, she finds a young girl waiting to do unto her what she, with a few exquisite pirouettes of the dagger, had done unto Margo Channing—but with more open aggressiveness. Mankiewicz then proceeds to turn a rather trite punchline into a tedious, totally redundant coda, which not only blunts his modestly ironic point but also reaffirms the filmmaker's failings. In screenwriting, the excessive destroys the incisive; the profuse negates the profound; the filibuster ruins the film.

The Barefoot Contessa (1954)

Mankiewicz's opposite number in the fifties is Samuel Fuller. Both were devoted to long talks and long takes, with Fuller's stationary camera seemingly trying to contain the hysteria always ready to erupt, and Mankiewicz's boom-mike following each character around like a devoted listener at a crucial but curiously uncharged debate. There the similarities end. Fuller played the Divine Primitive (though closer to Tarzan than to either of the Rousseaus), typing out his characters' dialogue with two raw fists, while Mankiewicz renounced the Hollywood laughter of a Wilder for the European languor of a Wilde. Neither role was completely convincing. Fuller's "delirious" pictures are not his most prepossessing, only his most preposterous; he is usually more effective in small, sensible films such as *Pickup on South Street* and *Forty Guns*, films that fit with surprising snugness into their respective genres of urban crime and the western.

As for Mankiewicz: the grace of his films' monologues won him a deserved reputation as a dinner-party wit (though somewhat eclipsed by the shadow of his brother Herman's tragicomic figure), but Joseph L.'s characters rarely evidenced the keener wit to know when to *stop* talking—the after-dinner quips would drone on into a Senate harangue. It may have been because JLM so desperately needed a severe, sympathetic editor for his own scripts that he worked so well as an editor of others' scripts: the MGM writers while he was a producer there in the late thirties and early forties, Philip Dunne when Mankiewicz did his directorial prenticework, Michael Wilson on *Five Fingers*, William Shakespeare on *Julius Caesar*, and Tennessee Williams on *Suddenly, Last Summer*. Fuller could have used a story editor, too; but he at least knew enough to punctuate his endless sentences with explosions of (often absurd) violence. At the end of a Mankiewicz sentence usually came a period, a pause, a deep breath—and then more, much more, of the same.

Even the itineraries of the two writer-directors can be mined for vagrant ironies. Both Mankiewicz and Fuller, along with many of their Guild colleagues, left Hollywood in the fifties to make movies on location. Mankiewicz's own productions took him (metaphorically or otherwise) on a cultured American's trek to Europe and points East: New York and New Haven for *All About Eve*, Germany for the source material of *People Will Talk*, Turkey for *Five Fingers*, Rome for *Julius Caesar*, Spain and the Riviera for *The Barefoot Contessa*, and finally Vietnam for *The Quiet American* —a bizarre vacation spot where Fuller, coincidentally, landed at about the same time on the end of a more direct route (his Pacific submarine cruising west toward Korea in *Hell and High Water*, with a stopover in Tokyo for *House of Bamboo*).

Appropriately, Mankiewicz approached the Vietnam "problem" from the decadent viewpoint of the corrupt French who were abandoning Saigon to concentrate on Algiers, whereas the Fuller "hero" was one of those lucky Americans whose love of killing, combined with a hatred of the Commies, cast them to perfection in the role of MCs for the *Götterdammerung* of U.S. optimism. Fifteen unpleasant years later, Mankiewicz's film is—for all its presumed ambiguities—permeated by an aura of innocent nostalgia; Fuller's wails with the siren of prophecy.

"Turn off the sound track," suggests Andrew Sarris, "and *The Barefoot Contessa* is closer to Lewin's *Pandora and the Flying Dutchman* than to Ophuls' *Lola Montès*." What a test! Turn off the sound track, and *Hamlet* is closer to *The House of Frankenstein* than to *King Lear*. Turn off the picture, and Ava Gardner sounds exactly like Annette Funicello. This is auteurism at its most audacious—judging a work of art by its least important component. As a matter of fact, *The Barefoot Contessa* does look remarkably like Albert Lewin's modernization of the Flying Dutchman legend; and not surprisingly, since both were photographed, on the beaches of Europe, in luxurious color, by the estimable Jack Cardiff. Lewin is distinctly out of favor at the moment, so it would seem like perverse vengefulness to make a tentative case for his rather admirable narrative over that elegantly embellished death's-head of Ohpulsian romanticism, *Lola Montès*. Suffice it to say that given the conventions of that pretentious genre, the Mythopoetic Allegory, *The Flying Dutchman* can be seriously preferred to *The Barefoot Contessa,* and that Ava Gardner as Pandora is bathed in a voluptuous mystique that completely evades Gardner as La Contessa Vargas.

Once Mankiewicz, the two-time Oscar winner, had escaped to Europe, he no longer felt the garlicky breath of a Mayer, a Lubitsch, or a Zanuck on his neck. He could now make the "film plays" he had always wanted to do. The change of environment proved disastrous. Just as the New York playwrights, novelists, and critics often went soft in the Hollywod sun, so did the Hollywood screenwriters when they made their move to Europe in the fifties. The films these talented writers directed—yes, Lewin's precious *arcana,* but also Samuel Taylor's *Monte Carlo Story*, Norman Krasna's *The Ambassador's Daughter*, the Mankiewicz *Contessa* and, most lamentably, Preston Sturges's *Les Carnets du Major Thompson*—all have the air of a too-casual business afterthought to a too-long European holiday. When the tension of the Hollywood hothouse evaporated, so did the dramatic tension these writers were capable of injecting into their films.

Ironically, some of the decline of American movies in the past twenty years can be traced to the rise of independent production, which forced powerful directors to spend too much valuable time on production details formerly left to the likes of Henry Blanke and Arthur Hornblow, Jr. Creative energies were wasted in contract haggling and location scouting. The further a director traveled from Hollywood, the longer it seemed to take him to return with a final print. In the thirties, George Stevens (a fairly typical example) averaged two films a year; in the forties, one film a year; in the fifties, one film every two years; in the sixties, one film every five years. In the years 1946 to 1950, Mankiewicz averaged two films a year; from 1951 to 1955, he made one a year; since then, he has made only six films, none of which have been Mankiewicz originals.

Sometime in the fifties—I believe it was around the time of *The Barefoot Contessa*—Mankiewicz lost the momentum, and he never regained it. With this "testament" film came the realization that audiences would sit through a Kirk Douglas diatribe in order to see a Linda Darnell cat fight; they'd tolerate a Hugh Marlowe monologue because a bit of Bette Davis bitchery awaited them; but they wouldn't go to a movie that offered little but a series of monologues —film essays, rather than a film play—even if Bogart, Edmond O'Brien, and Marius Goring were delivering them.

Mankiewicz's attempts, especially in the lead-footed *Contessa,* to bring Shavian dialogue to Hollywood films was a failure; but better, perhaps, the failure of Sisyphus than the victory of Pyrrhus. One is reminded of the ending of *Man and Superman,* in which Jack Tanner rails endlessly, charmingly, against the crushing banalities of conventional marriage. When he is interrupted, his loving, victorious fiancée purrs, "Never mind her, dear. Go on talking." Tanner explodes: "Talking!" We join the "universal laughter" of Shaw's stage description because Shaw and his characters were such superb talkers. They never stopped, and we never wanted them to. Unlike Mankiewicz, Shaw not only respected his characters' theses, but he respected their antitheses, and enjoyed making them attractive. Shaw created a dramatic form that only he could fulfill, let alone transcend. Mankiewicz bravely chose that form, only to become its slave—or rather, its faithful private secretary.

Herman J. Mankiewicz
(1897–1953)

1926   STRANDED IN PARIS (Herbert Rosson) screenplay
1927   FASHIONS FOR WOMEN (Dorothy Arzner) co-adaptation
      A GENTLEMAN OF PARIS (Harry d'Abbadie d'Arrast) titles
      FIGURES DON'T LIE (A. Edward Sutherland) titles
      THE SPOTLIGHT (Frank Tuttle) titles
      THE CITY GONE WILD (James Cruze) titles
      THE GAY DEFENDER (Gregory La Cava) co-titles
      HONEYMOON HATE (Luther Reed) co-titles
1928   TWO FLAMING YOUTHS (John Waters) titles
      GENTLEMEN PREFER BLONDES (Mal St. Clair) co-titles
      THE LAST COMMAND (Josef von Sternberg) titles
      LOVE AND LEARN (Frank Tuttle) titles
      A NIGHT OF MYSTERY (Lothar Mendes) titles
      ABIE'S IRISH ROSE (Victor Fleming) co-screenplay
      SOMETHING ALWAYS HAPPENS (Frank Tuttle) titles
      HIS TIGER LADY (Hobart Henley) titles
      THE DRAG NET (Josef von Sternberg) titles
      THE MAGNIFICENT FLIRT (Harry d'Abbadie d'Arrast) titles
      THE BIG KILLING (F. Richard Jones) titles
      THE WATER HOLE (F. Richard Jones) titles
      THE MATING CALL (James Cruze) titles
      AVALANCHE (Otto Brower) co-screenplay, titles
      THE BARKER (George Fitzmaurice) titles
      THREE WEEK ENDS (Clarence Badger) co-titles
      WHAT A NIGHT! (A. Edward Sutherland) titles
1929   MARQUIS PREFERRED (Frank Tuttle) titles
      THE DUMMY (Robert Milton) screenplay, dialogue
      THE CANARY MURDER CASE (Mal St. Clair) titles
      THE MAN I LOVE (William A. Wellman) story, dialogue

THUNDERBOLT (Josef von Sternberg) dialogue
MEN ARE LIKE THAT (Frank Tuttle) co-screenplay, dialogue
THE LOVE DOCTOR (Melville Brown) titles
THE MIGHTY (John Cromwell) titles

1930 THE VAGABOND KING (Ludwig Berger) screenplay, dialogue
HONEY (Wesley Ruggles) screenplay, dialogue
LADIES LOVE BRUTES (Rowland V. Lee) co-screenplay, co-dialogue
TRUE TO THE NAVY (Frank Tuttle) dialogue
LOVE AMONG THE MILLIONAIRES (Frank Tuttle) dialogue
THE ROYAL FAMILY OF BROADWAY (George Cukor and Cyril Gardner) co-screenplay

1931 LADIES' MAN (Lothar Mendes) screenplay, dialogue
MAN OF THE WORLD (Richard Wallace) story, screenplay

1932 DANCERS IN THE DARK (David Burton) co-screenplay
GIRL CRAZY (William A. Seiter) co-screenplay, co-dialogue
THE LOST SQUADRON (George Archainbaud) co-dialogue

1933 MEET THE BARON (Walter Lang) co-story
DINNER AT EIGHT (George Cukor) co-screenplay
ANOTHER LANGUAGE (Edward H. Griffith) co-screenplay

1934 THE SHOW-OFF (Charles F. Reisner) screenplay
STAMBOUL QUEST (Sam Wood) screenplay

1935 AFTER OFICE HOURS (Robert Z. Leonard) screenplay
ESCAPADE (Robert Z. Leonard) screenplay
IT'S IN THE AIR (Charles F. Reisner) co-screenplay (uncredited)

1937 THE EMPEROR'S CANDLESTICKS (George Fitzmaurice) co-screenplay (uncredited)
MY DEAR MISS ALDRICH (George B. Seitz) story
JOHN MEADE'S WOMAN (Richard Wallace) co-screenplay

1939 IT'S A WONDERFUL WORLD (W. S. Van Dyke) co-story

1941 CITIZEN KANE (Orson Welles) story, screenplay
RISE AND SHINE (Allan Dwan) screenplay
THE WILD MAN OF BORNEO (Robert B. Sinclair) from his and Marc Connelly's play
KEEPING COMPANY (S. Sylvan Simon) story
THIS TIME FOR KEEPS (Charles F. Reisner) based on the characters he created for *Keeping Company*

1942 THE PRIDE OF THE YANKEES (Sam Wood) co-screenplay

1943 STAND BY FOR ACTION (Robert Z. Leonard) co-screenplay
THE GOOD FELLOWS (Jo Graham) from his and George S. Kaufman's play

1944   CHRISTMAS HOLIDAY (Robert Siodmak) screenplay
1945   THE ENCHANTED COTTAGE (John Cromwell) co-screen-
       play
       THE SPANISH MAIN (Frank Borzage) co-screenplay
1949   A WOMAN'S SECRET (Nicholas Ray) screenplay
1952   THE PRIDE OF ST. LOUIS (Harmon Jones) screenplay

> Mankiewicz also co-scripted (without credit) and produced the
> following films: *Laughter* (1930, Harry d'Abbadie d'Arrast),
> *Monkey Business* (1931, Norman Z. McLeod), *Horse Feathers*
> (1932, Norman Z. McLeod), *Million Dollar Legs* (1932, Eddie
> Cline).

One look at Herman J. Mankiewicz's filmography and you think:
Orson Welles *must* have written *Citizen Kane*! How else explain that
film's audacious concept and rich, racy dialogue emanating from
the author of *Avalanche, Stamboul Quest, The Emperor's Candlesticks,* and *The Pride of St. Louis*? Many of Mankiewicz's early
films are lost in the mist of Pauline Kael's girlhood memories; but
the ones available for viewing, even the famous ones, suggest the
work of an occasionally happy hack whose career reveals, at best, a
dull consistency. A surprisingly large number of Mankiewicz's films
fit into the noble-melodrama mold that Miss Kael usually, and properly, reviles—from the 1929 *The Man I Love,* about a boxer who's
losing the big fight until his girl friend cheers him on from ringside,
to the fey, calculatedly uplifting 1945 film, *The Enchanted Cottage.*
   Nor was his *œuvre* much respected by the New York newspaper
critics, some of whom must have remembered him from his days at
the *Times* drama desk. They found Mankiewicz's dialogue for two
William Powell films "stilted and trite" (*Ladies' Man*) and insuf-
ficiently "vigorous and unhackneyed" (*Man of the World*). They
considered *Girl Crazy* weak, even for a Wheeler and Woolsey picture, and *Meet the Baron* a case of some good comics let down by a
poor script. The dialogue in *My Dear Miss Aldrich* was "close to
burlesque at times," and *John Meade's Woman* was "a thoroughly
absurd piece of theatrical claptrap." In 1942, a year after *Kane,*
John Mortimer reviewed *The Pride of the Yankees* and delivered the
final, lowest blow to Mankiewicz's undoubtedly tattered pride.
"Why," Mortimer asked, "are a couple of out-dated script writers
[Mankiewicz and Jo Swerling] assigned to the task of distorting a

natural scenario with honky-tonk vaude clichés, the sort that make old silents, seen today, look so banal."

Front-line critics of the thirties and forties were not especially noted for the ability to expand their perspectives to embrace a broader, more experimental vision, but there's little in Mankiewicz's career to suggest that his films lacked acceptance because they were too avant-garde. Indeed, the only excuse for looking at (or writing about) most of his non-*Kane* scripts is to identify thematic and stylistic footprints leading up to and away from the great work. There are a few. Several of his thirties films were set in a journalistic milieu; and one of these, *My Dear Miss Aldrich*, which concerns a Nebraska schoolteacher who inherits the ownership of a New York daily and tries to convince the editor that she deserves a reporter's byline, not only prefigures Charles Foster Kane's acquisition of the New York *Inquirer* but even sounds as if the lead would have been a good role for Marion Davies. And *John Meade's Woman* might just possibly be seen as the palest of blueprints for *Citizen Kane*, with lumber baron Edward Arnold in the Kane part, Gail Patrick as Emily Norton, and Frances Larrimore as Susan. Both *Christmas Holiday* and *A Woman's Secret* flash clumsily back and forward—but so, by the mid-forties, did practically every other murder mystery. Nothing in these films suggested what Mankiewicz could really do, given the time, the inclination, the subject . . . and Orson Welles.

Citizen Kane (1941)

For the restless shade of Herman J. Mankiewicz, 1971 marked the happy year when he was no longer only Joseph L.'s brother, and not yet only Frank's father. The occasion for this discovery of Herman in his own right was the publication of Pauline Kael's "Raising Kane," in which the *New Yorker* critic bestowed equal credit on Mankiewicz and Orson Welles as the prime creators of *Citizen Kane*. Mankiewicz's contribution had been almost completely ignored, by Bosley Crowther and his contemporaries in 1941, by Andrew Sarris and his more royalist acolytes three decades later, and by everyone in between—including Orson Welles. (For example, there are fewer than half a dozen references to Mankiewicz in the book-length *Focus on Citizen Kane*, and most of those are parenthetical.) So at the very least, Miss Kael's broadside had the cleansing effect of a strong disinfectant.

But if some saw her intention as restoring Mankiewicz, others saw it as desecrating the lovingly kept Welles monument—as a seventies version of the "Little Orson Annie" jibes made by small-minded cynics when the director first came to Hollywood. I think Miss Kael was fair to both Welles and Mankiewicz (though, ultimately, perhaps not to the film itself); besides, she had established her credentials as a Welles admirer back in 1967, with an eloquently sympathetic summary of his career up through *Falstaff*. What seemed to upset the Wellesians most were her remarks on his credit-mongering, which may have included a contractual agreement that Mankiewicz's name would not appear on *Kane*. The director's defenders have made much of his sharing of *Kane*'s final credit card with cinematographer Gregg Toland. But cinematography was the one craft Welles was known not to have mastered; a mantle of theatrical superman—actor, producer, director, writer—could still hang on his shoulders with impunity. Giving Mankiewicz credit was something else.

Imagine that, as the credits flashed by at the end of *Kane,* a high-pitched, gin-soaked, unprofessional voice is suddenly heard: "I conceived and wrote this film. My name is Herman J. Mankiewicz." What must we imagine then? Embarrassed glances across the Algonquin Round Table? Snickers at Chasen's? Of course, it's ridiculous to think of the bracingly (and consciously) unheroic Mankiewicz committing an act of pomposity on the Wellesian scale. Indeed, few Hollywood collaborators have had personalities so odd, and so at odds, as Mankiewicz and Welles—the one a comic journalist, with all of that breed's facile sarcasm and fire-engine-chasing romanticism; the other a melodramatic man of the theater, an egotist and a solipsist, a prodigal and a prodigy, a fake and a genius.

Their very names might have been coined by Central Casting, or by Charles Dickens. "Herman J. Mankiewicz!" (The "J." is particularly endearing, and the name as a whole has the oafish grace of a Preston Sturges creation.) "Orson Welles!" (A preposterously mellifluous stage name, the more so when we recall that his full name is George Orson Welles. Some sixth theatrical sense must have told the boy that George Welles was a common-clay name, whereas Orson Welles could be profitably writ with a neon finger across the Broadway sky.) Perhaps it was just this professional and personal

antipathy that helped produce *Kane*'s vital antiphonies of energy
and pessimism, audacious originality and arrogant eclecticism,
youthful *élan* and twilight malaise, past conditional and present imperfect, the epic and the intimate, the frankly literary and the blat-
antly theatrical, the Marx Brothers brightness in the dialogue and
Murnauvian shadow in the *mise-en-scène*.

What's ironic is that *Kane*'s youthfulness is almost certainly
Mankiewicz's contribution, while the elegiac sense of waste, loss,
decay, and death may be attributed to Welles. Andrew Sarris has
called *Kane* an early, supreme example of the "cinema of memory";
but, in Welles' own case, it was more aptly the cinema of prophecy,
dooming the director to travel down paths defined, to an eerie extent, by Mankiewicz's scenario for *Kane*. As Miss Kael has pointed
out, Kane is an amalgam of three people: Hearst, Welles, and Mankiewicz. One may be forgiven for seeing more of Mankiewicz in the
Jed Leland role, at least in the following exchange between Leland
and Welles' Kane during the "Declaration of Principles" scene:

> KANE (*reading as he writes*): I will also provide them . . .
> LELAND: That's the second sentence you've started with
> "I." . . .
> KANE: People are going to know who's responsible.

It took thirty years and Pauline Kael for people to learn that
Mankiewicz was as responsible for *Citizen Kane*. Unfortunately
(for Mankiewicz as well as for Miss Kael), in making a case for
Kane as both admirable *and* likable, she made no real distinction
between a "great fun" film and a great film. Is that all there is to
Kane? people asked; if it is, we can blame its shallowness on Mankiewicz. Miss Kael's more virulent critics simply denied the validity
of her research. For *Kane* to be great, Welles had to have written it.
This reasoning is not only willfully perverse, it's also a perversion
of auteur polemics. Is *Falstaff* not a Welles film (or a great film)
because he didn't write it? What about *The Magnificent Ambersons*,
Touch of Evil, *The Trial*, *The Immortal Story*? Welles' only original
screenplay filmed to date is *Mr. Arkadin*, a hollow echo of the very
theme *Kane* probed so brilliantly.

The obvious answer to the *Kane* dilemma is that Herman Mankiewicz wrote the film and Orson Welles directed it; and that, while
these two functions can be distinguished for research purposes, they
are really the inseparable halves of a work of art. It may be helpful

to see Welles as the actor-manager, and Mankiewicz as the play-wright, collaborating on a stage production. Did Welles play Frédér-ick Lemaître to Mankiewicz's dim-witted authors of *L'Auberge des Adrets*? Or was Mankiewicz a Bernard Shaw to Welles' Granville-Barker? This is a question that deserves to be settled only after the last insight has been wrung from the text (and subtext) of the most admired, most liked, most discussed work in cinema history—the *Hamlet* of film.

Dalton Trumbo
(1905–   )

1936   ROAD GANG (Louis King) screenplay
      LOVE BEGINS AT 20 (Frank McDonald) co-screenplay
      TUGBOAT PRINCESS (David Selman) co-story
1937   DEVIL'S PLAYGROUND (Erle C. Kenton) co-screenplay
      THAT MAN'S HERE AGAIN (Louis King) co-adaptation
1938   FUGITIVE FOR A NIGHT (Leslie Goodwins) screenplay
      A MAN TO REMEMBER (Garson Kanin) screenplay
1939   THE FLYING IRISHMAN (Leigh Jason) co-story, co-screenplay
      SORORITY HOUSE (John Farrow) screenplay
      THE KID FROM KOKOMO (Lewis Seiler) story
      FIVE CAME BACK (John Farrow) co-screenplay
      HEAVEN WITH A BARBED WIRE FENCE (Ricardo Cortez) co-screenplay
      CAREER (Leigh Jason) screenplay
1940   HALF A SINNER (Al Christie) story
      A BILL OF DIVORCEMENT (John Farrow) screenplay
      KITTY FOYLE (Sam Wood) co-screenplay
      CURTAIN CALL (Frank Woodruff) screenplay
      THE LONE WOLF STRIKES (Sidney Salkow) story
      WE WHO ARE YOUNG (Harold S. Bucquet) story, screenplay
1941   YOU BELONG TO ME (Wesley Ruggles) story
      ACCENT ON LOVE (Ray McCarey) story
1942   THE REMARKABLE ANDREW (Stuart Heisler) 'screenplay, from his novel
1943   TENDER COMRADE (Edward Dmytryk) story, screenplay
      A GUY NAMED JOE (Victor Fleming) screenplay
1944   THIRTY SECONDS OVER TOKYO (Mervyn Leroy) screenplay

1945   OUR VINES HAVE TENDER GRAPES (Roy Rowland)
       screenplay
       JEALOUSY (Gustav Machaty) idea
1950   EMERGENCY WEDDING (Edward Buzzell) remake of *You
       Belong to Me*
1951   THE PROWLER (Joseph Losey) co-screenplay (uncredited)
1954   CARNIVAL STORY (Kurt Neumann) co-screenplay (un-
       credited)
1956   THE BOSS (Byron Haskin) screenplay (uncredited)
       THE BRAVE ONE (Irving Rapper) story [1], screenplay (un-
       credited)
1957   THE GREEN-EYED BLONDE (Bernard Girard) screenplay
       (uncredited)
1958   COWBOY (Delmer Daves) co-screenplay (uncredited)
1960   SPARTACUS (Stanley Kubrick) screenplay
       EXODUS (Otto Preminger) screenplay
1961   THE LAST SUNSET (Robert Aldrich) screenplay
1962   LONELY ARE THE BRAVE (David Miller) screenplay
1965   THE SANDPIPER (Vincente Minnelli) co-screenplay
1966   HAWAII (George Roy Hill) co-screenplay
1968   THE FIXER (John Frankenheimer) screenplay
1971   THE HORSEMEN (John Frankenheimer) screenplay
       JOHNNY GOT HIS GUN (Dalton Trumbo) screenplay, from
       his novel
1973   EXECUTIVE ACTION (David Miller) screenplay

[1] Under the pseudonym "Marcel Klauber."
[2] Under the pseudonym "Sally Stubblefield."
[3] Under the pseudonym "Robert Rich."
[4] Under the pseudonym "Les Crutchfield."

Dalton Trumbo is a remarkable writer and, to judge from the evidence of his recently published letters, as remarkable a husband,
father, and friend. This would have to be a churlish century indeed
to blacklist *Additional Dialogue,* the magnificent collection of
Trumbo's correspondence, from a bookshelf far too heavy with tortured satyriasis and turgid self-analysis. Trumbo has been many
men, most of them fascinating, and *Additional Dialogue* reveals
them all at their witty and wise best. He was a literate raconteur
whose true "medium" was literally that: the tightrope between spontaneous conversation and considered prose that is known as the
letter. One thinks of Wilde, of Shaw.
    Trumbo was also a screenwriter—probably the best known ex-
ample of that talented, frustrated breed. In the middle forties, he

was Hollywood's highest-paid writer (possibly excepting Ben Hecht). Soon after, with the convening of the House Un-American Activities Committee search for Communists in Hollywood, he became that timid community's highest-paid unemployed writer, and the most famous member of the infamous Hollywood Ten. After 13 years in furtive but energetic exile, he received credit for the scripts of such message-spectaculars as *Exodus*, *Spartacus*, and *Hawaii*. At the beginning of the seventies he directed the film version of his 1939 novel, *Johnny Got His Gun*.

Unfortunately for curious bookshelf browsers of the twenty-first century, Trumbo's reputation as a top screenwriter is all but inexplicable. Those of his films that cannot be dismissed as sophisticated but uninspired hack work are inevitably cursed with either preachy self-importance or cheery (but still preachy) patriotism. His career virtually sets the mold for Hollywood's intellectual, left-wing screenwriters, who saw it as their mission to convert the very masses they despised writing down to. If Howard Koch exemplified the screenwriters who respected their movie work and made the most of it, and Ben Hecht the writers who hated the art but loved their craft, then Trumbo apotheosized the committed writer determined, in his own words, "to use art as a weapon for the future of mankind, rather than as an adornment for the vanity of aesthetes and poseurs." In Trumbo's hands, this weapon is a blunt, deadly instrument.

His movies (notably *A Man to Remember*, *A Guy Named Joe*, and *Lonely Are the Brave*) do boast occasional, vagrant behavioral charms—the kind of Trumbonian dialogue that sets one to laughing aloud at his letters and reading excerpts to anyone at hand—but these arrant insights of basically appealing characters get smothered in the glop of his movies' messages, be they The Indomitability Of The Human Spirit or The Destruction Of The Individual By An Unfeeling, Inhuman System.

The literary device (perhaps "weapon" *is* the proper word here) which he employed so relentlessly in his more personal, pessimistic films is irony. At its most subtle we have Kirk Douglas, the last cowboy in *Lonely Are the Brave*, getting run over by a truck. Other examples are not quite so artful. This is irony imposed with a sledge hammer—a far cry from its use in his letters, where he employed not the velvet irony of a Howard Koch (whose scripts for films as superficially different as *Casablanca* and *Letter from an Unknown Woman* purr with casual nobility and understated regret) but rather an irony with its root in iron. Though he indulges it, luxuriates in it, his tone masks a precise awareness of this world's divine and, more often, demoniacal absurdity. And while the content of his letters is often as bitter as anything in *Johnny Got His Gun,* the style has a perversely irresistible savor.

How could the same man write such rich, rewarding correspondence and such predictable, simple-minded scripts? The easy way out is to blame the old Hollywood, where I.Q. generally diminished as power increased, from writer to director to actor to producer to the studio president—"the hollow-headed big boss," as Hecht described him, with a "fixation on peddling trash." Writers who were also leftist intellectuals came West for ready access to the eyes and, mainly, the ears of the mass audience they loved—from a distance. Abraham Polonsky once defined the social conscience of the Left as "a sentimental attitude toward the goodness of man, and getting together and working things out right, and getting rid of injustice." Obviously, the Hollywood capitalists and their most activist employees were made for each other. Perhaps this explains why Communist and socialist writers were corrupted more easily than the uncommitted ones (Hecht, Preston Sturges, etc.) who went to Hollywood to have fun and make money; certainly the films that have endured are precisely those pulpy entertainments scorned by the Party-liners.

A Guy Named Joe (1943)

Power corrupts; but, for many well-paid assembly-line screenwriters, the absence of power coupled with the presence of untold wealth corrupted absolutely. And Trumbo, to compare his novel and letters with his movie scripts, was among the corrupted. Within four years of writing a novel denouncing World War I and, by extension, all wars, Trumbo was churning out chauvinistic screenplays to help propagandize World War II—the *good* war. His specialty was movies about American bomber units, and one of these films contains an irony that would have elicited pages of well-wrought cynicism from Trumbo-the-letter-writer: the protagonist of *Johnny Got His Gun* was a guy named Joe Bonham whose legs, arms, and face were blown off as he fought in the Great War; in 1943 Trumbo wrote a bomber film for smiling Van Johnson, called *A Guy Named Joe.*

Trumbo's letters indicate a writing talent so prodigious that it would be perverse beyond the demands of cinematic indifference if some of this talent had not crept into his scripts. The Trumbo correspondence is successful because his expansive, blustery style found the perfect medium for its expression; the Trumbo movies are fascinating because of the disparity between a natural warmth and an imposed message. As much as one wants to loathe *A Guy Named Joe* for the cheeriness of the good guys' racial and military hatred of the Japs and Krauts, one begins by discounting this as necessary wartime gung-ho, and ends up being uneasily sympathetic to Spencer Tracy's devotion to the Air Force cause.

Trumbo's most characteristic films are thinly disguised tracts, and it follows that the pedagogical function is one he highly values. These roles concentrate on teaching, and stop just short of preaching, to the extent that they are fashioned after Trumbo's father, whose love and wisdom the writer obviously cherished, and who serves as the model for Joe Bonham's father in *Johnny Got His Gun*. When Tracy chats with a group of English kids outside an airfield, lecturing them gently on the affinity of a pilot to his plane, we can almost see Trumbo's father hovering over the star's shoulder, and Trumbo himself looking up worshipfully amid the other children. For whole sections of *A Guy Named Joe,* this caring, generous mood overwhelms the ideological truculence of the film's theme, and informs the unusually adult love affair between Tracy and Irene Dunne. The impression is one of a knowledgeable creative team taking familiar material and, by respecting it and their ability to transform it into something more than familiar, making it into a respectable film that elevates the very conventions it adheres to so tenaciously.

A Guy Named Joe is another heavenly fantasy—a kind of politicized *Here Comes Mr. Jordan,* with Group-Captain Lionel Barrymore sending the deceased Tracy back to earth on a mission to teach guys named Joe to drop more and better bombs. If we cannot forget that some of these bombs devastated such "targets" as Dresden, Berlin, Hiroshima, and Nagasaki, we should also remember that, in 1943, the operative word was not "bombing" but "mission," a term that was less a War Department euphemism than a hope for the forceful conversion of Germany and Japan. Trumbo can hardly be singled out for limning hymns to American Air Power; as Lew Ayres and a few other lonely, brave souls discovered, pacificism in World War II was taken as treason. What now seems troubling is that Trumbo parlayed a facility for scriptwriting, and an ability to suppress his own best instincts, into a reputation as the screenwriter with the best contract a wary, reactionary industry and a wily leftist could negotiate.

The Brave One (1956)

In a letter written but not sent to the FBI around 1944, Trumbo denied that *Johnny Got His Gun* was pacifist (which it certainly is) and, implicitly, that he was a Communist (which at that time he was). And while his appearance before HUAC verged on the heroic, even this exhibition of courage was compromised ever so slightly, ever so crucially, by expediency. To refuse to admit that he was a Party member was undoubtedly perilous (he could, and did, go to jail for it); but to have publicly admitted his membership would have been almost as perilous to him (he probably would have been fired) and far less appealing to civil libertarians.

Trumbo's profile on the Mount Rushmore of political courage may be a trifle weak-chinned, but he probably qualifies for the rank of "Hero, 2nd Class"—a rank he might share, along with some other surprising qualities, with the late Lenny Bruce. Both of these men coaxed art out of venerable but profane forms—Trumbo the letter, Bruce the monologue. Both could assume a milder image when working for mass media—Trumbo for the movies, Bruce for TV. Both even wrote hilarious "confessions" on that once-taboo topic, masturbation. And both suffered a kind of martyrdom for crimes of which many sympathizers believed them to be innocent— Trumbo for Communism, Bruce for heroin addiction. That they were guilty as charged mitigates their heroism but does not revoke it, since the charges themselves were camouflage for more sinister accusations—that Trumbo dared to defy an Un-American inquest, and that Bruce attempted to purge America's social and sexual prejudices by cloaking them in the most pungent satire. Both men suffered from these pressures; Bruce succumbed to them, while the more resilient Trumbo finally overcame them.

The winning combination of businessman and craftsman, which had made Trumbo the most financially successful Hollywood screenwriter in the forties, kept his career alive in the blacklisted fifties. The ruin that other writers took as malefic destiny, Trumbo saw as a challenge. Should such a Dark Age again descend on the movie community, the middle chapters of *Additional Dialogue* will serve as a survival kit for the determined. Writing as quickly as ever, but for three thousand dollars per script instead of the seventy-five thousand he had earned a decade earlier, Trumbo did survive. It would be pleasant to think that Trumbo and his blacklisted brethren wrote, pseudonymously the finest fifties films. But with the exception of Michael Wilson (who had scripted *A Place in the Sun, Five Fingers,* and *Friendly Persuasion* before being blacklisted, and *Salt of the Earth, The Bridge on the River Kwai,* and *Lawrence of Arabia* afterward), their output was prolific but hardly profound. The political and administrative pressures that obsessed most leftist writers in the forties became murderously oppressive in the fifties, and most of the blacklisted screenwriters' work came through subterranean channels and went into substandard productions. None of Trumbo's scripts were turned into films of quality, and this applies even to his bizarre Oscar winner, *The Brave One.*

Mexico City was one of Trumbo's bases of operation during his exile, and the relative superiority of *The Brave One* over his other (identified) scripts of the period is attributable to Trumbo's knowledge of the physical and psychological terrain. But this mild vignette of a Mexican boy and his beloved bull—itself suspiciously similar to a Robert Flaherty story, "Bonito the Bull," which Orson Welles bought and filmed as part of his abortive 1942 Mexican documentary, *It's All True*—is perhaps worthier of publication in the *Reader's Digest* ("The Most Unforgettable Toro I Ever Met") than of an Academy Award for the Best Original Story of 1956. One plausible explanation may be that the Screenwriters Underground had been alerted to Trumbo's authorship, and united to vote the rascal in. The film does feature another of Trumbo's teacher figures (here an actual teacher) and, in its climactic demonstration of taurine heroics which result in a rare verdict of amnesty, it embodied Trumbo's hopes for a triumphant return to Hollywood. Perhaps the Academy's writers realized this, and were actually rewarding the admirable, inexhaustible doggedness of Dalton Trumbo—the cunning one, the persistent one, and, in a way Hollywood could best understand, the brave one.

Johnny Got His Gun (1971)

Trumbo's resilience is a bracing complement to his sense of compromise. He joined the System successfully; when ostracized, he beat It successfully. He knew the right tricks; he knew what would play to which audience. And this is, finally, the vital link between his letters and his scripts: Trumbo's acute sense of audience. When he could work to an audience of one intelligent friend, as in most of his correspondence, Trumbo could be—and was, incessantly—in complete possession of an eloquent comic prose style. When he wrote *Johnny Got His Gun* for what might have been a relatively small group of readers, form combined with feeling to produce a powerful novel that transcends the severe restrictions of agit-prop. But when he wrote scripts for thousands of dollars and millions of moviegoers, his sense of an audience he could not respect led him toward bathos and demagoguery.

Trumbo wrote the novel *Johnny Got His Gun* in his thirty-third year, and directed its adaptation in his sixty-sixth—yet the novel seems more mature. As a book, *Johnny Got His Gun* had two great strengths: its ability to transport the reader convincingly into the mind of a faceless quadruple amputee (no small technical achievement), and the warmth of its flashbacks into poor Joe Bonham's childhood. These flashbacks were wrenched out of Trumbo's own experience—the bucolic Colorado family, the shoe-selling, bee-keeping father, the boy's work on a section gang and, when the family moved to Los Angeles, in a bakery—and, in the novel, they have an immediacy all the more poignant for functioning as apolitical interludes in a "thesis" novel.

But Trumbo didn't make *Johnny Got His Gun* into a movie just to capture those blessedly irrelevant, privileged moments on film. Over three decades, the interludes have faded while the thesis remains, and Trumbo seems as removed in spirit from the boy's life-sustaining memories as he is in time from his own youth. It is Trumbo's misfortune that Luis Buñuel, who was once to have directed *Johnny Got His Gun*, could not. (Buñuel's *Los Olvidados* is not the most closely reasoned condemnation of juvenile delinquency imaginable, but it has an informed passion that is missing here.) Trumbo directs movies the way he writes them, with every gesture underlined, every glance portentous, the camera catching his actors only when they "act." Jason Robards' performance is instructive: in the book, Joe's father was both a sage and a failure, but Robards plays him only as a failure, with weight-of-the-world stooped shoulders and eyes filled with anticipated defeat. His performance deals, like the film itself, with things remembered but not felt. Dehumanized, *Johnny Got His Gun* becomes the pacifist equivalent of the hated war machine: a propaganda machine for peace. It is a measure of the film's ineffectiveness that Joe Bonham will inevitably be eclipsed in movie history by his opposite number, Harold Russell, the amiable amputee of *The Best Years of Our Lives*.

A long look at the nonmovie ephemera of Trumbo, Hecht, Harry Brown, Herman J. Mankiewicz, and others convinces me that half the screenwriters in Hollywood poured their talent into witty letters, fierce memos, and funny stories once they realized their scripts would not be filmed as they were written. Of the self-destructive Mankiewicz, Ben Hecht wrote: "I knew that no one as witty and spontaneous as Herman would ever put himself on paper. A man whose genius is on tap like free beer seldom makes literature out of it." The art of conversation is not only a dying art, it is one that dies anew as the embers of a witty evening's memory turn to the dust of gossip. Mankiewicz "put himself on paper" for the movies just once—when he wrote *Citizen Kane*. Trumbo's own genius was clandestine, conspiratorial, circulated only to special friends and formidable enemies. His screenplays deserve the oblivion most of them have already received; but his letters will live, for the true record of the man is there—in those florid, cantankerous, incandescent salvos.

IV. *The Chameleons*

JULES FURTHMAN	SIDNEY BUCHMAN	CASEY ROBINSON
MORRIE RYSKIND	EDWIN JUSTUS MAYER	DELMER DAVES
CHARLES LEDERER	CHARLES BRACKETT	FRANK S. NUGENT
RING LARDNER, JR.		

> A screenwriter is at best a stylistic chameleon: he writes in the style of the original source—or should, if he's worth his salt.
>
> —PHILIP DUNNE

A chameleon is not a hack. He is not one of those faceless back-lot boys who took whatever assignment the bosses gave him, polishing apples and dialogue with equal ease. If he were, he would not be in this book. The talented men represented in this section were often powerful, pioneering, important. Several of them can boast of long, productive associations with Hollywood's finest directors. Many earned the respect of moguls and movie stars alike for their ability to deliver actable, tractable scripts that could be shot as written. What would Columbia Pictures have been like without Sidney Buchman? Or Paramount without Jules Furthman? Or Warners without Casey Robinson?

Mostly, they transferred the stories, plays, and novels of others to the screen. Theirs was the task of paring and repairing, of adapting and adopting. Indeed, adaptability was both their strength and their limitation. A strong personal style like Ben Hecht's or Frank Tashlin's has derailed more than one streamlined Hollywood vehicle, but it has also provided some of the cinema's strangest and most sublime moments. The contours of a chameleon's career are

263

more elusive. Jules Furthman scripted *Morocco*, Frank S. Nugent scripted *The Searchers*; and yet these are surely directors' films as much as any the American cinema has produced. Neither Charles Lederer nor Charles Brackett was exactly an anonymous artisan; and yet, in their respective collaborations with Hecht and Billy Wilder, they were surely not the dominant party. To what extent *were* our chameleons responsible for their films (some of the finest in talkie history)? The following chapters attempt to answer that perplexing question.

JULES FURTHMAN
(1888–1960)

1915   STEADY COMPANY (Joseph De Grasse) story [1]
       BOUND ON THE WHEEL (Joseph De Grasse) story [1]
       MOUNTAIN JUSTICE (Joseph De Grasse) story [1]
       CHASING THE LIMITED (Henry McRae) story
       QUITS (Joseph De Grasse) story [1]

1918   THE CAMOUFLAGE KISS (Harry Millarde) story, co-screenplay
       MORE TROUBLE (Ernest C. Warde) screenplay
       JAPANESE NIGHTINGALE (George Fitizmaurice) screenplay
       ALL THE WORLD TO NOTHING (Henry King) screenplay [2]
       MANTLE OF CHARITY (Edward Sloman) screenplay [2]
       HOBBS IN A HURRY (Henry King) screenplay [2]
       WIVES AND OTHER WIVES (Lloyd Ingraham) story,[2] screenplay [2]

1919   WHERE THE WEST BEGINS (Henry King) story,[2] screenplay [2]
       BRASS BUTTONS (Henry King) story,[2] screenplay [2]
       SOME LIAR (Henry King) screenplay [2]
       A SPORTING CHANCE (Henry King) story [2]
       THIS HERO STUFF (Henry King) story [2]
       SIX FEET FOUR (Henry King) screenplay [2]
       VICTORY (Maurice Tourneur) screenplay [2]

1920   THE VALLEY OF TOMORROW (Emmett J. Flynn) story [2]
       TREASURE ISLAND (Maurice Tourneur) screenplay [2]
       WOULD YOU FORGIVE? (Scott Dunlap) story, screenplay
       LEAVE IT TO ME (Emmett J. Flynn) screenplay
       THE TWINS OF SUFFERING CREEK (Scott Dunlap) screenplay

[1] Under the name "Julius Grinnell Furthman."
[2] Under the pseudonym "Stephen Fox."

WHITE CIRCLE (Maurice Tourneur) co-screenplay
THE MAN WHO DARED (Emmett J. Flynn) story, screenplay
THE SKYWAYMAN (James Patrick Hogan) story, screenplay
THE GREAT REDEEMER (Clarence Brown) co-adaptation
THE TEXAN (Lynn Reynolds) co-screenplay
IRON RIDER (Scott Dunlap) screenplay
LAND OF JAZZ (Jules Furthman) story, co-screenplay
1921 THE CHEATER REFORMED (Scott Dunlap) story, co-screen-
play
THE BIG PUNCH (John Ford) story, screenplay
THE BLUSHING BRIDE (Jules Furthman) story, screenplay
COLORADO PLUCK   (Jules Furthman) story, screenplay
HIGH GEAR JEFFREY (Edward Sloman) story, screenplay [3]
SINGING RIVER (Charles Giblyn) screenplay
THE LAST TRAIL (Emmett J. Flynn) co-screenplay
THE ROOF TREE (John Francis Dillon) screenplay
1922 GLEAM O'DAWN (John Francis Dillon) screenplay
THE RAGGED HEIRESS (Harry Beaumont) story, screenplay
ARABIAN LOVE (Jerome Storm) story, screenplay
THE YELLOW STAIN (John Francis Dillon) story, screenplay
STRANGE IDOLS (Bernard J. Durning) screenplay
CALVERT'S VALLEY (John Francis Dillon) screenplay
THE LOVE GAMBLER (Joseph Franz) screenplay
A CALIFORNIA ROMANCE (Jerome Storm) story
PAWN TICKET 210 (Scott Dunlap) screenplay
1923 LOVEBOUND (Henry Otto) co-screenplay
ST. ELMO (Jerome Storm) screenplay
NORTH OF THE HUDSON BAY (John Ford) story, screen-
play
THE ACQUITTAL (Clarence Brown) screenplay
CONDEMNED (Arthur Rosson) story, screenplay
1924 TRY AND GET IT (Cullen Tate) screenplay
CALL OF THE MATE (Alvin J. Neitz) story, screenplay
1925 SACKCLOTH AND SCARLET (Henry King) co-screenplay
ANY WOMAN (Henry King) co-screenplay
BEFORE MIDNIGHT (John Adolfi) story, screenplay
BIG PAL (John Adolfi) story, screenplay
1926 THE WISE GUY (Frank Lloyd) story
YOU'D BE SURPRISED (Arthur Rosson) story, screenplay
1927 HOTEL IMPERIAL (Mauritz Stiller) screenplay
CASEY AT THE BAT (Monty Brice) screenplay

[3] According to the American Film Institute catalogue, this film is a "re-edited" version of *The Frameup* (1917).

FASHIONS FOR WOMEN (Dorothy Arzner) co-adaptation
BARBED WIRE (Rowland V. Lee) adaptation, co-screenplay
THE WAY OF ALL FLESH (Victor Fleming) screenplay
CITY GONE WILD (James Cruze) co-story,[4] screenplay

1928 THE DRAG NET (Josef von Sternberg) adaptation, co-screenplay [4]
THE DOCKS OF NEW YORK (Josef von Sternberg) screenplay

1929 ABIE'S IRISH ROSE (Victor Fleming) screenplay
THE CASE OF LENA SMITH (Josef von Sternberg) screenplay
THUNDERBOLT (Josef von Sternberg) co-story,[4] screenplay
NEW YORK NIGHTS (Lewis Milestone) screenplay

1930 COMMON CLAY (Victor Fleming) screenplay, dialogue
RENEGADES (Victor Fleming) adaptation, continuity, dialogue
MOROCCO (Josef von Sternberg) screenplay, dialogue

1931 BODY AND SOUL (Alfred Santell) screenplay
MERELY MARY ANN (Henry King)
YELLOW TICKET (Raoul Walsh) screenplay
OVER THE HILL (Henry King) co-screenplay

1932 SHANGHAI EXPRESS (Josef von Sternberg) screenplay
BLONDE VENUS (Josef von Sternberg) co-story, co-screenplay

1933 GIRL IN 419 (George Somnes and Alexander Hall) story
BOMBSHELL (Victor Fleming) co-screenplay

1935 CHINA SEAS (Tay Garnett) co-screenplay
MUTINY ON THE BOUNTY (Frank Lloyd) co-screenplay

1936 COME AND GET IT! (Howard Hawks, William Wyler) co-screenplay

1938 SPAWN OF THE NORTH (Henry Hathaway) co-screenplay
1939 ONLY ANGELS HAVE WINGS (Howard Hawks) screenplay
1940 THE WAY OF ALL FLESH (Louis King) remake of the 1927 film
1941 THE SHANGHAI GESTURE (Josef von Sternberg) co-screenplay
1943 THE OUTLAW (Howard Hughes) screenplay
1944 TO HAVE AND HAVE NOT (Howard Hawks) co-screenplay
1946 THE BIG SLEEP (Howard Hawks) co-screenplay
1947 MOSS ROSE (Gregory Ratoff) co-screenplay
NIGHTMARE ALLEY (Edmund Goulding) screenplay
1950 PRETTY BABY (Bretaigne Windust) co-story
1951 PEKING EXPRESS (William Dieterle) remake of *Shanghai Express*

[4] With Charles Furthman.

1957   JET PILOT (Josef von Sternberg) story, screenplay, producer
1959   RIO BRAVO (Howard Hawks) co-screenplay

Pauline Kael says that Jules Furthman "has written about half of the most entertaining movies to come out of Hollywood." Richard Koszarski makes a compelling case for Furthman's intensive co-authorship, if not auteurship, of such seemingly disparate films as *Morocco, Bombshell,* and *To Have and Have Not.* If these two eloquent apologists tend to overrate Furthman, it is certainly understandable, for most critics have not underrated this self-effacing screenwriter so much as they have simply ignored him—the better to sing the praises of those compleat creators, Josef von Sternberg (for whom Furthman wrote at least nine films) and Howard Hawks (for whom he wrote five).

But Furthman is not merely an enigma wrapped in the wet blanket of auteur criticism; he is also a pioneer craftsman whose roots are lost in Hollywood's prehistory. Although Furthman's career spans almost half a century—from *Steady Company* in 1915 to *Rio Bravo* in 1959—only about a quarter of his nearly a hundred film credits are talkies, and many films from his most prolific years have exploded or disintegrated into oblivion. As William K. Everson and others continue their invaluable excavations into the Fox vaults, the import of Furthman's five crucial years as scenarist and director at that studio—where, between 1920 and 1924, he wrote a couple of dozen films for, among others, John Ford—may become clearer. For now, film archaeologists will have to make do with plot summaries provided by the American Film Institute's Catalog of Hollywood Feature Films of the twenties. Even these scanty fossils offer circumstantial evidence of Furthman's lifelong devotion to a curious subgenre of American movies that might be called "the noble adventure film."

Over and over, in settings that ranged from a Colorado gold mine to the sands of Araby, Furthman wrote the story of a grizzled adventurer who, with great exertions of will and the love of an equally adventurous woman, finds salvation for himself and those around him. In *The Cheater Reformed,* an embezzler, disguised as a minister, reforms himself and a fellow crook, winning the minister's wife in the bargain. In *The Big Punch* (directed by Ford), a prospective theological student reforms his outlaw brother, who wins a Salvation Army girl in the bargain. In *The Wise Guy,* a fast-talking snake-oil salesman falls in love and is reformed by a girl who joins his show.

The scene of many of these films is a remote male enclave—gold-rush towns in *Colorado Pluck* and *North of Hudson Bay,* the Sahara in *Arabian Love,* the patent-medicine caravan in *The Wise Guy*—into which a plucky young woman comes to provoke disruption and eventual regeneration. This scene and theme may sound familiar, and well it should: it was the grid upon which Furthman designed some of the most characteristic works of Sternberg (*Docks of New York, Morocco*) and Hawks (*Only Angels Have Wings, Rio Bravo*)—not to mention such outside assignments as *Renegades* (Myrna Loy as a wartime spy), *Body and Soul* (Elissa Landi as another spy), *China Seas* (Jean Harlow on a clipper), *Spawn of the North* (Dorothy Lamour in Alaska), and possibly even *The Outlaw* (Jane Russell meets Billy the Kid).

What little controversy there is about Furthman centers on his association with *Underworld.* With disarming disingenuousness, Koszarski says that "it would seem unlikely that [Furthman] did not have at least an eye on the proceedings," and proceeds to catalogue the frequently remarked similarities between this would-be-first Furthman-Sternberg film and *Rio Bravo,* the final Furthman-Hawks —from identical opening sequence to identical nicknames for the female leads. Koszarski might have added that Arthur Rosson, whom Ben Hecht says "helped me to put the script together," had directed two earlier Furthman stories. And yet, as tempting as it is to bestow an almost classical symmetry on Furthman's career, I must admit I remain unconvinced that *Underworld* is Jules' work. The credits on the film read "Adaptation by Charles Furthman" (Jules' less prominent brother, with whom he occasionally collaborated), and it is unlikely that Jules, who in 1927 was Paramount's premier scenarist, would not have been given screen credit. At any rate, responsibility for this prototype gangster film belongs properly to Hecht, who wrote the original story, and Sternberg, who perversely brought Hecht's flesh-and-blood underworld figures to life by turning them into ethereal, otherworldly phantoms.

Unfortunately, as with so many distinctive but undistinguished American directors, it's easier to identify Furthman as an auteur than to establish him as an artist. In his talkies—the only work we have to judge him by—the vitality, to which Pauline Kael responds,

seems mechanical; the plotting, which Richard Koszarski so admires, is as predictable as a Kabuki scenario; and the dialogue,
which aims to be vigorous and racy, often comes across with a naïve
leer, like the tough talk of teen-agers. At his best, Furthman is a
Ben Hecht without the uppity polish; at his worst, he's a Dudley
Nichols without the uplifting message. The problem is that there's
not much difference between best and worst Furthman. He is always
competent, often compromising, rarely compelling, and never incomparable. In general, Furthman exemplifies the kind of screenwriter whose filmographic whole is greater than the sum of his
particular contributions to it, whose best work was done as the
"employee" of a directing or performing personality stronger than
his own, and whose career deserves to be resurrected but not adored.

Morocco (1930)

Morocco is spellbinding. But does its pendulous movement numb
the viewer with excitement in the presence of genius, or merely put
him to sleep? Is the film exotic or just bizarre? lapidary or languid?
austere or simple-minded? eloquent or talky? primitive or decadent?
all or none of the above? Morocco is so assertive in demanding to be
taken on its own terms that deciding whether or not to surrender to
it becomes a severe test of the critical will. A predisposition in Sternberg's favor, as well as a tolerance for Gary Cooper and all he embodies, may be necessary to accept Morocco with anything like the
enthusiasm its fondest devotees lavish on it.

Although Sternberg's mise-en-scène seems to evoke 1910 and
1984 with equal ease, Jules Furthman's screenplay is moored dis-
astrously to the early-talkie conventions of 1930. Sternberg's
achievement (and, possibly more conspicuous, that of his admirers)
is in ignoring the restrictions of trite plot and turgid dialogue even
while he honors them; he stretches out every line as if it were part
of a ritual he is daring the viewer to laugh at. Sometimes—especially when the dialogue is delivered by Marlene Dietrich, whose
tortuous pauses suggest an attempt to translate ideas and emotions
from some sublime, unknown language into words of one syllable
that Cooper can understand—Sternberg's audacity pays off: "I understand [pause] that men are never asked [pause] why they enter
the Foreign Legion. . . . There's a Foreign Legion of women [pause],
too. [Pause.] But we have no uniforms. [Pause.] No flags. [Pause.]

And no medals [pause] when we are brave. [Pause.] No wound
stripes [pause] when we are hurt." This is dialogue as confession, as
incantation, as litany, as a prayer for redemption. But Sternberg
gives the same emphasis to the doggerel Furthman wrote for
Cooper; and suddenly the delirious pratfalls into the ludicrous, as in
Cooper's midnight meeting with the amorous Mme. Cesar:

> TOM: Well, if it isn't Mme. Cesar!
> MME. CESAR: Tom—I must see you tonight.
> TOM: See me tonight? What if your *husband* sees you tonight?
> MME. CESAR: He isn't going to see me.
> TOM: Isn't he? What if he does?
> MME. CESAR: Cesar's wife is above suspicion.
> TOM: Yeah? You may know something about ancient history,
> but I know something about husbands. (*He waves goodbye.*)

Morocco's triangular tension is apportioned among Girl (Dietrich), Boy (Cooper), and Other, Older Man (Adolphe Menjou)—
the same trio around which, in *Desire,* Lubitsch & Co. (including
Dietrich and Cooper) will weave several baroque variations six
years later. Menjou is supposed to inhabit a world of sybaritic refinement somewhere between Claude Rains' Casablanca and Charlie
Kane's Xanadu (it is even said of Menjou's Le Bessier that "he
would be a great painter if he were not so rich," prefiguring Kane's
own self-pitying epitaph that "if I hadn't been very rich, I might
have been a really great man"). But, as Menjou plays him, Le Bessier has a depth neither of those formidable rascals can quite touch.
While Dietrich and Cooper begin circling each other, obsessed with
flirtation, and end up marching into the arid unknown, flirting with
obsession, Menjou remains suspended throughout the film in a per-
plexingly homely, if exquisitely stylish, devotion.

A hallmark of devotion is "making allowances" for one's beloved;
and Menjou allows Dietrich to meet, fall in love with, and finally
run off after Cooper, even though she is engaged to marry Menjou.
As he is all too aware, Dietrich resolved to join the "rear guard"
of camp followers the moment she heard the Legion tattoo announc-
ing the return from battle, and her pearl necklace fell apart, and she
rushed out of her betrothal dinner in search of her lost Legionnaire.
In *Morocco*'s minutes-long final shot, our attention is centered on
Dietrich's pursuit of her oasis-lover into ecstasy or oblivion—until
we realize we are watching her through Menjou's eyes as she recedes
out of his sight, his reach, and his life.

Sternberg's intense and productive collaboration with Dietrich encourages speculation about Menjou's Le Bessier as the director's alter ego, and about Cooper's Tom Brown as his alter libido. In this, the pair's first American film, Sternberg's guiding hand can be seen caressing and prodding Dietrich's every movement. She never convinces that her gestures and responses come from within herself or her character. Everything is imposed on her—although she is a dazzling presence, and often submits to these impositions gracefully. The difference between Garbo and Dietrich, at least at this point in their respective careers, is like that of Chaplin and Langdon: the one responding superbly to a serene spiritual choreography, the other taking tiny steps at the bidding of Svengali Frank Capra.

It hardly seems proper to intrude Furthman's name in the midst of these multiple symbiotic relationships. And, in fact, it's difficult to see Furthman here as much more than what Sternberg thought of him—which is hardly anything—even though the writer's previous film, *Renegades,* revolved around a Foreign Legion outpost in Morocco and another sultry triangle; and though a later Furthman-Sternberg effort, *Shanghai Express,* echoed *Morocco*'s male-female medals-and-bravery dialogue. For once, a screenwriter may be properly subsumed under the director's reputation. Such anonymity seemed to nourish Furthman, instead of stifling him—a working atmosphere other Sternberg associates usually found unbearable. The director might well have sympathized with Paul Porcasi, the sweaty café owner in *Morocco,* who complains to his customers, "For some reason, the artists I engage don't last very long. It may be the heat."

Only Angels Have Wings (1939)

Robin Wood defines two divergent strains in Howard Hawks's films as "Self-Respect and Responsibility" (*Only Angels Have Wings, To Have and Have Not, Rio Bravo*) and "The Lure of Irresponsibility" (*Scarface, His Girl Friday, Monkey Business,* among others). Hawks employed many regular screenwriters over a forty-five-year career—William Faulkner, Charles Lederer, Seton I. Miller, Dudley Nichols, and Leigh Brackett all wrote at least three films for him—but, for his most characteristic films, the director relied on Jules Furthman (who wrote or co-wrote the "Responsibility" films) and Ben Hecht (who co-wrote the "Irresponsibility" films mentioned above). This is an elegant if overschematic way of saying that Furthman's specialty was adventure films and Hecht's was comedies. And yet, there's usually a frenetic, not to say frenzied, physical force to Hecht's comedies, so that the distinction between adventure and laughter, between intensity and insanity, between the gasp and the guffaw, becomes blurred. Similarly, it's often difficult to tell when Furthman means us to take his characters' comically tough dialogue seriously.

Jean Harlow is probably the archetypal Furthman dame, with her blond hair, strident voice, and brassy manner. In *Bombshell* (a kind of comedy) and *China Seas* (a kind of adventure), she demolishes one movie stereotype of women only to reinforce another. Both the noble masochist of the weepie films and the ballsy comrade of the comedies and adventure films were turned into tedious puppets when their types were repeated without variation in countless Hollywood movies. Though Furthman wrote two Constance Bennett tearjerkers, he is popularly associated with the "man's woman," whether the subspecies is rarefied (as with Dietrich) or raunchy (as with Harlow). Rita Hayworth, in *Only Angels Have Wings,* not only continued the type established by Harlow—a young, sultry cartoon—but set the mold for Janet Leigh in *Jet Pilot,* Angie Dickinson ir·*Rio Bravo,* and especially Lauren Bacall in *To Have and Have Not,* even down to the same props: hair, door, come-hither look.

Cary Grant and Jean Arthur were, by 1939, past masters at the art of making snappy patter crackle with sexual flirtation and innuendo, and neither performer ever looked more attractive. But in *Only Angels Have Wings* Miss Arthur has trouble with the high-school histrionics Hawks and Furthman demanded of her; and Grant seems ill at ease when forced to suppress his natural exuberance and act sullen (as he must also do in *Notorious*). Grant's most successful roles exploit the childlike vulnerability beneath that manly profile. Indeed, part of our delight in *Holiday, Penny Serenade, An Affair to Remember, North by Northwest,* and *Charade* comes from seeing this handsome man's insecurity exposed. The one major Grant character who eludes this generalization is *His Girl Friday*'s Walter Burns. And there, pure style—the obsessive, perpetual forward motion that makes his excursions into highway robbery seem like genial hi-jinks—obliterates our scruples.

In *Only Angels Have Wings,* however, Grant's actions and attitude are supposed to justify themselves without resorting to questions of style. He bullies Jean Arthur, just as he does Rosalind Russell in *His Girl Friday,* but the dramatic point is Grant's nobility, not his raffishness. And the fliers who mock Jean Arthur's bereavement upon the death of Joe—a pilot who tried to land his plane in poor weather so he could date our heroine—are close relatives of the *His Girl Friday* pressroom gang, whose taunts drive a frenzied Molly Malloy out the nearest third-floor window. There, at least, the reporters' cruelty was "placed" by a lecture Miss Russell gives them with the full approval of her director. In *Only Angels Have Wings,* the penance is Jean Arthur's: she is made to confess that "I hadda behave like a sap." "Grown up?" asks Grant. "Hope so." "Good girl. . . . Who's Joe?" "Never heard of him."

Only Angels Have Wings is at its enjoyable best when it's indulging in preposterous coincidences, daredevil aerobatics, damnable strokes of ill fortune, and dialogue worthy of encasement in a Roy Lichtenstein balloon (Arthur: "Still carrying a torch for her?" Grant: "Got a match?"). When the film strains to touch some metaphysic of all-American stoicism—and when the film's most eloquent admirers, such as Robin Wood, invoke *The Nigger of the Narcissus* to explain one character's "meaning of life"—*Only Angels Have Wings* becomes a bore, for it can succeed only on the level of a razzle-dazzle air adventure. For literary analogues to Hawks and Furthman, one should turn, not to Joseph Conrad, but to Milton Caniff.

SIDNEY BUCHMAN
(1902–)

1931 DAUGHTER OF THE DRAGON (Lloyd Corrigan) dialogue
 BELOVED BACHELOR (Lloyd Corrigan) dialogue
1932 NO ONE MAN (Lloyd Corrigan) adaptation, dialogue
 THUNDER BELOW (Richard Wallace) adaptation
 THE SIGN OF THE CROSS (Cecil B. De Mille) adaptation, dialogue
 IF I HAD A MILLION (Ernst Lubitsch, Norman Taurog, Norman Z. McLeod, James Cruze, William A. Seiter, Stephen Roberts, H. Bruce Humberstone) co-screenplay
1933 FROM HELL TO HEAVEN (Erle C. Kenton) co-screenplay
 RIGHT TO ROMANCE (Alfred Santell) co-screenplay
1934 ALL OF ME (James Flood) co-screenplay
 WHOM THE GODS DESTROY (Walter Lang) co-screenplay
 HIS GREATEST GAMBLE (John S. Robertson) co-screenplay
 BROADWAY BILL (Frank Capra) co-screenplay (uncredited)
1935 I'LL LOVE YOU ALWAYS (Leo Bulgakov) co-screenplay
 LOVE ME FOREVER (Victor Schertzinger) co-screenplay
 SHE MARRIED HER BOSS (Gregory La Cava) screenplay
1936 THE KING STEPS OUT (Josef von Sternberg) screenplay
 THEODORA GOES WILD (Richard Boleslawski) screenplay
 ADVENTURE IN MANHATTAN (Edward Ludwig) screenplay
 THE MUSIC GOES ROUND (Victor Schertzinger) story
1937 THE AWFUL TRUTH (Leo McCarey) co-screenplay (uncredited)
 LOST HORIZON (Frank Capra) co-screenplay (uncredited)
1938 HOLIDAY (George Cukor) co-screenplay
1939 MR. SMITH GOES TO WASHINGTON (Frank Capra) screenplay

1940 THE HOWARDS OF VIRGINIA (Frank Lloyd) screenplay
1941 HERE COMES MR. JORDAN (Alexander Hall) co-screenplay
1942 THE TALK OF THE TOWN (George Stevens) co-screenplay
1943 SAHARA (Zoltan Korda) co-screenplay (uncredited)
1945 A SONG TO REMEMBER (Charles Vidor) screenplay, producer
       OVER 21 (Charles Vidor) screenplay, producer
1947 THE JOLSON STORY (Alfred E. Green) story (uncredited)
1948 TO THE ENDS OF THE EARTH (Robert Stevenson) co-screenplay (uncredited), producer
1949 JOLSON SINGS AGAIN (Henry Levin) story, screenplay, producer
1951 SATURDAY'S HERO (David Miller) co-screenplay
1961 THE MARK (Guy Green) co-screenplay
1963 CLEOPATRA (Joseph L. Mankiewicz) co-screenplay
1966 THE GROUP (Sidney Lumet) screenplay, producer
1972 LA MAISON SOUS LES ARBRES [THE DEADLY TRAP] (René Clement) co-screenplay

Sidney Buchman was Harry Cohn's favorite writer. If this fact doesn't seem impressive enough to admit Buchman into the Screenwriters Parthenon, it is only because the boss of Columbia Pictures was better known for his tantrums than for his keen intuition about which films would succeed. With surprising regularity, those films —*She Married Her Boss, Theodora Goes Wild, The Awful Truth, Mr. Smith Goes to Washington, Here Comes Mr. Jordan, The Talk of the Town, A Song to Remember, The Jolson Story*—sprang from the pen of the indispensable Mr. Buchman. Buchman had much in common with Robert Riskin, who had preceded him as Cohn's darling. Both Buchman and Riskin liked to write long and fast; both enjoyed building dramatic opposition between rural and big-city life; both were easygoing populists who would find their perfect director in Frank Capra. But, in drawing his moral, Riskin tended toward caricature, while Buchman's best work (*Theodora, Mr. Smith, Mr. Jordan, The Talk of the Town*) was subtle, eccentric, full-bodied—and enduring. Harry Cohn was right.

Theodora Goes Wild (1936)

The films that made Buchman's reputation—*Theodora Goes Wild, Mr. Smith Goes to Washington,* and *The Talk of the Town*—

share a common theme developed with such expertise and inexor-
ability that, with the exception of *Mr. Smith,* they can be considered
as projects closer to the writer than to the director. The protagonist
is in each case a good, modest person whom circumstances nudge
into the spotlight of notoriety. The plot is then complicated by the
hypocrisy of the protagonist's associates—to be resolved when the
hypocrite engages in dramatic self-criticism in front of his constitu-
ents. This sounds like Andrew Sarris's description of "the obligatory
scene" in a Frank Capra film: "the confession of folly in the most
public way possible." The most memorable of these *apologiae* can
be found in Claude Rains' condemnation and renunciation of the
political corruption that holds him—and, implicitly, the entire Senate—in thrall. And of course Buchman wrote *Mr. Smith. Theodora
Goes Wild* could be seen as a first draft of the Innocence-Over-
whelming-Hypocrisy situation in the Capra film, if it weren't so
winning and fully realized in itself.

Theodora (Irene Dunne), last descendant of the Lynns of
Lynnville, has secretly written a torrid romance that the local paper is serializing despite the objections of the Lynnville Literary
Circle—of which Theodora is a charter member. Only her New
York publisher knows that, beneath the pseudonym of a mysterious
lady novelist, resides the strait-laced but still fluttering heart of a
small-town girl. On one of her visits to New York, Theodora meets
and attracts a wealthy young layabout (Melvyn Douglas), who sub-
sequently comes to Lynnville and gains employment as a gardener
for Theodora and her snooty, moralizing aunts. He falls in love
with Theodora, and leaves her; he's married, you see, though
estranged. Brimming with love-hate, Theodora rushes to New York
and encamps in his apartment, the incarnation of his wildest dreams:
a vamp! But he preferred the mild Theodora to the wild one. This
dilemma is resolved when Theodora returns to Lynnville—a return
that the local editor builds into a triumph à la *Hail the Conquering
Hero*—and her aunts receive her with chastised warmth. (The film's
plot was the unofficial source for a Carry-On style comedy of the
late fifties called *Please Turn Over.*)

The story, especially as breathlessly retold here, is hardly as promising as its execution reveals. Buchman was a master at constructing
dialogue that delighted the audience while it developed the characters. This sounds like a definition of good screenwriting; if so,
good screenwriting is a rarer art than it should be. One has only to

compare Buchman's treatment of the extraordinarily dangerous *Mr. Smith* plot with Robert Riskin's attempt in the less audacious *Mr. Deeds*. It's the difference between manipulation (Riskin) and massage (Buchman), heat and warmth, the stark and the subtle, the grating and the graceful.

It's also the difference between Gary Cooper's naïve belligerence as Deeds and James Stewart's innocent perseverance as Smith. As fine as Buchman's major scripts are, the films made from them would hardly be as likable if they had not starred Irene Dunne, James Stewart, Robert Montgomery (*Here Comes Mr. Jordan*), and Cary Grant and Ronald Colman (*The Talk of the Town*). Ultimately, Irene Dunne is the reason for savoring *Theodora Goes Wild*. She provides an elegant tour de farce worthy of comparison with the best comic performances of Jean Arthur, Carole Lombard, Katharine Hepburn, and Rosalind Russell. And she set herself a particularly difficult challenge because, although the script isn't terribly "busy," her acting is. Unlike Arthur and Lombard, who carry *Easy Living* and *Hands Across the Table* with effortless charm, or Hepburn, who dominates *Pat and Mike* almost by an act of will, or Russell, who knows just when to break the furious pace of *His Girl Friday* with a winsome whine and when to stay out of the way of Howard Hawks's steamrolling direction, Miss Dunne holds *Theodora* together with a combination of star quality and a rich anthology of behavioral nuances. In her "seduction" of the unwary wolf Douglas, the execution of every raised eyebrow, every flirtatious hand gesture, every vocal modulation, every subtlety shifting mood, shows an awareness of ability and limitation, of timing and precision that evokes Hepburn's brilliance in the golf-store sequence of *Pat and Mike*. Buchman's script was crucial to the success of *Theodora Goes Wild*—certainly Miss Dunne could build a more coherent performance on the Theodora skeleton than she was able to do with Ray Schmidt in *Back Street*, just as John Gielgud could do more with *Hamlet* than with *Home*—but, whereas Buchman's conception of Theodora and his development of her milieu make the film lively, Miss Dunne's performance makes it live.

Mr. Smith Goes to Washington (1939)

One can easily imagine *Mr. Smith Goes to Washington* being cursed with the fate of so many other unofficial sequels of distin-

guished films: as *The Bells of St. Mary's* was to *Going My Way,* or
as *Passage to Marseille* was to *Casablanca,* the picture could have
been no more than a pallid imitation—and a pilfering exploitation
—of *Mr. Deeds Goes to Town,* with the usual slackening of creative energy in writing, direction, and acting. But the meeting of
Buchman's sensitivity and Capra's sensibility proved beneficial for
all concerned. The film is easily the high point of Capra's social
trilogy (*Mr. Deeds, Mr. Smith, Meet John Doe*). And its distinction is clearly attributable to Buchman—or at least to the sparks
his script struck with Capra and his cast—fitting securely within the
confines of Buchman's own social trilogy of *Theodora Goes Wild,*
Mr. Smith, and (in collaboration with Irwin Shaw) *The Talk of the
Town.* The Capra-Riskin streak of smug bullying, which fatally infected Longfellow Deeds and John Doe, and barely missed incapaci-
tating the stronger Peter Warne of *It Happened One Night,* is
transformed here into Capra-Buchman benignity and moral clarity.
By fleshing out the same sort of characters whom Riskin treated
with the contempt of morality-play simplicity, and by giving them
pasts and presence instead of letting them stew in the juices of their
respective humors, Buchman glides almost serenely through a plot
pocked with treacherous land mines, and ends up with his character—his protagonist—essentially uncompromised by the tyranny
of Capra's incorrigibly lovable majority.

All the *Mr. Deeds* pitfalls are enlarged, in accordance with the
unwritten law governing sequels: take everything successful in the
first picture and do it over, only more so. Once again the rube with
his rural rubrics does battle against the sinners and their city cynicism. Once again the Forces of Evil are etched in so much Goya-
esque venom that vanquishing them seems an impossible task. Once
again Our Hero tries to resolve philosophical differences with "a
sock in the jaw." Once again he is baited by a wicked Woman From
The City, whom he reforms into a Good Girl and takes as an ally.
Once again he is converted by his newfound madonna from passivist
into activist. Once again a roomful of sympathetic spectators act as
our surrogate audience during the final confrontation; indeed,
through them Capra orchestrates and conducts the feelings he wants
his movie audience to share. And once again the denouement rests
not on the will of the majority, but on the ability of that majority to
convey and impose its will on an elected representative—a three-

man panel of judges in *Mr. Deeds,* a corrupt but ultimately compassionate Senator in *Mr. Smith.*

Without distorting these Capran conventions, Buchman manages to enrich them through counterpoint detail, and thus to ennoble them. In *Mr. Deeds,* New York acts as a convenient contrast to Longfellow's New England village; but it can boast no greater icon of America's historical imperative than Grant's tomb. *Mr. Smith*'s Washington is a far more devious paradox. When Jeff arrives in the Capital it seems the apotheosis of his patriotism; but he soon comes to realize the gap between ideals—expressed in history books, tour guides' spiels, and monuments' inscriptions—and the facts of political life in Washington. Much of the film's power derives from the enormity of the corruption Smith faces. Boss Jim Taylor is not simply an extension of the character Edward Arnold had been portraying, with varying degrees of sympathy, for a decade; and Senator Paine is more than just the stooge of a capitalist tycoon. The film dared to characterize the Senate as a corrupt club, and to affix Jeff's state with accusations of a boss rule that controlled industry, the press, the governor, the state legislature, and both U.S. Senators.

His Girl Friday, released within a few months of *Mr. Smith,* took the immorality of politics and the press in stride; indeed, the film was a paean to the consummate style of corruption. When Ralph Bellamy wandered into Hildy Johnson's life, we knew he wouldn't be happy until he returned to Albany and the quiet life with his mother. James Stewart is far more naïve than Bellamy. His outlook amounts to criminal innocence, at least when faced with the complexities and compromises of the "grownup" world in Washington. But Stewart has more going for him than misdirected love for a tough-girl reporter: he has a child's idealism, a faith in Abraham Lincoln which encourages his belief that ideals can be transmitted into effective energy—and star billing.

This last quality isn't proposed cynically. It just means that the problem in *Mr. Smith* is "How can a nice-guy Boy Ranger reform a complacent Congress?" We never believed that Ralph Bellamy was a serious contender for Hildy's hand, except as a personification of her weariness with Walter Burns. In *His Girl Friday* love and opportunism play to a satisfying standoff, whereas in *Mr. Smith* Good must grind Evil into the dirt with the heel of its square-toed shoe. If, in the cynical seventies, we can respond to the two films with equal affection, then attention must surely be paid to Buchman's and Capra's talent for making the nearly incredible triumph of goodness seem as appealing as Hildy Johnson's surrender to stylish duplicity.

Boss Jim Taylor is powerful because he knows how to use the weakness of his associates. Everybody wants something, and Taylor can get something for everybody—for a price; the price is fealty. Senator Paine can be seen as a Taylor pawn, because he *is* one; but he can also be seen as a reasonable exponent of the practical politician, as a painter who renounces the garish chiaroscuro of black-and-white idealism for the pastels of the possible. "I compromised —yes!" he tells the crestfallen Jeff. "So that all these years I could stay in that Senate—and serve the people in a thousand honest ways." Robert Kennedy was merely living this credo when he campaigned as a conservative in the 1968 Indiana primary so that he might become a liberal President. The fact that Paine is an important cog in the Taylor machine tends to obscure the common sense of his argument. Jeff is, after all, a one-issue Senator: his proposal for a National Boys' Camp virtually defines his political program. Ambiguities are suspect; compromises are sinful. But Jeff's crusade would have meant nothing as a challenge to Senate duplicity if it had not succeeded. That it finally did succeed is attributable not to the effect Jeff's filibuster had on the Senate majority—there's no suggesting that it had any effect at all—but to Senator Paine's surrogate parenthood of this gawky idealist.

The argument of the entire film is for the purity of childhood and against the tarnished pragmatism of "grownups." Jeff, the publisher of *Boy Stuff,* is a hero to thousands of kids in his state. The suggestion to appoint him Senator derives from the seven children of the state's Humphreyesque governor (whose name, oddly enough, is Hubert "Happy" Hopper). His main support during the showdown, aside from Saunders, comes from the Senate page boys. When Taylor buys off the state's newspapers, the kids publish a special edition of *Boy Stuff* to spread the word of Jeff's filibuster.

The film's concurrent theme—of Jeff as an overgrown boy himself, and Paine as his ultimate father figure—is planted early, when Jeff reveals that his father and Paine had been close friends and colleagues: "a struggling editor and a struggling lawyer." His father's campaign against a powerful syndicate led to his death, "slumped over his desk . . . shot in the back." Senator Paine's past gives him a moral resonance which, as with Rick Blaine (and, for that matter,

Rains' own Captain Renault) in *Casablanca,* suggest hope for a climactic reformation.

Throughout the filibuster Jeff's only friend on the Senate floor is the languid President of the Senate; in a conference with Paine and a pride of hostile Senators, he says, "If you ask me, that young fellow's making a whole lot of sense." It is not until Taylor, who also seems to own Western Union, floods Washington with thousands of telegrams denouncing Jeff's behavior, and Jeff faints under the weight of what seems like popular adversity to his idealism, that Senator Paine reclaims his honorary parenthood and resolves to end his life just as Jeff's father's had been ended—with a bullet.

His suicide attempt must be unsuccessful, of course, because Jeff needs vindication. Paine's guilt can be purged only by purging himself from the Senate. "Expel *me!* Not him! Me! Willet Dam is a fraud. It's a crime against the people who sent me here—and *I* committed it. Every word that boy said is the truth!" This brief peroration reconciles "honor" with "power" even as it reunites "father" and "son." It is as emotionally satisfying as Paine's Declaration of Ambiguities had been intellectually convincing. But the essence of Capracorn was always the triumph of emotion over intellect. Buchman's achievement was in placing coherent dramatic reins on the director's rather base instincts about populist manipulation.

Once the antagonists' audacity has been established, the other Capra dicta fall into place without too much character distortion. Deeds' compulsion to knock out anyone whose motives he either condemns or can't understand is reduced to a flurry of punches Jeff Smith aims at the Washington press corps; he later atones. Jean Arthur is far less responsible for Jeff's humiliation than she had been for Longfellow's; here she merely chides him a bit and sends him into the clutches of Senator Paine's snide daughter. And once she begins to back Jeff, she also mobilizes the rest of the press corps in support.

Jeff, clearly, needs support, for he is opposed by the entire Senate in the wake of Paine's denunciation of him as a "contemptible young man" with a "contemptible scheme." Indeed, the other ninety-five Senators walk out on Jeff, thereby setting the stage for some historic (and occasionally hysterical) histrionics. Gary Cooper would simply have been embarrassing here. Until this role, Stewart's performances had relied as much as Cooper's on understatement; but unlike Cooper, whose heroic face and athletic form suggested tacit intimidation of anyone foolish enough to mistake pithiness for prissiness, Stewart had an awkward, gosling quality that made him more vulnerable, and thus more attractive, than Cooper.

In *Mr. Smith* this vulnerability lends a futile, winsome air to his attack on "Nosey," the aptly named reporter. And, notwithstanding Buchman's considerable talent for flesh-and-blood characterizations, this defenselessness is perhaps the most crucial element in making the frenetic climax believable. A more heroic persona would have made for a less heroic performance. One always suspected a concave chest beneath Stewart's ill-tailored suits; perhaps that accounted for his being billed second or third on the credit sheets, even after *Mr. Smith*. (It took a noble war record to convince moguls and viewers that he deserved star status.) There was, to be sure, the faintest trace of a know-it-all hidden in that know-nothing smile, which colored his roles whether he was playing a plunderer (as in *The Philadelphia Story*) or a blunderer (*Vivacious Lady*, for example). But this whiff of sophistication was redolent more of the cracker-barrel savant than of the beer-barrel wise guy. Its only effect on *Mr. Smith* was positive, for it gave his character the personal strength to back up his moral convictions.

This forcefulness was latent at best in Stewart's early roles; it is to Capra's eternal credit that he recognized the actor's potential, and it is to Buchman's greater glory that he converted this potential into action. The final process—turning the actions of Buchman's script into a sublimely sustained piece of acting—is a mystery that can be appreciated but not explained, since it resides somewhere in the rainbow arc between James Stewart's ineffable performance and its profound incarnation on the porous wall of the movie screen.

CASEY ROBINSON
(1903–   )

1928 BARE KNEES (Erle C. Kenton) titles
      CHORUS KID (Howard Bretherton) titles
      HAWK'S NEST (Benjamin Christenson) titles
      TURN BACK THE HOURS (Howard Bretherton) titles
      UNITED STATES SMITH (Joseph Henaberry) titles
      MAD HOUR (Joseph C. Boyle) co-titles
      WATERFRONT (William A. Seiter) co-titles
      DO YOUR DUTY (William Beaudine) co-titles
      COMPANIONATE MARRIAGE (Erle C. Kenton) titles
      THE PRIVATE LIFE OF HELEN OF TROY (Alexander
      Korda) co-titles
      HEAD OF THE FAMILY (Joseph C. Boyle) titles
      OUT OF THE RUINS (John Francis Dillon) titles
1929 TIMES SQUARE (Joseph C. Boyle) titles
1930 THE SQUEALER (Harry Joe Brown) continuity
1931 LAST PARADE (Erle C. Kenton) story
1932 LUCKY DEVILS (Ralph Ince) co-story
      IS MY FACE RED? (William A. Seiter) screenplay
1933 STRICTLY PERSONAL (Ralph Murphy) co-dialogue
      I LOVE THAT MAN (Harry Joe Brown) co-dialogue
      SONG OF THE EAGLE (Ralph Murphy) co-adaptation
      GOLDEN HARVEST (Ralph Murphy) adaptation
1934 EIGHT GIRLS IN A BOAT (Richard Wallace) co-screenplay
      SHE MADE HER BED (Ralph Murphy) co-screenplay
      HERE COMES THE GROOM (Edward Sedgwick) co-screen-
      play
1935 McFADDEN'S FLATS (Ralph Murphy) co-screenplay
      I FOUND STELLA PARRISH (Mervyn LeRoy) screenplay
      CAPTAIN BLOOD (Michael Curtiz) screenplay

284

1936   I MARRIED A DOCTOR (Archie Mayo) screenplay
        HEARTS DIVIDED (Frank Borzage) co-screenplay
        GIVE ME YOUR HEART (Archie Mayo) screenplay
        STOLEN HOLIDAY (Michael Curtiz) screenplay
1937   CALL IT A DAY (Archie Mayo) screenplay
        IT'S LOVE I'M AFTER (Archie Mayo) screenplay
        TOVARICH (Anatole Litvak) screenplay
1938   FOUR'S A CROWD (Michael Curtiz) co-screenplay
1939   DARK VICTORY (Edmund Goulding) screenplay
        YES, MY DARLING DAUGHTER (William Keighley) screen-
        play
        THE OLD MAID (Edmund Goulding) screenplay
1940   ALL THIS AND HEAVEN TOO (Anatole Litvak) screenplay
1941   MILLION DOLLAR BABY (Curtis Bernhardt) co-screenplay
        ONE FOOT IN HEAVEN (Irving Rapper) screenplay
        KING'S ROW (Sam Wood) screenplay
1942   NOW, VOYAGER (Irving Rapper) screenplay
1943   THIS IS THE ARMY (Michael Curtiz) co-screenplay
1944   PASSAGE TO MARSEILLE (Michael Curtiz) co-screenplay
        DAYS OF GLORY (Jacques Tourneur) screenplay, producer
        THE RACKET MAN (D. Ross Lederman) story, co-screenplay
1945   THE CORN IS GREEN (Irving Rapper) co-screenplay
        SARATOGA TRUNK (Sam Wood) screenplay
1947   DESIRE ME (George Cukor, Mervyn LeRoy) adaptation
        THE MACOMBER AFFAIR (Zoltan Korda) co-screenplay, co-
        producer
1949   FATHER WAS A FULLBACK (John M. Stahl) co-screenplay
1950   UNDER MY SKIN (Jean Negulesco) screenplay, producer
        TWO FLAGS WEST (Robert Wise) screenplay, producer
1952   DIPLOMATIC COURIER (Henry Hathaway) co-screenplay,
        producer
        THE SNOWS OF KILIMANJARO (Henry King) screenplay
1954   A BULLET IS WAITING (John Farrow) co-screenplay
        THE EGYPTIAN (Michael Curtiz) co-screenplay
1956   WHILE THE CITY SLEEPS (Fritz Lang) screenplay
1959   THIS EARTH IS MINE (Henry King) screenplay, producer
1964   THE SON OF CAPTAIN BLOOD (Tullio Demichelli) story,
        screenplay

Casey Robinson was Warner Brothers' master of the art—or craft
—of adaptation. Whether the property was a five-hundred-page
novel in need of drastic scenario surgery (*Now, Voyager*) or a so-

phisticated transatlantic comedy hit requiring the gentlest of nudges past the censors and into the mass-audience heart (*Tovarich*), Robinson brought to the task a chameleonic ability to "adapt" himself to the inner rhythms of the author's prose, as well as a remarkable sense for editing plots and dialogue into entertaining screenplays. It may be only "a talent to amuse"; it may be one of the cinema's minor, neglected art forms. But it is certainly one that has, with too few exceptions (Anthony Shaffer's adaptation of *Frenzy*), vanished along with the Golden Age of Studio Hollywood.

Robinson wrote his best scripts for Warners' romantics-in-spite-of-themselves, Errol Flynn and Bette Davis. (His temperament was less disposed to the studio's house existentialist, Humphrey Bogart, as *Passage to Marseilles* indicates.) Robinson's puckish wit, which even the conventions of a Bette Davis melodrama could not repress, found perhaps its aptest expression in Flynn, whose own good humor made his impudence delectable and his occasional self-righteousness tolerable. In the Robinson characters—and this applies especially to Davis and Flynn—a sense of humor meant a self-critical, but not masochistic, sense of proportion. When needed, they could step back and describe themselves, accurately, to others (as Davis does to George Brent in a brilliant *Dark Victory* monologue). This ironic detachment kept their sense of destiny, of superiority, under control and allowed the moviegoer both to idolize and to identify with them. At the same time, it made the films they appeared in more enjoyable than either the stodgy MGM swashbucklers or the many tearjerkers, of every studio, whose heroines lacked the neurotic resilience of the characters Robinson wrote (or rewrote) for Bette Davis.

Captain Blood (1935)

Robinson had been credited for toiling on eight "B" pictures at Paramount when Harry Joe Brown, who had directed a Robinson script there, took a producer's job at Warners and hired his old colleague. Their first effort, *I Found Stella Parrish*, was negligible, but their second, *Captain Blood*, proved crucial in turning Warners from a sausage factory, marketing low budgets and contemporary themes, into a more exclusive delicatessen, with a wide variety of genres on a more opulent scale. *Captain Blood* was the studio's first swashbuckler, Flynn's first starring role, the first pairing (of nine) for Flynn and Olivia deHavilland, and Robinson's first hit picture. It established for all time the image of the reckless, roguish hero, which Flynn was charmed—or condemned—to live out.

As Miss deHavilland herself has perceptively observed, Flynn's character was a boy's ideal of the revolutionary—handsome men, beautiful ladies, impeccably evil villains, clean-cut swordsmanship that relied more on grace than on force, the return to power of the rightful monarch, the revolutionary's return to the simple life—that surely helped a fated generation of teen-age boys prepare for battle against Hitler, the ultimate bad guy. In the two quintessential Flynn-deHavilland romances, *Captain Blood* and *The Adventures of Robin Hood* (the latter written by Norman Reilly Raine and Seton I. Miller), heroes Blood and Hood are interested less in revolution than in restoration. In *Captain Blood,* James II, the hated Catholic king, is considered a cruel usurper of the throne, ripe for a little selective resistance and benign anarchy. But, come the "Glorious Revolution" of 1688 (which actually restored the crown to a Protestant, albeit Dutch, head), Captain Blood renounces his title and his piracy; England is safe again.

The Raine-Miller script for *The Adventures of Robin Hood* cleaves remarkably close to Robinson's model. This time, Bad Prince John is the usurper. Robin steals from the rich and gives to the poor only until the true king, Richard the Lionhearted, returns from the Crusades. Then Robin, an undercover knight, returns to his castle with Maid Marian, and his Merry Men presumably go back to their jolly serfdom with a song in their hearts and a few vagrant coins in their purses. Peter Blood, a doctor, is also a nobleman of sorts; at Warners, it would seem, a popular revolution was O.K. as long as it was led—and ultimately subdued—by an upper-class liberal. In a way, the Flynn pictures were cheerful, remote versions of the studio's solemn social biographies of Zola and Juárez, with every injustice assuaged by a Flynn grin, and every political ambiguity resolved in a duel to the death between our winsomely arch hero and the arch-villain Basil Rathbone. Audiences of the thirties and the seventies could respond to Flynn's revolutions, because they were grounded in glistening, bloodless nostalgia—which Robinson himself must have responded to, since he contributed, thirty years later, to a film called *The Son of Robin Hood* starring Sean Flynn, the actor's son.

It's Love I'm After (1937)

This was the first of Robinson's six Bette Davis vehicles between 1937 and 1945 (the others were *Dark Victory, The Old Maid, All This and Heaven Too, Now Voyager,* and *The Corn Is Green;* on all but the last, Robinson was the only screenwriter of record). In a busy plot with some perplexing premonitions of *Casablanca,* Leslie Howard and Davis are a star acting team who play Romeo and Juliet on stage and the Bickersons off. Cow-eyed Olivia deHavilland moons over Howard who, in order to disillusion her so he can marry Davis, tries every shtick in the Samuel French catalogue— including a feigned rape, which deHavilland foils by encouraging it! Nothing works until an inadvertent screen scene convinces Olivia that Patric Knowles is the *jeune premier* for her, thus enabling Petruchio and Kate to reunite for a final lovers' row.

This is all so theatrical, and so actable, that it comes as a surprise to learn that Robinson's adroit screenplay was based not on a Broadway hit, but on a sketchy screen story by Maurice Hanline. His dialogue, especially in the early duels between Howard and Davis, is agreeably witty, with none of that sense of straining for a punchline that identifies too many stage comedies when transferred to the screen. Archie Mayo's direction turns a bit strident toward the middle—second-act slump?—and deHavilland is such a marplot that the incessant ingenuousness of her character threatens not only to mar the plot but to mire it in a welter of boring complications. When Davis re-enters, however, the lady saves the play as well as the day. Davis fits into this Lombard-Hepburn role with astonishing snugness. She is bitchy here, but not yet the bitch goddess whom Robinson and others will develop from her next film (*Jezebel*) onward and, ultimately, downward through the forties.

Now, Voyager (1942)

In adapting Olive Higgins Prouty's novel to the demands of Hal Wallis and Bette Davis, Robinson pulled off a fantastic juggling act with elements that included mother hatred, adoptive-mother love, three nervous breakdowns, two ill-starred engagements, one adulterous affair, one platonic relationship, one huge, hostile family, and enough peripheral characters, each with his or her own idiosyncrasies, to dazzle Charles Dickens. (Imagine this story being remade by Robert Bolt and David Lean. It would take three years to write, four years to film, and five hours to watch.)

Robinson managed it by some marvelously precise plot-parsing and reams of terse, witty dialogue. He traced Davis's metamorphoses —from a neurotic spinster with a domineering mother; through a stage as the *soignée* Boston belle, dispatching old enemies and new beaux with a cool that artfully conceals her lingering vulnerability; and finally, absolving herself from the guilty suspicion that she provoked her mother's death, to the point where she is mature enough to win the confidence and become the true mother of her lover's disturbed young daughter—all this with a sweep and compassion that Davis matches, and possibly surpasses, in her performance.

Nearly every major character in *Now, Voyager* is either a parent figure, a spouse figure, or a child figure—or a combination of all three. Davis's Charlotte Vale, for instance, is, at thirty-odd, still her mother's unwanted baby, as well as her lover's mistress and the lover's daughter's surrogate mother. Claude Rains, the psychiatrist, is both father to Davis and, if not a lover, certainly a very affectionate friend, just as Paul Henreid, the married lover, acts as both psychiatrist and father figure.

Even the love Davis and Henreid share is a schizophrenic business. Davis's equation for love could be oversimplified as "sex + friendship = happiness." For her and Henreid, the sexual love they experienced on an aptly named "pleasure cruise" is only "part of the happiness," according to Henreid. When Davis's therapeutic love for Henreid's unwanted daughter—a palpable image of her own painful childhood—reunites the lovers, Davis decides that sex is the less crucial factor in the equation, and that they can retain hold on "their" child only by renouncing sex. It may be Davis's Back Bay puritanism that makes sex, however lustrous, seem as cold and remote as the moon; but it is her new maturity that allows her to accept a continuing, loving relationship with a married man—a relationship as sparkling, as overwhelming as a galaxy of stars. Her final line ("Don't let's ask for the moon when we have the stars") is less a cop-out line imposed by Hollywood censors than a single thread of dialogue that ties together *Now, Voyager*'s complex weave of plots and themes.

In both script and performance, there are no waste motions, no false appeals to sympathy; yet no hesitation in tackling situations which, if poorly realized, might have evoked snickers and not tears.

The entire film is a tightrope walk above a tub of scalding bathos, but Davis, Robinson, and director Irving Rapper pull the act off with dignity intact. Davis's performance is so "right," technically and emotionally, that her character becomes morally right, with the adulterers happily together at the final fade-out. They are united as much by the smoldering memory of their affair (adroitly symbolized in Henreid's audacious cigarette-lighting ploy) as by the cleansing presence of "their" daughter. If writing scripts like this was proof of Casey Robinson's craftsmanship, getting them past the Hays Office gives evidence of some kind of artistry.

Morrie Ryskind
(1895–   )

1929 THE COCOANUTS (Joseph Santley and Robert Florey) screenplay, from his and George S. Kaufman's play
1930 ANIMAL CRACKERS (Victor Heerman) co-screenplay, co-dialogue, from his and George S. Kaufman's play
1931 PALMY DAYS (A. Edward Sutherland) co-screenplay, co-dialogue, from his play
1935 A NIGHT AT THE OPERA (Sam Wood) co-story, co-screenplay
       CEILING ZERO (Howard Hawks) co-screenplay (uncredited)
1936 MY MAN GODFREY (Gregory La Cava) co-screenplay
       RHYTHM ON THE RANGE (Norman Taurog) co-adaptation
1937 STAGE DOOR (Gregory La Cava) co-screenplay
1938 ROOM SERVICE (William A. Seiter) screenplay
       THERE'S ALWAYS A WOMAN (Alexander Hall) co-screenplay
1939 MAN ABOUT TOWN (Mark Sandrich) screenplay
1941 PENNY SERENADE (George Stevens) screenplay
       LOUISIANA PURCHASE (Irving Cummings) from his and B. G. DeSylva's musical play.
1943 CLAUDIA (Edmund Goulding) screenplay
1945 WHERE DO WE GO FROM HERE? (Gregory Ratoff) co-story, screenplay
1946 HEARTBEAT (Sam Wood) adaptation

Although Morrie Ryskind co-wrote four Marx Brothers epics (two as plays and two as films), the domineering personality of George S. Kaufman inevitably cast Ryskind in the role of silent partner. Consequently, his influence on *The Cocoanuts, Animal Crackers,* and *A Night at the Opera,* while undisputed, is difficult to distinguish; and Ryskind remains, undoubtedly to his chagrin, an enigmatic force on these films, a self-effacing I. A. L. Diamond to Kaufman's bilious and urbane Billy Wilder. Perhaps this explains the success with which Ryskind adapted himself to the collaborative frustrations of Hollywood moviemaking—especially with Gregory La Cava and George Stevens—while Kaufman returned only to direct Charles MacArthur's *The Senator Was Indiscreet,* with its perverse similarities to the torrid love affair Mary Astor recorded in her notorious diary. By this time (1947), Ryskind had retired to devote his time to anti-Marxist causes and columns—a pursuit which, twenty years earlier, he and Kaufman might have found ideal for burlesque by those other, anarchic Marxes.

My Man Godfrey (1936)

Gregory La Cava's association with Morrie Ryskind (on two pictures) was more fruitful and certainly longer than any ties the director made with the studio bosses with whom he feuded constantly. Each of the seven La Cava films beginning with *Gallant Lady* in 1933 and ending with *Stage Door* in 1937 was distributed by a different company; indeed, he ran through every one of the "Big Eight" but Warner Brothers. (Imagine how factory boss Jack Warner would have reacted to the independent intransigence of renegade La Cava!) It's not that his films weren't popular—*She Married Her Boss, My Man Godfrey,* and *Stage Door* were especially so—just that they weren't block-bustin' enough for studio executives to forget their vindictiveness and put up with the firebrand. And so, rather like the homosexual James Whale, La Cava was retired early from his trade for personal reasons.

He and Ryskind worked together at the peak of their respective reputations in Hollywood; *My Man Godfrey* and *Stage Door* were nominated for hosts of awards. Ryskind lost out both times to wordy Warners biopics, although La Cava was chosen as Best Director by the New York Film Critics Circle. Today, Ryskind's importance rests more on Marx Brothers farces in the early years and well-wrought weepies (*Penny Serenade* and *Claudia*) in the forties than on the bizarre La Cava films, while La Cava's residence within spitting distance of the auteurist's Pantheon remains a mystery. The inspired improvisation La Cava's admirers detect in his work is surely more strained and less restrained than that of such masters as Capra and McCarey; one thinks of Frank Tashlin. Even the comic pacing, which is admittedly whirlwind in *Stage Door*, takes its cue in *My Man Godfrey* from the stagy, wait-for-the-laugh tempo Sam Wood imposed on *A Night at the Opera*.

This is one screwball comedy in which almost everyone seems genuinely crazy—not nutty, not naughty, not even screwy, but really insane. And La Cava's matter-of-fact *mise-en-scène* imparts a kind of documentary detachment to the film. You get the feeling psychosis is being rouged up as humor. The screwball genre occupied a halfway house between knockabout farce and the more genteel brands of romantic comedy. So the slow, measured pace—not only *after* punchlines but before and during them—seems cruel here. We're to accept the Bullock family (Carole Lombard, Alice Brady, Eugene Pallette, and the rest) as potential human beings, a demand never made on us on behalf of Groucho, Harpo, and Chico; at the same time, we're led along with the attitudes and dialogue of farce. With these characters and this material, it's too much to ask.

Ryskind's adaptation of Eric Hatch's *Liberty* magazine story shifts its emphasis from the lunacy at "1101 Fifth Avenue" (the story's title) to the one sane character in it—the Brahmin/bum/ butler played by William Powell. If La Cava had directed the actors less pathologically, and paced the film to stress the human instead of the animal element personified by Mischa Auer's monkey business around the living room, it would be more difficult to recognize *My Man Godfrey* for what it is: a manic Messiah story, a very strange *Strange Cargo*. To put it bluntly, Godfrey is God come to free the people from selfishness and pretense. The family is lurching to hell on the wings of blustering impotence (Mr. Bullock), prodigality (Mrs. Bullock), vengefulness (Cornelia), and ill-directed whimsy (Irene). By the end—with La Cava's camera placed just below eye level and tilting slightly up at Godfrey with suitable reverence—the Boston Savior has transformed and transfigured the entire family with a *volte-face* swiftness that must have had Dudley Nichols drooling with envy. Mr. Bullock is made solvent, Mrs. Bullock learns the value of thrift, Cornelia is chastened, and Mischa Auer is kicked out. In return everyone falls in love with him and cries when he goes. Irene (Carole Lombard) is Powell's co-star, so she gets to marry him at the end.

All this is much more palatable in Ryskind's script, which, like a few misdirected comedies mentioned in this volume, reads better than it plays. La Cava's company delivers the lines as if every prospective moviegoer were functionally deaf, creating the impression that we are in Warrendale and not a Fifth Avenue mansion. In print the characters are actually likable, and so we are encouraged to laugh with them, rather than being dared to laugh at them. The script appeals to our sympathies, the film to our antagonisms; the script amuses us, the film alienates us.

My Man Godfrey plays like an early, primitive ancestor of the comedy-horror movie *Morgan* (which in plot derives more from *The Awful Truth*). Indeed, its maddest, yet most delightful moment comes when Mischa Auer apotheosizes the film's insanity in a gorrilla ballet that approaches the sublimity of Chaplin's global juggling act in *The Great Dictator;* both express, in the most graceful, entrancing terms, the ecstasy and artistry of madness—the kind of madness that would have made a more satisfying subject for La Cava and Ryskind. As Auer lopes over sofas and climbs the French windows, Irene weeps and Mrs. Bullock titters and preens, with the rest of the company directing philistine comments toward the "performer." Mr. Bullock tells Auer, in disgust, "Why don't you stop imitating a gorilla and try to imitate a man?" and Mrs. Bullock, ever the dilettante, replies, "You wouldn't know an artist if one came up and bit you." Here in two lines is the theme of a film that, unlike *My Man Godfrey,* might have investigated the liberating appeal of insanity, instead of treating mere eccentricity so clinically that it can be passed off as a grating version of the real thing.

Penny Serenade (1941)

Two *farceurs* met one day and decided to make a weepie. In itself this fact is not surprising: Hecht, Sturges, Lubitsch, and McCarey were a few of the many comedy writers and directors who had holidayed among the hankies. But that Morrie Ryskind (the Marx Brothers gagman) and George Stevens (honor graduate of the School of Laurel and Hardy) should produce, in *Penny Serenade,* the definitive Hollywood sentimental comedy-drama—*this* merits some investigation.

Both Ryskind and Stevens were midway down a road that led from elegant slapstick for both men to punditry (for Ryskind) and pretentiousness (for Stevens). An intersection of their careers ten years earlier would undoubtedly have resulted in an artificial, heart-less weepie of the kind Ben Hecht too often delivered. If they had met in the fifties, their concoction would have bubbled with right-wing politics and simmered with agonizingly long takes. In either decade, Ryskind and Stevens would have been simply too far removed from characters they had to sympathize with at first for the audience to believe in at last. *Penny Serenade* does resound with both echoes from the pair's earlier comedies and premonitions of their later, separate but equal declines, but these reverberations contribute to a satisfying whole—indeed, they enrich it.

The weepie genre, which *Penny Serenade* snugly inhabits even as it transcends it, is one pocked with pitfalls; and the few film-makers who have mastered it—Leo McCarey (with Delmer Daves as his writer on *Love Affair* and *An Affair to Remember*), Casey Robinson (in his sappy-snappy Bette Davis scripts), and Douglas Sirk (in his elegant comic-strips on the spoils of success, with Ross Hunter and Rock Hudson)—seem to accomplish the feat by a combination of delicate finesse and sheer force of will. Respect for the genre was also important. But conviction on the part of a forties director doesn't necessarily guarantee convincingness for a seventies viewer. Not only are the genre's conventions subject to current derision, but the beliefs they upheld (mother love, constancy, the holy family) have grown senile along with the last generation that accepted them. In the forties, *Penny Serenade* reinforced popular prejudices; today, it antagonizes them. For the film to live as art, and not merely survive as a historical artifact, the same elements must be made to appeal to different audiences for different reasons.

If *Penny Serenade* succeeds today, it is because Ryskind and Stevens avoided some of the genre's dangers while confronting others head on. The almost monastic humorlessness that makes so many weepies perversely laughable is tempered here by occasional early-Ryskind one-liners ("I wish April was here—so I could get an advance on my December salary") and by set pieces that might have been plucked from one of Stevens' gentler Hal Roach comedies (such as the winning sequence, done in virtually one take, of crotchety old Edgar Buchanan showing Irene Dunne the intricacies of diaper-changing). Even the casting might constructively mislead an audience, since Cary Grant and Irene Dunne are identified primarily as light-comedy players. In fact, Stevens' pairing of these two resourceful, aggressive performers is no mere box-office strata-gem; faced with situations as cataclysmic as any in *Bringing Up Baby* or *Theodora Goes Wild,* Grant and Dunne can be expected to react—as they do react—with almost comic resilience.

When it comes to the delirious absurdities of plot and character required by the weepie, Ryskind and Stevens don't shirk. Poor Miss Dunne may have been crippled by a speeding car on her way to a skyscraper rendezvous in *Love Affair,* but that misfortune is a drop in the hankie compared with her suffering in *Penny Serenade.* As Donald Richie describes it in his adroit monograph on Stevens, "hundreds are destroyed in an earthquake so that Irene Dunne's miscarriage may be successfully accomplished." For Miss Dunne, it seems, Fate (Hollywood-style) was less an instrument of divine frustration than a weapon of directorial assault. Stevens' treatment of the earthquake scene is even more brutal than Richie's précis would suggest. As the beams of the newlyweds' Japanese home are crashing portentously around Miss Dunne, Stevens' camera dollies in on a treasured fortune-cookie paper that reads: "You will get your wish—A BABY." Another huge beam demolishes both the prediction and (off-camera, thankfully) Miss Dunne's reproductive organs, while the sound track groans with a particularly sickening, dubbed-in *THUD!* After this carnage, the audience—if not Grant and Dunne—can face the mere loss of a beloved, adopted child with an equanimity bordering on torpor. The earthquake provides the film's most lumbering omen of the symbolism whose triteness will deface some of Stevens' later work.

This said, I must point out that *Penny Serenade*'s other confrontations with the absurd are handled with either charming discretion or disarming forthrightness—and that these melodramatic highlights are saved from plummeting into soggy bathos by the quiet conviction Stevens, Ryskind, Grant, and Dunne bring to the connecting scenes. To be sure, "warmth" in a film such as this is more difficult to define than "heat" or "friction," and the critic who tries to establish "warmth" as a criterion for the weepie genre may be fairly accused of substituting total emotional immersion for disinterested analysis.

Charged with this, the critic could retort that Ryskind's "placing" of intense, marginally ludicrous scenes within the framework of an estranged wife's melancholy reverie gives them not only a dramatic distance that makes them acceptable but also a sense of pastness that makes them more poignant. The critic could argue that Grant's almost hysterical energy—exhilarating even when we expect it, as in *His Girl Friday*, but weird and astonishing in a melodramatic context—turns his all-stops-out plea for permanent custody of their adopted child from a potential disaster into one of the glories of actor's cinema. He might even be able to sneak in a word of praise for Stevens' caressing camerawork, which sleekly smoothes off the rough edges of Miss Dunne's sporadically abrasive presence.

But, valid as these defenses are, they serve mainly as rationalizations for a gut-and-heart response. It may be said that films whose premises must be taken on faith engender criticism whose arguments must be considered with charity. In the last analysis (or immersion), a film like *Penny Serenade* demands to be approached with a certain tolerance, if not sympathy, for its conventions and convictions. Within these conventions—which it shared with nearly every Hollywood film made before 1950—*Penny Serenade* created situations, characters, an entire milieu that emerges three decades later as a haven of believability and (damn it!) warmth. A *farceur*'s tears may be as ridiculous as his laughter is sublime, but in this case at least, Ryskind and Stevens showed how to walk a thin line between the two extremes with nothing but faith, talent, and amazing grace.

EDWIN JUSTUS MAYER

(1896–   )

1928 BLUE DANUBE (Paul Sloane) co-titles
      MIDNIGHT MADNESS (F. Harmon Wright) titles
      DEVIL DANCER (Fred Niblo) co-titles
      LOVE MART (George Fitzmaurice) titles
      WHIP WOMAN (Joseph C. Boyle) titles
      MANMADE WOMAN (Paul L. Stein) titles
1929 THE DIVINE LADY (Frank Lloyd) titles
      NED McCOBB'S DAUGHTER (William J. Cowen) titles
      SAL OF SINGAPORE (Howard Higgen) titles
      UNHOLY NIGHT (Lionel Barrymore) co-screenplay
      THE LOVES OF CASANOVA (Alexandre Volkoff and Ru-
      dolph Klein-Rogge) titles
1930 IN GAY MADRID (Robert Z. Leonard) co-screenplay, co-
      dialogue
      ROMANCE (Clarence Brown) co-screenplay, co-dialogue
      REDEMPTION (Fred Niblo) dialogue
      NOT SO DUMB (King Vidor) dialogue
      LADY OF SCANDAL (Sidney Franklin) co-dialogue
      OUR BLUSHING BRIDES (Harry Beaumont) co-dialogue
1931 NEVER THE TWAIN SHALL MEET (W. S. Van Dyke)
      screenplay, dialogue
      THE PHANTOM OF PARIS (John S. Robertson) co-dialogue
1932 MERRILY WE GO TO HELL (Dorothy Arzner) screenplay,
      dialogue
      WILD GIRL (Raoul Walsh) co-screenplay, co-dialogue
1933 TONIGHT IS OURS (Stuart Walker) screenplay, dialogue
1934 I AM SUZANNE (Rowland V. Lee) co-screenplay
      THE AFFAIRS OF CELLINI (Gregory La Cava) from his
      play, *The Firebrand*

THIRTY-DAY PRINCESS (Marion Gering) co-screenplay
HERE IS MY HEART (Frank Tuttle) co-screenplay
1935   SO RED THE ROSE (King Vidor) co-screenplay
PETER IBBETSON (Henry Hathaway) co-screenplay
1936   GIVE US THIS NIGHT (Alexander Hall) co-screenplay
WIVES NEVER KNOW (Elliott Nugent) co-screenplay (un-credited)
DESIRE (Frank Borzage) co-screenplay
'TIL WE MEET AGAIN (Robert Florey) co-screenplay
1938   THE BUCCANEER (Cecile B. De Mille) co-screenplay
1939   EXILE EXPRESS (Otis Garrett) story
MIDNIGHT (Mitchell Leisen) co-story
RIO (John Brahm) co-screenplay
1941   UNDERGROUND (Vincent Sherman) co-story
THEY MET IN BOMBAY (Clarence Brown) co-screenplay
1942   TO BE OR NOT TO BE (Ernst Lubitsch) screenplay
1945   A ROYAL SCANDAL (Otto Preminger) screenplay
MASQUERADE IN MEXICO (Mitchell Leisen) remake of *Midnight*
1958   THE BUCCANEER (Anthony Quinn) remake of the 1938 film

For those who have read or seen performed Mayer's 1930 play, *Children of Darkness,* any investigation of his movie work is bound to be an exercise in frustration. Many of the films he tailored to the demands of Paramount, Metro-Goldwyn-Mayer, Fox, and First National have moldered in their vaults, depriving historians of any chance for sympathetic revaluation. But, for the most part, even Mayer's most prestigious projects (*Romance, Desire, To Be Or Not to Be, A Royal Scandal*), are more flat than frothy. None of them can approach the mordant, inexhaustible wit of the play whose success raises our hopes for Mayer's Hollywood career—and perversely seals his doom. The one possible, if not plausible, exception is *Midnight*, a delightful enterprise in which Mayer's "co-story" credit seems properly subservient to the Brackett-and-Wilder screenplay and Mitchell Leisen's direction—and thus is hardly the ideal test case for this most distinctive playwright's authorship of a successful Hollywood film.

Desire (1936)

In *Desire*, director Frank Borzage, under the firm guidance of "producer" Ernst Lubitsch, reunited the stars as well as the general situation of *Morocco*: the spider-woman (Marlene Dietrich) traps the unwary fly (Gary Cooper) in a web of intrigue, only to be ensnared—and thus freed from further web-weaving—by the fly's straightforward devotion. By making the female a vessel of duplicity and the male a gullible innocent, filmmakers were twisting one Hollywood convention while submitting to another. True, it was the bad, or weak, man who was usually redeemed by the love of a good woman; but there was always a genre devoted to the Evil Woman, be she vamp or tramp. The teens had Theda Bara, the twenties boasted Garbo, and Dietrich held the fort until the arrival of Rita Hayworth, Ava Gardner, Gene Tierney, and the hordes of other dark-tressed *femmes fatales* in the forties *film noir*. What better, the Hays Office must have thought, than to put Dietrich in a film that reformed the formula even as it revamped the vamp.

Before accusing Lubitsch & Co. of collusion with the Decent but ruthless Legions who tried to impose a flaccid moral tone on Hollywood's directors and writers, I should mention that the bad-girl-good-boy comedy would become as conventional in the forties as the poor-girl-rich-boy theme was throughout the thirties. In 1940 and 1941, Barbara Stanwyck virtually defined the type, first foiling and then falling for such nice guys as Fred MacMurray (in *Remember the Night*), Henry Fonda (in *The Lady Eve*), and Gary Cooper (in *Ball of Fire* and *Meet John Doe*). But Stanwyck's film persona had not been irreconcilably welded to her face, as Dietrich's had after her films with Sternberg. Her Svengali had bathed those lapidary contours in an inevitable essence of fraudulence and frigidity, the sense of which tended to overwhelm mere vagaries of plot and character development. How to domesticate the Ice Tigress who had, only the year before *Desire,* convinced everyone within walking distance of a Paramount theater that "the devil is a woman"?

The solution concocted by Lubitsch, Borzage, Mayer, and co-scenarist Waldemar Young is, unfortunately, as trite as it is truistic: have her fall in love with a good man. Cooper had won her in *Morocco,* but her climactic march into the Sahara after Cooper was less the result of a conversion than the fulfillment of an obsession, the mingling of debasement and pride in equal and intriguing measures. As for Cooper, his Foreign Legionnaire was neither good man nor bad man. He was just a man, uncomplicated (indeed, largely undefined) and thus the perfect desert mirage-image for a lady's fixation. By 1936 Cooper had proved he could be amusing in dramatic roles (*Lives of a Bengal Lancer*) and stolid in comedy (*Design for Living*); and in his next film (*Mr. Deeds Goes to Town*) he would win lasting identification as the noble blunderer whose ineptitude was his salvation. Charm is an intangible, perhaps unarguable quality, so it would be useless for me to try to explain my feeling that Cooper was probably the least likable major romantic actor of the Hollywood thirties. In *Desire*, however, Cooper's galumphing directness works to the film's advantage, because it exposes Dietrich's redemption as a capitulation to the sheer tenacity of a good man, and not to goodness wrapped in the seductive camouflage of a charismatic charmer.

What does Edwin Justus Mayer, co-author of the *Desire* screenplay, have to do with these meandering thoughts on film acting and star personalities? Simply this: the success of any film is determined to a certain extent—sometimes minimal, sometimes crucial—not only by the ability of its actors but also by the audience's career associations with them. Cooper was both a "type" and a star. No matter how sophisticated Mayer's dialogue may have been, no matter how intricate the relationships between characters, both dialogue and motivation had to be filtered through Cooper's rather crude acting equipment. Actors may be mere marionettes manipulated by the director, but once a scene begins, the puppet pulls the strings.

Cooper is an automotive engineer on vacation in France and Spain. Dietrich is an "international jewel thief" who has just made off with a two-million-two-hundred-thousand-franc pearl necklace. (What Gaston, the *Trouble in Paradise* robber baron, would have given to work with her!) Dietrich believes she has met her final "mark" in Cooper, who will unknowingly smuggle the necklace across the Spanish border in his luggage. She knows men's vanity, so her ruse—to plant the necklace and then seduce him into comradeship long enough to retrieve it—pays off, for the moment. But Cooper knows his car: if it makes a sudden jolt, his suitcase will fall out. Thus, when Dietrich gets him to check the car trunk, and then abruptly drives off without him, his suitcase falls out, with the necklace still inside. Ingenious continental sophistication has lost a round to ingenuous American pragmatism, and all Dietrich is left with is that last refuge of the European *nouveau* poor: a sense of irony.

Cooper's verbal trademark in this pre-*Deeds* film was no longer "Huh?" and not yet "Yup!" It was a spasm of nervous laughter that endeared him to Dietrich even as it alienated him from me. Through most of *Desire*, Dietrich has to pretend she is in love with Cooper; toward the end, she has to pretend she does not love him. The former attitude provokes a fascinatingly unpleasant sequence in which Dietrich sings a seductive number that has the emboldened Cooper preening while trying not to be too irresistible. The latter has her feigning sleep while Cooper whispers his lumbering love to her. Sheer persistance has done her in. "I'm neither a king nor a prince nor a count," Cooper says as he proposes marriage with clumsy grandiloquence. "I'm not even an Elk." And Dietrich accepts—perhaps because, whatever Cooper is, he is neither a false prince nor a real crook.

Cooper's rival for Dietrich's hand (or at least for the stolen bracelet on her lovely wrist) is Carlos, her partner in *haut monde* chicanery and the one character in *Desire* who suggests any spiritual similarity whatever to Mayer's *Children of Darkness*. Misanthropic and misogynistic, elegant and totally without trust, Carlos is a less bombastic, less philosophical Count LaRuse. In a prettily conceived and realized parlor game, Carlos gracefully robs Cooper of the necklace which Dietrich has spent most of the film trying to retrieve. Was this because Carlos really wanted it, whereas Dietrich kept delaying the transaction so as to keep Cooper near her? Or was it simply because Carlos's cool, clean execution perfectly fitted his cold and cutting intention, whereas Dietrich's romantic ploys proved too subtle for an American clod?

Whatever the reason, Carlos, upon discovering Dietrich's affection for Cooper, surrenders her with a bit less generosity and *noblesse oblige* than Mayer's Count LaRuse had shown in conceding his working-class wench to a salivating pup. But then, the Count's pessimistic eloquence was always so passionate, so voluptuous, that one kept suspecting some altruistic emotions lying, dormant, within. Carlos had long since injected avarice into his veins, as surely as Dietrich had pocked her arms with other women's jewels. For him, possession of the stones and possessiveness of their wearer were one and the same. Devotion may have suffused Cooper; love may have touched Dietrich; but the only thing approaching emotion in Carlos

—the thing that makes this film glisten intermittently—is stone-cold desire.

To Be Or Not to Be (1942)

How was it that Edwin Justus Mayer, whose play *Children of Darkness* displayed an almost oppressively opulent and sustained wit, wrote so many mediocre films? *That* is the question. His movie work is so generally undistinguished, even when he collaborated with respectable directors, that *Desire* and *To Be Or Not to Be* could easily be ignored, or attributed to other writers, if he had not written that one perversely magnificent play. The very richness of its dialogue suggested a burgeoning fountainhead at its source, one that would not dry up quickly, even after the flood of epigrams and epithets that were mixed with the mineral stream of a mordant philosophy. Perhaps Mayer considered the play his one attempt to achieve the brittle, biting tone of Restoration comedy; and that, entrenched in Hollywood, he would concentrate on mimicking other verbal styles—Gary Cooper's drawl, for example, or Jack Benny's pusillanimous prissiness. The stars of *To Be Or Not to Be* are Benny and Carole Lombard, but the writer and director seemed less interested in turning Benny into a William Powell, or even a Fred MacMurray, than in making Lombard the visual equivalent of Mary Livingstone.

Lubitsch apparently thought that the Nazi threat was formidable enough to justify accommodating his style to the demands of a script that assaulted the pomposity of the Third Reich in brutal, often farcical terms. Irony was the first victim in Hollywood's propaganda film production. Directors seemed to want all moviegoers, not just the intelligent ones, to know how patriotic they were, so most of them ran a little scared—even Lubitsch. In a less critical time, he undoubtedly would have let nuance carry the day, as in the line a Jewish actor delivers to his colleague: "What you are, I wouldn't eat!" But in *To Be Or Not to Be* we get an explanatory riposte: "I resent your calling me a ham!"

No Lubitsch film is without its grace notes and, even here, the Lubitsch world is one in which a man may be considered a spy if he confesses ignorance of a famous actress, and in which anyone who would ask for a copy of *Anna Karenina* must be a patriot. But, in a typical Lubitsch film, manners equal morals, and taste verges on theology. In *To Be Or Not to Be,* the director set himself a more

difficult problem. Andrew Sarris has written: "For Lubitsch, it was
sufficient to say that Hitler had bad manners, and no evil was then
inconceivable." True enough. The most interesting character, however, is neither Hitler nor Jack Benny, as an improbable Polish
Hamlet with very bad manners, but Professor Alexander Siletsky,
whose manners are as impeccable as Herbert Marshall's, whose
mannerisms are as debonair as Melvyn Douglas's—but who, nevertheless, is a traitor and a Nazi. Was his grace, which is both assured
and reassuring, inborn (like Marshall's in *Angel*) or acquired (like
Marshall's in *Trouble in Paradise*)? Is he, in other words, an aristocrat or an actor? This is an important question, because the film
suggests that the European Theater of War could be saved by the
European theatrical tradition, by an acting troupe posing as Storm
Troopers. And yet Siletsky is far more accomplished an actor than
either Joseph Tura (the star of the troupe, and his rival in this
particular war game) or Jack Benny (who plays Tura).

Lubitsch solved this problem in *Trouble in Paradise* by bestowing
more genuine nobility on Marshall, the bogus baron, than on any
of the "genuine" nobles, even though Marshall learned the rules of
the game only so he could win by cheating. Siletsky is not redeemed
by any interior nobility. He is merely the supreme professional, eligi-
ble for our admiration on a technical level. Ultimately, he is destroyed by the most primitive of plot maneuvers: his ruse is discovered
and he is overwhelmed by force. For once, Lubtisch has opted for
matter over manner, for ideology over idiosyncrasy. Siletsky is evil
and Tura is good—or rather, Siletsky is a sophisticated gentleman
working for the Nazis and Tura is a vain buffoon working for the
Resistance—and, in a time threatened by Hitler's spectral presence,
that is enough. The closest Lubitsch and Mayer come to removing
Siletsky's impeccable mask is an analysis, by Carole Lombard, of the
traitor's signature. She combines graphology with genetics in re-
marking that "Alexander" is distorted by a cruel, sword-like "x"—
but "Siletsky" ends with a romantic flourish: "I only hope you live
up to that 'y.' " With that one exception, however, the filmmakers
allow our emotional attitude toward Siletsky to be determined only
by his political affiliation.

Once Siletsky is killed, Tura acquires some vicarious *savoir-faire*
by posing as the Professor in front of some Nazis. Here Sarris's dictum is more appropriate, though its fits perfectly only when stretched
with a little unconscious irony. Tura and his opponents share the

same vulnerable trait: vanity. If Tura has a slight edge, it is because he is imitating Siletsky's imitation of pedagogical refinement. Tura/ Benny is such an inadequate actor that his pose is often imperiled, and his vanity compels him to heap praises on "that great actor, Joseph Tura." Fortunately, the Nazi Occupiers are also insecure in their roles (fear of the *Führer* being endemic on both sides), and just as vain. When a Nazi colonel hears that he is known among the Poles as "Concentration Camp Ehrhardt," he responds with childish delight, as if Hitler himself had just kissed him on both cheeks. "Yes," he effuses, "We do the concentrating and the Poles do the camping!"

This is the strain of humor that won *To Be Or Not to Be* its reputation as a "callous, tasteless effort to find fun in the bombing of Warsaw" (Mildred Martin of the Philadelphia *Inquirer*). There *is* a certain audacity in the equation of bad acting with genocide, as in a line spoken by the Nazi Colonel: "I saw Joseph Tura on the stage once. What he did to Shakespeare, we are doing to Poland." But comparing figurative "bombing" or the "murdering" of a play to literal bombing and murder becomes atrocious only if we forget who the speaker is—an inept but no less terrifying totalitarian, insensitive to both dramatic artistry and human suffering; and not Mayer or Lubitsch. This is, I think, the mistake Sarris makes in claiming that Hitler's megalomania could be inferred from his boorishness. Lubitsch certainly knew the difference between the verb "to be" and the verb "to seem"; indeed, this was the theme of some of his best films. His concern in *To Be Or Not to Be* was even more basic: the monstrous chasm between being and not being, between the life of a country and its imminent death under Hitler's boot.

To Be Or Not to Be is one of those maddening, provocative films that are more satisfying to talk or write about than to see. One can do a Brecht number . . . you're not *supposed* to be involved, Lubitsch has constructed an artistic barrier between movie and moviegoer, etc., etc. One can do a juxtaposition-of-trivial-plot-with-enormous-theme number. Or a Life-Imitates-Art number. The film does feature several Jewish actors who either portray Nazis or portray Jewish actors portraying Nazis. And Benny's severe limitations as an actor approximate those of Tura, which may be seen as turning a limitation into an advantage, in that Benny is obviously right for the role. But there is a point in criticism at which appreciation of a film's conception must be distinguished from satisfaction at its realization. As piquant as the conception and development of the Benny character may be to the intellect, it nonetheless fails to persuade or please the viewer (*this* viewer, anyway). We are never made to feel Benny's insecurity, to sympathize with him; we only know the insecurity exists. This is Mayer's fault. The idea is there, but the understanding is not, and thus *To Be Or Not to Be*'s tone is frequently that of a Benny vehicle, as creaky and consumptive as the comic's famous old Maxwell.

The character upon whom Mayer did lavish his sympathy is Felix Bressart's Jewish actor. Bressart all but epitomized the fondness and generosity of *Ninotchka* and *The Shop Around the Corner*; here he is again warm and wise, with a sense of his own status that makes him discreetly unheroic—until pricked. "If you prick us, do we not bleed?" he cries, throwing Shakespeare's words at Hitler. "What a Shylock you would have made!" says a fellow actor, and Bressart philosophically replies, "I could only carry a spear." "I hope," his colleague says proudly, "we can carry spears again." Here is the kernel of an idea Mayer and Lubitsch used fleetingly, when Bressart provokes arrest by playing the entire soliloquy to some outraged Nazis. It might have made a more rewarding, moving film, rooted more firmly in the Lubitsch tradition—and, incidentally, it would have given Bressart an overdue chance to carry more than his usual, secondary-character spear. But the aching warmth of Bressart dominates only a few scenes. The rest is silliness.

DELMER DAVES
(1904–   )

1929   SO THIS IS COLLEGE (Sam Wood) co-story, co-screenplay
1931   SHIPMATES (Harry Pollard) story, co-adaptation, co-dialogue
1932   DIVORCE IN THE FAMILY (Charles F. Reisner) screenplay, dialogue
1933   CLEAR ALL WIRES (George Hill) adaptation
1934   NO MORE WOMEN (Albert Rogell) co-story, co-screenplay
       DAMES (Lloyd Bacon) co-story, screenplay
       FLIRTATION WALK (Frank Borzage) co-story, screenplay
1935   STRANDED (Frank Borzage) co-screenplay
       PAGE MISS GLORY (Mervyn LeRoy) co-screenplay
       SHIPMATES FOREVER (Frank Borzage) story, screenplay
1936   THE PETRIFIED FOREST (Archie Mayo) co-screenplay
1937   THE GO-GETTER (Busby Berkeley) screenplay
       THE SINGING MARINE (Ray Enright) story, screenplay
       SLIM (Ray Enright) co-screeplay (uncredited)
1938   SHE MARRIED AN ARTIST (Marion Gering) co-screenplay
       PROFESSOR BEWARE (Elliott Nugent) screenplay
1939   LOVE AFFAIR (Leo McCarey) co-screenplay
       $1,000 A TOUCHDOWN (James Hogan) story, screenplay
1940   THE FARMER'S DAUGHTER (James Hogan) story
       SAFARI (Edward H. Griffith) screenplay
1941   THE UNEXPECTED UNCLE (Peter Godfrey) co-screenplay
       THE NIGHT OF JANUARY 16TH (William Clemens) co-screenplay
1942   YOU WERE NEVER LOVELIER (William A. Seiter) co-screenplay
1943   STAGE DOOR CANTEEN (Frank Borzage) story, screenplay
       DESTINATION TOKYO (Delmer Daves) co-screenplay
1944   THE VERY THOUGHT OF YOU (Delmer Daves) co-screenplay

HOLLYWOOD CANTEEN (Delmer Daves) story, screenplay
1947   THE RED HOUSE (Delmer Daves) screenplay
       DARK PASSAGE (Delmer Daves) screenplay
1949   TASK FORCE (Delmer Daves) screenplay
1951   BIRD OF PARADISE (Delmer Daves) story, screenplay
1953   TREASURE OF THE GOLDEN CONDOR (Delmer Daves)
       screenplay
1954   DRUM BEAT (Delmer Daves) story, screenplay
1955   WHITE FEATHER (Richard Webb) screenplay
1956   JUBAL (Delmer Daves) co-screenplay
       THE LAST WAGON (Delmer Daves) co-screenplay
1957   AN AFFAIR TO REMEMBER (Leo McCarey) remake of
       Love Affair; co-screenplay
1959   A SUMMER PLACE (Delmer Daves) screenplay
1961   PARRISH (Delmer Daves) screenplay
       SUSAN SLADE (Delmer Daves) screenplay
1962   ROME ADVENTURE (Delmer Daves) screenplay
1963   SPENCER'S MOUNTAIN (Delmer Daves) screenplay
1964   YOUNGBLOOD HAWKE (Delmer Daves) screenplay
1965   THE BATTLE OF THE VILLA FIORITA (Delmer Daves)
       screenplay

Delmer Daves spent most of his long career at Warner Brothers. While the studio evolved from a six-day-week sweatshop in the thirties to a Seven-Arts subsidiary in the sixties, Daves played it the company way—an attitude some new critics have mistaken for classicism. The pictures Daves wrote for Frank Borzage and Leo McCarey in the thirties were just as delirious, if not so hilarious, as his own efforts to revive an embalmed genre would be a quarter of a century later. It's just that the world—and the film world—had spun wildly off a course that Daves was still traveling. Without his knowing it, the craftsman had become camp. We respond to his best films (and the two *Affairs*-to-remember represent his very finest work) with an admiration inextricably mixed with nostalgia. If the nostalgia demeans Daves' own considerable contributions, it also makes them more memorable.

Love Affair (1939) and *An Affair to Remember* (1957)

Daves' is one of the four names credited with the screen story and screenplay of *Love Affair*. In remarks published in the *Hollywood*

Screenwriters Anthology, Daves claims that "I contributed the original story concept without credit" and that "I worked with Leo McCarey, the director, from the original concept throughout the making of the film, actually writing scenes as the film progressed, thus developing them from the already created (in continuity) scenes." Daves' assertions have the ring of truth to them because of his generous tribute to McCarey ("a great adventure in filmmaking with a very brilliant director . . . he would have more right to [the title of] 'author' than I alone") and because of the genuine exhilaration he conveys in describing the project ("we finished [writing] the last scene the night before it was shot . . . an exhausting but very rewarding experience in writing"). The remake, *An Affair to Remember,* is extraordinarily faithful to the original script, even to including several scenes that were written for the 1939 film but cut from the released print—a fact that accounts for most of the twenty-six-minute difference in running time. The dialogue in both films is almost word-for-word from Daves' script, and there are fewer of McCarey's typical paraphrases and digressions than can be found in, say, *Make Way for Tomorrow,* in which McCarey and his actors substantially altered and rearranged Vina Delmar's screenplay.

The films' counterpoint themes, as well as their two possible resolutions, are expressed in the pair of songs that run through *Love Affair.* One is "Plaisir d'Amour" ("The joys of love in one short moment pass; / The pain of love all my life will grieve me"), sung by the heroine, Terry McKay, on what she describes as "the loveliest day I've ever known." It portends a long, tragic epilogue to her shipboard romance with the notorious ladies' man, Michel Marnay. The other theme, "Wishing Will Make It So," had been composed by Michel when he was a child-prodigy pianist, and all but forgotten in the decadent decades to follow. Terry's vivacious innocence seems to help him remember it: "If you wish long enough in your mind, and if you wish strong enough in your heart, and if you keep on wishing long enough and strong enough . . ." Terry interrupts, piquantly: "You get what you want for Christmas?" The first theme suggests Michel's European fatalism, the second Terry's American optimism. That Terry is given the first song and Michel the second evokes both her reservations about falling in love with a playboy and his hope that he has found the woman who can transform him from a flirtatious home-wrecker into a faithful husband.

Both Terry and Michel are technically "committed" to other people. But if she marries her lusterless boss, Ken, it will be for convenience; and if he marries his colorless fiancée, Lois, it will be for money. Neither opportunity is precisely exalting. Terry and Michel will still be searching for the love they eventually find in each other.

Michel is characterized (by three radio broadcasters in the opening scenes of *Love Affair*) as a playboy, impure and simple. Our knowledge of movie conventions alerts us to the strong probability that he and Terry will wind up together, but for this to happen Michel will need to be either reformed (if he really is nothing but a playboy) or rehabilitated (if he is a good boy gone bad). The latter case applies here. Like Senator Paine in *Mr. Smith Goes to Washington,* like Rick and Renault in *Casablanca,* Michel has an idealist's past: he was an altar boy, he was a gifted pianist, he was a talented painter. Even as a lover Michel was idealistic.

> TERRY: I imagine you've known quite a few women, haven't you? Or maybe *few* is the wrong word . . . ? (*He nods.*) And I gather you haven't much respect for them. . . . (*He shakes his head.*) But of course, you've always been fair in your judgment. . . .
>
> MICHEL: I've been more than fair. I idealize them. Every woman I meet I put up there . . . (*holding hand up*). But the longer I know her . . . the better I know her . . . and the better I know her. . . . (*His hand has dropped below the table. He looks at it, lifting tablecloth to see; then shrugs.*)

Michel's attitude, which masquerades as the world-weariness of the continental lover, is not too different from that of the repressed American Catholic adolescent—the disillusioned altar boy—who believes that a girl is frigid if she says no and nymphomaniacal if she says yes. One imagines Michel's statement delighting the same audience that would later find McCarey's *The Bells of St. Mary's* and *My Son John* to their taste. Nevertheless, it adroitly establishes Michel as more of a Don Quixote than a Don Juan; and American movies always preferred heroic vulnerability (Quixote) to pathetic venality (Juan).

There's no hard and fast rule governing Hollywood remakes. Some are superior to the original film, as is *His Girl Friday* to *The Front Page.* Some are inferior, as is *Bundle of Joy* to *Bachelor Mother.* This applies even when the scripts are nearly identical, and the difference can be fairly easily traced to directors and actors.

McCarey is one of the few filmmakers who has remade an earlier film very closely. (Hitchcock made important changes in his second version of *The Man Who Knew Too Much,* for example, and when Hawks remade *Ball of Fire* it became a Danny Kaye musical, although the dialogue stayed pretty much the same.) Because McCarey treated his familiar material with something more than the contempt Hawks showed for *Ball of Fire* when remaking it, and because Cary Grant and Deborah Kerr were fully as palatable and compatible as Charles Boyer and Irene Dunne had been in the original, the two versions of Daves' script are almost equally successful, though they are hardly identical.

An Affair to Remember is suffused with the lush music and luscious color of so many Fox CinemaScope travelogues of the middle and late fifties. The opulence of the production suits Grant's impeccable coiffure, clothes, and charms to a tee—while Deborah Kerr's smile, unalterably ironic, suggests bemused acceptance of the fact that the physical nature of the film favors her co-star, even as the matter-of-fact *mise-en-scène* tends to validate her own earthy aristocracy.

The production of *Love Affair* is more restrained, though neither bleak nor really austere. There's less musical underscoring than in most McCarey romances, and this makes the characters a bit less sure of themselves and the film less deterministic. In many Hollywood tear-jerkers, the music seems contrived not only to inform the audience of the actors' motivations and to cue in the application of handkerchiefs, but also to drive the characters relentlessly down a river of plot to a predestined docking spot in each other's arms. The absence of violins trilling seductively in the background of *Love Affair* deprives Michel of one of the accouterments of seduction, makes him less overpowering and thus more likable. Michel's reputation is practically an albatross around his necking, and it can be assumed that he is retiring into marriage (with a woman who calls him "Michael"!) simply to escape the boring routine of conquest without involvement, and not to use his fiancée's philanthropy to finance more philandering.

Boyer could easily have let his winsome vulnerability be understood as a pose that makes him all the more attractive, and his interest in Irene Dunne could have been taken as an artist's response to a fresh challenge instead of an expression of his search for a savior. But his balance is perfect, giving Michel just enough charm for the audience to find him worthy of its trust. Miss Dunne is hearty, playful, morally confident as befits her character's Kansas upbringing; whereas Miss Kerr, who is supposed to be from Boston (invariably used as the home of British actors who play American roles, just as American actors who play Englishmen invariably come from Canada), has the reserve and the resilience typical of the finest cultivated Easterners.

What Boyer and Dunne, Grant and Kerr all possess is the power to convey conviction. An actor once said that the two most difficult phrases to read meaningfully were "I love you" and "I believe in God." McCarey's actors sell both these emotions beautifully in the demanding scene in the chapel of Boyer / Grant's grandmother. The visit to Janou's chapel unites the three positive strands of our hero's life: his religion (lapsed), his painting (dormant), and his love for Terry (budding). McCarey, in his best films, was able to make religious belief believable and "cute" Hollywood children tolerable. Few other directors could skate so close to propaganda and bathos and end up with ankles straight and poise intact.

Perhaps even more demanding is the final revelation scene, in which Boyer / Grant discovers that Terry, who had planned to meet and marry him on the top floor of the Empire State Building six months after their shipboard romance, had been hit by a car and crippled on her way to the assignation. Through no fault of Boyer's, the Grant version is superior. Grant has ambled through the film with such assured sophistication that his ultimate display of vulnerability comes as a poignant surprise. He prowls around Terry's apartment, ever the Hitchcock cat-burglar, looking for evidence that will convict Terry of transcendent selflessness and thus undying devotion. At last we see that his suavity is a nobleman's mask for understated compassion. But he reveals this only to the audience and not to Terry, for he is also noble enough not to embarrass her with his ardor in case her own may have cooled. Their ultimate embrace is the definitive moment in weepie cinema: every matron's tear—and every critic's—has been well earned by characters whose honesty turns conventions into convictions, and cardboard into flesh.

If *Love Affair* is an example of romantic comedy-drama at its peak, during its peak years, *An Affair to Remember* is a vibrant evocation of the genre, if not its elegy. Soon after, the form would be laid to rest, with Ross Hunter movies and television soap operas acting as zombified descendants. The denouement of *An Affair to*

Remember may mark the last time a writer, a director, and a pair of actors could plumb the ludicrous shallows of the weepie and emerge deliriously triumphant—and the last time Hollywood had the strength to believe in the dreams that made it great.

Charles Lederer
(1906–   )

1931   THE FRONT PAGE (Lewis Milestone) co-dialogue
1932   COCK OF THE AIR (Tom Buckingham) co-story, co-screenplay, co-dialogue
1933   TOPAZE (Harry d'Abbadie d'Arrast) co-screenplay (uncredited) [1]
1937   DOUBLE OR NOTHING (Jay Theodore Reed) co-screenplay
         MOUNTAIN MUSIC (Robert Florey) co-screenplay
1939   BROADWAY SERENADE (Robert Z. Leonard) screenplay
         WITHIN THE LAW (Gustav Machaty) screenplay
1940   HIS GIRL FRIDAY (Howard Hawks) screenplay [1]
         COMRADE X (King Vidor) co-screenplay [1]
         I LOVE YOU AGAIN (W. S. Van Dyke) co-screenplay
1943   SLIGHTLY DANGEROUS (Wesley Ruggles) screenplay
         THE YOUNGEST PROFESSION (Edward Buzzell) co-screenplay
1947   KISS OF DEATH (Henry Hathaway) co-screenplay [1]
         RIDE THE PINK HORSE (Robert Montgomery) co-screenplay [1]
         HER HUSBAND'S AFFAIRS (S. Sylvan Simon) co-screenplay [1]
1949   I WAS A MALE WAR BRIDE (Howard Hawks) co-screenplay
         RED, HOT AND BLUE (John Farrow) story
1950   WABASH AVENUE (Henry Koster) co-story, co-screnplay
1951   THE THING (Howard Hawks and Christian Nyby) screenplay [1]
1952   FEARLESS FAGAN (Stanley Donen) screenplay
         MONKEY BUSINESS (Howard Hawks) co-screenplay [2]
1953   GENTLEMEN PREFER BLONDES (Howard Hawks) screenplay

[1] With Ben Hecht.
[2] With Ben Hecht and I. A. L. Diamond.

1955 KISMET (Vincente Minnelli) co-screenplay, from his and
Luther Davis's Broadway musical adaptation of Edward Knob-
lock's play
1956 GABY (Curtis Bernhardt) co-screenplay
1957 THE SPIRIT OF ST. LOUIS (Billy Wilder) adaptation
TIP ON A DEAD JOCKEY (Richard Thorpe) screenplay
1959 NEVER STEAL ANYTHING SMALL (Charles Lederer)
screenplay
IT STARTED WITH A KISS (George Marshall) screenplay
1960 CAN CAN (Walter Lang) co-screenplay
OCEAN'S ELEVEN (Lewis Milestone) co-screenplay
1962 MUTINY ON THE BOUNTY (Lewis Milestone) screenplay
FOLLOW THAT DREAM (Gordon Douglas) screenplay
1964 A GLOBAL AFFAIR (Jack Arnold) co-screenplay

Lederer directed but did not write the following films: *Fingers at
the Window* (1942) and *On the Loose* (1951).

Charles Lederer's role in the Ben Hecht court-in-exile was that of
the nimble, prankish jester. The Lederer anecdotes Hecht recalls in
Letters from Bohemia and *A Child of the Century* evoke an elfin
spirit that reverberates through the films he wrote (either with
Hecht and/or for Howard Hawks). *The Front Page, Topaze, His
Girl Friday, I Was a Male War Bride, Monkey Business, Gentlemen
Prefer Blondes* all reveal a tendency to deflate pomposity by whatever means necessary, whether the weapon is quick-wittedness or
offhand malice. Like Hecht—and even more like Hawks—Lederer
enjoyed making his characters squirm in situations calculated to
rob them of dignity, as much as he did seeing them squirm out of
them. Malice is a legitimate comic tool only when accompanied by
inventiveness (as, gloriously, in *His Girl Friday*); alone, it suggests
a condescension toward the characters, the audience, and, ultimately, the genre itself.

The Front Page (1931) and *His Girl Friday* (1940)

Welcome to Chicago, the city of The Front Page, *with an outstanding tradition of competitive journalism. Another tradition
has been the excellent rapport between the Chicago police and
working newsmen. You can be assured of our continued cooper-*

> *ation as you report to the nation about the 1968 Democratic*
> *Convention.*
>   —press handout, Chicago, August 1968

Ben Hecht had died four years before the Democratic National
Convention of 1968, and he and Charles MacArthur had written
The Front Page forty years earlier—but Hecht's big, tolerant heart
might have warmed, even as his liberal blood would have curdled,
at this press release from the Chicago Police Department, with its
unconscious irony worthy of *The Front Page*'s own Sheriff "Pinky"
Hartwell. It proved that four decades of twentieth-century progress
had been powerless in altering Chicago's image from its traditional
one as the breezily medieval Gun City of Al Capone. An Irishman
might now be sitting on that estimable Sicilian's throne, but business
went on as usual. Even the Chamber of Commerce still seemed to
be controlled by Murder, Inc.

Hecht and MacArthur rose, or escaped, from the very milieu they
half-canonized and half-cauterized. Their cynicism, toward both
City Hall and those who would fight it, might be confused with
misanthropy if they weren't so cheerful, so energetic—and so compromising, for they were too much a part of Chicago not to love it
a little without hating themselves a lot. After all, the only game in
town was prostitution of one kind or another, so you might as well
lean back and enjoy it.

The reporters in *The Front Page,* play and movie, and in *His
Girl Friday* (the adaptation Charles Lederer and Howard Hawks
made a decade later), take it for granted that every aspect of life,
themselves included, is completely and gloriously corrupt. *His Girl
Friday*'s pair of idealists—Earl Williams (the convicted killer) and
Bruce Baldwin (reporter Hildy Johnson's fiancé)—are treated as
amiable fools. Earl Williams is considered a sympathetic, if psychotic, character because the man he'd killed was only a Negro
policeman, whose death the unscrupulous city government is using to whip up the "race vote," and because anyone who preached
radicalism in the twenties *must* be crazy. As for Bruce, he's so palpably out of place, a kitten in the lion cage, that *he* seems to be the
aberration; and he's such an obvious mismatch for the resourceful,
peripatetic Hildy that for once we don't want the nice guy to get the
girl. Hildy winds up with the man she deserves: her domineering
managing editor, Walter Burns.

As pungent and invigorating as it is, *The Front Page* is neither foolproof nor actorproof. The breakneck speed at which the play is usually staged cleverly conceals the fact that it rather sits back on its haunches for more than an act, cranking up the plot and character machinery that will explode once Walter Burns enters in Act III. And, while the fast pacing demands a certain technical facility of the actors who play those sarcastic denizens of the Criminal Courts pressroom, it's even more important that the actors be able to balance the antagonistic feelings of capriciousness and maliciousness that they are alternatingly to convey. The press gang must act both as a chorus and as conspirators, and it takes real finesse to juggle both functions without jumbling them.

(Cynicism and despair hung over the whole *Front Page* enterprise. Actor Louis Wolheim, who had worked for *The Front Page*'s director, Lewis Milestone, in *Two Arabian Nights* and *All Quiet on the Western Front,* was anxious to play the Walter Burns role for Milestone, and, according to a contemporary source, "dieted to bring himself down to a suitable weight, losing twenty-five pounds in a few days. At this time he underwent an operation for cancer, and his weakened condition caused his death"! One can easily imagine this appalling story being told during the *Front Page* poker game, and eliciting a cantata of wisecracks.)

The Milestone version, on which Charles Lederer worked as an itinerant dialogue-polisher, introduces Walter Burns earlier—even taking Burns and Hildy out for a drink—and boasts a competent group of scene-stealers as the poker-playing press corps. But it remained for Lederer and Howard Hawks, with an uncredited assist from Hecht himself, to get to the root of the problem and bring on Walter Burns in the first scene. If Burns had kept out of sight, an *éminence grise, noir, et bleu* pervading and shaping the smoky atmosphere of the Court pressroom, Hawks's other grand maneuver —switching Hildy Johnson, Walter's ace reporter, from a man to Walter's ex-wife—would have fallen flat.

A general rule of romantic comedy is that, in a triangle situation, the boy and girl who are to end up together must be seen together first, thus establishing the couple's iconographic unity before the intruding Third Party enters. If we had seen Bruce and Hildy together for half the film, without Walter's overbearing presence, it might have taken even more than Cary Grant's incomparable charms to alter our sympathies from poor schmuck Bruce to manipulative dervish Walter.

I'm considering *The Front Page* and *His Girl Friday* as part of Charles Lederer's career, rather than Ben Hecht's, because it was the Lederer screenplay for *His Girl Friday* that crystallized the themes and moods Hecht and MacArthur were really only fooling with. The first third of *His Girl Friday*—in which Walter begins to undermine Hildy's professed preference for Bruce and his plodding, domestic, Albany life style—is primarily Lederer's achievement. Though Walter bullies, lies to, and spills things on Bruce, the film convinces us that Walter and Hildy were made for each other, if only because angelic boredom is a greater movie sin than stylish corruption.

His Girl Friday is Hawks's best comedy, and quite possibly his best film. Robin Wood has perceptively analyzed the benefits Hawks accrued when he changed Hildy's sex. But the inspiration can be exaggerated, since literally dozens of thirties comedies featured man-woman reporting-romancing teams. Nor should Hawks's influence on what even Wood cites as "the film's chief virtue—its brilliant dialogue" be overemphasized. Even the overlapping dialogue perversely attributed to Hawks can be found in the Hecht-MacArthur playscript, as well as many of the film's delightful behavioral gestures—like the moment when Walter lifts the lid of the desk hiding Earl Williams, fans a little air Earl's way, and promptly shuts it again. Still, Hawks's realization of the Hecht-MacArthur-Lederer script does it the fullest possible justice, as can be seen by comparing his direction with that of Lewis Milestone in the 1931 version.

In nearly every scene, Hawks proves his superiority to Milestone as a director of both actors and camera. *His Girl Friday*'s famous, frenetic dialogue delivery is actually slower than *The Front Page*'s. But, whereas Milestone's performers tend to speak very loud and fast, with stagy pauses after each punchline, Hawks has his actors speak at a lower level and slightly slower, but with no pauses. On the most immediate level, Hawks makes it easier for the audience to catch what is being said, while *The Front Page* audience has to strain to make sense of the dialogue. (Milestone may have been trying to beat the record set by George S. Kaufman, whose direction of the stage version was notoriously fast-paced.) Moreover, Hawks's attitude suggests a respect for the dialogue *and* provokes a more benign state of exhaustion; in *His Girl Friday*, the dialogue is not faster-paced but the film is. What these newspapermen are saying, after all, often lurches past journalistic sarcasm into genuine misanthropy, and Walter Burns' ploys have a touch of the clever psychotic about them. Hawks's steady pace never gives us time to question the characters' motives. Molly Malloy jumps out the window and is promptly forgotten; Walter kidnaps Bruce's mother and is promptly forgiven. Only in retrospect does this delightful comedy reveal itself as possibly the most subtly cynical film Hollywood has produced.

Hawks's camera observes these inanities and insanities with the detachment of a visitor to the Marat-Sade play-within-a-play, again letting us concentrate on the dialogue and situations. But Milestone is so busy trying to make *The Front Page* "cinematic" that we often don't know who's speaking, let alone what he's saying. Great pains are taken to establish that the pressroom does indeed have four walls; there are meaningless shock cuts to the gallows outside; the camera is on the move far more than any of the characters. It's a case of too many tracks spoiling the froth. Milestone's greatest indulgence is a follow-the-bouncing-camera effect that accompanies the reporters in song, and which nobody I've asked can justify or even understand. Hawks hardly bothers with the pressroom's "fourth wall"; but by then the film has moved from Walter's office to his city room to a restaurant, so there's no need for a hyperthyroid *mise-en-scène* later on. Further, since almost everything in the pressroom is played against one wall, the desk in which Earl Williams hides, fearing for his life, is almost always in sight, and thus his predicament is kept in mind even as Walter courts Hildy in his own peculiar fashion.

Maybe it's unfair to compare *The Front Page* with *His Girl Friday,* since the only available print of the earlier film is cursed with a sound track that is, on occasion, maddeningly indistinct. According to Dwight Macdonald, *The Front Page* "was widely considered the best movie of 1931," and critics must have been grateful for a film that *moved,* though in the wrong direction and for the wrong reasons. But a Hawks picture of the same year, *The Criminal Code,* can be seriously preferred to *The Front Page* for its natural use of the moving camera and its sophistication of dialogue delivery. By 1939 Hawks had sharpened his sense of pacing and direction of actors, and Lederer had refined his own considerable talent for movie adaptation, to the point where they were ready to transform the liveliest stage play of the twenties into the finest, most anarchic newspaper comedy of all time.

Gentlemen Prefer Blondes (1953)

Most of the films Lederer wrote for Howard Hawks in the post-war decade—*I Was a Male War Bride, Monkey Business, Gentlemen Prefer Blondes*—are comedies of sexual discomfort. *I Was a Male War Bride* serves as the definitive, and certainly most extreme, example of the postponed-marital-consummation farce. Cary Grant is a Captain in the Free French Army, Ann Sheridan is the Frenchman's Lieutenant-woman, and the tone veers only from abrasive to abusive, culminating in a Cary-in-drag sequence worthy of Tashlin's *The Lieutenant Wore Skirts*. In *Monkey Business* Grant is stripped of civilization as well as manhood; and, though the genuine affection he shares with his wife (Ginger Rogers) gives the film an anchor in romantic reality, *Monkey Business* itself scrupulously follows, and matches, Grant's degeneration into savagery. Hawks, for all his comic inventiveness, reveals a dogged fidelity to the material that ultimately makes the film unfaithful to the sympathies of its audience. Even *The Thing* has a (generally controlled) substratum of sexual competition masked by its brisk, technological banter.

In the world of *Gentlemen Prefer Blondes*' Lorelei Lee, as Lederer and Howard Hawks have adapted it from the Anita Loos novel and play, all men are either predators or pansies. No wonder diamonds are a girl's best friend—what else does she have to turn to? Once again Hawks caricatures, unmercifully and unjustly, any men who can't match the barracks bravado of his more typical heroes. Once again he indulges in unsavory baiting of intellectual or ineffectual males by dressing them in drag (see also *Bringing Up Baby* and *I Was a Male War Bride*) or by submitting them to smug indignities (see also *Bringing up Baby* and *Monkey Business*; and contrast this with the affection and respect Brackett and Wilder afford the eight professors in *Ball of Fire*—not a "work of special interest," according to Andrew Sarris).

Hawks puts glasses on his men to suggest effeminacy. There's nothing cruel, or novel, about this; in Bergman's films, spectacles connote moral myopia. But the similarity ends there. For Hawks, identifying the "glass character" is enough; it obviates the need for any further delineation. Unfortunately, in *Gentlemen Prefer Blondes*, it also robs the heroines of any satisfaction in their triumph over such spineless spenders. The pairing of Marilyn Monroe and Jane

Russell with Tommy Noonan and Elliott Reed may well be the most ill-suited in American films.

Nonetheless, Monroe's presence and performance are remarkable. She transcends Lederer's lackluster script and Hawks's flippant attitude toward the film's characters, just as she would do (with much better material) in *Some Like It Hot*. She gives Lorelei Lee a generosity and warmth the character hardly deserves. And her solo of "Diamonds," ending with an incredible Marni Nixon trill, marks one of the highlights of her career. This is an ascent Monroe had to make on her own, unassisted by Hawks and Lederer, two spirits weighed down with the impedimenta of their own raffish misanthropy.

Charles Brackett

(1892–1969)

1934   ENTER MADAME (Elliott Nugent) co-screenplay
1935   COLLEGE SCANDAL (Elliott Nugent) co-screenplay
        THE LAST OUTPOST (Louis Gasnier and Charles Barton) co-
        screenplay
        WITHOUT REGRET (Harold Young) co-screenplay
1936   ROSE OF THE RANCHO (Marion Gering) co-screenplay
        PICCADILLY JIM (Robert Z. Leonard) co-screenplay
        THE JUNGLE PRINCESS (William Thiele) co-screenplay (un-
        credited)
        WOMAN TRAP (Harold Young) story
1937   LIVE, LOVE AND LEARN (George Fitzmaurice) co-screen-
        play
        WILD MONEY (Louis King) co-screenplay (uncredited)
1938   BLUEBEARD'S EIGHTH WIFE (Ernst Lubitsch) co-screen-
        play [1]
1939   WHAT A LIFE (Jay Theodore Reed) co-screenplay [2]
        MIDNIGHT (Mitchell Leisen) co-screenplay [1]
        NINOTCHKA (Ernst Lubitsch) co-screenplay [4]
1940   ARISE, MY LOVE (Mitchell Leisen) co-screenplay [1]
1941   HOLD BACK THE DAWN (Mitchell Leisen) co-screenplay [2]
        BALL OF FIRE (Howard Hawks) co-screenplay [1]
1942   THE MAJOR AND THE MINOR (Billy Wilder) co-screen-
        play [1]
1943   FIVE GRAVES TO CAIRO (Billy Wilder) co-screenplay, [2]
        producer
1945   THE LOST WEEKEND (Billy Wilder) co-screenplay, [2] pro-
        ducer
1946   TO EACH HIS OWN (Mitchell Leisen) story, co-screenplay,
        producer

1948 THE EMPEROR WALTZ (Billy Wilder) co-story,[2] co-screen-play,[2] producer
A FOREIGN AFFAIR (Billy Wilder) co-screenplay,[5] producer
MISS TATLOCK'S MILLIONS (Richard Haydn) co-screen-play,[3] producer

1950 SUNSET BOULEVARD (Billy Wilder) co-screenplay,[7] producer

1951 THE MATING SEASON (Mitchell Leisen) co-screenplay,[6] producer
THE MODEL AND THE MARRIAGE BROKER (George Cukor) co-screenplay,[6] producer

1953 NIAGARA (Henry Hathaway) co-story,[6] co-screenplay,[6] producer
TITANIC (Jean Negulesco) co-story,[6] co-screenplay,[6] producer

1955 THE GIRL IN THE RED VELVET SWING (Richard Fleischer) co-story,[2] co-screenplay,[2] producer

1956 TEENAGE REBEL (Edmund Goulding) co-screenplay,[2] producer

1959 JOURNEY TO THE CENTER OF THE EARTH (Henry Levin) co-screenplay,[2] producer

Brackett produced but did not write the following films: *The Uninvited* (1944, Lewis Allen), *Garden of Evil* (1954, Henry Hathaway), *Woman's World* (1954, Jean Negulesco), *The Virgin Queen* (1955, Henry Koster), *The King and I* (1956, Walter Lang), *D-Day, The Sixth of June* (1956, Henry Koster), *The Wayward Bus* (1957, Victor Vicas), *The Gift of Love* (1958, Jean Negulesco), *Ten North Frederick* (1958, Philip Dunne), *The Remarkable Mr. Pennypacker* (1958, Henry Levin), *Blue Denim* (1959, Philip Dunne), *High Time* (1960, Blake Edwards), *State Fair* (1962, Jose Ferrer).

---

[1] With Billy Wilder.
[2] With Walter Reisch.
[3] With Richard Breen.
[4] With Wilder and Reisch.
[5] With Wilder and Breen.
[6] With Reisch and Breen.
[7] With Wilder and D. H. Marshman.

As what might be called the distaff half of "the most successful marriage in Hollywood," Charles Brackett occupies that enigmatic half-life state shared by Charles MacArthur, Morrie Ryskind, Ruth Gordon, I. A. L. Diamond, Lamar Trotti, and other members of famous writing teams. The received opinion of the Charles Brackett—Billy Wilder division of labor on thirteen films stretching from *Bluebeard's Eighth Wife* in 1938 to *Sunset Boulevard* in 1950 is that Wilder wrote the scripts and Brackett typed them. What seems more likely, after a look at the films the two made on their own before, during, and after their long period of collaboration, is that Brackett acted both as a mellowing influence on Wilder's effusive sarcasm, and as author of the important but underrated "bridging" dialogue between Wilder's Berliner jokes.

Their mid-forties "separate vacation" films indicated the route each would take after their divorce. Wilder's *Double Indemnity* set the stage, thematically and visually, for the bitter *film noir* of the postwar era, and set the tone for his solo excursions into double-identity and double-dealing. *To Each His Own*, which Brackett produced and co-wrote, sparkled with Olivia deHavilland's nobly masochistic presence, and glistened with Mitchell's Leisen's glossy direction. Brackett's post-Wilder career took him into smoother, more easily charted waters. *The Mating Season, Niagara*, and *Teenage Rebel* are not without their appeal, but it is the appeal of anonymous craftsmanship. Brackett's decline was as graceful as was his gentle imprint on those films that will always be known, with probable justification, as "Billy Wilder scripts." Thus, their collaborative efforts noted here (*Ball of Fire, A Foreign Affair, Sunset Boulevard*) are grouped under Wilder's career—with the utterly arbitrary exception of *Ninotchka*, which is included here as much for a tip of the critic's hat to Brackett, the gentleman-craftsman, as for the internal evidence of a peculiar similarity between it and *Teenage Rebel*.

Ninotchka (1939)

In the continuing critical war between those unequal powers, the Directorial Empire and the Writer's Colony, there is one crucial faction often overlooked: the actor-auteur, who dominates and determines as many middle-ground Hollywood films as either of the behind-the-scenes "creators." Chaplin and Keaton may be fine directors (and gag inventors), but it is their screen personalities that we especially cherish; indeed, it is their awareness of, if not their identity with, these personalities that makes their direction seem so right. Given the choice, who would trade Keaton the actor for Keaton the director? And who would prefer analyzing the directorial styles of James W. Horne, Donald Crisp, Edward Sedgwick, or Charles F. Reisner to savoring that sublime bodily mechanism that Keaton controls so beautifully?

The unique cinematic personae of W. C. Fields, Mae West, Laurel and Hardy, and (to a lesser extent) the Marx Brothers also flourished with little regard for the director of record—although, quite naturally, the combination of these comedians with different scripts and directors produced varying results. The same can be said of such incandescent performers as Katharine Hepburn, Cary Grant, and Greta Garbo. Just as one can be drawn to an exercise in visual style like Blake Edwards' *Darling Lili* without finding it a completely successful film, so can one delight in the way Garbo dignifies and illuminates a hoary melodrama like *Mata Hari* with her beauty, her passion, and her ironic acceptance of an innate and tragic superiority.

It's instructive—indeed, it's often fun—to watch the way a great actor transcends ridiculous scripts and ponderous direction, and Garbo's films offer a virtual course in transcendent acting. But most of Garbo's vehicles were so ramshackle that Alice Faye could have risen above them, and after more than a dozen jobs of effortless transcendence, Garbo must have longed for a script that would challenge her instead of crumbling in dead homage at her feet. *Camille* offered such a challenge, and the actress responded with what Gary Carey has properly called "the single most beautiful performance in the American sound film." Her characterization of Ninotchka Yakushova may be less sublime, but it is just as demanding, for it asks that Garbo express Marguerite Gautier's tragic malaise through the guise of a rigid caricature of Communist femininity, and that she bring some Lubitsch charm to the easy sophistication and facile cynicism of a Brackett-and-Wilder script . . .

. . . except that *Ninotchka*'s charm sings out from the pages of that script, and that what we may identify as Lubitsch touches—the photograph of Lenin that becomes suddenly animated in a what-me-worry smile, the maneuvering of maids in and out of discreetly placed hotel doors, the final visual punchline which attempts to rob the lovers' reunion of any lasting impression on the audience by enclosing it within a substandard gag situation—demean the script as often as they improve it. Lubitsch enjoyed playing the shrewd editor-in-chief over his writers. As Brackett and Wilder described it in a posthumous tribute to Lubitsch: "Always he was there, saying, 'Is this the best we can do? Does it ring the bell? When it's right, it rings the bell.' " But, though Lubitsch was the judge, it was the writers whose function was to "ring the bell." One of the most felicitous collaborations between Lubitsch and his writers resulted in *Ninotchka*—a veritable symphony of romantic and comic chimes.

The three giant steps that Ninotchka and Leon d'Algout (her political, ethical, sexual, and personal opposite) take toward each other, finally melting in each other's arms and souls, are as clear in the script as they are in the film. At first sight, Ninotchka is the austere Communist who would deprive porters and butlers of their jobs, her subordinates in the Soviet Trade Agency of a little coun- terrevolutionary fun, and herself of her womanhood. Leon, the model voluptuary, seems ineffective as her romancer, with his con- descending tone and stale jokes. Parisian women might understand that lines like (in response to Ninotchka's "I am looking for the Eif- fel Tower") "Is that thing lost again?" were meant as code words for an unspoken proposition; but Ninotchka takes them as pathetic attempts at capitalist humor—until Leon tempers his suave lechery with a little deflated humanity, falling off a restaurant chair and sending Ninotchka into silent paroxysms of laughter.

By the time Leon has talked himself into falling in love with Ninotchka, his *bavardage* has become eloquently alive. "Ninotchka, Ninotchka, why do doves bill and coo? Why do snails, coldest of creatures, circle interminably around each other? Why do moths fly hundreds of miles to find their mates? Why do flowers open their petals? Oh, Ninotchka, Ninotchka, surely you feel some slight symp- tom of the divine passion—a general warmth in the palms of your hands—a strange heaviness in your limbs—a burning of the lips that is not thirst but a thousand times more tantalizing, more exalt- ing, than thirst?" Ninotchka still thinks Leon is "very talkative"; it takes a persuasive kiss to trigger erotic rapprochement between the aristocrat and the Bolshevik. But once Ninotchka enters Phase Two, she becomes more expansive, urging Comrades Buljanoff, Iranoff, and Kopalski to get haircuts, to open the windows (in honor of a romantic *aggiornamento*), to embrace the Paris of the man she loves.

The third and last step restores Ninotchka and Leon to the halt- ing innocence of adolescence. Ninotchka appears for the first time in Parisian *haute couture,* a little girl decked out in woman-of-the- world finery. In Soviet khaki she was an imposing cog in the powerful revolutionary machine, but in her new dress Ninotchka must stand on her own in capitalistic competition with the city's most fashionable women—specifically the Duchess Swana, her rival both for a treasure of Czarist jewels and for a different, more desired prize: Leon. If we feel that the jewels will eventually find their way back to the homeland, it is because we see that Leon himself is, probably for the first time, in the throes of a love so overwhelming that his seductive eloquence has deserted him. He can only stammer. She has become giddy and "talkative"—with inexpressible melancholy. He and Ninotchka are equals at last.

> NINOTCHKA: Leon, I want to tell you something which I thought I would never say, which I thought nobody should ever say, because I thought it didn't exist—and, Leon—I can't say it. . . .

If Ninotchka "can't say it," it is certainly not because, as John Baxter absurdly charges, "Garbo . . . in a grotesque self-parody . . . plays comedy with more enthusiasm than skill." As brilliantly inhabited by Garbo, Ninotchka is wary of declaring her love for Leon because she has once before experienced the sensation of kissing a mortal enemy. As a sergeant in the Revolutionary Army, she had been wounded in the shoulder by "a Polish lancer. I was sixteen." When Leon somewhat ironically expresses his sympathy, Ninotchka retorts, "Don't pity me. Pity the Polish lancer. After all, I'm alive." Later, when she has learned that Leon is acting as counsel to the Duchess Swana, she turns cold. "But, Ninotchka, I held you in my arms," he implores; "You kissed me." "I kissed the Polish lancer too," she answers, more in remorse than in rebuttal, "before he died."

Ninotchka has literally been wounded in a love which—aided immeasurably by Garbo's gestures and even her posture, heroic yet stoop-shouldered—explains her allegiance to a political system in which one can lead the way for others while losing oneself. Although the script satirizes Communism and Czarism with equal, impartial glee, *Ninotchka* is ultimately an ode to bourgeois individualism; for, while critics can point to an almost communal collaboration between writers and director, it required Garbo's artistry to find wistful wisdom in the Brackett-Wilder wisecracks and deep feeling beneath Lubitsch's touch, transforming the genial aura of a superior thirties comedy into the substance of acting—and cinematic —genius.

Teenage Rebel (1956)

Teenage Rebel would be of only minor interest in Brackett's career—and the interest would derive from tracing his decline after breaking up with Billy Wilder, as his screenplays and productions become less audacious, less entertaining, more *ordinary*—if it weren't for the fact that this little drama of a mother reclaiming her estranged daughter is, in many respects, an unnoticed and possibly unknowing remake of *Ninotchka*. Brackett is again collaborating with Walter Reisch, the third screenwriter of that exceptional Lubitsch comedy; and though the tone is altogether different, the romantic situations are uncanny in their similarity.

Both Greta Garbo in *Ninotchka* and Betty Lou Keim in *Teenage Rebel* are citizens of the uptight East (Garbo is a Russian, Betty Lou a New Yorker) making a reluctant visit to the decadent West (Paris and California, respectively). Both are serious girls who have repressed all thoughts of romance, but who are attracted to insouciant young men (Melvyn Douglas and Warren Berlinger). The men are vaguely attached (Douglas to his Czarist mistress, Berlinger to a vacationing "steady"), but these aren't serious enough to keep them from falling in love with their respective women from the East. In each case, the woman's reserve is broken when the man, after telling the woman jokes in a restaurant, with no success, falls off a chair onto the floor. (In the modern version, Betty Lou falls off *her* stool, too.) When the woman learns about the "other" woman, she returns, wounded, to the East, only to go West again when the dispute is settled.

Edmund Goulding (who had directed two of Garbo's better vehicles, *Love* and *Grand Hotel*) is no Lubitsch, however, and the Brackett-Reisch script doesn't approach the sustained wit of the Brackett-Wilder-Reisch screenplay for *Ninotchka*. For the most part the film is as stagy and stage-bound as the Edith Sommer play, *A Roomful of Roses*, on which it was based. Miss Keim's early demeanor is so forced that her redemption is all too inevitable; and the film ends with that most hackneyed of short-story cappers, the A-X-A line, in which the lead character says sagely, "[cliché], [name of character to whom the line is being spoken], [cliché]." Here the line is, "I wouldn't know, Mother, I wouldn't know."

There are certain felicities, in Warren Berlinger's charmingly natural performance, and in Miss Keim's plainness, which is con-trasted with the well-preserved freshness of her mother (Ginger Rogers), and which gives the girl a reason for resenting her. But should these touches be attributed to the director? I think not. Goulding was the beneficiary of many fine performances; *Love*, as fine as his direction is, would certainly be far less a success without Garbo's presence. In a lesser film like *Teenage Rebel*, Goulding seems merely to be presiding rather than actively directing, and the Keim-Rogers plain-pretty dichotomy is an aspect of the film he did little to enhance. It simply exists, unspoken and unalluded to. Perhaps we should credit producer Brackett, who chose Miss Keim over other, more attractive young actresses. Unfortunately, this would be one of the few real credits we could honestly bestow on Brackett in his post-Wilder years, when he forsook the glory of a superior collaboration for the undistinguished power of an amiable boss.

FRANK S. NUGENT
(1908–1965)

1948 FORT APACHE (John Ford) screenplay
      THREE GODFATHERS (John Ford) co-screenplay
1949 TULSA (Stuart Heisler) co-screenplay
      SHE WORE A YELLOW RIBBON (John Ford) co-screenplay
1950 WAGONMASTER (John Ford) co-story, co-screenplay
      TWO FLAGS WEST (Robert Wise) co-story, co-screenplay
1952 THE QUIET MAN (John Ford) screenplay
1953 ANGEL FACE (Otto Preminger) co-screenplay
1954 THEY RODE WEST (Phil Karlson) co-screenplay
      THE PARATROOPER (Terence Young) co-screenplay
      TROUBLE IN THE GLEN (Herbert Wilcox) screenplay
1955 MISTER ROBERTS (John Ford, Mervyn LeRoy) co-screenplay
      THE TALL MEN (Raoul Walsh) co-screenplay
1956 THE SEARCHERS (John Ford) screenplay
1957 THE RISING OF THE MOON (John Ford) screenplay
1958 GUNMAN'S WALK (Phil Karlson) screenplay
      THE LAST HURRAH (John Ford) screenplay
1960 FLAME OVER INDIA (J. Lee Thompson) remake of *Wagonmaster*
1961 TWO RODE TOGETHER (John Ford) screenplay
1963 DONOVAN'S REEF (John Ford) co-screenplay
1966 INCIDENT AT PHANTOM HILL (Earl Bellamy) co-screenplay

In all the commotion raised by the sudden pre-eminence of Peter Bogdanovich and Penelope Gilliatt in the arena of moviemaking, as opposed to movie reviewing, it was almost impossible to distinguish the persistent but soft voice of film history, whispering the forgotten name of Frank S. Nugent. Depressingly few of those critics who wrote seriously about film in its infancy and adolescence ever had the inclination or opportunity to write films themselves. Julien Johnson, a generous and farsighted critic for the early *Photoplay*, wrote titles for some of the finest late silent films: *Manhandled, Moana, The Sorrows of Satan, Wings, The Patriot, Beggars of Life, Docks of New York*, and others; but by 1930 he had dropped out of sight. James Agee's profiles in eccentric courage (*The African Queen, The Bride Comes to Yellow Sky, The Night of the Hunter*) are well-known but peripheral gestures to what, for Agee, was a sort of obsessive avocation. On the wide horizon of Hollywood history, only Nugent's sail stands out among those reviewers who have dared put their critical vision to the test of ungrateful producers and aggrandizing directors.

Nugent was luckier than most screenwriters in finding talented, sympathetic directors to realize his scripts. But his most miraculous symbiotic relationship was with John Ford, who molded the sleek, sophisticated style Nugent had developed during his tenure as the *New York Times* movie critic into the more direct, epic style Ford required for his postwar westerns. In the first of these—*Fort Apache* and *She Wore a Yellow Ribbon*—an unproductive tension is evident between *Times*man Nugent and the *Saturday Evening Post* stories he was adapting. Gradually, as Nugent explored the Ford world from Ireland (*The Quiet Man*) to Boston (*The Last Hurrah*) to Hawaii (*Donovan's Reef*), its monuments and valleys became almost intuitively clear to him. Nugent's work, written for a man who was his father in spirit as well as in-law, culminated in his brilliant and self-effacing script for *The Searchers*—that rare Hollywood film that can be called indisputably great, and a prime example of invisible screenwriting helping to produce ineffable cinema.

The Searchers (1956)

> "A man will search his heart and soul,
> Go searchin' 'way out there . . ."

For all the riotous pictorialism of *The Searchers'* landscapes—portraits unmatched for formal perfection and emotive power—the terrain over which Ethan Edwards leads his "search party" of one is ultimately interior. Ethan, the embittered Civil War veteran fight-

ing for a cause that was not really his, returns to a home that might
have been his but is no more. Although there is not one line of dialogue in *The Searchers* that mentions it directly, we realize from
glances, gestures, and camera angles—all oblique—that the only
positive force in Ethan's life is Martha (the woman who married
his brother Aaron while Ethan went off to war), that they still love
each other, and that, when she and her husband and two elder
children are slaughtered by Comanches, Ethan becomes as scarred
with vengeance as the savages whose pursuit he makes his decade-
long obsession.

Every civilizing influence on Ethan springs from either Martha or
her "children": Debbie, her younger daughter, and Martin Pawley,
the orphan Ethan saved and gave to Martha as a son—"their" son
(although Ethan mutters that "it just happened to be me [who
found Martin] . . . no need to make more of it"). Without Martin's
check on his vindictiveness, Ethan undoubtedly would have murdered Debbie as soon as he saw her dressed in the garb of a Comanche bride. Martin's own priority of loyalties leads him first to
defend Debbie (his "sister") against Ethan (the father figure whose
paternity loses its persuasiveness as he turns further and further
away from Martha's gentle justice), then to defend Ethan against
an Indian attack. And without the understanding that Debbie is the
last repository of her mother's goodness—indeed, is the same little
girl he lifted up in a hail-and-farewell embrace ten long, lost years
ago—Ethan would be unable to complete the movement, clinging to
her instead of killing her, and say, "Let's go home, Debbie." "Home"
means Martha specifically, and civilization in general; and the
moment is all the more poignant for our awareness that, in his home,
Ethan will always be a visitor. It takes the entire film for Ethan both
to recognize that his own "family" consists of Martha (his wife),
Martin (his son), and Debbie (his daughter), and to accept the
fact that, for all their spiritual and empirical closeness, this family
is destined to remain an achingly elusive ideal and not a consummated reality.

The Searchers reverberates with characters who act as living surrogates for Aaron, Martha, and Ethan. The Edwards' homesteading
neighbors—Lars Jorgenson, his wife, and their daughter Laurie—are
invested, respectively, with Aaron's docility, Martha's warmth, and
Debbie's perkiness. Laurie also possesses some of Martha's tenacity:
Martha kept Aaron on their farm when he wanted to go back East

(he says, "She just wouldn't let a man quit," without realizing that Martha may have stayed in Texas to wait for Ethan's return); Laurie keeps after Martin—who combines Aaron's gentleness with Ethan's strength—until he surrenders. In the process, Martin must defend himself against Charlie McCorry, a simple-minded rival who resembles a caricature of Aaron, with all Aaron's passiveness exaggerated. Even Charlie achieves some dignity when, in a love song delivered to Laurie, his hayseed tenor miraculously modulates into a tuneful, masculine baritone; and he becomes suddenly human when he and Martin engage in fisticuffs whose theatrical staging (complete with side entrances, a makeshift proscenium arch, a palpably phony stage floor, and enlarged, stylized poses) keeps Charlie from trading on our pity even as he is allowed to draw on our pathos.

Gradually, Mrs. Jorgenson *becomes* Martha Edwards in our eyes. The opening shot of *The Searchers* begins with Martha opening the door of her home to welcome Ethan back from the war; the first time we see Mrs. Jorgenson, the camera is again inside a home (the Jorgensons') as the surrogate Martha beckons Ethan and Martin in after five years of searching for Debbie. When Mrs. Jorgenson learns of the death of a dishonest trader, her sympathetic response ("Oh, poor man") reminds us immediately of Martha. When Mose Harper, a feeble, beloved old trapper, babbles news of the Comanche band to which Debbie belongs, Mrs. Jorgenson turns comfortingly maternal, answering his sad question ("You don't think I'm crazy, do you, ma'am?") with affectionate, understated understanding ("No, Mose, you're just sick and hurt"). The film ends with one last "door shot," as Mrs. Jorgenson (Martha) stands on the porch with her husband Lars (Aaron) and Debbie (Martha's daughter), while Martin (Ethan-Aaron) and Laurie (Martha-Debbie) complete the portrait of a family together again for the first time. Ethan is blessed to be the "creator" of this portrait, and condemned to stay outside the frame; his eternal joy and sorrow will be to carry that image with him through all the turnings of the earth.

The Searchers is the ultimate "door" movie, with more than a score of shots in which doors help describe or extend the psychological milieu. Doors bring characters together: Laurie is continually walking through doors in her flirtatious pursuit of Martin, but when Charlie McCorry comes courting we see the doors half-closed, or at unusual angles. Doors reinforce characters' separation: Ethan, on the Edwards' porch, glances through the front door to see Aaron close his bedroom door with Martha inside; Ethan's last view of the home shows Martha against the front door with her arm around Debbie, and it may be the memory of that tableau that "saves" him and Debbie a decade later; when Ethan finds the Edwards' home razed by Comanches, it is the door of their storm cellar, charred and disfigured by Indian torches, that suggests the terrible vision of Martha that Ethan sees, and explains the revulsion which will provoke his equally terrible revenge. For the members of a family, a door is a bridge. To Ethan, the outsider, it will always be an unspoken, unyielding barrier.

In 1956, John Wayne was still seesawing precariously between the roles of critic's pawn and box-office phenomenon. In the full maturity of his acting career—when he was no longer Singin' Sandy and not yet Rooster Cogburn—Wayne played many parts that were a far cry from the critical stereotype of the sullen, swaggering, implacable good guy. Sullen, yes: but also, in *The Man Who Shot Liberty Valance*, remorsefully melancholic. Swaggering, yes: but also, in *Red River,* homicidally overbearing. Implacable, yes: but also, in *The Searchers,* tragically willful. Good guy, yes: but also, in each of these films, possessed of a truculence that often made him wrong, that made the viewer turn against his actions while still sympathizing with the actor. In sum, Wayne's persona was that of a man obsessed. And, although much of the credit for this unique characterization goes to his directors and writers—and to the deceptive ambiguities of the western genre itself—Wayne has collaborated so crucially in the genre's evolution from a documentary form (the "real" Old West as seen through William S. Hart's you-are-there microscope) to an art form (Ford's and Hawks's evocation of the West less as a primitive territory than as a complex state of mind) that to ask, "Can he act?" is not merely an inquisition. It is a myopic imposition.

The Searchers is a film about families, actual and imagined, past, present, future, and conditional. It is appropriate, then, that the Ford family of actors and artisans make appearances on both sides of the camera. Frank S. Nugent was no sooner Ford's scenarist than he became Ford's son-in-law; more astonishingly, he was no sooner "adopted" by the Master than he adapted his breezy journalistic prose to the epic style of Ford's late westerns. Wayne's son Patrick plays a winsomely green Cavalry officer (Lieutenant Greenhill, in fact), and is honored with his very own door shot, as well as an inadvertant "son" that escapes from Duke Wayne's lips. Natalie Wood plays Debbie as a teen-ager; Lana Wood, Natalie's baby sister, plays Debbie as a little girl. And the usual Ford repertory—Ward Bond, John Qualen, Harry Carey, Jr., Ken Curtis, Hank Worden—gives the film the feel of a brilliant, vital chapter in the 135-film family saga of John Ford.

Most important, and most moving, is the casting of Olive Carey as Mrs. Jorgenson. Olive's late husband, Harry Carey, Sr., was the star of Ford's first pictures, and a guiding, shaping force in the director's career. If Harry Carey was not quite a westernized version of Chaplin's tramp, he did at least end many of his films by clasping one hand around his other elbow and walking off, alone, toward the horizon. Wayne's imitation of this action in the last shot of *The Searchers,* as he walks away from Olive Carey and her new family, is perhaps the purest, most deeply felt *hommage* the movies have produced. It is a gesture that melds the exaltation of reunion with an exquisitely painful acceptance of loss; for the door that locks in a happy family must lock out the lonely, unsatisfied, relentless searcher.

> ". . . His peace of mind he knows he'll find,
> But where, dear Lord, Lord where?
> Ride away . . . ride away . . .
> Ride away."

Ring Lardner, Jr.
(1915–   )

1937   A STAR IS BORN (William A. Wellman) co-screenplay (uncredited)
NOTHING SACRED (William A. Wellman) co-screenplay (uncredited)

1939   MEET DR. CHRISTIAN (Bernard Vorhaus) co-screenplay [1]

1940   THE COURAGEOUS DR. CHRISTIAN (Bernard Vorhaus) co-story,[1] co-screenplay [1]

1941   ARKANSAS JUDGE (Frank McDonald) co-adaptation [1]

1942   WOMAN OF THE YEAR (George Stevens) co-story,[2] co-screenplay [2]

1943   THE CROSS OF LORRAINE (Tay Garnett) co-screenplay [2]

1944   TOMORROW, THE WORLD (Leslie Fenton) co-screenplay
MARRIAGE IS A PRIVATE AFFAIR (Robert Z. Leonard) co-screenplay (uncredited) [2]
LAURA (Otto Preminger) co-screenplay (uncredited)

1946   CLOAK AND DAGGER (Fritz Lang) co-screenplay

1947   FOREVER AMBER (Otto Preminger) co-screenplay

1949   FORBIDDEN STREET (Jean Negulesco) screenplay
SWISS TOUR [Four Days Leave] (Leopold Lindtberg) dialogue

1959   VIRGIN ISLAND (Pat Jackson) co-screenplay [3]

1960   A BREATH OF SCANDAL (Michael Curtiz) co-screenplay (uncredited)

1965   THE CINCINNATI KID (Norman Jewison) co-screenplay

1970   M*A*S*H (Robert Altman) screenplay

1972   LA MAISON SOUS LES ARBRES [The Deadly Trap] (René Clement) co-screenplay (uncredited)

[1] With Ian McLellan Hunter.
[2] With Michael Kanin.
[3] With Ian McLellan Hunter, under the joint pseudonym "Phillip Rush."

Of all sad words flung through the Hollywood offices of the Screen Writers Guild, the saddest may indeed be "Ring Lardner, Jr." Lardner's movie career spans almost four decades, during which perhaps two of his scripts—for *Woman of the Year* and *M*A*S*H*—were filmed the way he wanted. Even in these instances, there were hitches: writer John Lee Mahin, producer Joseph L. Mankiewicz, and director George Stevens devised an alternate ending to the final ringside reunion of Tracy and Hepburn which Lardner and Michael Kanin had written into their *Woman of the Year* script; and, when critics started lavishing laurels on *M*A*S*H*, most of the bouquets wound up in the lap of director Robert Altman, who was perfectly willing to encourage the fiction that he and his cast created *M*A*S*H* wholly on the wing of inspired improvisation.

The rest of Lardner's career offers enough examples of studio manipulation and suicidal frustration to turn Candide into a misanthrope. His most talented hack work (*Marriage Is a Private Affair* and *Forbidden Street*) was inappropriately cast and given to untalented hack directors. His most personal scripts (*Trumpet in the Dust,* treating Custer's Last Stand from a pro-Indian point of view, and *The Kid from Kokomo,* from Dalton Trumbo's story) were never filmed. His most important projects (adaptations of Gwendolyn Graham's *The Earth and High Heaven* and Christine Weston's *The Dark Wood*) were never even written. Indeed, his testimony before the House Committee on Un-American Activities as a member of the Hollywood Ten provided one of the rare occasions when this screenwriter's dialogue received faithful public transcription.

When the blacklist ended, Otto Preminger, who had employed Lardner to rewrite *Laura* and *Forever Amber,* announced that he would film Patrick Dennis's novel, *Genius,* from a screenplay by Lardner—but nothing ever came of it. Sam Peckinpah worked with him on a script for *The Cincinnati Kid*—but when Peckinpah was fired, Lardner went, too. And in the afterglow of *M*A*S*H,* not only does Lardner still have difficulty in finding backers for a script on the Mexican-American War, but he received no screen credit for his work on René Clement's *The Deadly Trap.* The only sensible response to this incredible run of bad luck would seem to be a bullet in the brain . . . *anybody's* brain. That Lardner has survived is remarkable enough. That a certain jaunty cynicism can be distinguished in films as different as *Woman of the Year,*

Laura, The Cincinnati Kid, and *M*A*S*H* is a testimony to an incorrigibly resilient craftsman.

Woman of the Year (1942)

Herewith, Garson Kanin, in *Tracy and Hepburn:*

> I believed, at that time [1941], that I had discovered the formula for a Hepburn success: A high-class, or stuck-up, or hoity-toity girl is brought down to earth by an earthly type or a lowbrow or a diamond in the rough, or a cataclysmic situation. . . .
>
> The Hepburn formula works, possibly because the audience is drawn to her, yet wants reassurance that she is real—that she is not entirely unlike itself. Nothing more endears a Queen to her subjects than a hiccup in public, a slip on the ice, a fall from a horse, or best of all, a marriage to a commoner.
>
> Once, after I had spent an evening with Dorothy Thompson, and had received a letter in the following morning's mail from Jimmy Cannon, an idea for a movie struck me: lady political pundit and hardheaded sportswriter work on same newspaper; clash in print; meet; clash in person; both wrong, both right— not bad!
>
> Since I had just been greeted by the Selective Service System, I turned the germ over to two of the brightest screenwriters I knew: my brother Michael, and Ring Lardner, Jr. It infected them neatly and the result, *Woman of the Year,* won them an Academy Award for Best Original Screenplay of 1942.

Michael Kanin and Ring Lardner, Jr. had both served time on the RKO lot in the late thirties, at the same time Garson was there directing seven amiable, adroit films. *Woman of the Year* often glides under Garson's indirect influence, while George Stevens' comic inventiveness and attention to behavioral detail mark him among the most talented directorial craftsman. (One feels the Stevens personality lurking and working at the edge of every frame, an impression more passive directors like George Cukor, and Garson Kanin himself, rarely give.) Still, *Woman of the Year* lacks the easy camaraderie—the sense of a story being inhabited instead of merely being enacted—because the writers took Garson's "Hepburn formula" too seriously. Instead of domesticating the Queen, they practically beheaded her.

That formula, of course, could be applied to just about every rich-girl-poor-boy romance Hollywood has produced, from early

D. W. Griffith to late Erich Segal. But it didn't always apply to Hepburn. In *Holiday,* for example, it's Doris Nolan, not Katharine Hepburn, who plays the rich little bitch girl; Hepburn's Linda has both the style to move at ease in high society and the sense to appreciate its stultifying limitations. What audiences may have resented about Hepburn—and Garbo, and Dietrich—was an intensity that transcended sex; and because it wasn't exactly "feminine," this intensity was assumed to be masculine, almost perverse. The actresses' natural aristocracy made them competitors to men, and not just accessories. Pairing them with equally aristocratic male stars (though none come to mind, suggesting that the greatest Hollywood actresses belonged to the nobility while the greatest Hollywood actors were commoners) would be, paradoxically, too combustible and too rarefied. The only solution was to bring them down to the level of bourgeois audiences who were looking for objects of identification, not of veneration, in their movie stars.

Garson Kanin and Ruth Gordon recognized that Hepburn's superiority could be made acceptable if it was a matter of achievement, rather than of class. (*Pat and Mike* is the most successful demonstration of this formula.) Lardner and Michael Kanin preferred to contrast the masculinity of her shortsighted, self-important careerist—whose fall from a horse would be very welcome indeed—with a genuine sexiness Hepburn rarely allowed herself in other roles. One *Woman of the Year* image defines Tess Harding's character: behind her office desk, her back to the camera, her luscious gams resting on a side table whose distinctive ornament is a model of the globe, while she spouts fluent Spanish to Colonel Battista on the other end of an international phone call.

Because Hepburn is so sexy here, so feminine, she can get away with being ambitious, overbearing, businesslike—"masculine." And because Spencer Tracy (as sportswriter Sam Craig) possessed such a comfortable assurance of his own maleness, he could afford to play the "woman's role" in *Woman of the Year*. In his pursuit of Tess, Sam behaves reverently while waiting to speak with the busy executive; sits, fumbling and docile, while the champion of woman's rights delivers an important speech; cooks her meals; answers her phone; and even strains to win her approval of a pretty hat he's just bought himself. And yet, in their love scenes, Tracy and Hepburn share a sexual magnetism so strong that the viewer begins to feel like a voyeur. The Lardner-Kanin script sets them against each other, toe to toe, but Stevens' direction crowds them into an intimate, almost claustrophobic frame and, tête à tête, all professional rivalries momentarily vanish in a smoldering, personal romance.

Whether oversexed or overachieving, Tess tends to emasculate every man she comes in contact with. A newspaper ad reads: WHAT DO YOU THINK? TESS HARDING TELLS YOU. And, unless she's trapped in a male enclave (the Yankee Stadium press box, the corner bar) or desperately trying to squeeze her formidable frame into a subservient, female role (as kitchen magician), Tess remains firmly in control—if only because she is too insecure to accept men in positions of equality. Her male secretary is prissy and feline. Her colleagues in politics and diplomacy are either withered or withering. She smothers her father and ignores her adopted son. It's hard not to see the scene in which she steals the boy away from his homey orphanage as the revenge male filmmakers enjoy taking on an uppity woman; certainly Garson Kanin and Ruth Gordon, themselves a professional, married couple, never wrote similar scenes for *their* Tracy-Hepburn movies. In its vagrant vehemence against a willful female, *Woman of the Year* suggests a benign precursor of *M*A*S*H*, Lardner's most fully developed (if unconscious) anti-career-woman statement. If Hot Lips Houlihan's "screen scene" seems crueler and more calculating, it is both because her humiliation is devastatingly public, whereas Tess's climactic failure to cook a decent breakfast is seen only by her husband, and because Hot Lips is far less able to cope with humiliation than is the resourceful Tess.

The preceding may seem like a flight of rhetorical frenzy to those whose memories of *Woman of the Year* are suffused with the Tracy-Hepburn glow—a glow Lardner and Michael Kanin were instrumental in kindling. Their bias in favor of Sam Craig doesn't deprive Tess of some zingy, stinging dialogue; and they make it clear that Sam doesn't want a fawning housewwife (a Mrs. Sam Craig) any more than he wants a self-centered philosopher-queen (a Tess Harding). He—as well as the audience—wants a Tess Harding Craig, who can keep a job and a home with equal ease. Whether or not Tess could sustain this delicate balance is a question Tracy and Hepburn answered in their eight succeeding films, in which they and their characters grew older and wiser together. The balance of Ring Lardner's own career was a maddening series of declines and ascents —and declines—that traced a course from Hollywood to jail to European anonymity and, finally but not quite triumphantly, back to Hollywood for an amazingly popular war comedy and a second Academy Award.

*M*A*S*H* (1970)

As the vehicle of Ring Lardner, Jr.'s return to the top of his profession—and as a film that received almost unanimous critical praise—*M*A*S*H* deserves two viewings, or none. At first sight, this comedy about a group of medics just behind the lines in Korea may seem cruel but very funny. The second time, *M*A*S*H* seems funny but very cruel. Granted that the surprise of a joke is part of its appeal; but *M*A*S*H* has, in its writing and direction, a style so relaxed and assured that it isn't lost on second viewing. What does become obvious is that this smooth style disguises a bludgeon, which the main characters in the film employ on anyone who disagrees with them.

M*A*S*H follows the surgical and sexual exploits of three lovable medics, known as the Swampmen, and their virtuoso outfit, the 4077th Mobile Army Surgical Hospital. Besides the knitting and purling usual in an operating room, their exploits include saving the life of a Korean baby through an emergency operation, saving the self-respect of a well-equipped dentist through the ministrations of a shapely *dea ex machina,* and winning a football game for the outfit by drugging the opposing team's star player. Grand, fun-loving guys with quick wits and hearts of gold, right?

Not exactly. *M*A*S*H*'s trio of "heroes" (Andrew Sarris's phrase) are also bully boys. Any admiration their coolness may inspire—a coolness that is suggested by having them all act as if perpetually stoned—is tempered by the ruthlessness they show in imposing their style on the recalcitrant uncool. It's true that, like hip vampires, they'll go for the jugular only when they see it exposed (preferably on a red-neck). Thus, their Lieutenant Colonel —a benign, befuddled, absent-minded-professional soldier who galumphs rather than glides—is spared the Swampmen's more vicious japes because he takes their hi-jinks and low-blows calmly. But their first tentmate is not no lucky.

Frank Burns is a high-strung surgeon of the Don Knotts variety, who does bad things like pray out loud and bite at the Swampmen when they bait him. When Burns conspires with Margaret Houlihan, the pretty, pompous Chief Nurse, to inform the nearest general of the loose-limbed life style at the 4077th Mobile Army Surgical Hospital, our heroes decide to teach them a lesson in being cool: they bug the tent where Majors Burns and Houlihan are making violent love, and feed their orgasmic groans over the P.A. system! Beautiful? A scream? And then, the next morning, hero Donald Sutherland goads Burns into a rage by asking him if Hot Lips Houlihan is a moaner or a screamer, and if the session was "better than self-abuse"—whereupon Burns lunges at Sutherland and is led off the base in a strait jacket! Fun-ny?

If our laughter at this practical joke sticks in our throat—if we find it impossible to laugh at all—it may not be because we, like Major Burns, can't take a joke. Perhaps we simply don't like to see human beings—even self-righteous or shortsighted ones, even those meant as butts of a general military joke—tortured in such a smug, pesudo-moralistic way. In most comedies, where the dialogue, situations, and characters are stylized to create a critical distance between actor and audience, we don't worry about the pain one character inflicts on another. Charlie Chaplin can fit Eric Campbell's Bluto head into the vise of a Victorian streetlight and turn the gas on; John Wayne can throw a pitcher of scalding water on a stubborn trapper in the burlesque *North to Alaska*; and we accept it without flinching, as a convention of the genre. The broadness of comic style is the film's assurance to its audience that nobody, least of all these fleshed-out cartoon villains, is really being hurt.

But *M*A*S*H* mixes comedy situations with a documentary rigor almost worthy of Fred Wiseman. When a patient in the operating room spurts a vigorous stream of blood, we're meant to gasp, not laugh, and to think it's real. The tendency also applies to the characters: they're not caricatures, they're meant to be real. And, of course, pain and humiliation are two different things. So our reaction to *M*A*S*H*'s first "humiliation" scene is closer to what it would be in a drama or melodrama, as it is in the gas suffocation in *Torn Curtain* or the scalding coffee Lee Marvin throws at Gloria Grahame in *The Big Heat*. Our sympathy inevitably goes to the humiliated majors in *M*A*S*H*, as it does to the victims in films as disparate as *Mr. Smith Goes to Washington* and *The Naked Night*. The heroes of *M*A*S*H* are guilty of a prank that, because of its effect on Major Burns, turns into an atrocity. In what other movie have we been expected to sympathize with the torturers (however likable) and against the victims (however ludicrous)?

This is only Phase One of the neat little trick our boys plan to spring on Hot Lips. As a penance for no particular transgression, the Swampmen rig a falling-screen device to determine Major Houlihan's "natural" color. When the ploy is realized, Hot Lips becomes hysterical and runs to the Colonel's tent to threaten resignation. But the Colonel is in bed with his secretary. "Goddammit, Hot Lips," he shouts, "resign your goddammed commission!" The virulence of this second humiliation—the most horrifying "shower scene" since *Psycho*—and the sense of claustrophobic persecution that Sally Kellerman conveys as Hot Lips, remove it entirely from the relaxed atmosphere of the rest of *M*A*S*H*. Miss Kellerman's (possibly misplaced) conviction as a pent-up, full-bodied woman being pecked at by a kindergarten full of Katzenjammer starlings forces us into the kind of paranoid identification we feel for Stefania Sandrelli, the pregnant girl in *Seduced and Abandoned*. It occurs to us that the MASH surgeons "maintain sanity in the rampant insanity of war" (as Lardner himself put it) simply by driving other people insane. Surely therapy has its limits.

But surely, Lardner would argue, the Swampmen are performing radical therapy on Hot Lips. And, to be sure, Nurse Houlihan is soon liberated—by sleeping with one of the heroes. The effects of this liberation are not entirely positive, however: a woman who, when repressed, displayed a tremulous but real dignity, suddenly becomes an idiot when freed. The movie's idea of redemption is to turn her, and all the other women in the outfit, into affable imbeciles who are only trusted with passing the scalpel, cheerleading at a ballgame, and acting as bedmates. *M*A*S*H* may be the first war film that rejects the back-home female fantasy of What Our Nice Boys Are Doing Over There (a dream necessary for civilian morale during World War II) for the male locker-room and barracks fantasy where all the guys are cool studs, all the chicks are succulent nymphets, all the officers are cheerfully corrupt, and all the troublemakers are "dealt with." Lardner, and Robert Altman even more so, are guilty of failing to "place" the Swampmen's sexism—a failure that suggests the filmmakers simply weren't aware of it.

Pauline Kael, only a shade more enthusiastic than her colleagues, called *M*A*S*H* "the best American war comedy since sound came in"—in other words, since Raoul Walsh's 1926 version of the

Anderson-Stallings play, *What Price Glory?* That sounds like a pretty sweeping recommendation, until you stop to examine that genre, "American war comedy." Subtract all the subgenres, those films dealing with noncombat aspects of the military like P.O.W. escapes (*Stalag 17*), civilians in wartime (*Hail the Conquering Hero*), basic training (*No Time for Sergeants*), peacetime "service" missions (*Operation Mad Ball*); throw out the comedy-series fillers (*Buck Privates, Sailor Beware, Francis Joins the WACs, McHale's Navy Joins the Air Force*), and you're left with a handful of combat comedies hardly substantial enough to be considered a genre: Bill Mauldin's *Up Front* movies, the John Ford remake of *What Price Glory?, Mr. Roberts,* and a very few others. It's like calling a movie the best horror musical, or the most exciting Negro western.

I think the critics liked *M*A*S*H* for a lot of the same reasons they and the public latched on to *The Graduate* a few years earlier: it's a comedy that looks different. *The Graduate* wasn't the best "generation-gap" comedy of the sixties. It was the first. And *M*A*S*H* is neither a great antiwar comedy nor even an antiwar comedy. Like *The Graduate*, it is a very funny movie—and Lardner deserves credit for the multilayered, mostly humorous dialogue that makes *M*A*S*H* sporadically appealing—whose characterizations lack the depth and consistency we demand when looking for a movie that's more than very funny. As with *The Graduate*, its tone is too distinct and erratic (The Hardy Boys one moment, Satan's Sadists the next) to fit it easily into a genre. And as with *The Graduate*, most critics tended to review a film they wanted to see instead of the film in front of them.

The Mike Nichols movie arrived at a time when opinionmakers like *Time* magazine and the U.S. Census Bureau were beginning to convince us that the half of America under twenty-five was gazing at the half over twenty-five across that infamous chasm, the Generation Gap. It mattered little that *The Graduate*'s Benjamin Braddock was an inert, inarticulate schlemiel right out of the Silent Fifties, or that his girl friend Elaine was a one-cylinder coed with all the smarts of Connie Francis in *Where the Boys Are*. Audiences needed a cuddly, acceptable totem for the rebellious Now Generation, and Benjamin was probably as radical a youth image as Mom and Baby Sis could accept.

M*A*S*H is a hip, unsolemn "antiwar" movie that ends with a crazy football game (a surefire irrelevant climax, as Harold Lloyd and the Marx Brothers could verify) and makes everybody feel good on the way out—just the way Ben's and Elaine's escape from marital catastrophe did at the end of *The Graduate*. But, despite *M*A*S*H*'s clear implication that the war under consideration is not Korea but Vietnam (long hair, "groovy," marijuana), the film is no more antiwar than *The Graduate* was antibourgeois. Both tell how a cluster of individuals adapts to an unpleasant environment: the MASH surgeons to the chaos of army life, Ben and Elaine to middle-class "maturity." Neither group is even vaguely political; neither film is remotely radical.

Indeed, *M*A*S*H*'s heroes are experts at beating the system, not Smashing The System. They are saving lives because it's their job, as driving a tank would be if they'd been teamsters back home. Their civilian counterparts are the publishing, pop-music, and advertising executives who look and talk weird, but get the job done. Their surgeons' manual is not *The Strawberry Statement* but *How to Succeed in the Army by Being Really Trying*. And the aura they exude is less the crackling atmosphere of an SDS meeting than the stale beer smell of a fifties frat party. All the sideburns, swish gestures, and scatological jive can't conceal their panty-raid sensibilities. The Swampmen aren't cleansing Hot Lips of fascist sympathies when they pull aside her shower curtain; they're just initiating her. The 4077th MASH is an overseas Sigma Nu with unsavory hazing policies. While it's not wrong to find these antics funny—they often are—it *is* dishonest to justify casual cruelty by associating it with antiwar activities.

A look at Richard Hooker's novel, *MASH* (no asterisks), suggests how the brutalizing of the characters took place. In the book, war is just as insane, but the heroes don't respond to it by torturing the officers they find pompous or incompetent. The film's two "humiliation" scenes are hardly recognizable, so subdued are they in the book. (Lardner has said that he wrote in the first sequence, involving Burns and Hot Lips, while Altman "improvised" the shower scene.) Hooker also includes a scene in which Hawkeye, the supercool hero, blows his cool during difficult surgery—just like the movie's bad old Major Burns. Hawkeye's fellow surgeons are far more understanding to Major Burns in the book than they are in the film. Now, there's no reason why the movie *M*A*S*H* should be faithful to the book. But Hooker's original makes the same points without any captious brutality. Even assuming the film's heroes were justified in purging the unit of Major Burns, I can find no reason for them to humiliate Hot Lips a second time. And isn't it being overly generous to assume that their motives were any more elevated the first time? They certainly seemed to be enjoying their work.

A case might be made for *M*A*S*H* as a clinically ambiguous study of the way Joe College and Fred Premed adjust—sell out— to the pervasive and corrupting system called War. But this would certainly not be the cute and cruel mish-MASH which most critics, anxious for a piece of old-fashioned entertainment with the look of "now, baby," prematurely propelled into the vault of great films. Nor would it be the subtly reactionary film that brought Ring Lardner, Jr.—the tenacious leftist—back into the limelight toward the end of what may be remembered as the most frustrating career of a major screenwriting talent.

V. *A New Wind from the East*

TERRY SOUTHERN   ERICH SEGAL   BUCK HENRY   JULES
FEIFFER   DAVID NEWMAN and ROBERT BENTON

Since the movies' prehistory, when the first moguls imported Maurice Metterlinck and Rex Beach to bestow a cultural pedigree on the bastard medium, New York playwrights and novelists have embarked on missionary safaris out west with the idea of converting the natives—and ended up, as often as not, being cannibalized. The new breed is different. Where the essential ingredient (and ultimate curse) for many displaced Easterners in the thirties was 86-proof condescension toward the commercial cinema, today's young screenwriters know and love movies of all kinds and all countries. And they've used their fond knowledge in making, and remaking, what we know as the contemporary Hollywood movie.

In temperament and level of achievement, the men represented here vary wildly. What they do share is the distinction of having revived the concept of "writer's cinema" in an era of auteur hype, for they have crucially influenced some of the past decade's most important and popular films. The next few years should tell us whether these and other screenwriters will imitate their Guild predecessors of the early forties, and assume directorial authority over their films as well as *de facto* authorship of them. One thing is certain: directors will always need talented storytellers like Feiffer, Henry, and Benton and Newman. In a narrative art form, it cannot be otherwise.

347

TERRY SOUTHERN
(1928–   )

1964   DR. STRANGELOVE, OR: HOW I LEARNED TO STOP
       WORRYING AND LOVE THE BOMB (Stanley Kubrick) co-
       screenplay
1965   THE LOVED ONE (Tony Richardson) co-screenplay
       THE CINCINNATI KID (Norman Jewison, Sam Peckinpah)
       co-screenplay
1968   BARBARELLA (Roger Vadim) co-screenplay
       CANDY (Christian Marquand) from his and Mason Hoffen-
       berg's novel
1969   EASY RIDER (Dennis Hopper) co-screenplay
1970   END OF THE ROAD (Aram Avakian) co-screenplay
       THE MAGIC CHRISTIAN (Joseph McGrath) co-screenplay

Remember the Silent Fifties, when Terry Southern was considered
shocking and, we thought, cleansing? He performed a valuable
service back then in his role as Merry Prankster for the Eisenhower
Generation. His novels (and whatever happened to Mason Hoffen-
berg?) comprised a series of practical, or sick, jokes that acted as
joy buzzers pressed against the hand of the body politic. But unlike
Lenny Bruce, to whose bleak and blue humor Southern's bore a superficial resemblance, his moral vision was both wide-eyed and
myopic. As the situation-comedy fifties gave way to that decade-
long horror movie known as the sixties, Bruce expanded his outlook
and insights to encompass his love-hate relationship with a legal
system symptomatic of America's complexities and absurdities.
Southern just kept jabbing away at national targets that had already
become soft from the sharper punches of so many others. His humor,

at first welcome because of its little-boy viciousness, refused to mature. Stunted, it was no longer offensive but cute, and then fashionable and thus trite. Now it is dull, and thus offensive.

Dr. Strangelove, Or: How I Learned to Stop Worrying and Love the Bomb (1964)

Southern was in his Welcome phase—*Candy* had finally been published by a reputable American firm—when his name appeared on the writing credits of Stanley Kubrick's *Dr. Strangelove, Or: How I Learned to Stop Worrying and Love the Bomb,* and he was given credit for turning a straight novel about nuclear destruction into a bold satire of the Bomb, the Military, venal Russkies, and effeminate Liberals. Kubrick denied that Southern's contribution was crucial, but "deviated prevert" and "purity of essence" had entered the language, and Terry Southern had entered the gates of Hollywood.

Lost in the Kubrick-Southern squabble were co-screenwriter Peter George, who had written the novel (called *Red Alert*), and star Peter Sellers, whom Kubrick himself credited with many of the film's funniest lines. To attempt acting as a one-man Writers Guild arbitration board, by assigning individual credit based on internal evidence, would seem to suggest programmatic madness worthy of Dr. Strangelove himself. Nevertheless, familiarity with the other work of Kubrick, Southern, and Sellers prompts a few educated guesses:

• Peter George's novel provided the basic plot thrust, which Andrew Sarris indirectly praised when he remarked that, "with the fate of the world riding on every twist and turn of the plot, suspense is virtually built into the theme of the film." George's work on the first drafts of the screenplay undoubtedly helped retain these vital elements.

• Kubrick made the equally vital decision to turn the suspense novel *Red Alert* into the black-comedy film *Dr. Strangelove.* He also developed and controlled the roles of General Jack D. Ripper, the low-key madman who orders the bombers under his command to attack Soviet defense installations, and General Buck Turgidson, the Pentagon apologist who argues that, although "the human element seems to have failed us here," it's not "quite fair to condemn the whole program because of a single slip-up."

• Southern is probably responsible for Major Kong, the bomber pilot who, upon realizing that his crew is heading for "Nuclear Combat toe to toe with the Russkies," drawls that their sortie will result in promotions and personal citations for "ever' last one of ya, regardless of yer race, color or yer creed," and for Colonel Bat Guano, who arrests a gallant British officer because "I think you're some kind of deviated prevert, and I think General Ripper found out about your preversion and that you were organizing some kind of mutiny of preverts." It's also likely that he contributed to Ripper's character the famous lines about allowing "the international Communist conspiracy to sap and impurify all of our precious bodily fluids," and about women who "sense my power and they seek the life essence. I do not avoid women . . . but I—I do deny them my essence."

• Sellers was largely responsible for the dialogue of the three characters he played. Group-Captain Mandrake, the audience's lone anchor of sympathy that keeps this buoyantly bilious satire from taking off into the nether regions of caricature, is a very gentle exaggeration of Trevor Howard's wartime persona, which Sellers had parodied back on the Goon Show. President Merkin Muffley, who has generally been identified as a weak Stevensonian liberal (but without a shred of the late Governor's epigrammatic grace), actually looks both backward to Eisenhower's homey know-nothingness and forward to Hubert Humphrey's garrulous say-nothingness. Muffley's big scene, a telephone conversation with the Soviet Premier, delivered with the concern and cadence of a soothing first-grade teacher, is strikingly close to a Nichols-and-May routine in which a nervous wife tries to break to her husband the news of an expensive auto collision. Sellers' great creation, though, is Dr. Strangelove himself, the humanoid Nazi scientist, the Doomsday Machine incarnate.

Herman Kahn has observed that Strangelove combined the popular images of himself, Wernher von Braun, and Henry Kissinger: Kahn thinking about the unthinkable aftereffects of thermonuclear war, von Braun putting irrational and irreducible human eccentricities into a computerized read-out, and Kissinger speaking of a human holocaust in an inhuman, unspeakable German accent. Strangelove and Ripper share that old Nazi optimism about "purifying" the race, through either genocide or cybernetics; and the joke, popular in the wake of Sputnik, that "their German scientists are better than our German scientists," lurks near enough to the surface of this film that Strangelove-duplicates can be assumed to have programmed Soviet politicians with the same devastating information.

Sellers was originally to have also played the Major Kong role, which would have given him control of the three varyingly impotent protagonists as well as the mechanical monster who personifies and seals their doom. With Slim Pickens giving the same odd intensity to his comic-pathetic role that Sterling Hayden invests in the tragi-comic apparition of General Ripper, the film loses its formal balance —although Pickens, riding that huge phallic rocket to Armageddon like a hopped-up rodeo star, and yahooing with the down-home excitement he must have brought to such low-budget westerns as *Border Saddlemates* and *Down Laredo Way,* achieves a poignant, all-too-American insanity that would simply have been foreign to Sellers, and beyond his reach.

It's a shame Sellers couldn't have assumed the Buck Turgidson role that went instead to George C. Scott. Though Scott looks right, with the popeyes of a borderline psychotic who has been watching a TV test pattern for three days straight, his performance vacillates between an O.K. impression of Eddie Mayehoff and a cacophony of gestural low-comedy, replete with primping and pratfalls. To be sure, Kubrick is to blame for this reckless, directionless hammery; at one point, he even simulates cartoon rays of anger emanating from Scott's head. But the feeling persists that Sellers might have brought to this role a few of the inventive nuances he bestowed on Mandrake, Muffley, and Strangelove.

What Sellers might have lost in his incarnation of Major Kong, he more than makes up for during Strangelove's final moments. As the DM (Doomsday Machine) begins to go haywire, so does DM (Doktor Merkwurdichliebe, Strangelove's real name). Fighting off the steel fingers that threaten to choke him, slipping into a halluci-nation that Muffley is *"Mein Führer,"* sputtering like a phonograph that has just been unplugged, and finally rising from his wheelchair "like old gray mad Nijinsky" (Nabokov's description of the death throes of Clare Quilty, the character Sellers played in the Kubrick *Lolita*), Sellers transcends mimickry, or even satire. He defines mad-ness; he embodies it. His miraculous cure—which Sellers' perform-ance makes miraculous—cues the arrival of the Biblical Day of Judgment. Except that, here, the Hand of Judgment obliterates the Mandrakes of the world along with the Strangeloves and Turgidsons of the War Room.

By now, the reader will have made an educated guess of his own, and will infer that my assignation of credit to the four writers is meant in ascending order of importance. This is true. But it may be wise to return to George and Kubrick, and reaffirm that the popular success of *Dr. Strangelove* derives basically from the simple device of cross-cutting (from Ripper's office to the Bomber to the War Room and back) and the closing-off of successive alternatives. This tremendous dramatic logic propelling the film to its eschatological climax, like the irresistible force of the plots of *The Manchurian Candidate* and *Planet of the Apes,* was a structure strong enough to bear the weight of Southern's satirical gargoyles. But the films that have followed—*The Loved One, Candy, Easy Rider, End of the Road,* and, most noticeably, *The Magic Christian*—have had little discernible structure, of either propulsive plot or sympathetic characterization, and Southern himself hasn't been strong enough to carry them by force of personality. *Dr. Strangelove*'s madness was nourishing, fulfilling as well as filling. The subsequent Southern films have been all icing and no cake, leaving the viewer sicker than Southern's discomforting jokes ever were.

The Magic Christian (1970)

The Magic Christian, an amiable enough jape when Random House published it at the end of the fifties, was a sort of spin-off from *Mad* comics' "Movie Scenes We'd Like to See." With absolutely no plot thrust, and lots of chapters and big print (which must have endeared it to reviewers in an era when no novel could be considered serious unless it outweighed the Sunday *Times*), *The Magic Christian* strung beads of nastiness—a championship fight between two gay boxers, a safari stocked with a 75-mm. howitzer, a man who eats a parking ticket for money, men who jump into a tub of dung for money, a world dying to pawn its soul for some easy green —on the fragile frame of an American billionaire named Guy Grand. If Southern's *Candy* was a modern Candide, receiving her *éducation sensuelle* at the hands and other appendages of the worst of all possible males, Guy Grand was the Old Testament God masquerading as David Rockefeller, dispensing a plague whenever he felt puckish or peevish. (These analogies to classical literature can be made, incidentally, without at all inflating the already gaseous reputation of Southern's revue-skit books.)

For satire to have any resonance, it needs a wall of normalcy to bounce off. The Hollywood creators of the thirties screwball comedies knew this. Why don't Peter Sellers and Joseph McGrath? Sellers, who plays an anglicized Guy Grand, has invested most of his larger parts with humanity as well as eccentricity; his characterizations in *Battle of the Sexes, Only Two Can Play, Lolita,* and *I Love You, Alice B. Toklas* show it. McGrath directed the most attractive segments of *Casino Royale*—the parts with Sellers, especially a lovely, funny seduction scene, in which Ursula Andress seduces Sellers' James Bond. With his next two films, the Dudley Moore musical-comedy showcase, *Thirty Is A Dangerous Age, Cynthia,* and the triumphantly graceful farce, *The Bliss of Mrs. Blossom,* McGrath soldered his standing as an extraordinarily inventive and stylish entertainer. Unfortunately, the graceful comedy genre is as neglected today as the western was in the fifties. In our reappraisal of the postwar westerns of Budd Boetticher, John Ford, Sam Fuller, Howard Hawks, Anthony Mann, Nicholas Ray, and Jacques Tourneur, we tend to forget that studio economics forced most of these men out of the genre, and out of work as well. In another decade critics may rediscover the comedies of McGrath, Philippe de Broca, Frank Tashlin, and George Axelrod. But their films were not immediately appreciated, and studios preferred to finance a "searing satire" in the Southern style instead of McGrath's small, subtle comic gems. As a result, critics of the future will have far fewer films to rediscover. At its apogee, the McGrath cult numbered about three—hardly enough to back his next picture—and it shrank with the release of *The Magic Christian.*

There's an unpleasant strain evident in McGrath's work here: the tension between a graceful, tasteful artist and the gross, small-minded material he has to work with. McGrath's forte—like Sellers' and, for that matter, Southern's—is embellishment. Give him an agreeable script (Dennis Norden's and Alec Coppel's for *The Bliss of Mrs. Blossom*) and a few charming actors (James Booth, Shirley MacLaine, and Richard Attenborough in the same film), and McGrath can *realize,* or *direct,* an enchanting film. But he can't *create* out of whole cloth; certainly not from Southern's motley quilt. McGrath is an interpretive, not a creative, artist. In *The Magic Christian* he is charged not with shaping and stylizing an idea already suited to his taste, but with inventing ideas around a scheme he probably finds unsympathetic. McGrath, Sellers, and Southern—the scriptwriters of record—are not up to it.

After beginning beautifully, in a generous, lyrical McGrathian tone completely removed from that of the book, the movie settles down to a screen translation, and slight expansion, of the book. As Christ "went about doing good," Guy Grand goes about "making it hot for people." For the viewer, it's not so hot. Invention, even of the outrageously sick sort that made parts of the *Candy* film memorably repulsive, is lacking, and an air of desperation begins to hang over the film. When in doubt—which is almost always—McGrath indulges his already too highly developed taste for fag humor. Or Sellers mugs, out of character, in his Oxonian swish accent. Or Ringo Starr, who has absolutely nothing to do, looks balefully into the camera. Or Paul McCartney's infectious signature tune, "Come and Get It," is played for the fifth time. Or Yul Brynner, in drag, sings "Mad About the Boy" to Roman Polanski.

This fearless, cheerless film mocks nearly every aspect of Western Civilization the book did—except for two, the movies and television. Evidently, Southern decided that even satire had to be sold—to the movies and television. Everyone, as Guy Grand would say, has his price. Or did it get just a bit too hot for him?

Erich Segal
(1937–   )

1968   YELLOW SUBMARINE (George Dunning) co-screenplay
1970   THE GAMES (Michael Winner) screenplay
       R.P.M. (Stanley Kramer) story, screenplay
       LOVE STORY (Arthur Hiller) story, screenplay
1971   JENNIFER ON MY MIND (Noel Black) screenplay

What can you say about a Love Story that more than ten million people read and loved? That its Beauty consists in manipulating the reader's heart—long untouched by contemporary novelists—as mechanically as a Pacemaker. That its Romanticism consists in exploiting a vital family conflict without really exploring it. And that no critics' warning could keep five times as many people from seeing the Paramount movie version of Erich Segal's phenomenal weepie.

Segal is the youngish Yale classics professor whose public personality combined the optimism of Hubert Humphrey in his recent Politics-of-Joy period with the opportunism of Abbie Hoffman in his early Politics-of-Joy-Buzzer period. This would be unobjectionable if his novel—a shimmering reflection of the Segal sensibility—hadn't made record-breaking numbers of jocks weep, housewives read, booksellers solvent, and reviewers claim it as the novel that bridges our Grand Canyon of a generation gap. Even all *this* folderol would be of little concern to movie critics if it hadn't helped vault Segal into the Parthenon of Most Powerful Screenwriters, a residence which until then had been occupied only by Terry Southern and Buck Henry. That these three vastly overrated scribes comprise the front line against the onslaught of Omnipotent Directorism in Hollywood is a cause for more weeping and gnashing of typewriters than *Love Story* itself ever provoked.

Segal began his ascent to the Parthenon with a rewrite job on the *Yellow Submarine* script. I'd be happy to credit him with such puntifications as "We're in the Sea of Holes—the Hole-y Sea." But the success of that animated Beatles film was due almost entirely to its designers' play with images and ideas, which dazzled the viewer into a benign toleration of the script's play on words.

The Games, Segal's adaptation of the Hugh Atkinson novel, appeared and submerged with the speed, if not the grace, of a yellow submarine. Still, the movie deserves notice because, in a year of thumpingly tasteless disasters, it reached the nadir of ineptitude without being at all dirty. Segal mixed the form of *Intolerance* with the content of his own obsession: long-distance running. But instead of building four stories from different historical epochs into one grand, polyphonic chase, Segal built four stories of cross-country runners from different countries into one bland, phony race. The dialogue is a virtual anthology of Harry Purvis's great movie clichés, delivered with so meager a sense of absurdity that one suspects Segal believed the bilge he was putting on paper, and the actors (among them Ryan O'Neal, as a Yale track star) look too confused to do anything about it.

In *R.P.M.,* Segal teamed up with two icons of Hollywood liberalism, Stanley Kramer and Anthony Quinn, to produce a funeral oration over the corpse of campus liberalism. True to Segal's form, the movie burbled these last rites with extreme unction, bluntly stating the premises of gut issues only to use the night stick of evasiveness to evict any moral ambiguity from the premises. It was as far from any genuine spirit of youthful rebellion as balding Gary Lockwood and pendulous Ann-Margret were from the youth of the grad-school radicals they were supposed to embody.

Like *Jennifer on My Mind,* Segal's exploitation-sounding successor to *Love Story, R.P.M.* tries to palm off sophomoric soporifics as professorial profundities. (In *Jennifer on My Mind,* the following Socratic exchange takes place: "What is a Jew?" "A guy who thinks too much to ever be happy." This may help explain why, in his TV appearances, Segal always seemed so happy.) Segal's vacuous idealizing of troubled, troubling young people may make life easier for him at Yale, but is only laughable when Old-Hollywood Kramer or New-Hollywood Noel Black attempts to transfer it to celluloid. Lines that should be smart sound smart-alecky instead; emotions that should be acutely felt are too cutely felt-tipped. Anyone who believes that, in response to a thankful "God bless you, Mr. Dolci!", the retort "Did I sneeze?" is a punchline strong enough to end a scene, needs a crash course in Screenwriting I. And anyone who believes Segal's glib collegiates have the faintest resemblance to contemporary students needs to spend a few days outside the Yale placenta.

R.P.M. did have two affecting sequences. One was a short scene in which Ann-Margret serves Quinn his dinner along with a few sarcastic volleys on the precariousness of his academic and sexual reputation. The other was Quinn's final, defeated walk through an angry, disappointed crowd of students, which inevitably called to mind Gary Cooper's showdown as the victorious liberal in Kramer's *High Noon*, and served as the director's admission of the failure of the stolid social-consciousness that had carried him through twenty years of Hollywood do-gooding. Neither of these scenes had much to do with Segal's screenwriting abilities. They were amusing or moving because of our sympathy with the actors or identification with the director. But they did indicate some of the factors that would make the movie *Love Story* superior to the book.

Love Story (1970)

Segal's novel (which was derived from his film script) trades on several notable movie genres: the tyrannical-father melodrama, the rich-boy-poor-girl romance, and the dying-heroine tragedy. In movies of the thirties, these plots implied conflicts—Power vs. Devotion, Irresponsibility vs. Hardheaded Idealism, Love vs. Death—that were occasionally profound, often superficial, but usually persuasive. *Love Story* attacked these genres with all the facility of daytime soap opera, but without the soapers' density of detail. It established a problem (such as Ollie Barrett's strained relationship with his father) in the vaguest outline, and then left it up to the reader to fill in the color, the tone, the nuance, the blanks. The reader eagerly did all this by dredging up material from his own experience, and this is what made the book seem so personal, so "beautiful" to so many people. It was a mirror that reflected the reader at least as much as it did Segal—except that the reader saw himself (as Ollie) or herself (as Jenny) through a glass darkly,

and completed the sketch by trying to fit into the appropriate silhouette.

When Segal attempts to flesh out his characters with dialogue,
he reveals himself as a hopeless novice in comparison with Old
Masters like Sidney Buchman, Howard Koch, Norman Krasna, and
Delmer Daves. These men could write dialogue that advanced the
plot *and* developed the characters *and* was witty besides. (See *Mr.
Smith Goes to Washington, Casablanca, Bachelor Mother,* and *Love
Affair* for delightful proof.) Segal tries too hard to be clever. His
"well-made" scenes begin and end on the same line but have nothing
in between. He indulges in the comedy of obvious contradictions.
(Jenny's father to Jenny: "Don't use profanity in this house. What
the hell's he gonna think?") As a result, Segal undermines his characters' likability, making them seem self-conscious and cutesy-poo.
Despite all protestation from the Consciousness III kids, Segal's
incorrigibly linear plotting and the effusive sentimentality of his dialogue demonstrate that he is much closer to McKuen's message
than he is to McLuhan's medium.

But never mind the sparsity of detail. Forget the naïve screenplay.
If a guy starts out with a story that combines *The Barretts of Wim-
pole Street* with *Easy Living* and *Camille,* adds the American
dream-milieu of a Harvard-Radcliffe romance, and puts it all into
a format that any lip reader can digest in less time than it takes to
have her hair done, he's bound to touch a lot of nerves. When some
Eli of the twenty-first century runs *Love Story* through a computer
as part of his doctoral dissertation, we'll find out just how close all
those parallels are between Oliver Barrett IV and Elizabeth Barrett Browning; certainly there are enough clues to claim it as an unofficial *hommage.* But the most interesting comparison may be
among the actresses who have portrayed Elizabeth Barrett in her
screen incarnations, for all were the wives of prominent Hollywood
production chiefs. Norma Shearer, wife of MGM's Irving Thalberg,
starred in the first adaptation—after beating out Marion Davies, the
mistress of William Randolph Hearst, whose Cosmopolitan Productions had originally planned the film. In 1957 the part was played
by Jennifer Jones, wife of independent producer David O. Selznick.
And *Love Story* itself was turned down by most of the major studios
until Ali MacGraw, later the wife of Paramount's production boss
Robert Evans (who had played Thalberg in *The Man of a Thousand*

Faces), read it and wept. Thus was Jennifer Cavilleri Browning Oliver Barrett reborn.

Arthur Hiller's direction is pretty trashy, emphasizing Segal's low-blow punchlines with shock cuts to the next scene, undercutting characters like Oliver's mother with more abrupt cuts, zooming in with TV-show predictability. And Miss MacGraw plays Jenny with one continuous smirk, which is not the subtlest way to suggest an insouciant irony that eventually encompasses a metareligious fatalism. Ray Milland (Oliver Barrett III) looks great without his toupee, like grouchy, senile Charles Foster Kane, or like the petrified old man with the lion in Magritte's "Memory of a Voyage"; and seeing the young star of *Easy Living* thirty-three years later, in a role similar to the one played by Edward Arnold (as *his* father) in the same film, stirs the movie buff's pleasantest kind of career associations. But Hiller does little with Milland except to end scenes with unflattering close-ups of his distinguished, fallen face.

Why, then, is the movie *Love Story* superior to the book? Because the dominant visual motif—snow—manages to bleach a lot of repulsiveness out of the lovers. Because Francis Lai's luscious score would evoke hot tears even if it were used as the background music for *Hee Haw*. But mainly because of Ryan O'Neal's remarkable performance. O'Neal's Ollie is as different from the snide egotist of the book as his Rodney Harrington (on TV's *Peyton Place*) was from Grace Metallious's Rodney, a spoiled brat who got—and deserved—a knee in the crotch from poor but resilient Betty Anderson. O'Neal replaces Ollie's vapidity with vulnerability, and gives an apologetic air to Ollie's selfish comments that absolves them of all malice. He carries himself with exactly the sort of easy assurance that Miss MacGraw lacks, and convinces the stingiest viewer of Ollie's suppressed nobility. In the last part of the film O'Neal accepts his fate as a "merry widower" with a sadness, grace, and dignity that recall Cary Grant's understated compassion in the sublime *An Affair to Remember*.

O'Neal is so substantial and resonant as Ollie that he tends to expose *Love Story* for what it is, even as he eloquently suggests what it might have been . . . if someone else had played Jenny, and someone else had directed the film, and, most of all, if Erich Segal were content to be a Renaissance man back on the Machiavellian East Coast instead of—for one brief, shiny moment—the hottest screenwriter in Babylon West. *Love Story*'s box-office success may have made Segal too arrogant to apologize to the critics who accused him of manipulating his audience's worst instincts. But, as the popular failure of *Jennifer on My Mind* proved, moviegoers are fickle enough to want Segalesque treacle one Christmas, and Bondian sadism the next. In the long view of film history, only Talent means never having to say you're sorry.

Buck Henry
(1930–   )

1964　THE TROUBLEMAKER (Theodore J. Flicker) co-story, co
　　　　screenplay
1967　THE GRADUATE (Mike Nichols) co-screenplay
1968　CANDY (Christian Marquand) screenplay
1970　CATCH-22 (Mike Nichols) screenplay
　　　　THE OWL AND THE PUSSYCAT (Herbert Ross) screenplay
1972　WHAT'S UP, DOC? (Peter Bogdanovich) screenplay
1973　THE DAY OF THE DOLPHIN (Mike Nichols) screenplay

Buck Henry came out of cabaret and television comedy, and most of his work has never escaped the aura of his origins. If some of *The Graduate* sounds sophomoric today, if *Candy* fails to transcend its black-out format, if *The Owl and the Pussycat* plays like nothing so much as a horny sitcom, and if *What's Up, Doc?* seems in desperate need of a laugh track, the reasons may be traced back to Henry's formative days in "The Premise" and on *Get Smart*. These are the training grounds—the minor leagues—of comedy; when so much material has to be manufactured so quickly, one solid laugh in four times at bat is a pretty good average. Unlike Paul Mazursky and Larry Tucker, Henry (so far) hasn't created characters; instead he's written lines for a character someone else has created. And unlike David Newman and Robert Benton, he rarely has been able to inhabit his characters. He just seems to be passing through, on the way to another gag-writing assignment.

The Graduate (1967)

The Graduate brought Dustin Hoffman fame, Joseph E. Levine money, and Buck Henry power; as the film's director, Mike Nichols was naturally showered with all three. Henry shares screenplay credit with Calder Willingham, but the word was quickly passed that Willingham had delivered an unacceptable script which was then completely reworked by Henry. (John Simon wrote: "The final script, we hear, is almost all Henry's.") Soon, Henry was one of the handful of screenwriters about whom *New York Times Magazine* articles are written, an honor never bestowed on such anonymous grinds as Jules Furthman, Sidney Buchman, or Howard Koch. Celebrity had attached itself to Buck Zuckerman.

And all this for a job of adaptation so close that it was less re-writing than retyping. Andrew Sarris correctly observes that Charles Webb's novel is "almost all dialogue, with the intermittent straight prose passages functioning as visual tips for the director." Yet he concludes that *"The Graduate* is a director's picture because even its mistakes are the proofs of a personal style." To be sure, most of the film's mistakes—the casting of swarthy New York actors in svelte California parts, the obtrusive *hommages* to just about every influential filmmaker of the past generation, the absence of a per-suasive, pervasive milieu, the straining to end each scene with a gimmicky "touch"—can be attributed to the director. But what audiences responded to, and what saves *The Graduate* from its ex-cesses and simplifications, are Webb's characters, situations, and dialogue. The original and defining creative impulse was his; Nich-ols and Henry were little more than adroit message carriers.

This is not to deny Henry's perspicacity in knowing a good thing when he read it—we can assume that his screenplay *was* superior to Willingham's precisely because Henry suppressed any desire to in-flict his own personality on the material—or Nichols' ability with actors and his generally correct sense of camera placement, which is usually stage-center. Critics who ascribed the director's deep-focus long-takes to the influence of Orson Welles had evidently forgotten that Nichols was fresh from the Broadway stage (as was Welles in 1940), and earlier from cabaret theater. Surely these are his major influences. Three of his films (*Who's Afraid of Virginia Woolf?*, *The Graduate*, and *Carnal Knowledge*) have, literally, a three-act structure, complete with a fade-out at the end of each "act." Most of his stage assignments dealt with small casts, with any peripheral characters reduced to the merest caricatures. Nichols won a reputation for devising ingenious bits of "business" to underline the comic points, and for getting extra mileage out of his actors. Most of all, he trusted his playwrights. *The Graduate* is strongest when, like Henry, Nichols goes with the material, and weakest when he feels the need to goose it.

The Graduate would be more satisfying if Nichols had been able to translate his talent for staging "business" into a flair for creating a realistic environment. His three "play" movies seem to exist in a vacuum that turns the cameras into so many footlights, and the screen into an invisible fourth wall. This isn't a real flaw in *Who's Afraid of Virginia Woolf?*, where George and Martha are staging a ritual that could just as easily take place on a deconsecrated altar or in a fraternity hazing room; and it's a positive decision—indeed, it is crucial to Jules Feiffer's theme—that the backgrounds in *Carnal Knowledge* be flat, white, bare, and barren. But Benjamin Braddock, the graduate, is supposed to be responding to a hostile, frustrating environment. And yet all we see are his parents, his swimming pool, and his hotel room. Benjamin tells Mrs. Robinson: "I think you're the most attractive of all my parents' friends"—and, from the information Nichols gives us, these jaded, jejune middle-agers are Ben's only companions. If Ben doesn't trust anyone over thirty, it is because he doesn't seem to know anyone under forty.

This was just barely acceptable in the novel. Webb was concentrating exclusively on his protagonist; in a way, the novel was a monologue in the third person, and Benjamin could be taken as a young man so enshrouded in self-doubt that he doesn't recognize, or respond to, his surroundings. But this concentration is a right not accorded the filmmaker. We expect to see a little life seep in around the edges—especially when this life, or the lack of it, affects the leading character. Instead, Nichols chose to *emphasize* the novel's identification with Benjamin, and to force a sympathetic identification onto the viewer in the simplest way possible: by turning all the other characters (except Ben's eventual true love, Elaine) into easily recognizable villains.

Webb's Mr. Braddock is an understandably vexed father, and in the scene where he asks Ben to tell him what's wrong we are clearly led to question Ben's Bartlebian inertia. But Nichols and Henry remodeled Mr. Braddock to fit William Daniels' prissy, pompous, fake-palsy personality. As a result, we are allowed to pigeonhole the father-son impasse into that of superior-son-vs.-close-minded-fossil. And Dad becomes the inept situation-comedy buffoon whose only use is feeding straight-lines to his witty children. (Mr. Braddock: "Ben, this whole idea seems pretty half-baked." Ben: "No, it's not. It's completely baked.") Again, in the book, Mr. Robinson retains a parcel of human dignity that Murray Hamilton is denied in the film. The scene in which Mr. Robinson tells Ben he can never see Elaine again is scripted and shot word for word from the novel—until the end of the scene, when Mr. Robinson shouts at Ben: "I think you are filth. I think you are scum. You are a degenerate!"

The most important distortion is saved for Mrs. Robinson, the vessel for Ben's *éducation sentimentale*. Because Webb scrupulously avoided cuing the reader by means of descriptive adjectives, we were free to infer a degree of tolerance, even of protectiveness in the older woman's attitude toward Ben. If Nichols had allowed Anne Bancroft a wry smile here and there, Mrs. Robinson might have emerged from the shadows of her caricature as the neurotic Black Widow—and would have made it more difficult for the audience to switch its allegiance so guiltlessly to her daughter Elaine. Instead, Bancroft plays Mrs. Robinson as a predatory bitch until her last big scene in the hotel room, when Nichols suddenly gives her a juicy close-up for instant empathy, and we see her suffering away while callous Ben screams at her from far back in the shot.

When *The Graduate* first appeared, critics accused Nichols of betraying the satirical tone of the Mrs. Robinson section for the romantic comedy of the Elaine part. But the changes Nichols and Henry made from the book could result only in a pleasant romantic comedy with a few iconoclastic trimmings. Ben and Elaine are the ideal hero and heroine of traditional romantic comedy, and Mrs. Robinson is the evil "fiancée" the hero always had to ditch in order to win the heroine's love. Even so, the final sequence in which Elaine turns from her brand-new, plaster-saint husband to scream, "Ben!" at her true love trapped in the choir loft, succeeds as one of the genre's genuine cathartic moments, synthesizing and releasing all of Elaine's jumbled emotions about the boy who's been screwing her mother and screwing up her own life.

Everything else—the alienation, the overtones of incest, the vague references to politics and generation gaps—is irrelevant. The movie Benjamin is not even recognizable as an icon of the socially involved sixties. He doesn't leave graduate school in order to work for SNCC or SANE; he doesn't let his hair grow and join a commune; he doesn't try to politicize his parents and their bourgeois friends. His "revolution" is pure fifties: like the best minds of the Eisenhower-McCarthy era, he simply withdraws.

In 1962, when Webb wrote *The Graduate*, the novel could still function as a valedictory address to the Silent Generation. In 1967, Ben was less an apotheosis than an anachronism. And this, of course, is what gave the film such wide appeal. The most reactionary middle-American could sit back comfortably and think that, if marrying a pretty girl is all my subversive son wants, maybe the kid isn't so bad after all. Henry could have tried to update Ben's predicament, given him the guerrilla appearance and rhetorical skills of the late-sixties collegiate, and just possibly written a film that would have deserved the praise *The Graduate* actually received. Instead, he simply doctored Webb's novel—padding his own role (as a suspicious hotel desk clerk), and adding clever tag lines to several scenes—and was given credit for writing the largest-grossing comedy of all time.

Jules Feiffer
(1929–   )

1971   LITTLE MURDERS (Alan Arkin) screenplay, from his play
         CARNAL KNOWLEDGE (Mike Nichols) story, screenplay

All of Jules Feiffer's cartoon characters, from Bernard Mergen-
dieler to Richard Nixon, from Harry the Rat with Women to Jonathan the Ball-Busted Bastard, are amateur, anachronistic logicians,
groping for simple reason in an age that has chosen to embrace the
circuitous and the casuistic. The old answers don't apply; the new
questions haven't yet been devised. But the Feiffer characters plod
on, coping with the absurdities of the urban life-death, and occasionally vaulting into hysteria or sinking into catatonia when the pressure becomes intolerable. Those who say Feiffer's vision is simplistic
because he is a cartoonist are wrong; it is simple because he is a
moralist. That vision is a creation unique in its comic pessimism. It
is also remarkably consistent, which may explain why *Little Murders,* conceived as a novel, succeeded as a play—and why *Carnal
Knowledge,* conceived as a play, stands as the most personal and
perceptive film to emerge from the new breed of screenwriters.

Carnal Knowledge (1971)

   Carnal Knowledge is a dirge to American male impotence. Its
message is that men have substituted the trappings of visual and
verbal sexual stimulation for the tactile reality of sexual contact.
And its medium is that vessel of vicarious sex, the American movie.
Jonathan and Sandy, the protagonists, are both victims and villains

366

of the male tribal mystique: they get aroused by talking about, reading about, watching, and thinking about sex, instead of by experiencing it. They not only share fantasies; they share the girl who personifies those fantasies. Sandy's marriage and subsequent affairs are "living" sex manuals, with his women acting as so many professors of the artful orgasm. And Jonathan's reliance on word-and-picture stimulation leads him to the brink of impotence. Finally, he can "get hard" only by gazing at the slides of his former conquests, or by listening to a hundred-dollar whore deliver an erotic litany in praise of his penis: "More beautiful, more powerful, more perfect—you're getting hard—more strong, more masculine, more extraordinary, more robust—it's rising, it's rising!—more virile, more domineering, more irresistible—it's up! *It's in the air!*"

The "heroes" of the past few years' most important films (*Midnight Cowboy, Easy Rider, Alice's Restaurant, M*A*S*H, Loving, Diary of a Mad Housewife, Five Easy Pieces, Electra Glide in Blue, The Last Picture Show,* and *Blume in Love* among them) comprise a gallery of young adults in protracted adolescence, either living out adolescent fantasies or waking up to their limitations. *Carnal Knowledge* is the brutal, conscious summation—and condemnation—of this subgenre, in which women function as props for the men's sexual and psychical apparatus. Because it concentrates its magnifying glass on its characters' sex lives, burning a hole in their most cherished, destructive illusions, the film has been called cold and two-dimensional. If the film is cold, it is because it remains faithful to its characters—by following them in their predetermined degeneration—even as it refuses to absolve them through either spiritual regeneration or apocalyptic disaster. Like *The Graduate, Carnal Knowledge* charts a young man's withdrawal, or wilting; unlike the earlier Nichols comedy, it doesn't cop out with an exhilarating chase sequence and the evanescent triumph of idealism. What seems like Feiffer's conventional comic affection for Jonathan and Sandy in the college section of the film is really the top of a dramatic slope that leads them into psychological depression and sexual regression. It is enough that Feiffer grants Jonathan one last erection before the film ends; the author would have betrayed his theme if he had given Jonathan a resurrection too.

Critics who charge that *Carnal Knowledge* is two-dimensional are cheating: they know Feiffer is a cartoonist whose panels consist of talking heads and no background at all. Mike Nichols adapted this purity, or sterility, for his design of the film. Whole sequences take place in the dark, or in background-obliterating close-up, or against blank, white walls. The various milieux—Amherst and Smith in the forties; New York offices, night clubs, and bedrooms in the sixties; a bachelor apartment in the seventies—are sketched in as economically as the background of a UPA cartoon (some of which Feiffer drew). The women are defined only as they relate to the men, and the men are defined only as they relate to sex. *Carnal Knowledge* is no Elizabethan drama, or Dickensian novel, packed with everything you wanted to know about its characters. But this is not a fault of the film; it's a sensible, radical, formal decision of Feiffer's, which Nichols has meticulously realized.

Feiffer's dating game is a senseless ritual which men observe and women have no choice but to follow. It is also a ritual without the saving graces of nostalgia (as in *Summer of '42*), preciosity (*Le Souffle au Coeur*) or affection (*American Graffiti*). Whereas these "warm, human" comedies treat the role-playing of their young men as a rite of passage into mature sexuality, Feiffer sees it as the first taste of an addictive delusion which some American men can never completely kick. Before we ever see Jonathan, we hear him describe his ideal woman: "I'd want her sexy-looking. . . . Big tits." Later, when he's begun to doubt his potency, he meets Bobbie—"and I get one look at the size of the pair on her and I never had a doubt I wouldn't be all right again." When Sandy cautions Jonathan that looks aren't everything, Jonathan replies, "Believe me, looks are everything." A sex life that began by responding only to looks and words ends in an inability to respond to anything else, to anything deeper.

The ritual makes Jonathan suspicious of easy girls like Gloria ("I started to be in love. And then she let me feel her up on the first date. And it turned me right off"), and disappointed with aloof girls like Gwen ("I was really getting crazy about her, but she was stuck-up. She wouldn't let me lay a hand on her. So I went back to Gloria"). The ritual demands a chess-like progression to necking on dates: "If I could kiss you once last week, I should be able to kiss you at least twice tonight." It demands that conversation be less a form of communication than of strategy: "Most girls I talk to, it's like we're both spies from foreign countries, and we're speaking in code. Everything means something else. Like I say, 'Would you like to take a walk?' and it means something else. And she says, 'I can't,

I've got a French test tomorrow,' and it means something else." It demands that you despise a girl who puts out and resent a girl who doesn't. (Jonathan: "You feel her up?" Sandy: "Come on, I like this girl.") Boys are your friends, your confidants, your equals. Girls are your adversaries, your defensive players, your "goals"; you make a girl the way you make a goal in sports: through cunning, deception, and force.

Later, in "adult" life, the rules are just as strict. Women must meet a bachelor's exact specifications. ("A good pair of tits on her but not a great pair; almost no ass at all and that bothered me; sensational legs—I would've settled for the legs if she had two more inches here [*indicates height*] and three more inches here [*indicates bust*].") The man must always shower after sex. (Jonathan takes four showers during the film, and after losing his virginity jumps fully clothed into the Amherst swimming pool.) When on the prowl, he must play the good-natured letch. (Bobbie: "You always know your own mind." Jonathan [*leers*]: "Right this minute anyway.") If married, he must pretend that the routine of sex never turns into a boring ritual, even when it does. (Sandy: "We don't believe in making a ritual of it. . . . Maybe it's just not meant to be enjoyable with women you love." Jonathan: "Sandy, you want to get laid?" Sandy: "Please.") And, in the matter of mate-swapping, it's the men who make the decision, as if their women are bubblegum cards to be traded. *Plus ça change, plus c'est la même chose maudite*.

This is Feiffer's bleak-and-white vision of modern manhood. Since, in this film, the vision dominates the images, *Carnal Knowledge* is unarguably a Jules Feiffer film—and not Mike Nichols', as the credits arrogantly state. Feiffer originally offered the script to Nichols as a play, and the film still has a recognizable three-act structure (or, as Arthur Miller might describe it, two acts and a requiem), with Sandy's and Jonathan's image of the perfect girl—a graceful figure skater, "young, beautiful, incredibly built"—functioning as a dreamlike entr'acte. Nichols may be said to have "staged" Feiffer's play on the screen. For the third time, Nichols has made a bravura choice of casting (Ann-Margret as Bobbie, following Elizabeth Taylor in *Who's Afraid of Virginia Woolf?* and Dustin Hoffman in *The Graduate*) and won critical praise for himself and the performer. As with Miss Taylor, the kudos result as much from taking a previously underrated actress, telling her to put on ten or twenty easy pounds, and handing her some pungent, actable dialogue, as from the director's mystical talent with actors.

In fact, in casting Jack Nicholson as Jonathan, the Jewish boy up from the Bronx, Nichols made a serious error. (The part was first offered to Elliott Gould.) Nicholson is a low-key actor whose Mandarin eyes and Aryan features give most of his characters a reasonableness they might lack if played by other actors. But with Jonathan, Nicholson made two mistakes. In his more choleric moments, he tries too hard to "act Jewish," with broad gestures and exaggerated inflections: this is something Nicholson is unused to, and it makes him uncomfortable, and Jonathan unconvincing, in these scenes. Secondly, like Richard Benjamin in *Diary of a Mad Housewife,* Nicholson seems to want everyone to know that he's not really like Jonathan. So he stands outside the character, satirizing him, making him into a gargoyle instead of a troubled human being. There's very little of Jack Nicholson's appeal in Jonathan because, the actor would have us believe, there's very little of Jonathan's self-delusion in Jack Nicholson.

Jules Feiffer was brave enough to admit that there's a lot of his characters in him, and perceptive enough to see that there's at least a bit of them in every American male. If *Carnal Knowledge* at first seems as cold as its title (the legal definition of sexual intercourse), it is finally as honest as Feiffer's sympathy and empathy for Jonathan, Sandy, and the rest of us aging little boys.

DAVID NEWMAN (1937–   )
and
ROBERT BENTON (1932–   )

1967 BONNIE AND CLYDE (Arthur Penn) story, screenplay
1970 THERE WAS A CROOKED MAN (Joseph L. Mankiewicz)
story, screenplay
1972 WHAT'S UP, DOC? (Peter Bogdanovich) story (uncredited),
co-screenplay [1]
BAD COMPANY (Robert Benton) story, screenplay
OH, CALCUTTA (Jacques Levy) From the revue, including
the Benton-and-Newman sketch, "We Will Answer All Sincere
Replies"
1974 MONEY'S TIGHT (David Newman) story, screenplay
19 — ? HUBBA-HUBBA story, screenplay

[1] With Peter Bogdanovich and Buck Henry.

Benton and Newman rode out of the East—magazines (*Esquire*) and
Broadway (*Superman*)—with a script turned down, according to
instant movie legend, by every director from Truffaut to Godard and
every actress from Lesley Ann Warren to Tuesday Weld. When
Bonnie and Clyde was finally filmed and released, the credit went
to Arthur Penn. Penn's direction was forceful and meticulous, but
the success of the film's mixture of colloquial humor with ignorant
terror, and the use of the Bonnie Parker–Clyde Barrow story as the
frame for an essay on the limitations of movie genres, are clearly
Benton and Newman's. Their next film, *There Was a Crooked
Man*, revealed the same preoccupations in a more relaxed vein. Refreshingly cynical, it nonetheless bore a real affection for its devious,
eccentric characters and a respect for that elastic, almost elegiac
genre, the western.

Bonnie and Clyde (1967)

Millions of thoughtful words have been written about *Bonnie and Clyde,* but the slogan of the film's publicity campaign—"They're young. They're in love. And they kill people"—came close to saying it all with the simplicity of a deranged syllogism. In standard movie code, "young" means beautiful, and "in love" means good; in traditional movie morality, the beautiful and the good don't kill people without extreme provocation. So how do we reconcile our early sympathies for the Barrow gang with the random horror of their crimes? The answer lies in the use Benton and Newman make of conventions shared for so long by moviegoers and moviemakers alike.

For the first half of the film Bonnie and Clyde take us on a jaunty jalopy ride through the Depression-parched Dust Bowl region. We're like the anxious, bemused couple whose car the gang steals, and who trade some beautifully written (funny, tense, tragicomically ominous) dialogue with the engaging outlaws. Suddenly, this backwoods vehicle backfires, with a shotgun blast that bloodies an innocent man's face, and we find ourselves smack up against what might be called "an American pathedy" (since Bonnie and Clyde don't possess the exalted status or state of mind to be tragic heroes). From then on, our necks and sensibilities have been so twisted that we feel guilty for having laughed. This brutal reversal has broken our shock absorbers.

In *Jesse James*, Nunnally Johnson led us gently from an acceptance to a questioning of the gang's values, and even provided an audience surrogate to cue us how to react. This doesn't indicate any condescension on Johnson's part, because Jesse himself is as aware of his revenge-turned-obsession as he is unable to subdue it. Bonnie and Clyde retain a childlike moral myopia about their escapades; the success of the film lies in forcing us to share their criminal ignorance while all along indicating the fatal fork this particular dirt road will lead to. And, again like Johnson's *Jesse James*, it shapes our responses by manipulating our awareness of movie clichés. The rags-to-riches stories of the early talkie era primarily involved gangsters (*Public Enemy, Scarface*) and performers (*42nd Street,* the *Gold Diggers* series). Bonnie and Clyde are both. Their models are the fast talkers and snappy dressers whose appealing arrogance defined the man on the move, whether his ultimate destination was Broadway or San Quentin.

It's a truism that contemporary audiences found Cagney and Robinson "an ideal for emulation," as Richard Griffith says in *The Movies,* and never mind the cop-out, crime-does-not-pay ending. Everybody knew that crime paid a hell of a lot better than any available employment. Bonnie and Clyde knew it, and so did the average Joe who applauded their sudden celebrity. Cagney and Robinson had spurted from anonymity to stardom by playing gangsters; Parker and Barrow would do the same.

Thus, their bank-robbing *modus operandi* is pure show biz: some professional choreography (Clyde's brother Buck clears a teller's window in three graceful steps, catching Clyde's satchel with one hand), a touch of Hollywood humanism (they steal only from the institutions, not from the people), and a catchy punchline ("We're the Barrow gang!"). Bonnie even writes a scenario in verse: "The Ballad of Bonnie and Clyde." They all seem more interested in building an acceptable movie image than in accumulating a bankroll; they're auditioning for roles in their own celluloid biography— roles already defined by the concepts of Central Casting.

If we (the audience) hadn't accepted the movies' idealizing of the gangster as completely as had Bonnie and Clyde, we wouldn't be as shocked as they are when reality—in the form of blood, death, and instant, inadvertent guilt—intrudes to turn fantasy into horror, dream into nightmare. If the purpose of the farmhouse murder in *Torn Curtain* was to show, as Hitchcock says, "that it was very difficult, very painful, and it takes a very long time to kill a man" when that's the intention, *Bonnie and Clyde* demonstrates how easy it is to kill a man when you *don't* want to. In all their movie-made exhilaration, the Barrow gang forgot to load their shotguns with blanks. Nothing in *Public Enemy* (their equivalent of a how-to book) seemed to cover this contingency; no wonder they respond with fits of hysteria and depression.

From now on, every comic action will have an opposite and deadly reaction. When a rural admirer says, "They did right by me —and I'm gonna take Mrs. Flowers to their funeral"; when a little boy "plays dead" in slow motion; when the fellow whose car they stole tops—and stops—their jokes with the line, "I'm an undertaker," the laughs catch in our throat because they're coated with portent. As Fritz Lang (director of *You Only Live Once,* a thirties version of the Bonnie and Clyde story) might say, they are inhabiting an imaginary garden filled with real *tod*. Buck is systematically surrounded and mechanically slaughtered, his hand trembling in a death spasm that recalls Gromek's death in *Torn Curtain*—or the rabbit, shivering with the approach of death, in *The Rules of the Game*. Buck, Bonnie, and Clyde played by the rules, as defined by Hollywood; the posse that guns them down ignores those conventions, or, rather, adheres to a different set: those of the western, with the honest ranchers consolidating to protect their kin. Bonnie and Clyde earn our sympathy at their death almost as much because "the law" has deviously switched genres on us as because it represents an ill-defined, inhuman force massacring two likable, pathetic individuals.

The Barrow gang's role-playing extends, naturally enough, to the actors playing those roles. Warren Beatty (Clyde), Faye Dunaway (Bonnie), Gene Hackman (Buck), Estelle Parsons (Buck's wife Blanche), and Michael J. Pollard (C. W. Moss) often convey less a sense of submerging themselves in their roles than the fun a quintet of New York–trained actors are having pretending to be smart-ass Texas hicks. In a film "about" acting, this isn't necessarily a flaw. Gene Hackman's successful attempt to "be" Buck approximates Buck's attempt to "be" a bank robber; and Faye Dunaway's Bonnie—a high-fashion model whose smile is just too ironic, whose voice drips with just too much sarcasm—is a pretty girl with delusions of impending grandeur that might goad her to make a pilgrimage to the Schwab's soda fountain, but without the star quality to get her more than a quickie screentest and a producer's proposition.

Clyde (Beatty) is the best Pygmalion-producer Bonnie could hope to meet. He sculpts her "image" in the true, resourceful Sternberg-Dietrich fashion correcting her make-up, instructing her in the care and handling of firearms, giving her lessons in bank-robbing etiquette—making her the showpiece of his bucolic, one-man Actor's Studio so that, by the time they go on the road, they'll make a lasting impression on their audience. She's a triumph of semblance over substance; and so is Clyde, the handsome leading man who's really impotent. Bonnie tells him: "Your advertising's great. People'd never guess you got nothing to sell." Clyde's "advertising"— his blazing six-shooter—is a substitute for the flaccid sex life he shares with Bonnie, an analogy of impotence made clumsily obvious by Bonnie's fondling of his pistol. (This facile Freudian slop is as much a fault of the writers as of the director.) In Clyde's climactic comeuppance, the symbolism turns from pistol to peach; the movie drops (like an anvil) the hint that, were it not for the intervention of the law, Bonnie and Clyde might have driven into the sunset to live a happy, normal life.

The final shoot-'em-up, which combines the brutality of *Titus Andronicus* with the Dresden delicacy of *Swan Lake,* triggered a slew of critics' essays on violence. Pauline Kael waxed rhapsodic; Bosley Crowther waned apoplectic. Five years later, *Bonnie and Clyde*'s repellent carnage now seems like restrained classicism. Action directors like Sam Peckinpah and Don Siegel, and intellectuals like Stanley Kubrick and Roman Polanski, have embraced the balletics of violence so rigorously (if not pathologically) that Arthur Penn's meticulously constructed sequence can now be charged with siring an entire subgenre.

Repetition and exaggeration of Penn's effects have inevitably led to a coarsening of our response to set pieces of violence. What was awesome has degenerated into the merely awful. If not that, then at the very least we no longer react with cathartic wonderment, but only with irrelevant wondering: when Andy Robinson pulls a long, blood-soaked knife blade out of his leg (in *Dirty Harry*), we wonder how they did it. The violent sequences in an action movie have become the seventies equivalent of the mammoth production numbers in a Busby Berkeley musical—the province of special-effects men and not filmmakers, of artisans and not artists. And when, as with later Berkeley, our only question is "How are the special-effects men going to top themselves?" we are surrendering to the mechanics of moviemaking instead of the magic.

In the cinema's prehistory, audiences cringed when a train chugged toward the screen; imagine what their reaction must have been to the astonishingly life-and-death-like decapitation in *The Execution of Mary Queen of Scots* (1895). Today's audience is more sophisticated (read: jaded). We don't respond to violence—except on some muddled aesthetic level—because we know it isn't really happening. Andy Robinson will live to walk another day. All that's left is sex; at least that *could* be happening. Pauline Kael wrote that *Bonnie and Clyde* "has put the sting back into death." Its successors have removed that sting, just as, inevitably, some venereal

Peckinpah of the future will produce a movie that takes the savor out of sex.

Bad Company (1972)

Of Peter Bogdanovich, David Newman once remarked: "Everyone else in Hollywood wants to be Fellini. Peter wants to win the Irving J. Thalberg Award." Thalberg, of course, was notorious for having a scenarist's work rewritten by successive teams of equally powerless hacks; and Bogdanovich's handling of the Newman-Benton original script of *What's Up, Doc?* was frustrating for all concerned. But Bogdanovich should be seen simply as the point of Newman's lovely one-liner, and not as the butt. Benton and Newman may not want to be Thalbergian moguls, but I suspect they don't want to be Europeanized icons in the Fellini mold either. Their goal, which they have reached with surprising sure-footedness, is to make good *American* films that both celebrate and scrutinize the values of the genres and milieux their films inhabit.

Benton and Newman are certified movie nuts. This is obvious from looking at their films; it was evident in their work for *Esquire,* from the annual "college" issues through the "Dubious Achievement" awards to their famous article on the New Sentimentality; it is gloriously manifest in any conversation with them lasting more than thirty seconds. They love movies of all kinds and all countries. But, to their credit, they know they're neither SoHo structuralists nor *Cahieriste* surfers on the *nouvelle vague.* Thus, they have chosen to work from within traditional Hollywood genres, bending them ever so slightly to an angle that accommodates their own modern perspective. Unless it's encased in the condescending quotation marks of "camp," a contemporary audience's response to senile genre-conventions is one of impatience, suspicion, contempt. So Benton and Newman create characters who fail trying to "live" (or relive) those conventions.

This decision, to be faithful to the demands of realistic (if convoluted) plots and naturalistic (if colorful) dialogue, places a difficult restriction on the writers' work. Their characters must at all times be believable as *people*—not as paper symbols of, say, Universal Brotherhood, and not as corporeal stickmen standing on one leg to balance the Panavision image. Each scene must "work" as both experience and, if possible, a comment on that experience; and to accomplish this, Benton and Newman must work harder. I could never imagine them saying, on being told that a certain sequence falls flat, "Well, of course, it was *meant* to fall flat." It's pleasantly perverse of them to decide to write sonnets in an age when poetry reads like prose; it's also rather audacious. Their modest ambition —to recapture, and then recast, the spirit of the great American movies—seems nothing less than heroic.

Bad Company fits snugly into two traditions: the "westward ho!" theme so richly mined by Howard Hawks and Anthony Mann (and Borden Chase), and the "likable losers" theme of the earlier Newman and Benton films. Jake Rumsey (Jeff Bridges) and Drew Dixon (Barry Brown) lead a gaggle of ragtail youths across the American plains of the Civil War years armed only with big dreams in their heads and petty larceny in their hearts. As with the Barrow Gang, Jake & Drew & Co. are not exactly equal to the task. What was planned as a boys' adventure straight out of nineteenth-century romantic fiction—"huntin', fishin', livin' off the land," as Jake describes it—turns into a maturing lesson in disillusionment for Jake and Drew, and an American Gothic nightmare for the others. Their urge for some ultimate destiny has been frustrated by the need for immediate survival, and movement toward a divine potential boomerangs into movement away from a demonic posse. But our heroes are still alive, they're still together, and they're still moving west!

Jake Rumsey is a prime example of the Benton-Newman conartist who's forever spoiling to match wits against the local Establishment (cf. Warren Beatty's Clyde, Kirk Douglas in *There Was a Crooked Man*, Barbra Streisand in *What's Up, Doc?*); Drew Dixon is his wily accomplice-adversary (cf. Faye Dunaway, Henry Fonda, Ryan O'Neal). All the usual polarities attendant to such relationships—active-reactive, teacher-student, protective-possessive, masculine-feminine—apply to *Bad Company*, including the subterranean antagonisms of sexual role-playing. With his blustering manner and frank, smiling eyes, Jake is the take-charge, frontier male to Drew's virginal female. Where Jake will bluff and bully, Drew will flirt and whine. The film is full of whispered confidences, threats of desertion, even a "lovers' quarrel" when Jake enthusiastically engages a traveling whore as Drew watches with resentment and envy. In this light, *Bad Company* can be seen less as a *Wild Boys of the Road* than as an *It Happened One Night*. And the "walls of Jericho" in *Bad Company* don't fall until the climactic moment when Drew realizes that he and Jake share parts of the same mendacious soul. A virgin dies; a scoundrel is born; a partnership is made.

It's hard not to see Benton and Newman in these roles. Part of the fun in watching their movies comes from digging the spectacle of two street-smart Manhattanites trying to immerse themselves in rural, past-tense arcana—and from smiling with satisfaction when they bring the charade off. Of course, they can't *be* Jake and Drew any more than Jake and Drew can *be* Western desperadoes; and their films can't be duplicates of the old movies they cherish any more than Peter Fonda can be Henry Fonda. But their respect for Ford and Hawks and the Joe Mankiewicz of *There Was a Crooked Man* (who receives an *hommage* in *Bad Company*, in the person of a fat, languid old bandit called "Big Joe") can be translated into respect for the characters in their own films, can help them to de-mythologize a genre without debunking it—and to transform eccentricity into elegy. As director, Benton has realized this. His stylistic tributes to other directors—for example, a dazzling three-minute tracking shot down a Western main street that recalls similar shots from Jean-Luc Godard's *Weekend* and Samuel Fuller's *Forty Guns* —never break the dramatic mood-spell he is trying to create. And he handles actors and images with a relaxed assurance worthy of the best American directors at their very *American* best.

At the end of *Bad Company*, Jake and Drew walk nervously into a Wells Fargo office, gulp down their apprehensions, and blurt out: "Stick 'em up!" There must be times when Benton and Newman suspect that what they're doing—getting paid for writing (and now directing) the kind of movies they've always enjoyed watching—is pure highway robbery. Not true. Any plot turns or character-types they may have pilfered from the bank of Hollywood clichés are more than repaid by the understated richness of *Bad Company*.

Hubba-Hubba (19 - - ?)

Throughout their screenwriting career, Benton and Newman have been able to embrace the narrative vitality of traditional movie genres even as they remain at a disinterested (but fascinated) arm's length from Old-Hollywood character stereotypes—and this knowledgeable ambivalence extends to their work habits as well. The very idea of team movie-writing seems an anachronism from the Thalberg days of screenplay-by-committee; but Benton and Newman have not only adopted this system for their own, they have flourished under it to the extent that, as Newman (or is it Benton?) says, "We really don't know who does what." Their Manhattan office is probably no larger than an average writer's cubicle on the old Monogram back lot; but they are there almost every day, working as intensely as if some mini-mogul were breathing down their necks. And, in the great screenwriter tradition of unproduced masterpieces, only three of their dozen or so projects since *Bonnie and Clyde* have been brought to the screen.

A few of their ideas were aborted in the business-lunch stage, such as a deal for them to do an adaptation of *Little Murders* for Jean-Luc Godard, and an original screenplay, called *Lover*, to be directed by themselves. Other properties were scuttled after the team had written a treatment (such as *Choice Cuts*, from the Boileau-Narcejac novel). But most of them have been completed as screenplays, including three which Newman himself hopes to direct: *Money's Tight*, about a trio of Manhattan co-op dwellers who plan to rob Bloomingdale's on Christmas Eve; *Floriana*, to star Jeanne Moreau and Leonard Rossiter, and which Newman describes as a film "about mysticism, based on a true story about a series of murders that took place on an island in the Galapagos in 1934, in a Utopian colony founded by a German dentist with stainless steel teeth"; and *The Crazy American Girl*, about emotional dissipation in Paris and St. Tropez. This last script was written by Newman and his wife Leslie, and with any luck it will have begun filming in France by the time this book appears.

If Benton and Newman haven't succumbed to the cynicism or rage of many of their predecessors, it may be because they have never felt that mixture of condescension and impotence that numbed men like Scott Fitzgerald and Ring Lardner, Jr., and Budd Schulberg and Harry Brown, who saw what they considered to be their best scripts declared stillborn by timid bozoes and front-office philistines. It may also be due to Benton and Newman's view of the director as a collaborator, and not as either enemy or employee. Still, neither Benton and Newman nor I would discount the older screenwriters' attitudes as merely so many cases of perennial pessimists stewing in their own bile. The writer's job is to write a script; the director's job is to direct it. When, in the old days, the production chiefs decided not to film a given script, its assigned director

would simply move on to something else, while the writer ground
his teeth down to the gums over lost power, forfeited glory, wasted
time, misplaced creativity, and a ruptured ego. If you hear enough
stories like this, you begin to think that a collection of Great Hollywood Screenplays should be researched, not by watching old movies,
but by rummaging through the Dead Scripts files at MGM, Warners,
and Fox. And in the back of your mind you can hear Cliff Robertson, the unwary fly in Joseph L. Mankiewicz's *Honey Pot,* saying
philosophically, "I write my little scripts like everybody—'til life
louses them up."

It is prosaically ironic that Benton and Newman should have
written a script featuring just such a suicidal screenwriter (in a bit
part, of course). And it is poetically apt that this particular script,
Hubba-Hubba, written in 1970, has yet to be filmed—even though
it is still under option to the Kaufman-and-Hart of TV sitcoms,
Norman Lear and Bud Yorkin. *Hubba-Hubba,* a Hollywood farce
in the distinguished tradition of *Bombshell, Once in a Lifetime,* and
Singin' in the Rain, brings the Benton-and-Newman obsessions with
role-playing and genre-bending upfront for the first time. It substan-
tiates every stargazer's base beliefs by suggesting that most actors'
award-winning performances are given behind the scenes and between the sheets. In *Hubba-Hubba* Hollywood, all moviefolk may be
divided into letches and kvetches, hustlers and hasslers, putters-out
and putters-down, Sodomites and cynics. And this most "Hollywood"
of Benton-and-Newman movies (one imagines it costing a lot of
money to make, and making a lot more back) is simultaneously their
brightest and bitterest—a tempermental juggling act that brings us
back, past 1941, and into the sticks-and-stones age of Ben Hecht and
His Merry Misanthropes.

Though its tone and setting represent something of a *volte-face*
from the team's "Westerns," the characters in *Hubba-Hubba* have
the same problem living up to the demands of genre conventions.
What is more difficult, after all, than "being" a movie star? Or a
director? Or a studio boss? Or (need we say?) a screenwriter? Hopes
are frustrated, ideals turn sour, energies become misdirected, erec-
tions go limp. And for the most ambitious, the Janus mask conceals
a grim-grinning corpse. Three leading characters (man, wife, and
son in the Schindell family, breeder of movie moguls) go to their
deaths in moments of ecstacy (two sexual, one careerist). Only
ninety-five-year-old Grandma Schindell survives, perhaps because

she alone has never taken part in the Hollywood game of ordering, pleading, pushing, grabbing, wanting, caring, living. At least the other Schindells lived for something (however venal or venereal), and died happy.

The fourth death in this steamroller farce goes to Willie Ryan, screenwriter extraordinaire, who is bequeathed a suicide scene that half the scenarists in Hollywood would love to have written—and the other half love to have played. Ryan's big joke on the movie colony is that "I've got the greatest screenplay in the world, and nobody gets it! It goes down with me!" And, true to an alcoholic's word, he proceeds to kill himself—after telephoning his wife to say she was a lousy lay, his agent to say he's a pimp, and his mother to say she screwed up his childhood. As it happens, his script of *A Woman's Shame* is put into production at Famous Players–Schindell Studios, but Willie has the last grimace: the picture turns out to be a critical and financial fiasco, and is responsible for closing down the studio. Herman J. Mankiewicz, rest in peace.

It's worth mentioning here that *Hubba-Hubba,* for all its mordant irreverence, is an achingly funny screenplay, with three or four sequences that audiences will long remember—if they ever get to see them. It could be exactly the kind of movie Hollywood desperately needs: a *funny* comedy. I say "could be" because the success or failure of any movie, however successful the screenplay, ultimately depends on the director. Whether he's considered Michelangelo or midwife, the director is responsible for shaping the finished product. Nothing in this book disputes that truism. What needs to be discussed (and my intention has been to open discussion, not close it) is the degree to which the director, like executives in other fields, orchestrates the creativity of those who work with him. In this context, a Howard Hawks can be seen as the Hollywood equivalent of an authentic American genius like Thomas Edison, who exploited and enhanced the ideas of his unsung "screenwriter," William K. L. Dickson. Thus was the cinema born, and its tradition of dubious authorship launched.

The past decade has seen the auteur theory "transformed from heresy to cliché." Its acceptance in Hollywood might have triggered a Renaissance; but too many one-shot Fellinis came up empty-handed the second time around, and now a more cautious period of Restoration has set in. The bosses have realized that moviegoers still prefer a good story to a freaked-out fresco. As a result, they are beginning to give the crucial money and power to screenwriters, who can be expected to protect both their script and their investment by signing less erratic directors. It may seem here as if aesthetic considerations are degenerating into market analysis. But such dollars-and-sense speculation is unavoidable. The American cinema is a most peculiar child: conceived in the shotgun marriage of art and industry, raised in a circus, brought to maturity under the whole world's watchful eyes—and then abandoned in its prime. It costs money to make movies, especially for the dwindling audience of the seventies; and unless self-enlightenment and self-interest can continue to intersect, the talking picture will die out like the Schindell family—but with agony instead of ecstacy.

Perhaps this newest Hollywood tendency—"enthroning screenwriters where once not so long ago only directors reigned"—will indeed blow the wind of reaction across briefly-liberated movie screens. Perhaps, too, the trend will have proven to be a fad, with a new monarch (the cinematographer?) to be anointed next Tuesday. Kingmakers and studio bosses are notoriously eager to opt for *realpolitik* over an ideal *politique*. But if early returns from key precincts are any indication, we may hope for a consolidation of writer and director. The emerging power elite is a group of young screenwriters (Terry Malick, John Milius, W. D. Richter, Rudy Wurlitzer, Paul Schrader, and half-a-dozen others) who grew up looking at movies as well as listening to them, and who have learned to think in images as well as in words. Like Benton and Newman, they write *original* screenplays, with a mastery of regional dialects and mannerisms, that explore forgotten backwaters of funky Americana. In time, of course, this group portrait will be seen as an informal collage of individual talents and ambitions. Already, in first-director features by Milius (*Dillinger*) and Malick (*Badlands*), we can distinguish between the one's carnivorous classicism and the other's beautifully controlled, eye-level elegy.

Now other Young Turks—or, as they may prefer to be called, Young Punks—are turning to direction as both the only way to preserve what they want to say and an excitingly new way to say it. Will this combustion spark a new cinema, in which critics will no longer need to argue over the respective contributions of writer and director, but will concentrate on the filmmaker—and the film? If so, the next Hollywood generation will have to prove their talent as authors before claiming status as auteurs; and the work of their gifted, frustrated predecessors will have been vindicated at last.

CAST & CREDITS OF THE FILMS
DISCUSSED INDIVIDUALLY IN THIS BOOK

Discussion of the film in question may be found in the chapter of the screen-writer whose name is in bold face.

ADAM'S RIB   1949, MGM, 101 min.

Story and screenplay by Ruth Gordon and **Garson Kanin**. Directed by George Cukor. With Spencer Tracy (*Adam Bonner*), Katharine Hepburn (*Amanda Bonner*), David Wayne (*Kip Lurie*), Judy Holliday (*Doris Attinger*), Tom Ewell (*Warren Attinger*), Jean Hagen (*Beryl Caighn*).

AN AFFAIR TO REMEMBER   1957, Fox, 119 min.

Screenplay by **Delmer Daves** and Leo McCarey. From a story (for the film *Love Affair*) by Delmer Daves (uncredited), and Mildred Cram and Leo McCarey. Directed by Leo McCarey. With Cary Grant (*Nickie Ferrante*), Deborah Kerr (*Terry McKay*), Cathleen Nesbitt (*Grandmother Janou*), Richard Denning (*Ken Bradley*), Neva Patterson (*Lois Clarke*), Fortunio Bonanova (*Courbet*).

ALL ABOUT EVE   1950, Fox, 138 min.

Screenplay by **Joseph L. Mankiewicz**. From "The Wisdom of Eve," a short story by Mary Orr. Directed by Joseph L. Mankiewicz. With Bette Davis (*Margo Channing*), Anne Baxter (*Eve Harrington*), George Sanders (*Addison DeWitt*), Celeste Holm (*Karen Richards*), Gary Merrill (*Bill Sampson*), Hugh Marlowe (*Lloyd Richards*), Thelma Ritter (*Birdie*), Marilyn Monroe (*Miss Caswell*), Gregory Ratoff (*Max Fabian*), Barbara Bates (*Phoebe*).

ANGEL   1937, Paramount, 98 min.

Screenplay by **Samson Raphaelson**. From the play by Melchior Lengyel, as adapted into English by Guy Bolton and Russell Medcraft. Directed by Ernst Lubitsch. With Marlene Dietrich (*Lady Maria Barker*), Herbert Marshall (*Sir Frederick Barker*), Melvyn Douglas (*Anthony Halton*), Edward Everett Horton (*Graham*), Laura Hope Crews (*Grand Duchess Anna Dmitrievna*).

ANGELS OVER BROADWAY   1940, Columbia, 78 min.
Story and screenplay by **Ben Hecht**. Directed by Ben Hecht and Lee
Garmes. With Douglas Fairbanks, Jr. (*Bill O'Brien*), Rita Hayworth
(*Nina Barone*), Thomas Mitchell (*Gene Gibbons*), John Qualen
(*Charles Engle*), George Watts (*Hopper*), Ralph Theodore (*Dutch
Enright*).

BACHELOR FLAT   1962, Fox, 91 min.
Screenplay by **Frank Tashlin** and Budd Grossman. From the play by
Budd Grossman. Directed by Frank Tashlin. With Tuesday Weld
(*Libby*), Richard Beymer (*Mike*), Terry-Thomas (*Professor Bruce*),
Celeste Holm (*Helen*), Francesca Bellini (*Gladys*), Jessica Dachshund
(*Herself*).

BACHELOR MOTHER   1939, RKO, 80 min.
Screenplay by **Norman Krasna**. From a story by Felix Jackson. Directed
by Garson Kanin. With Ginger Rogers (*Polly Parrish*), David Niven
(*David Merlin*), Charles Coburn (*J.B. Merlin*), Frank Albertson
(*Freddy Miller*), Ferike Boros (*Mrs. Weiss*), Ernest Truex (*Man from
the Foundling Home*), Elbert Coplen, Jr. (*Little Johnnie*).

BAD COMPANY   1972, Paramount, 93 min.
Story and screenplay by **David Newman and Robert Benton**. Directed
by Robert Benton. With Jeff Bridges (*Jake Rumsey*), Barry Brown
(*Drew Dixon*), Jim Davis (*Marshall*), David Huddleston (*Big Joe*),
John Savage (*Loney*).

BALL OF FIRE   1941, RKO, 111 min.
Screenplay by Charles Brackett and **Billy Wilder**. From a story by Billy
Wilder and Thomas Monroe. Directed by Howard Hawks. With Gary
Cooper (*Professor Bertram Potts*), Barbara Stanwyck (*Sugarpuss
O'Shea*), Oscar Homolka (*Professor Gurkakoff*), Henry Travers (*Pro-
fessor Jerome*), S.Z. Sakall (*Professor Magenbruch*), Tully Marshall
(*Professor Robinson*), Leonid Kinskey (*Professor Quintana*), Richard
Haydn (*Professor Oddly*), Aubrey Mather (*Professor Peagram*), Dana
Andrews (*Duke Pastrami*).

THE BAND WAGON   1953, MGM, 112 min.
Story and screenplay by **Betty Comden and Adolph Green**. Directed by
Vincente Minnelli. With Fred Astaire (*Tony Hunter*), Cyd Charisse
(*Gaby*), Oscar Levant (*Lester*), Nanette Fabray (*Lily*), Jack Buchanan
(*Jeffrey Cordova*), James Mitchell (*Paul Byrd*).

THE BAREFOOT CONTESSA   1954, UA, 128 min.
Story and screenplay by **Joseph L. Mankiewicz**. Directed by Joseph L.
Mankiewicz. With Humphrey Bogart (*Harry Dawes*), Ava Gardner
(*Maria Vargas*), Edmond O'Brien (*Oscar Muldoon*), Marius Goring
(*Alberto Bravano*), Valentina Cortese (*Eleanora Torlato-Favrini*),
Rosanno Brazzi (*Vincenzo Torlato-Favrini*), Warren Stevens (*Kirk
Edwards*).

THE BELLS OF ST. MARY'S 1945, RKO, 126 min.
Screenplay by **Dudley Nichols**. From a story by Leo McCarey. Directed by Leo McCarey. With Bing Crosby (*Father O'Malley*), Ingrid Bergman (*Sister Benedict*), Henry Travers (*Mr. Bogardus*), Ruth Donnelly (*Sister Michael*), Joan Carroll (*Patsy*), William Gargan (*Patsy's Father*).

BODY AND SOUL 1947, UA, 104 min.
Story and screenplay by **Abraham Polonsky**. Directed by Robert Rossen. With John Garfield (*Charlie Davis*), Lilli Palmer (*Peg Born*), Hazel Brooks (*Alice*), Anne Revere (*Anna Davis*), William Conrad (*Quinn*), Joseph Pevney (*Shorty Polaski*), Canada Lee (*Ben*), Lloyd Goff (*Roberts*).

BONNIE AND CLYDE 1967, Warners, 111 min.
Story and screenplay by **David Newman and Robert Benton**. Directed by Arthur Penn. With Warren Beatty (*Clyde Barrow*), Faye Dunaway (*Bonnie Parker*), Gene Hackman (*Buck Barrow*), Estelle Parsons (*Blanche Barrow*), Michael J. Pollard (*C.W. Moss*), Gene Wilder (*Eugene Grizzard*), Evans Evans (*Velma Davis*), Denver Pyle (*Frank Hamer*).

THE BRAVE ONE 1956, RKO, 100 min.
Screenplay credited to Harry Franklin and Merrill G. White, but actually written by **Dalton Trumbo**. From a story by Robert Rich (pseudonym for Dalton Trumbo). Directed by Irving Rapper. With Michel Ray (*Leonardo*), Rodolfo Hoyos (*Rafael Rosillo*), Elsa Cardenas (*Maria*), Carlos Navarro (*Don Alejandre*), Joi Lansing (*Marion Randall*).

CAPTAIN BLOOD 1935, Warners, 119 min.
Screenplay by **Casey Robinson**. From the novel by Rafael Sabatini. Directed by Michael Curtiz. With Errol Flynn (*Dr. Peter Blood*), Olivia de Havilland (*Arabella Bishop*), Lionel Atwill (*Colonel Bishop*), Basil Rathbone (*Captain Levasseur*), Guy Kibbee (*Hagthorpe*).

CARNAL KNOWLEDGE 1971, Embassy, 95 min.
Story and screenplay by **Jules Feiffer**. Directed by Mike Nichols. With Jack Nicholson (*Jonathan*), Art Garfunkel (*Sandy*), Candice Bergen (*Susan*), Ann-Margret (*Bobbie*), Cynthia O'Neal (*Cindy*), Rita Moreno (*Louise*).

CASABLANCA 1942, Warners, 102 min.
Screenplay by Julius J. Epstein, Philip G. Epstein, and **Howard Koch**. From *Everybody Comes to Rick's*, a play by Murray Burnett and Joan Alison. Directed by Michael Curtiz. With Humphrey Bogart (*Rick Blaine*), Ingrid Bergman (*Ilsa Lund*), Paul Henreid (*Victor Laszlo*), Claude Rains (*Captain Louis Renault*), Conrad Veidt (*Major Strasser*), Sydney Greenstreet (*Señor Ferrari*), Peter Lorre (*Ugarte*), S.Z. Sakall (*Carl*), Madeleine Le Beau (*Yvonne*), Dooley Wilson (*Sam*), Joy

Page (*Annina*), John Qualen (*Berger*), Leonid Kinskey (*Sascha*), Helmut Dantine (*Jan*), Curt Bois (*The Dark European*), Marcel Dalio (*Emil, the Croupier*).

CHARADE   1963, Universal, 123 min.

Screenplay by **Peter Stone**. From a story by Peter Stone and Marc Behm. Directed by Stanley Donen. With Cary Grant (*Carson Dyle/Alexander Dyle/Peter Joshua/Adam Canfield/Brian Cruikshank*), Audrey Hepburn (*Regina "Reggie" Lambert*), Walter Matthau (*Hamilton Bartholomew/ Carson Dyle*), James Coburn (*Tex Penthollow*), George Kennedy (*Herman Scobie*), Ned Glass (*Leopold Gideon*), Jacques Marin (*Inspector Grandpierre*).

CITIZEN KANE   1941, RKO, 119 min.

Story and screenplay by **Herman J. Mankiewicz**. Directed by Orson Welles. With Orson Welles (*Charles Foster Kane*), Joseph Cotten (*Jedediah Leland*), Dorothy Comingore (*Susan Alexander Kane*), Everett Sloane (*Bernstein*), George Coulouris (*Walter Parks Thatcher*), Ray Collins (*Boss Jim Gettys*), Ruth Warrick (*Emily Norton Kane*), William Alland (*Thompson*).

DESIGN FOR LIVING   1933, Paramount, 90 min.

Screenplay by **Ben Hecht**. From the play by Noël Coward. Directed by Ernst Lubitsch. With Fredric March (*Tom*), Gary Cooper (*George*), Miriam Hopkins (*Gilda*), Edward Everett Horton (*Max*), Franklin Pangborn (*Mr. Douglas*).

DESIRE   1936, Paramount, 89 min.

Screenplay by **Edwin Justus Mayer** and Waldemar Young. Adaptation by Samuel Hoffenstein. From the play by Hans Szekely and R.A. Stemmle. Directed by Frank Borzage. With Marlene Dietrich (*Madeleine de Beaupré*), Gary Cooper (*Tom Bradley*), John Halliday (*Carlos Margoli*), William Frawley (*Mr. Gibson*), Ernest Cossart (*Aristide Duval*).

DIAMOND JIM   1935, Universal, 93 min.

Screenplay by **Preston Sturges**. Adaptation by Harry Clork and Doris Malloy. From the biography by Parker Morell. Directed by Edward Sutherland. With Edward Arnold (*Diamond Jim Brady*), Jean Arthur (*Jane Matthews/Emma*), Binnie Barnes (*Lillian Russell*), Cesar Romero (*Jerry Richardson*), Eric Blore (*Sampson Fox*), William Demarest (*Harry Hill*), Alan Bridge (*Man on Train*).

DR. STRANGELOVE, OR: HOW I LEARNED TO
STOP WORRYING AND LOVE THE BOMB   1964, Columbia, 93 min.

Screenplay by Stanley Kubrick, **Terry Southern**, and Peter George. From *Red Alert*, a novel by Peter George. Directed by Stanley Kubrick. With Peter Sellers (*Group Captain Lionel Mandrake/President Merkin Muffley/Dr. Strangelove*), George C. Scott (*General Buck Turgidson*), Sterling Hayden (*General Jack D. Ripper*), Keenan Wynn (*Colonel Bat Guano*), Slim Pickens (*Major T.J. "King" Kong*).

EASY LIVING   1937, Paramount, 87 min.

Screenplay by **Preston Sturges**. From a story by Vera Caspary. Directed by Mitchell Leisen. With Jean Arthur (*Mary Smith*), Edward Arnold (*J.B. Ball*), Ray Milland (*John Ball, Jr.*), Luis Alberni (*Louis Louis*), Mary Nash (*Mrs. J.B. Ball*), Franklin Pangborn (*Van Buren*), William Demarest (*Wallace Whistling*), Esther Dale (*Lillian*), Robert Greig (*Butler*).

THE FIRST TIME   1952, Columbia, 89 min.

Screenplay by Jean Rouverol, Hugo Butler, **Frank Tashlin**, and Dane Lussier. From a story by Jean Rouverol and Hugo Butler. Directed by Frank Tashlin. With Robert Cummings (*Joe Bennet*), Barbara Hale (*Betsey Bennet*), Bill Goodwin (*Mel Gilbert*), Jeff Donnell (*Donna Gilbert*), Carl Benton Reid (*Andrew Bennet*).

FORCE OF EVIL   1948, MGM, 78 min.

Screenplay by **Abraham Polonsky** and Ira Wolfert. From *Tucker's People*, a novel by Ira Wolfert. Directed by Abraham Polonsky. With John Garfield (*Joe Morse*), Beatrice Pearson (*Doris Lowry*), Thomas Gomez (*Leo Morse*), Roy Roberts (*Ben Tucker*), Howland Chamberlin (*Bauer*).

A FOREIGN AFFAIR   1948, Paramount, 115 min.

Screenplay by Charles Brackett, **Billy Wilder**, and Richard Breen. Adaptation by Robert Harari. From a story by David Shaw. Directed by Billy Wilder. With Jean Arthur (*Congresswoman Phoebe Frost*), Marlene Dietrich (*Erika Von Schluetow*), John Lund (*Captain John Pringle*), Millard Mitchell (*Colonel Rufus J. Plummer*), Stanley Prager (*Mike*), Bill Murphy (*Joe*).

THE FORTUNE COOKIE   1966, UA, 125 min.

Story and screenplay by **Billy Wilder** and I.A.L. Diamond. Directed by Billy Wilder. With Jack Lemmon (*Harry Hinkle*), Walter Matthau (*"Whiplash Willie" Gingrich*), Ron Rich (*Luther "Boom Boom" Jackson*), Cliff Osmond (*Purkey*), Judi West (*Sandy Hinkle*), Lurene Tuttle (*Mother Hinkle*), Sig Ruman (*Professor Winterhalter*).

THE FRONT PAGE   1931, UA, 101 min.

Screenplay by Bartlett Cormack. Dialogue by Bartlett Cormack and **Charles Lederer**. From the play by Ben Hecht and Charles MacArthur. Directed by Lewis Milestone. With Adolphe Menjou (*Walter Burns*), Pat O'Brien (*Hildy Johnson*), Mary Brian (*Peggy*), George E. Stone (*Earl Williams*), Mae Clarke (*Molly Malloy*).

GENTLEMEN PREFER BLONDES   1953, Fox, 91 min.

Screenplay by **Charles Lederer**. From the play by Anita Loos and Joseph Fields. Directed by Howard Hawks. With Jane Russell (*Dorothy*), Marilyn Monroe (*Lorelei Lee*), Charles Coburn (*Sir Francis Beekman*), Elliott Reid (*Malone*), Tommy Noonan (*Gus Esmond*), George Winslow (*Henry Spofford III*).

THE GIRL CAN'T HELP IT   1956, Fox, 96 min.
Screenplay by **Frank Tashlin** and Herbert Baker. From "Do Re Mi,"
a short story by Garson Kanin. Directed by Frank Tashlin. With Tom
Ewell (*Tom Miller*), Jayne Mansfield (*Jerri Jordan*), Edmond O'Brien
("*Fats*" *Marty Murdock*), Henry Jones (*Mousie*), Julie London, Ray
Anthony, Little Richard, Fats Domino, The Platters, The Treniers, Gene
Vincent, Eddie Fontaine, Abbey Lincoln, The Chuckles, Johnny Olenn,
Nino Tempo, Eddie Cochran (*Themselves*).

THE GRADUATE   1967, Embassy, 105 min.
Screenplay by Calder Willingham and **Buck Henry**. From the novel by
Charles Webb. Directed by Mike Nichols. With Anne Bancroft (*Mrs.
Robinson*), Dustin Hoffman (*Benjamin Braddock*), Katharine Ross
(*Elaine Robinson*), William Daniels (*Mr. Braddock*), Murray Hamilton
(*Mr. Robinson*), Elizabeth Wilson (*Mrs. Braddock*), Buck Henry
(*Room Clerk*).

THE GREAT MOMENT   1944, Paramount, 83 min.
Screenplay by **Preston Sturges**. From the biography by René Fulop-
Miller. Directed by Preston Sturges. With Joel McCrea (*Dr. W.T.G.
Morton*), Betty Field (*Elizabeth Morton*), Harry Carey (*Professor
Warren*), William Demarest (*Eben Frost*), Louis Jean Heydt (*Dr.
Horace Wells*), Julius Tannen (*Dr. Jackson*), Porter Hall (*President
Franklin Pierce*), Edwin Maxwell (*Vice President of the Medical So-
ciety*), Franklin Pangborn (*Dr. Heywood*), Grady Sutton (*Homer
Quinby*), Harry Hayden (*Judge Shipman*), Torben Meyer (*Dr. Dahl-
meyer*), Vic Potel (*Dental Patient*), Thurston Hall (*Senator Borland*),
J. Farrell MacDonald (*Priest*), Robert Dudley (*Cashier*), Reginald
Sheffield (*Young Father*), Robert Greig (*Morton's Butler*), Harry
Rosenthal (*Mr. Chamberlain*), Frank Moran (*Porter*).

A GUY NAMED JOE   1943, MGM, 118 min.
Screenplay by **Dalton Trumbo**. From a story by Chandler Sprague and
David Boehm. Directed by Victor Fleming. With Spencer Tracy (*Pete
Sandidge*), Irene Dunne (*Dorinda Durston*), Van Johnson (*Ted Ran-
dall*), Lionel Barrymore (*The General*), James Gleason ("*Nails*" *Kil-
patrick*).

HAIL THE CONQUERING HERO   1944, Paramount, 101 min.
Story and screenplay by **Preston Sturges**. Directed by Preston Sturges.
With Eddie Bracken (*Woodrow Truesmith*), Ella Raines (*Libby*), Ray-
mond Walburn (*Mr. Noble*), William Demarest (*Sergeant Julius Heffle-
finger*), Franklin Pangborn (*Chairman of the Reception Committee*),
Elizabeth Patterson (*Libby's Aunt*), Georgia Caine (*Mrs. Truesmith*),
Freddie Steele (*Bugs*), Harry Hayden (*Doc Bissell*), Jimmy Conlin
(*Judge Dennis*), Alan Bridge (*Political Boss*), Esther Howard (*Mrs.
Noble*), Robert Warwick (*Marine Colonel*), Vic Potel (*Progressive
Party Band Leader*), Torben Meyer (*Mr. Schultz*), Chester Conklin
(*Western Union Man*), Arthur Hoyt (*Reverend Upperman*), George
Melford (*Sheriff*), Frank Moran (*Town Painter*), Paul Porcasi (*Cafe
Manager*), Pauline Drake (*Telephone Operator*).

HANDS ACROSS THE TABLE 1935, Paramount, 81 min.

Screenplay by **Norman Krasna**, Vincent Lawrence, and Herbert Fields. From a story by Vina Delmar. Directed by Mitchell Leisen. With Carole Lombard (*Reggie Allen*), Fred MacMurray (*Theodore "Ted" Drew III*), Ralph Bellamy (*Allen Macklyn*), Astrid Allwyn (*Vivian Snowden*), Ruth Donnelly (*Laura*).

HIS GIRL FRIDAY 1940, Columbia, 92 min.

Screenplay by **Charles Lederer** and (uncredited) Ben Hecht. From *The Front Page*, a play by Ben Hecht and Charles MacArthur. Directed by Howard Hawks. With Cary Grant (*Walter Burns*), Rosalind Russell (*Hildy Johnson*), Ralph Bellamy (*Bruce Baldwin*), John Qualen (*Earl Williams*), Helen Mack (*Molly Malloy*).

HOLY MATRIMONY 1943, Fox, 87 min.

Screenplay by **Nunnally Johnson**. From *Buried Alive*, a novel by Arnold Bennett. Directed by John M. Stahl. With Monty Woolley (*Priam Farll/Henry Leek*), Gracie Fields (*Alice Challice*), Laird Cregar (*Clive Oxford*), Una O'Connor (*Mrs. Leek*), Eric Blore (*Henry Leek/Priam Farll*).

HUBBA-HUBBA 19??, Warners, ??? min.

Story and screenplay by **David Newman and Robert Benton**. To be directed by Bud Yorkin. Cast of characters: Lou Schindell (*The Studio Boss*), Nora Duke (*A Star*), Dennis Blanchard (*An Aging Ex-star*), Sylvia Schindell (*Lou's Mother*), Jack Tilton (*Tyro Director*), Willard "Choo-Choo" Zale (*Hero's Gravel-voiced Sidekick*), Penny Lane (*Ingenue*), Grandma Schindell (*Mother of the Founder of Famous Players–Schindell*), Willie Ryan (*Misunderstood, Self-destructive Screenwriter*), Larry Stone (*Penny's Agent*), Adolph Schindell (*Founder of Famous Players–Schindell*), and Fong (*Himself*).

IT HAPPENED ONE NIGHT 1934, Columbia, 105 min.

Screenplay by **Robert Riskin**. From "Night Bus," a short story by Samuel Hopkins Adams. Directed by Frank Capra. With Clark Gable (*Peter Warne*), Claudette Colbert (*Ellie Andrews*), Roscoe Karns (*Oscar Shapeley*), Walter Connolly (*Alexander Andrews*), Jameson Thomas (*King Westley*).

IT'S LOVE I'M AFTER 1937, Warners, 90 min.

Screenplay by **Casey Robinson**. From a story by Maurice Hanline. Directed by Archie Mayo. With Leslie Howard (*Basil Underwood*), Bette Davis (*Joyce Arden*), Olivia de Havilland (*Marcia West*), Patric Knowles (*Henry Grant*), Eric Blore (*Digges*).

JESSE JAMES 1939, Fox, 105 min.

Story and screenplay by **Nunnally Johnson**. Directed by Henry King. With Tyrone Power (*Jesse James*), Henry Fonda (*Frank James*), Nancy Kelly (*Zee*), Randolph Scott (*Will Wright*), Henry Hull (*Major Rufus Cobb*), Brian Donlevy (*Barshee*), John Carradine (*Bob Ford*), Donald Meek (*McCoy*).

JOHNNY GOT HIS GUN   1971, Cinemation, 100 min.
Screenplay by **Dalton Trumbo**. From his novel. Directed by Dalton
Trumbo. With Timothy Bottoms (*Joe Bonham*), Kathy Fields (*Kareen*),
Marsha Hunt (*Joe's Mother*), Jason Robards (*Joe's Father*), Donald
Sutherland (*Jesus*), Diane Varsi (*Nurse*).

THE LADY EVE   1941, Paramount, 97 min.
Screenplay by **Preston Sturges**. From a story by Monckton Hoffe. Di-
rected by Preston Sturges. With Barbara Stanwyck (*Jean Harrington/
Lady Eve McGlennon Keith*), Henry Fonda (*Charles "Hopsy" Pike*),
Charles Coburn ("*Colonel*" *Harrington*), Eugene Pallette (*Mr. Pike*),
William Demarest (*Muggsy*), Eric Blore (*Sir Alfred McGlennon
Keith*), Melville Cooper (*Gerald*), Robert Greig (*Burrows*), Luis Al-
berni (*Mr. Pike's Chef*), Jimmy Conlin (*Steward*), Alan Bridge (*Stew-
ard*), Vic Potel (*Steward*), Frank Moran (*Bartender*), Pauline Drake
(*Social Secretary*), Harry Rosenthal (*Piano Tuner*), Julius Tannen
(*Lawyer*), Arthur Hoyt (*Lawyer*), Torben Meyer (*Purser*), Robert
Warwick (*Bank Manager*), Reginald Sheffield (*Professor Jones*), Robert
Dudley (*Husband on Boat*).

LETTER FROM AN UNKNOWN WOMAN   1948, Universal, 80 min.
Screenplay by **Howard Koch**. From the novella by Stefan Zweig. Di-
rected by Max Ophuls. With Joan Fontaine (*Lisa Berndl*), Louis Jour-
dan (*Stefan Brand*), Mady Christians (*Frau Berndl*), Marcel Journet
(*Johann Stauffer*), John Good (*Lieutenant Leopold von Kaltnegger*),
Leo B. Pessin (*Stefan Jr.*).

A LETTER TO THREE WIVES   1949, Fox, 103 min.
Screenplay by **Joseph L. Mankiewicz**. Adaptation by Vera Caspary.
From the novel by John Klempner. Directed by Joseph L. Mankiewicz.
With Jeanne Crain (*Deborah Bishop*), Linda Darnell (*Laura Mae Hol-
lingsway*), Ann Sothern (*Rita Phipps*), Kirk Douglas (*George Phipps*),
Paul Douglas (*Porter Hollingsway*), Jeffrey Lynn (*Brad Bishop*), Ce-
leste Holm (*voice of Addie Ross*).

THE LIEUTENANT WORE SKIRTS   1956, Fox, 98 min.
Screenplay by Albert Beich and **Frank Tashlin**. From a story by Albert
Beich. Directed by Frank Tashlin. With Tom Ewell (*Gregory Whit-
comb*), Sheree North (*Kathy Whitcomb*), Rita Moreno (*Sandra*), Rick
Jason (*Captain Barney Sloan*), Les Tremayne (*Henry Gaxton*).

LORD LOVE A DUCK   1966, UA, 105 min.
Screenplay by Larry H. Johnson and **George Axelrod**. From the novel
by Al Hine. Directed by George Axelrod. With Roddy McDowall (*Alan
"Mollymauk" Musgrave*), Tuesday Weld (*Barbara Ann Greene*), Lola
Albright (*Marie Greene*), Martin West (*Bob Barnard*), Ruth Gordon
(*Stella Barnard*), Harvey Korman (*Weldon Emmett, the Principal*),
Max Showalter (*Howard Greene*), Martin Gabel (*Harry Belmont, the
Producer*).

LOVE AFFAIR   1939, RKO, 87 min.
Screenplay by **Delmer Daves** and Donald Ogden Stewart. From a story
by Delmer Daves (uncredited), Mildred Cram, and Leo McCarey. Di-

rected by Leo McCarey. With Charles Boyer (*Michel Marnet*), Irene
Dunne (*Terry McKay*), Maria Ouspenskaya (*Grandmother Janou*),
Lee Bowman (*Ken Bradley*), Astrid Allwyn (*Lois Clarke*), Maurice
Moscovich (*Colbert*).

LOVE IN THE AFTERNOON   1957, Allied Artists, 126 min.

Screenplay by **Billy Wilder** and I.A.L. Diamond. From *Ariane*, a novel
by Claude Anet. Directed by Billy Wilder. With Gary Cooper (*Frank
Flannagan*), Audrey Hepburn (*Ariane Chavasse*), Maurice Chevalier
(*Claude Chevasse*), John McGiver (*Mr. X*), Olga Valery and the
Gypsies (*Themselves*).

LOVE STORY   1970, Paramount, 100 min.

Story and screenplay by **Erich Segal**. Directed by Arthur Hiller. With
Ali MacGraw (*Jennifer Cavilleri*), Ryan O'Neal (*Oliver Barrett IV*),
Ray Milland (*Oliver Barrett III*), John Marley (*Phil Cavilleri*), Kath-
erine Balfour (*Mrs. Oliver Barrett III*).

MADIGAN   1968, Universal, 101 min.

Screenplay by Henri Simoun, **Abraham Polonsky**, and (uncredited)
Harry Kleiner. From *The Commissioner*, a novel by Richard Dougherty.
Directed by Don Siegel. With Richard Widmark (*Detective Dan Mad-
igan*), Henry Fonda (*Commissioner Anthony X. Russell*), Inger Stevens
(*Julia Madigan*), Harry Guardino (*Detective Rocco Bonaro*), James
Whitmore (*Chief Inspector Charles Kane*), Susan Clark (*Tricia Bent-
ley*), Michael Dunn (*Midget Castiglione*), Steve Ihnat (*Barney Be-
nesch*), Don Stroud (*Hughie*), Sheree North (*Jonesy*), Warren Stevens
(*Ben Williams*), Bert Freed (*Chief of Detectives Hap Lynch*), Harry
Bellaver (*Mickey Dunn*).

THE MAGIC CHRISTIAN   1970, Commonwealth, 92 min.

Screenplay by **Terry Southern**, Joseph McGrath, and Peter Sellers. Ad-
ditional dialogue by Graham Chapman and John Cleese. From the novel
by Terry Southern. Directed by Joseph McGrath. With Peter Sellers
(*Sir Guy Grand*), Ringo Starr (*Youngman Grand*), Isabel Jeans (*Aunt
Agnes*), Wilfrid Hyde-White (*Captain Klaus*), Richard Attenborough
(*Oxford Coach*), Leonard Frey (*Ship's Psychiatrist*), Laurence Harvey
(*Hamlet*), Christopher Lee (*Ship's Vampire*), Spike Milligan (*Traffic
Warden*), Raquel Welch (*Slave Priestess*), John Cleese (*Director in
Sotheby's*).

THE MARRYING KIND   1951, Columbia, 93 min.

Story and screenplay by Ruth Gordon and **Garson Kanin**. Directed by
George Cukor. With Judy Holliday (*Florence Keefer*), Aldo Ray (*Chet
Keefer*), Madge Kennedy (*Judge Carroll*), Mickey Shaughnessy (*Pat
Bundy*), Barry Curtis (*Joey*).

M*A*S*H   1970, Fox, 116 min.

Screenplay by **Ring Lardner, Jr.** From the novel by "Richard Hooker"
(joint pseudonym for Dr H. Richard Hornberger and William Heinz.
Directed by Robert Altman. With Donald Sutherland (*Hawkeye*), Elliott Gould (*Trapper John*), Tom Skerritt (*Duke*), Sally Kellerman

(*Major Margaret "Hot Lips" Houlihan*), Robert Duvall (*Major Frank Burns*), Jo Ann Pflug (*Lieutenant Dish*), Roger Bowen (*Colonel Henry Blake*), John Schuck (*Painless Pole*).

MEET JOHN DOE   1941, Warners, 135 min.
Screenplay by **Robert Riskin**. From a story by Richard Connell and Robert Presnell. Directed by Frank Capra. With Gary Cooper (*Long John "John Doe" Willoughby*), Barbara Stanwyck (*Ann Mitchell*), Edward Arnold (*D.B. Norton*), Walter Brennan (*The Colonel*), James Gleason (*Henry Connell*), Regis Toomey (*Burt Hanson*).

MIRACLE IN THE RAIN   1956, Warners, 107 min.
Screenplay by **Ben Hecht**. From his novel. Directed by Rudolph Maté. With Jane Wyman (*Ruth Wood*), Van Johnson (*Art Hugenon*), Eileen Heckart (*Grace Ullman*), Josephine Hutchinson (*Agnes Wood*), William Gargan (*Harry Wood*), Barbara Nichols (*Arleene Witchy*), Alan King (*Sergeant Gil Parker*).

THE MIRACLE OF MORGAN'S CREEK   1944, Paramount, 99 min.
Story and screenplay by **Preston Sturges**. Directed by Preston Sturges. With Eddie Bracken (*Norval Jones*), Betty Hutton (*Trudy Kockenlocker*), William Demarest (*Officer Kockenlocker*), Diana Lynn (*Emmy Kockenlocker*), Brian Donlevy (*McGinty*), Akim Tamiroff (*The Boss*), Porter Hall (*Justice of the Peace*), Emory Parnell (*Mr. Tuerck*), Alan Bridge (*Mr. Johnson*), Julius Tannen (*Mr. Rafferty*), Vic Potel (*Newspaper Editor*), Almira Sessions (*Justice's Wife*), Esther Howard (*Sally*), J. Farrell MacDonald (*Sheriff*), Georgia Caine (*Mrs. Johnson*), Torben Meyer (*Doctor*), George Melford (*U.S. Marshall*), Jimmy Conlin (*Mayor*), Harry Rosenthal (*Mr. Schwartz*), Chester Conklin (*Pete*), Frank Moran (*First MP*), Budd Fine (*Second MP*), Byron Foulger (*McGinty's Secretary*), Arthur Hoyt (*McGinty's Secretary*).

MR. DEEDS GOES TO TOWN   1936, Columbia, 115 min.
Screenplay by **Robert Riskin**. From "Opera Hat," a short story by Clarence Buddington Kelland. Directed by Frank Capra. With Gary Cooper (*Longfellow Deeds*), Jean Arthur (*Babe Bennett*), George Bancroft (*MacWade*), Lionel Stander (*Cornelius Cobb*), Douglass Dumbrille (*John Cedar*), H.B. Warner (*Judge Walker*), Ruth Donnelly (*Mabel Dawson*), John Wray (*Farmer*), Gustav von Seyffertitz (*Dr. Frazier*), Wryley Birch (*Psychiatrist*).

MR. SMITH GOES TO WASHINGTON   1939, Columbia, 125 min.
Screenplay by **Sidney Buchman**. From a story by Lewis R. Foster. Directed by Frank Capra. With Jean Arthur (*Saunders*), James Stewart (*Jefferson Smith*), Claude Rains (*Senator Joseph Paine*), Edward Arnold (*Boss Jim Taylor*), Guy Kibbee (*Governor Hubert Hopper*), Thomas Mitchell (*Diz Moore*), Eugene Pallette (*Chick McCann*), Beulah Bondi (*Ma Smith*), H.B. Warner (*Senator Fuller*), Harry Carey (*President of the Senate*), Astrid Allwyn (*Susan Paine*), Ruth Donnelly (*Emma Hopper*), Charles Lane (*Nosey*).

THE MORE THE MERRIER   1943, Columbia, 104 min.

Screenplay by **Garson Kanin** (uncredited), Robert Russell, and Frank
Ross. Additional dialogue by Richard Flournoy and Lewis R. Foster.
From a story by Garson Kanin (uncredited), Robert Russell, and Lewis
R. Foster. Directed by George Stevens. With Jean Arthur (*Connie
Milligan*), Joel McCrea (*Joe Carter*), Charles Coburn (*Benjamin
Dingle*), Richard Gaines (*Charles J. Pendergast*), Bruce Bennett
(*Evans*).

MOROCCO   1930, Paramount, 90 min.

Screenplay by **Jules Furthman**. From *Amy Jolly*, a play by Benno Vigny.
Directed by Josef von Sternberg. With Gary Cooper (*Tom Brown*),
Marlene Dietrich (*Amy Jolly*), Adolphe Menjou (*Le Bessier*), Eve
Southern (*Madame Cesar*), Paul Porcasi (*Cafe Owner*).

MY MAN GODFREY   1936, Universal, 95 min.

Screenplay by **Morrie Ryskind**. From "1101 Park Avenue," a short
story by Eric Hatch. Directed by Gregory La Cava. With William
Powell (*Godfrey*), Carole Lombard (*Irene Bullock*), Alice Brady
(*Angelica Bullock*), Eugene Pallette (*Mr. Bullock*), Gail Patrick (*Cor-
nelia Bullock*), Alan Mowbray (*Tommy Gray*), Jean Dixon (*Molly*),
Mischa Auer (*Carlo*).

NINOTCHKA   1939, MGM, 110 min.

Screenplay by **Charles Brackett**, Billy Wilder, and Walter Reisch. From
a story by Melchior Lengyel. Directed by Ernst Lubitsch. With Greta
Garbo (*Comrade Nina Ivanovna "Ninotchka" Yakushova*), Melvyn
Douglas (*Leon d'Algout*), Ina Claire (*Swana*), Sig Ruman (*Iranoff*),
Felix Bressart (*Buljanoff*), Alexander Granach (*Kopalski*).

NORTH BY NORTHWEST   1959, MGM, 137 min.

Story and screenplay by **Ernest Lehman**. Directed by Alfred Hitchcock.
With Cary Grant (*Roger Thornhill*), Eva Marie Saint (*Eve Kendall*),
James Mason (*Phillip Vandamm*), Jessie Royce Landis (*Clara Thorn-
hill*), Leo G. Carroll (*The Professor*), Martin Landau (*Leonard*), Brion
O'Dow (*George Kaplan*).

NOTHING SACRED   1937, UA, 75 min.

Screenplay by **Ben Hecht**. Additional dialogue by Ring Lardner, Jr.
and Budd Schulberg. From "Letter to the Editor," a short story by
James H. Street. Directed by William A. Wellman. With Carole Lombard (*Hazel Flagg*), Fredric March (*Wallace Cook*), Charles Winninger (*Dr. Downer*), Walter Connolly (*Oliver Stone*), Sig Ruman
(*Dr. Eggelhoffer*), Maxie Rosenbloom (*Max*).

NOW, VOYAGER   1942, Warners, 117 min.

Screenplay by **Casey Robinson**. From the novel by Olive Higgins Prouty.
Directed by Irving Rapper. With Bette Davis (*Charlotte Vale*), Paul
Henreid (*Jerry Durrence*), Claude Rains (*Dr. Jaquith*), Gladys Cooper
(*Mrs. Vale*), Janis Wilson (*Tina*).

OH, MEN! OH, WOMEN!   1957, Fox, 90 min.

Screenplay by **Nunnally Johnson** (uncredited). From the play by Edward Chodorov. Directed by Nunnally Johnson. With Dan Dailey (*Arthur Turner*), Ginger Rogers (*Mildred Turner*), David Niven (*Dr. Alan Coles*), Barbara Rush (*Myra Hagerman*), Tony Randall (*Cobbler*).

ONLY ANGELS HAVE WINGS   1939, Columbia, 121 min.

Screenplay by **Jules Furthman**. From a story by Howard Hawks. Directed by Howard Hawks. With Cary Grant (*Jeff Carter*), Jean Arthur (*Bonnie Lee*), Richard Barthelmess (*Bat McPherson*), Rita Hayworth (*Judith*), Noah Beery Jr. (*Joe*).

PAT AND MIKE   1952, MGM, 95 min.

Story and screenplay by Ruth Gordon and **Garson Kanin**. Directed by George Cukor. With Spencer Tracy (*Mike Conovan*), Katharine Hepburn (*Pat Pemberton*), Aldo Ray (*Davie Hucko*), William Ching (*Collier Weld*), Sammy White (*Barney Gray*).

PENNY SERENADE   1941, Columbia, 125 min.

Screenplay by **Morrie Ryskind**. From a story by Martha Cheavens. Directed by George Stevens. With Irene Dunne (*Julie Gardiner Adams*), Cary Grant (*Roger Adams*), Beulah Bondi (*Miss Oliver*), Edgar Buchanan (*Applejack*), Eva Lee Kuney (*Trina, age six*), Baby Biffle (*Trina, age one*).

THE POWER AND THE GLORY   1933, Fox, 73 min.

Story and screenplay by **Preston Sturges**. Directed by William K. Howard. With Spencer Tracy (*Tom Garner*), Colleen Moore (*Sally*), Ralph Morgan (*Henry*), Helen Vinson (*Eve Borden*), Clifford Jones (*Tom Jr.*), Henry Kolker (*Mr. Borden*), Sarah Padden (*Henry's Wife*).

THE PRISONER OF SHARK ISLAND   1936, Fox, 95 min.

Story and screenplay by **Nunnally Johnson**. Directed by John Ford. With Warner Baxter (*Dr. Samuel Mudd*), Gloria Stuart (*Peggy Mudd*), Joyce Kay (*Martha Mudd*), Harry Carey (*Commandant*), John Carradine (*Sergeant Rankin*).

THE PRIVATE LIFE OF SHERLOCK HOLMES   1970, UA, 125 min.

Story and screenplay by **Billy Wilder** and I.A.L. Diamond. Based on characters created by Arthur Conan Doyle. Directed by Billy Wilder. With Robert Stephens (*Sherlock Holmes*), Colin Blakeley (*Dr. Watson*), Genevieve Page (*Gabrielle Valladon*), Christopher Lee (*Mycroft Holmes*), Tamara Toumanova (*Petrova*), Clive Revill (*Rogozhin*).

RED RIVER   1948, UA, 125 min.

Screenplay by **Borden Chase** and Charles Schnee. From *The Chisholm Trail*, a serialized novel by Borden Chase. Directed by Howard Hawks. With John Wayne (*Tom Dunson*), Montgomery Clift (*Matthew Garth*), Joanne Dru (*Tess Millay*), Colleen Gray (*Fen*), John Ireland (*Cherry Valance*).

REMEMBER THE NIGHT
1940, Paramount, 93 min.

Story and screenplay by **Preston Sturges**. Directed by Mitchell Leisen. With Barbara Stanwyck (*Lee Leander*), Fred MacMurray (*Jack Sargent*), Beulah Bondi (*Mrs. Sargent*), Elizabeth Patterson (*Aunt Emma*), Sterling Holloway (*Willie*), Snowflake (*Rufus*), Tom Kennedy (*Fat Mike*), Georgia Caine (*Lee's Mother*), George Melford (*Brian*), Fuzzy Knight (*Bandleader*), Ambrose Barker (*Customs official*).

SCARFACE
1932, UA, 90 min.

Screenplay by Seton I. Miller, John Lee Mahin, and W.R. Burnett. Adaptation by **Ben Hecht**. From the novel by Armitage Trail. Directed by Howard Hawks. With Paul Muni (*Tony Camonte*), Ann Dvorak (*Cesca*), Karen Morley (*Poppy*), George Raft (*Guido Rinaldo*), Purnell Pratt (*Publisher*), Harry J. Vejar (*Louie Costillo*).

THE SEARCHERS
1956, Warners, 119 min.

Screenplay by **Frank S. Nugent**. From *The Searcher*, a novel by Alan Le May. Directed by John Ford. With John Wayne (*Ethan Edwards*), Jeffrey Hunter (*Martin Pawley*), Vera Miles (*Laurie Jorgenson*), Ward Bond (*Captain Reverend Clayton*), Natalie Wood (*Debbie Edwards*), Lana Wood (*Debbie as a child*), John Qualen (*Lars Jorgenson*), Olive Carey (*Mrs. Jorgenson*), Ken Curtis (*Charlie McCorry*), Pat Wayne (*Lieutenant Greenhill*), Hank Worden (*Mose Harper*), Walter Coy (*Aaron Edwards*), Dorothy Jordan (*Martha Edwards*).

THE SHOP AROUND THE CORNER
1940, MGM, 97 min.

Screenplay by **Samson Raphaelson**. From the play by Nikolaus Laszlo. Directed by Ernst Lubitsch. With Margaret Sullivan (*Klara Novak*), James Stewart (*Alfred Kralik*), Frank Morgan (*Hugo Matuschek*), Joseph Schildkraut (*Ferenc Vadas*), Felix Bressart (*Pirovich*), William Tracy (*Pepi*), Edwin Maxwell (*The Doctor*).

SINGIN' IN THE RAIN
1952, MGM, 103 min.

Story and screenplay by **Betty Comden and Adolph Green**. Directed by Gene Kelly and Stanley Donen. With Gene Kelly (*Don Lockwood*), Donald O'Connor (*Cosmo Brown*), Debbie Reynolds (*Kathy Selden*), Jean Hagen (*Lina Lamont*), Millard Mitchell (*R.F. Simpson*).

SISTER KENNY
1946, RKO, 116 min.

Screenplay by **Dudley Nichols**, Alexander Knox, Mary E. McCarthy, and (uncredited) Milton Gunzburg. From *And They Shall Walk*, an autobiography by Elizabeth Kenny with Martha Ostenso. Directed by Dudley Nichols. With Rosalind Russell (*Elizabeth Kenny*), Alexander Knox (*Dr. Aeneas McDonnell*), Dean Jagger (*Kevin Connors*), Beulah Bondi (*Mary Kenny*), Philip Merivale (*Dr. Brack*).

SKIN GAME
1971, Warners, 102 min.

Screenplay by Pierre Marton (pseudonym for **Peter Stone**) and (uncredited) David Giler. From a story by Richard Alan Simmons. Directed by Paul Bogart. With James Garner (*Quincy Drew*), Lou Gossett (*Jason*), Susan Clark (*Ginger*), Brenda Sykes (*Naomi*), Edward Asner (*Plunkett*).

SOME LIKE IT HOT   1959, UA, 120 min.
Screenplay by **Billy Wilder** and I.A.L. Diamond. From a story by
Robert Thoeren and M. Logan for the German film *Fanfare of Love*.
Directed by Billy Wilder. With Marilyn Monroe (*Sugar Kane Kowal-
chek*), Tony Curtis (*Joe/Josephine*), Jack Lemmon (*Jerry/Daphne*),
George Raft (*Spats Columbo*), Pat O'Brien (*Mulligan*), Joe E. Brown
(*Osgood E. Fielding III*), Nehemiah Persoff (*Little Bonaparte*).

SON OF PALEFACE   1952, Paramount, 95 min.
Story and screenplay by **Frank Tashlin**, Robert L. Welch, and Joseph
Quillan. Directed by Frank Tashlin. With Bob Hope (*Junior*), Jane
Russell (*Mike*), Roy Rogers (*Himself*), Bill Williams (*Kirk*), Lloyd
Corrigan (*Dr. Lovejoy*).

STAGECOACH   1939, UA, 96 min.
Screenplay by **Dudley Nichols**. From "Stage to Lordsburg," a short
story by Ernest Haycox. Directed by John Ford. With John Wayne
(*Ringo Kid*), Claire Trevor (*Dallas*), Thomas Mitchell (*Dr. Boone*),
George Bancroft (*Curley Wilcox*), Andy Devine (*Buck*), John Carradine (*Hatfield*), Louise Platt (*Lucy Mallory*), Donald Meek (*Mr. Pea-
cock*), Berton Churchill (*Gatewood*), Tim Holt (*Lieutenant Blanchard*).

SULLIVAN'S TRAVELS   1942, Paramount, 90 min.
Story and screenplay by **Preston Sturges**. Directed by Preston Sturges.
With Joel McCrea (*John L. Sullivan*), Veronica Lake (*The Girl*),
Robert Warwick (*Mr. Le Brand*), William Demarest (*Mr. Jones*),
Franklin Pangborn (*Mr. Casalsis*), Porter Hall (*Mr. Hadrian*), Byron
Foulger (*Mr. Valdelle*), Vic Potel (*Cameraman*), Torben Meyer (*Doc-
tor*), Robert Greig (*Butler*), Eric Blore (*Valet*), Alan Bridge (*Mr.
Carson*), Esther Howard (*Miss Zeffie*), Almira Sessions (*Ursula*),
Frank Moran (*Tough Chauffeur*).

SUNDAY IN NEW YORK   1963, MGM, 105 min.
Screenplay by **Norman Krasna**. From his play. Directed by Peter
Tewksbury. With Cliff Robertson (*Adam Tyler*), Jane Fonda (*Eileen
Tyler*), Rod Taylor (*Mike Mitchell*), Robert Culp (*Russ Wilson*), Jo
Morrow (*Mona Harris*).

SUNSET BOULEVARD   1950, Paramount, 110 min.
Screenplay by Charles Brackett, **Billy Wilder**, and D.M. Marshman, Jr.
From a story by Charles Brackett and Billy Wilder. Directed by Billy
Wilder. With William Holden (*Joe Gillis*), Gloria Swanson (*Norma
Desmond*), Erich Von Stroheim (*Max Von Mayerling*), Nancy Olson
(*Betty Schaefer*), Cecil B. De Mille, Hedda Hopper, Buster Keaton,
Anna Q. Nilsson, H.B. Warner (*Themselves*).

SWEET SMELL OF SUCCESS   1957, UA, 99 min.
Screenplay by **Ernest Lehman** and Clifford Odets. From *Tell Me About
It Tomorrow*, a novella by Ernest Lehman. Directed by Alexander
Mackendrick. With Burt Lancaster (*J.J. Hunsecker*), Tony Curtis
(*Sidney Falco*), Susan Harrison (*Susan Hunsecker*), Martin Milner
(*Steve Dallas*), Emile Meyer (*Harry Kello*).

TEENAGE REBEL 1956, Fox, 94 min.

Screenplay by Walter Reisch and **Charles Brackett**. From *A Roomful of Roses*, a play by Edith Sommer. Directed by Edmund Goulding. With Ginger Rogers (*Nancy Fallon*), Michael Rennie (*Jay Fallon*), Betty Lou Keim (*Dodie*), Warren Berlinger (*Dick Hewitt*), Mildred Natwick (*Grace Fallon*).

TELL THEM WILLIE BOY IS HERE 1969, Universal, 96 min.

Screenplay by **Abraham Polonsky**. From *Willie Boy*, a novel by Harry Lawton. Directed by Abraham Polonsky. With Robert Redford (*Cooper*), Katharine Ross (*Lola*), Robert Blake (*Willie*), Susan Clark (*Liz*), Barry Sullivan (*Hacker*).

THEODORA GOES WILD 1936, Columbia, 94 min.

Screenplay by **Sidney Buchman**. From a story by Mary E. McCarthy. Directed by Richard Boleslawski. With Irene Dunne (*Theodora Lynn*), Melvyn Douglas (*Michael Grant*), Thomas Mitchell (*Jed Waterbury*), Thurston Hall (*Arthur Stevenson*), Rosalind Keith (*Aunt Adelaide Perry*), Spring Byington (*Aunt Rebecca Perry*).

THIS LAND IS MINE 1943, RKO, 103 min.

Story and screenplay by **Dudley Nichols**. Directed by Jean Renoir. With Charles Laughton (*Albert Lory*), Maureen O'Hara (*Louise Martin*), George Sanders (*George Lambert*), Walter Slezak (*Major Von Keller*), Kent Smith (*Paul Martin*), Una O'Connor (*Mrs. Emma Lory*).

TO BE OR NOT TO BE 1942, UA, 99 min.

Screenplay by **Edwin Justus Mayer**. From a story by Melchior Lengyel and Ernst Lubitsch. Directed by Ernst Lubitsch. With Carole Lombard (*Maria Tura*), Jack Benny (*Joseph Tura*), Robert Stack (*Lieutenant Stanislaus Sobinski*), Felix Bressart (*Greenberg*), Stanley Ridges (*Professor Siletsky*), Sig Ruman (*Colonel Ehrhardt*).

TROUBLE IN PARADISE 1932, Paramount, 83 min.

Screenplay by **Samson Raphaelson**. From *The Honest Finder*, a play by Laszlo Aladar. Directed by Ernst Lubitsch. With Miriam Hopkins (*Lily*), Kay Francis (*Madame Colet*), Herbert Marshall (*Gaston Monescu*), Edward Everett Horton (*François*), C. Aubrey Smith (*Giron*), George Humbert (*Waiter*).

UNDERWORLD 1927, Paramount, 90 min.

Screenplay by Charles Furthman (and, uncredited, Jules Furthman?). Adaptation by Charles N. Lee. From a story by **Ben Hecht**. Directed by Josef von Sternberg. With George Bancroft (*Bull Weed*), Evelyn Brent (*Feathers McCoy*), Clive Brook (*Rolls Royce*), Larry Semon (*Slippy Lewis*), Fred Kohler (*Buck Mulligan*).

UNFAITHFULLY YOURS 1948, Fox, 105 min.

Story and screenplay by **Preston Sturges**. Directed by Preston Sturges. With Rex Harrison (*Sir Alfred de Carter*), Linda Darnell (*Daphne de Carter*), Barbara Lawrence (*Barbara Henschler*), Rudy Vallee (*August Henschler*), Lionel Stander (*Hugo*), Kurt Kreuger (*Anthony*), Edgar

Kennedy (*Sweeney*), Alan Bridge (*House Detective*), Julius Tannen (*Dr. Schultz*), Robert Greig (*Jules*), Georgia Caine (*Dowager*).

WILL SUCCESS SPOIL ROCK HUNTER?   1957, Fox, 94 min.

Story and screenplay by **Frank Tashlin**. Suggested by the title of a play by George Axelrod. Directed by Frank Tashlin. With Jayne Mansfield (*Rita Marlowe*), Tony Randall (*Rock*), Betsy Drake (*Jenny*), John Williams (*Irving LaSalle, Jr.*), Mickey Hargitay (*Bobo Braniganski*), Groucho Marx (*Georgie Schmidlap*).

WOMAN OF THE YEAR   1942, MGM, 112 min.

Story and screenplay by **Ring Lardner, Jr.** and Michael Kanin. From an idea by Garson Kanin. Directed by George Stevens. With Spencer Tracy (*Sam Craig*), Katharine Hepburn (*Tess Harding*), Fay Bainter (*Ellen Whitcomb*), Reginald Owen (*Clayton*), William Bendix (*Pinkie Peters*), Dan Tobin (*Gerald, Tess's secretary*), Minor Watson (*William Harding*), Roscoe Karns (*Phil Whittaker*).

Some other books published by Penguin
are described on the following pages.

Peter Bowen, Martin Hayden, and Frank Riess

SCREEN TEST
A Quiz Book about the Movies

This volume offers a unique opportunity to test knowledge of films. Sixteen chapters of questions cover every aspect of the cinema—from silent films to science fiction. A sample: Who played the flute and who conducted the orchestra in *Hot Millions*? What films do these lines come from?— Peter Lorre: "We may be rats, crooks, and murderers . . . but we're *Americans*." James Cagney: "I'm from the collection agency . . . I've come to collect my wife." Illustrated with 188 photographs.

Peter Harcourt

SIX EUROPEAN DIRECTORS

This is a sympathetic and well-informed review of the work of six masters of the European cinema: Sergei Eisenstein, Jean Renoir, Luis Buñuel, Ingmar Bergman, Federico Fellini, and Jean-Luc Godard. Peter Harcourt holds that film criticism ought to be more accurately descriptive but also that the critic must not repress his enthusiasms or mask his preferences. By limiting himself to the cinema of Europe, Harcourt is able to apply these standards in the light of a common cultural background. Peter Harcourt has established a program in film studies at Queen's University, Ontario, Canada.

Ralph Stephenson and J. R. Debrix

THE CINEMA AS ART

In recent years the motion-picture director has
taken on the stature of an artist. How the director
exploits all of the cinematic techniques—script
planning, camera movement, costume, sound, editing—to isolate what is mentally and emotionally
significant and create a work of art is fully explained here by two professional moviemakers.
Illustrated with fifty-four photographs.

Roy Armes

FILM AND REALITY
An Historical Survey

This survey of the relationship between historical context and artistic achievement in films begins with a look at film realism—from the early documentaries of Dziga Vertov to cinema verité—and at the progress of fictional realism in film—from Erich von Stroheim's *Greed* to the works of Jean Renoir and Roberto Rossellini. It then considers the significance of Hollywood and shows how the films of D. W. Griffith and Charles Chaplin gave rise to the system of studios, stars, and genres. Finally, it asks how film, as an important twentieth-century art form, is related to such movements as expressionism and surrealism.

Jean Cocteau

TWO SCREENPLAYS

Here are the complete screenplays of Jean Cocteau's first film, *The Blood of a Poet*, and his last, *The Testament of Orpheus*—as well as some of his most important writings on the cinema and his philosophy of filmmaking. Illustrated with sixty photographs from the two films and views of the writer-director at work.

V. F. Perkins

FILM AS FILM
Understanding and Judging Movies

Here is a new set of criteria for judging the movies. *Film as Film* looks at actors, critics, technicians, and directors from the D. W. Griffith of *The Birth of a Nation* to the giants of today's international cinema. This book's unique approach is based neither on accepted classics nor on fashionable triumphs of recent years but on films that represent what the movies mean to their public. V. F. Perkins is in charge of film studies at the Berkshire College of Education in England.

Edited by W. R. Robinson

MAN AND THE MOVIES

In this study of the motion picture as an art form, twenty well-known writers and critics explore movies from various points of view—that of the director, the critic, the screenwriter, and most of all, the viewer Among the contributors are Leslie Fiedler, David Slavitt, Richard Wilbur, Joseph Blotner, and R. V. Cassill. W. R. Robinson is Associate Professor of English at the University of Florida